Crit

"HISTORICAL FICTION
IN THE GRAND TRADITION"
Nashville Banner

"RICH, ROBUST HISTORICAL FICTION ...
wonderfully plotted and magnificently written"
Chattanooga Daily Times

"There is everything
in HERE BE DRAGONS but dragons:
princesses held captive in stone towers,
bloody wars, princes scheming to
dethrone their own brothers,
castles under siege, maidens in distress,
power struggles for half of civilization ..."
The Washington Post Book World

"A tapestry of panoramic dimensions ...
lavish with romance"
Grand Rapids Press

"Penman has written
something wonderful here."
Arizona Daily Star

Here Be Dragons

SHARON KAY PENMAN

AVON
PUBLISHERS OF BARD, CAMELOT, DISCUS AND FLARE BOOKS

AVON BOOKS
A division of
The Hearst Corporation
105 Madison Avenue
New York, New York 10016

The Holt, Rinehart and Winston edition contains the following Library of
Congress Cataloging in Publication Data:

Penman, Sharon Kay.
  Here be dragons.

  1. Llewelyn ab Iorwerth, d. 1240—Fiction. 2. Wales—History—To
1536—Fiction. 3. Great Britain—History—Plantagenets, 1154–1399—
Fiction. I. Title.
PS3566.E474H4   1985   813'.54   84-23480

First Avon Printing: August 1987

To my parents

ACKNOWLEDGMENTS

I would like to thank the following people for their support and encouragement and understanding: My parents. Julie McCaskey Wolff. My agent, Molly Friedrich of the Aaron M. Priest Literary Agency. My dear friend Cris Arnott, who helped me to track down the elusive Richard Fitz Roy. Betty Rowles and Jean and Basil Hill, who showed me so many kindnesses during my research trips to Wales. Olwen Caradoc Evans and Helen Ramage, who shared with me their knowledge and love of Welsh history. Above all, my editor at Holt, Rinehart and Winston, Marian Wood. And lastly, the staffs of the National Library of Wales, the British Library, the Caernarfon Archives, the University College of North Wales Library, the research libraries of Cardiff, Llangefni, and Shrewsbury, the Brecknock Borough Library, the County Archives Office in Mold, and in the United States, the University of Pennsylvania Library.

PROLOGUE

Theirs was a land of awesome grandeur, a land of mountains and moorlands and cherished myths. They called it Cymru and believed themselves to be the descendants of Brutus and the citizens of ancient Troy. They were a passionate, generous, and turbulent people, with but one fatal flaw. They proclaimed themselves to be Cymry—"fellow countrymen"—but they fought one another as fiercely as they did their English neighbors, and had carved three separate kingdoms out of their native soil. To the north was the alpine citadel of Gwynedd, bordered by Powys, and to the south lay the realm of Deheubarth. To the English kings, this constant discord was a blessing and they did what they could to sow seeds of dissension and strife amongst the Welsh.

During the reigns of the Norman Conqueror, William the Bastard, and his sons, the English crown continued to gain influence in Wales; Norman castles rose up on Welsh soil, and Norman towns began to take root in the valleys of South Wales. As the Normans had subdued the native-born Saxons, so, too, it began to seem that they would subdue the Welsh.

Henry Plantagenet, King of England, Lord of Ireland and Wales, Duke of Normandy, Count of Anjou, ordered a wall fresco to be painted in his chamber at Winchester Castle. It depicted a fierce, proud eagle being attacked by four eaglets; as the great bird struggled, the eaglets tore at its flesh with talons and beaks. When asked what this portended, Henry said that he was the eagle and the eaglets were his sons.

And as the King's sons grew to manhood, it came to pass just as Henry had foretold. Four sons had he. Young Henry, his namesake and heir, was crowned with his sire in his sixteenth year. Richard, the second son, was invested with the duchy of Aquitaine, ruling jointly with Eleanor, his lady mother. Geoffrey became Duke of Brittany. The youngest son was John; men called him John Lackland for he was the last-born and the Angevin empire had already been divided amongst his elder brothers.

But John alone held with his father. The other sons turned upon Henry, seeking to rend him as the eaglets had raked and clawed at the bleeding eagle on the wall of Winchester Castle. In the year of Christ 1183, the House of Plantagenet was at war against itself.

BOOK ONE

1

SHROPSHIRE, ENGLAND

July 1183

He was ten years old and an alien in an unfriendly land, made an unwilling exile by his mother's marriage to a Marcher border lord. His new stepfather seemed a kindly man, but he was not of Llewelyn's blood, not one of the Cymry, and each dawning day in Shropshire only intensified Llewelyn's heartsick longing for his homeland.

For his mother's sake, he did his best to adapt to the strangeness of English ways. He even tried to forget the atrocity stories that were so much a part of his heritage, tales of English conquest and cruelties. His was a secret sorrow he shared with no one, for he was too young to know that misery repressed is misery all the more likely to fester.

It was on a Saturday morning a fortnight after his arrival at Caus Castle that Llewelyn mounted his gelding and rode north, toward the little village of Westbury. He had not intended to go any farther, but he was bored and lonely and the road beckoned him on. Ten miles to the east lay the town of Shrewsbury, and Llewelyn had never seen a town. He hesitated, but not for long. His stepfather had told him there were five villages between Westbury and Shrewsbury, and he recited them under his breath as he rode: Whitton, Stony Stretton, Yokethul, Newnham, and Cruckton. If he kept careful count as he passed through each one, there'd be no chance of getting lost, and with luck, he'd be back before his mother even realized he was gone.

Accustomed to forest trails and deer tracks, he found it strange to be traveling along a road wide enough for several horsemen to ride abreast. Stranger still to him were the villages, each with its green and market cross, its surprisingly substantial stone church surrounded by a cluster of thatched cottages and an occasional fishpond. They were in truth little more than hamlets, these Shropshire villages that so intrigued Llewelyn, small islands scattered about in a sea of plough-furrowed fields. But Llewelyn's people were pastoral, tribal, hunters and herdsmen rather than farmers, and these commonplace scenes of domestic English life were to him as exotic as they were unfamiliar.

It was midday before he was within sight of the walls of Shrewsbury Castle. He drew rein, awed. Castle keep and soaring church spires, a fortified arched bridge spanning the River Severn, and the roofs of more houses than he could begin to count. He kept his distance, suddenly shy, and after a time he wheeled the gelding, without a backward glance for the town he'd come so far to see.

He did not go far, detouring from the road to water his horse at Yokethul Brook, and it was there that he found the other boy. He looked to be about nine, as fair as Llewelyn was dark, with a thatch of bright hair the color of sun-dried straw, and grass-green eyes that now focused admiringly upon Llewelyn's mount.

Llewelyn slid to the ground, led the gelding forward with a grin that encouraged the other boy to say, in the offhand manner that Llewelyn was coming to recognize as the English equivalent of a compliment, "Is that horse yours?"

"Yes," Llewelyn said, with pardonable pride. "He was foaled on a Sunday, so I call him Dydd Sul."

The other boy hesitated. "You sound . . . different," he said at last, and Llewelyn laughed. He'd been studying French for three years, but he had no illusions about his linguistic skills.

"That is what Morgan, my tutor, says too," he said cheerfully. "I expect it is because French is not my native tongue."

"You are not . . . English, are you?"

Llewelyn was momentarily puzzled, but then he remembered. The people he thought of as English thought of themselves as Norman-French, even though it was more than a hundred years since the Duke of Normandy had invaded and conquered England. The native-born English, the Saxons, had been totally subdued. Unlike us, Llewelyn thought proudly. But he knew the Normans had for the Saxons all the traditional scorn of the victors for the vanquished, and he hastened to say, "No, I am not Saxon. I was born in Gwynedd, Cymru . . . what you know as Wales."

The green eyes widened. "I've never met a Welshman

before," he said slowly, and it occurred to Llewelyn that, just as he'd been raised on accounts of English treachery and tyranny, this boy was likely to have been put to bed at night with bloody tales of Welsh border raids.

"I'll show you my cloven hoof if you'll show me yours," he offered, and the other boy looked startled and then laughed.

"I am Llewelyn ab Iorwerth . . ." He was unable to resist adding, "Ab Owain Fawr," for Llewelyn was immensely proud that he was a grandson of Owain the Great, proud enough to disregard Morgan's oft-repeated admonition against such bragging.

But the younger boy did not react, and Llewelyn realized with a distinct shock that the name meant nothing to him. He seemed to want to respond to Llewelyn's friendliness, but there was a certain wariness still in his eyes. "I am Stephen de Hodnet." He hesitated again. "You do not live in Shropshire, do you? I mean, if you are Welsh . . ."

The implication seemed clear: if he was Welsh, why was he not in Wales where he belonged? Llewelyn was more regretful than resentful, for this past fortnight had been the loneliest of his life. "I'm staying at Caus Castle," he said coolly, and reached for Sul's reins.

"Caus Castle!" The sudden animation in Stephen's voice took Llewelyn by surprise. "Lord Robert Corbet's castle? You're living there?"

Llewelyn nodded, bemused. "For now I am. My lady mother was wed a fortnight ago to Sir Hugh Corbet, Robert's brother. You know them?"

Stephen laughed. "Who in Shropshire does not know the Corbets? They are great lords. My papa says they have more manors than a dog has fleas. In fact, he hopes to do homage to Lord Robert for the Corbet manor at Westbury." And he then proceeded, unasked, to inform Llewelyn that he was the youngest son of Sir Odo de Hodnet, that the de Hodnets were vassals of Lord Fulk Fitz Warin, holding manors of Fitz Warin at Moston and Welbatch, that he was a page in Fitz Warin's household at Alberbury Castle.

Llewelyn was a little hazy about the intricacies of English landholding, but he did know that a vassal was a tenant of sorts, holding land in return for rendering his overlord forty days of military service each year, and he was thus able to make some sense of this outpouring of names, places, and foreign phrases. What he could not at first understand was Stephen's sudden thawing, until he realized that the name Corbet was his entry into

Stephen's world. It was, he thought, rather like that story Morgan had once told him, a tale brought back by the crusaders from the Holy Land, of a man who'd been able to gain access to a cave full of riches merely by saying the words "Open Sesame!"

This realization gave Llewelyn no pleasure; it only reinforced his conviction that English values were beyond understanding. How else explain that he should win acceptance not for what truly mattered, his blood-ties to Owain Fawr, the greatest of all Welsh princes, but for a marriage that he felt should never have been? All at once he was caught up in a surge of homesickness, a yearning for Wales so overwhelming that he found himself blinking back tears.

Stephen did not notice, had not yet paused for breath. ". . . and my papa says Caus is the strongest of all the border castles, that it could withstand a siege verily until Judgment Day. Tell me—is it true that Lord Robert has a woven cloth on the floor of his bedchamber?"

Llewelyn nodded. "It is called a . . . a carpet, was brought back from the Holy Land." He could see that Stephen was on the verge of interrogating him at tiresome length about a subject that interested him not at all, and he said quickly, "But I know naught of castles, Stephen. Nor do I much like living in one. We do not have them in my land, you see."

Stephen looked incredulous. "None at all?"

"Just those that were built by the Normans. Our people live in houses of timber, but they're scattered throughout the mountains, not all clustered together like your English villages."

It was obviously a novel thought to Stephen, that not all cultures and societies were modeled after his own. They were both sitting on the bank by the stream and he rolled over in the grass, propped his chin in his hands, and said, "Tell me more about the Welsh."

Llewelyn no longer had any reservations about boasting of his bloodlines. Stephen was so woefully ignorant that it was truly a charitable act to enlighten him, he decided, and proceeded to acquaint Stephen with some of the more legendary exploits of his celebrated grandfather, giving his imagination free rein.

"And so," he concluded, having at last run out of inspiration, "when my grandfather died, his sons fought to see who would succeed him. My father was deprived of his rightful inheritance, and Gwynedd is now ruled by my uncles, Rhodri and Davydd."

Welsh names were falling fast and free—to Stephen's unfamiliar ears, much like the musical murmurings of Yokethul Brook.

But one fact he'd grasped quite clearly. A prince was a prince, be he Welsh or Norman, and he looked at Llewelyn with greatly increased respect. "Wait," he begged. "Let me be sure I do follow you. Your grandfather was a Prince of . . . Gwynedd, and your lady mother is the daughter of a Prince of . . . ?"

"Powys. Marared, daughter of Prince Madog ap Meredydd. My father was killed when I was a babe, and ere my mother wed Hugh Corbet, we lived with her kin in Powys . . ."

Llewelyn had not begun talking until he was nearly two, and since then, his mother often teased, he seemed bound and determined to make up for all that lost time. Now, with so satisfactory an audience as Stephen and a subject that was so close to his heart, he outdid himself, and Stephen learned that among the Welsh there was no greater sin than to deny hospitality to a traveler, that Welshmen scorned the chainmail armor of the English knight, that Llewelyn's closest friends were boys named Rhys and Ednyved, and the ancient Welsh name for Shrewsbury was Pengwern.

The sun had taken on the dull, red-gold haze of coming dusk as Llewelyn obligingly gave Stephen a lesson in the basics of Welsh pronunciation. "Say Rhys like this: Rees. And Ed-*nev*-ed. Now try Gruffydd; it sounds like your Griffith. In Welsh, the double 'd' is pronounced as 'th.' So my little brother's name is spelled A-d-d-a, but we say it as Atha, Welsh for Adam." He paused, his head cocked. "Do you hear that? Someone is calling your name."

Stephen scrambled to his feet so fast he all but tumbled down the brook embankment. "My brother! Jesú, but he'll flay me alive!"

"Why?"

"I coaxed him into taking me with him to Shrewsbury this morn. We agreed to meet at St George's bridge and I . . . I just forgot!"

"Well, cannot you say you're sorry and . . ."

Stephen shook his head, staring at the boys now mounting the crest of the hill. "No, not with Walter. He . . . he's not much for forgiveness . . ."

The approaching boys looked to be about fourteen. The youngster in the lead had Stephen's butter-yellow hair. He strode up to Stephen and, without a word, struck the younger boy across the face, with enough force to send Stephen sprawling.

"We've been looking for you for nigh on two hours! I've a mind to leave you here, and damned well should!"

As Walter reached down and jerked Stephen to his feet, Llewelyn came forward. He'd taken an instant dislike to Walter de Hodnet, but for Stephen's sake, he sought to sound conciliatory as he said, "It was my fault, too. We were talking and . . ."

Walter's eyes flicked to his face, eyes of bright blue, iced with sudden suspicion. "What sort of lowborn riffraff have you taken up with now, Stephen?"

Llewelyn flushed. "I am Llewelyn ab Iorwerth," he said after a long pause; instinct was now alerting him to trouble. At the same time Stephen burst into nervous speech.

"He is a Welsh Prince, Walter, and . . . and he's been telling me all about Wales . . ."

"Oh, he has?" Walter said softly, and Stephen, who knew his brother well enough to be forewarned, tried to shrink back. But Walter still had a grip on his tunic. With his other hand he grasped a fistful of Stephen's hair and yanked, until Stephen's head was drawn back so far that he seemed to be staring skyward, and was whimpering with pain.

"That's just what I could expect from you. No more common sense than the stupidest serf, not since the day you were born. So he's been telling you about Wales? Did he tell you, too, about the crops burned in the fields, the villages plundered, the women carried off?" Releasing Stephen, he swung around suddenly on Llewelyn.

"Suppose you tell him about it now. Tell my lack-wit brother about the border raids, tell him how brave your murdering countrymen are against defenseless peasants and how they run like rabbits when we send men-at-arms against them!"

Sul was grazing some yards away, and for several moments Llewelyn had been measuring the distance, wanting nothing so much as to be up on the gelding's back and off at a breakneck run. But with Walter's taunt, he froze where he was, pride temporarily prevailing over fear. He'd never run like a rabbit, never. But there was a betraying huskiness in his voice as he said, "I have nothing to say to you."

Walter was flanked by his two companions; they'd moved closer to Llewelyn, too close, and he took a backward step. But he dared retreat no farther, for the brook embankment was at his back and he did not know how to swim. He stood very still, head held high, for he'd once seen a stray spaniel face down several larger dogs by showing no fear. They stepped in, tightening the circle, but made no move to touch him. He was never to know how long the impasse might have lasted, for at that moment one of the boys noticed Sul.

"Damn me if he does not have his own mount! Where would a Welsh whelp get a horse like that?"

"Where do you think?" Walter, too, was staring at the chestnut, with frankly covetous eyes. "You know what they say. Scratch a Welshman, find a horse thief."

Llewelyn felt a new and terrible fear, for he'd raised Sul from a spindle-legged foal; Sul was his pride, his heart's passion. He forgot all else, and grabbed at Walter's arm as the older boy turned toward Sul. "He's mine, to me! You leave him be!"

It was a grievous mistake, and he paid dearly for it. They were on him at once, all three of them, and he went down in a welter of thudding fists and jabbing elbows. He flailed out wildly, desperately, but he could match neither his assailants' strength nor their size, and he was soon pinned down in the trampled grass, Walter's knees on his chest, his mouth full of his own blood.

"Misbegotten sons of Satan, the lot of you!" Walter panted. "Bloody bastards, not worth the hanging . . ." And if the profanity sat self-consciously on his lips, flaunted as tangible proof of passage into the mysteries of manhood, the venom in his voice was not an affectation, was rooted in a bias that was ageless, breathed in from birth.

"Know you what we mean to do now, Welsh rabbit? Pluck you as clean as a chicken . . ." He reached out, tore the crucifix chain from Llewelyn's neck. "Spoils of war, starting with that chestnut horse you stole. You can damned well walk back to Wales, mother-naked, and just thank your heathen gods that we did not hang you for a horse thief! Go on, Philip, I'll hold him whilst you get his boots . . ."

Sul. They were going to take Sul. His bruised ribs, his bloodied nose, hurt and humiliation and impotent fury—all of that was nothing now, not when balanced against the loss of Sul. Llewelyn gave a sudden frantic heave, caught Walter off guard, and rolled free. But as quick as he was, the third boy was quicker, and before he could regain his feet, an arm had crooked around his neck, jerking him backward. And then Walter's fist buried itself in his midsection and all fight went out of him; he lay gasping for breath, as if drowning in the very air he was struggling to draw into his lungs.

"Walter, no!" Stephen had at last found his voice. "He's not a nobody, he's highborn and kin by marriage to Lord Corbet of

Caus! He's stepson to Hugh Corbet, Walter, and nephew to Lord Robert!''

Suddenly, all Llewelyn could hear was his own labored breathing. Then one of the boys muttered, ''Oh, Christ!'' and that broke the spell. They all began to talk at once. ''How do we know he's not lying?'' ''But Walter, do you not remember? Lord Fulk was talking at dinner last week about a Corbet marriage to a Welshwoman of rank, saying the Corbets hoped to safeguard their manors from Welsh raids with such a union.'' ''Will he go whining to Corbet, d'you think?'' ''Since you got us into this, Walter, you ought to be the one to put it right!''

After a low-voiced conference, they moved apart and Walter walked back to Llewelyn. The younger boy was sitting up, wiping mud from his face with the sleeve of his tunic. He was bruised and scratched and sore, but his injuries were superficial. His rage, however, was all-consuming, blotting all else from his brain. He raised slitted, dark eyes to Walter's face; they glittered with hatred made all the more intense by his inability to act upon it.

''Here,'' Walter said tersely, dropping the crucifix on the ground at Llewelyn's feet. The conciliatory gesture was belied by the twist of his mouth, and when Llewelyn did not respond, he leaned over, grasped Llewelyn's arm with a roughness that was a more honest indicator of his true feelings.

''Come, I'll help you up.'' Walter's voice softened, took on a honeyed malice. ''You need not be afraid,'' he drawled, and Llewelyn spat in his face. It was utterly unpremeditated, surprising Llewelyn almost as much as it did Walter, and he realized at once that his Corbet kinship would avail him little against an offense of such magnitude. But for the moment the incredulous outrage on Walter's face was worth it, worth it all.

Walter gasped, and then lunged. Shock slowed his reflexes, however, and Llewelyn was already on his feet. He sprinted for Sul, and the gelding raised its head, expectant, for this was a game they often played, and Llewelyn had become quite adroit at vaulting up onto the horse's back from a running jump. But as he chanced a glance back over his shoulder, he saw he was not going to make it; Walter was closing ground with every stride. Llewelyn swerved, tripped, and sprawled facedown in the high grass. There was no time for fear, it all happened too fast; Walter was on top of him, and this time the older boy was in deadly earnest, he meant to inflict pain, to maim, and his was the advantage of four years and fully forty pounds.

"Walter, stop!" The other boys had reached them, were struggling to drag Walter off him. Llewelyn heard their voices as if from a great distance; there was a roaring in his ears. His right eye was swelling rapidly, and an open gash just above the eyelid was spurting so much blood that he was all but blinded. Through a spangled crimson haze, he caught movement and brought his arm up in a futile attempt to ward off the blow. But the expected explosion of pain did not come; instead the voices became louder, more strident.

"Jesus God, Walter, think what you do! Did you not hear your brother? The boy's not fair game, he's kin to the Corbets!"

"He's talking sense, Walter. You've got to let the boy be!"

"I intend to . . . as soon as he does beg my forgiveness." Walter was now straddling Llewelyn, holding the boy immobile with the weight of his own body, and he shifted his position as he spoke, driving his knee into Llewelyn's ribcage until he cried out in pain. "We're waiting on you. Tell me how sorry you are . . . and whilst you be at it, let's hear you admit the truth about your God-cursed kinfolk, that there's not a Welshman born who's not a thief and cutthroat."

Pain had vanquished pride; Llewelyn was frightened enough and hurting enough to humble himself with an apology. But it was unthinkable to do what Walter was demanding.

"Cer i uffern!" It was the worst oath Llewelyn knew, one that damned Walter to the fires of Hell. The words were no sooner out of his mouth than his face was pressed down into the dirt and his arm twisted up behind his back. He'd been braced for pain, but not for this, searing, burning, unendurable. The shouting had begun again. Walter's mouth was against his ear. "Say it," he hissed. "Say it, or by Christ I'll damned well break your arm!"

No. No, never. Did he say that aloud? Someone was gasping, "Sorry . . ." Surely not his voice. "Welshmen are . . . thieves . . ." No, not him.

"Again . . . louder this time."

"Enough, Walter! It was different when we did not know who he was. But Philip and I want no part of this. You do what you want with him, but we're going home . . . and straightaway!"

The pain in his arm subsided so slowly that Llewelyn did not at once realize he was free. Time passed. He was alone in the meadows now, but he did not move, not until he felt a wet muzzle on the back of his neck. It was Sul, nuzzling his tunic, playing their favorite game, seeking out hidden apple slices. Only then did tears well in Llewelyn's eyes. He welcomed them, needing to cry, but it was not to be; this was a hurt beyond tears, and they trickled into the blood smearing his cheek, dried swiftly in the dying heat of the setting sun.

Priding himself on his horsemanship, Llewelyn had never felt the lack of a saddle before. Now, with his right arm all but useless, with no saddle pommel to grip, the once-simple act of mounting was suddenly beyond his capabilities. Again and again he grasped Sul's mane, struggling to pull himself up onto the gelding's back. Again and again he slid back, defeated. But Sul's placid temperament stood him in good stead; the chestnut did no more than roll its eyes sideways, as if seeking to understand this queer new game Llewelyn was set upon playing, and at last, sobbing with frustration, Llewelyn was able to pull himself up onto Sul's withers. He was promptly sick, clinging to Sul's mane while his stomach heaved and the sky whirled dizzily overhead, a surging tide of sunset colors spinning round and round like a child's pinwheel, until the very horizon seemed atilt and all the world out of focus.

He headed the gelding back toward Caus Castle; he had nowhere else to go. Village life ceased at dusk, for only the wealthy could afford the luxury of candles and rushlight, and the little hamlets were deserted, his passage heralded only by the barking of dogs. It was well past nightfall by the time he approached Westbury. He had a hazy, half-formed hope that he might somehow sneak unseen into the castle bailey, and then up into the keep, to the upper chamber where Robert Corbet's three young sons slept. How he was to accomplish this miraculous feat, he had no idea, and it was rendered irrelevant now by the sudden appearance of a small body of horsemen.

Llewelyn drew rein, for he'd recognized the lead rider. Hugh Corbet, his mother's new husband.

"Llewelyn! Where in the name of Jesus have you been, boy? Your mother's frantic and little wonder. We've been out looking for you since Vespers!"

The search party carried lanterns, and as Hugh reined in beside Llewelyn, a glimmer of light fell across the boy's face, only a flicker of illumination, but enough. Hugh drew in his breath sharply. "My God, lad, what happened to you?"

There was some talk of summoning a doctor from Shrewsbury, but it was finally decided that Llewelyn's need was not so great as that. As the lady of the manor, Emma Corbet was, of necessity, a skilled apothecary, as adroit in stitching up wounds, applying poultices, and brewing healing herbs as any physician. It was she who applied a salve of mutton fat and resin to Llewelyn's bruised ribs, bathed his swollen eye in rosewater, and washed the blood and dirt from his face.

No, his shoulder was not dislocated, she said soothingly. If it were, he'd be unable to move the arm at all. She did feel certain, though, that his wrist was sprained; see how it was swelling? She'd need cold compresses for the eye, hot towels for the wrist, and her cache of herbs, she directed, and her maids speedily departed the bedchamber, leaving Llewelyn alone with Emma and Marared, his mother.

Voices sounded beyond the door. Llewelyn recognized one as his stepfather's; the other belonged to Robert Corbet, Hugh's elder brother. "Do you not think you're making too much of this, Hugh? Boys will get into squabbles. Look at my Tom, how he—"

"You have not seen him yet, Rob," Hugh said grimly, and pushed the door back.

Robert Corbet, Baron of Caus, was only twenty-eight, but he was decisive by nature and long accustomed to the exercise of authority. At sight of Llewelyn, his face hardened. Kneeling by the boy, he said, "Who did this to you, lad?"

Marared was standing behind her son. She reached out, let her hand rest on his shoulder. Emma shook her head and said, "It is no use, Rob. He's not said a blessed word so far. Mayhap if we left him alone with Hugh and Margaret . . ."

Llewelyn's head came up at that. Her name is Marared. Marared, not Margaret. The words hovered on his lips; he bit them back with a visible effort, and turned his face away, staying stubbornly silent.

Servants had carried bedding into the chamber, were spreading blankets down on the floor by the bed, and Hugh smiled at Llewelyn, said, "Margaret and I thought it would be best if you passed the night here with us. Now why do we not see about getting you out of those begrimed clothes?"

Llewelyn rose obediently, let his stepfather strip off the blood-ied, torn tunic, his shirt, chausses, linen braies, and the knee-length cowhide boots. But as Hugh pulled the blanket back and the boy slid under the covers, he said, very softly yet very distinctly, "My mother's name is Marared."

Hugh stood looking down at his stepson. He did not say anything, but Llewelyn had an unsettling suspicion that he under-stood, understood all too well.

Left alone at last, Llewelyn sought in vain to make himself comfortable on the pallet. He held the compresses to his injured eye, tried not to think of anything at all. When the door opened, he did not look up, believing it to be his mother. But the footsteps were heavier, a man's tread. Llewelyn raised himself awkwardly on his elbow, and his heart began to thud against his sore ribs, for it was Morgan.

Marared had been only fifteen when Llewelyn was born, widowed the following year while pregnant with his brother. With Adda, small and frail and maimed, she was fiercely protective, but she'd tended from the first to treat her eldest son as if they were playfellows rather than mother and child. Llewelyn adored the dark, beautiful girl who teased him, laughed at his misdeeds, and taught him to view their troubles with lighthearted abandon. But it was Morgan who set the standards that structured his life, it was Morgan's approval that mattered. Instinctively he knew that his mother would forgive him any sin, no matter how great. Morgan would not, and that made his good opinion the more precious. He shrank now from revealing his shame to Morgan; that the youthful priest should look upon him with contempt was a greater punishment than any pain Walter de Hodnet had inflicted.

Morgan was carrying a platter. Setting it down, he tossed a cushion on the floor by Llewelyn's pallet, and spreading the skirt of his cassock as if it were a woman's gown, he settled himself beside the boy.

"The Lady Emma has sent up some broth, and your lady mother thought you might like a slice of seedcake."

Llewelyn smiled wanly at that; his mother's invariable remedy for any childhood hurt was to offer sweets. Morgan leaned forward, spooned some broth into Llewelyn's mouth, and then turned the boy's head to the side, his eyes moving slowly over the bruises, contusions, and swellings.

"You're likely to have a scar over that eye," he observed dispassionately and, not waiting for a response, fed Llewelyn another spoonful of soup. Putting the bowl aside, he turned toward the tray, handed Llewelyn a fresh compress.

"Are you ready now to tell me about it?"

Llewelyn flushed, shot Morgan a look of mute entreaty. But Morgan's grey eyes were unwavering, expectant. Llewelyn could not lie, not to Morgan. He swallowed, began to speak.

Shrewsbury. Stephen. The meadow. Walter de Hodnet, his fear, and "Welshmen are thieves . . ." He held none of it back, spared himself nothing. But he could not meet Morgan's eyes, could not bear to see Morgan's dawning disgust. He looked instead at Morgan's hands, linked loosely in his lap; they were beautifully shaped, fingers long and supple, a symmetry marred only by the bitten, gnawed nails, chewed down to the very quick, an incongruous quirk in one with such a disciplined nature. Llewelyn kept his gaze riveted on those hands, saw them flex, tense, and then slowly unclench.

When Llewelyn had at last run out of words, one of the hands reached out, touched his hair in what seemed strangely like a caress. But Morgan's caresses were sparingly doled out and surely would not be given now, not after what he'd just confessed. And yet the hand had not been withdrawn; it was brushing the hair back from his forehead, lingering.

"Morgan . . ." Bewildered, utterly at a loss.

"I'm proud of you, lad."

"Proud?" Llewelyn choked. "I shamed you, shamed us all. Did you not understand? I did what he demanded, I dishonored my blood, groveled before him."

"And would you rather he'd broken your arm, mayhap maimed you for life?"

"No, but . . ."

"Listen to me, Llewelyn. Courage is a commendable quality, and a true test of manhood. You showed that today, and may rightly take pride in it. But for a prince of our people, courage alone is not enough; it must be tempered with common sense. You showed that too, today, lad, showed you were able to make a realistic recognition of superior strength. There's no shame in that, Llewelyn, none whatsoever. Be thankful, rather, that in a world full of fools, Our Lord Saviour has blessed you with brains as well as boldness of spirit."

"I was so ashamed . . ." Llewelyn whispered. "Not for the apology, but for the other, for saying my countrymen are thieves and cutthroats."

"And does saying it make it so?" Morgan shook his head. "Do you know what the English say of us, Llewelyn? They say a Welshman's word is worth spit in the wind. And they are right, lad. An oath given to an enemy is made to be broken; we understand that. We use what weapons we have available to us, and when we fight, we fight on our terms, not theirs.

"These are lessons you must learn, Llewelyn, and learn well. The day will come when you'll return to Gwynedd, lay claim to the lands your uncles now rule. You must be ready to win back what is yours by right, and above all, to deal with the English.

"We are not a numerous people. For every Welshman born, the Lord God has seen fit to beget twenty of English blood. Our princes have been forced to accept the English king as their liege lord. But we have not been subjugated as the Saxons were, we have not become a nation of serfs and bondsmen. These Norman lords who rule England, and would rule Wales if they could, hate us above all others. And still we live free, with our own princes, our own ways and customs."

Llewelyn nodded eagerly, intent on a lesson he'd long ago learned.

"This is because when the English come onto our lands," Morgan continued, "our people drive their livestock up into the hills and then they hide themselves. The English burn our houses, but we are not bound to the land like the English peasants, and when they withdraw, our people rebuild. Nor do we despair when we fight the English and find ourselves outnumbered. When we see ourselves losing, we retreat—and hit them again on the morrow. When they send armies into our land, we fade away into the woods, and they cannot find us.

"If you understand this, Llewelyn, you must understand, too, that you've no reason to reproach yourself, no reason to feel shame."

It seemed nothing less than miraculous to Llewelyn that Morgan could heal the worst of his hurts with so little effort, and he gave the priest a grateful smile. Morgan smiled back and then said briskly, "Now . . . is it your wish that I tell the Corbets about this boy?"

Llewelyn hesitated. Although he was feeling more and more comfortable about the role he'd played in that frightening encounter by Yokethul Brook, he still did not relish the prospect of confiding in his Corbet kin. "No," he said slowly. "No matter what they did to him, he'd just take it out on Stephen afterward. I'd rather we let it lie, Morgan." For now, he added silently. Walter de Hodnet. Not a name to be forgotten.

Morgan watched as Llewelyn touched his fingers to the puffy, discolored skin over his eye, to the swelling bruise high on his cheekbone, almost as if he were taking inventory of his injuries. And that, the priest knew, was precisely what the boy was doing, making a private acknowledgment of a debt due. Morgan sighed. Vengeance is mine, saith the Lord. On that, Holy Church spoke quite clearly. But his people parted company with their Church on this issue; they did not believe in forgiving a wrong, forgetting an injury—ever.

"Here," he said, handing Llewelyn a brimming goblet. "The Lady Emma mixed some bryony root in wine, to ease your pain and help you sleep. Drink it down and I'll stay with you till it does take effect. I have something of great importance to tell you. We learned this noon of a death, a death that will change the lives of us all."

Llewelyn sat up. "Who, Morgan?"

"Young Henry, the English King's eldest son and heir. We had word today that he died in France on the eleventh of June, of the bloody flux. He knew he was dying and pleaded with his father to come to him so they might reconcile ere he died. But Henry did not believe him, fearing it was a trick. They are an accursed family, in truth, the Devil's brood." He shook his head, made the sign of the cross.

"What will happen now, Morgan?"

Ordinarily the priest would have insisted that Llewelyn be the one to tell him that. But it was late and the boy was bruised and sore, in no condition to be interrogated about lessons of history and statecraft. "You know, Llewelyn, that the English give all to the firstborn son. Since young Henry had no son of his own, the heir to the English throne is now his brother Richard. So this means that Richard will one day be King."

"That is not good for us, is it, Morgan? If Richard is as able a soldier as men say . . ."

"He is."

Llewelyn swallowed some more wine. "I'm sorry Henry died," he said regretfully. "Since he was to be King one day, you made me learn as much as I could about him. And now all that effort goes for naught and I have to begin all over again with Richard!"

That triggered one of Morgan's rare laughs. "It is even worse than you know, lad. It is very likely that one of Richard's brothers might one day be King after him, so that means you must familiarize yourself with Geoffrey and John, too."

"All three? But why, Morgan? Richard will surely marry and beget a son. How, then, can Geoffrey or John ever be King?"

Morgan did not respond at once, seemingly lost in thought. "Aye," he said at last. "I reckon you are old enough to know. I take it that your mother and her brothers have spoken to you of carnal matters, explaining how a woman gets with child?"

"Of course! Mama and my Uncle Gruffydd told me what I needed to know ages ago."

A youngster growing up around livestock could not remain sheltered for long, and Llewelyn's were an uninhibited people who viewed sex as a natural urge and a very enjoyable pleasure; nor was theirs a society in which the stigma of illegitimacy carried much sting. Morgan was not surprised, therefore, by the boy's emphatic answer.

Actually, Llewelyn knew far more about carnal matters than Morgan suspected, for he knew about Gwynora. The average parish priest, be he Welsh or English or French, was not a well-educated man; Morgan was an exception. Most were simple villagers, and the burden of celibacy was one that not many could shoulder with equanimity. It was not at all uncommon for these lonely men to take to their hearths wives and live-in concubines, and while the Church officially decried these liaisons, they were tacitly accepted by most people as inevitable and even natural. Unlike so many of his fellow clerics, Morgan had never taken a wife or hearthmate, and the occasions were few when he'd found his vow of chastity too onerous for mortal flesh. He was always quite discreet, and it was purely by chance that Llewelyn had found out about Gwynora. He had told no one, and would never have dreamed of saying a word to Morgan; it gave him a warm glow of pleasure to keep a secret for this man he so loved.

"I know all about carnal matters, Morgan," he said loftily. "But what has that to do with one of Richard's brothers becoming King?"

Morgan hesitated. "Richard is a brilliant battle commander, one of the best in Christendom. Nor, for all his tempers, is he an impious man. It is well known that he yearns to take the cross."

"You mean go on pilgrimage to the Holy Land?"

Morgan nodded and then hesitated again. "The fact remains, however, that Richard has been known to indulge in an unnatural vice. He would rather satisfy his lust with men than with women."

Llewelyn's eyes widened. "But . . . but how?" he blurted out, then saw Morgan frown, and lapsed into a chastened silence. Men laying with other men? How was that possible? He'd seen enough animals mating to be able to envision a coupling between a man and woman, but when it came to coupling between men, his imagination failed him.

"Morgan . . . do Richard's brothers share this sin?"

"It is not a hereditary vice, Llewelyn; it does not pass with the blood," Morgan said dryly. "Young Henry was happily wed, though childless. Geoffrey's sins are beyond counting, but he does confine those of the flesh to adultery. As for John, his

wenching is notorious. As young as he is, he has at least one
bastard and seems destined for a life of debauchery and lechery.''
His mouth tightened.

"They are not admirable men, lad, but one of them will one
day be England's King, and your lives will be inextricably
entwined, yours and his. Know thine enemy, Llewelyn. I can
teach you no more valuable lesson than that.''

"Lessons? At this time of night? Good God, Morgan, have
you no mercy?'' Marared had come quietly into the room. Laughing at Morgan, she bent over Llewelyn's pallet, enveloping him
in a perfumed cloud.

"Here, darling, I thought you should have a pillow tonight.
And I brought you this . . ." She opened her palm. "See? It's a
coral pater noster. You put it under your pillow and you'll not be
troubled by bad dreams.''

She began to adjust the covers, tucking him in, all the while
keeping up a running commentary about his "battle scars,''
telling him of fights his father had gotten into as a youngster. He
had reached the age where he'd begun to shy away from caresses,
and she confined herself to a playful kiss on the tip of his nose,
saying cheerfully, "Get some sleep now, sweeting, and when
next there is a full moon, we'll go out by the moat and catch a
frog. Then we'll draw a circle around it, throw a handful of salt
about, and you whisper to the frog the name of the wretch who
gave you that fearsome black eye . . . and within a month he'll
find himself covered with loathsome, hairy warts!''

She got the response she was aiming for; her son grinned. But
as she straightened up, Morgan touched her elbow, drew her
away from the pallet.

"I do wish, Madame," he murmured, "that you would refrain
from filling the boy's head with such fanciful thoughts. Supersti-
tions of that sort are rooted in pagan rites and have no place in
Christian belief.''

Marared laughed, unrepentant. "Do not be such a stick, Morgan!" But then her amusement chilled as if it had never been.
The dark eyes narrowed, the full red mouth thinned noticeably. It
was as if he were of a sudden looking at a different woman
altogether.

"I want the names, Morgan.''

"Names, Madame?''

"The names of the hellspawn who did that to my son,'' she
hissed. "I know he told you, he tells you everything.''

"He does not want you to know, Madame. It's better forgotten.''

"Forgotten? That is my son, flesh of my flesh! I'll not let—"

"Mama?"

They both turned back toward the bed. Mararéd leaned down, smiled at her son. "Are you not sleepy yet, sweeting?"

"Yes . . ." The day's trauma and the medicinal wine had loosened Llewelyn's tongue at last. "Mama, I do hate it here. So does Adda. I'm so homesick, Mama. I miss Rhys and Ednyved and Uncle Gruffydd and—"

"Ah, Llewelyn . . ." Mararéd's eyes filled with tears.

"Please, Mama, can we not go back where we belong? Can we not go home?"

"You will, lad," Morgan said quietly. "I promise you that the day shall come when you will."

Llewelyn stared up at him and then turned his head aside on the pillow. "You mean we have to stay here for now."

"Yes . . . for now." Morgan stepped back, stood looking down at the boy. "But you will go back to Wales, Llewelyn. You will go home."

2

SHROPSHIRE, ENGLAND

June 1187

"Think you, then, that there'll be war?"

Hugh Corbet hesitated. It was no easy thing to be a younger brother in an age in which all passed by law to a man's eldest son. But Hugh had been luckier than most. His was a family of considerable wealth; the Corbets held lands not only in Shropshire, but in Normandy, Warwickshire, Worcestershire, and Wales. Robert Corbet had inherited the barony of Caus, but there were manors to spare for Hugh, too, and his relationship with his brother was blessedly free of the poisonous jealousy that bred such strife between a fortunate firstborn and his landless siblings.

Much of the time they were in harmony, working in tandem for the common Corbet good. But in this they were at odds. In this they were a House divided, much like the rival royal masters they served, for Robert's loyalties lay with Richard, King Henry's eldest son and heir, and Hugh's sympathies went out to the beleaguered, aging King.

Hugh was silent, considering Robert's grim query. "I would hope to God it will not come to that, Rob," he said at last. "Father against son—that is the ugliest of all feuds; it goes against the natural order of things."

Robert took this as a veiled jab at Richard, the unfilial son. "It would never have come to this if Henry would but formally recognize Richard as his heir!"

Hugh had to concede the truth of that. Finding himself forced to defend the indefensible, he at once took the offensive, saying sharply, "Be that as it may, Richard had no right to ally himself with the King of France—not against his own sire!"

"You know damned well why he felt that need, Hugh! With

21

their brother Geoffrey dead in France last summer, that does leave but Richard and John in line for the succession, and Richard knows all too well that his father loves him not. He knows, too, that Henry has ever favored John. What else can Richard think, except that his father means to raise John up to the place that is rightfully his?''

''And a right fine fear that be,'' Hugh scoffed, ''one to cover a multitude of sins. You know fully as well as I that Henry could anoint John as the very King of Heaven for all it'd avail him. The lords of this realm would never countenance so flagrant a breach of the laws of inheritance. Nor can you doubt the outcome. Whatever John might be given, he'd not long hold—not against Richard. No, Rob, if that be the balm Richard uses to soothe his conscience, he is a man much in need of absolution.''

Robert's face was mottled, splotched with resentful red. ''Richard is to be our next King, should God so will it, and I'll not have you speak ill of him in my hearing.''

Hugh sighed. By now he could recite the dialogue verbatim for these acrimonious exchanges. Rob was as blind as a barn owl in a noon-bright sun, dazzled by Richard's celebrated skill with a sword. Mayhap it was true that he was the finest soldier in Christendom, but if he had in him the makings of a good King, Hugh had yet to see any signs of it. Like as not, he'd pawn London itself to raise the gold he needed for his foreign wars. And John . . . would John be any better? Hugh thought not.

He came abruptly to his feet. Why offend Rob and unsettle himself? To what end? Let it lie.

They were sequestered in the uppermost chamber of the castle keep, alone but for a bored page and a dozing mastiff, Robert's faithful shadow. The window was unshuttered; in winter it would be screened with oiled and thinly scraped hide, but this was summer and it was open to sun and sound from the tiltyard below. Hugh went to it and watched for a while.

''What do you watch?'' The question was polite in tone, conciliatory in intent; Robert thrived on family discord no more than Hugh.

''Llewelyn and some of his friends.'' As Robert joined him, Hugh gestured toward a small group of youngsters gathered below. Llewelyn was mounted on a burnished chestnut gelding; as the boys watched, he lowered his lance, took aim, and sent the gelding cantering across the tiltyard. He hit the target off-center and the quintain swung about in a wide arc, the sandbag slicing through the air like an opponent's counterblow. It should have sent him tumbling from the saddle to the straw meant to soften youthful falls. But Llewelyn twisted sideways in the saddle, leaning so far to his left that it seemed inevitable he'd be unhorsed, and the sandbag swept by harmlessly overhead.

Hugh grinned. It was a showy stunt, an undeniably impressive feat of horsemanship, one that Hugh had seen before. Robert had not, however, and he swore in startled wonder.

"How in Christ did he do that without breaking his neck?"

Hugh laughed. "You'd not credit what I've seen that lad do on a horse. I truly believe the Welsh do learn to ride even ere they're weaned."

Below them, Stephen de Hodnet was taking his turn upon Llewelyn's gelding. He, too, hit the quintain awry and, seconds later, went sprawling into the straw, with a bruising impact that earned him no sympathy from the two watching men; they had suffered too many such spills themselves during their own years as knightly apprentices.

Reclaiming Sul, Llewelyn led it over to the fence, held out the reins to his brother. Adda shook his head, but Llewelyn persisted, maneuvering the gelding up to the fence so the younger boy could mount. Once securely in the saddle, Adda shed much of his awkwardness, and while he did not attempt the quintain, he put the gelding through several intricate maneuvers, showing himself to be a better rider than most of Llewelyn's friends.

Robert frowned. No matter how often he told himself that it was unchristian to feel such abhorrence of deformity, he could not control his distaste, could not keep his eyes from Adda's twisted leg. Thank the Lord Jesus that his Tom was sound of limb, that the younger boys, too, were whole.

"He lacks for spirit, that one. If not for Llewelyn's coaxing, I daresay he'd never stir from the hearth."

"Well, it's hard on the lad, Rob, being lame. What future has he, after all? Under Welsh law, that crooked leg bars him from any claim to his father's lands."

Robert shrugged. "He's not like to starve. Their law also holds that he must be provided for."

"True, but would you want to be taken care of—like a woman? At thirteen, Adda's old enough to feel the shame of it."

"I suppose," Robert agreed, without interest. It was not that he wished Adda ill, merely that he regretted his engrafting onto the Corbet family tree. It was fortunate indeed that Llewelyn was of more promising stock. "Tell me, Hugh, what plans have you made for Llewelyn's future?"

"Well, it is the custom in Wales for boys to be placed with a local lord when they reach fourteen or so. Whilst in his service, they learn the use of arms, the tactics of warfare, much like our youths do whilst serving as squires. Margaret thought to send Llewelyn back to her brothers for such training, but I think I've persuaded her that we should place him as a squire in a Norman household. I daresay the boy will balk at first, but I feel such a move would be in his best interest."

"That is just what I'd hoped you'd say, Hugh. You see, when I was in London at Whitsuntide, I had the good fortune to encounter his Grace, the Earl of Chester. Naturally the conversation turned to our common interests, protecting our respective lands from Welsh raids. He was most interested to learn that your stepson is the grandson of Owain Fawr, and he suggested that he find a place for the boy in his household."

"Jesú!" This was so far above Hugh's expectations that he was, for the moment, speechless, and Robert grinned, well pleased with himself.

"I see I need not tell you what an opportunity this will be for the boy, for us all. Chester is one of the greatest lords of the realm, and as shrewd as a fox for all his youth. He saw at once the advantage of befriending a boy who might one day rule in his grandfather's stead. Llewelyn has the blood-right, after all, and most assuredly the spirit. With luck . . ." He shrugged again and said, "But a chance like this, to come to manhood in an Earl's household! Loyalties given in youth often last for life. As Chester's squire, the brilliance of Llewelyn's world cannot help but eclipse all he's learned in the woodlands of Wales. He'll find himself amongst the greatest Norman lords, at the royal court, and in time he'll come to embrace Norman values, to adopt Norman traditions as his own."

Robert paused. "Do not misunderstand me, Hugh. I know how fond you are of the boy, and I find him a likable lad myself. But I cannot help feeling a certain disappointment that, after four years, he clings so tenaciously to the teachings of an undeniably primitive people. Despite all the advantages you've given him, Llewelyn remains so stubbornly—"

"Welsh?" Hugh suggested dryly, and Robert laughed. He'd actually been about to say "untamed" before thinking better of it, and he did not demur now at his brother's interpretation; they were, he thought, merely different ways of saying the same thing.

"Well, I shall talk to Margaret this forenoon, tell her about

Chester's offer—'' Hugh began, and then turned toward the opening door.

"Ah, Margaret, we were just speaking of you. Rob has— Margaret?''

Upon seeing Marared for the first time, Hugh had blessed his luck, suddenly found himself eager to consummate their political alliance in the marriage bed. Marared was a beautiful woman, if rather exotic by English standards, and after four years of marriage, he still took considerable pleasure in the sight of her. But she had no smile for him now, and the golden glow that owed so little to the sun was gone. Bleached of color, her face was ashen and her lashes were sooty thickets, smudged with the kohl bleeding into a wet trail of tears.

She paid no heed to Robert, crossed to her husband. "Hugh, we must go home. We must go back to Powys at once. It is my brother Owain. He . . . he's been murdered.''

There was a word in Welsh, *hiraeth*, that translated as "longing,'' but it meant much more, spoke of the Welsh love of the land, of the yearning of the exile for family, friends, home. Whenever he was claimed by *hiraeth*, Llewelyn would flee to the heights of Breiddyn Craig, and there he would spend hours in sun-drenched solitude, gazing out over the vales of the rivers Hafren, Vyrnwy, and Tanat. Now he was back at last, sitting Sul before the grey stones and slate roof of Llanfair, the church of St Mary.

This ancient church in the vale of Meifod was the traditional burial place for the princes of Powys; here his mother's father had been entombed and here his slain uncle would be laid to rest. He sought to summon up grief for this uncle he could little remember, but to no avail. He'd come back for a funeral, to mourn a man who was his blood kin, and yet as he looked upon the wooded hills that rose up behind the church, he felt only exhilaration, felt like a caged gerfalcon, suddenly free to soar up into the sun-bright azure sky.

Here he'd passed the first ten years of his life. Seven miles to the south was Castell Coch, the ancestral seat for the princes of Powys. His mother's family had a *plas*—a palace—less than a mile away, at Mathraval. The woods of mountain ash and oak and sycamore, the river teeming with trout and greyling, dappled by summer sun and shadowed by willow and alder—each stone was known to him, each hawthorn hedge rooted deep in memory. He was home.

He glanced sideways at his companion, one of his stepfather's squires. Should he tell Alan of his family's *plas*, he knew what the other boy would expect, a Norman edifice of soaring stone and mortar, for while most castles were timbered fortresses, the word "palace" conjured up images of grandeur and luxury. Llewelyn had been to London, had seen the Tower and the palace at Westminster, and he'd heard of the splendors of Windsor Castle. He knew there was nothing in Wales to compare to the magnificence of the Norman court, and he cared not at all that this was so.

He laughed suddenly, and when Alan shot him a curious look, he slid from Sul, handing the squire the reins.

"I'd be obliged if you looked after Sul, Alan. Should my lady mother or my stepfather ask for me, concoct what excuse you will."

Alan grinned. "Consider it done. But are you sure you'd not want company?"

Llewelyn was tempted, but only briefly. He thought of Alan as a friend, but his were memories, emotions, sensations that no Norman could hope to understand.

The Vyrnwy was free of the mud and debris that so often polluted English rivers, for there were no towns to despoil its purity with refuse and human waste. Llewelyn could see chalk-white pebbles glimmering on the shallow river bottom, see the shadows cast by fish feeding amidst the wavering stalks of water weeds. He forgot entirely that his uncle had died by this very river, his *plas* at Carreghova besieged by a man who was Llewelyn's own first cousin, Gwenwynwyn, Prince of southern Powys. He forgot his mother's tears, forgot his stepfather's ambitious plans for his future, forgot all but the here and now.

He'd walked these woods so often in memory, hearing the rustle of woodmice and squirrels, the warning cries of overhead birds, sentinels ever on the alert for the intrusion of man into their domain. A fox come to the river to drink was slow to heed the alert and froze at sight of Llewelyn, muzzle silvered with crystal droplets of river water, black eyes bright as polished jet. Boy and fox stared at one another in rapt silence, and then Llewelyn snapped his fingers, freeing the fox to vanish into the shadows as if by sorcery; not a twig cracked, not a leaf rustled to mark its passing. Llewelyn laughed and walked on.

He felt no surprise when he broke through a clearing in the wood and came upon the boys by the river; somehow he'd known that he would find them here. The Vyrnwy had always been their favorite fishing stream.

Shyness was an alien emotion to Llewelyn, but he found himself suddenly ensnared by it now, reluctant to approach the youths who'd once been like his brothers. They were not talking, theirs the companionable silence born of the intimacy of blood and a bonding that had begun in the cradle. Watching them, Llewelyn felt an unexpected emotion stir, one closely akin to envy. He belonged here, too, fishing on the banks of the Vyrnwy with Ednyved and Rhys, but how to surmount the barriers built up by four years of English exile?

They were lounging on the grass in positions as characteristic as they were familiar: Rhys sitting upright, utterly intent upon the trout to be hooked, Ednyved sprawled on his back in the sun, fishing pole wedged into a pyramid of piled-up rocks. And as ever, Llewelyn found himself marveling that two boys so unlike could share the same blood. First cousins they were, but none seeing them together would ever have guessed the kinship.

Rhys shared with Llewelyn the pitch-black hair so common to their people, but while Llewelyn's eyes were dark, too, Rhys had the eyes of a Welsh mountain cat, purest, palest green. His unusual coloring, thick sable lashes, and features so symmetrical as to draw all eyes were, for him, a burden rather than a blessing. He loathed being fussed over, and yet his startling beauty of face doomed him to be forever fending off the gushing compliments and effusive embraces of his doting female relatives, who considered him quite the handsomest male child ever born and took great pride in showing him off to mothers and aunts of less favored youngsters, to Rhys's utter disgust and the vast amusement of his friends.

It was possible to look upon his beauty—for there was no other word for it—and to note his slightness of build and conclude that there was a softness, a fragility about the boy. That was, Llewelyn had long ago learned, an impression so erroneous as to be utterly ludicrous, and not a little dangerous. Rhys was as hard, as unyielding as the flint of his native land; there was no give in him, none at all.

As for Ednyved, in all honesty he could only be described as homely. Lanky brown hair, deepset eyes of a nondescript color that was neither brown nor hazel but a murky shade somewhere in between, a mouth too wide and chin too thrusting, too prominent. Big-boned even as a small boy, he seemed to have sprouted up at least a foot since Llewelyn had seen him last, and Llewelyn had no doubts that when fully grown, Ednyved would tower head and shoulders above other men.

As he watched, Llewelyn suddenly found himself remembering a childhood game he'd long ago liked to play with his mother, in which they sought to identify people with their animal counterparts. Llewelyn had promptly pleased his sleekly independent and unpredictable mother by categorizing her as a cat. Hugh, whom he liked, he saw as an Irish wolfhound, a dog as bright as it was even-tempered. Robert Corbet, whom he did not like, he dubbed another sort of dog altogether, the courageous but muddle-headed mastiff. Morgan, too, was easy to classify, for Morgan was a priest with the soul of a soldier, a man who'd chosen of his own free will to fetter his wilder instincts to the stringent disciplines of his Church. Morgan, Llewelyn had explained to Marared, could only be a falcon, for the falcon was the most predatory of birds, a prince of the skies that could nonetheless be tamed to hunt at man's command. Adda, too, was a bird, a caged sparrow hawk, tethered to earth whilst his spirit pined only to fly; when he'd told his mother that, tears had filled her eyes. But when she wanted to know how he saw himself, Llewelyn grew reticent, evasive. From the day she'd taken him to the Tower of London to see the caged cats, he'd known what animal he wanted to claim as his own, the tawny-maned lion, but that was a vanity he was not willing to confess, even to his mother.

He had never tried to characterize Rhys or Ednyved, but it came to him now without need for reflection, for Rhys had the unpredictable edginess of a high-strung stallion and Ednyved all the latent power, the massive strength and lazy good humor of the tame bear he'd seen at London's Smithfield Fair.

Ednyved yawned and stretched, reaching for the woven sack that lay beside their bait pail. He shook several apples out onto the grass, tossed one to Rhys.

"I daresay you want one, too, Llewelyn?" he asked nonchalantly and, without looking up, sent an apple sailing through the air. It was remarkably accurate for a blind pitch, landing just where Llewelyn had been standing seconds before. He was no longer there, however, having recoiled with such vehemence that he bumped bruisingly into the nearest tree. Rhys, no less startled, spun around so precipitantly that he overturned the bait pail, and, as he cursed and Llewelyn took several deep breaths, trying to get his pulse rate back to normal, Ednyved rolled over in the grass and laughed and laughed.

"How in hellfire did you know I was there?" Llewelyn demanded, and Ednyved feigned surprise.

"How could I not, with you making enough noise to bestir the dead? Is that the English style of woodland warfare?"

He'd always been a lethal tease, and Llewelyn was not normally thin-skinned. But they'd not yet established the boundaries of their new relationship. Llewelyn opened his mouth to make a sharp retort, but Rhys was quicker. Rhys's pride was prickly and unpredictable, easily affronted, and he'd been embarrassed by his failure to take notice of Llewelyn. Glaring at his cousin, he snapped, "And Llewelyn might well ask if this is the Welsh way of welcome!" Turning back to Llewelyn, he smiled, said, "We thought you'd be home for your uncle's funeral, were watching for you."

Llewelyn smiled back, and coming forward, he settled himself beside them on the grass. A silence fell between them, one that seemed likely to swallow up any words they could throw into the void. It was broken at last by Llewelyn; he heard himself making courteous queries about the health and well-being of their families, falling back upon all the obligatory conversational gambits to be shared between strangers. Nor did Rhys ease the awkwardness any by offering Llewelyn formal condolences for the death of his uncle.

Llewelyn would have liked to speak freely, to explain that he'd not known his Uncle Owain all that well. But he felt constrained to respond with a conventional politeness, and thus found himself flying false colors, coming before them in the guise of a grief that was not his.

Rhys offered him an apple. "Did your stepfather come with you?" he asked, as if he could possibly have had any interest in Hugh's whereabouts.

Llewelyn nodded. "Hugh came on behalf of the Corbet family, as a gesture of respect to my mother's kin . . ." He stopped, for Ednyved had leaned forward, was regarding him with exaggerated attention.

"Why do you look at me like that? Has my face of a sudden turned green?"

"I was trying to decide," Ednyved drawled, "whether or not you'd picked up a French accent."

Llewelyn tensed, but then he looked more closely at the other boy, saw that Ednyved's eyes were bright with friendly laughter.

"No French accent," he said, and grinned, "but I did spend some right uncomfortable days this spring, worrying that I'd picked up the French pox!"

Ednyved's mouth twitched. "Llewelyn!" With a frown toward

his cousin. "If you please, no bawdy talk—not before the lad here!" Ducking just in time as an apple whizzed past his head.

Seconds later, Rhys followed up his aerial assault with a direct frontal attack, and Ednyved, caught off balance, was knocked flat. Rhys's anger was more assumed than not, and their scuffling soon took on an almost ritualistic quality, for this was an old game, rarely played out in earnest, and likely to continue until one or the other of the combatants lost interest. In this case the mock battle lasted until they noticed that Llewelyn had appropriated the rest of the apples and stretched himself out comfortably on the turf to watch, for all the world like a front-row spectator at a bearbaiting.

"Go to it, lads," he said airily, and by common consent, they both pounced on him at once. For a few hectic moments all three boys were tumbling about on the riverbank, until at last they lay panting in a tangled heap, lacking breath for anything but laughter.

After that, there seemed to be too much to say and not enough time in which to say it, and they plunged into the past as if fearing it might somehow be forgotten if it was not shared immediately, interrupting each other freely, trading insults and memories, laughing for laughter's sake alone.

Rhys had gone to the river to drink. Returning, he threw himself down in the grass, and broke into Ednyved's monologue to demand, "When must you go back to England, Llewelyn?"

"I'm not going back," Llewelyn said, at once capturing their undivided attention.

"You both know the history of my House, know how my uncles Davydd and Rhodri cheated my father and my other uncles of their rightful share of my grandfather's inheritance. They carved Gwynedd up between them as if it were a meat pie, forced my father, Owain Fawr's firstborn, into exile, brought about his death whilst I was still in my cradle. His blood is on their hands and they've yet to answer for it. I think it time they did."

"You mean to avenge your father's death?" Rhys's green eyes were luminous, aglitter with sudden excitement, but Ednyved seemed far more dubious.

"All know the English are born half mad," he said slowly, "but I wonder if the madness might not be in the water they drink or the air they breathe. How else explain that four short years amongst them could have so scattered your wits?"

Llewelyn was amused. "Your faith in me is truly wondrous to

behold, Ednyved. Think you that I'm such a fool as to challenge my uncles on my own, with only God on my side? I had a long talk this morn with my Uncle Gruffydd, and he has sworn to give me his full backing, men who know war well and the money to pay them; he even offered the services of no less a soldier than Gwyn ab Ednywain. It is my intent, too, to join forces with my Uncle Cynan's two grown sons. They were denied their inheritance just as I was, giving us common cause against Davydd and Rhodri."

"When you do put it that way, it does not sound quite so crackbrained," Ednyved conceded. "But how in the name of the Lord Jesus did you ever get your lady mother and stepfather to give their consent?"

Llewelyn hesitated. "Well, to be honest, I have not told them yet," he admitted, and flushed when they both laughed.

"Can you truly blame me?" he protested. "We'll be bound to have a godawful row. I know not with whom my mother'll be more wroth, me or my Uncle Gruffydd, for aiding and abetting me in this. As for Hugh, he's like to have an apoplectic fit. You see, he'd arranged for me to enter the household of a Norman Earl."

Llewelyn shook his head in mock regret. "Poor Hugh, how he has struggled to make of me a proper Norman. I once overheard his brother grumbling about turning a sow's ear into a silk purse, and I daresay Hugh has had moments when he's in heartfelt agreement!"

This last was said without rancor. Llewelyn never doubted that Hugh's fondness for him was genuine, but he'd come to understand that affection and bias could take root in the same soil. In this he had the advantage of Rhys and Ednyved, and they looked so offended that he felt compelled to come to Hugh's defense.

"Yet he is a good man for all that. My mother has been quite content with him, and I"—he grinned suddenly—"I even did come to forgive him for his greatest sin, that of not being born Welsh!"

But here they had no common meeting ground; neither Rhys nor Ednyved had English friends, English kin. Both looked blank, and then Rhys dismissed what he did not understand, saying, "You'll not let them talk you out of it?"

"No." Llewelyn sat up, his eyes searching their faces with sudden sober intent. "I shall have men to counsel me, men well lessoned in the ways of war. But no matter how much help I get from my Uncle Gruffydd or my cousins, I shall have to stand or fall on my own efforts. If I cannot convince people that my claim be just, if I cannot win their allegiance . . . nor can I expect my blood to count for aught should I fall into Davydd's hands. And the risks will be no less for those who follow me." He paused. "My Uncle Gruffydd has agreed to speak with your fathers, should you—"

"You want us to help you overthrow Davydd and Rhodri, to fight with you?" Rhys could wait no longer, and burst out eagerly, "Jesú, Llewelyn, need you even ask?"

Llewelyn smiled. "What of you, Ednyved? Does Rhys speak for you, too?"

"I'd as soon speak for myself," Ednyved said, sounding quite serious for once. "I want to be sure I fully understand. We'd be camping out in the mountains of Gwynedd, harassing your uncles howsoever we could, living like outlaws, sleeping in the open, eating on the run, rebels with prices on our heads. Is that a fair summing up of what we could expect?"

"Very fair," Llewelyn agreed, and a slow grin began to spread over Ednyved's face.

"Who could possibly turn down an offer like that?"

"It is settled, then," Rhys said briskly, never having doubted what his cousin's answer would be. As he spoke, he was rolling up the sleeve of his tunic. Before Llewelyn and Ednyved realized what he meant to do, he unsheathed his dagger and, without the slightest hesitation, drew it swiftly across the bared skin of his forearm.

"This is too important for mere words," he explained composedly, watching the flow of his own blood with indifferent eyes. "For this, we must swear in blood."

It was a gesture as irresistible as it was melodramatic, at least to Llewelyn. Ednyved looked rather less enthusiastic, and when Rhys passed him the bloodied dagger, he took it with such reluctance that Llewelyn burst out laughing.

"Since you share the same blood as Rhys, mayhap you could swear, too, in his," he gibed, and Ednyved grimaced, drew a few drops of blood.

"Here, my lord princeling," he grunted. "Your turn."

Llewelyn made a far more modest cut than Rhys had, saying, "If I'm to spill my blood, I'd as soon spill it in Gwynedd." Rising, he searched the clearing until he'd gathered a handful of rock moss. This he brought back to Rhys, and leaning over, he applied it to the other boy's arm.

"Hold this upon the cut till the bleeding ceases, or you might

well end up as the first casualty of my war," he said, and
laughed again, realizing that he was as happy at this moment as
he'd ever been in his life.

Hugh Corbet was surprised to find the great hall all but deserted;
as in England, the hall was the heart of Welsh home life. But
then he heard the voices, angry, accusing, and he understood. At
the far end of the hall his wife and her elder brother Gruffydd
were standing, and even Hugh, who knew no Welsh other than a
few endearments Marared had taught him in bed, could tell at
once that they were quarreling, quarreling bitterly. Gruffydd's
retainers and servants had wisely fled the battlefield; only Llewelyn,
Adda, and Morgan ap Bleddyn, his wife's chaplain, were still in
the hall.

   As Hugh moved up the center aisle, Gruffydd turned on his
heel and stalked out the door behind the dais, slamming it
resoundingly behind him. Hugh was secretly amused that his
wife should be giving her brother such grief. He had discovered
early in his marriage that Welshwomen were more outspoken and
less submissive than their Norman sisters, and while he'd learned
to accept Marared on her own terms, it pleased him to see
Gruffydd reaping what he had sown. For certes, a society in
which women were not taught their proper place was bound to
lack harmony, a natural sense of order.

   But he was taken aback by what happened next. Marared
swung around on her eldest son, put a question to him, and when
he shook his head, she slapped him across the face. Hugh was
astonished, for he'd never seen her raise her hand to Llewelyn
before, not even on occasions when the boy richly deserved it.
He hastened toward them, wondering what sins would loom so
large in her eyes.

   Could Llewelyn have set his heart upon trading his gelding for
an untamed stallion? No, Margaret was a doting mother, not a
foolish one; she'd never sought to wrap the boy in soft wool.
What, then? Had he gotten some village lass with child? That
was likely enough. He was an attractive lad, and having discovered where his sword was meant to be sheathed, he seemed set
upon getting as much practice as possible. But no, why should
Margaret fret over a peasant wench ploughed and cropt? She was
too sensible for that, would not blame Llewelyn for so small a
sin.

   Marared had turned away abruptly, sitting down suddenly on
the steps of the dais. Llewelyn followed at once, hovering uncer-

tainly at her side, his face troubled. But when he patted her
shoulder awkwardly, she pushed his hand away. Hugh quickened
his step, no longer amused.

"Margaret? What is wrong?"

"Ask Llewelyn," she said tautly, and then, "He says he's not
going back to England with us. He wants to stay in Wales, to try
to overthrow his uncles in Gwynedd."

Her answer was so anticlimactic that Hugh felt laughter well
up within him, dangerously close to the surface. He gave an
abrupt, unconvincing cough, knowing she'd never forgive him if
he laughed. But how like a woman, to let herself get so distraught over a boy's caprice, a whim of the moment that bore
little relationship to reality. Doubtless, too, she'd been seeking to
scare Llewelyn with horror stories of the hardships he'd be
facing, the dangers and deprivations, the hand-to-mouth existence
of a rebel on the run. And what could be better calculated to
appeal to a foolhardy fourteen-year-old?

"Is this true, Llewelyn?"

Llewelyn nodded, but his eyes were wary and Hugh hesitated,
recognizing the need to tread lightly, not wanting to trample the
boy's pride into the dust.

"That is a rather ambitious undertaking, lad, too much so. In
saying that, I do not mean to belittle your courage in any way.
But courage alone is not enough, not when we are talking of
rebellion."

"I know." Llewelyn slanted a sudden glance toward Morgan.
"Courage without common sense is the least of God's gifts."

"It's glad I am to hear you say that, Llewelyn. For should you
go up against your uncles now—on your own—I fear the only
ground in Gwynedd you'd claim would be enough to fill a grave."

"I know," Llewelyn said again, and when Hugh smiled, so
did he. Before adding, "That is why I did appeal to my Uncle
Gruffydd for advice and assistance. He thinks I'm of an age to
lay claim to what is mine, has promised to help me do just that."

Hugh's jaw dropped. "He what?" Jerking around to stare at
his wife. "Your brother has agreed to this, to aid him in this
madness?" he demanded, incredulous, and she nodded grimly.

Christ, no wonder Margaret was so wroth! "Of all the damned
fool . . . ! I am sorry, Llewelyn," he said curtly, "but you must
put this scheme from your mind. There is no way on God's earth
that I'd ever give my consent."

"I'm sorry, too," Llewelyn said softly. "I should've liked to
have your approval."

He'd spoken so politely that it was a moment or so before Hugh realized he'd just been defied.

"You're not being offered a choice, Llewelyn! I'm telling you that you're to forget this lunacy, you're to return to Shropshire with your mother and me, and that will be the end of it. As for your uncle, I'd not speak ill of a man in his own house, but he had no right to encourage you in this, to go against our wishes. You are not his son, after all."

"I am not your son, either."

Hugh stiffened. The boy's matter-of-fact reminder hurt more than he'd have expected or Llewelyn had intended. It was a hurt that camouflaged itself in rage, and he clenched his fist, his face darkening with a sudden surge of blood. But while Llewelyn felt that his mother had a perfect right to hit him if she chose, he did not accord Hugh the same privilege, and he'd prudently put distance between them.

"No, you are not my flesh and blood. But when I wed your mother, your wardship passed into my hands. That means, Llewelyn, that you are answerable to me, and will be until you do come of legal age. Once you reach your majority, you may do what you damned well please, may sell your life as cheaply as you like. But for the next seven years you'll do what I say. Is that clear?"

"Very."

It was Llewelyn's composure that struck the first false note. The boy was too calm, was arguing more like an adult than a youngster with a head full of fanciful dreams, and Hugh said warningly, "If you think to run away once we're back in Shropshire, Llewelyn . . ."

Llewelyn was shaking his head. "I've heard you out, Hugh. Now I'd have you do as much for me. I'd not have you think me ungrateful . . . and I do not deny your right of wardship over me until I come of legal age. As we both know, in England that is twenty-one. But what you plainly do not know is that in Wales it is fourteen . . . and I did turn fourteen in February."

Hugh stared at his stepson. Llewelyn's dark eyes were shining with triumph; a smile he could not quite repress quirked one corner of his mouth. Hugh caught his breath, swore softly. Little wonder the lad had been so cocky; he'd known from the first that he was playing with loaded dice.

Hugh was swallowing bile, spat into the floor rushes. Rob was right; there was no reasoning with the Welsh, they were all mad, beyond redemption or understanding. What were they to tell

Chester? The opportunity of a lifetime lost to them, all because a
headstrong boy wanted to play the rebel!

"And what of your brother? Would you leave him without a
qualm, knowing he has such need of you, knowing you go where
he cannot follow—"

"Adda hears just fine! Do not speak of him as if he were not
even here!"

There was a strained silence. Adda had gone very pale, but he
said, quite evenly, "I want Llewelyn to go, want him to claim
what is his. So would I, had God not willed otherwise."

Hugh felt a touch of shame; it was Llewelyn he'd wanted to
wound, not the innocent Adda. Llewelyn was staring at him,
accusing, defiant. Whatever chance he might have had of prevailing was utterly gone now. Llewelyn might, he knew, forgive a
slight on his own behalf, but on Adda's, never. He'd not yield in
this, knowing he had the full backing of his Welsh kinsmen. All
their plans set at naught, their hopes of an alliance with Chester
now gall and wormwood, ashes in his mouth.

"Go to Gwynedd and be damned, then!" he said bitterly, and
turned away.

They watched in silence as Hugh strode from the hall. But
when Marared rose to follow him, Llewelyn stepped in front of
her. "Mama . . ."

"No, Llewelyn. Do not expect my blessings. Do not expect
my forgiveness, either."

He'd won. But he could take no pleasure in it, not now.
Llewelyn sank down on the dais steps, passed some moments
disconsolately sliding his dagger up and down its sheath. The
excitement he'd experienced in sharing his plans with Ednyved
and Rhys had gone suddenly sour, tarnished by his mother's tears.

"Adda?" Marared let her hand linger on her younger son's
shoulder. "Are you coming, lad?"

"Yes, Mama."

As Adda rose, Llewelyn looked up, said, "Hugh did not mean
that, Adda. He was angry, just did not think . . ."

"People never do, do they?" Adda smiled thinly. "Yet we'd
be apart, too, once you were sent off to serve as Chester's squire.
Better you should follow your heart."

Their eyes caught, pulled away. Marared was waiting. Adda
reached for his crutch and angled it under his armpit. Watching
his brother limp toward the door, Llewelyn felt a protective pang.
What Adda had just said was true. It was also true that he was
being left behind.

"Morgan . . . Morgan, am I doing the right thing?"

"If I said no, would you heed me?"

Llewelyn considered, and then gave the priest a rueful smile. "No," he conceded. "Gwynedd is my birthright. But it's like to take years to claim it. Years I can ill afford to squander in Shropshire. I have to do this, Morgan. I have to."

Morgan nodded slowly; he'd expected no less. He, more than anyone else, had nurtured in Llewelyn a love for his heritage, his homeland, had molded youthful clay into adult ambition. He was proud of what he had accomplished, proud of Llewelyn's resolve, his daring. But he could not help feeling fear, too, for Llewelyn was the son he'd never have.

"I cannot say I approve, lad." And then, very softly, "But I do understand."

3

CHINON CASTLE, PROVINCE OF TOURAINE

June 1189

"What is your name, girl?"

"Lucy . . ." She added "my lord" for safety's sake; a fort-night at Chinon had not been long enough for her to absorb the intricacies of the castle hierarchy. She knew only that this man was a bailiff, a being as far above her as stars in the firmament, and she was trembling with dread that she'd somehow dis-pleased, that she might be dismissed in disgrace.

"Turn around," he directed, and as she complied in bewilder-ment, he gave a satisfied nod. "Yes, you'll do once you're cleaned up some; he's right particular about such niceties. Agnes, see that she has a bath first. I expect it is too much to hope that you would still be a virgin?"

Lucy gasped so audibly that several men laughed, and the bailiff looked at her with the first flicker of genuine interest. "Well, well. That is a stroke of luck for you, girl. How many wenches get to lose their maidenheads in a royal bed?" He laughed, moved on to other matters, and Lucy was forgotten.

She stood there, rooted, until Agnes stepped forward and slipped a supportive arm around her waist. "Shall we get you that bath?" she said, and giving Lucy no chance to balk, she guided the girl toward the door. "Do not look so stricken, lass. It'll not be as bad as you think; you might even enjoy it."

"But . . . but he's so old and sickly!" Lucy shuddered. She'd seen the old King infrequently since his arrival at Chinon. There was in his face the haggard, grey gauntness of coming death; it would, she thought with horror, be like embracing a corpse.

"Old?" Agnes echoed and then laughed. "You need not fear, Lucy, you're not for poor King Henry. God pity him, he's beyond feeling the itch that only a woman can scratch. No, his son rode in within the hour, and it is a rare night when that one does not want a wench to warm his bed.''

"Lord John?"

"Well, for certes not Richard!" Agnes giggled, but thought better of pursuing that particular brand of high-risk humor; instead, she took it upon herself to allay Lucy's fears. "He's handsome, is Lord John. Not as tall as Richard, of stocky build like his father, although dark as a Barbary pirate. And young, one and twenty against his sire's six and fifty, a far better age for bedding!"

But Lucy did not seem to appreciate her good fortune; she looked dazed. Agnes thought she knew why, and glanced about to make sure no others were within earshot.

"You must not believe all you hear, child. It is true John does have men about him who'd make even Hell the fouler for their presence. He might not rein them in as he ought, but he does not seem to be one for sharing their nastier sport. In the five years I've been at Chinon, I've never heard it said that he takes pleasure in a woman's pain, and whilst I cannot speak firsthand, mind you, I've been told he has no quirks a woman would not enjoy, too. And he's ever been generous in the past, will be sure to give you something after."

She hesitated. "But in all honesty, his temper's like to be on the raw. God knows, he has reason and more, with his father ailing, with Richard and the French King encamped outside Tours, just a day's march from here. Richard has much to answer for, in truth. To war upon his own father . . ." She shook her head. "At least John is loyal."

Henry moaned, turned his face into the pillow. His shirt was soaked with sweat; so, too, were the sheets, damp and darkly splotched. A servant had removed his shoes and chausses, and his legs looked absurdly white and frail, utterly incongruous supports for that barrel chest, those massive shoulders. But even that once-mighty chest seemed somehow shrunken, diminished. It was impossible for John to recognize in this bedridden invalid the father who'd cast so colossal a shadow, larger than life, omnipotent: King of England, Lord of Ireland and Wales, Duke of Normandy and Gascony, Count of Anjou, Touraine, and Maine, liege lord of Brittany, Auvergne, and Toulouse.

Henry was breathing through his mouth, gulping air as if each breath might be his last. Saliva had begun to dribble down his chin, but John could not bring himself to wipe it away, shrank from touching that wasted flesh. He was profoundly shocked that in a mere fortnight his father's illness should have made such lethal inroads; until this moment he'd not acknowledged that the illness might be mortal.

"John? Thank God you've come. He's done little but fret over you. Could you not have sent word that you'd gotten away safe from Le Mans?"

Two weeks ago the town of Le Mans had fallen to the forces of John's brother Richard and Philip, the young French King. Henry and his followers had escaped the burning city just as the French army moved in, and in the confusion John had gotten separated from the others, had passed some harrowing days himself, in consequence. But he was not about to explain that now to the speaker, his illegitimate half-brother Geoffrey. Like all of his brothers, Geoffrey was much older than John, well into his thirties, a tall, powerfully built man with sandy hair, Henry's flint-grey eyes, and an acerbic tongue. John did not feel for Geoffrey the consuming, corrosive jealousy that he did for Richard, but he had no more liking for this Geoffrey than he'd had for the dead brother who'd borne the same name. Ignoring the accusatory, querulous tone of the other's question, he said, "Christ, but he looks bad. Is he in much pain?"

Geoffrey nodded. "All the time," he said bleakly, and then turned toward the bed as Henry stirred.

The grey eyes opened, focused on John. "At last," he said huskily, held out his hand. "You did give me some bad moments this past week, lad."

John was much relieved at the hot, dry feel of the hand in his, having steeled himself for a touch cold and clammy. "You need not have worried, Papa. Are you not the one who always said I had more lives than a cat? Or was that the morals of a cat?" he added, coaxing from his father a grimacing smile, a cough masquerading as a chuckle.

"Johnny . . . I had William de Mandeville and William Fitz Ralph swear to me . . . swear that should any evil befall me, they'll surrender my castles to you, and to you alone. Not to Richard, God rot him, not to Richard . . ."

To John, that sounded more like a concession of defeat than a declaration of trust. "Surely you do not expect it to come to that, Papa?"

There was a wine flagon on the bedside table, and Henry gestured, waited till John poured out a cupful. "Of course not, lad. You'll never see the day dawn when I let them get the better of me," he said, with a bravado that might have been more convincing had John not needed to help him up in order to drink. "Le Mans was not the first town I've lost in my life, will not be the last . . ." He drank deeply, signaled for John to lower him back against the pillows.

"Johnny . . . listen, lad. I have not forgotten my promise to you. I do mean to give you the earldom of Mortain, give you the revenues from Cornwall . . ."

John's mouth twisted. For how many years had he been hearing this? Promises he had in plenty, but little else. His brother Henry had been the heir apparent, Geoffrey had been Duke of Brittany, and Richard was Duke of Aquitaine, Count of Poitou. But him? John Lackland. He'd been betrothed since age nine to his cousin Avisa, a bride to bring him the rich earldom of Gloucester, but that, too, was proving to be an empty expectation; the very least that could be said of a twelve-year-old betrothal was that his father was in no tearing hurry to have him tie so lucrative a nuptial knot. It was John's private suspicion that his father denied him incomes of his own for the same reason he'd refused to name Richard as his heir, to keep them close, puppet Princes who'd dance to his tune only.

"I think you should rest now, Papa," he said, and Henry nodded; sweat was breaking out again on his forehead, trickling into his beard.

"The fever is worse at night," he mumbled. "Stay with me till I sleep."

The chamber was heavy with the fetid odors of illness, with stifling summer heat. John soon began to sweat, too, began to yearn for a lungful of the cooling night air so fatal to the sickroom. At last Henry found relief in sleep; his hold slackened, fingers no longer clutched. John gently disengaged his hand, wiped his palm against the sheet, and came to his feet.

He stood for some moments looking down at his father, until joined by Geoffrey.

"He's dying, is he not?"

"Yes." Geoffrey gave John a thoughtful look. "You surprise me, John; you sound as if you care."

John caught his breath. "Damn you, of course I care!"

Henry groaned, fumbled with the blankets, and Geoffrey at once bent over the bed, making soothing sounds, lulling the older man back into sleep. John watched until Henry quieted again, then turned away with such haste that, to Geoffrey, it seemed not so much an exit as an escape.

                              *   *   *

Entering his own chamber, John was reaching for a wine flagon
when he caught movement from the corner of his eye, spun
around to see the girl cowering in the shadows.

"Who are you?"

"Do not be angry, my lord," she pleaded, stumbling forward
to make an exceedingly awkward curtsy. "I . . . I am Lucy, and
I am here because Master Randolph . . . he thought . . ."

Her painful stammer, her flaming face told John quite clearly
what Master Randolph thought. His first impulse was to get rid
of her, but even as the dismissal was forming on his tongue, he
changed his mind. What better way to exorcise the horrors of the
sickroom than with flesh that was smooth and whole and healthy?
Moreover, he had ever hated to be alone. Tonight of all nights,
even the company of this timid little maidservant was preferable
to his own.

"Remind me to thank Master Randolph," he said and smiled
at her. "Be a good lass now and fetch me some wine."

But the wine did not help as he'd hoped. Instead of dulling his
anxieties, it acted as a stimulant, spurring his imagination into
unpleasant excesses, conjuring up half-forgotten fears of boyhood
and projecting them into a future that suddenly seemed fraught
with menace.

"He's dying, Lucy. Did you know that?"

"Yes, my lord," she whispered. Hastening to refill his wine
cup, she approached the bed and then skittered back out of range,
putting him in mind of a squirrel caught between trees.

He'd sent Lucy down to the buttery for another wine flagon
when he heard a commotion in the stairwell. He sat up on the bed
as Martin Algais and Lupescaire burst into the chamber.

"Look what we found in the stairwell." Shoving Lucy forward into the room. "What is that saying about a bird in the
hand?"

John was not amused. Algais and Lupescaire were Brabançons,
men who sold their swords to the highest bidder. In the past he
had permitted, even encouraged, familiarity, dicing and drinking
with them, treating them as intimates. But tonight he had no
desire for their company, and he found himself resenting the way
they were making free with what was his, Lupescaire helping
himself to the wine while Martin Algais backed Lucy into a corner,
laughing at her ineffectual attempts to fend off his roving hands.

"I do not recall summoning you," John said irritably, as
Lupescaire handed him a brimming wine cup.

"The talk amongst our men is that the old King is in a bad way. You did see him, my lord; how does he, in truth?"

John could not, in fairness, fault them for their concern; their future, like his own, rose and fell with each labored breath Henry drew. But they were servants, companions, handpicked hirelings—not confidants.

"Well enough," he said, had his cup halfway to his mouth when Lucy screamed. His hand jerked, and wine splashed onto the bed, splattered his tunic. John jumped to his feet with an oath. "Damn your soul, Martin, look at this!" He stared down at the wine spill in disgust, then turned to glare at Algais. "Must you ever have your hand up a woman's skirts? If you want to tumble a wench, you can damned well do it someplace else than in my chamber. Let that girl be, and get a servant up here to change these bedcovers."

But Algais did not move. Holding the weeping girl with one hand, with the other he reached for the neck of her gown, jerked until the material tore, baring her breasts.

"Did you not hear me?" John demanded, astonished. "I told you to let the girl alone."

"Why?" Algais sounded sullen, defiant. "We've shared women before; why not now?"

Lupescaire put his wine cup down, eyes suddenly aglitter, cutting from John to Algais and back again. John's mouth went dry; never had either of them dared to defy him before. "Because I say so, Martin. You take what I choose to give you, no more and no less."

Algais had very pale eyes, an unblinking, feral stare. But after a few frozen breaths, he loosened his hold on Lucy. "You want me to ask? Then I'm asking. I have taken a fancy to this one; let me have her for an hour."

It would be so easy to agree, a face-saving solution for them both, and John was very tempted; he'd never had a stomach for confrontation. But he knew better, knew it had to be all or nothing with a man like Martin Algais.

"No," he said.

Algais's fingers clenched, dug into Lucy's upper arm, and she sobbed anew. But then he pushed her away.

John's breathing slowed, steadied. "Go down to the great hall," he said. "Send a servant up to me. You need not come back after. I've no use for you tonight."

He'd won. They did as he bade, if not docile, at least unrebelling. John moved to the table, poured the last of the wine with a shaking hand. He knew them for what they were, his pet wolves, but he'd never thought they might turn on him. He knew why, of course. For the same reason that Geoffrey had suddenly dared to voice his dislike. The scent of blood was in the air.

Lucy was still sobbing, and he snapped, "Will you stop your whimpering, girl? You were not hurt, after all!" But as he turned toward her, he saw that was not true. There was an angry red welt upon her left breast; there would soon be an exceedingly ugly bruise.

"Do not cry, lass," he said, more gently, and then she was on her knees before him, clinging to his legs, weeping incoherently. It was some moments before he could make sense of her sobbing, before he realized that she was feverishly, hysterically thanking him for saving her from Martin Algais. John choked back an unsteady, mirthless laugh, raised her up.

"Lucy, listen to me. Dry your tears and go down to the hall. Find my squire, tell him to get up here. Then go to the kitchen, tell the cooks I said to give you mutton fat for that bruise." As he spoke, he was steering her toward the door. "After that, lass, go to bed . . . your own."

Giving him an incredulous look, she fled. Within moments his squire was panting up the stairs. "My lord, what is amiss? That girl acted so strange . . ."

"Get our men together. I want us ready to ride within the hour."

"Ride where? My lord, it's full dark. Where would we go? At such an hour, we might well have to bed down by the roadside—"

"I was giving you a command, not inviting a debate. I want to be gone from here as soon as we can saddle up, and if you make me repeat that, you'll have more regrets than you can handle. Now see to it!"

Hastily the man said, "I will, my lord, indeed. But . . . but what of your lord father? I've been told he sleeps; is it your wish that he be awakened ere you depart?"

"No," John said. "Let him sleep."

"I know you Angevins have ever been short of brotherly love, but surely John is not as worthless as you think? Admittedly, I know him not well, but he never struck me as a fool."

"Oh, John is clever enough. But what do brains avail a man if he does lack for backbone?"

In Richard's lexicon of insults, that was the most damning accusation he could make, and to Philip, it cast a revealing light upon Richard's relationship with his younger brother. He found himself feeling a touch of sympathy for John, who'd been weighed against Richard's exacting standards of manhood and found wanting, for he knew that he, too, had failed to measure up in Richard's eyes; their friendship had never been the same since Richard discovered that he had an irrational fear of horses, rode only the most docile of geldings.

"But to be fair," Richard said grudgingly, "my father has ever played the same game with John as he did with me and, whilst they lived, Geoffrey and Henry, promising all and delivering nothing. Although the one time he did entrust John with power of his own, sent him to Ireland, it was an unmitigated disaster. So badly did John bungle his rule that he achieved the all but impossible; he got the Irish chieftains to stop squabbling with one another and unite against him!"

"Surely that was Henry's blunder as much as John's. You do not send a boy of seventeen to do a man's work."

"When I was seventeen, I was putting down a rebellion in Poitou," Richard said pointedly, and Philip, conceding defeat with a wry smile, signaled to a servant.

"We'll see Lord John now."

John had rarely been so nervous; eleventh-hour allies were not always welcomed with open arms. He was much relieved, therefore, when the French King smiled as he knelt, at once motioned him to rise.

"Your Grace," he said, with an answering smile that lost all spontaneity, all sincerity, at sight of his brother. Even in the dim light of a command tent, Richard's coloring had lost none of its vibrancy, eyes blazingly blue, hair bronzed even brighter now by a summer in the saddle. Most likely, John thought sourly, he did glow in the dark. "Richard," he said, as if they'd been parted just that morning, and Richard gave him an equally indifferent greeting in return.

"You did surprise me, John," he said dryly. "I'd expected you to turn up weeks ago. Cutting it rather close, were you not, Little Brother?"

Fortunately for John, hatred choked all utterance. He stared at Richard, reminding himself this was but one more grievance to be credited to Richard's account, promising himself that payment would be in the coin of his choosing.

Philip had been watching the Angevin brothers with covert amusement. Now he asked the question John most dreaded. "John . . . how does Henry?"

John had given this a great deal of thought in the hours since his midnight flight from Chinon. He had no way of knowing if Philip and Richard were aware of the gravity of Henry's illness, could only hope they were not; an infidel who converted at knife-point had, of necessity, to count for less than one who willingly renounced his heresy.

"I do not know, Your Grace. I've not seen my father since we fled Le Mans."

Richard and Philip exchanged glances, and then Richard said, "Rumor has it he is bedridden, but I expect it's yet another of his damnable tricks; he could teach a fox about slyness."

John said nothing, concentrated his attention upon a nearby fruit bowl. Picking out two apples, he tossed one to Richard, a sudden, swift pitch that disconcerted Richard not in the least. He caught it with the utmost ease, his the lithe coordination, the lazy, loose grace of the born athlete. John doubted that Richard had made a careless misstep, a clumsy move in all of his thirty-one years.

Richard crunched into the apple. "Let's talk about you, Little Brother. What is the going price for—" He caught himself, but not in time.

"Betrayal? What game are we playing now, Richard? If we are tallying up sins, I rather doubt you're in any position to cast the first stone."

There was a silence, and then Richard gave a short laugh. "Fair enough. I deserved that. Let me put it another way. What do you want for your support?"

"Only what be my just due," John said cautiously, "what I've been promised since boyhood. The county of Mortain, the earldom of Gloucester, the incomes from the lordship of Ireland, Nottingham Castle."

Richard did not hesitate. "Done," he said, so readily that John regretted not asking for more.

He murmured a perfunctory expression of appreciation, and then said, "You might want to do something for our brother Geoffrey, too. If I were you, Richard, I'd keep Geoffrey in mind when it comes time to fill the next vacant bishopric."

Richard frowned, but after a moment he began to laugh. "An excellent thought, Little Brother. I shall do just that."

Philip looked from one to the other in bemusement. "I seem to have missed something. Correct me if I be wrong, but I never thought either one of you to be overly fond of Geoffrey. Why, then, do you want to make him a bishop?"

"Geoffrey has no more calling for the priesthood than I have,"
Richard said with a grin. "Some years ago, our father sought for
him a career in the Church, tried to make him Bishop of Lincoln,
but he balked, refused to be ordained. So we'd be doing him no
favor."

"Brother Geoffrey has ambitions ill befitting his base blood,"
John added softly. "Too often have I heard him remind people
that William the Conqueror was himself bastard born."

Philip saw the light. "And as a priest, he would, of course, be
barred from ever laying claim to the crown. Clever, John, very
clever. But risky. What's to keep Richard from concluding that
Holy Orders might do your soul great good, too?"

Richard laughed until he choked, sputtering something
unintelligible about "Father John." John laughed, too, but his
eyes narrowed on Philip with sudden speculation. Philip, he
decided, was one for muddying the waters. That would indeed
bear remembering.

"You did arrive just in time, John. We are about to lay siege
to Tours, for its fall is sure to force the old fox from his lair. This
campaign has dragged on far too long. It's nigh on two years
since I did take the cross; I'd hoped to be before the walls of
Jerusalem months ago." Richard paused, then said with sudden
seriousness, "Philip will be leading a French army, and we
expect men to flock to our standards. You ought to give some
thought to taking the cross yourself, John. What better quest can
a man have than pledging his life to the delivery of the Holy City
from the infidels?"

John was appalled, forced a strained laugh. "The truth now,
Richard," he said with what he hoped would be disarming
candor. "Can you truly see me as a pious pilgrim on the road to
Damascus?"

Philip laughed; so did Richard. "No," he admitted, "I confess
I cannot, Little Brother. You'd disappear into some Saracen
harem, never to be heard from again!"

John smiled thinly, marveling that Richard should dare to
sneer at another man's sexual habits, given Richard's own vulnerabilities in that particular area. There were, he thought scornfully, worse vices than liking women overly well. But all at once
he found himself thinking of that ugly scene at Chinon, remembering the fear he'd felt when facing down Martin Algais. That
would, he knew, never have happened to Richard. Men did not
defy his brother. The foolhardy few who'd dared were dead. He
had a sudden wild impulse to tell Richard that their father was

dying, wondering what Richard would say or feel. Nothing, he suspected. Everything was always so damnably easy for Richard.

John was the youngest of the eight children born to Henry Plantagenet and Eleanor of Aquitaine. His sisters had been bartered as child brides to foreign Princes, were little more to him now than time-dimmed memories. His brothers had been, by turns, indifferent and antagonistic to this last-born of the Angevin eaglets—with one exception. William Longsword was, like Geoffrey, a bastard half-brother. But Will had somehow missed his share of the Angevin temperament; his was a placid, unimaginative nature, sentimental and straightforward, an unlikely drab grey dove in that family of flamboyant hawks. Will had been amiably interested in the little brother born within days of his own tenth birthday, had taken it upon himself to wipe John's nose, to pick him up when he fell, to be for John a good-natured guide through the pitfalls and passages of childhood. He'd become quite fond of the dark little boy so eager to please, had watched rather sadly as John was utterly ignored by his mother, overly indulged by his father, as the twig was bent, twisted awry, seeing the distortion but not knowing how to set it right. Yet the bonds of boyhood had proven to be enduring ones, and Will and John did to this day enjoy a relationship remarkably free of strain in a family notorious for its internecine rivalries.

It was nightfall by the time Will reached Rouen and was escorted up to John's chamber. John greeted him with a grin, with genuine pleasure, at once sent to the castle buttery for wine, even dismissed an uncommonly pretty bedmate so they could talk alone.

Richard had that day departed Rouen for Gisors, where Philip awaited him, and John and Will joked now about the exorbitant price Philip was likely to claim for his support in securing Richard the crown. Will could not help thinking that John, too, had profited handsomely. Richard had wasted no time in investing his younger brother as Count of Mortain; John's marriage to Avisa of Gloucester was to take place on August 29, and Will had heard that Richard meant to bestow upon John the incomes from the English counties of Cornwall, Devon, Dorset, Somerset, Nottingham, and Derby. Will thought Richard had been surprisingly generous, and said as much to John.

"That," John said cheerfully, "is because I am—by the vagaries of fate—Brother Richard's heir. And Richard's more peculiar proclivities do make it at least likely that I'll be the only heir."

Will sighed, feeling much like a parent with a loved but wayward child. "Bear in mind, lad, what Scriptures say about coveting," he said mildly, and John laughed.

"What we need to do now, Will, is to get Richard to find an heiress for you ere he goes galloping off to find martyrdom in Messina—or was it sainthood in Syria? Can you believe the man, Will? He's not even set the date for his coronation yet, and all he can talk about is how he cannot wait to risk his life in some infidel hellhole. I truly think he must be mad," John said, with such sincerity that Will had to laugh.

"If you can coax Richard into giving me a landed wife, I'll be much in your debt. But now we do need to talk. I rode in from Fontevrault with Geoffrey. He's right bitter, John, like to say that which would be better left unsaid. I thought I'd best get to you first, tell—"

"My lord? My lord, your brother—"

Geoffrey did not wait to be announced, but shoved the servant aside, and strode into the chamber. "I do want to talk to you, John."

"How lucky for me," John said coolly, signaled to the servant to pour them wine. "What shall we drink to, Geoffrey? Your good fortune? Did he tell you, Will, that Richard has ordered the canons of York to elect Brother Geoffrey as their Archbishop? Of course, there is still a minor matter of taking vows, but that is a small price to pay to become a Prince of the Church, is it not?"

"I rather thought I had you to thank for that," Geoffrey said. "But that is not why I'm here, and you damned well know it, John. I'm going to tell you how our father died, and you're going to listen."

"Am I indeed?" John's eyes had gone very green. "I think not. If you want to lay blame about, lay it where it belongs—on Richard's head. Not mine. If you have anything to say, say it then to Richard!"

"I did . . . at Fontevrault. He at least was man enough to hear me out. Are you?"

John had half risen from his chair. With that, he sank back. "Say what you have to say and then get out."

"Gladly." Geoffrey reached over and, without asking, helped himself to one of the wine cups. "I would to God I knew what Papa saw in you. He kept faith to the end, you know. Even your cowardly flight from Chinon did not open his eyes. Almost to the last, he kept expecting you to come back, even worried about you, if you can credit that!"

"Geoffrey," Will said uneasily, "this does serve for naught . . ."

"Keep out of this, Will. On July third, Tours fell, and Philip and Richard summoned Papa to Colombières. He was sick unto death, made it only as far as the Knights Templars at Ballan. But when he sent word to Philip, Richard insisted he was malingering, playing for time. By then he could barely stay in the saddle, but he refused a horse litter, somehow got himself to Colombières. Even Philip was moved to pity at sight of him, even Philip, offered to spread a cloak on the ground for him. But he would not agree. He was too proud, you see . . ." Geoffrey's voice had thickened; he drank, keeping his eyes all the while upon John.

"They told him he was there not to discuss terms, but to yield to their demands. They dared to speak so to him, and he could do nothing about it. Then they told him what they wanted. He must do homage to Philip for his lands in Normandy and Anjou, accept Philip as his overlord. He must pay Philip twenty thousand marks, must have all his barons swear fealty to Richard, must promise not to take vengeance upon those who'd betrayed him. All this they demanded—and more. By then the noonday sky was black as ink, sweat ran off him like rain, and how he ever kept to his saddle, the Lord Christ Jesus alone does know. But they were not through yet. He must publicly give Richard the kiss of peace, they said. Even that he did, even that . . . and then hissed in Richard's ear, 'God grant I do not die ere I have revenged myself upon you.' Of course, you may already know that, John. I understand Richard told one and all at the French court, as if it were some droll joke!

"We brought him back to Chinon by horse litter, and I watched through the night as his fever burned ever higher. The next day Roger Malchet rode in from Tours with a list of rebels, those men who'd gone over to Philip and Richard. Need I tell you, John, that your name did head the list?"

Geoffrey paused, but John said nothing. "He did not believe it at first, cursed Roger, me, all within hearing, accused us of lying, of trying to poison his mind against you, his 'dearest born.' And when he could deny it no longer, he turned his face to the wall, said no more. Within hours he was dead. His last words to me were, 'You are my true son. The others—they are the bastards.'

"There were only a few of us with him at the last; most had already taken themselves off to Richard's encampment. Whilst I was in the chapel, his servants stripped his body, stole rings, clothing, whatever they could find. We'd have had to bury him

mother-naked had not one of his squires let us wrap the body in
his cloak, and as it was, we had not even money for alms.

"So died the greatest Prince in Christendom, our lord father.
You think on that, John, think on how he died, and then tell me
again that you bear no blame. Well? Have you nothing to say?
Passing strange, neither did Richard."

Geoffrey drained the wine cup very deliberately, turned and
walked to the door. "Richard forced him from a sickbed, broke
his power, his pride. But you, John, you broke his heart. I truly
wonder which be the greater sin."

Will shifted uncomfortably as the door slammed, slanted a
surreptitious look toward John. It may have been the dim lighting, but John seemed to have lost color. He'd turned his head
away; his face was in profile, utterly still, masklike. Will fidgeted, opened his mouth, and then sat back, defeated. What,
after all, was there to say?

4

SOUTHAMPTON, ENGLAND

February 1192

Will was frowning as he followed a servant up the stairwell to his brother's chamber, dreading the scene that was sure to follow. He was almost tempted to stand aside, to let John rush headlong to his own destruction. Almost.

His mouth softened somewhat at sight of the man and boy together on the settle. John was surprisingly good with children, could not be faulted when it came to the care of his own, and whenever Will found himself despairing of his brother's flexible measurements of morality, he took comfort in remembering how conscientious John was in acknowledging and providing for the children born of his bedsport. That was no small virtue to Will, himself born of Henry's passing lust for a green-eyed milkmaid with well-turned ankles.

He was as yet unnoticed. John was holding out his hands, fists clenched. "Now tell me, Richard. Which hand holds the fig?" The little boy pointed. "Sorry! This hand, then? No, wrong again. Where did it go? Ah, there it is . . ." Reaching out, he seemed to find the fig behind the child's ear, to Will's amusement and Richard's utter delight.

"One more time, Papa!" he pleaded, as John turned at sound of Will's chuckle. For an unguarded moment, his face showed sudden unease, and then he smiled, beckoned Will into the room.

" 'One more time,' " he mimicked. " 'One more time.' Mayhap we ought to call you that rather than Richard!" He then plucked the fig from Richard's sleeve, while Will watched and wondered, not for the first time, what perverse impulse had prompted John to name his son after the brother he so hated. As with much of what John did, the answer eluded him. Will had

52

long ago recognized that his imagination was rooted in barren soil; no matter how he strained, it brought forth only a meagre crop, never the sort of creative conjecture he'd have needed to track the twisting byways of his brother's brain.

Richard was munching on the elusive fig; now he offered the uneaten half first to John and then to Will, with a gravely deliberate courtesy that was both unexpected and poignant in one so very young. He was, Will knew, just shy of his third birthday, a date well etched in Will's memory because of the scandal attached to that birth. For Richard's mother was quite unlike John's other bedmates, was no impoverished knight's daughter, no Saxon maidservant. Alina was the daughter of Hamelin de Warenne, Earl of Surrey, half-brother to King Henry, albeit baseborn.

That was the first and only time Will could remember Henry showing concern for one of his sons' sexual escapades. He had even taken it upon himself to rebuke John for seducing a first cousin, a girl of high birth. Unfortunately, his own moral armor was particularly vulnerable to that very charge, and he succeeded only in arousing in John an indignation that was, Will conceded, not altogether unjustified. John's involvement with Alina was of minor moment, after all, when compared to Henry's seduction of the Princess Alais.

Will did not like to think of Alais; he was by nature protective of women, and he could not deny that Alais had been ill used, first by his father and now by Richard. Sister to Philip, the French King, she had been betrothed to Richard in childhood and, at age seven, was sent to England to be reared at Henry's court in accordance with custom. It was hardly customary, though, Will thought grimly, for a man to bed his son's betrothed, and yet his father had done just that, had taken Alais to his bed when she was sixteen. It was scarcely surprising, Will acknowledged, that upon Henry's death Richard refused to honor the plight troth, telling Philip bluntly that he'd not wed his father's whore. Will saw no justification, however, for keeping Alais in close confinement, and yet for almost three years now, Richard had held Alais prisoner in Rouen.

But Will had troubles enough of his own without taking on those of a captive French Princess, and he shifted impatiently in his seat, waiting for John to send Richard off to bed so they could talk.

"You did that trick with the fig very adroitly. Where did you learn it?"

"From a juggler at the French court. He told me that I have a rare gift for sleight of hand!"

John looked at him, eyes alight with laughter, and Will felt a dull ache, a wrenching realization that he was too late, years too late. Yet he had to try, and as soon as Richard's nurse came to collect the boy, he said very quietly, "John . . . do not do this."

"Do what, Will?"

"I know why you are here in Southampton. You mean to sail for France, to meet in Paris with the French King."

"Is that why you came racing from London? Poor Will . . . you did bruise your bones for naught, in truth." John's smile was wry, faintly reproachful. "I am about to sail as soon as the weather does clear, but for Normandy, not France."

He was more than plausible, he was thoroughly convincing, and he was lying. Will leaned over, grasped his wrist. "John, do not play me for a fool. You owe me better than that. If I cared enough to make an eighty-mile ride in weather as foul as this, then you can damned well hear me out!"

"All right, Will," John said slowly, taken aback by this uncharacteristic outburst. "What makes you think I mean to ally myself with Philip?"

"Because Philip and Richard buried what was left of their friendship in the Holy Land. Because Richard is still in Acre and Philip is now back in Paris, nursing a mortal grudge. Because you'd barter your very soul for a chance to do Richard ill. Because Philip has of a sudden invited you to Paris. Need I go on?"

"If disliking Richard be grounds for accusing a man of conspiracy, I daresay you could implicate half of Christendom in this so-called plot," John scoffed. "Richard endears himself easiest to those who've yet to meet him." Rising, he moved to the table, gained time to think by pouring himself a cupful of cider. He poured, too, for Will, stood for a moment looking down at the older man. So, he thought suddenly, must their father have looked at thirty-four, for Will had Henry's reddish gold hair, his ruddy coloring, even the same scattering of freckles across the bridge of the nose.

"Just suppose, Will, that you are right, that I do mean to throw my lot in with Philip. If you had proof of that, what would you do? Go to my lady mother? Betray me to Richard?"

Will's shoulders slumped. "No," he mumbled, full of self-loathing. "You know I could not."

"Do not begrudge me your loyalty, Will. I deserve it more

than Richard, for he loves you not and I love you well." John
thrust a dripping cider cup into Will's hand, took the closest seat.
"I even love you enough to trust you with the truth. Did you by
chance see a monk in the great hall when you arrived? That is
Brother Bernard de Coudray, Philip's man. You were right, of
course; Philip has indeed made me an offer. 'All the lands of
England and Normandy on the French side of the Channel.' I
need only swear homage to him as overlord, and once we get his
sister Alais out of Richard's power, take her to wife."

Will choked on his cider, began to sputter. "Christ Jesus,
John! You cannot mean that? You'd truly agree to wed Alais?"

"Why not?"

Will drew a strangled breath. "For one thing," he snapped,
"you already do have a wife! Or did that somehow slip your
mind?"

John drank to conceal a grin; his brother's ponderous attempts
at sarcasm never failed to amuse him, but he did not want to
offend Will by laughing outright. "Have you forgotten that Avisa
is my second cousin? Or that we neglected to get a papal dispensation for our marriage? Nor need your heart bleed for Avisa, the
abandoned wife. We may not agree on much, but we do share a
deep and very mutual dislike."

"But Alais! She bedded with Papa for years and all know it,
even bore him a stillborn son!"

John shrugged. "Being Papa's concubine does not make her
any less Philip's sister, and if she's the price for Philip's support
. . . at least we'd be keeping her in the family!"

"That's not amusing, John! How can you jest about betrayal
and treason, a marriage all but incestuous?"

John set his cup down with a thud. "What would you have me
do? It's been sixteen months since Richard named our dead
brother Geoffrey's son as his heir, nine months since my lady
mother coerced him into taking a Spanish wife. Nine months,
Will. For all I know, she could already be with child. What if she
is, if she manages a miracle, keeps Richard in her bed long
enough to give him a son?"

"Ah, John . . . you'd still be Count of Mortain, Earl of
Gloucester, with an income of four thousand pounds a year. Can
you not content yourself with that?"

John stared at him, and then gave a short, incredulous laugh.
"God help you, Will, I truly think you're serious!"

Until that moment, Will had been slow to see the magnitude of
his mistake. Had he really thought he could talk sense into John?

All he'd done was to take on a share of the guilt, to compromise himself in the complicity of silence.

"Do not leave on the morrow, Will. Stay till week's end. How is your manor at Kirton? This was a bad year for crops; if you're in need of money . . ."

Will had no false pride, saw no reason to refuse aid from John, not when he had only the manors of Kirton and Appleby, and John had the revenues from six shires. He made a point, though, of not abusing John's generosity, never asking unless there was a specific need. "Thank you, lad, no. I do not—"

"My lord!" A flustered servant stumbled into the chamber. "My lord, the Queen has just ridden into the bailey!"

John spilled his cider. "That cannot be! My mother is in Normandy."

"No, my lord, she's in the great hall."

"You both are wrong," a cool voice said from the doorway. "I'm out in the stairwell."

Will jumped to his feet. He was very much in awe of John's mother, for Eleanor of Aquitaine was more than the widow of one King, mother to another. She was a creature rarer even than the unicorn, a woman who, all her life, had been a law unto herself, as Duchess of Aquitaine, then as Queen of France, and finally as Queen of England. She had in her past two failed royal marriages, a crusade, scandal and lovers, even a rebellion, for when Henry betrayed her, she'd incited their sons to civil war, had spent sixteen years in confinement as a result. But she'd won in the end, had outlived the husband who'd shut her away from the world, from her beloved Aquitaine. Moreover, she had somehow survived those bitter years with her soul unscarred, her spirit unbroken.

Upon regaining her freedom, she had, at age sixty-nine, journeyed to Navarre to fetch a bride for her favorite son, brought the girl across the Alps to Richard in Sicily. She was now in her seventy-first year, and in the high, elegantly hollowed cheekbones, the posture that conceded nothing to age, and the slanting green-gold eyes, Will could still see traces of the great beauty she'd once been. He was both fascinated and repelled by this woman who'd dared to outrage every tenet of the code governing proper female behavior, but he was glad, nonetheless, to see her now, for she was the one person John might not dare to defy.

Will watched as John greeted her with guarded formality, did not mind in the least when she made it pleasantly yet perfectly plain that his presence was not required. In a contest of wills between John and his mother, he did not think John would prevail, indeed hoped he would not. But he did not care to be a witness to their confrontation; he suspected Eleanor's methods would be neither maternal nor merciful.

Eleanor snapped her fingers and the last of the servants disappeared. As John handed her a goblet of mulled wine, she sipped in silence for some moments, then confirmed his worst fears. "I do hope you have not entangled poor Will in your intriguing, John. That would be rather unsporting, like spearing fish in a barrel."

"Should I know what that means, Madame?"

She leaned back against the settle cushions, eyed him reflectively. "Do you have any memories of Gwendolen, John? No, I see not. She was a young Welsh girl, nurse first to your sister Joanna and then to you. I liked her, found the Welsh to be much like my own Poitevins, a people passionate yet practical. There was one Welsh proverb in particular that Gwendolen was fond of quoting: 'Better a friend at court than gold on the finger.' " She smiled faintly, glanced down at her hands, at the jeweled fingers entwined loosely in her lap. "As you can see, I have gold rings in profusion. But I also have friends at court, John . . . at the French court."

She waited, but John continued to look at her blankly, with the suggestion of a quizzical smile. "Why is it," he asked, "that I suddenly feel as if I've stumbled into the wrong conversation?"

"You do that very well, John. Honest bewilderment, with just the right touch of humor. I do not doubt your indignation will be equally impressive. And if you insist, we can play the game out to the end. I'll tell you exactly what my informants at the French court revealed, and you can deny any and all knowledge of Philip's intrigues. I'll confront you with the fact that I know you've coerced the constables of Wallingford, Berkshire, and Windsor to turn over the royal castles to you, and you can then concoct some perfectly innocent explanation for that.

"But eventually, John, we'll get to the truth. It may well take all night, but we will, that I promise you. So why do you not make it easy on both of us? It has been a very long day. I'm tired, John, am asking you to keep this charade mercifully brief . . . for my sake if not your own."

John could not say with which precise word she hit a nerve; it may have been the tone as much as the content. But by the time she stopped speaking, he was rigid with rage. "For your sake?

There was a time when I'd have done anything on God's earth for you, just to get you to acknowledge I was even alive! But now? You're too late, Mother, years too late!''

There was a sudden silence. John rose, retreated into the sheltering shadows beyond the hearth, but he could not escape her eyes, could feel them following him all the while. What had ever possessed him? Fool! In lashing out like that, he'd only shown her where his defenses were weakest, most vulnerable to attack.

"What would you have me say, John?" she said at last. "That you are my flesh and blood, my last-born, that I care, care more than you know? It would be easy enough to say, and I admit I might be tempted . . . if I thought you'd believe me."

"I would not," he said hastily, and she gave him an unexpected smile, a look of sardonic and surprising approval.

"Why should you? You were not yet six when Henry confined me in Salisbury Tower, sixteen when next I saw you, twenty-one when Richard ordered my release. How could I love you? I do not even know you. You were ever Henry's, never mine."

"That's a lie," John said bitterly. "You never cared for me, never! Not from the day I was born. You think I do not remember how it was?"

"You exaggerate," she said, but there was that in her voice which he'd never heard before, a faintly defensive note. "Mayhap I did not have you with me as often as I should in those early years; I'll concede that. I'll concede, too, that I could take no joy in a pregnancy at forty-five. Why should I? I had just found out about Henry and that Clifford slut. He'd even dared to install her at Woodstock—Woodstock, my favorite manor!" She stopped abruptly, and John saw that she, too, had been goaded into saying that which she'd not meant to share.

"It is a pretty fiction that mothers must love each child in equal measure . . . a fiction, no more than that. There is always a favorite. With me, it was Richard. With Henry, it was you."

"No," John said, too quickly. "I was not his favorite. It was rather that I was the only son he had left. Have you forgotten? My brothers sided with you."

Again, John had the disquieting sense that he'd have done better to hold his tongue. Eleanor's eyes were too probing, too knowing. Cat's eyes, ever on the alert for movement in the grass, he thought uneasily, not reassured when she shrugged, said, "If that's how you'd rather remember it. But I did not mean that as a reproach. I do not, in truth, think less of you for having the common sense to abandon a ship once waves began to break over the bow. Nor, after sixteen years shut away from the sun, am I likely to find tears to spare for Henry Plantagenet.''

Without warning, she came abruptly to her feet, crossed swiftly to John. ''But Richard—that is another matter altogether, John. Did you truly think I'd stand idly by whilst you plotted with Philip to usurp Richard's throne?''

When he sought to move away, she caught his arm. ''Of my children, I have ever loved Richard best, have never made a secret of it. My first loyalties are to him, will always be to him. But what you do not seem to realize is that they are then given to you. You want to be Richard's heir. Well, I, too, want that for you, am willing to do what I can to make it so.''

She sounded sincere, but John knew how little that meant; neither of his parents had ever held veracity to be a virtue. ''Why?'' he said warily. ''The soul of sentiment you're not . . . Mother.''

She laughed. ''To your credit, neither are you. I've always thought sentimentality to be one of the cardinal sins, second only to stupidity.''

That afforded John a certain ironic amusement, for it was his private conviction that his brother Richard was decidedly stupid, in all but killing, at which he excelled. But he said nothing, let Eleanor lead him back to the settle.

''Richard's marriage is not working out. Unfortunately, the girl is as insipid as she is innocent, and so absurdly sweet-tempered that I suspect if you cut her, she'd bleed pure sugar. She and Richard . . . well, it's been like pairing a butterfly with a gerfalcon. I do not think it likely she'll give him a son.''

''And if she does not, that leaves only me . . . or Geoffrey's son. Richard prefers the boy; why do you not, Madame?''

''Arthur is not yet five; you're twenty and four. That in itself would be reason enough to favor you. And you are my son; that's another. Lastly, I think you have it in you to be a better King than your past record would indicate. At least you're no fool, and most men are.''

''Even if you do favor me over Arthur, what of it? Richard has already made his choice.''

''No choice this side of the grave is irrevocable. Richard named Arthur as a means of keeping you in check whilst he was on crusade. Once he does return from the Holy Land, he may well reconsider, especially if I urge him to do so. I'm sure you'll agree that if there be one voice he heeds, it is mine. If I speak for you, he's like to listen. But it does cut both ways, John. If I speak against you, he's apt to listen then, too. So it is up to you."

"What do you want me to do?"

"It is rather what I want you to refrain from doing. No intrigues with Philip. No pleasure jaunts to Paris. No conniving with the Welsh or the Scots." She paused, hazel eyes holding his own. Satisfied with what she saw in them, she rose, stifling a yawn. "I expect a bedchamber has been made ready for me by now, so I'll bid you good night. I'm glad we did reach an understanding. But I rather thought we would, Johnny."

"Do not call me that!" John said sharply, startling himself even more than Eleanor. She stared at him, eyebrows arching, and he flushed.

"I'd almost forgotten," she said softly. "That was what Henry always called you, was it not?"

John said nothing, and she moved toward the door, where she paused, turned to face him. "If you should happen to suffer a change of heart in the night, John, decide that Philip's offer is a better gamble than mine . . . I think it only fair to tell you that, on the same day you sailed for France, I would personally give the command to seize all your lands, castles, and manors in England, confiscate them on behalf of the crown." And closing the door quietly behind her, she left him alone.

5

GWYNEDD, WALES

January 1193

They left Hawarden Castle in the early hours of a cloud-darkened dawn. A week of unrelenting rains had reduced the road to a mere memory, and as they headed west into Wales, they found themselves trudging through mud as thick and clinging as molasses. It spattered their legs and tunics, squished into their boots, made them fight for every footprint of ground gained. Exhaustion soon claimed Edwin; so, too, did disillusionment. Stumbling after his companions, blinded by gusts of wind-driven rain, chilled and utterly wretched, he could only wonder where the glory had gone.

All of his eighteen years had been passed in the Cheshire village of Aldford. He had never even seen Chester, a mere five miles to the north. But three months ago his cousin Godfrey had come back to Aldford. Godfrey was a legend in their family, the youth who'd willingly abandoned home and hearth for the alien world waiting without. Godfrey was a solidarius, a man who fought for pay, and he told his awestruck kin that he was now being paid by no less a lord than Ralph de Montalt, Lord of Hawarden and Mold, Seneschal of Chester. And then he told them why he'd come back: for Edwin.

There was no question of refusal; any village lad would have pledged his soul for such a chance. Much envied, Edwin had accompanied Godfrey back to Hawarden, eager to learn about war and women and the world beckoning beyond Aldford. But at Hawarden he'd found only long hours, loneliness, scant pleasure. Garrison guard duty was monotonous and dreary. But this was far worse, this was unmitigated misery, and as he tripped and sprawled into the mud, blistered and sore and soaked to the skin,

Edwin wished fervently that he'd never even heard of Godfrey, that he'd never laid eyes upon Hawarden Castle.

Of their mission, he knew only that the young knight they were escorting had an urgent message for Davydd ab Owain, a Welsh Prince who had allied himself with the Normans. Godfrey had told him the Welsh Prince was encamped at Rhuddlan Castle, some twenty-five miles from Hawarden, and he wondered how long the journey would take. He wondered, too, why they were no longer following the coast, why they'd swung inland at Basingwerk Abbey.

"Godfrey?" He quickened his pace, caught his cousin's arm. "Godfrey, why did we change our route? Are we not more vulnerable to attack in the hills?"

"You'd bloody well better believe it!" Godfrey tripped, cursed as the mud sucked at one of his boots. "But our guide told de Hodnet that this is a quicker way, a road made long past by the Romans. And that Norman whoreson is set upon getting us to Rhuddlan as fast he can, no matter the risk."

Edwin had been about to ask who were these Romans, but with his cousin's last words, he forgot all else, stared at Godfrey in amazement. De Hodnet was a Norman, a knight; to Edwin, that made him a being beyond criticism. He glanced ahead at the knight, his eyes lingering admiringly upon the man's roan stallion, the silvery chain-mail armor. He felt no resentment that de Hodnet should ride while they walked. That was just the way of it, and now he ventured a timid protest.

"But Godfrey, surely he knows what he's doing. After all, he's a knight."

"So? Does that make him the Lord Jesus Christ come down to earth again?" Godfrey sneezed. "Think you that no man Norman-born can be a fool? As for his Norman knighthood, that'll count for naught against a Welsh longbow."

"Should you speak so?" Edwin asked uneasily, provoking a snort of derisive laughter from his cousin.

"You think he'll hear? Nay, he knows just enough English to order us about." Godfrey reached out, grasped Edwin's arm. "If a man is like to lead you over a cliff, Little Cousin, you'd best see him for what he is. De Hodnet wears a long sword and sits a horse well, but he's no more fit to wage war against the Welsh than our Aunt Edith. He's as green as grass, lad, and as arrogant as Lucifer, and there are no more dangerous traits known to man or God."

Edwin stared at him, dismayed. "But . . . but he's been taught the ways of war. All knights . . ."

"Aye, and I daresay he'd fare well enough on a battlefield in France or Flanders. But what does he know of the Welsh? He was in service with Lord Fitz Warin for a time, did garrison duty at Fitz Warin's manor of Lambourne in Berkshire. After that, he found a place with a Wiltshire lord. Then his lord took the cross like King Richard, and de Hodnet had no urge to see the Holy Land." Godfrey sneezed again, spat into the road. "Shropshire, Berkshire, Wiltshire. But not Wales, Edwin, not Wales."

He shook his head, said bitterly, "Giles tried to tell him, warned him that the risk be too great, what with Llewelyn known to be in the area. But what Norman ever heeded Saxon advice? He does not know his arse from his elbow when it comes to fighting the Welsh, but he gives the orders, we obey, and if we reach Rhuddlan Castle, it'll be only by the grace of the Almighty."

Edwin glanced over his shoulder at the shadowed, wet woods that rose up around them, dark spruce and pine blotting out the sky, giving shelter behind every bush to a Welsh bowman. The Welsh scorned the crossbow, preferred a weapon called a long-bow, and they used it with deadly skill. According to Godfrey, a Welsh bowman could fire twelve arrows in the time it took to aim and fire one crossbow; he swore he once saw a Welsh bowman send an arrow through an oaken door fully four inches thick. Remembering that, Edwin hunched his shoulders forward, suddenly sure that even at that moment a Welsh arrow was being launched at his back.

"Who is Llewelyn?" he asked at last, and at once regretted it, for Godfrey gave him an incredulous look.

"God keep me if you are not as ignorant as de Hodnet!" But Edwin's discomfort was so painfully obvious that he relented somewhat. "You do know that Davydd ab Owain claims to rule most of North Wales? Well, Llewelyn ab Iorweth is his nephew and sworn enemy. They've been warring for nigh on six years, and were I to wager on the outcome, I'd want my money on Llewelyn. He's not much older than you, I hear, yet he's been able to get the people on his side, has forced Davydd on the defensive. Davydd still holds a few strongholds like Rhuddlan Castle, but Llewelyn now controls the countryside, owns the night."

Edwin decided he did not want to hear any more, lapsed into a subdued silence. The rain had ceased, but the small patches of sky visible through the trees were an ominous leaden grey.

Although it was unusually mild for January, Edwin shivered each time the wind caught his gambeson. Stuffed with rags, quilted like eiderdown, it suddenly seemed a poor substitute for de Hodnet's chain-mail hauberk. He ran his hand over the padding, trying to convince himself that it could deflect a lance.

As the men moved deeper into the woods, so, too, deepened their sense of unease. They were bunching up, all but treading upon each other's heels, moving at an unusually brisk pace for men who'd been on the march all day. Edwin paused to fish a pebble from his boot, sprinted to catch up. Panting, he slowed, came to a bewildered halt. The men had stopped, were gathered around Giles. Edwin squeezed into the circle, straining to hear.

Edwin was very much in awe of Giles. A dark, saturnine man in his forties, laconic and phlegmatic, he was renowned for his icy composure, and Edwin was stunned now to hear the raw emotion that crackled and surged in his voice.

"We've taken too great a risk as it is, should have followed the coast road. But if we take this path, we are begging to be ambushed!"

"I do not agree. We're losing the light, are wasting time even now that we can ill afford to squander. I have an urgent dispatch for Davydd ab Owain, a message that comes from His Grace, the Earl of Chester. I swore to my lord Montalt that I'd get it to Rhuddlan without delay, and that is what I mean to do."

Giles stepped forward, stopped before the roan stallion. "Sir Walter, I urge you to heed what I say. You do not know the Welsh, you do not know how they fight. This is not war as you learned it. It is bloody, brutal work, with no quarter given. Let me tell you about the battle of Crogen. The old King, Henry of blessed memory, led an army into Wales, went up against Owáin Fawr. The Welsh won the day, and King Henry was forced to retreat back into England. But ere he did, he had a number of Welsh hostages brought before him, wellborn men all, including two of Owain's own sons. He ordered them blinded, Sir Walter."

The other's face did not change. "That battle was fought nigh on thirty years ago. Why tell me this now?"

"Because you may be sure the Welsh do remember. Because that's how war is waged in Wales—on both sides. I've fought in Normandy, in Scotland, even in Ireland, and I tell you true when I say the Welsh do make the worst enemies. They do not play by your rules, they win when they are not supposed to, and they do not know when they're beaten. They're wild and cunning and treacherous, not to be underestimated. It's been only a week since we captured one of Llewelyn's men not a mile from Hawarden. When we put the knife to him, he admitted that Llewelyn was encamped in these woods. Knowing that, we'd be mad to take yon path, no matter how much time we'd save.''

"Our guide assures me that this rebel you seem to fear so much is not in the area, that he's known to be in Arfon. He also assures me that this is the quickest way to Rhuddlan.'' Walter de Hodnet paused, his eyes moving from Giles to the encircling men. Although most of them spoke only rudimentary French, it was evident that they'd followed the argument; their faces were flushed, hostile. He stared them down and, turning back to Giles, said curtly, "Give the order to move out.''

Giles had black eyes, flat and shallow-lidded. They flickered now, glittering with impotent fury. And then he nodded, signaled the men to fall into line. There was hesitation, but only briefly. From the cradle, they were taught obedience to rank; rebellion was utterly beyond their ken.

But although they obeyed, they did not like it. Walter could hear them muttering among themselves in the guttural English he found so harsh upon the ear. Saxon swine. As a boy, he'd thought it was one word, Saxonswine. Stupid and sly, the lot of them. It was always his accursed ill luck to have such oafs under his command. Little wonder he'd yet to win the recognition he craved, to find his niche. But this time would be different. By getting Chester's message to Rhuddlan by nightfall, he'd stand high in Montalt's favor. It was not inconceivable that Montalt might even make mention of him to Chester.

A smile softened his mouth at that, and for a happy moment he indulged in a gratifying daydream, imagining himself summoned by the mighty Earl, friend to King Richard, one of the most powerful lords of the realm. A knight in Chester's service would be a made man. He'd have no reason then to envy his elder brother Baldwin; Baldwin might even envy him.

His smile faded; thoughts of Baldwin were always sure to sour his mood. There was less than a year between them, but Baldwin was the eldest born, Baldwin was his father's heir, would inherit all when Sir Odo died. For Walter, for his brothers Will and Stephen, there would be nothing, only what they could win with their wits or their swords. And a younger son's options were limited. If he was fortunate, he might find a place for himself in some lord's household. Or he might try his luck in the tournament lists, but that was a risky way to earn a living. For those who'd failed to find service with a lord, or lost in the lists, there

was little left but banditry. Of course, one could become a clerk,
like his brother Will. But a clerk had no social status; he was a
nonentity, of no account. Walter's mouth tightened. Was he any
better off, in truth? What had he except his horse, his armor, and
a shilling a day in wages?

But if he could do this for Montalt and Chester . . . he glanced
back over his shoulder, at Giles's dark, sullen face. He'd managed to infect them all with his damned fool fears; they were
shying at every sound, as jumpy as cats. As little as he liked to
admit it, it was even getting to him. He tilted his head back,
studied the sky with narrowed eyes. Dusk was falling fast. But if
their guide was right, they were less than seven miles from
Rhuddlan.

Walter slid his fingers under the noseguard of his helmet,
rubbed the chafed skin across the bridge of his nose. What was
the guide's name? Martin? A quiet sort, half-Welsh, half-Saxon,
an outcast in both worlds. But he knew these hills as few men
did, and he—

"Sir Walter!" Giles had come up alongside his stallion. Keeping his voice pitched for Walter's ear alone, he said tensely,
"You hear it—the silence? Suddenly there is not a sound, no
birds, nothing."

Walter stiffened, listened. Giles was right. "Oh, Christ," he
whispered. He swung about in the saddle, peering into the surrounding shadows, saw nothing.

"Martin!" he called sharply. A few yards ahead, the guide
turned, his face questioning. But as he did, a low humming noise
cut through the eerie stillness. Walter gasped, flinched as a rush
of hot air fanned past his face. His stallion leapt sideways, and he
jerked on the reins, turned the animal in a circle. Only then did
he see Giles. The other man had dropped to his knees in the road.
As Walter watched, he tugged at the arrow shaft protruding from
his chest, and then fell forward, slowly slid into the mud churned
up by Walter's stallion.

For a moment frozen in time, nothing happened. And then
one of Walter's men, the one called Godfrey, dropped to the
ground, rolled toward a fallen log, shouting, "Take shelter!" An
arrow slammed into the log, scant inches from where he crouched,
followed by an earsplitting, wordless yell, and Walter's men
panicked, whirling about, slipping in the mud, crashing into one
another in their haste to escape the trap.

Walter jerked his sword from its scabbard. Godfrey's action
had been instinctive, but Walter knew it was also futile. The

Welsh were firing from both sides of the road, with savage-sounding battle cries that only panicked his men all the more. The woods offered no refuge, only shafted death, and he shouted, "Make haste for the castle!" An arrow burned past his thigh, grazed his stallion's mane, and he spurred the animal forward. The horse stumbled over Giles's body, righted itself, and lengthened stride. In the fading light, Walter never saw the rope stretched across the road. It caught him in the chest; he reeled backward, hit the ground with jarring impact.

When he came to, dazed and disoriented, he did not at first remember where he was. He groaned, started to move, and a knife blade was at once laid against his throat. Behind the knife were the coldest green eyes he'd ever seen. The man was young, twenty at most. He said something in Welsh, and Walter said, "I do not understand."

The youth spoke again, harshly, and Walter shook his head, tried to sit up. His coif was jerked off, and the knife nicked into his throat; a thin red line appeared upon his neck. He froze, scarcely breathing, and the pressure eased slightly.

From the corner of his eye he could see several figures huddled on the ground: a freckle-faced, frightened youngster, Godfrey, and a third man smeared with his own blood. Beyond them a body lay sprawled in the mud, and nearby was a young Welshman, seeking to soothe Walter's roan stallion.

Another man was now bending over him, a huge youth with a scarred cheek and deepset brown eyes. He reached for the neck of Walter's hauberk, and as Walter recoiled, he grinned. "Easy, English," he said, in accented but understandable French. "The Lord loveth a cheerful giver!"

He drew out the rolled parchment, eyes widening at sight of the Earl of Chester's seal. "Chester," he murmured, passing the scroll to his companion. "Well, well. You fly high, English."

Walter drew a deep breath, thanking God for this French-speaking, amiable giant. Surely he could reason with this one. But the other . . . he glanced at the glinting blade, swallowed, and said in a rush, "My name is Sir Walter de Hodnet, son of Sir Odo de Hodnet of Welbatch in Shropshire. My father is a man of means, and will pay dear for my safe return."

"Indeed?" The Welshman smiled at him. "Horses? Gold?"

"Yes, both," he said, knowing his father would not part with so much as a shilling on his behalf.

"You hear, Rhys? We've a man of wealth in our midst. Tell me, English, what of your men there? Who ransoms them?"

Walter stared up at him, perplexed. Who'd pay money for men-at-arms? "I do not see—"

"No, I know you do not. But I'd wager your men do." He was no longer smiling, and Walter's mouth went dry. Giles's voice was suddenly thudding in his ears: He blinded them. Blinded them. Blinded them.

He was barely twenty, his face contorted with pain, sweat beading his upper lip, his temples. A dark stain was spreading rapidly across his tunic. Llewelyn knew few injuries were as dangerous as an upper-thigh wound; all too often the man died before the bleeding could be checked. Drawing his dagger, he split the tunic, set about fashioning a rude tourniquet. It was with considerable relief that he saw it begin to take effect.

"You're a lucky lad, Dylan," he said, and grinned. "Half a hand higher and you'd have lost the family jewels."

Dylan was chalk-white, but he managed a weak smile at that, whispered, "Jesú forfend."

Two men were bringing up a blanket stretched across two poles, and Llewelyn rose, watched as Dylan was lowered onto it. A flash of movement caught his eye. He turned, saw the guide, Martin, standing several feet away. Llewelyn unfastened a pouch at his belt, sent it spinning through the air. Martin caught it deftly, tucked it away in his tunic. for a moment their eyes held; then he silently saluted Llewelyn and vanished into the wooded darkness beyond the road.

Ednyved was now at his side. He said, "Well?"

"Three dead, including one gutshot so badly that I thought he'd count death a mercy. Four captured. The rest fled. One horse taken. And this." Handing Llewelyn the parchment roll.

Llewelyn, too, was startled at sight of the seal. "Chester, no less!" He turned, beckoned to the closest man. "Rosser, fetch a torch."

"One of those taken is the lack-wit who led them right to us. A fool of the first order, but you might want to talk with him nonetheless, Llewelyn. He says his name is de Hodnet. Is that not what an English friend of yours be called, too?"

Surprised, Llewelyn nodded. "Yes, Stephen de Hodnet. Yet the last I heard, Stephen was attached to Fulk Fitz Warin's household, not Montalt's. Of course, Stephen does have several brothers—" He broke off and, after a moment, laughed and shook his head. "But no, I could not be that lucky!"

*   *   *

Godfrey was cursing under his breath. Edwin sat stunned and silent beside him. They both stiffened at Llewelyn's approach, watching warily as he stopped before them and then moved toward Walter de Hodnet.

Walter waited no less warily. The man standing before him was quite young, nineteen or twenty, dressed in the same home-spun as his comrades, and Walter was startled when he said, in fluent French, "I'm Llewelyn ab Iorwerth. Welcome to Wales."

Walter flushed; even as frightened as he was, he did not miss the mockery in the other's voice. But he could not afford pride, not now, and he said hurriedly, "It's glad I am that you speak French, my lord. If I may say so, you're young to have made such a name for yourself." He summoned up a smile, was encouraged when Llewelyn smiled back. "My lord Llewelyn, may I speak plainly? I can pay for my release; you need only name your price. My father—"

"You do not remember me, do you?"

Bewildered, Walter shook his head. "We've met? My lord, I think not. I would—"

Llewelyn was still smiling. "A pity your memory is so poor, Walter de Hodnet. For I do remember you, all too well."

This was no pretense, Llewelyn saw; Walter was genuinely baffled. He stood looking down at the Norman knight, and then, abruptly tiring of this cat-and-mouse game, he said, "I think you'll remember if you put your mind to it. Think back some years, to a summer noon and a meadow beyond Shrewsbury, to a chestnut gelding and a fearful ten-year-old boy."

"I still do not—" Walter began, and then sucked in his breath.

Llewelyn saw his face twitch, saw his eyes glaze over with horror, and he said, "You see? You have not forgotten me, after all."

Rhys and Ednyved had been following this exchange with increasing curiosity. Now Rhys demanded, "What is this English to you, Llewelyn?"

"A man who has long owed me a debt." Speaking rapidly in Welsh, Llewelyn gave them a terse summary of that long-ago encounter by Yokethul Brook, concluding in French, "So what say you? What shall I do with him?"

Rhys's eyes flicked to Walter. "Need you ask? Kill him," he said, without hesitation. He'd answered in Welsh, for he used French only under duress, but it was obvious that Walter under-stood; he was ashen.

"Ednyved?"

Ednyved shrugged. "This English is such a dolt, it would be almost a shame to lose him; never have I seen a man so eager to be ambushed. And he is the brother of your friend. Would his death grieve Stephen?"

"I very much doubt it," Llewelyn said dryly, saw Walter flinch, and thought that Stephen had just unknowingly gained vengeance for a childhood of beatings and intimidation.

"Well, I can think of no other reasons to spare him, Llewelyn. There are too many English as it is; one less would be no loss. This grievance you hold against him, how deep does it fester?"

Llewelyn smiled at that. "Is there ever a time when you do not go right to the heart of the matter? The answer is, of course, that it does not . . . not anymore."

He gazed down at Walter, his eyes thoughtful. And then he turned, for Rosser was approaching with a burning pine torch.

"Ah, at last." Breaking the seal, he held the parchment up to the light. "Let's see what message is worth the lives of three men." Beginning to read, he laughed aloud, beckoned to those within hearing range.

"It seems King Richard had more to fear from his fellow Christian crusaders than he did from the infidels. On his way back from the Holy Land, he fell into the hands of his erstwhile ally, the Duke of Austria, and is being held for ransom by the German Emperor!"

His men had gathered around to listen. They burst out laughing, too, began to exchange markedly unsympathetic quips about the English King's plight.

Llewelyn was rapidly scanning the rest of the letter. "Wait, you've yet to hear the best of it. When word reached England, Richard's brother John did himself proud in the finest tradition of Cain and Abel, at once set about gaining the crown for himself. He's sailed for France, where he means to ally himself with the French King Philip. It seems they plan to offer the Emperor an even larger ransom not to let Richard go!"

Llewelyn was elated, for nothing better served Welsh interests than English discord. God had indeed been good to Wales, he thought, in giving Richard a brother as untrustworthy as John. With Richard languishing in some Austrian castle and John scheming to steal the throne, the English would be too taken up with their own troubles to have time to spare for Welsh conquest. That meant he'd have a free hand to move against Davydd, to force a battle that would break his uncle's power once and for all.

"One good turn deserves another, so I wish John well," he

said, and laughed again. "For although he does not know it yet, he's going to give me Gwynedd."

"I do not doubt it, my Prince," Ednyved said with mock servility, "but at the moment you're a rebel on the run, and we'd best be gone ere any of those English soldiers reach Rhuddlan. Now," jerking his head toward their captives, "what mean you to do about them?"

"To tell you true, Ednyved, I have not made up my mind." Llewelyn walked over, looked down at his prisoners.

Godfrey tensed, and then blurted out in broken French, "My lord, spare my cousin. He's but a lad of eighteen; do not put him to the knife, I beg you."

"Why should I put any of you to the knife? There are but two legitimate times for torture, when a man has information you must have or when he has committed a sin so great that justice demands he suffer for it." But Godfrey did not fully believe him, Llewelyn saw.

And what of Walter de Hodnet? A rare jest of God, in truth, that de Hodnet should fall into his hands now, years too late. Walter was mute; but his eyes pleaded with anguished eloquence.

"You fear more than death, do you not?" Llewelyn said slowly. "You think I mean to extract every ounce of mortal suffering for a boyhood wrong. A pity, Walter, you know so little of the Welsh. You see, we have a saying amongst my people: *O hir ddyled ni ddylir dim.* 'From an old debt, nothing is due.' "

Walter stared up at him in utter disbelief. Rhys looked no less startled, but Ednyved laughed, as if at some private joke.

"I thought it was your ambition to be Prince of Gwynedd, Llewelyn. Are you seeking sainthood, too?"

"I know you're woefully ignorant of the Scriptures, Ednyved, but even you must have heard: 'Vengeance is mine, saith the Lord.' " Llewelyn paused, and then added in Welsh, "Of course, we do have another proverb I rather fancy: 'The best revenge, contempt.' "

Ednyved nodded, eyes alight in amused understanding. "Now that sounds more like you," he said, as Walter found his voice.

"You truly mean to let me go?" Walter sounded more suspicious than relieved, for magnanimity to an enemy was an alien concept to him.

"Yes, I do, but I rather doubt you'll thank me for it. For I mean to release your men, too. I should think they'll have a most interesting tale to tell Montalt. You've hardly endeared yourself to them, have you?''

Walter opened his mouth, shut it abruptly, but he was unable to keep his eyes from shifting toward Godfrey. Llewelyn saw, smiled.

''Of course you will have time to think up an explanation for your appalling ineptitude . . . on your walk to Rhuddlan. For although you are free to go, we'll be keeping your horse and armor. Spoils of war . . . remember?''

Five minutes ago, Walter would have bartered anything on God's earth for his life and not counted the cost. But his were now the changed priorities of reprieve, and he gave a gasp of dismay. ''If I do reach Rhuddlan like that—naked, alone, on foot—Christ, I'll be a laughingstock!''

''Yes,'' Llewelyn agreed. ''I know.'' And signaling to two of his men, he said, ''Strip him of his armor.''

Walter scrambled to his feet, began to back away. In that instant his fear of humiliation was greater than his fear of death, and his eyes darted to the dagger in Llewelyn's belt. For a mad moment he saw himself lunging for it, plunging the blade into Llewelyn's chest, and racing for the woods.

But his was an easy face to read. Llewelyn felt a sudden surge of excitement. ''It is your choice, Walter,'' he said softly, almost encouragingly.

Walter's throat muscles contracted; he had not enough saliva to swallow. The realization that Llewelyn wanted him to go for the knife was a lifeline back to sanity. Appalled by what he'd almost done, he sagged against the nearest tree.

''I swear by all the saints that you'll regret this day,'' he said, choking on his hatred, and Rhys lost all patience. In three strides he'd crossed the clearing, had his dagger poised at Walter's throat.

''Are you so eager to die, English?'' he demanded. ''Think you that we need an excuse to claim your life?''

''He does not speak Welsh, Rhys,'' Llewelyn said, amused, and Rhys smiled grimly.

''Mayhap not, but he understands me well enough.''

Walter had lost all color; a vein showed at his temple, throbbing wildly against skin damp with sweat.

''Yes,'' Llewelyn conceded. ''I daresay he does!'' Glancing up at the darkening sky, he realized that they'd already tarried here too long, and he moved toward Walter's men. ''You understand what was said?''

Godfrey had been staring at Walter de Hodnet, eyes glittering. Now he looked up at Llewelyn, nodded, and then grinned. *"Merci,"* he said, and then gestured toward Walter, adding something in English which Llewelyn did not understand; he caught only a name, Giles.

But time was on his uncle's side; some of the fleeing soldiers might have reached Rhuddlan by now. He still held Chester's dispatch. Unsheathing his dagger, he slashed at the parchment until it hung in tattered ribbons. Handing it to the wide-eyed Edwin, he said in slow, deliberate French, "Here, lad. Give this to Montalt. And tell him that Llewelyn ab Iorwerth has a message for Chester: Stay out of Wales."

Edwin could not envision himself ever giving a message like that to a Norman lord, and he was much relieved when his cousin said, "I'd like nothing better, my lord!"

Edwin released his breath, clutched the shredded parchment to his chest. Godfrey would keep faith with the young Welsh lord, and he was glad, for they owed this man their lives. He doubted that the Earl of Chester would heed the warning, would stay out of Wales. But he would, he thought, with sudden resolve. He was going home. Home to Aldford.

6

LISIEUX, NORMANDY

May 1194

In January 1194, Queen Eleanor reached Germany with the one hundred thousand silver marks demanded as ransom for her son's freedom. Richard was finally released on February 4, one year and six weeks after he'd been taken captive in Austria. By March he was once more upon English soil, where he set about extinguishing the embers of his brother John's rebellion. John's castles of Tickhill and Nottingham fell to him within a fortnight, and on March 31 he summoned John to appear before his great council. John was given forty days to answer the charges of treason. He defied the summons, did not appear, and on May 10 he was outlawed, declared to have forfeited any claims to the Angevin crown, and then stripped of the earldoms of Gloucester and Mortain, of his castles, estates, and manors in England and Normandy.

Two days later, Richard and Eleanor sailed from Portsmouth. Landing at Barfleur, they headed south into Normandy. After lingering a few days at Caen, they moved on to Lisieux, where they were greeted with excessive affability by Archdeacon John de Alençon, Richard's vice-chancellor, and there joined by Joanna Plantagenet, sister to Richard, daughter to Eleanor, young widow of William the Good, King of Sicily.

". . . and after I set up a gallows before the walls of Nottingham Castle, hanged a score of John's men, and left them for the ravens, the others lost their taste for treason, moved out even faster than the ravens moved in!"

"What of Johnny, Richard? Have you any word as to his whereabouts?"

"Oh, I know exactly where John is, Joanna—skulking about the French court. He fled to Paris months ago, after Philip sent him warning that my release was imminent. 'Look to yourself; the Devil is loose,' " Richard quoted with relish, and then laughed.

Joanna laughed, too. "This has not been one of Philip's better years, what with your return and his troubles with the Pope."

"What is the straight of that, Jo? The garbled account I heard did not seem likely to me, that Philip sought to repudiate his Queen the day after their marriage."

"Likely or not, it's true enough. They were wed at Amiens last August, and the very next day Philip disavowed the marriage, refused to recognize Ingeborg as his Queen. When she balked at being shipped back to Denmark like defective goods, Philip convened a council of French bishops at Compiègne, got them to declare the marriage null and void, then confined Ingeborg to a nunnery. But the Danish King did not take kindly to this, and he appealed to the Pope on his sister's behalf. I expect His Holiness will order Philip to take Ingeborg back, but Philip is nothing if not stubborn, and I'm not sure he'll yield even if the Pope does lay France under Interdict."

"Jesú, the idiot, the utter idiot!" Richard shook his head in amused amazement. "Mayhap I ought to ask him if he wants to send Ingeborg to me at Rouen. We could pen her up with Alais, split the cost of their upkeep!"

He laughed again. In the shadows behind him, Archdeacon Alençon could not hide his disapproval. After a moment, his eyes shifted from Richard to the woman at his side. Eleanor was watching her son, a faint smile curving her mouth. It was not a smile to give Alençon comfort, reminding him what an implacable enemy this woman made. Upon gaining her own freedom, one of her first acts had been to declare an amnesty for those imprisoned in English jails, declaring that she knew from personal experience "how irksome it was to be a prisoner." And yet she'd shown no pity at all for the woman confined for five years now at her son's command, the unfortunate Alais, who'd been raised at her court, had come to womanhood in her husband's bed.

But it was too late to worry about Eleanor's enmity. He'd chosen to gamble, could only hope he'd not made a fool's wager. Moving closer, he murmured, "Madame, might I have a few moments alone with you? I've a matter most urgent to discuss."

Eleanor felt no surprise. She had a sharp eye for the unease of others, and Alençon's overly hearty welcome put her in mind of a man whistling his way past a graveyard. She asked no questions, came unobtrusively to her feet and followed Alençon from the hall.

The Archdeacon's manor was a substantial structure of stone and timber, rising up two stories on the bank of the River Touques. It was to an upper chamber that Alençon led Eleanor, stepping aside so she could enter first. As she did, he closed the door quietly behind her. Eleanor stood very still, staring at the man by the unshuttered window, silhouetted against a twilight sky of soft, shadowed lavender.

"Mother," he said at last, so low she could not be sure he'd spoken at all.

There was an oil lamp sputtering on a trestle table. She reached for it, took several strides forward into the room, held it up so that the smoky light fell across his face.

John blinked, flinched away from the sudden illuminating glare. His mother's face was impassive, but her eyes pinned him to the wall, amber ice in which he could read the reflection of his every sin, could read accusation and indictment, but no hint of absolution.

He forgot entirely his carefully rehearsed plea of explanation and atonement. When the silence had become more than he could endure, he blurted out, "You know why I'm here. I need you to speak for me. You're the one person Richard would be likely to heed."

"I daresay you're right. But whatever makes you think I would?"

Eleanor set the lamp on the table, turned back to her silent son. "At least you've shown you're not the utter coward Richard thinks you to be; he was sure you'd not dare leave the sanctuary of the French court. Although how you'd have the nerve to face him after all you've done—allying yourself with your brother's sworn enemy against your own House; promising to wed your father's harlot and to cede the Vexin back to Philip in return for his support; hiring Welsh mercenaries and seeking to stir up a rising in England; doing your damnedest to sabotage the collection of Richard's ransom. And when all else failed, joining with Philip in offering to better Richard's ransom if the German Emperor would but hold Richard for another year. Have I left anything out?"

"No," he said shortly, unwillingly.

"Well, then, suppose you tell me why I should want to help you escape the punishment you so deserve, why I should raise even a finger on your behalf. And do spare me any maudlin pleas about you being flesh of my flesh; you'll have to do better than that, John . . . much better."

John drew an uneven breath. "Nothing has changed since that night we talked in Southampton. Your hopes for an Angevin dynasty are not going to take root with Richard's seed. He's not laid eyes upon his wife in nigh on two years, did not even bother to summon her to England upon his return. Unless you are counting upon another Virgin Birth, Madame, I suggest that leads us right back to Arthur or me, a child of seven or a man grown of twenty-six."

"Yes," she said icily. "But the child is as yet unformed clay; who knows what manner of man he may become? Whereas we already know the man you are, John."

John was not as impervious to insult as he'd have her think; he betrayed himself with rising color. "Yes, you do—a man who knows what he wants and will fight to keep what is his. Can you say as much for Arthur? I might make use of Philip's help if it serves my need, but we'll see the Second Coming ere I'd trust him out of my sight. But Arthur? His advisers wax fat on French gold, look to Paris for guidance the way infidels do look to Mecca. He'd be Philip's puppet and you well know it, Madame. Just as you know I would not."

"What I want to know," she said, "is how you can be shrewd enough to see all that and yet stupid enough to fall in with Philip's schemes, to so disregard my promise . . . and my warning."

Her tone was barbed; each word carried a separate sting. And yet John sensed he'd gained some ground. "For what it's worth, I fully meant to hold to our understanding."

"Why did you not, then?"

"The truth? Because Richard's capture unbalanced the equation. I truly did not think he'd ever come back, not with the enemies he's made. I saw the crown up for the taking, and so . . ." He shrugged. "I put in my bid. What more can I tell you?"

Eleanor's mouth twitched. "Credit where due, you can surprise. I was curious as to what your last line of defense would be. But I admit I did not expect you to fall back upon honesty!"

With that, John no longer hesitated. "Well?" he said. "Will you help me, Mother? Will you intercede with Richard on my behalf?"

She gave him a look he could not interpret. "I already have."

John's relief was intense but ephemeral. So this whole scene had been yet another of her damnable games, he thought resentfully, a stupid charade as meaningless as it was malicious.

"Richard can be unpredictable, so there are no guarantees. But he did agree that if you came to him, he'd hear you out. It might help," she added dryly, "if you sought to appear somewhat contrite."

She started toward the door, stopped when he made no move to follow. "What are you waiting for? Richard's below in the great hall; now would be as good a time as any."

"The great hall?" John echoed in dismay. He thought it penance enough to have to humble his pride before Richard, was not about to put on a performance for a hall full of witnesses. But as he opened his mouth to protest, he caught the contempt in his mother's eyes. She was like Richard, he knew, in that she, too, was one for setting tests and traps for people, measuring their worth by standards that made no allowance for frailties or failure. Richard judged a man by his willingness to bleed, to risk his life upon the thrust of a sword. With his mother, the test was more subtle and yet more demanding. She might forgive deceit and betrayal, but never weakness, would expect above all else that a man be willing to answer for the consequences of his actions.

"I suppose you're right." He moved away from the window, gave her a crooked smile. "What was it the Christian martyrs always said before they were thrown to the lions? *Morituri te salutamus?*"

"Your command of Latin is not bad, but your grasp of history is rather weak. 'We who are about to die salute you' was the battle cry of the Roman gladiators, not the Christian martyrs. We can safely say you have no yearning whatsoever for martyrdom, but it will be interesting, nonetheless, to see how you handle yourself in the lion's den." Eleanor's laugh was not in the least maternal, but John knew he'd pulled back from the brink in time, had scrambled to safety even as the ground seemed sure to crumble under his feet.

Men stared at sight of John, fell suddenly silent. Eleanor stepped aside so that he stood alone. Richard was sitting on the dais at the far end of the hall. John hesitated, then began the longest walk of his life. So quiet it was that he could hear the scuffling sound his boots made as they trod upon the floor rushes, hear the clinking of his sword in its scabbard—even hear, or so he imagined, the thudding of his own heart. Richard had not moved, was watching him approach, eyes narrowed and utterly opaque. John stopped before the dais, slowly unbuckled his scabbard, and laid it upon the steps. Then he knelt.

"My liege." In the brief time allotted to him for calculation, he'd decided that candor was his best hope. It had served him well with his mother, and might, if he was lucky, appease Richard, too. In truth, what other choice did he have? For what could he possibly say that Richard would believe?

"I can offer you no excuses, Richard. I can only ask for your forgiveness. I know I've given you no reason to—" He stopped in mid-sentence, for he'd just recognized the woman seated at Richard's left, a slim woman with green eyes and reddish gold hair gleaming under a silvery gossamer veil, a woman he'd not seen for eighteen years. His sister Joanna.

"I'm surprised to see you here, John. Frankly, I did not think you'd have the nerve. I was not surprised, however, by your treachery, by your willingness to snap at Philip's bait. You're as easily led astray as any child, have never learned to say no. It's lucky you were not born a woman, Little Brother. You'd have been perpetually pregnant!"

Richard laughed, and so did most of the others in the hall. The color drained from John's face; he bit down on his lower lip until it bled, sought to focus upon the pain to the exclusion of all else.

Rising, Richard bent down, picked up John's sword. "But you're here; that counts for something. And our lady mother would have me forgive you; that counts for much. I suppose I should just be thankful that since you are so much given to treachery, you're so reassuringly inept at it!" He stepped forward, held out John's sword. "Your betrayals are forgiven, Little Brother . . . if not forgotten. But though your blood buys you a pardon, the price is higher for an earldom, higher than you can pay. I've no intention of restoring your titles and lands, not until I'm damned well sure that you're deserving of them . . . if ever."

John came to his feet, reached for his sword. Richard was some inches the taller of the two, and now, standing on the dais stairs, he towered over the younger man. As their eyes met, John said, quite tonelessly, "I shall remember your generosity, Brother. You may count upon that."

Supper was generally an afterthought, but that evening's meal was an unusually bountiful one; in his relief that his risky role as peacemaker had met with such success, Archdeacon Alençon

emptied his larders, set before Richard a succession of meat and
fish dishes, highly seasoned venison and salmon swimming in
wine gravy. The salmon Richard dispatched to John's end of the
table, with a good-humored but heavy-handed jest about the Prod-
igal Son and the Fatted Calf. To John, the taste was bitter as gall,
and as soon after the meal as he could, he escaped the hall, out
into the dark of the gardens.

He was alone but a few moments, however, Joanna had
followed, came forward to sit beside him on a rough-hewn oaken
bench. "Here," she said, thrusting a wine cup into his hand. "I
think you're in need of this."

They'd gotten on well as children; she was only two years
older than he, and he'd been sorry when their father had sent her
off to Sicily as an eleven-year-old bride for William the Good.
When he thought now upon his humiliation in the great hall, it
was Joanna's presence there that he minded the most, and he said
sharply, "If you've come to offer pity, I do not want any!"

"You need not worry; I do not think you're deserving of any.
You were not 'led astray,' knew exactly what you were doing
. . . and got what you deserved." But then she gave him a
direct, searching glance. "Does that offend you, Johnny?"

"No," John said, surprised to discover that he actually preferred her matter-of-fact rebuke to Richard's contemptuous pardon, and when she smiled at him, he smiled back.

"I'm glad," she said simply. "I can tell you, then, that I think
Richard erred. A pardon should be generously given or not at all.
For all that Richard has a fine grasp of tactics, he's always been
woefully lacking in tact!"

And what was he expected to say to that, John wondered,
agree and incriminate himself? But after a moment to reflect, he
dismissed the suspicion as unwarranted. For all the love that lay
between them, he could not truly see Joanna as Richard's spy.
Nor, were he to be fair, was that Richard's way, either. Richard
would not take the trouble.

"I'd rather not talk of that, Jo." The childhood name came
without thought, was curiously comforting, evoking echoes of an
almost forgotten familiarity. "You're beautiful, you know, you
truly are. Not at all the skin-and-bones sister I remember! Joanna
Plantagenet, Queen of Sicily, Duchess of Apulia, Princess of
Capua. Were you happy, Jo, in Sicily?"

"Not at first. I was too young, too homesick. But William
meant well by me, gave me no cause for complaint. He was
some thirteen years older, treated me like a daughter until I was

ready to be a wife. Yes, I was happy enough. But at thirty-six
he died, leaving no heirs, and as you know, his bastard cousin
Tancred seized the throne. Tancred not only denied me my dower
rights, he put me into close confinement at Palermo. I sometimes
wonder what would have become of me, Johnny, if not for
Richard. He landed at Messina on his way to the Holy Land, and
when Tancred balked at releasing me, restoring my dower, Richard laid siege to the town, forced Tancred into submission.''

Yes, John thought, and then he took you with him to the Holy
Land, where he offered you to the brother of the infidel Prince
Saladin. But he said nothing.

''Richard's arrival at Messina was a godsend, in truth, and I
will be ever grateful to him. Yet I do not doubt you'd have done
as much for me, too, Johnny. So would our brother Henry. Even
Geoffrey, provided it did not inconvenience him unduly. Any
one of you would have come to my aid, I know that. And
yet none of you would ever have come to the aid of each other.
I've often thought on that.''

''When I was sixteen, Jo, Papa sought to persuade Richard to
cede the Aquitaine to me. Our brother Henry was a year dead,
and Papa promised to name Richard as his heir, but he thought it
only fair that Richard should then yield up Aquitaine in return.
Richard did not see it that way, flared into a rage and swore he'd
be damned ere he'd agree. Papa flew into an equal rage, told me
that Aquitaine was mine if I could take it from Richard. A
sixteen-year-old boy has no money for troops. But the Duke of
Brittany does, and Geoffrey offered to provide the men and
money, told me this was the chance of a lifetime. So Geoffrey
and I led an army into Poitou, and Richard burned damned near
half of Brittany in retaliation . . . until Papa made haste to
summon us all to London, told us he had not meant to be taken
seriously.''

They were both silent for a time after that. John leaned over,
plucked a primrose from the closest bush, and presented it to
Joanna with self-mocking gallantry. ''Tell me, Jo, why did you
follow me out to the gardens? What did you want to say to me?''

''Do you remember what I would call you whenever we'd
have a falling-out? Johnny-cat, because you were always poking
about where you had no right to be.''

''I remember. I never liked it much.''

''I could not help thinking of that as I watched you and
Richard in the great hall. You offered up your eighth life in
there, Johnny-cat. You do know that?''

"Christ, Joanna, of course I do. Do you think anything less than that could have brought me to Lisieux?"

"Thank God you see that," she said somberly. "I was so afraid you would not. Because I know Richard; he'd not forgive you again, Johnny. The next time you fall from grace will be the last time. For your sake, I do hope you never forget that."

7

YORKSHIRE, ENGLAND

September 1196

Too excited to sleep, Joanna awakened just before dawn on the morning of her fifth birthday. Taking care not to disturb her mother, she slid from their bed, pulled her gown over her head, and ran a wooden comb through her tangled dark hair. She knew she should wash her face, clean her teeth with a hazel twig, but she could not wait; the day, her very own, was beckoning.

In the outer room, Maud still slept, rolled up in blankets by the hearth. Joanna tiptoed around her, searching for food to break the night's fast. The only furniture the room contained was a trestle table, a coffer chest, and several stools, but it was cluttered with household utensils: her mother's distaff and spindle, a pile of reeds that Maud meant to plait into baskets, the hand mill that Maud used to grind their corn, several letten pots and pans. In the corner an armful of peeled rushes was being steeped in tallow fat; Joanna's nose wrinkled at the pungent smell. Reassured by Maud's steady snoring, she broke off a chunk of thick, black rye bread, smeared it with cheese, and headed for the door.

Outside, she detoured by the hen roost, soothed her conscience by scattering a handful of seeds in among the chickens. Joanna very much wanted her mother to think her responsible, did not mean to shirk her household duties. But the morning sky was clear and cloudless, the brilliant blue of her mother's eyes, and the wind rippled through the moorland grass, stirring up a billowing green sea that swept all before it as it raced for the distant silver of the River Ure. Joanna let the wind take her, too; breaking into a run, she skimmed the grass, arms outstretched and hair streaming behind her like an ebony sail, and for a moment or two she actually was a small boat, bound for exotic, alien shores.

She slowed as she approached the cottage, home to Cedric, the young Saxon farmer who did for them those chores that required a man's hand. Cedric's cottage looked, at first glance, much like their own: thatched roof and timber framework, covered with clay, chopped straw, and cow dung. But it was much smaller, contained a single room for Cedric, his wife, Eda, and their three children. Joanna had once sneaked a look inside, knew they all slept on pallets around the hearth, lacking the straw mattress and wooden bedframe she shared with her mother. Nor did they have the feather pillows, the embroidered coverlets, or the hand mirror of polished metal, all of which Joanna's mother had brought with her from her home to the south, the home Joanna had never seen.

As early as it was, Cedric's family was already up and about. He was disappearing into the distance, on his way to the fields he worked with the other villagers. Eda was toting a bucket of milk toward the cottage, and the children were chasing the chickens out of the garden. They were making a noisy game of it, herding the hens in a circle, and Joanna felt a pang of envy, yearning to join in. She'd watched Cedric's children for months, knew the boy was called Derwin and his sisters Rowena and Elfrida, names strange and foreign-sounding to Joanna. She knew, too, that they were not proper playmates for her; Maud had warned her often enough of that. Saxon peasants, she'd said scornfully, bound to the land, who could be bought and sold and were born to serve. That had confused Joanna somewhat, for she knew that Maud, too, was a servant. Maud had nursed her mother, called her "lamb" and "sweeting," and yet she was still a servant; Joanna had heard her mother remind Maud of that more than once. So why, then, did she look upon Cedric and his family with such contempt?

No, Joanna did not understand. It mattered little to her that Cedric's children were serfs, that they spoke an alien tongue. She would even have dared her mother's wrath, so lonely was she, so eager for friends. But Rowena and Elfrida had shied away from all her overtures, stared at her with suspicious, wary eyes, and at last she'd stopped trying. Yet she still wondered why they would not play with her. Was it because she was Norman? Because Cedric addressed her mother as "my lady"? Or because she was "different"?

As young as she was, Joanna was aware of the irregular aspects of her homelife. She had no family but her mother. They had no friends, no visitors, and the past was a forbidden terrain, a land of dark secrets, secrets Joanna instinctively feared. There was so much she did not understand, but she sensed that what was wrong in their lives was somehow her fault.

Now the other children had noticed her, were whispering among themselves, laughing. Joanna turned, walked away.

But her spirits lifted, as always, at sight of the castle. She spent hours here some days, watching the people passing in and out of the bailey. Four times a year Maud would mount the steps into the keep, would pay the rent for their cottage to Guy, the bailiff for Robert Fitz Ranulf, Lord of Middleham. Joanna had begged in vain to accompany Maud on these quarter-day visits, and the world hidden away behind those timbered outer walls remained a mystery to her.

Stretching out in the grass, she picked up a stick and cleared a space. Her mother was different from the villagers in yet another way; she could read and write. Very few women had such a skill, she'd told Joanna one night when wine had loosened her tongue, but her father—Joanna's grandfather—had permitted her to be taught with her brothers. "He was so proud of me, Joanna . . . once," she whispered, and when she began to cry, Joanna cried, too; she dreaded her mother's tears even more than her slaps.

Now she patted the earth till it was smooth, took the stick and laboriously scrawled her mother's name in the dirt: CLEMENCE. Then she traced JOANNA below it. But that was the extent of her knowledge; Clemence had neither the patience nor the aptitude to instruct, and her sporadic attempts to teach Joanna the alphabet had come to naught.

A solitary child is more given to daydreaming, and Joanna was no exception. She lost track of time; the morning drifted away on an easterly breeze. Yawning, she sat up in the grass, and then saw how high the sun was in the sky. It was nigh on ten o'clock; she was perilously close to being late for dinner. Joanna scrambled to her feet, began to run.

Sprinting through the village, with several barking dogs at her heels, she raced for home. Maud kept a water bucket outside the door and, proud that she'd remembered, she conscientiously washed the dirt from her face and hands. But she'd splashed water about too freely, and looked with dismay now at the splotches darkening the skirt of her gown. She was always displeasing her mother and Maud, and yet she tried so hard to be good, she truly did.

She hoped the mud stains would pass unnoticed, but at sight of her, Maud set down her bowl with a thud. "And where have you been, rooting about in the pigsty? For the love of the Lord, look at the child!''

Clemence, thus appealed to, turned from the hearth. "Oh, Joanna!" Ruefully. "What a slovenly little beggar you are."

There was no anger in her voice, though, and Joanna's tension dissipated in a rush of relief. But the bewilderment remained. The same misdeed that would, on one day, earn her a slap in the face might, at another time, be shrugged off with indulgent laughter. Her mother's erratic tempers were baffling to the little girl, but they were disquieting, too. There was a perverse security in the constancy of Maud's dour disapproval, none whatsoever in her mother's quicksilver moods.

A special birthday dinner had been cooked for Joanna: a rabbit stew, flavored with onions, saffron, and wine; a thick bean pottage; stewed apples. There was cider for Joanna, red wine for Clemence, ale for Maud, and plum tarts for the final course. Sitting in the place of "honor," Joanna was flushed with happiness. Their dinner usually consisted of soup or fish, bread and cheese, and she took this rich fare as proof that she was loved, in favor. She even dared to hope that her mother might have heeded her pleading, have gotten her the dog she so wanted. She held her breath in excitement now as Maud cleared away the stale bread trenchers that served as plates, as her mother rose, moved toward the bedchamber.

"Joanna, these are for you." Her mother was smiling, holding out her presents: several scarlet hair ribbons and a wooden top.

Joanna bit her lip, blinked back tears. "Thank you, Mama," she mumbled, and Clemence frowned.

"I told you we'd be having no dogs in this house. I thought you understood that."

Joanna swallowed. If only Mama knew how much she wanted a puppy! She'd tried so hard to make Mama understand.

"Joanna! Joanna, I like it not when you sulk; you know that."

"I'm not sulking, Mama, I'm not," Joanna said hastily, and after a long moment, Clemence nodded.

"See that you do not. Now come here and get your birthday kiss."

Joanna did.

Joanna sat on a stool, watching in awe as her mother loosened her thick blonde braids, shook her head in a swirl of brightness. Joanna was fascinated; when unbound, her mother's hair cascaded down her back in a silky tumble of light, reaching well below her hips. She smiled over her shoulder at Joanna, held out the brush, and Joanna reached eagerly for it; she loved brushing her mother's hair, took pride in making it gleam like gold.

"Mama . . . when is your birthday?"

"In less than a fortnight." Clemence seemed to sigh. "My twenty-first. I expect that sounds very old to you?"

"Yes," Joanna admitted, and they both laughed.

"Then I was almost born on your birthday, was I not, Mama? Mama . . . was I not?"

She felt her mother stiffen. "Yes," Clemence said at last, a grudging one-word answer that thudded between them like a stone, and Joanna suddenly wanted to cry. Once again she'd managed to say the wrong thing.

"You have pretty hair, Mama," she said imploringly. "So pretty, it is like looking at the sun."

"That's sweet, Joanna." Clemence reached over, patted Joanna's hand, and then picked up the mirror. As she shifted, Joanna saw her own eyes staring back at her. Not blue like her mother's, but a strange color neither brown nor green, what her mother called hazel, slanting queerly at the corners. Joanna hated her eyes, just as she hated the straight, coarse hair that even now was defying her birthday ribbons.

"Mama . . . why do I not look like you? Why do I have hair black like a crow?"

"Because you take after him." Clemence turned on the stool, gazing upon her daughter, the blind inward look that Joanna most feared, for she knew it meant her mother was remembering, not seeing her at all.

"That was all I asked of God, that I need not see him each time I looked into your face. Little enough to ask, I should think." She laughed suddenly, unsteadily. "But we do pay and pay for our sins, it seems, and you grow more like him with each day that passes."

Joanna shrank back. She knew who "he" was, the father who had not wanted her, who had made Mama so unhappy. "Mama . . ."

"Oh, God, how like him you are!"

Clemence's eyes were not blind now; they were riveted on Joanna's face with an emotional intensity that terrified the child; she thought she could read revulsion in them, and she sobbed, "No, Mama, I'm not! Please, Mama, I'm not!"

This was not the first time her mother had accused her of this blood-sin, but for once her tearful denial proved stronger than the pull of the past. Clemence blinked, sagged back on the stool.

"Do not weep, Joanna," she said, with an effort. "Hush now. It matters not if you've his coloring, as long as you've not his accursed, evil soul."

Joanna's tears dried; once more her mother had forgiven her for a sin beyond her understanding. But when she came back from the garden privy, she found the bedchamber door barred to her. Maud was already asleep, and she scratched softly on the door. "Mama? Mama, it's me."

There was no response. After a few moments she gave up, found a blanket, and dragged it over to the hearth next to Maud. This had happened before; there were times, Maud explained, "when your lady mother needs to be alone." But as she edged closer to Maud's bulky shelter, Joanna wished her mother had not felt such a need on this, her birthday.

The next morning, Clemence was moving about the kitchen by the time Joanna awakened. She was pale, hollow-eyed, and as she bent over to kiss Joanna, there was a sour-wine smell on her breath. But she seemed to have laid her ghosts to rest, at least for a time, and Joanna asked for no more than that. Nor did Maud, who set about cooking breakfast with unusual cheer.

It was midmorning. Joanna was weeding midst their cabbages and onions, chanting under her breath, "Plant a seed, pull a weed," when she looked up and saw the cart moving slowly down the road.

The coming of the cart was an occasion in their lives, much like Christmas or Easter week, and she dashed to meet it. Three or four times a year, a tight-lipped driver she knew only as Luke pulled up at their door. When Joanna had been younger, she'd confused him with St Nicholas, for, like the celebrated saint, Luke brought riches, food, and blankets, and sometimes a pouchful of small silver coins. Dancing with excitement, Joanna sought now to see what the cart held. Two crated geese. Sacks of salt and flour. A barrel of salted pork. Bundles of flax stems; Maud would soak them to separate the fibers, and her mother would then spin them into linen for sheets and clothing. Jars of honey and flagons of wine.

"Mama! Luke's come, and with so much food! Can we have a goose for Michaelmas, can we, Mama?"

Clemence did not answer; she was staring at the object Luke was holding out toward her, a sealed parchment. Joanna slid down from the cart wheel. Mama had never gotten a letter before. She shivered suddenly, watched her mother break the seal with clumsy fingers.

"No! Oh, God, no . . ." The letter fluttered to the ground, and Joanna grabbed for it. But her mother had whirled, was fleeing back into the house.

"Luke? Why did the letter make my mama cry?"

He rarely acknowledged her, generally acted as if she were invisible to adult eyes. But he looked down at her now, said, "Her father is dead."

The bedchamber door was ajar. Joanna gave it a push and it swung open. Her mother and Maud were on the bed, Maud cradling the younger woman as if she were no older than Joanna.

"I always thought . . . thought someday he'd forgive me. I had to believe that, had to . . . but he did not, died believing me to be a whore . . . and I'm not, I'm not!"

"I know, lovedy, I know." Tears were streaming down Maud's face. "My little girl, do not. I beg you . . ."

"And George . . . he'll inherit all, will not pay the rent on the cottage . . . you know he will not! And what will we do, Maud? Mother of God, what will we do?"

Joanna could bear no more. "Mama . . . Mama, do not cry!" But her mother was beyond any consolation she or Maud could offer. She continued to weep as the day dragged on, sometimes silently, hopelessly, sometimes with deep, shuddering sobs that convulsed her in gasping spasms, until at last her body rebelled and she retched miserably into the floor rushes around the bed.

At dark, Maud made pallets for Joanna and herself by the hearth. But the bedchamber door could not completely shut out the sounds of sobbing. At last Joanna cried herself to sleep. She was awakened well past midnight by a dull thud. Sitting up, she saw her mother standing by the table, two of Luke's wine flagons clutched to her chest. She put her fingers to her lips, backed stealthily toward the door. Her face was waxen in the moonlight, her eyes swollen to slits, blonde hair spilling down her breasts and shoulders in a colorless, tangled snarl. Joanna's breathing quickened; this glassy-eyed, swaying stranger was not her mother.

By the time she wriggled free of the blankets, Clemence had retreated back into the bedchamber. As Joanna reached the door, she heard the bolt slide into place. When Maud awoke at dawn, she found the little girl asleep on the floor, huddled against the bedchamber door.

The day seemed endless. Joanna wandered about the cottage like a ghost; not even Middleham Castle could lure her away from that closed bedchamber door. Maud made periodic attempts to coax Clemence out. Sometimes her entreaties provoked curses and slurred abuse; at other times her pleas echoed into an eerie silence. At dusk, Maud set a plate of cheese and bread before Joanna, stood over the child until she choked down a few mouthfuls, and then put her to bed by the hearth. Exhausted, Joanna slept.

But the next morning the bedchamber door was still bolted. Maud sent Joanna for Cedric, and as they hastened back up the path toward the cottage, they could hear Maud's fists thudding against the oaken door.

"My lady, I beg you, open the door. You've not eaten for two full days."

Maud's hands were raw, knuckles bleeding, but she continued to beat futilely on the door until shouldered aside by Cedric. He tested the latch several times, and then said, "Where is your axe?"

Maud gave a low moan and gestured, but a shudder passed through her body each time the axe connected with the wood. As the door gave way, Cedric put his shoulder to it, shoved inward, and stumbled into the room. Joanna heard him gasp, and then he had spun around, was seeking to block Maud's entry with an outstretched arm. She lunged past him, and then began to scream.

There was a strong stench in the room, of wine and vomit and urine. Joanna could see part of the bed, see the overturned flagon on the floor. Wine dripped from the rim, had gathered in a sodden pool midst the rushes. Her mother's blonde hair swept the floor; the ends were trailing in the wine, matted and dark. The wine looked like blood to Joanna. She tried to take a step closer, but her knees gave way.

"A doctor, name of God, fetch a doctor!"

A white arm dangled over the side of the bed, fingers tightly clenched. Cedric reached out, reluctantly grasped the wrist and quickly let it drop. "Nay, we do need a priest," he said huskily, and Maud fell to her knees by the bed, began a high keening wail. Cedric crossed himself, backed toward the door.

Joanna found herself sitting on the floor by the hearth. She slid along the ground until she reached the table, crawled under. There she crouched, putting her hands up to her ears to shut out Maud's screams.

Maud had yet to move away from Clemence's body. She looked up as Cedric reentered the bedchamber, and her face contorted in fear, for he'd not summoned the village priest; the white-garbed monk at his side was John Brompton, Abbot of Jervaulx Abbey. He looked at the woman on the bed, shook his head slowly, and Maud sobbed, grabbed his arm.

"A mischance, Reverend Father, that is all . . . I swear it! She wanted only to sleep . . ."

He disengaged her clutching fingers, gazed down at the empty wine flagons. "She did take a sleeping draught?"

Maud sobbed again. "Her nights were so bad, Abbot John. Last spring I went to the castle leech; he gave me henbane and white poppy. But she meant no harm to herself. You must believe that, must let her be buried in consecrated ground, I beg you . . ."

Her voice rose shrilly, and the Abbot said hastily, "Calm yourself, woman. You do disturb yourself for naught, I assure you. It is plain enough what happened. She was distraught, did misjudge the potion."

Maud nodded dumbly, then snatched up his hand and, before he could withdraw, pressed it to her lips. He patted her shoulder, said, "Do you wish Cedric to see the wainright about building a coffin?"

She'd buried her face in her apron, only wept the harder, and he sighed, unfastened the crucifix that dangled from his belt, and approached the bed. As he did, he happened to glance toward the outer room, and for the first time he noticed Joanna, cowering under the table.

"God in Heaven, did you never think of the child?"

Joanna watched as he knelt beside her, held out his hand. "Come to me, little one. That's a good lass . . ."

He smelled of sweat and horses and garlic, but his voice was soft, coaxing. Joanna wrapped her arms around his neck. She was trembling so violently that her teeth were chattering, and she bit down on her thumb, tasting blood in her mouth. "Mama . . ."

"She's in God's keeping now, lass. She's dead."

Clinging to the Abbot's hand, Joanna entered into the bailey of Middleham Castle. Ahead of her rose the limestone ashlar keep. She stared up at it, openmouthed, for it seemed to reach straight toward Heaven. A wooden stairway extended out into the bailey, led up into the keep, and she hesitated, dizzy at the thought of scaling those heights, but the Abbot gently propelled her forward, and she grasped the railing, began a slow, cautious climb.

The great hall could easily have accommodated their entire cottage, so vast it was, with windows soaring toward the roof and an open hearth in the center of the floor. A woman was moving toward them, dressed in the softest blue wool Joanna had ever seen.

"I've been expecting you, Reverend Father. Is this the child?"

"Aye. Joanna, this is the Lady Helweisa, wife to Lord Robert. Make your curtsy and then await me in the window seat."

He watched as the child moved away, said, "She has not cried, not even yesterday when we buried her mother." Turning, he gratefully took the wine cup a servant was offering, followed Helweisa to the hearth.

"Tell me, Madame, what do you know of the girl's mother?"

"Nothing, if truth be told. Guy, our bailiff, rented them the cottage, and all their dealings were with him. Neither my husband nor I concern ourselves with such minor matters. I did assume that the woman was a young widow or, more likely, a foolish girl who'd listened to the wrong man's blandishments."

He nodded. "An all-too-common tale, I fear. The girl was very young, and the man was married. When her family discovered she was with child, they cast her out in disgrace."

"How, then, did she pay the upkeep on the cottage?"

"From what the old woman, Maud, told me, the girl's father paid the rent, saw that her needs were met. Not so much out of charity, I fear, as to keep her from bringing further shame upon the family name. He knew enough to realize that a girl turned out to starve will buy her bread with all she has left to barter, her body. But although they put food on her table, they denied her their forgiveness. The father said she was dead in his eyes, and held to that, even upon his deathbed. The elder son was no less rigid. The younger son was more sympathetic, but he could not gainsay his father and brother, although he did take it upon himself to write her of their father's death. The rest you know."

"As you say, Reverend Father, a common tale, and likely to remain so, as long as there be born men with glib tongues and silly chits willing to pay them heed. What mean you to do about the child? A pity she is not a boy; it might be easier to find a family willing to take in a lad."

"That is why I've come to you, Madame. You see, the girl was wellborn, of Norman stock. I got the family name from Maud: d'Arcy. The father held his manor from no less a lord than William de Ferrers, Earl of Derby."

"Ah, that does put a different light upon it," Helweisa conceded. "If the child's mother be of gentle birth, then a villein's hut is no fitting place for her, bastard or no. What would you have me do, write to the family?''

The Abbot nodded. "Aye, to the younger brother, Sir Roger d'Arcy. He should be told of his sister's death . . . and of her child's need."

"I shall be glad to oblige you, of course, Abbot John." Helweisa's eyes strayed across the hall to where Joanna sat, very still, in the window seat. "Poor little lass, I wonder what shall become of her."

"She is in God's hands, Madame. As are we all."

There was no reality in Joanna's time at Middleham; it left little imprint upon her memory. She did as she was bade, spoke when spoken to, and when left to her own devices, she sat for hours staring out at the dales, now burnished with bracken. To the other children of the castle, pages and playmates of Lord and Lady Fitz Ranulf's young son Ralph, she was a curiosity and, provoked by her eerie indifference, they baited her with words learned from their elders: "bastard" and "sideslip." They were the first to put a name to it, to the sin of birth that somehow made her different from other children. A fortnight ago, she'd have been devastated by their mockery. But now their taunts had no power to hurt. What mattered if they called her "bastard"? She had so much more grievous wrongs to answer for. Mama was dead because of her. In her grieving, Mama had sobbed out the truth at last, had cried, "If only she'd never been born!"

Mama had not wanted her, and now Mama was dead, and it was her doing, would not have happened if not for her. She did not wonder that Maud did not come to the castle to see her. How could there be forgiveness for a sin so great?

On her ninth day at Middleham, she was awakened by a young maidservant, and to her astonishment and apprehension, was told to attend Lord and Lady Fitz Ranulf in the solar.

She'd seen Lord Fitz Ranulf only in passing, was much in awe of him, a heavyset man in his fifties, with the brusque, no-nonsense manner of one who does not suffer fools gladly, and prides himself inordinately upon that impatience. Lady Helweisa was more familiar to Joanna. A plump, complacent woman much her husband's junior, she would stop and talk to Joanna whenever they happened to meet in the bailey or great hall, but Joanna did not think Lady Helweisa truly heard her answers.

Her nervousness eased somewhat, though, at sight of Abbot John, for he had been kind to her. The fourth man in the chamber was young, dressed in starkest black, with a long sword at his left hip. But it was his hair that held Joanna's eyes; it was blond, the same sunlit shade as her mother's.

"Come here, Joanna." Lady Helweisa beckoned her into the solar. "There's one here to meet you, your uncle, Sir Roger d'Arcy."

Joanna gasped, stared up at this man who was her kin, her family. As her gaze reached his face, she saw he had her mother's sapphire-blue eyes.

"Jesú!" His breath hissed through his teeth; the blue eyes widened. "Christ, if she's not his very image!"

For the briefest moment, hope had flickered in the dark of Joanna's world. Her uncle had come for her. But with his words, that faint hope guttered, died. There was on his face the same expression that had been on her mother's the night she'd cried, "Oh, God, how like him you are!"

Seeing they all were staring at him, Roger d'Arcy drew a deep breath, said, "I'd never seen her, you see . . ." There was a wine cup on the table, and he reached for it, drank until he began to cough. "I expect you think my father was a hard man. Mayhap he was. He put family honor above all else, taught us to do likewise. He taught us, too, that a woman of rank must be chaste, must go to her marriage bed a virgin. When my sister confessed she was with child, he felt betrayed. Shamed."

"And you?" Abbot John asked quietly.

"It was my duty to obey my father's wishes." Roger drank again, not meeting their eyes. "But . . . she was so pretty, my sister. So quick to laugh. And so young. Just fifteen when she came to court. Fifteen . . ." He turned back to face them, said tautly, "I always did blame him, not her. She was such an innocent, such easy prey. I'd have killed him if I could." His voice sounded suddenly muffled, as if he were swallowing tears. "But I could not. I could only watch my sister suffer for his accursed lust."

Helweisa and her husband exchanged glances. Roger d'Arcy had just unwittingly confirmed a growing suspicion of hers. Why had not the d'Arcys taken vengeance upon the man? As bitter as they were, one thing alone could have stayed their hand; the man had to be highborn. Very highborn.

"What of the child's father, Sir Roger? Would he do nothing for your sister?"

He shook his head. "She'd have died ere she asked him for so much as a shilling. My sister was a d'Arcy, Madame; she, too, was proud."

Helweisa hesitated, and then decided that the best tactic might be a direct frontal assault. "Sir Roger, who is the child's father?"

He looked at her, then down at Joanna, and she said, "Your sister is beyond slander. If you keep silent now, you do but protect the man."

"You're right," he said abruptly. "By God, you're right. The man who seduced my sister, the man I blame for her death—he is the Count of Mortain."

There was a shocked silence; even Helweisa had gotten more than she'd bargained for. Her husband whistled softly, as Abbot John echoed, incredulous, "The Count of Mortain? John, the King's brother?"

Roger nodded. "Mayhap you understand now why we could not . . ." His voice trailed off.

"Joanna," Abbot John said hastily, "go and sit in the window seat," and held up his hand for silence till she was out of earshot. "That does explain much. But there is one thing I do not understand. For all his vices, Lord John has never failed to acknowledge his bastards. He may spill his seed without care, but he's then willing to claim the crop as his; he has at least five baseborn children, and they lack for little. Why would he not do as much for Joanna?"

"My sister hated him, Abbot John, blamed him for her plight. She took her vengeance the only way she could, by denying him his daughter. We gave it out that the child was stillborn." Roger saw the Abbot's disapproval, added defensively, "My sister feared, too, that John might take Joanna from her if he knew. Christ curse him, he had the power."

He drained the wine cup, set it down. "I am in your debt for what you did for my sister, Abbot John. I shall be taking Maud back with me. She nursed us all; we'd not have her starve. I shall send Luke for the furnishings of the cottage." As he spoke, he was taking a pouch from his belt, spilling several silver pennies onto the table. "Take these, Abbot John, and have Masses said for my sister on her month-mind."

The Abbot nodded, but then realized that Roger d'Arcy meant to depart. "Sir Roger, wait! What of the child?"

Roger seemed no less taken aback. "Surely you do not expect us to take her in? John's spawn? My brother would sooner shelter a leper, and in this I do agree with him. There are always villagers in want of children; place her with one of them."

"Sir Roger, these be hard times; few of our serfs have food to spare for their own. And what of your sister? Joanna is her child, too."

Roger was shaking his head. "We cannot take her. My brother would never consent, and I— Do you not see? Every time I did look upon her, I'd remember the Hell that was my sister's life these five years past. Christ, you cannot ask that of us. She'd be a living, festering sore in our midst, and we will not take her. We cannot!" But he did not move, and after a moment, he shook additional coins out onto the table.

"There; use that for her corrody, place her with the nuns at St Clements. I can do no more than that." Not waiting for their response, he moved swiftly toward the door, did not look back.

Abbot John approached the table, looked down at the silver pennies. "Well, mayhap it is for the best. May the lass stay with you, my lord, until I can make arrangements with the sisters in York?"

Robert Fitz Ranulf nodded, then turned in surprise as his wife said, "No, Reverend Father. We can put that money to better use. Why not send the child to her father, to John?"

"Madame, you would undertake that? Lord John is in Normandy, and to be truthful, I think such a journey would cost more than d'Arcy's grudging offering."

"No matter, we will pay the difference," Helweisa said placidly, and her husband stared at her in outraged astonishment.

"That is indeed a kindness, Madame, and you shall not go unrewarded for it. God sees . . . and approves."

"I do not doubt it, Abbot John." Helweisa smiled, shepherded the Abbot toward the door.

"Have you lost your senses, woman? Whatever possessed you to make an offer like that? You do not even know that John would accept her as his!"

"Ah, Rob, that is a false fear. Whatever other evils may be credited to his account, John does tend to his own, and that child is his. Once he sees her, he'd be the last to deny that."

"Even so, you do not expect him to reimburse us for our trouble, do you? What prince ever paid back a debt?"

"That is true enough," she conceded readily. "But it will be a cheap price to pay for the favor of a King."

"And what makes you so sure that John will ever be King?"

"My dearest, can you doubt it? It's been five years now since Richard's mother badgered him into taking a Spanish wife, and she's yet even to set foot in England! Richard will give England no son of his loins; nor is he a man to die peacefully in bed. He has but two possible heirs, his brother John or his nephew Arthur. Arthur is a child of nine. John is twenty-eight, and has Lucifer's own luck. Did we not all think he'd ruined himself with his scheming when Richard was taken by his enemies in Austria? Remember what happened when Richard's ransom was finally paid? John was banished from England, had the earldoms of Mortain and Gloucester taken from him. And then? He did meet with Richard in Normandy, somehow got Richard to forgive him and, within a year, even to restore his titles. Any man who could work a miracle like that is no man to wager against, Rob.''

Her husband nodded slowly. ''Mayhap I was overhasty in objecting. Very well, you do have my permission.''

Helweisa, who'd never doubted that for a moment, nonetheless gave him a grateful smile, a dutiful kiss. ''I think I know just the one to escort the child, Rob. Simon, our bailiff's eldest. He's a likely lad, and can be trusted to keep his wits about him.''

Across the solar, Joanna sat, forgotten, in the window seat. She understood now why her mother had not wanted her, why her uncle and Maud did not want her. There was something shameful in her birth, so much so that her uncle had looked upon her with loathing.

''Joanna?'' Lady Helweisa was standing by the window seat, smiling at her. ''I do have wondrous news, child. You are to go to Normandy, to go to your lord father.''

Joanna's breath stopped. She could only stare up at the woman, too stricken for speech, for more than a whispered, ''Please, no . . .'' that none heard, or would have heeded.

Joanna's fear of her father was soon eclipsed by the utter misery of her journey. Perched precariously behind Simon's saddle, she slowly overcame her panicked conviction that each dip in the road would jar loose her hold on Simon's belt, send her sprawling into the dirt, to be trampled by the horses of Simon's escort. But the jouncing soon raised blisters and welts upon her thighs and buttocks. As Simon was under orders to make haste, some days they covered thirty miles, and Joanna's muscles would be so cramped and sore that she could barely crawl into bed at night. Bed was generally no more than a scratchy woolen blanket, and on those nights when they could find no monastery or inn to take them in, they bedded down in the fields, Joanna huddling against Simon in a futile search for warmth, for it was October now and the nights were chill.

The days blurred, one into the next. They would be on the road at dawn, moving south through ghostly hamlets and silent villages, for plague and famine were abroad in the land. Simon's men kept swords loose in their scabbards, for all knew that in troubled times the roads abounded with highwaymen and brigands. Joanna's anxieties were more immediate; too shy to ask Simon to stop when she needed to relieve herself, she suffered agonies of discomfort, and once, the ultimate humiliation, as urine trickled down her legs, stained her skirt. Her world was taking on more and more the aspects of a terrifying dream, one that offered no escape.

They reached London on the tenth day. Joanna had not thought there could be so many people in all of Christendom. The streets were never still. Heavy carts rumbled by; men led overladen pack animals; women rode sidesaddle and in horse litters; the activity never seemed to cease. Nor did the noise. She was glad when, after a night passed in a seedy Cheapside inn, Simon led her toward the wharves.

The docks were crowded with vessels, large galleys manned by oarsmen, smaller esneques rigged with canvas sails. It was one of these that was to convey them across the Channel, and Joanna found herself squeezed into a dark, foul-smelling canvas tent already overflowing with pilgrims, merchants, and mercenaries. Joanna had never even seen the sea, and she became seasick almost at once. Most of the passengers were experiencing the same distress, and the fetid, airless tent soon became unbearable for all entombed within.

It took several days to navigate the River Thames and turn south into the Channel. They reached the Seine estuary on the third day, began the slow passage upriver toward Rouen, not dropping anchor until dusk on the following day. It was dark by the time they disembarked. Joanna had long since passed the limits of her endurance. She stumbled after Simon in a daze, clutching his hand as if it were her only lifeline. When he dragged her into a riverside alehouse, she simply sat down on the floor at his feet. Snatches of his conversation drifted to her. ". . . in Rouen for the wedding of his sister Joanna, the Queen of Sicily, to the Count of Toulouse . . . bringing his baseborn daughter . . ." Joanna at once was surrounded by strangers, suddenly the center of attention. She heard someone say, "He is at Le Vieille, at the castle." That was the last thing she remembered. There on the dirt floor of the tavern, she fell into an exhausted sleep.

When she awakened, she found herself in a large, torchlit chamber, again encircled by strangers. The smoke from the hearth stung her eyes; she rubbed them with the back of her hand, tried to focus on her surroundings.

"I suppose we must take your word that there is a child hidden underneath all that grime. Has she ever, in all her life, had a bath?"

The voice was scornful, belonged to the most beautiful woman Joanna had ever seen, fair-skinned and flaxen-haired, a flesh-and-blood embodiment of ideal womanhood, as extolled in Clemence's bedtime chansons. But this bewitching creature was looking at her with such distaste that Joanna flushed, pressed back against Simon, who seemed no less flustered. He stammered something about the hardships of the road, and the woman laughed.

"I daresay you never even noticed how she looked. God knows, you're filthy enough yourself!"

Joanna did not like this woman, not at all. "My mama gave me baths," she said, and was bewildered when those around her laughed.

But then the door was opening, and two enormous dogs were rushing at her, barking furiously. They towered above Joanna; when one lunged at her, hot breath brushing her face, her nerves gave way and she began to scream, could not stop even after someone had lifted her to safety.

Joanna's screams soon gave way to choked sobs. Her rescuer let her cry, having silenced the dogs with a one-word command. His tunic seemed wondrously soft to her, fragrant with orris root. She rubbed her cheek against it, felt his hand moving on her hair.

"Do you not like dogs, lass?" he asked, stirring an immediate, indignant denial.

"I love dogs! But they were so big . . . ." Peering down from his arms, she saw that the dogs were not quite so monstrous after all, were merely large, friendly wolfhounds. "I love dogs," she repeated. "But my mama would never let me have one."

He laughed, and touched his finger to a smudge on her nose. "Well, you are a surprise package, if a rather bedraggled one. How would you fancy a bath?"

A pallet had been made up by the bed; they stood looking down at the sleeping child.

"Do you remember the mother at all, John?"

"Yes, I do; does that surprise you? Clemence d'Arcy. A very pretty girl . . . and a very stupid one."

Joanna's clothes lay on the floor by the bathing tub, and John touched them with the toe of his boot. "Have these rags burned, Adele. I assume there is a seamstress in the castle? See that she has enough material, from your own coffers, if need be."

"But John . . . it's nigh on ten; she's abed for certes."

"Not for long. I want a new gown for Joanna by morning, something soft, in green or gold." Reaching for the corner of the blanket, he rubbed gently at Joanna's wet hair. She stirred, but did not awaken.

"I'm amazed, in truth, that she does not seem to fear me. I rather doubt that Clemence spoke tenderly of me. Until I can engage a suitable nurse, I'll expect you to care for her," he added, and Adele's mouth dropped open.

"Me?"

"Yes, darling—you. Passing strange about the name. Joanna was Clemence's mother; I recall now. I think I shall tell her that she was named after my sister Joanna. She is my first daughter, Adele; all the others have been sons."

Adele laughed. "I've never seen this side of you before, John. You remind me of nothing so much as a lad with a new toy!"

John raised his head, gave her a long, level look. "I begin to think you might be as stupid as Clemence," he said, very softly, and Adele paled.

"I did not mean to offend you, my lord."

"Well, then, you'd best think how to make it up to me, darling," he said, still softly, and she nodded.

"It shall be my pleasure."

"Not entirely yours, I hope!" He laughed then, and after a pause, she laughed, too.

Joanna slept till midmorning, awakening, bewildered, in a huge curtained bed as soft as a cloud. There was a fox-fur coverlet pulled up over her, and at the foot of the bed lay the most beautiful clothes she'd ever seen: a linen chemise, an emerald wool gown, and a bliaut over-tunic of green and gold. But her own gown was nowhere in sight.

Wrapping herself in the fur coverlet, she moved cautiously from the bed, began to search the chamber for her clothes. Never had she been in a room like this. The walls were covered with linen hangings, glowing with color. Thickly laid floor rushes, intermingled with sweet-smelling basil and mint, tickled the soles of her feet. There was a table covered with a clean white cloth, an enormous oaken coffer, even a large brass chamber pot.

Joanna was at a loss. But she was remembering more now, remembered being bathed and put to bed, remembered a man with a reassuring smile, green-gold eyes, and the beautiful, unfriendly woman he called Adele. She remembered, too, how, when she'd awakened in the night, not knowing where she was, he'd taken her into bed with him and Adele; nestled between them, she'd soon slept again, feeling safe for the first time since her mother died.

The door opened; Adele entered. "Well, you're up at last. John's awaiting you in the great hall, so hurry and dress."

"My clothes are gone," Joanna said reluctantly, suddenly afraid that she'd be blamed for their loss.

"They're right there on the bed." Adele pointed impatiently when Joanna merely looked at her, uncomprehending. And only then did Joanna reach out, timidly touch the soft lace edging the chemise, not truly convinced such clothes could be hers until Adele snapped, much as her mother had so often done, "Are you going to tarry all day? Put them on."

Following Adele down the winding stairwell, Joanna discovered it led to a great hall, much like the one at Middleham. Dogs were rooting in the floor rushes for bones; servants were carrying platters of food; men seated at long trestle tables laughed and joked as they ate, the overall atmosphere one of cheerful chaos. Joanna hesitated, daunted by the sight of so many people, but Adele pushed her forward, into the hall. "Go on in. Would you keep him waiting?"

At the end of the hall a dais had been set up, and Joanna recognized the man who'd been so kind to her the night before. She was gathering up her courage to approach him when he beckoned to her. She came at once, realizing, with a jolt of astonished happiness, that he was as glad to see her as she was to see him. Within moments she found herself seated beside him, being urged to share the food ladled onto his trencher. She was dazzled both by the size of the portions and the amazing variety: roasted venison, lampreys in sauce, a rissole of beef marrow, pea soup, glazed wafers, pancake crisps, and a sweet spiced wine he called hippocras.

John let her sip from his cup, named each food for her—even let her choose for herself which dishes she wanted to try, and by the end of the meal, Joanna was utterly captivated by him. He had a low, pleasant voice, never raised it, and yet was obeyed with celerity. It was obvious to Joanna that he was a man of importance. That made it all the more wondrous that he should take such an interest in her. She watched him closely, eating what he ate, and laughing when he did, so intent she did not at first notice what would normally have claimed all her attention, the small spaniel puppy being led toward the dais.

"You said your mother would allow you no dog, Joanna. Well, I will," John said, depositing the squirming spaniel in her lap. He heard her catch her breath; she looked up at him with eyes so adoring that he laughed. "I think you shall be cheaper to content than the other women in my life; they yearn for pearls and silks, not puppies."

"For me? Truly for me?" The puppy was a soft silver grey; it wriggled as Joanna ruffled its fur, swiped at her fingers with its tongue.

"Have you a name in mind, Joanna?" When she shook her head, John smiled. "I've one for you, then. Why not call her Avisa?"

Joanna thought that a very pretty name, wondered why so many of the men laughed. One, wearing a priest's cassock, said, "Despite your differences, the Lady Avisa is still your wife, my lord, in the eyes of both man and God."

"And precisely because she is, Father, I can say for certes that Avisa is an uncommonly apt name for a bitch," John said dryly, and again those around the dais laughed.

Joanna did not understand this byplay, but she reached out, shyly stroked John's sleeve. "I do like Avisa for the puppy," she said, seeking to please him, saw by his smile that she had.

After the meal was cleared away, the men sat down at one of the tables and unrolled a large map of Normandy. Joanna hovered in the background, playing with her puppy. When her curiosity drew her toward the table, John did not chase her away; instead he sat her on his lap, spent several moments pointing out places on the map, showing her a French town called Gamaches and telling her how he had taken and burnt the town that August past for his brother the King. Joanna did not understand about battles or campaigns; what mattered to her was that he should take the time and trouble to explain.

She was so happy that she went quite willingly when Adele came to fetch her. Back in the bedchamber, she sat docilely upon the coffer while Adele brushed her hair, wondering why Adele, who obviously did not like her, should care if her hair was combed or not. When Adele put the brush away, she went to the window, climbed onto the seat to gaze down into the bailey. And panicked at what she saw.

"Simon!" She'd actually forgotten all about him.

"Who is Simon?"

"He brought me here." Joanna jerked at the shutters, tugged until she'd blocked Simon from view. "When does he go?"

Adele shrugged. "On the morrow, I expect."

On the morrow. On the morrow Simon would take her away, to her father.

As soon as Adele departed the chamber, Joanna scrambled from the window seat. Never before had she thought to rebel, but never before had so much been at stake. She quickly settled upon the coffer. Rooting in the hearth for a suitable stick of firewood, she tucked the puppy under her arm, lowered herself into the coffer, and jammed the stick under the lid so she'd not be utterly in the dark. On the morrow Simon would search for her in vain, would have to leave without her.

"Joanna?"

She tensed, heard her name called again. Avisa had begun to whimper. She shivered, kept very still. And then the coffer lid was thrown back, her hiding place exposed.

"Why did you not answer me, Joanna? What foolish game is this?" But at sight of her tearstained face, John's annoyance ebbed away. Reaching down, he lifted her out, set her beside him on the bed.

"Now, tell me what is wrong."

"I was hiding from Simon," she confessed. "So he could not take me to my father."

There was a silence. She slanted a glance through wet lashes, saw he was watching her, with a very strange look on his face. "Please," she entreated. "Do not make me go with him."

Still he said nothing. As hope faded, tears began to streak her face again.

"I thought you understood. Joanna . . . I am your father."

He saw her eyes widen, pupils dilate with shock. He started to touch her, stopped himself. "Joanna . . . what did your mother tell you of me?"

She swallowed. "That you were wicked, that your soul was accursed, that you did not want me."

The corner of John's mouth twitched. "She lied to you, lass. I do want you."

Joanna stared down into her lap. "Mama did not want me," she whispered.

"Did you love your mother, Joanna?"

She nodded, and then said, almost inaudibly, "I was afraid of Mama sometimes."

John reached out, tilted her chin up. "Do you fear me?"

She did not answer at once, and he was later to tell Adele that he'd actually been able to see it in her eyes, that moment when loyalty given to a dead woman was given to him.

"No," she said, and as the wonder of that realization registered with her, she shook her head vehemently. "No, oh, no . . ."

"You're flesh of my flesh, Joanna, of my blood. You understand what that means?"

"That I belong to you?" she ventured, and he smiled.

"Just so, Joanna. Just so." And then she was in his arms, clinging, and he was laughing, hugging her back.

That was the beginning of the good times for Joanna.

8

POITIERS, PROVINCE OF POITOU

January 1199

"So you've come. I was not sure you would."

"Of course I came, Madame. You sent for me, did you not?" John's smile faded. "What is wrong? Why do you look at me like that?"

"As if you do not know!" Eleanor had stood motionless by the hearth as John crossed the chamber. But as soon as he moved within reach, she took two quick steps forward and struck him across the mouth. "You fool! You utter fool!"

John gasped, grabbed her wrist when she raised her hand as if to strike him again. His face was stinging; her signet ring had scratched his cheek. "Christ Jesus, Mother, what is the matter with you? Why should you be wroth with me?"

"Why, indeed? Betrayal is as natural to you as breathing, is it not? More fool I, for imagining it could ever be otherwise!" Eleanor jerked her wrist free, began to pace. "Five full years without a misstep, five years of fidelity. Besieging Evreux, burning Gamaches, taking the Bishop of Beauvais prisoner—all for one reason only, to win Richard's favor. And you were more successful than you know. Not that Richard would ever trust you again, in this life or the next, but you had shown him you could do more than intrigue, that you were not as worthless as he once thought. Five years, John, all for naught. Name of God, why?"

"Why what? Just what am I supposed to have done?"

"Oh, enough! We know, you see, know of your latest scheming with the French King. Philip told Richard all when they met on Wednesday last to declare a truce. And how fitting that you should be betrayed to the very one you did mean to betray!"

"And Richard believed this?" John was incredulous. "What

joy it must give Philip, that he has only to dangle the bait and
Richard invariably lunges for it like a starving trout! But you,
Madame, God's truth, I'd have expected better of you!"

"Philip claims to have a letter that proves your complicity in
this intrigue, a letter in your own hand."

"Oh, for the love of Christ! What better proof of my innocence could you ask for than that? If I were involved in some
scheme to betray Richard, do you truly think I'd ever be so stupid
as to incriminate myself in writing? Are you sure Philip does not
have a convenient confession, too, that I somehow happened to
sign and leave in his safekeeping?"

Eleanor felt the first flickers of doubt. "Your denial has the
ring of truth to it," she said slowly. "But then your denials
always do, John."

"If you and Richard believe this lunatic accusation, it can only
be because you want to believe it, Madame. You yourself said it;
five full years I've devoted to regaining Richard's goodwill.
Think you that I've enjoyed being at his beck and call, being
subject to his erratic tempers, his every whim? Or that I'd gamble
those five years on something so worthless as Philip's word?
Jesus God, Mother! What would I gain by intriguing with Philip?
We both know he has no hope of ever defeating Richard on the
field."

He was as angry as Eleanor had ever seen him, too angry for
either artifice or discretion. His was not a defense calculated to
endear, and would have found little favor with Richard. But there
was an ice-blooded, unsparing honesty to it that was, to Eleanor,
more persuasive than any indignant avowals of good faith. It was
the very amorality of John's argument that carried so much
conviction. "You're saying, then, that Philip was merely seeking
to stir up trouble between you and Richard?"

"And succeeding, from the sound of it. Know you where
Richard is now? Will I find him still at Castle Gaillard?"

Eleanor no longer doubted. There could be no better indication
of John's innocence than this, that he would willingly seek
Richard out. When he was in the wrong, the last thing he ever
wanted was to face his accusers, to confront those he'd betrayed.

Eleanor's relief was inexpressible. Her easy acceptance of
John's guilt had been prompted as much by fear as by her son's
dismal record of broken faith and betrayals, the fear that she had
misjudged him, after all, that he was not the pragmatist she'd
thought him to be. Had he indeed been intriguing with Philip,
that would mean to Eleanor that his judgment was fatally and

unforgivably flawed, flawed enough to taint any claim he might
have had to the crown. That was a conclusion she shrank from,
for it would signify the end of all her hopes for an Angevin
dynasty, and that was the dream which had somehow sustained
her even when she'd had nothing else to hold on to.

She sat down abruptly in a cushioned chair. "Thank God,"
she said simply, with enough feeling to soothe John's sense of
injury.

"But of course I do accept your apologies, Mother," he said,
very dryly. Righteous indignation was not an emotion indigenous
to his temperamental terrain; he had too much irony in his
makeup to be able to cultivate moral outrage, and now that he no
longer feared being called to account for a sin that truly was not
his, he was beginning to see the perverse humor in his predicament. " 'Be not righteous overmuch,' " he quoted, and grinned.
"But how can I help it? After all, how often have I been able to
expose my conscience to your exacting eye . . . and lived to tell
the tale?"

Eleanor could not help herself, had to smile, too. "By what
strange alchemy do you manage to make your vices sound so
much like virtues?" She shook her head, gestured toward the
table. "Fetch me pen and parchment. Better that I be the one to
assure Richard of your innocence."

The ancient river port of Rennes was the capital of Brittany. It
was, as well, the favorite residence of Arthur, the young Duke
who bore the name of a fabled Celtic King and never doubted
that one day he, too, would be a King.

The April wind had suddenly shifted and servants were hastening to shutter the windows on the leeward side of the great hall.
A juggler was making a manful attempt to entertain, but only
Arthur was finding his antics amusing; the adults were far more
interested in speculating upon the provocative presence of the man
seated at Arthur's right. John had arrived in Rennes at dusk the
preceding day, bearing lavish gifts for his "dear nephew" and
"sweet sister-by-marriage." While all agreed that he must have
an ulterior motive in mind, none could agree upon what it was,
and after twenty-four hours of unbridled conjecture, rumors were
rampant, the Breton court was in turmoil, and John was enjoying
himself immensely.

Growing bored now with the amateurish efforts of Arthur's
juggler, John appropriated a ruby ring from the prettiest of the
women. Showing off the sleight of hand that never failed to

delight his daughter, Joanna, he soon had an appreciative audience, and when he at last pretended to find the ring in the girl's bodice, she blushed midst all the laughter, but then slanted him a long-lashed look of unmistakable invitation.

"I want to learn how to do that trick, would have you teach me." After a nudge from his mother, Arthur grudgingly added, "If you will, Uncle."

"It would give me great pleasure to lesson you, lad," John said pleasantly. "On the morrow, shall we say?" Knowing that Arthur was a typical twelve-year-old in that what he wanted, he wanted at once.

Arthur was not that much older than John's son Richard, but the two cousins had nothing whatsoever in common beyond a blood bond. Richard was an unusually introspective youngster, conscientious and cautious, but quietly stubborn, too; John was fond of his youngest son, but he never knew what Richard was thinking. Arthur was Richard's opposite in all particulars. Boisterous, cocky, imperious as only a cherished only son can be, Arthur was not accustomed to sharing the limelight, and he'd taken John's unexpected arrival with exceedingly poor grace. He could not comprehend why he must welcome his only rival for the Angevin crown, and at first he'd not even made a pretense of civility. But the ruder he was, the more courteous John became, indulgently affectionate, playful, answering insult with an exaggerated solicitude that stopped just short of parody. Arthur was spoiled, but by no means stupid, and he was not long in realizing that John was getting much the best of these exchanges. He was too young, however, to understand that he was, in effect, making a fool of himself. Now he opened his mouth to protest, thought better of it, and lapsed into a sulky silence.

But John had lost all interest in baiting the boy. A woman was approaching the dais. Making a graceful curtsy before Arthur, she then curtsied to John. She had utterly compelling eyes the shade of purest sapphire; she looked briefly into his face, and turned away. John waited a discreet interval, announced he was retiring for the night, and made an ostentatious departure for his own chambers.

The gardens were deserted. Although early April, it was as if spring were being held in abeyance that year; the trees were barren, the grass still browned and sere. John hesitated, stepped off the path.

She was waiting for him in the arbor, came quickly into his

arms. He slid his hands under her mantle, kissed her mouth, her throat, and she sighed, pressed close against him.

"I heard you'd come, but did not believe it. What devious game are you playing now, John? Why are you here?"

"To see you again, why else?" John said, in part because he thought it was expected of him, and in part because he was curious to see if she was naïve enough to believe him.

She laughed softly. "How gallant! But have you forgotten how well I know you, my love? Have you some specific troublemaking in mind, or are you merely seeking to muddy the waters?"

"The latter," John admitted; he, too, was laughing now. "Philip could find conspiracy in a convent of Cistercian nuns, and his favored pastime is jumping to conclusions. Need I tell you what dire plots he'll read into my visit to Arthur's court? And whilst Philip is convincing himself that Arthur and I must be up to no good, Arthur's advisers are unable to sleep for worrying over what I've got in mind. It's not often I've been able to sow so much discord with so little effort!"

"I cannot blame you for wanting to give Philip some grief. My husband told me about the good turn he tried to do you. There were more than a few here in Rennes who were right disappointed that Philip's ploy came to naught."

"That I do not doubt, sweetheart. It's lucky, in truth, that Richard and I have such pure and perfect trust between us . . . is it not?" John began to kiss her again. "I hear your husband is in Nantes; how long will he be gone?"

"A fortnight, at least. How long can you stay?"

"Till the week's end. Richard's been besieging some godforsaken castle near Limoges; one of his vassals found a Roman treasure on his lands and was then idiotic enough to refuse when Richard claimed it all as his liege lord. Richard expects to need just a week to wreak utter havoc upon the poor fool's lands, told me to meet him and our lady mother at Fontevrault Abbey for Easter. But ere I do, I want to pass some time in Rouen; I've a lass there most eager for the sight of me."

"Indeed?" Feigning anger, she dug her nails into the back of his hand. "If you think I came out into the cold to listen to you boast about your other bedmates . . ."

"She's my daughter, darling. I do not have her with me as often as I ought, but I do try. With my sons, it is different. Save for Richard, they're old enough to fend for themselves. And, bastard or no, many would envy Richard. He's highborn, after all; his mother is a Warenne. But Joanna is just seven, has no one but me. And now that I've satisfied you, when can you do the same for me? Can you come to me tonight?''

"John, it's so risky . . .'' But after he devoted some moments to increasingly intimate persuasion, she sighed again, murmured, "Yes . . . yes, I will. But we dare not tarry here any longer; we might be seen." She pulled away, set about rearranging her clothing, and then turned back, gave him one last kiss, biting his lip and taking his breath.

John waited, giving her time to depart unseen. But as he emerged onto the garden path, a shrouded figure detached itself from the shadows, barred his way. The man was garbed all in black, his face hidden by a deep cowled hood. He was no apparition to encounter on a moonless night—a stark, spectral embodiment of the most irrational and elemental of mortal fears—and John recoiled violently.

"My lord, I must talk with you.''

John took a second look, recognized the habit and mantle of a Benedictine monk, and swore, fluently and with considerable feeling.

The monk listened in stolid silence, and when John had exhausted every abusive possibility in an uncommonly extensive vocabulary, he repeated stubbornly, "We must talk, my lord.''

But as the monk moved closer, John happened to glance down, saw the dusty boots protruding from the hem of the monk's habit. For a moment he froze, and then jerked his sword free of its scabbard.

"Indeed, we'll talk. We'll begin by you telling me who you are, in whose pay, and just why you went to so much trouble to find me alone like this. And Christ save you if I do not like your answers.''

The man burst out laughing, "And I thought I made a truly admirable monk! What gave me away?'' He reached up, pulled back his hood, and John swore again.

"De Braose!'' Slowly he lowered his sword. Suspicions were coming too fast for him to take them all in. "I thought you were at Châlus with my brother Richard.''

"I was.'' De Braose was fumbling at his belt. "Your mother the Queen bade me give you this, so you'd not doubt I came at her behest.''

John stared down at the ring de Braose had pressed into his hand; it was indeed his mother's. Sheathing his sword, he followed de Braose off the path.

"My lord, you do not know how very lucky you are. Word

has not gotten out yet. If it had, you'd not live to see the morrow.''

John caught his breath. "Do you mean what I think you do?''

William de Braose nodded. "I do . . . my liege.''

"Richard . . . he's dead?''

De Braose nodded again. "He was near death when your lady mother commanded me to get to you, to warn you away from Rennes ere Arthur learns the crown is up for the taking. Too many of his men know my face, hence this monk's cowl. I've men and horses waiting; they are at your disposal, my lord.''

"I still cannot believe it. That it would happen like this, so sudden . . .''

"You're not alone in your disbelief, my lord. Your brother was so sure of victory that he had not even bothered to arm himself. He'd ridden out to inspect the siege's progress with only a shield, took an arrow in his left shoulder. It was full dusk, and his men did not see him hit. He made no sound, turned and rode back to his tent, had his surgeon cut it out. He took the castle, ordered every living soul in it hanged—servants, women, children, all—sparing only the man who shot him, for God knows what fate. But the wound festered. When he realized it was like to be mortal, he pardoned his killer and sent for your mother the Queen.''

" 'Near death,' you said. Are you sure he could not recover?''

De Braose's mouth twitched in a grim smile. "My lord, I could scarce bear to enter the tent for the stench of rotting flesh.'' He stiffened suddenly; so did John. But they'd heard only echoes on the wind, were still alone in the gardens. De Braose loosened his grip on his sword hilt. "I think it best, my lord, if you do not return to your chambers, make no farewells. If we leave now, we can put a good thirty miles between us and Rennes by dawn.''

"Jesú, yes! My life would not be worth spit should this get out whilst I'm still in Brittany.'' John gave an abrupt laugh, both exultant and unsteady. "But you have no idea, Will, what I'll be passing up!''

"You still have not asked it, what I expected to be the first question you'd put to me—if Richard named you as his heir.''

"He did . . . did he not?''

"Yes,'' de Braose admitted, and John grinned.

"You did say my lady mother was at his deathbed, no? Well, as soon as you told me that, there was no need to ask. For even if he had not named me, she would have told the world that he had!''

*   *   *

A woman was walking alone in the cloisters of Fontevrault
Abbey, a frail, forlorn figure swathed in deep mourning. She
turned at sound of John's footsteps, and he recognized Berengaria,
his brother's neglected Queen.

He'd gone out of his way to befriend her, motivated as much
by a malicious desire to vex Richard as by pity for her plight, and
now he found himself cast in an unfamiliar role, giver of comfort
and solace.

"Juan!" Berengaria held out her hands, gave him a shy,
sisterly kiss, and burst into tears.

"*Calma, querida, calma.*" That was, however, the extent of
John's Spanish, and he could do no more than pat her consol-
ingly on the shoulder, wait for her to regain her rather uncertain
grasp of French.

"Forgive me," she sobbed. "But it's been so hard . . . so
hard. I was at Beaufort-en-Vallée, would have gone to him at
once, Juan. But I did not know, not till he was dead. He sent for
his mother, but not for me. Not for me . . ."

"But of course he would not! He was in great pain, *querida*.
He knew you could never bear to see him suffer so, wanted to
spare you that. Any husband would."

"Truly you think it so?" Fawn-brown eyes beseeched him to
convince her. "If I could but believe . . ."

Hugh of Avalon, Bishop of Lincoln, had followed John into
the cloisters, reached them just in time to hear this exchange.
His eyes softened, and he watched with approval as John gently
disengaged himself from his sister-in-law's tearful embrace. But
no sooner were they alone on the cloister walkway than John
shook his head, said wryly, "Damn me if those tears were not
genuine. And yet she could count herself lucky that Richard even
remembered her name from one day to the next! That girl is a
born martyr if ever there was one. But, to be fair, there's
something to be said for Richard, too. All that Madonnalike
purity and goodness would be enough to put any man off; who
wants to bed a saint?"

The Bishop jerked his head up, gave John a look of poorly
concealed dislike. "Such talk is most unseemly, my lord," he
said, so stiffly that John laughed. He'd been almost continuously
in the aged churchman's company on the ride from Chinon, and
he was wearying of the Bishop's homilies on virtue, his exhorta-
tions about sin and salvation; it was all too plain that he thought
John's soul to be in mortal peril, thought John to be the most

ungodly of a family never noted for its piety; and John, who'd begun by good-naturedly seeking to placate, was now deliberately doing all he could to confirm the priest's worst fears.

"You seem to be laboring under a misconception, my lord Bishop," he said cheerfully. "I mean to be crowned, not canonized." But by then they were entering the abbey church, and he sobered abruptly, did not at once move into the sunlit stillness of the nave.

Eleanor stood before the marble tombs of her husband and son, John's father and brother. Her face was tearless, all but bloodless; her grieving was painful to look upon, but intensely private, had in it a fierce pride that conceded little, asked for even less.

"Mother." John stopped before her, hesitated, and kissed her on the cheek. He could discern the faintest stiffening of her body at his touch, an almost imperceptible pulling away, so slight he might have imagined it. Releasing her at once, he stepped back. For a long moment they looked at one another, and then he said, "I am sorry I could not get here in time for the funeral."

The others had tactfully withdrawn, giving them some degree of privacy, and he could risk asking, very low, "Did Richard truly name me?"

"Yes . . . he did." Eleanor glanced down at Richard's tomb, back to her surviving son's face. "But that alone will not make you King," she said tonelessly. "You're likely to have to fight for the crown, John. Whilst you'll have no trouble winning acceptance in England and Normandy, the barons of Brittany, Maine, and Touraine will hold fast for Arthur. Already his partisans are moving on his behalf. We had word this morn that Angers has been taken in Arthur's name, that Le Mans is likely to fall to his forces, too. Angers is not ten leagues from here, John."

"Your point is taken, Madame. You need not worry; I mean to head north on the morrow, to raise an army in Normandy if need be."

Eleanor searched his face, found what she sought, and nodded. "I've done what I could. It is up to you now."

"Yes," John said coolly. "I know."

Eleanor watched as he departed the crypt, pausing for only the briefest of moments before the tombs of their dead. She did not move until the Bishop of Lincoln came to stand beside her.

"Do you know why he missed the funeral, Madame? As soon as he learned Richard was mortally stricken, he rode straight for

Chinon. Not Châlus, where his brother lay dying, or Fontevrault, where he would be laid to rest, but Chinon . . . where the royal treasury is kept.''

"I know," Eleanor said wearily, and he presumed upon an old and enduring friendship to put a supportive hand upon her arm.

"Madame . . . I would not add to your griefs for the very surety of my soul. But I cannot deny my fears, not even for you. If John does prevail over Arthur, it will be in large measure your doing, Madame . . . and your responsibility. Are you sure you're making the right choice?"

"Choice?" Eleanor echoed, with such bitterness that he shrank back. "Think you that I'm blind, that I do not see John as he is—as Henry's son?" She drew a labored breath, then said softly, "But he is still my son, too. And at least he'll not be Philip's puppet, as Arthur would. At least he'll not be that . . ."

9

POWYS, WALES

April 1199

Never having been in Wales, Aubrey de Mara looked about with interest when Thomas Corbet informed him that they'd just crossed from Cheshire into Powys.

"I hear Wales is a wild, beautiful country, deeply wooded and right mountainous." But Thomas just grunted, and Aubrey cast a sideways glance at the other man, a big-boned, burly youth in his early twenties. He had no liking for Thomas Corbet, would not of his own accord have chosen Thomas as a traveling companion. But in his passage through Shropshire, he'd twice enjoyed the hospitality of the Corbet family, first with Thomas's uncle, Walter Corbet, Prior of Ratlinghope Priory, and then with his father, Robert Corbet, at the latter's castle of Caus, and when Thomas decided he would accompany Aubrey into Cheshire, Aubrey could think of no graceful way to escape Corbet's company.

He'd hoped Thomas would turn back once they reached Hawarden, but he showed no signs of homesickness, spent a month as the guest of Aubrey's cousin, Ralph de Montalt, and when Aubrey announced his intention to move on to the Montalt castle of Mold, Thomas nonchalantly allowed that he, too, would stop over at Mold.

"Your cousin at Mold, Lord Ralph's brother . . . you've never met him, either?" Thomas now asked idly, and Aubrey shook his head.

"No. Their grandfather and my great-grandfather were brothers, but they settled here in England with William the Bastard whilst my family kept to Normandy." Turning in the saddle, he signaled to his squire, was handed a wineskin. "Are you sure, Tom, we needed no escort from Hawarden?"

"Damned sure. Mold is but six miles from Hawarden. More-over, the Welsh dare not trespass in these parts; they're not ones to risk their necks unless the odds are rigged in their favor. So you need not fret, I'll get you there safe enough." Thomas smiled, to signify that he was, of course, joking, and Aubrey smiled sourly back; he did not doubt that Thomas could merely wish a man good morning and yet manage to give offense.

"Tell me of the Welsh," he said. "Who rules in these parts? Was there not a Welsh prince named David, who was wed to a half-sister of old King Henry?"

"Yes, although the Welsh do pronounce that as *Dav*-ith. But Davydd was dethroned nigh on five years ago. The man who now wields the greatest power in Gwynedd is Llewelyn ab Iorwerth."

"Ah, yes, I recall hearing some talk about him. He sought to overthrow Davydd at a rather young age, did he not?"

"At fourteen." Thomas was frowning. "When he was twenty-one, he defeated Davydd in a bloody battle at the mouth of the River Conwy, and since then has ruled Gwynedd with his cousins and allies; they hold the lands west of the Conwy and he all that lies east . . . for now. Sooner or later, he'll find a pretext to claim all of Gwynedd. Nor would I—were I a prince of Powys—sleep well nights with him for a neighbor; I'd sooner bed down with a snake."

Aubrey grinned. "Still, though, few men gain so much so young. How old is he now?"

"Twenty-six this February past," Thomas said flatly, and Aubrey's eyes shone with sudden curiosity.

"You seem uncommonly well informed about the man, even to his very birthdate."

"He's my cousin," Thomas said reluctantly, and then made haste to add, "by marriage," lest Aubrey think he had Welsh blood. "My uncle Hugh did wed with Llewelyn's mother."

"I gather there is no love lost between you," Aubrey said wryly, and Thomas leaned over, spat into the road.

"What of Llewelyn's uncle Davydd? Was he put to death?"

"No," Thomas said grudgingly. "Llewelyn banished him into English exile."

Aubrey was thoroughly enjoying the turn the conversation had taken. "Most magnanimous," he murmured, much amused when Thomas rose at once to the bait.

"Do not fool yourself," he snapped. "He knows no more of mercy than he does of honor. If he spared Davydd's life, it was only so as not to make a martyr of the man; I'd wager my birthright on that."

Aubrey laughed. "It sounds as if the poor man cannot win with you, Tom. If he'd claimed Davydd's life, I daresay you'd have scorned him for a coldblooded murder; yet because he did not, you scorn him even more!"

"If that is a jest, I see no humor in it." Thomas lapsed into a sullen silence, and they rode without speaking for a time, Aubrey congratulating himself upon having discovered so effective a burr for Thomas's saddle.

"Where mean you to go after our stay at Mold?" Thomas asked at last, and Aubrey, grimacing at "our stay," shrugged.

"I thought I might venture down into South Wales, the lands under Norman control. Whilst serving with King Richard in Normandy a few years past, I became friendly with a Marcher border lord, and I should like to renew that friendship, to spend some days with him at Abergavenny Castle."

"Aber—Jesú, man, are you talking of William de Braose?"

"Yes, Lord of Brecknock and Upper Gwent. Why does that so surprise you?"

"Because de Braose's name stinks like a mackerel in the sun; I'd have thought the foul smell sure to've reached even as far as Normandy."

"You speak of a man I call friend," Aubrey said stiffly. "I'd advise you to choose your words with care."

"You are an innocent, Aubrey, in truth," Thomas said impatiently. "Ere you unsheath your sword, you'd best hear me out, hear how de Braose avenged the death of his uncle. The man responsible was a Welsh lord, Seisyll ap . . . whatever. De Braose summoned this Seisyll and his followers to Abergavenny to hear a royal proclamation, set out for them a rich table, as much wine as they craved. When the Welsh were off guard, de Braose's men fell upon them, killed them all. Then, ere word could get out, he dispatched others to Seisyll's camp, there abducted Seisyll's wife and, right before her eyes, murdered her seven-year-old son." Thomas reined in, looked challengingly at Aubrey. "I bear no love for the Welsh, but vengeance such as that does no man honor."

Aubrey was shocked. "But he had such an agreeable nature, was quick to jest, to open his purse to his friends. And he seemed truly pious, never passed a wayside cross without offering up a prayer . . ."

"Farsighted of him, I daresay, given how greatly he'll be in need of prayers come Judgment Day. Although, to be fair, there are those who say de Braose was urged to it by his kin. There are even those who think the old King was not displeased. And that bloody night at Abergavenny is twenty years past. But none would deny that de Braose is a hard man, a man not overburdened with scruples." Thomas laughed suddenly. "Little wonder his greatest friend at court is none other than Lord John!"

Aubrey was not surprised that Thomas should be so indiscreet, not after some six weeks in the latter's company. But he had no intention of compromising himself, of sharing his political prejudices with Thomas. "Indeed?" he said coolly, and then, "Tom, look at the sky. There must be a fire ahead."

Thomas stared at the smoke spiraling up through the trees, and then spurred his stallion forward. Rounding a bend in the road, he came to an abrupt halt. Aubrey and the squire reined in, too.

"Christ Jesus!" Thomas sounded stunned, turned to Aubrey in disbelief. "The whoreson's besieging Mold!"

Aubrey searched in vain for an identifying banner. "Who?"

"Llewelyn, you fool! Who else would dare?"

Smoke from the smoldering palisades drifted across the outer bailey, set Llewelyn's men to coughing. Most of the faces around him were well smudged with soot, but he saw only jubilant smiles, for they'd broken through the first ring of the castle defenses. Ahead lay the deep ditch that separated the inner and outer baileys, and beyond, the castle curtain wall, a far more formidable obstacle than the timber palisades, which had been easily set afire with brushwood and flaming arrows. But the curtain wall was stone, the gateway shielded by a portcullis grille.

The drawbridge meant to link the two baileys still blazed, torched by retreating soldiers. Llewelyn glanced about at his captains, said, "We can do nothing till we fill in the ditch; see to it. But we'll need cover. Remember, their crossbows may be more cumbersome than our bows, but they have a greater range."

As if to prove his point, behind him a man screamed, fell forward into the dirt. Up on the walls, an English bowman gave a triumphant shout. Encouraged, his comrades loosed their own arrows down into the bailey. The Welsh drew back, retreating behind a wall of upraised shields.

When enough wood, sand, and fagots had been thrown into the ditch, Llewelyn signaled and the battering ram was brought up, a huge tree trunk capped in iron, sheltered by a large-wheeled shed fireproofed with raw cowhide.

Ednyved ducked behind the shed, gave the battering ram an approving pat. "What are your orders?"

"Whilst we seek to break through with the ram, turn the mangonels upon the walls. Now I want every bowman we have aiming up at the walls. Have the scaling ladders ready."

Ednyved gave a pleased grunt. "Consider it done," he said, crawled under the shed to confer with the men crouching within. Llewelyn raised his right arm, dropped it sharply. At once the air throbbed with the twanging of Welsh longbows, and the battering ram began creaking across the bailey.

By the time the shed reached the curtain wall, the castle defenders were raining every possible sort of missile down upon it: stones, lances, lit torches, even quicklime. But it continued to creep inexorably forward, like a huge shelled turtle, leaving a trail of deflected weaponry in its wake. Once within range, the men inside jerked on the ropes, straining until the massive log began to swing back and forth, gathering momentum and smashing into the portcullis. There was a splintering; the iron reinforcements held, but the wood buckled, and the Welsh raised a cheer.

The capture of Mold Castle would be a signal victory for the Welsh, and Llewelyn had left little to chance; his army was equipped both with the huge crossbow machines known as ballistas and with the even larger mangonels, catapultlike devices capable of launching boulders of considerable size. He watched as his largest mangonel was dragged forward, as a windlass was wrenched to pull the beam back, as it was loaded with heavy rocks, and then released. The beam jerked back to a vertical position, propelling the rocks into a deadly overhead arc. Some shattered against the castle walls; others plummeted down into the inner ward. Not waiting to savor their success, his men were already reloading the mangonel. Llewelyn paused long enough to shout, "Good lads!" and then sprinted across the open ground toward the lean-to being set up by the ditch. "Bring out the second mangonel," he panted. "And keep your shields up. They're launching red-hot bolts from the walls; I just saw one go clean through a man's belly."

So far, all was going according to Llewelyn's expectations. The battering ram continued its relentless thrusting. Up on the walls, men were lowering large hooks, desperately fishing for the ram, but the arrow fire was too intense for any man to risk exposure for long, and they were grappling blindly.

"Llewelyn!" Rhys raced for the lean-to, flung himself down a split second before an arrow buried itself in the wood above his head. It had all but grazed his hair, yet he said only, "Close, that one. Llewelyn, they signal from the ram. They've broken through the portcullis, have reached the door."

"Now!" Again Llewelyn raised his arm, let it fall. "Do not let up, drive them off the walls!" And as his bowmen obeyed, launching arrow after arrow with eye-blurring speed, he pulled his sword from its scabbard, brought his shield up.

With wild yells, the Welsh rushed the castle walls. Those up on the battlements threw down stones, flaming pitch; more than one Welshman was engulfed in fire, rolled screaming upon the ground. But Llewelyn's bowmen had achieved their aim, forcing many of the English to retreat, and the Welsh headed now for these exposed areas, threw scaling ladders against the walls, and began to scramble up, trailing light thong ladders over their shoulders.

By the time Llewelyn reached the walls, the battering ram was smashing through the oaken door. He was among the first to plunge through, fought his way clear of the gatehouse to find many of his men already within, clambering down their thong ladders to head off the English retreat. Of the buildings ranged along the curtain walls, only one was not of wood: a squat, two-story tower. Seeing themselves overwhelmed, the English soldiers were running for this, their last refuge, and Llewelyn shouted, "Christ, cut them off!"

But even as he raced for the keep, he knew they'd be too late. Men with torches were standing in the doorway. When most of the soldiers had made it to safety within, they scattered brushwood upon the stairs, tossed their torches onto the pile. The stairs ignited at once. One of the torchbearers was too slow, took a Welsh lance in his chest, and tumbled down into the flames, but the other ducked back inside; the door was slammed and bolted behind him.

Smoke hung heavy over the inner ward; the wooden buildings had been put to the torch. Llewelyn and his captains had gathered in the gatehouse, were measuring the keep with speculative eyes.

Rhys gestured toward the charred ruins of the wooden stairway. "Even if we built a platform and then forced the door, all the advantages would lie with them; they could smite us down one by one as we sought to enter. Better we should build a mine, tunnel under the wall, and bring it down about their ears. Or else use the battering ram to smash into the cellar.''

"The River Alyn sinks underground here; the ground is like to be too wet for tunneling.'' Ednyved took up a flask, drank, and passed it around. "But we could use the battering ram, though it'd be slow going. What say you, Llewelyn?''

Llewelyn considered. "If we go across the battlements, we can enter onto the roof of the keep. If we then stuff burning brushwood down the louvres, mayhap we can smoke them out. But ere we decide, I'd see if I cannot talk them out.''

Moving to the door of the gatehouse, he raised his voice. "I would speak with your castellan or constable!''

There was a silence, and then a shutter was cautiously drawn back. "I am Sir Robert de Montalt. Identify yourself.''

Llewelyn and his friends exchanged surprised looks; they'd not expected to hook so large a fish. "I am Llewelyn ab Iorwerth, Prince of Gwynedd below the Conwy.''

The silence was even longer this time. "What would you say to me?''

"Just this. I shall take your keep. If nothing else, I need only wait, starve you out. You can neither escape nor hope for succor. Your overlord, the Earl of Chester, is in Normandy with your King. The Lord de Montalt, your brother, is known to be ailing; nor has he the men to break my siege. Remain mewed up within the keep and you do but prolong your own suffering, do only delay what is writ in blood. Yield now and with honor. Your lives shall be spared, and you may ransom your freedom, with no shame to you, for a fight well fought.''

The shutter opened wider. "And if I refuse to yield?''

"Need you ask? You know full well what's like to befall a besieged garrison that persists in holding out after all hope is gone. My people call this place Yr Wyddgrug: the burial mound. If need be, I'll turn this ground into a burial mound in truth. I shall take this keep, easy or hard, but take it I shall, and when I do, all within shall be put to the sword. So the choice is yours. I do give you two hours to decide.''

Llewelyn passed the next hour conferring with his captains, getting reports on the casualties suffered, the prisoners taken, and planning for their assault upon the keep, should it become necessary. There was still an hour remaining upon his deadline when Ednyved appeared at his side.

"Well, my lord, once more your silver tongue triumphs!'' He

pointed toward the keep. The door was opening. As they watched, elated, a ladder was slowly lowered over the side.

"My grandfather took Mold Castle, too, Rhys. The garrison held out for three months before yielding, and he later said it was his sweetest victory ever."

"My lord!" Llewelyn and Rhys turned from the window, toward the man just entering the solar. He was carrying a large bolt of emerald velvet; this he held out to Llewelyn, saying, "As soon as I saw this, my lord, I knew your lady should have it. Nothing better becomes a woman with red hair than the color green."

Llewelyn fingered the cloth. "Indeed, you are right, Dylan. It shall please her greatly to make a gown of this."

"Llewelyn?" Ednyved paused in the doorway. "Is it your wish to see de Montalt now? And our men captured two English knights up on the road. I'll fetch them, too."

Sir Robert de Montalt was no longer young, had advanced well into his fifties, time enough to have acquired a philosophical approach to the vicissitudes of fortune. If he felt any resentment now at being ushered, a prisoner, into his own solar, he was too politic to let it show in his face.

"My lord Llewelyn," he said, stiffly correct. "I assume, of course, that you mean to raze the castle."

"Of course," Llewelyn agreed politely, secretly amused, as always, at the Norman insistence upon preserving the amenities. As if war were a game of sorts, to be played according to recognized rules.

Robert de Montalt gestured toward the table. "I will, with your permission, write to my brother, tell him that our men shall be set free once your forces withdraw. May I ask what price you mean to put upon my freedom?"

Llewelyn calculated rapidly. "I think seven hundred marks to be a fair sum."

It was steep, but not exorbitant, and de Montalt nodded. "You will take partial payment in cattle and horses, I trust?"

"Naturally," Llewelyn said, no less gravely, not daring to meet Ednyved's eyes lest he laugh, reveal what a charade he thought this to be.

The other men were now being escorted into the solar. The first was a flaxen-haired youth, expensively armed. He did not look particularly pleased by his predicament, but neither did he look all that worried. Here, Llewelyn saw, was another games-player, confident that men of rank would always make common cause against those of inferior birth, acknowledge their membership in an international aristocracy of class. They would never understand, Llewelyn knew, that he felt a greater kinship to the least-born Welshman than to the highest-born Norman lord.

His eyes narrowed, though, at sight of the second man. "Well, Tom," he said coolly, "you're a long way from home."

Thomas was not cowed. "So are you," he shot back. "This is Powys, not Gwynedd."

Aubrey decided Thomas Corbet was indeed mad. All knew the Welsh were as unpredictable a people as could be found in Christendom, and common sense dictated that a man did not bait a bear in its own den. "You are, of course, Prince Llewelyn," he said hastily. "I am Sir Aubrey de Mara of Falaise, cousin to Lord Ralph and Sir Robert de Montalt." He turned then to de Montalt, smiled ruefully. "I regret I must impose upon our kinship, Cousin, must request that your brother pay my ransom. My lord father will, naturally, reimburse you."

With such a victory, Llewelyn could afford to be generous. "Add another hundred marks for your cousin, Sir Robert, and I shall be content."

Aubrey grinned. "I do not know whether I should be thankful to escape so cheaply," he confessed, "or insulted that you do not value my worth more highly!"

Llewelyn laughed, and upgraded Aubrey in his estimation; generally, when a man was bested in combat, his sense of humor was the first casualty.

"Well, you two can barter what you will for your freedom, but I'll be damned ere I pay so much as a penny for mine," Thomas said truculently, and Aubrey and de Montalt jerked their heads about, stared at him in astonishment. There was on Aubrey's face grudging admiration for so bold a stance, yet resentment, too, for his own easy acceptance of his plight suddenly seemed less than honorable when contrasted with Thomas's defiance.

Llewelyn was regarding Thomas with unconcealed contempt, but it was to Aubrey that he said, "*Mwyaf trwst llestri gweigion.* In your language that translates as, 'Empty vessels make the most noise.' Your heroic friend knows full well that his release is already secured, bought with his Corbet blood. I do owe Hugh Corbet too much to claim the life of his nephew, and, as ever, he does trade upon that."

Thomas had flushed angrily. "I accept no favors from Welshmen!"

Llewelyn, too, was angry now. "You're an even bigger fool than I once thought . . . Cousin. That does not, however, alter the debt I owe your uncle. But come the day when he's gone to God, I shall be sorely tempted to burn Caus Castle around your head. I'd think on that, if I were you."

Thomas opened his mouth, and Aubrey jabbed him with an elbow. "For Christ's sake," he hissed, "do not stretch your luck!"

"My Prince!" It was Dylan again, pushing before him a fearful youngster of eighteen or so. "This one ran right into our scouts, claims he has an urgent message for de Montalt."

The boy fumbled within his tunic and withdrew two rolled parchments. With an apologetic glance toward Robert de Montalt, he knelt and handed the messages to Llewelyn.

De Montalt had stiffened. He watched tensely as Llewelyn broke his brother's seal. He saw surprise upon the latter's face; Llewelyn said something in Welsh, and the others looked no less startled.

"Cousin?" Aubrey had sidled closer. "See the second dispatch? Does it not bear His Grace of Chester's seal? The news, then, is from Normandy."

The Welsh were still talking among themselves, with considerable animation. Several were smiling, but Llewelyn looked suddenly pensive. He walked toward them, said to de Montalt, "Your brother has just received a letter from the Earl of Chester. Your King Richard was sore wounded whilst besieging Châlus Castle; he died on the sixth of April."

Thomas did not appear overly affected by the news of his King's demise, but de Montalt was stunned and Aubrey stricken. He sagged back against the wall, whispered, "Jesú have mercy upon his soul."

Thomas dutifully crossed himself at that, then blurted out, with the single-mindedness of the true pragmatist, "Whom did he name as his heir, John or Arthur?"

"His brother John." Llewelyn's eyes flicked from the letter to the ashen-faced de Montalt. "If you wish," he said, "your chaplain may offer up prayers for Richard's soul."

De Montalt swallowed, nodded. "He . . . he was a great soldier."

Llewelyn nodded, too; that he could acknowledge in all honesty.

*   *   *

As soon as the Welsh were alone in the solar, Llewelyn's companions crowded around him. "What of Arthur, Llewelyn? Did he not put in his claim, too?"

Llewelyn glanced again at the letter. "Indeed he did, Ednyved. Chester says rebel barons of Brittany and Touraine laid siege to Angers and Le Mans, proclaimed Arthur as Richard's rightful heir. He says John almost fell into their hands at Le Mans, but he was able to reach safety at Rouen, and there the Norman lords did rally to him, answering his call to arms. He led an army back into Anjou, razed the castle at Le Mans, and burned the city. Arthur escaped, fled to the French court, and John seems like to prevail. Chester writes that he was invested as Duke of Normandy on the twenty-fifth, that he sails for England within the fortnight."

"Llewelyn?" Rhys was frowning. "What means this to us? Are we the better or the worse for his death?"

"I would that I knew, Rhys. For certes, I'd rather have seen Arthur crowned over John; a twelve-year-old lad would cast no great shadow in Wales. As for John . . . I hope I am wrong, but he may well prove to be more troublesome than ever his brother was. For all his vaunted skill with a sword, Richard never bothered much with Wales. Or with England, either, if truth be told. He was King for ten years, and how often was he even on English soil? Twice, I do believe! But John has no interest in crusades or foreign campaigns, is like to make England the central jewel in his crown. And he knows our ways better than most; he was, as Earl of Gloucester, himself a Marcher border lord. No, I suspect we've no reason for rejoicing that John is to be King."

"King John," Llewelyn repeated softly. "Morgan is a better prophet than even he knows. Once, years ago, he told me our lives should entwine, John's and mine. And, so it now seems, they shall."

10

FONTEVRAULT ABBEY,
PROVINCE OF ANJOU

June 1200

The royal abbey of St Mary of Fontevrault was young in years
when measured against the timeless span of stone and mortar, but
few religious orders were as influential or as wealthy. Matilda de
Boheme, the proud, pious woman who ruled as Abbess, was
related both by blood and marriage to the great Houses of Cham-
pagne and Blois, and the thriving community within Fontevrault's
walls included a convent for wellborn nuns, a monastery for
monks and lay brothers, a hospital for lepers, a home for those
nuns and monks grown too old to serve God in other than prayer,
even a shelter for penitent prostitutes. At Fontevrault were buried
the Plantagenet dead of Henry's House, and Eleanor was often an
honored guest of the Abbess. Taken ill that spring, she had
chosen to convalesce in the white-walled stillness of the abbey,
and lingered there weeks later, having found an unexpected
contentment in the cloistered and placid peace, so utterly lacking
in the turbulence and high drama that had marked her life for
almost eight decades.

The Abbess Matilda welcomed her with heartfelt gladness;
theirs was a friendship of genuine affection, if not genuine
intimacy. She wondered, though, how long it would be before
Eleanor's restless spirit would begin to yearn for the pleasures of
the world that was truly hers, the glittering court at Poitiers,
where for almost sixty-five years she had reigned in her own
right as Duchess of Aquitaine. Eleanor was not, she knew, a
woman ever to renounce power, no matter the accompanying
pain . . . and pain there had been in plenitude.

Looking pensively at Eleanor's sculptured profile, at the face so familiar and yet so unrevealing, Matilda found herself thinking of all the griefs Eleanor had endured in recent months. Death had claimed four of her children in a heartbreakingly brief span. Both the daughters born of her marriage to the French King were now dead; Richard had died in her arms, and not five months later, she'd stood a ghastly vigil over yet another child, as Joanna died giving birth to a stillborn son. She had, Matilda thought, been no luckier as a mother than she had been as a wife. Of the ten children she'd borne, she'd buried eight, had only a daughter in distant Castile and the son she was even now awaiting, the last of her eaglets—and the least loved.

And yet Matilda knew she had labored tirelessly for that same son to gain for him the Angevin crown, had then exhausted herself seeking to win recognition of his right. She'd traversed the length and breadth of her domains on his behalf, formally designated him as heir to her duchy of Aquitaine, and, lastly, undertaken for him a grueling journey that would have daunted a woman half her age. This past January, Philip and John had come to terms, sought to secure peace with the marriage of Philip's son and John's niece. Eleanor took it upon herself to fetch the young Spanish bride, child of the daughter sent so long ago to wed the King of Castile. Daring a dangerous winter crossing of the Pyrenees, she'd brought her granddaughter to Normandy for the wedding that would one day make her Queen of France. But however indomitable her spirit still was, her body was in its seventy-ninth year, and she'd fallen gravely ill upon her return, had been forced to miss the royal wedding she'd done so much to bring about.

Eleanor rose, moved restlessly to the window and back again. John had sent word that he'd be arriving at noon; he was already two hours late.

"This will be the first time that you've seen your son since the wedding, will it not, Madame?" Matilda would have liked to discuss the controversial peace that the wedding was meant to warrant. The treaty was not proving popular in England, where men long accustomed to Richard's readiness to wage war for honor and profit looked askance at any resolution not bought with blood. Among those most eager for plunder and among those who'd have cheered the campaign on from the battle lines of London alehouses, John had earned himself a derisive sobriquet, one utterly at odds with the admiring "Richard Lion-Heart" that had been bestowed upon his brother: "John Softsword." But

Matilda knew better than to broach the subject; Eleanor did not share confidences, least of all about her youngest son.

"Madame . . ." A young novice nun stood in the doorway. "Madame, the King's Grace has just ridden into the garth."

" . . . and we celebrated the wedding the day after Philip and I concluded the treaty. We had to hold it across the border in Normandy, of course, what with France being under Interdict, and Philip had to get a secondhand account of the ceremony, since he's barred from all the Sacraments."

At that, John and Eleanor exchanged identical amused smiles, for the French King's marital troubles had only grown more tangled with time, had now embroiled him in a confrontation with the Holy See. It was seven years since he'd rejected Inge-borg, four since he'd defiantly wed the Duke of Meran's daugh-ter, and the Pope had at last lost patience. Six months ago he had turned upon Philip one of the more effective weapons in the papal arsenal, laying France under Interdict until the King agreed to set aside his present wife and recognize the long-suffering Ingeborg as his Queen.

"A pity you had to miss all the festivities, Madame . . . especially that memorable moment when Philip compelled Arthur to do homage to me for the duchy of Brittany, to acknowledge me as his King and liege lord. If I'd gained nothing else from the treaty, the look on Arthur's face would be recompense enough!"

This last was said with a trace of defiance. John knew what was being said in alehouse and army encampment—that his brother Richard would never have made such a peace—and he'd come prepared to defend himself with irrefutable logic and com-mon sense. But his relationship with his mother was too tenuous, too fraught with ambivalence and inconsistencies to be governed by the detached dictates of reason.

Instead of citing the very material advantages of peace with Philip, he found himself saying sarcastically, "But I'm discover-ing that a truce not won at swordpoint is somehow suspect. People crave glory, I give them peace, and they fancy themselves the poorer for it. What of you, Madame? Do you, too, fault me for renouncing glory in favor of crops in the fields and money in my coffers?"

Eleanor gave a startled laugh. "Good God, no! Do you know me as little as that? War is the least productive of men's pas-times, and the most indulgent. Why should I want you to fight for what you can gain at the bargaining table?"

John was pleased, but still wary. "I yielded to Philip only that which I could not hope to hold on the field," he said cautiously. "The truth of it, Mother, is that I cannot afford a war. The money is just not there."

They both knew why: because Richard had depleted the royal treasury with his wars, his crusade, his ransom. Eleanor said nothing, and John, disarmed by her unexpected approval, forbore for once to criticize the son she still mourned.

"Not that I expect the peace to last," he admitted. "But it will give me the time I need to replenish my coffers, to checkmate Arthur, and to deal with trouble from a source I had not expected— you have heard? Despite years of rivalry and bad blood, the Count of Angoulême means to wed his daughter to that whoreson de Lusignan. It is a marriage guaranteed to give me naught but grief."

Eleanor's mouth twisted; in their dislike of Hugh de Lusignan, she and John were in rare and full accord. That past January, as Eleanor was setting out for Castile, she'd been intercepted by Hugh de Lusignan, compelled to accept the hospitality of his stronghold at Lusignan Castle. Just as de Lusignan's invitation could fairly be termed an abduction, the favor he sought from Eleanor was more in the nature of extortion than appeal: that she yield to him the county of La Marche. Eleanor was proud, but hers was a pride tempered by pragmatism; making a grimly realistic assessment of her predicament, she acted to cut her losses, gave de Lusignan what he demanded, and, within hours, was free to resume her journey westward. John, on the verge of making peace with Philip, could do little but acquiesce in the *fait accompli*, accept de Lusignan's homage as the new Count of La Marche. But he knew that de Lusignan would never have dared to commit such an audacity while Richard lived, and that was a raw, ulcerous sore, a grievance beyond forgiving.

"Yes," Eleanor said flatly, "I heard. That is why I summoned you to Fontevrault. We know what Hugh de Lusignan is; the man has the scruples of a snake. But the Count of Angoulême is another malcontent who serves only his own interests, and both of them are hand-in-glove with Philip. Should they put an end to their feuding, ally their Houses in this marriage, that would one day give Hugh both Angoulême and La Marche. We cannot allow the marriage to take place . . . although I confess I'm at a loss as to how to prevent it. You dare not forbid it outright; as

jealous as my barons be of their rights, every lord in Aquitaine
would rally to their support.''

"If I forbid it, yes.'' John leaned back in his chair. "Yesterday I summoned the Count of Angoulême to do homage to me on
July fifth . . . at Lusignan Castle.''

"You what?'' Eleanor's eyes widened. "The three of you
under one roof? That is a volatile mix if ever I heard one! What
mean you to do, John?''

"I mean to stop the marriage.''

"But how? I do not see . . .''

"I'd rather not say just yet. I will tell you this much, that if I
succeed, Aymer of Angoulême and Hugh de Lusignan will be
blood enemies till the day of mortal reckoning and beyond, and
I'll have made of Aymer a steadfast ally—which is more, Madame, than Richard could ever do. And if it also happens that
Hugh de Lusignan should find himself a laughingstock, the butt
of every jest from Poitiers to Paris—well, that's not like to break
my heart. Nor yours, either, I'd wager.''

Eleanor did not respond as he had expected. After some moments of silence, she said thoughtfully, "If you are asking
whether I'd like to see Hugh de Lusignan humiliated, of course I
would. If you are asking whether I think it would be wise, I'd
have to say no. With all the enemies you have, John, vengeance
is an indulgence you can ill afford right now.''

John was irked, disappointed, too. "Life at Fontevrault is
making you very pious, Mother. Next you'll be quoting Scriptures.''

"I'm talking of foresight, not of forgiveness," Eleanor snapped,
but John was already on his feet. She tensed, but did not protest.
With Richard, she could have insisted that he stay, hear her out.
She had no such leverage with John, and well she knew it.

"I do not know what sort of devious scheme you have in
mind. I can only tell you this: Whilst stupidity may indeed be a
sin, it is also possible to be too clever. I sometimes fear, John,
that you are too clever by half.''

John shrugged. "At least," he said, "you might wish me
luck.''

Will Longsword was seated at a table in his brother's chamber,
laboring over a letter to his girl-wife. He wielded the pen awkwardly, for his was a hand more accustomed to grasping a sword
hilt, and he swore under his breath as he searched for words to
put to parchment.

Done this sixth day of July in the Year of Our Lord 1200, at the castle of Hugh de Lusignan, Count of La Marche and Lord of Lusignan and Couhé.

To the Lady Ela, Countess of Salisbury, my dear wife, greetings.

And that was as far as he'd gotten. Will had no idea why they were at Lusignan. Neither, he suspected, did Hugh de Lusignan. It was well known that John never forgave a wrong or forgot a grudge, and Hugh had made ready for his lord's goodwill visit with skeptical wariness, much like a man who'd just been assured that the wolf wandering midst his flocks was in fact a domesticated dog. But whatever John's ultimate intentions, he was presently on his best behavior. Even his enemies never denied he had a certain scapegrace charm when he cared to exert himself, and he'd been drawing upon that charm so lavishly that Hugh had begun to relax somewhat, to let down his guard. The workings of Hugh's brain were too broadly meshed for subtlety. He knew Richard would not have rested until his head rotted on a pike over his own gatehouse, until his castles were reduced to rubble and his lands to charred embers, his womenfolk despoiled and his brother hanged. But John drank with him, diced with him, swapped bawdy jokes, and hinted at royal favors to come. Such a man was not to be feared. Once Hugh reached that fateful conclusion, he was hard put to hide his disdain; there was a bluff heartiness in his manner that was a shade too familiar, a swaggering assumption of intimacy that filled Will with foreboding.

Now Will sighed. Even if he had been privy to John's plans, he could not have shared them with Ela. She was just fourteen, all elbows and knees and sudden blushes, a sweet child, he thought fondly, who'd brought him an earldom and deserved in turn to be sheltered and protected until she outgrew her little-girl awkwardness. But what to tell her, then? Will gazed at the parchment as if willing words to materialize of their own accord, at last gave up and elected instead to watch the game of tables in progress between John and Aymer Taillefer, Count of Angoulême.

Aymer was staring down at the gameboard with unblinking blue eyes. He played as he did all else, with a competitive intensity that knew no quarter, and he sucked in his breath when the dice roll gave the game to John, paused too long before saying, "What do I owe Your Grace?"

"Shall we play again? Only this time let's double the stakes." John smiled as if oblivious to the other man's ill humor, and reached for the wine cup by his elbow. "Hugh tells me you've set a date for the wedding."

"August twenty-sixth." Aymer tossed the dice onto the table. His were eyes as hard as stones, empty of all save suspicion. "Shall we speak plainly, Your Grace? Hugh de Lusignan may be a fool, but I am not. I know full well that Hugh's coming marriage to my daughter is not to your liking, that you would prevent it if you could. It is your right as my liege lord to speak against it, and if it is your wish, I will hear you out. But I think it only fair to tell you that I shall not change my mind, that I mean to see Isabelle as Countess of La Marche."

John drank, studying Aymer all the while. "It is said that your daughter is uncommonly pretty. Is that true?"

"She is a beauty, Your Grace. Why?"

"Your daughter is a great heiress, will one day inherit all of Angoulême. And she is of high birth, her mother a first cousin to the King of France. Now you say she is a beauty in the bargain. What escapes my understanding is why you would waste such a girl on Hugh de Lusignan. I should think you'd aim higher—much higher."

"Your Grace?" Aymer was no longer feigning disinterest. "Just what are you saying?"

"I am saying that you'd be doing your daughter a grave disservice if you settled for Hugh de Lusignan." John paused; there was faint mockery now in his smile. "Unless, of course, you have no interest in seeing her as Queen of England."

Aymer's intake of breath was audible even to Will. He hastily cast his eyes down, but not in time; John caught the sudden hot light, the glimmer of bedazzled greed. "You overwhelm me, my liege, and do my daughter great honor. But you already have a Queen, have you not?"

"No," John corrected amiably, "I have a wife, not a Queen. Think you that I neglected to have Avisa crowned with me through sheer oversight? It has long been my intent to end the marriage; I've merely been awaiting the opportune time."

Aymer swallowed, so caught up in John's spell that he absentmindedly helped himself to John's wine. "You do not foresee any difficulty in casting off the Lady Avisa?"

John laughed. "Unlike Philip, who's likely to be yoked to the martyred Ingeborg for all eternity, I happen to be able to satisfy the most scrupulous papal conscience. Avisa and I are second cousins, you see, well within the prohibited degree of consanguinity, and we never did bother to get a papal dispensation for our marriage. Need I say more?"

Aymer laughed, too, in that moment vulnerable as only a man could be who suddenly found reality exceeding all expectations, even the fantasy world of dreams. "It will afford me great pleasure, Your Grace, to give you my daughter. But what of de Lusignan? He makes an ugly enemy, is one to nurse a grudge to the grave. How shall we manage it?"

"Easily enough, I think. I understand the girl is now at Hugh's castle of Valence, no? Well, after you depart here, you need only ride to Valence, tell the de Lusignans you wish to take her back with you to Angoulême for a final visit with her mother ere the wedding. In the meantime I shall find some distant task for Hugh and his kin to undertake on my behalf. I daresay you've noticed that Hugh's acting much like a cat that got into the cream. He's sure that he's basking in my royal favor, will see this charge as proof positive that he's truly won my trust, my friendship."

"Indeed," Aymer said approvingly. "And then?"

"From here I go to Bordeaux, where I'll have the Archbishop declare my marriage void *ab initio*. As you know, I plan to pass the summer on progress in my lady mother's domain. What would be more natural than to accept your hospitality when I reach Angoulême, at which time I shall right gladly plight troth with your pretty daughter . . . on the twenty-sixth of August, mayhap? After that, we need only decide whether we want to invite de Lusignan to the wedding!"

This time, however, Aymer did not join in John's laughter. "A plight troth," he echoed sharply. "Why not a wedding?"

John hesitated. This was the only weakness he could see in his scheme. A plight troth would give him all the political benefits of a marriage—would, as well, enable him to disavow Isabelle without difficulty should a better marital prospect appear at a later date. But the advantages of a plight troth were so blatantly one-sided that he was not at all sure Aymer would ever agree.

"Because of your daughter's extreme youth," he said earnestly. "She's but twelve, is she not? I think it only fair to give her time to adjust. It will be bound to come as a shock, to arrive in Angoulême expecting to marry Hugh, a man she knows well, only to be told she's to wed a total stranger."

Aymer reflected upon this in silence, then gave John an oblique smile. "Your concern for my daughter is commendable." He rose as John did, made a perfunctory obeisance, and suddenly burst into malicious laughter. "Damn me if de Lusignan's not going to look a right proper fool when word gets out!"

"Yes," John agreed complacently. "I expect he will."

He waited till they were alone, but no longer, at once turning to Will and demanding, "Well? What think you?"

"It is brilliant, John," Will said admiringly, "in truth, it is. That marriage would have been a disaster for us, and you've hit upon the one way you could stop it. But . . . but would it not be better to let Hugh de Lusignan save face? You need not do it this way, could let Aymer end the betrothal, then wait a discreet interval ere you claimed the girl. I fear that if you steal her out from under Hugh's nose—" John was smiling and Will stopped in mid-sentence. It had baffled him that a man as bright as his brother could be so blind to consequences; now John's sardonic smile brought it all into focus for him. "You want to humiliate Hugh de Lusignan, do you not?" he said slowly. "Fully as much as you want the girl, if not more. John . . . are you sure you've thought this through, that the game be worth the candle?"

"Shall I tell you, Will, why you always lose to me when we play at hazards or tables? Because you're so cautious it damned near cripples you! Poor Will, just once in your life have you never wanted to risk all upon one throw of the dice?" John moved back to the table, gestured for Will to pour them wine.

"Only one thing does puzzle me," he confessed. "Aymer is right; he's no fool. So why, then, did he agree to a plight troth? Why did he not insist upon a wedding?"

From Bordeaux, John moved south into Gascony, and then began a slow circuit back into Poitou. On Wednesday, August 24, he crossed the River Charente, and the next morning was welcomed into the walled capital city of Angoulême.

The great hall of Aymer's ancient castle had been swept clean, strewn with fresh rushes and sweet-smelling herbs, hung with embroidered wall hangings of red, green, and gold. Aymer's Countess, a striking, statuesque woman who bore no resemblance to her cousin the French King, insisted upon personally acting as John's guide, proudly pointing out her favorites among the hangings: the Five Joys of the Blessed Mary, and the Story of Paris and Helen. John made the proper admiring responses, but he was impatient to see the girl he'd one day be taking to wife and, sensing that, the Lady Alice excused herself, went to fetch Isabelle.

"You have told her, I assume?" John asked, and Aymer nodded.

"But of course. She was both awed and honored that Your Grace should think her worthy of a crown, and she vowed that you should never repent your choice."

John gave Aymer a skeptical smile, and winked at Will. He had enough experience with children to know that no twelve-year-old was likely to harbor such lofty sentiments, much less express them aloud. He only hoped the girl was truly reconciled to the plight troth; England must seem as distant as Cathay to a girl who'd never been anywhere but Angoulême and Valence. Will's little Ela had been a twelve-year-old bride, too, and remembering how fearful she had been, approaching the altar like a lamb led to the slaughter, John hoped Isabelle would be of sturdier stock. But the memory of Ela's unease gave him an idea, and he beckoned to Will. "What say you we send the lass to Ela at Salisbury?"

Will beamed. "An excellent thought. I daresay she'd be less homesick with Ela and me than at your court. She'd be good company for Ela, too . . ."

He stopped, for John was no longer listening. He'd taken an involuntary step forward; Will heard him murmur, "Good God." Turning to see what had so transfixed his brother, Will found himself staring, too, at the girl coming toward them. His mouth dropped open; the shock was all the greater because he'd instinctively cast Isabelle in Ela's image. Expecting an endearing, coltish clumsiness, bitten nails, and shy, sidelong glances, he saw, instead, a slender vision in turquoise and silver silk, a delicate oval face framed in a cascade of shimmering light. Will had occasionally seen young girls who'd matured too early, overly ripe and knowing beyond their years. Isabelle d'Angoulême was not one of these, had not forfeited the touching and poignant appeal of innocence. And yet she held the eye of every man in the hall. It was the first time in his life that Will had ever seen a woman who could truly be called "unforgettable," and it was with a vague sense of shame that he acknowledged the sheer physical impact of the girl, reminding himself hastily that she was not a woman—was, for all her startling beauty, still a child of twelve.

What amazed him even more than her appearance was her poise. She approached John without a trace of nervousness, sank down before him in an eye-pleasing curtsy. But after a moment to reflect, Will realized why; no girl who looked as this one did could long remain ignorant of her advantages. For the first time he glanced toward his brother. John was staring at Isabelle so avidly that Will decided John, too, needed to be reminded of Isabelle's extreme youth.

"Your Grace," she said, her French attractively enhanced by the soft accents of Provençal, the *langue d'oc* spoken throughout Eleanor's domains.

"No, darling, the grace is yours," John said huskily. "I'd have you call me John."

Aymer had been standing to one side, watching with an odd little smile, one Will had seen once before, that July night at Lusignan Castle. Stepping forward now, he said, "I explained to Isabelle that you thought it would be a kindness to delay the marriage. She assured me, however, that will not be necessary, told me she would like to be wed at once. Is that not so, Isabelle?"

"Yes, Papa." Isabelle gave John a dazzling smile. "That is indeed my wish." But only Will noticed as she then surreptitiously wiped the palms of her hands against her elegant silk skirt. Poor little lass, he thought; so she was not so different from his Ela, after all. And his heart went out to her in a surge of protective, paternal tenderness.

"Is that agreeable to Your Grace, then? Have I your permission to make plans for the wedding? As the Archbishop of Bordeaux is in your entourage, he could officiate. On the morrow, shall we say?"

John had yet to take his eyes from Isabelle. "By all means, Aymer," he said, and smiled at Aymer's daughter. "The sooner the better."

"Oh how beautiful! Is it truly for me?"

John smiled. "Truly. Here, turn around and I'll fasten the clasp for you."

Isabelle did as he bade, sitting beside him on the garden bench. Because of her youth, she wore no wimple or veil, but let her hair fall free down her back. John brushed it aside, fastened the necklet about her throat; even in the moonlight, the stones glowed, opals the shade of twilight and amethysts of deepest purple. "Emeralds would suit you better, I think. Do you like emeralds, Isabelle?"

"They are green, no? I've never owned much jewelry. I do have a betrothal ring from Hugh. But I suppose I must give it back now, must I not?" she said impishly, and John laughed.

"Indeed not; consider it a keepsake. You have no regrets, then? About not marrying Hugh?"

"Oh, no! I would have tried to be a dutiful wife, truly I would. But . . . but I did not want to marry him." Isabelle hesitated, not sure whether such candor was permissible. "He was so much older than me, older even than my papa. He had salt-grey hair, not black and glossy like yours, and his eyes were always bloodshot and he . . . he made me uncomfortable sometimes, the way he looked at me . . ."

"As if he were starving and you were on the menu?" John suggested, and she gave a startled giggle.

"But I look at you that way, too; have you not noticed?"

"I do not mind it with you," she said softly, lowering her lashes to cast silky shadowed crescents upon skin so perfect it looked like porcelain. John reached over, stroked her cheek. When she did not pull away, he leaned closer still, touched her mouth with his. Her breathing quickened; he could see the rise and fall of her small breasts, budding against the bright silk of her bodice. He kissed her again, this time as a man would kiss a woman, and found that the entrancing flirt who'd invited such intimacies was but an illusion born of the moonlight and his own desire, found himself holding a fearful little girl. She submitted docilely to his embrace, let him explore her mouth with his tongue, but her body had lost all pliancy, was rigidly unresponsive under his hands. John released her, frowning, and tears filled her eyes.

"I did not please you?" she faltered. "Papa said I must, said I—"

"Isabelle, hush. There is nothing about you that does not please me. I do not expect you to know how to pleasure a man, will teach you all you need to know." He began to caress her hair, let his fingers trail across her throat. "And they'll be lessons much to your liking, that I can promise you."

There was no anger in his voice, and Isabelle was emboldened to confide, "Papa told me I must not let Hugh touch me till we were wed, but . . . but he said I should let you do what you will. And I was so afraid . . . because if we bedded together and then you did not want me as a wife, Papa would have blamed me for that, would have been so wroth . . ."

"Isabelle, listen to me. Forget what your father told you; it does not matter. You do not belong to him any longer. You belong to me, and I do want you. I want you as my Queen, I want you in my bed, and right now I want you on my lap." John smiled, but she reacted as if to a command, at once settled herself upon his knee, and put her arms shyly about his neck.

Her obedience delighted him, and he realized suddenly that he wanted her as much for her youth as in spite of it; she was still unformed, as malleable as she was beautiful, soft clay to be molded and shaped as he desired. "You are so fair to look upon," he murmured, then began to laugh. "And I've done Hugh de Lusignan an even more grievous hurt than I dared hope for!"

The great hall was in utter chaos, as the entire household of the Count of Angoulême labored to make ready for the wedding on the morrow. When Will could abide the confusion no longer, he escaped out into the gardens. It was becoming increasingly apparent to him that this wedding had been planned weeks in advance, so sure was Aymer of his daughter's power to enchant. He wondered briefly if he should mention this to John, decided it was pointless; John was not being shoved to the altar at swordpoint, after all.

He was approaching an intricate arbor of white thorn and willow, walled by trellises and fragrant with summer honeysuckle. As he came nearer, he heard a man's voice, low and coaxing. "You have to trust me, love. You do, do you not?" The girl's voice came even more clearly to Will's ears, an innocent accomplice in her own seduction. "Oh, but I do, truly I do." Will was genuinely shocked; he'd recognized the male voice at once as his brother's, but he found it almost impossible to believe that John could be so reckless, so unforgivably ill-mannered as to debauch one of Aymer's womenfolk on the very eve of his marriage to Aymer's daughter. What if it had been Aymer who'd come upon them? he thought, and strode forward, a warning hot on his lips, only to stop, dumbfounded, at sight of Isabelle.

Isabelle gave a little gasp of dismay, flushed bright red. It was one thing to tell herself that John had every right to fondle and caress her as he chose, that it was proper to allow him such intimacies. It was quite another for his brother, the Earl of Salisbury, to discover her sitting on John's lap, her hair in telling disarray and her bodice partially undone.

She came hastily to her feet, jerking at her gown, so flustered she might have fled had John not reached out, caught her hand. Rising unhurriedly, he said soothingly, "You've no cause for embarrassment, love. It is not for Will—or any other—to pass judgment upon you."

And with that, Isabelle suddenly and fully comprehended just what marriage to John would mean. That she would get to wear a crown and enjoy unknown luxury, that a son of hers would one day be King of England—all of that she'd already grasped, though it was not quite real to her, not yet. The awareness that came to her now was more immediate, and therefore more easily understood. All of her life she'd been taught it was her duty to obey, to please others, first and foremost the father whose expectations she could never quite satisfy. But no more. She need not ever worry again about her father's anger. Nor about her mother's sharp-tongued reprimands, or Hugh de Lusignan's hot rages, or the jealousy and spite of girls less favored than she. She had only to please one man and one man alone, and as long as she was secure in his approval and affections, no one else's disapproval mattered.

Isabelle drew a deep breath, giddy with the realization that she who'd had so little power would now have so much. When I am Queen of the English, she thought in awe, it will be Papa who'll have to please me—me! And she looked at John in wonderment, Will all but forgotten.

They could hear other voices in the gardens now, women's voices. Isabelle cocked her head, listening. "My mother . . . She's calling for me." But she did not move, looked to John for guidance. "Would you have me go to her?"

John nodded, bringing her hand up to his mouth and kissing her palm. "It is late; you'd best be in." Watching as she gathered up her skirts and ran lightly up the garden path, he said admiringly, "Lord God, what a beauty she's going to be, Will! To think she almost ended up in Hugh de Lusignan's bed; talk about casting pearls before swine!"

He was turning to follow after Isabelle when Will grasped his arm. "John, wait. I want you to tell me I misinterpreted what I just saw. I want you to tell me that you do not mean to bed that little girl."

John's eyes narrowed, took on sudden green glints. "Are you worrying that I shall dishonor her ere the wedding? How quaint. But you can put your mind at ease. I do intend to wait till the morrow . . . though that be no small sacrifice!"

"Christ Jesus, John, she is but twelve years old—a child! You do not think I'd have touched Ela, do you? Nor will I, not till she's of a proper age for bedding. As you must wait with

Isabelle. Her father would expect no less; he's entrusting her to your care, your keeping. If he even suspected you—''

John gave an angry, incredulous laugh. ''There are times when your innocence truly defies all belief! Who do you think sent us out into the gardens? You fool, I could lay with Isabelle at high noon atop a table in the great hall, and Aymer would cheer us on!''

But John did not truly want to quarrel with Will. Those very elements of Will's nature that made him champion Isabelle so stubbornly were also those that made him the only man John had ever been able to trust. He paused, then said impatiently, ''Will, you are my brother, my companion, even my confidant. But my conscience you are not, and thank God for it. I suspect you'd put a saint to shame! Good Christ, man, what do you think I mean to do, go after her like a stag in rut? You know me better than that, Will, or you bloody well should! I admit I've forced a woman or two in my life, but you name me a man who has not. I'm no Will de Braose, and you know it. I prefer a willing bedmate, prefer a woman who wants what she's getting.''

He grinned suddenly. ''I assure you, Isabelle will be in good hands. I had my first woman at fourteen, have long since lost count. You think I did not learn from all those couplings? That I'd not make Isabelle's deflowering as easy for her as I could? She's more woman than you know; I'd wager it'll take no more than a fortnight ere she's not only willing, but eager.''

''John, you must not—''

''Sweet glory of God, enough! Better me than de Lusignan. Now let that be an end to it.''

Will knew his brother well enough to read the danger signals, but he felt honor-bound to persevere. ''I do not doubt that de Lusignan would have wasted no time dragging the lass into bed. But you know better, John. The very fact that you feel the need to justify yourself proves that. It would be wrong to bed a twelve-year-old girl, no matter how fair she is. It's not . . . not decent. And it's dangerous, as well. What if you get her with child? I need not tell you how many women die in childbirth . . . and the younger the mother, the greater the risk.''

John caught his breath and then swore. ''Will, I'm warning you for the last time! You've pushed to the very limits of my patience. I'm heartily sick of this, will hear no more on it.''

But as he swung about, Will followed him onto the path, hastening to keep pace. ''What of your own daughter, what of Joanna? Can you tell me you'd want to see her as a man's

bedmate at twelve, a mother at thirteen? John, I know what I'm
saying! My Ela could not have—''

"Pox take your Ela, and you, too! I see nothing noble in your
forbearance; I've met Ela, remember? I do not wonder that
you're in no hurry to claim her maidenhead. But I doubt you'd be
so saintly if it were Isabelle naked and eager in your bed!''

Will recoiled violently, backed away. John did not wait for a
response, stalked up the path. He did not look back, but Will
watched, unmoving, until he was out of sight.

As deeply offended as Will was, even greater was his sense of
hurt. Never before had he felt the full lash of John's Angevin
temper. His was a uniquely privileged position; he alone dared
speak his mind utterly and freely to his brother, with no fear of
incurring the King's disfavor. Will was honest enough to admit
to himself that he relished the many tangible benefits he derived
from John's kingship, but even more did he relish his special
status as the King's brother and confidant. He prided himself on
his candor, told himself that even if John did not always heed his
advice, at least John was always willing to hear him out, liked to
think he alone knew how to appeal to John's better instincts, and
in consequence, he'd been slow to feel the ground shifting under
his feet.

He stood there alone for a time in the darkness, half expecting
John to return, seeking to make amends. But John did not come
back, and Will was left with the envenomed echoes of that last
lethal exchange, with the unhappy understanding that his influence over John was more illusory than not, that he must take
John on his own terms . . . or not at all.

Picking up a brush, Joanna parted her hair and then began to plait
it into two thick braids. Impatience made her clumsy, and the
strands kept slipping through her fingers. But she persevered; she
was nine now, too old for wild, unkempt hair, especially on the
day of her father's return from Normandy.

Never before had he been gone so long, five lonely months.
Always before, he had taken her with him; in the past four years
Joanna had learned to look upon a Channel crossing as noncha-
lantly as a Londoner viewed an outing across the Thames into
Southwark. But when John had sailed for Normandy that past
April, he'd left Joanna at Conisbrough, the Yorkshire castle of
his uncle Hamelin de Warenne, Earl of Surrey, home, too, to
Hamelin's grandson, her half-brother Richard.

Now it was October and Joanna was back at Westminster

Palace, awaiting John's arrival. All around her, women were sleeping; she shared a chamber with the ladies-in-waiting to the noblewomen of John's court. Snapping her fingers to attract Avisa, she unlatched the door, moved into the stairwell, the spaniel at her heels.

Emerging out into the sunlight of the New Palace yard, she was just in time to collide with a man coming around the corner of the old hall. He stumbled, caught her as she reeled backward.

"I'm sorry, my lord."

"No matter, Joanna. If I cannot sustain a bruising from a little lass like you, I'd best retire to my hearth and give my lands over to my sons," he said and smiled at her. William de Braose, Lord of Brecknock, was an attractive man, fit and sun-browned, blond hair and beard only lightly touched by grey although she knew he was well into his fifties. He was one of her father's closest friends, and was unfailingly pleasant to her. There was no reason why she should be so ill at ease with him, and yet she was. It was with relief now that she saw de Braose was not alone, was accompanied by her father's half-brother Will, Earl of Salisbury.

Will was family; with him, she need not stand on formality. "Papa's come?"

Will nodded. "We rode in from Freemantle late last night, so I expect he's still abed."

"I'd wager the surety of my soul on that!" de Braose said and laughed.

Will frowned and Joanna edged closer. "Uncle Will . . . Papa's new wife, is she comely?"

"Very comely, Joanna." Will looked intently into her face, and then put his arm around her shoulders, drew her aside. "Does it bother you, lass, that John has wed again?"

Joanna shook her head swiftly. "No, but . . . but I did not think he would wed again so soon." She fidgeted and then blurted out, "Uncle Will, I heard some men talking last month after we had word of Papa's marriage. They . . . they said Papa's new wife was plight-trothed to another lord, that Papa stole her away from this lord. That is not true, is it?"

Will did not answer at once. Joanna was, he knew, normally well insulated from rumors and gossip; no rational man would dare criticize the King in the hearing of his daughter. But this marriage had been virtually guaranteed to stir up controversy. It was said that Hugh de Lusignan had gone berserk with rage, raving and ranting and swearing to avenge himself upon John, even if it took a lifetime. And Hugh found some sympathizers among the Poitevin nobility, men who disapproved of the clandestine, underhanded nature of the marriage, others who'd willingly seize upon any pretext for rebellion. The result was that a marriage which should have solidified John's hold upon Poitou was in itself proving to be a source of dissension, while John had alienated the more pious of his subjects by his lustful infatuation with a girl of Isabelle's tender years.

Will shook his head slowly, wondering just how to answer Joanna. "Yes, it is true, lass. Isabelle was betrothed to as untrustworthy a man as you could find in all of Christendom, and her marriage would one day have put into his hands all of Angoulême. Your father could not let that happen."

Joanna was quiet. "Is she truly only twelve?" she asked at last, and Will nodded.

"I think I do know what frets you. But she is a lively, good-natured lass, and I'm sure you shall like her."

That was not what was fretting Joanna at all. She was quite prepared to like Isabelle, although she did think it distinctly odd to have a stepmother only three years older than she. Her fear was that Isabelle would not like her. She had long since accustomed herself to her father's women. Most were kind to her, sometimes cloyingly so; Adele alone had not been friendly, and Adele's reign had been brief. One day she was gone and Joanna had learned a valuable lesson: Whilst Papa's ladies came and went, her own place in his heart was constant. But a wife . . . a wife was not like a mistress.

Brooding on this as she crossed the bailey, she was pleased to see Richard coming toward her. She'd gained more than a father at Rouen, she'd gained six brothers, too. Most were well into their teens by now, and she saw them but seldom. With Richard it was different. He was only two years older than she, and from their first meeting he had appointed himself her protector, her guide and mentor. She could ask Richard what she could not ask Will, and as he fell in step beside her, she said, "Richard . . . what if she does not like us?"

Richard was eating manchet bread glazed with honey. He took a large bite, handed what remained to Joanna. "Papa will not love us any the less if she does not, Joanna. My mama says not to worry, that Papa is no man to be swayed by a woman's cajoling."

It occurred to Joanna that Richard was not as confident as he sounded, else he'd not have felt the need to consult his mother.

But she took comfort, nonetheless, from his assurance. His mother was more than a onetime mistress. Alina was John's first cousin, and had remained on friendly terms with him to this day, was often at court. Hers was a voice to be heeded.

"Richard . . . when your mama's family found out she was with child, were they shamed?"

"Angry, yes, but shamed . . . no. After all, Papa was a Prince. And then, too, my grandpapa Hamelin is baseborn himself; he was a bastard brother to King Henry. Mama told me that Grandpapa and my uncle did berate her some at first, but they know women are weak vessels. They could hardly blame her for being true to her nature."

"My mama was not so lucky," Joanna said softly. "Her family shunned her for her sin." She hesitated. "I told you that my mama died. But I never told you that I did think it was my fault."

Richard had been reaching to reclaim the honeyed bread. He stopped, gave her a look of sudden interest. "You did? Why?"

The memories of her mother's death were so fraught with pain even now that Joanna had never been able to share them with anyone but John, and she said evasively, "Oh, because she was so unhappy. But Papa explained it all to me, told me that the blame did lie with my mama's family, not with me."

Richard's interest waned. "Well, you're— Joanna, look. There's Uncle Will."

Will raised an arm, beckoned. "Joanna, Richard, make haste. Your lord father is ready to see you now."

St Edward's chamber had been for well over a hundred years the traditional bedchamber of the King, was still used even though it was part of the old palace of the Confessor. John was sitting on a coffer as his barber carefully trimmed his beard, but he waved the man away at sight of his children.

Joanna ran to him, into his arms. "Papa, I missed you so!"

"I missed you, too, sweetheart. But keep your voices down. Isabelle is still asleep."

Joanna and Richard quieted at once, cast subdued glances toward the curtained bed. John smiled at them, gave Richard a playful poke. "You need not act as if you're in church! Come over here and see what I brought back for you."

Lifting the coffer lid, he fished around, at last unearthed their presents: spurs for Richard, a carved ivory comb for Joanna. "I do have a second gift for Joanna, lad, but that is because I did miss her birthday. Here, sweetheart.''

Joanna gave a delighted gasp, slipped the ring onto her finger. It was a perfect topaz, set in silver, but too big, was sliding over her knuckle until she made a quick fist.

''John . . . John, where did you go?'' The voice was young, sleepily content. Richard and Joanna turned as a tousled head poked through the bed hangings. Joanna felt a sharp pang of envy; as she'd suspected, Isabelle's hair was a lustrous swirl of sunlight. She yawned like a lazy kitten, blinked at them with long-lashed, lavender-blue eyes. Joanna could not, of course, begin to comprehend the complicated sexual cravings that made this beautiful child-woman so desirable to a man with jaded sensibilities, a man in need of novelty. But she could see how undeniably lovely Isabelle was, and her fear came rushing back. How could Papa not be influenced by Isabelle?

''You must be Joanna and Richard.'' Isabelle jerked the bed hangings aside and, wrapping herself in the sheet, accepted a servant's offering, a cup of watered-down wine. ''I guess I'm now your mother!'' She laughed suddenly. ''But do not dare call me Mama!''

''What shall we call you, Madame?'' Joanna asked, at a loss, and Isabelle gave a comical grimace.

''How serious she is, John! I am Isabelle, of course. Come, sit beside me on the bed and I shall tell you of my first meeting with your father. I can tell her, can I not, John? It is six weeks to the day; we were wed without even posting the banns! John said he knew as soon as he saw me, knew he would have me for his Queen and no other.''

Joanna and Richard exchanged bemused glances. Both quiet by nature, they were overwhelmed by Isabelle, who seemed able to talk without even pausing for breath. But her friendliness set their fears at rest, and Joanna gladly did as Isabelle bade, settled herself upon the foot of the bed. She should have had more faith in Papa, she thought, should have known he would not have chosen a wife who'd scorn his children.

11

GWYNEDD, WALES

August 1201

After passing the night at Basingwerk Abbey, Baldwin de Hodnet and his brother moved cautiously westward, keeping to the narrow coastal road. The sea was frothed with whitecaps, the sky flaming to the east in a sunburst dawn that promised a day of surpassing beauty. But Baldwin had no eye for God's wonders; he was too much taken up with man-made troubles.

"How do you know where he is, Stephen?"

"I do not. The Welsh court moves about no less frequently than John's. Llewelyn has palaces at Aber, at Aberffraw on the isle of Môn, at Caer yn Arfon, has palaces and hunting lodges scattered throughout the Eryri Mountains."

"Well, then, how shall we find him?"

"We will not. He'll find us," Stephen said, and withdrew from his saddle pouch a brightly painted silk banner: quartered lions passant, red on gold. "Llewelyn's arms. What better way to make known that we seek him?"

"Clever," Baldwin said grudgingly. "But to what avail? I'm damned if I know why I let you talk me into this. We'll find no welcome at his court, Stephen. How can we? Just last month he did sign a truce with King John, did agree to do homage to John as his overlord, and, in return, was recognized as ruler of Gwynedd. Why should he risk angering John by aiding men branded as rebels?"

Stephen laughed. "You do not understand the Welsh, Baldwin. You share all the common misconceptions about Llewelyn's people. Ask any lord at John's court to describe the Welsh character, and what is he like to say? That the Welsh are impulsive, quick-tempered, easily stirred by passion. That may well be true. But it is also true that in matters of statecraft, no people in Christendom are as pragmatic as the Welsh princes. They have to be, with England more than twenty times the size of Wales. Since the reign of Owain Fawr, their princes have sworn allegiance to the English kings, because they were shrewd enough to see they had no choice. The Welsh are realists, Baldwin, and an oath of allegiance is cheaper than blood as the price of sovereignty. Do not ever think, though, that Llewelyn sees himself as a vassal of John's. He does not.''

Stephen grinned. ''The great weakness of the Welsh has always been their penchant for fighting amongst themselves, a weakness our kings have been quick to exploit. But Llewelyn has a rare gift for fishing in troubled waters. John may well find—''

''I'd as soon you spared me a lesson in Welsh history,'' Baldwin interrupted impatiently. ''All that does concern me at the moment is whether we're likely to find refuge at Llewelyn's court. And you've yet to convince me that we will.''

Now it was Stephen who showed impatience. ''We always knew it might come to this, Baldwin. When Fulk Fitz Warin rose up in rebellion against John, and we decided we could not do otherwise than support him as our kinsman and liege lord, we had no illusions about the risks, or the likely outcome. Tell me, would you rather seek exile in France?''

''No,'' Baldwin conceded. ''I ought not to be taking out my foul temper on you, Little Brother. As you say, better Llewelyn than Philip. How long has it been since you saw him last?''

''Three or four years, I think,'' Stephen said, and Baldwin let out an explosive oath.

''Blood of Christ! You expect him to incur John's wrath for a man he has not even seen in years?''

Stephen was unperturbed. ''The Welsh make bad enemies, better friends. Your trouble, Baldwin, is that you have so little faith!''

''My trouble is that I have a price upon my head, and an ingrate of a brother set upon laying claim to my inheritance,'' Baldwin said sourly.

''What else would you expect from Walter?''

''Better than this. Did I not persuade Fulk to give him a place in his household? And when he came to me, claiming he'd had his horse and armor stolen, did I not lend him the money for another mount and hauberk?''

''And I thought you were mad to do it; I still do. As the eldest, you never knew him, Baldwin, not as Will and I did.''

"What else could I do, Stephen? He's still blood kin."

"If he were drowning, I'd throw him an anchor," Stephen said flatly, and Baldwin gave his brother a surprised, speculative look.

"You truly mean that, do you not? I did not realize—" He stiffened suddenly, and then said softly, "Stephen, to your left."

"I know. I think we're about to be welcomed into Wales."

There was a flash of movement through the trees; a lance thudded into the path a few feet ahead, quivered like a snake coiled to strike. They both drew rein, waited.

A man emerged from the woods, came to a wary halt. Stephen tilted his lance up so that Llewelyn's banner caught the breeze. *"Tangnefedd,"* he said loudly. *"Rydu i Stephen de Hodnet, cyfaill o Llewelyn ab Iorwerth, o Tywysog Gwynedd."*

There was a silence; other men were now coming out of the shadows. Stephen ventured a few more sentences in halting Welsh, then turned to Baldwin, smiling. "Did I not tell you? These are Llewelyn's men, will take us to him. I told them that I am his friend, that he will want to see me."

"You hope," Baldwin said.

They were traveling south, through a well-wooded river valley. Stephen was carrying on a disjointed conversation with their guides, partly in his rudimentary Welsh and partly in their fragmented French, and from time to time he'd translate for Baldwin's benefit. "We have to ford the River Conwy up ahead, and then veer west."

"Did you, by any chance, think to ask where we're going?"

"Dolwyddelan Castle." Anticipating Baldwin, Stephen grinned, said with exaggerated precision, "Dole-with-*ell*an. I'd hoped Llewelyn would be at Aber or Aberffraw, wanted you to see the Welsh court. But Dolwyddelan should be of interest, too; it's one of the few Welsh-built castles, belonged to Llewelyn's father Iorwerth."

That did interest Baldwin. So, too, did the countryside once they were across the River Conwy. It was far more mountainous now; on all sides the sky was silhouetted by snow-capped crags. Baldwin was impressed in spite of himself, forbore to mock as Stephen shared the knowledge gleaned from their guides. "They say snow is sometimes found all summer long upon the highest peaks. The steepest is that one to the south, Yr Wyddfa. And over to your right is Moel Siabod, which all but overshadows Dolwyddelan."

"Little wonder the Welsh are so hard to dislodge," Baldwin said, and shook his head. "Their whole wretched country is a fortress of sorts!"

They reached Dolwyddelan Castle at dusk. It appeared without warning, seemed to spring suddenly from the rough-hewn rocks overlooking the River Lledr. Baldwin, appraising it from habit, with an eye to assault, saw at once that it would be no easy prize for the taking. On the south, the ground fell away sharply, and deep ditches had been cut into the rock to the west and east. But what impressed Baldwin was the high curtain wall. Most castles were enclosed by timber palisades, but Dolwyddelan was encircled by stone.

Stephen, too, was regarding the curtain wall with surprise. "When last I was here, that was a wooden enclosure."

"He's doing right well for himself if he could undertake an expense like that," Baldwin said thoughtfully, and Stephen frowned.

"He's not just another Marcher border lord, Baldwin. He's Prince of Gwynedd. Power is power, be it Welsh or Norman; you'd best bear that in mind."

Passing through a gateway in the north wall, they dismounted in the bailey. Baldwin's eyes catalogued the wooden buildings clustered along the walls, focused upon the two-story rectangular keep, its entrance protected by a wooden forebuilding. He noted with satisfaction that the stairs leading up into the forebuilding were of stone; a miscalculation for certes. But as he reached the top, he abruptly revised his opinion of the keep's defenses. A wide pit lay between the stairs and the door of the keep, a gap that could be spanned only by drawbridge.

"Clever," he murmured to Stephen. But his brother was already hastening across the drawbridge, utterly sure of his welcome within. Following more slowly, Baldwin discovered that the entire first floor of the keep contained one large chamber. By the hearth, his brother was kneeling. As Baldwin watched, Llewelyn raised Stephen to his feet, and the two men then embraced. Stephen turned, gave Baldwin a smile shot through with triumph.

Baldwin leaned back in the window seat, only half listening to his brother's conversation with Llewelyn. He was more interested in his surroundings than in Stephen's boyhood reminiscences, and he glanced about with frankly curious eyes. They were in Llewelyn's bedchamber; a large curtained bed stood at the far

end of the room. The furnishings startled Baldwin, in that they
were so familiar: rushes for the floor, a trestle table, coffers,
even a privy chamber tucked away into the thickness of the
southeast wall. He could, Baldwin mused in surprise, quite easily
have been in the bedchamber of any Norman lord.

He did not realize how nakedly his thoughts showed upon his
face until Llewelyn looked at him, said, "Did you think to find
us living in caves?"

Although said with a smile, it carried a sting nonetheless, and
Baldwin flushed. He was honest enough, however, to acknowledge he'd been fairly caught, and he summoned up a smile of his
own. "To tell you true, my lord, I knew naught of how the
Welsh do live."

"We have our own ways, but we are not too proud to learn
from others." Llewelyn grinned, gestured toward the bed. "Take
yon feather bed. That is one Norman custom I'm quite willing to
adopt for Wales."

"Papa even sleeps on a pillow," a voice said, right at Baldwin's elbow, and he jumped, turned to find himself under the
unblinking scrutiny of a small boy. He looked to be about five,
an unusually handsome youngster with dark red hair, wide-set
green eyes, and a rather remarkable assurance for his years,
volunteering now without waiting to be asked, "I'm Gruffydd ap
Llewelyn."

Llewelyn laughed. "My son Gruffydd, who does delight in
giving away all my guilty secrets!"

Gruffydd thrived upon attention, and he moved closer to
Baldwin, confiding, "Papa has two pillows. But he lets my
mama use one."

Baldwin was not comfortable with children. "Does he indeed?" he said lamely. Adding, since the boy was obviously
cherished, "You speak French very well, lad."

"I know," Gruffydd said. "Are you English? Do you know
what Papa says of the English? He says, 'Poor Wales, so far
from Heaven, so close to England!' "

"Gruffydd!" Llewelyn frowned, sought without success to
look disapproving. "Where are your manners, lad?"

Not in the least amused, Baldwin managed a thin smile.
Stephen, who *was* amused, diplomatically piloted the conversation toward safer waters, saying swiftly, "How is your lady? She's
not here with you, I take it?"

"No, she's at Aberffraw. Her babe is due next month . . . our fourth.'' A man now leaned over Llewelyn's chair, murmured a few words, and he rose.

"Alun will escort you to the great hall, where our cooks have set out a meal for you. I'll join you directly I put this hellion to bed.'' Gruffydd at once darted for the door, but Llewelyn was quicker, grabbed the boy and swung him up into the air, making him shriek with laughter.

Baldwin signaled for another helping of stewed eels. ''Your friend does feed his guests well,'' he admitted. ''But tell me— whilst we're alone—you asked after his 'lady.' A concubine, not a wife?''

Stephen hesitated. "Llewelyn is not wed to Tangwystl. But do not be misled by that, Baldwin. Tangwystl is highborn, daughter to Lord Llywarch of Rhos. Less than a wife, mayhap, but much more than a mere bedmate. Theirs is looked upon as an honorable liaison. The Welsh have their own ways, as Llewelyn told you, and I confess I find none stranger than their attitude toward bastard-born children. They see no sin attaching to the children; under Welsh law, Gruffydd is fully equal to any sons Llewelyn may later have in wedlock.''

Baldwin was shocked. "You mean that even though he's a bastard, he's Llewelyn's heir?'' And when Stephen nodded, he could only shake his head in astonishment. ''The Welsh are mad, in truth. You've met her then, this Tang . . . ?''

"Tang-oo-*is*-til.'' Seeing Llewelyn enter the hall, Stephen smiled a welcome, said, ''I was telling Baldwin; Tangwystl does mean 'pledge of peace,' does it not?''

"And never was a woman more aptly named, Stephen. She claims I like to ride the whirlwind, but she's managed to make of our home a veritable haven of peace.'' Llewelyn tasted the mead set before him, and then said, ''I understand Fulk Fitz Warin has rebelled against King John—a dispute over a castle, I believe?''

Baldwin stiffened; he'd not expected so abrupt an exposure of their need. Stephen seemed unfazed, however. ''Yes,'' he said. ''John did unjustly deny Fulk's claim to Whittington Castle. Baldwin and I . . . we felt honor-bound to support him. But John has passed Bills of Attainder against us all, and we've been hard pressed these weeks past, Llewelyn. Will you help us?''

"Of course. You are welcome at my court, for as long as you wish. So, too, is your lord, Fulk Fitz Warin. Did you doubt that?''

Stephen shook his head. "No, I know you too well, know the ways of Welsh hospitality.''

Baldwin was still unable to believe salvation was being offered so casually. "Why?" he blurted out. "Why should you risk John's enmity for us?"

Llewelyn looked amused. "Scriptures set forth Commandments for all Christians to honor. But my people honor other commandments, too, those that speak to the difficulties of dwelling in England's shadow. Let not an enemy be thy neighbor. It is no deceit to deceive a deceiver. And the enemy of my enemy is my friend."

Baldwin nodded slowly. "So you see John, then, as your enemy?"

Llewelyn smiled. "I said that?" Reaching over, he clinked his cup against Stephen's. *"Croeso i Gymru, Steffan.* Welcome, Stephen, to Wales."

The man seated at Baldwin's left had been introduced to him as Rhys ap Cadell, but he seemed little inclined to polite conversation. The man on his right was Gwyn ab Ednywain, Llewelyn's Seneschal; he was friendly enough, but at the moment was concentrating all his attentions upon the food being ladled from chafing dishes: venison baked in coffyn pies; boiled pears flavored with honey, dates, and cinnamon; oatcakes; roast heron. It was, Baldwin acknowledged, a meal fit to grace any Norman table. He was beginning to think his stay in Wales would not be so great a hardship after all.

He glanced around the hall with interest. Except that it was a ground-floor structure, it looked exactly like any Norman hall: three parallel rows of wooden pillars, the side aisles occupied by beds and partitioned off by screens. He and Stephen had slept here last night, as comfortably as ever they had in Fulk's Alberbury Castle, had been given places of honor near the hearth.

Llywarch, Llewelyn's court bard, now moved toward the center aisle, carrying a small harp. The hall quieted at once. Men laid down their knives and spoons to listen as he began a haunting ballad, not a word of which Baldwin understood. He was rather surprised that Llywarch had so much standing at Llewelyn's court, being treated by all as a man of importance. Bards and minstrels enjoyed no such privileged status in England. There was much that Baldwin found odd in Llewelyn's world, but gratitude was proving stronger than bias, and he was determined to adapt as best he could. When the song ended, conversation resumed again, and he leaned forward with interest when he heard Stephen say, "You expect war with your cousin, Meredydd ap Cynan, my lord Llewelyn?"

"It may well come to that. When my cousin Gruffydd— Meredydd's brother—did die last year of a wasting fever, I laid claim to his lands. As that gave me most of Gwynedd above the Conwy and all of Gwynedd below the Conwy, Meredydd took it amiss, and there's been naught but discord between us for months now."

Llewelyn did not sound particularly grieved about this, and Baldwin smothered a smile with his napkin. He did not know Meredydd ap Cynan, but he had a strong suspicion that, having snapped at the bait, Meredydd was about to bite down upon the hook.

Llewelyn drained his wine cup. "I was sorry to hear of your lord father's death, Stephen."

"Thank you, my lord. His death was a tragedy twice over for us, as Walter is now laying claim to my father's estates, lands that should by rights have passed to Baldwin."

"I see. Baldwin is under attainder, so Walter moves in for the kill."

Stephen nodded glumly. "And there is little we can do to stop him."

"Mayhap not. But I rather think I can. Shall I?"

"You mean that? Jesú, we'd be ever in your debt! Baldwin, did you hear?"

Baldwin did not share Stephen's excitement. "That would be very kind of you, my lord," he said slowly, "but in truth, I do not see how you can help."

Llewelyn's smile was suddenly cool. "You'd not care to wager upon that?"

Stephen laughed. "I'd not take him up on that, Baldwin. You see, Walter has long owed him a debt!"

Llewelyn laughed, too. "Not so, Stephen. That debt was discharged in full some eight years ago; did Walter never tell you? No, this I do for you."

Stephen did not reply; he was staring across the hall, at the man standing in the door. A slender, silver-haired priest in his mid-forties, he looked somehow familiar to Stephen. "My lord Llewelyn, I may be wrong, but is that not your chaplain, Morgan ap Bleddyn?"

Llewelyn turned at once. "Yes, it is. Strange, he knew I'd be back at Aberffraw by week's end. I wonder what could not wait . . ."

"My lord . . ." Morgan knelt, rose stiffly to his feet. "A word with you, if I may . . . alone."

Llewelyn pushed his chair back. "Morgan, are you ill? I've seen corpse candles with more color. Here, take some wine . . ."

"Llewelyn . . ." The priest waved the cupbearer away. "If we might retire behind the screen . . ."

Llewelyn moved around the table, grasped the older man by the arm. "Tell me," he said. "Tell me now."

"It happened yesterday morn. Tangwystl was entering the chapel; somehow she stumbled, fell upon the stairs. As soon as your doctor saw her birth pangs had begun, he did summon the midwives." Morgan stopped, drew a deep breath. "You have a daughter, Llewelyn. I'll not lie to you; she's fearfully tiny and frail. But with our prayers . . ."

"I'll leave for Aberffraw as soon as the horses can be saddled. You told Tangwystl you were coming to fetch me?"

"Llewelyn . . . she began to bleed. The midwives, they did what they could, but . . . they could not save her, lad."

"She's dead?" Llewelyn's was the calm of utter disbelief. He stared at Morgan, saw tears well in the priest's eyes. He was aware now of the others. The hall was very quiet, but all else looked as it had only moments before. Dogs still lurked under the tables, snarling over bones. Summer sun still spilled through the unshuttered windows. Out in the bailey a curlew cried, a rising mournful plaint that went unanswered.

Morgan pressed a crucifix into Llewelyn's hand. "Come with me to the chapel. I'll say a Mass for her soul, and afterward, we'll talk . . ."

Llewelyn looked at the crucifix, let it drop into the rushes. Turning away from Morgan, from them all, he walked rapidly across the hall.

Unlike Baldwin, who'd been listening in utter bafflement, Stephen had grasped enough for appalled understanding. He took a quick step toward the door, but Ednyved caught his arm.

"No," he said. "Let him be. There is nothing any man can say now that will ease the pain. I know; I did lose my wife in childbed, too."

Morgan retrieved the crucifix. "It is God's will," he said, sounding very tired, and Ednyved turned upon him with something much like anger.

"I can tell you, Father, that is but little comfort to a man who's just lost his wife!"

"It is all we do have, Ednyved." Morgan's grey eyes met

Ednyved's brown ones, held them steadily. ''I know Llewelyn, better even than you do. All his life he has always gotten what he wanted, has shrugged at obstacles that would have daunted other men. It has been his strength, that utter assurance, the certainty that he can shape his own destiny. But you see, he's never learned to deal with defeat. He's never had to—until now.''

Ednyved nodded. ''Yes,'' he said softly. ''You do understand.''

The air was cool and damp against his face. Llewelyn slid from the saddle. The sky was no longer visible, stars hidden by leafy clouds of oak, birch, and hazel. Here was no woodland quiet; the night echoed with the white-water sounds of river raging against rock. Llewelyn could see a ghostly gleam of white through the trees as the cliffs rose up above the bank. The roaring was louder now. Rhaeadr Ewynnol, his people called it, the Foaming Fall. Even at midday the water was always dark near the rocks, lightening to a paler green in the shallows. Now it was the blackest of blacks, faintly silvered by moonlight. Above the pool surged the River Llugwy, spilling down onto the rocks in a wild, white cascade of foam.

Llewelyn did not know how long he stood there, scant inches from the cliff. Instinct alone had drawn him to Rhaeadr Ewynnol, where he'd so often come with Tangwystl, just as instinct had guided him during those hours alone on the heights of Moel Siabod. He had no memory of where he'd been, merely a blurred awareness of time passing, darkness blotting out the light. There was only numbness, an inability to accept Morgan's words as true. Tangwystl was dead. He knew that. And yet how could she not be waiting for him at Aberffraw? How could she be gone forever from his life?

Exhaustion at last led him back to Dolwyddelan Castle. They were watching for him; the drawbridge was lowered by the time he rode up the north slope, and a groom was waiting to take his stallion. He crossed the bailey, noting with dull surprise that the sky showed pale grey along the horizon. Mounting the steps into the keep, he all but stumbled over his son.

''Gruffydd? Gruffydd, lad, what are you doing out here?''

The boy blinked sleepily, looked about him as if he, too, wondered why he was not in bed. His face was puffy, streaked with dirt from the stairs. ''I was waiting for you, Papa.''

Lifting Gruffydd in his arms, Llewelyn carried him into the keep. Rushlights burned in wall sconces, the bed coverlets were turned back, a large flagon of mead and a loaf of manchet bread had been set out on the table. But the chamber was empty; the servants who normally slept on pallets were nowhere to be seen. Mead and solitude—all his friends could think to offer him.

"Sit beside me, Gruffydd. There is something I must tell you . . . about your mother."

Gruffydd had Tangwystl's green eyes; they were, Llewelyn now saw, swollen and rimmed in red. "Uncle Rhys told me, Papa, told me Mama is dead."

Llewelyn touched the boy's cheek, stroked his hair. "You understand what that means, lad?"

Gruffydd nodded. "That I will not see her anymore." Tears escaped his lashes, smudged a grimy path down his face. "Uncle Rhys said Mama's soul has gone to God. But . . . but when my dog died, Papa, you buried him in the ground. Will Mama be buried, too? I do not want her buried, Papa, do not want her in the ground . . ."

"Oh, Christ . . ." Llewelyn stumbled to his feet, backed into the table. Gruffydd had, with those few words, made Tangwystl's death real at last. The merciful numbness, the stunned sense of disbelief gave way before the image now burning into his brain— Tangwystl covered with dirt, lying alone under cold, dark earth, Tangwystl who'd so loved light and summer warmth.

The flagon rocked as he bumped the table, and his fingers closed of their own accord around the handle. The earthenware jug shattered on impact against the hearthstones, scattered clay fragments into the rushes. The flames sputtered and hissed; fingers of fire shot upward, feeding upon the sudden surge of air.

Gruffydd still sat upon the bed, staring wide-eyed at the wreckage strewn about the floor. And then he scrambled down, ran to Llewelyn. "Do not cry, Papa, please . . ."

Llewelyn knelt, and Gruffydd wrapped his arms around his father's neck, sobbed into his shoulder. "Hush, lad, hush. I did not mean to frighten you." Gruffydd's tears were wet upon Llewelyn's face; his son's breath, hot and gasping, rasped against his ear. "It is all right to weep for her, Gruffydd. But the pain will ease, I promise you . . ." And in seeking to comfort his stricken son, Llewelyn finally found a small measure of comfort for himself.

12

ROUEN, NORMANDY

June 1202

"When do you depart for Fontevrault Abbey, Joanna?"

"At week's end, Papa said." Joanna sat on the bed, began to brush her stepmother's long, silky hair. "Will you tell me about her, Isabelle?"

"About Eleanor? What could I add that you have not long since heard by now?"

"But I have not . . . heard that much, I mean. People rarely tell me about scandals," Joanna said regretfully.

Isabelle needed no further coaxing. "You do know, of course, that she was the greatest heiress of her time, Duchess of Aquitaine and Countess of Poitou. So great a marital prize was soon taken, and when she was fifteen, she became Queen of France. They say Louis doted upon her, could deny her nothing, even to allowing her to accompany him on crusade."

"In truth?" Joanna asked, having learned the hard way to be rather dubious of Isabelle's more extravagant claims, and Isabelle crossed herself with a dramatic flourish.

"Upon the soul of Blessed Mary, ever Virgin, I swear it so. And whilst in the Holy Land, she did bring great scandal to her name. Her Uncle Raymond was Prince of Antioch, a most handsome man only eight years older than she. Eleanor had not seen him since childhood, and he welcomed her right lovingly . . . too much so, men thought. Whilst none can prove they did bed together, it is known that Eleanor told Louis she wanted to end their marriage. But he was still besotted with her, had her taken from Antioch by force!

"Theirs had always been a marriage of fire and milk. Eleanor was once overheard to say she'd thought to marry a King, but

157

found she'd married a monk! The Pope sought to reconcile them, but when Eleanor gave birth to a second daughter, even Louis began to think their union was not blessed in the eyes of God. And then, in the fall of 1151, Henry Plantagenet, Duke of Normandy, came to the French court. Eleanor was eleven years older than he, but still surpassingly beautiful. We do not know what passed between them, but as soon as Henry left Paris, Eleanor again besought Louis to annul their marriage. This time he agreed, and the marriage was declared invalid in March 1152. She at once withdrew to her own lands in Poitou, and there stunned all of Christendom by taking Henry Plantagenet as her husband.

"Louis would never have let her go had he suspected her intent, would rather have seen her wed to the Devil, so deeply did he fear Henry's ambitions. And with cause. With Eleanor's backing, Henry pushed his claim to the English crown, and within three years of their marriage, Eleanor became the only woman ever to wear the crowns of both France and England."

Joanna was, as usual, proving to be a highly satisfactory audience, and Isabelle plunged ahead, scarcely pausing for breath. "In fifteen years as wife to Louis, Eleanor had given him but two daughters. But as Queen of England, she bore Henry a rich crop, eight children in fourteen years. Four healthy sons she gave Henry; what king could ask for more?"

"How, then, did she fall out of favor with Henry?"

"I'd say, rather, that Henry fell out of favor with her! He'd never been faithful, but that is a wife's lot, and she'd turned a blind eye to his straying. Rosamond Clifford, however, could not be ignored. He brought Rosamond into his bed, even to his table, honored her as if she were Queen, not concubine. Most husbands are more discreet than that, praise God, for the truth of it is, Joanna, that even if a man sets up his harlot right in the keep, there is little his wife can do about it. But Eleanor . . . Eleanor was not like other women; when Henry shamed her so, she left him, withdrew to her own Poitou, and raised the standard of rebellion against him!"

Joanna had been listening, openmouthed. Indeed, her grandmother was *not* like other women! "What happened then?" she prompted, as if listening to some improbable minstrel's tale.

"John was just a little lad, but their other sons were well nigh grown, and they sided with Eleanor. So, too, did Louis, the French King, who was only too eager to turn Henry's own sons against him. In the fighting that followed, Henry ravaged Eleanor's lands, took her prisoner. She was," Isabelle said with relish, "not waiting meekly by the hearth for capture, but had dressed as a man and was seeking to escape into Anjou. Henry sent her back to England under guard, imprisoned her in Salisbury Tower, kept her closely held until his death . . . nigh on sixteen years, Joanna."

"Oh, no!" Joanna had utterly forgotten these were events from a long-gone past; her sympathy for Eleanor, the captive Queen, was as immediate as it was unlawful. She knew she should feel only disapproval toward a wayward wife, a rebel Queen, but she was aware, instead, of a sharp, piercing regret, an ache for that wild spirit caged at last within Salisbury Tower.

"They were bitter years for Henry, too," Isabelle conceded, "years of strife with his sons. Henry, the eldest-born, died of a bloody flux. Geoffrey was killed in a tournament in France, leaving his wife with child, that wretched boy Arthur who now gives John such grief. Richard allied himself with Louis' son Philip, and between them they brought Henry to bay, forced him to accept their terms for peace. He died days later, muttering, so they say, 'Shame upon a conquered King.' "

But Joanna's imagination was still fired by Salisbury Tower. "What of Eleanor?"

"Oh, Richard at once dispatched William Marshal to free her. They were always close; when Richard was taken captive by the Holy Roman Emperor, she labored day and night to raise his ransom."

"Have you ever met her, Isabelle?"

"Yes, two years ago. John took me to Fontevrault soon after our marriage. She was most generous, dowered me with the cities of Niort and Saintes. But I confess I am ever so thankful that she divides her time between Poitiers and Fontevrault, that she dwells not at John's court!"

Joanna had heard few fables as enthralling as this factual account of a flesh-and-blood woman, her own kindred. But she had noted one strange omission in Isabelle's narrative. "But where was Papa in all this, Isabelle? Did he not help to raise the ransom, too?"

Isabelle laughed. "Oh, indeed! He and Philip pledged one hundred thousand silver marks—if the Emperor would but hold Richard for yet another year. Does that shock you? It should not; you know John loved Richard not."

Joanna nodded slowly. While her father spoke but rarely of his family, he did occasionally relate sardonic stories about his brother, stories that were far from flattering to Richard: how, when he and the Saracen Prince Saladin failed to come to terms over the ransom of prisoners at Acre, Richard had given the command to slaughter them all, some twenty-five hundred captives; how it had cost every man in England one-fourth of his year's income to pay Richard's ransom; how, when Issac, the Emperor of Cyprus, had surrendered to Richard, he'd done so on the promise that he would not be put in irons, only to have Richard fetter him in chains made of silver.

"Papa had no reason to love Richard," Joanna said defensively. "He was not a good King. Papa is a better one."

"I can guess who taught you that!" Isabelle teased.

"And do you find fault with it, Isabelle?"

Isabelle turned a startled face toward the door, said hastily, "Of course I do not, John! I think you're a far more able King than your brother; surely you do know that, my love?"

Joanna waited as Isabelle crossed to John, sought to placate him with a long, lingering kiss. Then she, too, rose, moved to greet her father.

"Isabelle was telling me about your lady mother, Papa," she explained, watching him all the while with anxious eyes. Never had she seen him so tense, so quick to take offense as he'd been in recent weeks. Since the spring, since the outbreak of war with France.

Watching unhappily as her father's nerves frayed under the dark strains of the coming campaign, Joanna sought to cheer him in small ways, engaging him in talk of his cherished falcons, memorizing a verse he'd much admired, obeying his every whim with the alacrity of a command. But all her efforts had so far gone for naught. She knew her father to be deeply troubled, and every night she prayed for God to smite his enemies, Philip, King of the French, and the youth to whom Isabelle always referred as "that wretch Arthur."

Three years ago, when her father had claimed the crown, Joanna had been too young to realize how close a thing it had been, his prevailing over Arthur. Now she understood all too well. The Angevin Empire remained dangerously divided over the succession, with England and Normandy favoring John, and the barons of Brittany, Anjou, Maine, and Touraine preferring Arthur. Time had not reconciled them to John, and Arthur, Breton-born, was casting a long shadow indeed. He was fifteen now, old enough to assert his own claims to what he'd been taught was his birthright, and he had a valuable ally in the calculating King of France. Just as he'd once sought to advance his own interests by turning Richard against Henry and, later, John against Richard, Philip now saw in Arthur the means of John's downfall. In May he'd accepted Arthur's oath of homage, had betrothed his five-year-old daughter to the young Duke of Brittany. And that meant, Joanna knew, the stakes for her father were all or nothing. A loss to Philip and Arthur would cost him his crown, his realm, his life.

She hastened now to pour a cup of wine, offered it to him with exaggerated care. "What is she like, Papa . . . your lady mother?"

John was quiet for so long that she thought he was not going to reply. "A legend," he said softly. "A living legend . . . like my illustrious brother, the Lion-Heart." His eyes, shadowed by weariness, shone with a hard green glitter.

"You want to win her favor, Joanna? Talk to her of Richard, then." He'd drained the cup already, set it down with a thud. " 'I have lost the staff of my age, the light of my eyes.' Those were her words, what she cried out upon his capture. Yes, talk to her of Richard."

Joanna did not know how to answer him. Nor, she saw, did Isabelle. They looked at each other helplessly.

"I would rather talk to her of you, Papa," she ventured, and John gave a sudden laugh, a staccato sound that had in it little of mirth.

"I'd not advise that, lass. My mother has never been one to feign interest where she has none."

Joanna's eyes filled with tears. She was aware by now that he was drunk, and that only made her all the more uneasy, for he generally had a good head for wine.

Isabelle, no less at a loss than Joanna, reached out to steady his hand as he refilled the cup. "Come to bed, beloved," she coaxed, knowing no other comfort to offer, knowing only what he'd taught her.

He touched her cheek, brushed aside the bright hair falling free about her face. "You're such a child, Isabelle, a lovely child. I do not want you tonight. Go away. Both of you, go away."

Isabelle started to speak, and he put his fingers to her mouth. "I would not take out my demons on you, Isabelle. But if you stay, I shall. Take Joanna and go."

She nodded, retreated toward the door, pulling Joanna after her. In the antechamber she sank down, white-faced, upon the nearest coffer. "Mayhap I should not have left him . . . Joanna, Joanna, was I wrong? Should I have stayed?"

Joanna was accustomed to Isabelle asking her questions better put to an adult, but that did not make the answers come any easier. "I do not know," she confessed. "I never saw Papa like that before . . ."

"He's afraid," Isabelle said, almost inaudibly. "God knows, he has reasons enough for fear. So many enemies. So few he can trust." She shivered. "He's afraid, Joanna . . . and so alone."

The Benedictine abbey of Fontevrault was situated in the province of Anjou, not far from the crossing of the Rivers Vienne and Loire. It was a rich land, famed for its vineyards, lush and green in the summer sun, and Joanna's journey from Rouen should have been a pleasant one. But the threat of war overhung the countryside, hovering like woodsmoke along the horizon, and Joanna soon discovered that distance did little to ease her fears for her father's safety. She was nervous, moreover, about meeting her grandmother.

Eleanor was entering her eighty-first year, an age no less vast to Joanna than that of the ancient, gnarled oaks shadowing their path. Joanna's craving for family, for belonging, was the mainspring of her being, but as Fontevrault Abbey came into sight, she found herself beset by misgivings. She had no right to her father's name, was accepted at court only on his sufferance. Would Eleanor welcome a grandchild born of sin?

The room was in shadows, shielded from the sun by heavy linen hangings. Joanna groped her way forward, blindly, knelt before the woman sitting in an oaken, upright chair, much like a throne.

"Come closer, child, so I might see you." The voice was not at all the croaking whisper Joanna had been expecting; it was clear, perfectly pitched, made her long to hear it again.

Joanna rose shyly, took the hand outstretched to her. It was hot and dry, so frail she could think only of the time she'd held a captive bird within her palms; her grandmother's bones seemed no less fragile, to be broken by a breath. But then the fingers, long and tapering, ablaze with emerald and opal and turquoise, closed around her own, firmly, drawing her forward. For a moment she felt a cheek pressed against her own; it, too, was hot, crinkled like parchment. An exotic, beguiling fragrance perfumed the air; as her grandmother embraced her, she heard the whisper of silk. She lifted her lashes, looked into hazel eyes much like her own.

"So you are Joanna," Eleanor said, and when she smiled,

Joanna, caught like so many others before her by the potent pull of that sudden, capricious charm, gave up her heart with reckless and innocent abandon.

July skies were cloudless, shimmering metallically above vines scorched beyond renewal by the unrelenting sun. Joanna rarely ventured out into the midday heat, having adapted her habits to those of her grandmother. Eleanor was that rarity in an age of dawn-risers, a creature of the night. She flowered in those hours after dusk, not going to her bed until the world was long stilled and hushed, sleeping away the bright, hot afternoons under the soft swishing of her ladies' fans. That was, she told Joanna, one of the advantages of age, that she could at last follow her own inner clock.

"What other advantages does age offer, Madame?"

"Precious few, child. The sweet satisfaction of outliving all my enemies, of burying my mistakes, of remembering and savoring my triumphs. Memory is merciful, Joanna, more so than man. It fades past pain, yet holds bright the colors in recalled joy."

Joanna was not long in discovering that Eleanor's memory was no less remarkably preserved than her small white teeth. It was rare to reach such an age without gaping blank spaces in the mouth and mind; most ancients were reduced to gruel and muddled memories in which time blurred all boundaries. But Eleanor had somehow triumphed over the vagaries of age, just as she'd somehow triumphed over the confines and constraints of womanhood. Her past was very much with her, vivid and precisely drawn, a treasure trove of memories ripe for sharing. And share them she chose to do, in those sultry summer nights when sleep would not come and her yesterdays seemed so very close, just beyond reach.

She told Joanna of her long-ago girlhood, conjured up the ghosts of her marital bed: Louis, so mild, so pious and softspoken, so utterly unlike the Angevin great-grandson of the Conqueror, the youth who'd dared to seek her out at her husband's court, caressing her boldly with hot grey eyes as he talked of empires. "I was twenty-nine and Henry was eighteen, but more of a man than any I'd ever known, in bed or out," Eleanor said softly, startling Joanna by the nonchalance with which she confessed to adultery, but then she gave the girl a self-mocking smile not entirely free of bitterness. "I must have loved him, in truth, else I could not have hated him so much after."

She told Joanna of Henry's bitter quarrel with Thomas à Becket, how Henry had sealed Becket's doom by crying out in a fit of rage, "Will none rid me of this turbulent priest?" Told her the legend that the royal House of Plantagenet came from the Devil; told her, too, how her sons had laughed at their Angevin heritage, turning aside criticism with jests about the demon Countess of Black Fulk of Anjou.

Some of her memories were tragic: her daughter Joanna's death in childbed at thirty-four; Richard's foolish and fatal bravery before the walls of Châlus. Others were fraught with menace: Eleanor's perilous journey from French territory into her own lands in Poitou after her divorce from Louis; two separate attempts had been made to ambush and abduct her, for landed women were often forced into marriage against their wills, and Eleanor was the greatest heiress in Christendom.

And some of her stories were tales of horror, none more so than that of the massacre of the Jews the year before Joanna's birth: "Richard had forbidden all Jews to attend his coronation, but some wealthy merchants brought gifts to the banquet following. Members of his court, the worse for wine and having no liking for Jews even when sober, expelled them from the hall, and the citizens of London took this to mean all Jews in the city were fair game. Rioting broke out, the ghetto burned, and many died. Other cities were soon caught up in the same violence, as it swept like plague across the realm, but nowhere was the outbreak worse than in York. There the Jews had sought refuge in the castle keep, and when it appeared certain they'd be taken by the besieging mob, the men, women, and children trapped within, numbering in the hundreds, did kill themselves."

Joanna, dutifully crossing herself, felt no real surprise; death seemed to follow her uncle Richard like a lover. The thought was not her own, of course, but had its seeds in a caustic comment once made by John, that Richard's lust was sated on the battlefield, not in the bedchamber.

But in these weeks at Fontevrault, slowly another image of Richard was taking shape. Richard loomed large in his mother's memories. From Eleanor, Joanna learned that Richard, having to withdraw from the Holy Land, denied himself even a glimpse of Jerusalem from the heights of Nebi Samwil, saying, "Those not worthy to win the Holy City are not worthy to behold it." She learned of the celebrated exchange between Richard and Philip, the French King, over Richard's great fortress, Castle Gaillard, Philip boasting, "If its walls were made of solid iron, yet would

I take them," and Richard's mocking rejoinder, "If its walls were made of butter, yet would I hold them." Richard had indeed been a great soldier, Joanna reluctantly acknowledged. But she did not understand why her grandmother should have preferred him above her other children, and wished she could summon up the nerve to ask Eleanor why she spoke so often of Richard and so rarely of John.

She never did, though, sensing that such a question would not be to Eleanor's liking. As bedazzled as Joanna was by Eleanor, she was very much in awe of her, too, and uneasily aware of the fragile foothold she'd gained in her grandmother's life. There was indeed iridescent magic in Eleanor's spell, but no security. Eleanor could be amusing, indulgent, utterly captivating. She was also impatient, unpredictable, easily bored. On any given evening, Joanna might find herself welcomed into Eleanor's presence with genuine pleasure; Eleanor would share confidences both intimate and adult in nature, tutor Joanna in the intriguing complexities of politics and statecraft, and at such moments Joanna knew happiness in full and abiding measure. But on the morrow she might find her grandmother preoccupied, pensive, with no interest whatsoever in a child's companionship. Joanna did not resent Eleanor's mercurial mood swings; her sense of self was too tenuous, too vulnerable, to allow for the indulgence of wounded pride. She only tried all the harder to earn her grandmother's goodwill, and when she did not, she accepted the failing as her own.

On this particular night in late July, Eleanor was in markedly good spirits, relaxed and responsive to Joanna's eager queries about times long past and people long dead. But as midnight approached, Joanna's energy began to ebb; she sought to stifle a yawn, was relieved when Eleanor said, "You'd best get to bed."

Joanna rose obediently. "May I go and light a candle first for the French Queen, Madame?"

"If you wish." Joanna's impassioned partisanship for Philip's unfortunate Queen was a source of some amusement to Eleanor, but she was touched, too, suspecting that Joanna's pity for Ingeborg's plight could be traced to her own years of confinement, that it was the captive Eleanor whom Joanna was mourning as much as it was the hapless Ingeborg, whose luck had yet to change for the better. Philip had held out against the Pope's Interdict for seven stubborn months, and then agreed to set aside his second wife, to recognize Ingeborg as his Queen. But he'd

then confined her in Étampes Castle, and rumor had it she was
not being treated kindly.

Joanna's sympathies went out to the Danish Princess, Queen of
France in name only, being made to suffer for no sin of her own,
and she'd been lighting nightly candles on Ingeborg's behalf.
Now she hastened back from St Magdalene's chapel, stripped,
and crawled into the pallet made up for her at the foot of her
grandmother's bed.

Lights still burned, and the constant murmur of conversation
sounded around her; Eleanor's ladies could not retire until she
did. But Joanna had learned to block out background noises, and
she fell at once into a fitful sleep. Her dreams were troubled,
reflecting the tenor of her waking hours. Eleanor had recently
had a letter from John, in which he'd told her that he'd broken
Philip's siege of Radepont, just ten miles southeast of Rouen.
But that was the only good news the letter held. Isabelle's father,
Aymer, Count of Angoulême, had died suddenly that past month,
but John had not dared to risk her attendance at the funeral;
Angoulême bordered upon La Marche, and Hugh de Lusignan
still nursed a bitter grudge over Isabelle's loss.

Tossing and turning on the pallet, Joanna attracted the attention of the Abbess Matilda. Matilda was intrigued by her friend's
unexpected rapport with Joanna; she'd never before known Eleanor to show more than the most perfunctory interest in children.
It was, she decided, probably because Joanna was such a serious
child. The questions she asked were invariably sensible, of the
sort Eleanor had always encouraged in her own daughters; she
had nothing but scorn for the prevailing viewpoint that women
should abjure interest in such masculine concerns as power,
policy, and tactics.

Matilda was surprised, too, that Eleanor should suddenly evince
a hitherto unexpressed interest in looking back, in dwelling upon
yesterday; at last she attributed this to the twin crosses of age and
illness, for Eleanor was not well, had not been well for months.
Her spirit still blazed so brightly that those around her did not
always notice how frail the shell enclosing that spirit had become. Matilda did. For all that Eleanor was fiercely private about
her ailments, Matilda saw with sorrowing eyes how easily she
tired in this summer of her eighth decade, how she'd begun to
lean upon a companion's arm when walking, to place a hand over
her breast as if willing away the heart palpitations she'd not
acknowledge. And as Matilda watched on recent evenings as
Eleanor pieced together her past with the gossamer strands of

memory while Joanna listened, intent and enthralled, she found herself wondering if Eleanor was not reaching out to right a wrong, seeing in this hazel-eyed, dark-haired granddaughter the son she'd never loved.

This was sheer speculation, she knew; Eleanor was the least fanciful of women, little given to regrets. The thought lingered nonetheless, and she laughed soundlessly now, envisioning what Eleanor's reaction would be should she be so foolish as to confess what she suspected. Joanna sighed, mumbled something unintelligible, and Matilda stooped, touched her hand to the sleeping child's forehead. "She does not feel feverish, but her sleep is not a restful one."

Eleanor sat down on the bed. "She fears for her father."

"As well she might, poor lass. She's utterly devoted to him."

Eleanor looked up at that. "Need you sound so surprised?" she said dryly. "Or think you, as do John's enemies, that he is incapable of loving or being loved?"

"No, Madame, indeed not. I would not presume upon our friendship to speak ill of your son. But I must admit to being troubled by some of his acts, such as how infrequently he does partake of the Holy Sacraments."

"That is rash of him, I agree, and I daresay he'll pay a high price for it."

"I would hope, Madame, that he will repent in time; God forbid that he should go unshriven to his Maker," the Abbess said with fervor, and Eleanor gave her a thin, ironic smile.

"Indeed. But I was not thinking of his immortal soul, Matilda. I was thinking that history is chronicled by monks."

Joanna had begun to whimper in her sleep, and Eleanor leaned over, shook the girl's shoulder. Joanna awoke with a gasp, eyes wide and staring. She had been dreaming of her father, abandoned and alone before Philip and Arthur, but she was reluctant to admit it; it seemed somehow disloyal to John, almost as if she'd be revealing his own fears. She hesitated, and then turned aside Eleanor's query with the first lie to come to mind. "Yes, a bad dream . . . of Ingeborg."

"You must not dwell upon her, Joanna. Hers is a sad fate, yes, but common to women of rank. Would you pity the swan that ends up swimming in gravy upon your father's table? Well, princesses, too, are bred to be sacrificed, as pawns in the marital game. That is just the way of it. Be grateful, rather, that you were spared such a fate, that you need not fear a foreign marriage

in a far-off land. Unless, of course, you do yearn for a crown . . ."
Eleanor smiled, shrewdly certain that Joanna did not.

Joanna had long been thankful that her tainted birth so severely
reduced her value on the marriage market; her ambitions rose no
higher than a manor and children of her own, a husband of
respectable rank, ideally a knight of her father's household, so
that they might be often at court.

"No, I would not want a crown, Madame. I would that Papa
had not one, either, would that he were still Count of Mortain.
Mayhap then he'd be safe . . ."

She was hoping for some sort of assurance from her grandmother, an expression of faith that all would go well for John.
But Eleanor was turning away, frowning at the woman standing
in the antechamber doorway.

"Your Grace, Sir Aubrey is without, requests an urgent word
with you."

Joanna sat up on the pallet, pulling the sheet up to her chin.
Aubrey de Mara was the captain of her grandmother's guards,
but Joanna had never known him to seek Eleanor out at such an
hour. She watched uneasily as he entered the chamber, knelt
before the Queen.

"Madame, forgive me, but a courier has ridden in, sent by
your son. The King's Grace wants you to leave Fontevrault on
the morrow, to withdraw with all speed into your own lands in
Poitou."

"Arthur and the de Lusignans?"

"They've been encamped at Tours, not forty miles to the
north, are now known to be on the road south. The King has left
Queen Isabelle in Rouen, is heading for Le Mans. But he fears
for you, Madame, as well he should. You'd be a most tempting
prize, in truth."

Eleanor nodded slowly. "My son is right. We depart for
Poitiers at first light. See to it, Sir Aubrey."

Their journey south proved to be a slow, arduous one. The road
was rutted and rock-strewn, the soil cracked and seared by weeks
of burning sun, and their horses churned up clouds of thick red
dust. Jolted from side to side in her swaying horse litter, Eleanor
at last called for a halt. As her servants began to set up a tent so
that the Queen might shelter a while from the heat of high noon,
Joanna slid from her mare, hastened to join Eleanor in the shade
of several elms. In addition to his midnight message for her
grandmother, her father's courier had carried two letters for her,

a brief dispatch from John instructing her to accompany Eleanor
south for safety's sake, and a longer communication from her
brother Richard. Clutching this letter, she settled herself in the
grass next to Eleanor.

"Shall I fan you, Madame? I've a letter from my brother; may
I read it to you? Richard is serving as squire to the eldest son of
Lord de Braose, is with his household in South Wales. He says
there is trouble between the de Braose sons and a Welsh Prince,
Gwenwynwyn of Powys, that Gwenwynwyn—what queer names
the Welsh have—is set upon war."

"I'd say, rather, that the de Braoses are the ones set upon
war." Eleanor leaned back against the tree, closed her eyes.
"Your father did grant them the right to any Welsh lands they
could gain by conquest. And they know that there has been a
shift in our Welsh policy, that John has decided it is more to his
advantage to back Gwenwynwyn's chief rival, Llewelyn, Prince
of Gwynedd."

"Richard makes mention of him, too . . . Prince Llewelyn. He
says Fulk Fitz Warin is still in rebellion against Papa, that he has
taken refuge at this Llewelyn's court. He says, too, that Llewelyn
has been pulling strings in Shropshire on behalf of the rebels, that
he did prevent a younger brother of one of Fitz Warin's vassals
from laying claim to his father's manors. The family—de Hodnet,
they're called—did hold land of the Corbets, and Robert Corbet,
as overlord, refused to recognize the younger de Hodnet's claim.
Richard says all do know the Corbets were acting at Llewelyn's
behest, he being kin."

Joanna frowned. "I met Lord Corbet once, when we were at
Worcester two years past. Papa granted him the right to hold a
weekly market at Caus. I do not think he should be so quick to
do a Welsh Prince's bidding, not when that Prince is aiding men
outlawed, men who are Papa's sworn enemies."

Getting no response, she glanced up, saw that Eleanor was no
longer listening. Sweat was glistening at her temples; her face
was bleached of color, as white as the linen wimple that hid her
hair. "Two years ago," she said, bitterly amused, "I did ride a
mule across the Pyrenees, and in the dead of winter, too. But
who'd believe that, seeing me now . . ."

"Madame!" Aubrey was coming toward them at a run. "Madame, our scouts report a large armed force on our trail. I'd
wager my life it is the Duke of Brittany and the de Lusignans,
that you are the prey."

Joanna was amazed to see how rapidly her grandmother seemed

to shake off her fatigue. She at once held out her hand for Aubrey's assistance, came quickly to her feet. "If my memory serves," she said coolly, "we are but a few leagues distant from Mirebeau. It's not much of a refuge, but beggars, as they say, cannot be choosers."

Aubrey nodded grimly. "Madame, can you ride astride?"

"I shall have to, shan't I?" Some of her servants were struggling now to dismantle the tent they'd just erected, and Eleanor said impatiently, "For Jesú's sake, let it be!" Seeing Joanna still standing immobile, she gave the girl a push. "Go on, child, make haste to mount. Sir Aubrey . . . which of your men do you most trust?"

Aubrey did not hesitate, beckoned to a slight bandy youth, one who looked to have been born in the saddle. "Edmund, take my stallion. Kill him if you have to, but get to Le Mans, get to the King."

Edmund did not even pause to acknowledge the command. Vaulting up onto Aubrey's roan, he set off across the fields at a dead run, and within moments was lost from view.

Mirebeau was a walled town in the marches between Anjou and Poitou, having sprung up around a small border castle. It was little more than a village, and the sudden arrival of the Queen created a sensation. Men and women abandoned their daily labors, crowded into the street to catch a glimpse of the legendary Eleanor of Aquitaine. Aubrey at once set about conscripting men to guard the walls, gave orders to bar the town gates as the Queen and her party passed on into the castle bailey. There the exhausted Eleanor was assisted from her mare, up into the keep.

Relief at having reached Mirebeau was not long in giving way to dismay. Even to Joanna's untrained eye, it was all too clear that the castle was in a ruinous state. The moat was clogged with debris and weeds, silted and foul-smelling. The outer curtain walls were constructed of aging timbers, looked likely to tumble down in a stiff wind. The keep itself was a stone-and-mortar tower, but it, too, showed the effects of long neglect. Aubrey, assuming command in the name of the Queen, put the small garrison to work shoring up the walls as best they could, sent men into the town to appropriate food supplies. The women did what they could to convert the solar into a suitable bedchamber for the Queen. And then they waited for the inevitable to occur, waited to be found by the pursuing army, an army led by Eleanor's own grandson.

They appeared before the town gates as summer twilight slowly darkened the Poitevin countryside, flying high the banners of Arthur, Duke of Brittany, Hugh de Lusignan, Count of La Marche, and his uncle Geoffrey, Lord of Vouvant. A peremptory demand for surrender was rejected with equal dispatch by Aubrey. Negotiations dragged on for a futile time under a perfect crescent moon, and then both sides settled down to pass the night.

Soon after sunrise the next day, the negotiations resumed. Arthur and the de Lusignans wanted Eleanor alive, and she exploited that, her only advantage, to the fullest, feigning belief in their goodwill, playing desperately for time. They, in their turn, promised whatever they thought likely to lure her out, swore she could continue unmolested on her journey, that she need only agree to cede Poitou to Arthur. Back and forth the lies flew, until Hugh de Lusignan lost patience and gave the command to assault the town walls. The townsmen, unwillingly impressed into a quarrel not of their making, put up only feeble resistance, and by day's end Mirebeau was in enemy hands. The ancient castle alone held out, ripe for the taking.

The keep was stifling, its shuttered windows barring entry to cooler night air. Joanna huddled on a bench in the great hall, a plate of food untouched upon her lap. It was quiet now, but her ears still echoed with the cries of the wounded and dying, the screams of the women claimed as spoils of war by Arthur's jubilant soldiers. When the assault was first launched, she'd climbed with Eleanor up to the battlements atop the keep, had watched as the town's defenders sought to push aside the scaling ladders, as men plunged screaming to their deaths. Hours later, the horror of it was still very much with her; unable to sleep, she kept inconspicuously to the shadows, watching as her grandmother and Aubrey sought a viable plan of defense.

It was very late when Aubrey rose, sent a man to the kitchens for his first food of the day. Joanna slipped from the bench, crossed to Eleanor.

"Madame . . . what will happen on the morrow?"

"They shall assault the castle."

"Can we hold?"

"No, child, we cannot, not for long."

Joanna swallowed, sought to emulate her grandmother's composure. "But . . . might not Papa come in time?"

"No, Joanna. I'd not give you false hope. We cannot be sure my courier made it to John's camp. And even if he did, Le Mans is well over eighty miles away. John could not reach us before

Friday, Thursday night at the earliest . . . and by then it shall be too late.''

Joanna knelt on the floor by Eleanor's chair. ''Aubrey is a brave knight. Surely God will not favor Arthur over Aubrey, Madame?''

Eleanor did not reply.

Wednesday dawned hot and overcast. The sky was leaden, and for a time it did seem as if God meant to favor Aubrey. A rainstorm swept in from the east, denying the attacking army the potent weapon of fire. Aubrey's outmanned force struggled to keep the enemy off the walls, casting down boiling water and stones from the curtain battlements. The de Lusignans responded with mangonel bombardments, set about filling in the overgrown moat so they could make use of a battering ram.

In the top floor of the keep, Eleanor stood at an arrow loop, watching as Aubrey waged a gallant, futile battle below. His courage was contagious, and his men offered up their lives with desperate abandon, until overwhelmed at the last by the sheer numbers of their attackers. Forced off the walls, they fell back toward the keep. Eleanor, hastening down into the great hall, signaled the guards to stand ready. As Aubrey and the surviving defenders plunged into the hall, they torched the stairs, bolted the door.

The great hall was overflowing with exhausted men. They lay sprawled in the rushes, some seeking sleep while they could, others clutching wine flagons close. There was little eating, less talking. In the corner, one youth sat alone, softly strumming a gittern. Aubrey, grey-faced with fatigue, was slumped in the window seat. He raised his head only after Joanna plucked repeatedly at his sleeve, regarding her with bloodshot blue eyes.

''Sir Aubrey, when they take the keep, what will they do to us?''

''They want the Queen . . . only the Queen. They might let my men go . . . or they might put them to the sword.'' Aubrey was slurring his words like one drunk, yet he still thought to add, ''But not you, not a little lass like you . . .'' He leaned forward, cradled his head in his arms, and Joanna backed away.

Taking a candle, she groped her way up the stairwell. The solar door was ajar, but as she reached for the latch, she heard her grandmother's voice.

''The de Lusignans must not know that Joanna is John's

daughter. I've already discussed this with Aubrey, mean to claim her as a niece of the Abbess Matilda.''

"But Madame, might it not be a greater protection for her . . . that she is the King's daughter?''

"Are you truly as naïve as that, Cecily? I should not think I'd need to remind you that Hugh de Lusignan is not a man of honor. They do need me; I shall not be harmed. But they might well see John's bastard-born child as . . . fair game, shall we say? And that is a risk I am not prepared to take.''

Joanna sank down upon the stairs. She sat there for a long time, alone in the dark, not wanting them to know she wept.

Joanna awoke in her grandmother's bed, with only a vague memory of how she got there. Had she fallen asleep upon the stairs? She still wore her chemise, but someone had removed her gown and bliaut, folded them over the foot of the bed. She reached for the gown, pulled it over her head. As she did, she saw the light filtering through the unshuttered solar window. For a moment, her breath stopped. They'd lost the night, their last shield. Even now, men might be gathering below, preparing for the final assault upon the keep.

All around her, her grandmother's ladies slept on makeshift pallets. Threading her way between their bodies, she reached the window, climbed up onto the seat. Although to the west a few stars still glimmered, the sky was slowly and inexorably paling, taking on the dull pearl color of coming dawn. The bailey was enveloped in an eerie quiet, men just beginning to stir, to crawl, groaning, from their bedrolls. A few castle dogs prowled about. A sleepy soldier relieved himself against the chapel wall, provoking curses from some of the blanket-clad forms downwind. Up on the curtain wall, guards dozed by empty wine flasks. The aroma of roasting pigeon wafted across the bailey from the gatehouse, where Arthur and the de Lusignans had set up their command post. The scene below her resembled not so much a siege as the morning after a drunken carouse, and that, Joanna knew, was what the night had been. So sure of victory were these men that they'd already begun to celebrate their triumph, for they, no less than those trapped within, knew there could be but one outcome. The only question as yet unanswered was how many men would die in the capture of the aging Queen.

Footsteps sounded behind Joanna, and she turned as her grandmother and Aubrey de Mara entered the solar, joined her at the window. The soldier who'd just urinated glanced up, saw them standing there, and raised his voice in a mocking shout. "We've been wagering upon the hour when the keep falls. Think you that you can try to hold out till noon? If so, you'll win me a right fair sum!"

The window was faced with an iron grille, but Joanna shrank back, grateful when Aubrey reached out, jerked the shutters into place. "I've set men to bringing up water buckets from the cellar well, Madame. I expect they shall seek to fire the outer door, so I had it well soaked. I had additional bolts attached, too, but the wood is so warped and rotted that I do not doubt even the little lass here could force it."

As Joanna watched, marveling at the lack of emotion in his voice, he walked over to the solar door, tested the bolt's strength. "You'd best barricade yourself here within the solar, Madame. We'll hold them as long as we can below."

Eleanor nodded. "I expect we've a few hours' wait. They do not seem in much of a hurry, do they?"

"Why should they be? Does a cat rush in for the kill when it has its prey secure within its paws?" Aubrey's mouth twisted. "I would to God that—" He broke off abruptly, as a shout echoed down from the battlements. Joanna flinched, started to tremble. Was it to begin as soon as this? They heard now a clatter upon the stairs. Aubrey reached the door just as a man lurched into the solar, all but fell into his arms.

"Under attack . . ." he gasped. "Hurry . . ."

Aubrey whirled toward the window, and the soldier caught his arm. "No," he panted, "not the keep . . . the town!"

The stairs were in a dangerous state of disrepair, and Eleanor had to lean heavily upon Joanna for support, compelled to caution when they both yearned to run. Emerging at last out onto the battlements, Joanna froze for a moment, grappling with her fear of heights, and then edged along the walkway. The men were leaning recklessly over an embrasure, suddenly heedless of enemy bowmen, gesturing toward the town. The wind was gusting; Joanna found herself blinded by her own hair. Clutching Eleanor's hand, she nerved herself to look over the battlements, down into the bailey.

Men were stumbling to their feet, shouting groggy questions none could yet answer, groping hastily for weapons. Dogs were barking frantically as soldiers staggered, bewildered and bleary-eyed, from the buildings ranged along the curtain walls; a rider-less horse galloped in panicked circles, adding immeasurably to the confusion. The more wide awake were running for the gatehouse, only to encounter comrades retreating from the town, where a wild melee had broken out.

"Could it be des Roches, Madame, and the garrison from Chinon Castle?"

Eleanor, no less bemused than Aubrey, shook her head. "He has not the men to raise a siege. I confess I do not—"

Joanna could wait no longer, tugged at her arm. "It's Papa, is it not? He's come for us!"

"I do not see how it could be John," Eleanor said slowly, "and yet—"

"It is Papa," Joanna interrupted. "I know it is!"

"She's right, look at the banner they fly!" Aubrey gestured toward the armed knights now surging into the narrow streets of Mirebeau, cutting off escape into the castle. "Gules, three lions passant guardant in pale or—the Royal Arms of England, Madame!"

Aubrey's soldiers raised a cheer as the door was unbarred, squabbling good-naturedly over who should lower the ladders, reaching out eager hands to assist the men climbing up into the keep. Joanna squirmed among them, hopelessly hemmed in, until one young soldier swung her up into the air, and she found herself passed from man to man to be deposited, breathless and dizzy, within sight of the door, just as William de Braose scrambled up into the keep.

She almost did not recognize him. De Braose had always prided himself upon his elegance, and this man looked as if he'd not had a bath in months, so grimy and disheveled was he, blond hair matted and dark with dirt, eyes reddened and dust-swollen. But his smile was a dazzle of radiant white, and when he demanded, "Good Christ, give me a drink," fully a dozen flasks and flagons were thrust at him from all directions.

The next man up was William des Roches, Seneschal of Anjou and Touraine. But then the soldiers surged forward, shoving and pushing, and Joanna could no longer see the door. By the time she'd managed to squeeze through the press, her father had mounted the ladder into the keep. Like de Braose, he was utterly filthy, and like de Braose, too, his smile was blinding. Joanna had meant to curtsy, but John held out his arms to her. The chain links of his hauberk scratched her cheek, and he was holding her so tightly that it hurt, but she made no objections; it was only when she saw the dark wet stain across his surcoat that she recoiled, with a cry of fright.

"Papa, you are bleeding!"

"No, sweetheart, it is not mine," he said soothingly. "There's nothing wrong with me that a bath and a week in bed will not cure!"

There was a sudden stir among the men; a path was opening. John set Joanna back on her feet, moved toward his mother. For a long moment, they looked at one another, and then Eleanor said incredulously, "You're truly here; I know my eyes do not lie. But eighty miles! How in God's name did you do it, John?"

John laughed. "I daresay that's what Arthur and the de Lusignans are asking themselves, too, about now! Your man caught up with me late Tuesday, outside Le Mans. We set out at once for Mirebeau, rode day and night, spurred our horses till they foundered, till men reeled in the saddle like drunkards, stopping only at Chinon for William des Roches and fresh mounts." Someone handed him a flask; he drank deeply, all but choked. "They'd barred all the city gates but one, which they left open for supplies . . . and for us. By the time their besotted guards awoke, we were in the town. Upwards of two hundred knights captured, none escaping."

Eleanor had never seen him so elated; there was about him an intense, surging excitement, an intoxication of the senses bordering upon euphoria. "And Arthur? What of Arthur, John?"

John's eyes showed suddenly gold. "Arthur and Hugh and Geoffrey de Lusignan, all taken. They were breakfasting on pigeon pie, had not even time to draw their swords. And their faces . . ." He laughed again. "Ah, Madame, to see their faces!"

"You have indeed won a great victory," she said, then put her hand upon his arm. "Come now, sit and I'll send for food. Do you even remember when you've last eaten?"

"No," he admitted. "Why? Think you that I'm in need of sobering up?" He grinned, let her lead him toward the table, and then stopped without warning, swung about to face her. "Arthur and the de Lusignans were not alone in their disbelief . . . were they?" he challenged. "You never expected me to come to your defense, never expected me to reach you in time, never expected much of me at all, did you . . . Mother?"

Eleanor saw now how exhausted he truly was; his voice was slurred, husky with fatigue, his eyes hollowed and feverishly bright, at once triumphant and accusing. "It was not a question of faith, John," she said carefully. "Do you not realize the extent of your victory? You have done what most men would swear to be impossible, covered some eighty miles as if you'd put wings to your horse, arrived in time to save me from capture, to take the town, all your enemies. That is a feat more than remarkable, it is well nigh miraculous.'' She paused, and then said that which she knew he'd waited all his life to hear, what she could at last say in utter sincerity: "Not even Richard could have hoped to equal what you did this day.''

John looked at her, saying nothing for a time. "I should have known that the highest praise you could offer would be a comparison with my sainted brother. Well, that is an honor I think I'll decline, Madame. I've no longer any inclination to compete with a ghost.''

"Ah, Johnny . . .'' Eleanor was suddenly and overwhelmingly aware of her own exhaustion, of the toll these last days had taken. "I am proud of you, I swear it,'' she said softly. But she'd waited too long; John had already turned away.

John's triumph was even more conclusive than he had at first thought, for his nephew Arthur was not the only prize to be taken in Mirebeau. Arthur's sister had been with him when he joined forces with the de Lusignans, and rather than risk leaving her behind in Tours, he'd chosen to have her accompany him, for safety's sake. As ill-fated as was his decision to besiege Mirebeau, this was to be an even greater blunder, for he thus delivered into John's hands both remaining heirs of the Angevin House, the two people with a rival claim to the English crown.

Joanna watched with sympathetic interest as the girl was escorted into the great hall. Ironically named Eleanor after the grandmother Arthur had been seeking to capture, she was slender and blue-eyed, looked to Joanna to be about seventeen or so. She also looked terrified. Approaching the dais, she sank down before John in a deep, submissive curtsy, but he at once raised her up, drew her toward him. He spoke softly and earnestly for several moments, and then smiled at her, pulling from his own finger a topaz ring. Topaz, he murmured, was a known talisman against grief. It would please him greatly if she would accept it, as his niece and kinswoman.

None knew better than Joanna how reassuring her father could be when he so chose, and she was not surprised now to see color coming back into Eleanor's face, to see that Eleanor's hands were no longer shaking as she let John slip the ring onto her finger. Pouring a cupful of Madeira from the sideboard, Joanna carried it across the hall, presented it to her father. He already had a cup, but he set it aside, accepting Joanna's, instead.

"Thank you, lass," he said, and then smiled at her. "What say you, Joanna? Should you like to meet your cousin Arthur?"

Joanna was shocked by her first sight of Hugh de Lusignan. A huge, shambling bear of a man, stout and greying, he seemed the least likely of mates for the exquisite Isabelle, and Joanna decided her grandmother was right. There was great risk in being born a swan.

Both Hugh de Lusignan and his uncle seemed stunned by the sudden reversal of their fortunes. Shoved forward, shackled at the wrists, they knelt awkwardly before the dais, watching John warily, as if they still could not fully credit their own senses.

If Hugh de Lusignan did not fulfill Joanna's expectations, her cousin Arthur did. He truly looked like a Prince, she conceded grudgingly, taller already, at fifteen, than her father, with bright chestnut hair and blue eyes like his sister. He, however, showed none of her fear; unlike the de Lusignans, he refused to kneel, had to be forced by his guards.

John continued to drink, measuring his nephew with thoughtful eyes. "Well?" he said at last. "Have you nothing to say to me?"

"No," Arthur said sullenly.

"Do not be a fool, boy," Hugh de Lusignan said, out of the corner of his mouth, and Arthur gave him a scornful look.

"I am no boy. I am a belted knight, Duke of Brittany, Count of Richmond, rightful heir to the Angevin crown, and I ask no man's pardon for seeking what is rightfully mine."

"Boldly spoken," John said, very dryly. "That speech might sound more effective, however, if you were not fettered in irons, having just bungled an assault upon your own grandmother."

There was laughter at that, and Arthur flushed. "At least I was open and honest in my quest for the crown. Unlike you, Uncle, you who'd have sold his own brother to the Saracens if he could, who did betray his dying father—"

"That is quite enough, Arthur!" Eleanor said sharply. "For all your posturings, you are very much a child, and I, for one, am weary of listening to you."

"So am I." John's voice was quite even, devoid of emotion. He raised his hand, and guards at once stepped forward, dragged Arthur from the hall. Eleanor ignored the struggles of her defiant grandson, kept her eyes riveted on John. Her husband's most dubious legacy to his offspring was the wild Angevin temper; his sons were notorious for the violence of their rages. But she had

learned that John was most dangerous when he did not shout or
threaten, and she leaned forward, laid her hand upon his arm. As
she feared, the muscles were corded, rigid with tension.

"He's a stupid, willful boy," she said softly, "foolish and
headstrong. But he is a boy, John . . . and blood kin."

John exhaled a breath too long held, slowly unclenched his
fingers from the stem of his wine cup. "As you say, Madame, a
foolish boy."

Hugh and Geoffrey de Lusignan still knelt stiffly before the
dais, and John's eyes now came to rest upon Hugh. Hugh's face
was streaked with sweat and grime, an unhealthy ashen grey;
under John's mocking gaze, color began to stain his cheekbones,
the dull, blotched red of impotent rage. But he was forty-five,
not fifteen, knew enough to hold his tongue.

Geoffrey de Lusignan cleared his throat. "Your Grace, what
mean you to do with us?"

"What would you do if you were in my place?" John asked,
saw the other man flinch. "So . . . as bad as that? I can see
we're going to have a great deal to talk about, and I'll make time
for it, you may be sure. But you're luckier than you deserve, for
you happen to be worth more to me alive than dead. If not, I'd
have hanged you both higher than Haman, and might yet."

He signaled, did not bother to watch as his guards pushed the
de Lusignans toward the door. Glancing about the hall, he beckoned to William de Braose. "Since you had the honor of taking
my nephew prisoner, Will, you shall have the honor of looking
after him. I hereby remand him into your custody."

De Braose did not appear surprised. "As it pleases Your
Grace."

William des Roches, however, appeared distinctly taken aback.
"But . . . but my liege!" He stepped forward, toward the dais.
"You did assure me that the Duke of Brittany would be put into
my keeping. Your Grace . . . you gave me your word!"

"Did I?" John sounded quizzical. "I recall no such promise.
Do you, Will?"

"No, Your Grace," William de Braose said blandly, and des
Roches opened his mouth, shut it again. But he seized his first
opportunity to speak to the Queen, drawing Eleanor aside as
servants began to set up trestle tables, to prepare the hall for
John's victory dinner.

"Madame, I did not lie; upon my oath, I did not."

"No one has accused you of lying, my lord."

"Your Grace . . . may I speak plainly? I did support your son

against Arthur, have been his loyal subject. But I do understand
the loyalties your grandson commands amongst many in Anjou,
in Touraine, in Brittany. I sought to explain this to the King, to
make him understand the risk, and he promised me I should have
the care of his nephew. I do not think it wise to give the lad over
to de Braose, Madame, in truth I do not.''

Eleanor agreed with him, but she responded with so glacial a
stare that des Roches's warning froze in his throat; he swallowed,
not daring to say more, realizing he'd already said too much.

Joanna, hovering within earshot, wondered why Lord des Roches
should be so concerned about Arthur. Each time she remembered
the outrageous way he'd dared talk to her father, she felt anger
stir anew. Arthur was arrogant and hateful, deserved to be punished for his malice. She hoped her father kept him close, for a
long, long time. She did feel sorry, though, for Arthur's sister,
and pushing through to John's side, she waited patiently till she
caught his eye. He leaned down, listened as she whispered in his
ear, then nodded. ''If that be your wish, sweetheart, by all
means.''

Joanna did not wait, made her way across the hall, toward the
girl sitting forlorn and forgotten in the window seat. Eleanor was
staring down at her lap, twisting the ring John had given her. She
did not look up, not until Joanna said, ''Lady Eleanor? I am your
cousin Joanna, the King's daughter. My father wants you to dine
with us, says you shall have a place of honor, as his kinswoman.''

''That's most kind of him,'' Eleanor said tonelessly.

Joanna had hoped to cheer Eleanor, was disappointed by the
girl's tepid response. ''I know you are afraid. I was afraid, too,
when I thought we'd be taken by your brother. But there's no
need to fear, in truth there's not. My father does not blame you
for what Arthur did, would not ever maltreat you. Please believe
me, he would not.''

Eleanor studied the child. ''I do believe you, Cousin Joanna,''
she said, and managed a wan smile, even as her eyes filled with
tears. ''But what of my brother? What of Arthur?''

13

SOUTHAMPTON, ENGLAND

April 1204

Following a servant into the solar, Will found his sister-in-law conferring with her almoner. Isabelle was always friendly, but now she greeted Will with such unfeigned delight that he flushed with startled pleasure. He was not at ease with lovely women, and Isabelle's beauty was particularly intimidating and ethereal to him. Try as he might, he could not imagine her afflicted with such ordinary, mundane ailments as chilblains, blisters, or cramps, could not envision her nose red with cold, her eyes swollen with sleep, her hair in uncombed, early-morning disarray—as he'd so often seen Ela, who was not glamorous or exotic, but reassuringly real.

"John and I did break our Lenten fast by eating meat yesterday, and so today I've instructed our almoner to feed one hundred of the city's poor," Isabelle explained, linking her arm in Will's and drawing him toward the privacy of a window recess. "How glad I am that you've come, Will. Have you seen John yet?"

"No, I was told he'll be hearing appeals from the shire courts for the rest of the day."

"You'll sup with us, of course, and you must stay awhile with the court, Will. John has need of you, and so have I. I am relying upon you to cheer his spirits. He's in a right foul temper, has been brooding for more than a fortnight about the fall of that wretched castle."

"Well, Castle Gaillard is of great defensive importance, guards the approach to Rouen . . ." Will began, quite willing to educate Isabelle in the finer points of military strategy.

His efforts were wasted. Isabelle heard him out, but murmured only a tepidly polite, "How very interesting." She glanced about to make sure all others were out of earshot. "Will . . . tell me in honesty. Is Normandy well and truly lost to John?"

"We still hold Rouen and Falaise, Chinon Castle . . ." Will hedged. "But even if the tide continues to run against us, and Normandy, too, falls to Philip, you must not fear, lass. Angoulême, Gascony, and Poitou still hold fast for John."

He waited glumly for her to remind him, though, that Maine, Anjou, Brittany, and Touraine had all been lost to Philip within the past twelvemonth. He could recite the reasons why it had happened, a litany of ill luck, blunders, and betrayal. John's chronic and crippling lack of funds. The disloyalty of his Norman barons, who thought it safer to defy a distant English King than a neighboring French one. John's errors of judgment and his indecision, his unfortunate penchant for turning allies into enemies; William des Roches had ridden away from Mirebeau as a rebel. But to understand why Philip had prevailed was not to accept it, and Will did not want to discuss their disastrous Normandy campaign with anyone, least of all with his brother's wife.

Isabelle fidgeted with her rings; John might be short of money to pay his troops, but he still found the means to indulge his young Queen's love of jewels. "I suppose," she said, "that it was a great mistake for John to have ever let Hugh de Lusignan buy his freedom."

Will winced. When John had decided to set the de Lusignans at liberty, he'd encountered opposition from an unexpected source, his mother. Eleanor had been adamantly against the idea, insisting that the time to make peace with Hugh de Lusignan had been before John's marriage to Isabelle, that it was now too late. Will had not agreed with her, unwilling to believe it was ever too late to right a wrong; while he cared not a whit for Hugh de Lusignan's sense of injury, he hoped a conciliatory gesture on John's part would favorably impress other Norman lords wavering in their loyalty. Convinced that they could keep Hugh in check by demanding hostages for his good faith, Will had added his voice to those arguing for release. Hugh and Geoffrey de Lusignan had been freed five months after their capture at Mirebeau, had at once joined William des Roches and the rebel barons of Brittany and Anjou, leaving Will a legacy of guilt out of all proportion to his small share of the responsibility.

"The de Lusignans offered up such an extravagant sum for their freedom that John could not afford to turn it down," he said defensively, "not with so pressing a need for money."

"I know; John explained it all to me at the time. But shall I tell you what I think, Will? That John was goaded as much by his mother's opposition as he was swayed by the money. It's said she can be right clever at getting men to do her bidding, but with John, she's ever been brutally blunt. They had a fearful row about it, and I think that was when John truly made up his mind to set Hugh free, to prove to Eleanor that he was in the right."

Will stared at her, all at once seeing Isabelle with new insight. John had never been known for constancy, and Will's expectations for his marriage were minimal. Greatly to his surprise, John's passion for his girl-wife had not been slaked by possession; Isabelle was his constant companion and bedmate on his travels around his realm. Will had attributed Isabelle's continuing bewitchment over his brother to her uncommon beauty. Now he suddenly wondered if he'd underestimated her.

"I think," he said slowly, "that you do content John so well because you do understand him so well," stating the obvious with such a solemn sense of discovery that Isabelle had to stifle a giggle.

"I doubt that anyone understands John all that well! But I do know when he is troubled. I truly think he'd not long mourn the loss of his continental domains in and of themselves. He has ever seen England as the heart of his inheritance, has oft told me how easy it is to safeguard an island kingdom, how difficult to defend a far-flung empire. But that empire was Richard's, and so he cannot bear to let it go." Isabelle leaned forward, put her hand on Will's sleeve. "I would help him if I could, but I do not know how. I was so hoping that you did," she said, giving Will a look of such irresistible appeal that he felt a lump rise in his throat.

He'd wondered if Isabelle loved his brother, was pleased now to conclude that she did. And yet he felt a certain surprise, too. He had few illusions about John, knew what John had done and what he was capable of doing, but the bond of brotherhood was one to last from the cradle to the grave. The bond between husband and wife he believed to be more fragile. Women were known to be the lesser sex; Will thought they were also the purer sex, softer of heart and more innocent of mind than men. As Isabelle lay with John in their vast marital bed, was her sleep never disturbed by uneasy thoughts of Arthur?

Will could not be sure, of course, that the rumors were true, that Arthur was dead. But his suspicions were strong enough to keep him from confronting his brother, from insisting that John tell him what he'd rather not know. It was not that he was

shocked; while he would never have chosen himself to claim
Arthur's life, he recognized John's right to do so. Treason warranted death. Scriptures said that plainly, said rebellion was as
the sin of witchcraft. And Arthur had remained defiantly unrepentant. Will had been present when John confronted Arthur at
Falaise in January 1203, had come away from that turbulent,
ugly encounter with the grim realization that Arthur was doomed;
if he would not bend, he'd have to be broken. The French King
had been putting about lurid rumors for months, contending that
Arthur had been murdered in a number of grisly ways—drowned,
stabbed, blinded and castrated—rumors that found ready believ-
ers among Arthur's Bretons, but few in England, where Arthur's
fate was a matter of supreme indifference. But that past Easter,
John had paid a second visit to Arthur, then being held at Rouen
Castle, and soon after, rumors again began to circulate that the
sixteen-year-old Duke of Brittany had been put to death at his
uncle's command, some even said by John's own hand. That
last, Will dismissed as nonsense; he knew John too well, knew
his brother had ever preferred to keep distance between himself
and his darker misdeeds. Yet the sinister silence that descended
over Rouen Castle after that Easter visit convinced Will that these
rumors were well grounded in reality, and he could only wonder
at John's genius for self-sabotage. However deserved was Arthur's death, it was still a drastic, draconian step to take, and
even a political novice like Will understood that it had to be done
in the fullest light of high noon—or not at all.

"Will . . . why are you staring at me like that?"

Will blinked, lost Arthur's ghost in the deep blue of Isabelle's
eyes. She was truly a sweet lass, he thought, and not for the
world would he see her lose her faith in John. "It gladdens my
heart to know that you are happy in your marriage, and I shall
indeed do what I can to ease John's discontent."

"Why would I not be happy in my marriage?" Isabelle echoed,
surprised. "John denies me nothing. Richard's poor Berengaria
might well have been invisible, for the notice people took of her.
But when I enter a chamber, all conversation hushes, all eyes are
upon me—because people know John cares whether I am content
or not. Oh, I grant you he is not always an easy man to live with,
has tempers and black moods and shadowy places in his soul
where I cannot follow. But we'll be wed four years come August, Will, and not once has my womb quickened with life. Yet
not once has John ever reproached me for that. How many barren
wives could say as much?"

Will was both embarrassed and touched by the unexpected intimacy of this glimpse she'd just given him into her married life. "I am sure you'll conceive in God's time, lass," he said awkwardly, and Isabelle smiled.

"So am I," she assured him, sounding faintly amused. "But it is kind of you to try to ease my mind. You are a good man, Will, you truly are. John . . . John is good to me," said with just enough emphasis on the last two words to tell Will that she was not so innocent as he'd first thought, as he'd like to believe. He looked at her, at the wide-set eyes utterly clear and untroubled by ghosts, at the mouth so soft and sweetened by laughter, and decided he must have misread her meaning.

"You must not fret," he said soothingly. "I'll stay as long as John has need of me, I promise you."

"It is your move, John," William de Braose prompted, sounding so smug that John gave him a cold stare before resuming his very deliberate study of the chessboard.

Will shifted in his seat. He was a mediocre chess player at best, but even he could see that John had allowed himself to be maneuvered into an utterly untenable position. That realization gave Will almost as much exasperation as it did John, for Isabelle had not exaggerated; he'd rarely seen his brother in such a grim mood, a mood not likely to be improved by a loss to William de Braose. De Braose was as ungracious a winner as John was a loser. Already there was gleeful anticipation in his grin. He would win, then magnanimously waive payment of their wager stakes, gloating thinly guised as jest; Will had seen de Braose win before.

Will had known de Braose for some ten years, for he was one of the few men who'd managed to be friendly with both Richard and John. Will had watched disapprovingly as de Braose insinuated his way into John's inner circle, becoming, in time, one of John's favorite carousing companions. He'd never lacked for confidence—as shy as a timber wolf, as scrupulous as a Barbary pirate—but Will had noted an increasing familiarity in his friendship with John, a familiarity that Will found offensive, that seemed to go beyond their mutual pursuit of what de Braose jokingly called "the three aitches . . . hunting, hawking, and 'horing." A familiarity that Will had first noticed in the past year, in the weeks after John's Eastertide visit to Rouen.

Will was not alone in his critical appraisal of the chess game's unhappy consequences. Joanna knew how her father hated to lose. Lord de Braose would revel in his victory, she knew, and Papa would be in ill humor for the rest of the night. It was not fair. Papa was so disquieted, much in need of distraction. Joanna thought it only just that he should be able to forget his troubles for a few hours. She knew suddenly what she must do, took a moment or so to nerve herself for it. Rising, she reached for a bowl of candied fruit, carried it across the chamber to John.

"Would you like a fig, Papa?" she asked, and then bumped into the trestle table, upsetting the chessmen and knocking the board onto the floor.

"Papa, I'm so sorry! I truly do not know how I could have been so clumsy."

"Divine Providence?" John suggested, straight-faced, but his eyes were laughing.

"That is one explanation, I suppose," William de Braose said, favoring them both with a sour smile, and Joanna saw that he, too, knew her action had been deliberate. But John was looking at her with such amusement, such affectionate approval that nothing else mattered to her. She groped hastily for a topic of conversation likely to hold his interest, to exclude de Braose.

"Did you hear any uncommon appeals today, Papa?" she asked, knowing as soon as she spoke that her question was inspired, for John shared his father's fascination with the law. He genuinely enjoyed hearing court appeals, arguing points of law with his justices, issuing writs to right perceived wrongs, and he saw to it that the Exchequer published his itinerary weeks in advance so that petitioners might know where he'd be on a given day, so they could appeal to the royal court for justice denied in the shire courts.

"Indeed I did, Joanna. A youth not much older than you, calling himself Roger of Stainton. He'd been amusing himself by throwing stones across a stream. By ill luck, one struck a young girl. She died and he was sentenced to be hanged."

"Shall you pardon him, Papa?" Joanna asked, pleased when John nodded.

"How could I not? It was death by misadventure; a man should not hang for that." John paused, looking up as an usher came into the chamber.

"Your Grace, a courier has just arrived from Fontevrault."

John tensed; his good humor chilled into icy wariness. He'd been dreading this, his mother's reaction to the loss of Castle Gaillard, Richard's pride and joy, the castle he'd boasted he could hold even if the walls were made of butter. John did not want to be reminded of this by Eleanor; even if she did not reproach him directly, he did not doubt her disappointment would echo between every line. It was with considerable reluctance, then, that he said curtly, "Send him in."

The monk was young and visibly ill at ease. The black habit of the Benedictines camouflaged the grime of his journey, but the parchment he clutched was soiled from much handling, slashed and threaded through with a braided grey cord that might once have been white. He knelt, thrust the letter at John as if he longed only to be rid of it.

John looked down at the wax sealing the cord ends; it was intact, but unfamiliar. "This is not my mother's seal."

"The letter is from the Abbess Matilda, Your Grace. She bade me tell you . . ." The monk swallowed, no longer meeting John's eyes. "Your lady mother . . . she is dead, my liege."

John heard his daughter cry out, plaintively denying death with an indrawn breath that broke on a sob. No one else spoke. John found himself staring at the monk's clasped hands; they were rawboned, knuckles roughened, nails caked with dirt. Never had he been so aware of detail; he saw a sheen on the man's habit, where kneeling had worn the material thin, saw the damp splotches under his armpits, the telltale signs of sweat, of fear. But he felt nothing, only a stunned sense of disbelief.

Utterly unnerved by John's silence, the monk squeezed his knees tightly together to stop his trembling, and stammered, "It . . . it did happen on Thursday last, soon after Vespers. But it may comfort you, my lord, to know that hers was a peaceful and Christian passing. She died in God's grace, with our lady Abbess and Abbot Luke of Turpenay at her bedside; he'd been with her when your brother King Richard died, you may recall, and when she knew her end was nigh, she sent to St Mary's Abbey for him."

Still John said nothing, and the monk drew several shallow breaths, speaking now almost at random. "It was your mother's wish that she be buried at Fontevrault with King Richard and your sister, the Lady Joanna. Our Abbess saw that it was done. I hope that meets with your approval, my liege . . ."

"Did she leave any word . . . any message for me?"

"No, my lord."

Another silence fell. John crumpled the letter, unread, let it drop into the rushes at his feet. The monk made an instinctive grab for it, then jerked his hand back as if burned. Will cleared his throat, seemed on the verge of speech. John forestalled him, said without any intonation whatsoever, "Leave me. All of you."

The men did not need to be told twice; even Will obeyed at once. But Joanna's discipline took her only as far as the door. There she whirled, ran back, and knelt by John's chair. "Let me stay, Papa," she pleaded. "Please . . ."

The face upturned to his was waxen, wet with tears. John put his arm around her, and she began to sob in earnest. He drew her closer, let her weep against his shoulder, and after a brief time her sobs subsided, gave way to sighs and hiccups. Joanna's first flow of tears had been for herself, for her own loss. But now she wiped her face with her sleeve, ready to share that loss, recognizing that her father's sense of bereavement might be even greater than hers.

"Papa . . . I'm so sorry." Joanna remembered, too vividly, what it had been like to lose her mother, remembered not so much her grieving as her sheer terror. Did men and women grown ever experience blind, suffocating panic like that? She did not know. Her father's face was shuttered, unreadable.

"Papa . . . you have not said a word, not one. Do you not want to talk? How do you feel?" She looked up at him anxiously, no longer a child, not yet a woman, tears still glistening in the slanting hazel eyes, Eleanor's eyes, and John was suddenly glad he'd allowed her to stay.

"How do I feel?" He found that was not an easy question to answer, at last said, "Alone . . . very alone. And angry, so angry I can think of nothing else."

Adult emotions were no longer as mysterious or inexplicable to Joanna as they'd once been, but this was utterly beyond her comprehension. "Angry . . . at your mother? Because she died? But why? I do not understand, Papa."

"Neither do I, Joanna." And in that moment John sounded no less bewildered than his twelve-year-old daughter. "Neither do I."

14

WINCHESTER, ENGLAND

September 1204

Summoned by her father, Joanna left London on Tuesday morning of Michaelmas week. Traveling in the company of her Aunt Ela, Countess of Salisbury, they reached Winchester at dusk on Thursday. There they found other ladies of the court—like them, summoned to attend the King. But John had not yet arrived from Clarendon, had still not come by noon the next day.

With so many people to be sheltered, beds were scarce, and Joanna's aunt was given a cramped chamber musty with the rancid odors rising up from the castle moat. It was a far less desirable room than those taken by Maude de Braose and Isobel, Countess of Pembroke, but Ela voiced no objections. Although she had brought her husband an earldom, his fief was neither large nor lucrative; Will held only fifty knights' fees, and no castles, although John did allow him to make use of Salisbury Castle. In contrast, William de Braose held no less than three hundred fifty knights' fees and some sixteen English and Welsh castles. Ela, a shy, self-effacing young woman, accepted the realities of power without a murmur of protest, would never have dreamed of contesting wills with so aggressive a personality as Maude de Braose. It did occur to Joanna, who liked Maude not at all, but her youth and illegitimacy effectively rendered her mute.

Joanna was standing now on the stairs outside their bedchamber, frozen with rage. The door was only slightly ajar, but the voices within came quite clearly to her ears, so audibly that she recognized the speakers without difficulty: Maude de Braose, Maude's daughter Margaret de Lacy, wife to the Lord of Meath, and Isobel, wife to the powerful William Marshal, Earl of Pembroke. She had yet to hear her aunt's voice, however, and while that did not surprise her, it did anger her. Ela was her father's sister by marriage; common courtesy, if not loyalty, should compel her to speak up for him.

"I had a letter from my husband today, Mama. Word reached Ireland a fortnight ago that Poitiers fell to the French on August tenth, but Walter refuses to believe it."

"After the defeats of the past year? After losing all of Normandy in less than a twelvemonth? You could tell me tomorrow that Philip had taken London itself, and I'd not think to doubt you!"

"Ah, Maude, that's not strictly fair. I grant you the King made some grave errors of judgment. My husband warned him it was folly to release the de Lusignans, no matter how many hostages they offered up as pledges for their loyalty. Nor did John help himself by relying upon so brutal a captain as Lupescaire; a man does not gain himself a name like 'the Wolf' without cause, and I doubt not he affronted many who might otherwise have stayed loyal to John. But—"

"Yet men such as that do have their uses. In Wales we—"

Most people found themselves at a distinct disadvantage when competing with Maude de Braose for conversational control, but Isobel of Pembroke was a remarkably single-minded woman, little given to self-doubt. "If I may finish, Maude," she said, placidly overriding Maude's interruption with one of her own, "not all of his troubles were of the King's making. His lack of money—you know as well as I that Richard drained the royal treasury dry. And in all honesty, some of John's difficulties with his Norman barons can be traced, too, to his brother's reign. Richard laid a heavy hand upon the land, and there were many who chafed under it."

"I daresay there's some truth in what you say, Isobel. But that changes not the fact that within two years of his triumph at Mirebeau, John did lose Normandy, Anjou, and Touraine, and now most of Poitou. Say what you will about Richard, but think you that he would have stayed in England whilst Castle Gaillard was under siege? Not if he had to swim the Channel with his sword in his teeth! Mayhap he, too, would have lost Normandy, but we may be sure that Richard would have lost his life, as well, would have died ere he'd yield up so much as a handful of Norman soil to Philip. You can scarcely say the same for John!"

Joanna had not meant to confront them; girls of thirteen did not challenge their elders. But with Maude's taunt, she forgot all else, grabbed for the door latch. The women within turned

startled faces toward her; even Maude looked somewhat disconcerted. Recovering quickly, however, she said curtly, "I trust
you were not eavesdropping, Joanna."

"I need no lesson in manners, Madame. Not from you."

Maude's mouth tightened. "If you were my daughter, I'd slap
you silly for that," she snapped. "No child of mine would dare
speak so insolently to her elders."

"But I am not your daughter, Madame. I am the King's
daughter," Joanna said, and saw that she'd achieved the all but
impossible, had the last word in an argument with Maude de
Braose. Never had she been so rude to an adult, but now she
turned her back upon Maude, crossed to her coffer chest. No one
spoke, watching in silence as she knelt, retrieved a willow basket. She could feel their eyes upon her, all the way to the door.

The lower bailey was awash in sun. A postern gate in the north
curtain wall opened out into the gardens, and it was toward this
door that Joanna hastened, almost running in her need to put the
bedchamber scene behind her. Reaction to her rage had set in,
and she was flushed, trembling. But she was proud, too, that she
had stood up to Maude de Braose.

Joanna had long since passed the stage where she thought
every adult was all-knowing. Some were quite clever. Others
were not. And some could be remarkably shrewd and yet surprisingly foolish, too. Joanna was slowly realizing that her young
stepmother was one such, insightful about that which interested
her—relationships between men and women—and unabashedly
uninformed about all else. Now, as much as she disliked Maude
de Braose, Joanna did not dismiss Maude as a fool. No, Maude
and Isabelle were reverse sides of the same coin. Maude was
quick-witted about that which interested Isabelle least. She could
add up long columns of figures in her head, knew the names of
all her vassals, could talk of Welsh border warfare as well as any
man. But she had no understanding of people's hearts.

Joanna smiled. Precisely because she was so ignorant of emotional needs, Maude would be sure Joanna would repeat all to her
father, would have some uneasy moments in consequence, for
even Maude, who prided herself upon her outspoken, careless
candor, even she would not want such a tale to reach the King's
ears.

Not that she would ever tell Papa. He had burdens enough,
needed no more. He was—Joanna calculated rapidly—only in his
thirty-seventh year, but his hair was increasingly flecked with
grey, and there were lines around his mouth that had not been

there a year ago. Worst of all, his temper was honed to a sharp
edge. He rarely shouted, as his father and brothers had done, but
sarcasm, too, could scar. Even in good humor, he'd always trod
that fine line between jest and mockery, and these days he was
all too quick to turn upon others the sardonic lash of an unbridled
tongue.

Joanna sighed. Papa was so good to her, so good to Isabelle.
And he was very clever, in truth he was. So why, then, did he
offend people so needlessly? For he did, he was too suspicious,
too quick to read the worst into men's motives. Not, she added
loyally, that he had no cause for mistrust. Many of the Norman
barons had gone over to Philip at the first chance.

Joanna had spent much time in the past year seeking to puzzle
it out, how her father's luck could have soured so swiftly in the
months after Mirebeau. She'd even attempted to discuss it with
John, but had been rebuffed with unwonted sharpness. And
Isabelle had been no help whatsoever. She was interested only in
consoling John for his loss, not in analyzing the whys and
wherefores.

It was from her Uncle Will that Joanna had gotten most of her
answers. He'd admitted that John had blundered in freeing Hugh
de Lusignan and in alienating William des Roches. But he'd told
her, too, that John's mistakes were threads woven into a larger
pattern. "In some ways, Joanna, John is reaping the crop Richard sowed. Mayhap Richard could have held on to the lands for a
while longer, but that is all. What is writ is writ. You remember
that, lass, whenever you hear ignorant tongues wag."

Joanna did remember, sought now to dismiss Maude's mockery as her uncle had advised. But anger was not so easy to
subdue; resentment remained, and regret that others could not see
into her father's soul, could not know him as she did. Yet there
was, as well, a realization that had no place within the borders of
childhood, that was rooted in an adult understanding: that her
father could make mistakes, could suffer from uncertainty and
indecision, could share all the failings of mortal men. He was
not a saint, after all, not the all-powerful knight without peer,
Lancelot and Roland and Gawain, a child's champion in the lists,
her favor on his lance and her name on his lips.

"He was a burning and shining light," Joanna murmured,
with some self-mockery, but not much. Why should she scorn
the bedazzled child she had been? She had loved Papa when, in
her innocence, she'd thought him to be perfect, and she loved
him no less now that she knew he was not.

* * *

Winchester had been a favorite residence of Joanna's grandfather, the old King, and in days gone by, when he'd still cared about pleasing his Queen, he'd built for Eleanor vineyards to remind her of her native Poitou, chains of fishponds, a garden arbor. It was to these gardens that Joanna retreated.

From her basket she fished out her lesson tablet and the bone stylus she used to mark the wax coating. But this was just a sop to her conscience, for she did not intend to study. Unrolling a sheet of scraped parchment, she smoothed it with a pumice stone, then dipped her pen into her inkhorn.

> To the Lady Eleanor, my cousin, greetings.
>   I write to you from the gardens at Winchester Castle, on this, the Friday after Michaelmas, whilst I await my lord father the King to ride in from Clarendon. I have not seen him since he did meet last month with the Welsh Prince . . .

Here she paused, having no idea how to spell Llewelyn. After some thought, she opted for a phonetic spelling, although she was not even sure if her pronunciation was correct.

> . . . Lliwelin. He had sworn to do homage to my father more than three years ago, but he was not overeager to make good his word, did only this summer agree to meet with Papa at Worcester. I hope their meeting did go well, hope, too, that I shall have more time with my father now. I saw him but little this twelvemonth past, as you know. He was occupied in defending his lands against the French King, and I spent part of the year with my grandmother in Poitiers . . .

Again she paused, remembering that her cousin, too, was Eleanor's grandchild. Inking out "my," she wrote "our" above it, and then added in an uneven hand, "may God assoil her." It lacked one day of being five months since Eleanor had died at Fontevrault, but Joanna's grieving was still green, her loss still keenly felt.

She sat for a time, staring down at the parchment. Letters to her cousin were never easy, invariably written with a faltering, hesitant pen. But she felt compelled to persevere, knowing how lonely Eleanor must be. And then, too, Joanna liked to write letters. There was something almost mystical to her about the process. She enjoyed signing her name with a flourish, using large blobs of sealing wax, paying couriers with the silver pennies hoarded for such a purpose, remembering the little girl who could do no more than draw her name in the dirt with a stick.

Did you get the saddle my father ordered for you? I do not yet know where Papa shall keep his Christmas court, but I am sure he will want you to join us. Since I saw you last, I have acquired a dog. I had one once before; she died when I was ten, was run over by a cart, and I swore I would never have another. But my stepmother the Queen gave me a puppy for my New Year's gift. She is no bigger than a cat, with long, silky fur, comes from the island of Malta. My father suggested I name her Sugar because she was so costly!

What to say now? Should she mention Arthur? Was Eleanor aware of the vile lies put about by Papa's enemies, that Arthur was dead? It was so unfair. He'd been nothing but kind to Eleanor, saw that she had every comfort, even brought her occasionally to his court. Why, then, would he put her brother to death? Joanna shook her head, reaching for the inkhorn. Pray God Papa would soon be able to mount his campaign to win back Normandy and Poitou, to punish Philip as he deserved.

"Joanna!"

The voice was Richard's. Joanna scrambled to her feet, ran to meet him. "Richard, how glad I am to see you! Has Papa come, then? Did the council with the Welsh Prince go well? Did you meet him?"

"Yes, to all your questions. Hurry now, get your things together. Papa is asking for you, wants to see you straightaway."

"Indeed?" Joanna was delighted. Her father's arrivals were inevitably chaotic; sometimes hours passed before she had the chance to see him alone. "He truly wants to see me first?"

Richard nodded. "You know, it was rather queer. When Papa asked after you, Aunt Ela and the other ladies acted right peculiar, almost as if they were reluctant to have you found. Even Lady de Braose professed ignorance of your whereabouts, and she most generally has an opinion on everything!"

"Lady de Braose has a viper's tongue," Joanna said emphatically, "and I care not a pin for her good opinion. Need I comb my hair first?"

"No, but your face is dirty." Richard spat on his fingers, wiped away a smudge on her cheek, and then pleased Joanna by giving her a quick, awkward hug.

"The last time I remember you doing that," she laughed, "I'd spilled ink on Papa's favorite book, was about to be called to account for my sin!"

Richard gave her a look she could not interpret, reached down for her basket. "Come, I'll take you back to the castle."

Joanna fumbled with the cloth, unwrapped an exquisitely engraved ivory case. At the touch of her fingers, it flew open to reveal a thin sheet of glass over brightly polished metal.

"Papa, what a beautiful mirror!" Setting it down beside her other present, a bolt of deep blue linen, she gave John a grateful kiss. "But you sent me a book for my birthday, do you not remember?"

"And can I not give you more than one gift? A pity my men in the Exchequer are not as frugal as you; mayhap I'd not then be so deeply in debt!"

They were alone in John's bedchamber. Much to Joanna's surprise, her father had dismissed all others upon her arrival, even Richard, who seemed strangely reluctant to leave, glancing back over his shoulder with the same enigmatic look he'd given her in the garden.

"I think, lass, that you're now old enough to have a lady in attendance, to assist you in dressing and the like. So I've told Isabelle to choose someone suitable for you."

"Thank you, Papa!" Joanna wondered if this was how Richard had felt when he'd learned he was to be squire to William de Braose the younger, was to take that first step over the threshold toward manhood.

"I have one more gift for you, sweetheart—a crown."

Joanna giggled. "And a halo, too, Papa?"

John laughed, shook his head. "I'm not jesting, Joanna. I've made a brilliant marriage for you. I've agreed to betroth you to Llewelyn ab Iorwerth, Prince of Gwynedd."

"Papa?"

"In truth, sweetheart. I've offered the castle and manor of Ellesmere in Shropshire as your marriage portion, will yield it to Llewelyn next spring, although I would not have the marriage take place till after you do pass your fourteenth birthday." John reached over, took Joanna's hand. "You realize what this will mean, Joanna? You'll be a Princess, lass. This goes so far beyond what I ever hoped to gain for you. It is a rarity, indeed, when needs and wants do mate in such harmony. But . . . but have you nothing to say to me? I would have thought you'd be besieging me with questions. Are you not curious about the man you shall marry?''

Too stunned for coherent thought, Joanna could only stare at her father in dazed disbelief. "He . . . he does speak French?'' she whispered at last.

That was not what John had been expecting. "Of course, and quite well. He knows much of our ways, did live in Shropshire as a lad.''

"Is he . . . is he a Christian, Papa?''

John frowned, torn between amusement and annoyance. "What sort of foolish question is that, Joanna? Wales has been a Christian country since the days of St Patrick. To whom have you been listening?''

To you, Papa. How often I've heard you say the Welsh were barbarians, that theirs was an accursed land fit only for mountain goats, that the Welsh were as bad as the Scots and worse than the Irish. Joanna said nothing, though, watched as John rose, moved to the table. Her hands were icy; she laced her fingers together, locked them around her drawn-up knees.

"This Welsh Prince . . . how old is he, Papa?''

"I'd reckon about thirty or thirty-one.''

Joanna could not hide her dismay. "As old as that?'' she gasped.

"He happens to be at least five years younger than I, Joanna,'' John said dryly. He was smiling, but Joanna remembered, just in time, that her father was fully twenty years older than Isabelle.

"I . . . I did not mean it like that, Papa,'' she stammered, and then a sudden thought came to her, a faint glimmer of hope. "But Papa, I am your natural daughter. What Prince would want a wife born out of wedlock?''

"A Welsh Prince,'' John said and laughed. "The stigma of illegitimacy counts for little amongst Llewelyn's people. If a father recognizes a child as his, that child then enjoys full rights under Welsh law. Llewelyn had his son with him at Worcester, a lad about eight or so, born of a Welsh concubine, and yet looked upon by all as his heir. In fact, if a Welsh woman swears a holy oath that a certain man fathered her child, he must then deny her charge under oath, too, or the child is held to be his. Moreover, even if he does make such a denial, if she can show he gave her money for the child, her word counts against his! I have to admit, they do have some queer customs, but . . .''

Joanna was no longer listening, was trying to envision herself as a stepmother to an eight-year-old boy. She could not, and with to him for what she was . . . or was not. She was the King of England's daughter, and he had wanted this marriage, had been no less eager than her father to make the match. And yet . . . and yet why should she feel such surprise? She had a mirror, had she not? Did she truly need to be told once again that beauty was to be found in skin lily-white, in hair like flax, in eyes like Isabelle's? Not in slanting cat eyes, ink-black hair, and the dusky skin of a Saracen . . . sallow skin.

"My lord? You asked me . . . what?"

"If you have always lived with your father the King."

"Since I was five," Joanna said swiftly, grateful that he seemed willing to do what she could not, to exercise some control over the conversation.

"And your lady mother?"

Normally, Joanna was very reluctant to discuss her mother; those memories were like imperfectly healed wounds, painful if probed too deeply. But now she was quite willing to talk of Clemence, so great was her dread of silence, and she answered readily. He continued to feed her questions, about her childhood, her father, and slowly she began to relax somewhat, to follow his lead.

". . . and then these enormous dogs did rush in, barking fit to wake the dead. I was so fearful, but my father picked me up, all dirty and ragged as I was, held me out of harm's way. I did not yet know, of course, who he was, but—" Joanna stopped suddenly, in some confusion. What had ever possessed her to tell this man something so very personal? Isabelle was right; he was, indeed, a good listener, too good.

"I did not mean to talk so much of myself," she said, suddenly self-conscious again. "Will you not tell me about yourself, my lord?"

"What would you most like to know?"

Joanna considered. She knew next to nothing about him, but there was one question in particular she yearned to ask. "I would like to know about your children, my lord. Would you tell me of them?"

"With pleasure. I have six, two boys and four girls . . . by two mothers," Llewelyn added, with a faint smile, and Joanna blushed, taken aback that he should have read her thoughts so easily. Her father's seven children had all been born to different women.

"Do they all live at your court?"

"The four eldest do. Gruffydd, my firstborn, is ten. Gwladys is eight, Marared six, and Gwenllian nigh on five.'' Llewelyn paused, and then again answered an unspoken question. ''Their mother is dead.''

''And the other two?''

He smiled. ''Tegwared and Anghared, the twins. They lack but a fortnight of their first birthday.''

Joanna raised startled eyes to his face. It was a rather common belief that for a woman to give birth to twins, she must have lain with two men. Yet Llewelyn seemed neither embarrassed nor defensive. Was it, she wondered, that he had such faith in the woman? Or in himself?

''I was most fortunate in that my lord father married a woman who showed me naught but kindness. I shall not do less for your children, my lord,'' she said earnestly.

She'd sought to please him, was bewildered to see that she had not. He looked suddenly somber, pensive. For the first time, a prolonged silence fell between them.

''Tell me, have you begun to learn Welsh, as I suggested in my last letter?''

Joanna tensed again. ''No, my lord,'' she admitted reluctantly, watching him anxiously for signs of anger.

''Well, there will be time enough.''

Indeed, she thought bleakly. A lifetime.

''Joanna.'' It was the first time he'd called her by name. ''Now that I've satisfied your curiosity, I would have you do the same for me. I should like to see the color of your hair. Will it distress you if I remove your veil and wimple?''

Caught completely off balance, she could only shake her head mutely. She willed herself to sit very still, not to flinch as he leaned over, unpinned her veil. His fingers were quite sure, barely touching her cheek. Joanna continued to stare down into her lap. After a time, she felt his hand under her chin, gently forcing her face up to his. As their eyes met, he smiled. ''You do look very Welsh.''

''Do I?'' she whispered. He was much more sympathetic than she'd expected him to be. He'd been kind to seek to put her at ease, and he was being kinder now in trying to mask his obvious disappointment. But she could think only that in less than twenty-four hours he would have the right to strip away her clothing as he had just stripped away her veil, to bare her body as he'd bared her hair.

''My lord . . . would you think me unforgivably rude if I did

ask your leave to withdraw? I . . . I have so much still to do ere
the wedding . . .''

"I understand, Joanna," he said slowly. He rose as she did,
brought her hand up to his mouth. "Until the morrow."

Ednyved ap Cynwrig made his way across the great hall, to
where Llewelyn stood by the window seat. "What, has the bride
fled so soon, and ere I could get more than a glimpse of her?
Well? Is she fat, thin, plain, pretty? From the look on your face,
I'd wager that she was not much to your liking."

"And you'd lose." Llewelyn was frowning after Joanna's retreating figure. "She has the makings of a beauty. But Jesú, how
very young she is! I'd not expected that, in truth."

"To thirty-three, fourteen is bound to seem close to the cradle." Ednyved gave Llewelyn a shrewdly appraising look, said,
no longer flippant, "Many girls are wed at fourteen, Llewelyn,
are ripe for the marriage bed even at that age."

"Not this one. She's a child, Ednyved, a child being forced
into a marriage she greatly fears." Llewelyn glanced down, saw
that Joanna had, in her haste, forgotten her veil and wimple. He
picked up the veil, fingered the fragile silk weave. "Poor little
lass, trying so hard to do what her elders expect of her . . .''

Joanna's bridal clothes were the loveliest she'd ever had. Everything was new, even the garters for her stockings. Her chemise
was of soft white linen, the gown of finest Florentine silk, as was
the embroidered bliaut. Joanna knew they were becoming. Isabelle had insisted upon choosing the colors herself, and Isabelle
had an unerring eye, selecting a deep emerald for the gown, a
much paler shade of green for the tightly laced bliaut, delicately
threaded through with gold. Since Joanna would wear her hair
loose and flowing down her back, to proclaim she came to her
marriage bed a virgin, there was no wimple, but merely a thin,
circular veil, as light as air, to be held in place by a gold circlet.

Joanna smoothed the skirt of her gown, remembering another
outfit of green and gold, laid out at the foot of John's bed that
first morning she'd awakened in Rouen. She stood for a moment,
staring into the mirror Blanche was holding up for her inspection,
and then turned toward Isabelle and Ela. "I am ready."

Custom decreed that a bride's father or guardian be the one to
lead her mount to the church. Since both John and Joanna's
Uncle Will were in Winchester, the Earl of Chester had offered
to act in John's stead, and it was he who lifted Joanna up into the

saddle. The mare, a glossy, small-boned chestnut, was Llewelyn's bride-gift to Joanna. She'd never had a horse of her own before, and such a gift would normally have transported her into a state of high excitement. Now, however, she felt nothing. The prancing mare, the crowds lining Bridge Street, the sunlight so bright upon the banners above her head, all lacked reality for her. There was a strange, dreamlike quality to the day, as if she were watching from afar as a girl very like her rode to her wedding with a Welsh Prince.

The precincts of the abbey of St Werburgh were already filled to overflowing with the people of Chester, eager for the spectacle of a royal wedding. Llewelyn was awaiting Joanna by the south door of the church, for it was there that their wedding vows would be exchanged; weddings were traditionally performed out in the open before as many witnesses as possible. He came forward to meet her, smiling. Time took an abrupt lurch forward, and with bewildering suddenness she found herself standing before Geoffrey de Muschamp, Bishop of Chester, holding hands with a stranger.

Almost before she knew it, Llewelyn was pledging her his troth. She drew a deep breath, said in a clear, carrying voice, "I, Joanna, do take thee, Llewelyn, in holy Church, as my wedded husband, forsaking all others, in sickness and health, in riches and poverty, in well and in woe, till death us do part, and thereto I plight thee my troth."

The Bishop having blessed the ring, Llewelyn took Joanna's left hand, slipped the ring in turn upon each of her fingers, saying, "In the name of the Father and of the Son and of the Holy Ghost . . ." Sliding it then upon her third finger, he gave her hand a gentle squeeze. "With this ring, I thee wed."

The crowd was cheering, surged forward as Llewelyn and Joanna dipped into the alms dish, scattered coins in their midst. Joanna was then embraced in turn by Isabelle, Ela, and the Countess of Chester. But it was Llewelyn now, not Chester, who led her into the church, for with her marriage she had passed from her father's control to that of her husband.

As little as she remembered of the wedding ceremony, Joanna remembered even less of the Mass of Trinity that followed. It was cool and dark within, pleasantly scented with incense. At one point she heard the Bishop intone, "Let this woman be amiable as Rachel, wise as Rebecca, faithful as Sarah," and she realized, with bemusement, that he was speaking of her. She was shamefully ignorant of the Scriptures, could not for the life of her swallow; the wine was warm, so heavily sugared that she all but gagged.

"There are men who be born lucky. All their lives, fortune does favor them, does play the whore for them. My brother Richard was one such. Llewelyn ab Iorwerth is another. And he is clever enough, ambitious enough, and ruthless enough one day to rule all of Wales if he is not reined in. Already he looks beyond Gwynedd, dares to send envoys to the French court, to treat with Philip as if they were brother sovereigns. Should he ever forge an alliance with the French . . . ."

John had wandered to the window, speaking almost as if to himself. He turned now, back toward his daughter, gave her a sudden smile of coaxing charm. "Are you not pleased, sweetheart, that you shall be Princess of Gwynedd?"

Joanna swallowed. "Indeed, Papa," she said tonelessly. "If it be your wish that I wed with Prince Llewelyn, I am content."

Leaving her father's bedchamber, Joanna stood for a moment in the darkened stairwell, not knowing where to go. So caught up was she in her own thoughts that she did not at once notice the young page.

"Lady . . . lady, will you come? The Queen does want you."

Joanna looked blankly at the child. "Yes," she said with an effort. "Of course." But the summons was not all that unwelcome. Isabelle might be the one person who could understand how she felt.

Isabelle was awaiting her in her bedchamber, welcomed her with a perfumed embrace. "Ah, Joanna, how happy I am for you, love! Is it not wondrous? Think, you shall be a Princess!"

"A Welsh Princess," Joanna said, and with that, tears welled in her eyes, began to spill silently down her face.

Isabelle blinked. "Are you as unhappy as that? Ah, Joanna . . . ." Putting an arm around the younger girl, she led Joanna toward the bed.

"You just need time to accustom yourself to it. Do you not think I felt the same qualms when my father sent me to live in Hugh de Lusignan's household? Of course, that marriage was not to be, and glad I am for it. But if fate had decreed otherwise, I do not doubt I could have learned to be content as Hugh's Countess. As you will be content with Prince Llewelyn. Once the surprise of it does fade, you'll be quite reconciled, you'll see.

"Now sit on the bed, and I'll tell you all about your husband, tell you what John should have and likely did not, men having no that realization, some of her panic began to ebb. She could not make this marriage. She could not. To leave Papa, Richard, Isabelle, all that was known and familiar to her, to live out her life amongst strangers, an exile in an alien land . . . no, she was not strong enough, had not the courage. Somehow she must make Papa see that, make him understand that he asked too much of her.

John had poured wine into two cups, gave one to Joanna. "Ah, lass, I cannot tell you how pleased I am about this marriage. Mayhap I should not say this to you, but of all my children, you are the dearest, the closest to my heart. I can think of no greater gift to give you than this, a crown."

"Papa, you have been so good to me, and I would do anything for you, I swear I would. But this marriage—"

"—is the answer to so much, Joanna." John leaned forward, his eyes shining; it had been months since she'd seen him so animated, so enthused. "Before God, it was an inspired solution to the Welsh problem. I do gain a gold coronet for you and a secure border for England, all for the price of one castle and a wedding ring. Rarely has a war been so cheaply won, sweetheart!"

"A war . . ." Joanna echoed numbly. "Is the marriage as important to you as that?"

John's smile faded. "Yes, it is. You want the truth, Joanna? I do not know if I shall ever be able to reclaim the lands lost to the French—Normandy, Anjou, Touraine. Now Poitou is slipping away, being swallowed up by that whoreson on the French throne. I'll not let it go, not lose the lands that were my mother's, that Richard held before me—by Christ, I will not. But I cannot fight a war on two fronts, cannot deal with the Welsh and the French, too."

He rose abruptly, began to pace. "They are a strange people, the Welsh. Man for man, the best fighters in the world, for you cannot defeat a foe who has not the sense to know when he's beaten! We'd never have been able to keep them from laying claim to Shropshire and Cheshire, much less conquer so much of South Wales, had it not been for their one fatal weakness, that they are such a quarrelsome, passionate people. They kill one another as readily as they do Normans, engage in blood feuds, nurse grudges for years, and thank God, but they have ever lacked a Prince capable of uniting them against England . . . until now."

Joanna stared down at her wine cup as if at some utterly alien and exotic object. Raising it to her lips, she took a tentative remember what Rachel, Rebecca, and Sarah had done. She could think only of Ruth—Ruth, who'd gone forth into an alien land, who'd said, "Whither thou goest, I will go, thy people shall be my people, and thy God my God."

Llewelyn was approaching the altar now, to receive from the Bishop the kiss of peace. And then he was back at her side, lifting her veil. She raised her face obediently for him to transmit the kiss to her, felt his lips upon hers, a light, warm touch, almost impersonal.

Chester had always suffered a reputation as one of the most violence-prone cities of the realm; Cheshiremen were notorious for their thin skins, their ready swords. The Welsh were no less renowned for the touchiness of their tempers, for the ease with which they took affront. It was a volatile mixture, and Llewelyn and the Earl of Chester had done what they could to minimize the dangers. It was for this reason that Ascension Day had been chosen for the wedding; men who'd care little about breaking the King's Peace might think twice before breaking God's Peace, as well. For the same reason, the wedding feast was served immediately upon their return from the church, in hopes that men well wined and dined would be lulled into goodwill, be less likely to yield to age-old antagonisms.

Joanna had never before eaten from the dais, except on that long-ago day in Rouen, sitting on John's lap. Now she sat between Llewelyn and the Earl of Chester, did her best to feign interest in the food being offered her, venison and roast partridge, fresh herring, each course crowned with an elaborate sugared subtlety. She was grateful that the conversational demands being made upon her were minimal. Llewelyn was being monopolized by Isabelle, seated at his left, and Chester, a dour, taciturn man, already balding although only in his thirties, was not much given to small talk. Joanna knew he'd only recently been restored to her father's favor; John had suspected him of conspiring with the Welsh Prince, Gwenwynwyn of Powys. If it was true, he could not be deriving much pleasure from playing host to Llewelyn, Gwenwynwyn's chief rival. But mayhap it was not true; Papa's suspicions were not always grounded in fact. Pray God his campaign would go well. Joanna laid down a tart, untasted. How would she even know? Whilst he was fighting a war in Normandy, she would be deep in Wales, utterly isolated from those she most loved.

Across the great hall, voices rose suddenly. Joanna saw both

Llewelyn and Chester stiffen. Sharing a trencher and wine cup with Llewelyn, she was not long in becoming aware that her husband was not drinking. Joanna was puzzled; such abstinence was highly unusual at a wedding feast, where male guests seemed to feel a social obligation to drink themselves into oblivion. Her unease grew as she realized that Chester, too, was cold sober.

The voices were growing louder. A bench was tipped over; a woman screamed. Joanna gasped as a man pushed away from the table, fumbled for the hilt of his sword. Llewelyn was already on his feet, shouting in Welsh. The man turned, reluctantly let his sword slide back down its scabbard. By then, Llewelyn had reached them, with Chester right on his heels. A brief angry exchange followed, with Llewelyn tongue-lashing the Welshman and Chester berating the Norman. The offenders lapsed into a sullen silence, but tension gripped the hall, spread by murmurs of discontent, voiced in two tongues. Joanna bit her lip, watched as Llewelyn took Chester aside, spoke in an urgent undertone. Chester nodded, stepped back, and sent a servant hastening from the hall.

Joanna gave Llewelyn a questioning look as he resumed his seat, but he said only, "I thought it time for a diversion."

Joanna was not long in finding out what he had in mind. Servants were entering the hall, carrying several huge baked pies. As all watched, they cut carefully into the crusts, freeing more than a dozen small birds. The birds soared upward, circling and swooping over the tables as the men and women below laughed and cheered, eagerly awaiting the finale, the release of three sleek sparrow hawks. What resulted was utter chaos, with dogs barking in berserk frenzy, and men clambering up on benches to better view the kills, laying tipsy wagers upon the outcome, animosities forgotten in the excitement of the hunt.

"That was indeed clever, my lord," Joanna said approvingly, and Llewelyn laughed.

"It was my man's fault. There is a hamlet across the Dee called Hanbridge, but it's been taken so often by the Welsh that we call it Treboeth, 'the burned town.' It is one thing to do so amongst ourselves, quite another to do so midst a hall full of Normans . . . as Rosser should have known."

"I see." Joanna watched as a feather wafted slowly downward, came to rest in a tureen of sorrel soup. If the Welsh had such a hatred for Normans, how would they ever accept her as Llewelyn's wife?

*   *   *

Once the trestle tables were cleared away, there was dancing, but after there'd been two spills, caused by overexuberant dancers whose coordination was rather the worse for wine, Chester signaled for less risky entertainment: jugglers, a man with trained marmosets, several minstrels eager to sing for their supper. The song requests were becoming increasingly bawdy, and Joanna was once more growing tense. It was not that she found the suggestive lyrics objectionable in themselves, but that they reminded her of what still lay ahead, the bedding-down revelries and the consummation of her marriage.

Turning away from a group clustered around the wittiest of the minstrels, she collided with Maude de Braose, spilling some of her drink upon the sleeve of Maude's gown.

"I am sorry, Madame. I did not see you." It was a listless apology, indifferently offered, but the best she could do under the circumstances.

"Obviously." Maude's voice was tart, her eyes unfriendly. "You've been wandering about the hall like a ghost. Can you not at least make a pretense that this marriage be to your liking?"

The unfairness of that took Joanna's breath away; she'd been trying so hard to hide her true feelings. "I assure you this marriage is very much to my liking, Madame." Even had she believed Llewelyn ab Iorwerth to be the veritable Antichrist, nothing on earth could have induced her to admit that to Maude. But she was never to know what imp then took possession of her tongue, was even more startled than Maude to hear herself add, "Your advice I can well do without, Madame. I do, however, need a fresh cup of wine."

Maude's eyebrows shot upward. "You want me to fetch it for you?" she demanded, openly incredulous.

"Yes." But Joanna had never in her life given an order to a man or woman of rank, and there'd been a brief hesitation, a hesitation that did not escape Maude.

"I think not," she said coolly, and turned away.

"Lady de Braose!" Joanna's voice had carried; others were looking her way. Still not sure how she'd gotten herself into such a predicament, she stared helplessly at the older woman, knowing neither how to enforce her command nor how to extricate herself without loss of face. Maude was looking at her mockingly, and she crimsoned, going hot with humiliation and impotent anger. She opened her mouth, having no idea what she was going to say, and then saw Maude's face change, saw her smile splinter into frozen fragments. Joanna spun around, to find Llewelyn standing just behind her.

"What are you drinking, Joanna? Hippocras?"

She nodded, watched wide-eyed as he held the wine cup out to Maude. "Lady Maude, if you will," he said, smiling. Maude was of a sudden as deeply flushed as Joanna, but she managed a stiff smile of her own.

"As it pleases Your Grace, it would be my pleasure."

"No, Lady Maude. As it pleases my wife."

Joanna wanted nothing so much as to sit down in a quiet corner; she felt as if her knees had turned to butter. She drew several uneven breaths, nerving herself to look up into Llewelyn's face. No matter how harshly he might treat her in time to come, she'd ever be grateful for what he'd just done, would never forget it. But what must he think of her, that she would make such a fool of herself? If he was furious, she could scarce blame him, and she said, very low, "Thank you, my lord. I'm so sorry, in truth I am. I did not mean to make a scene. I just wanted to . . ."

"To settle an old score?" he suggested softly, and as she raised her eyes to his, she saw in them only amused understanding.

If the Normans were indifferent and the Welsh aloof, there were wedding guests present who were absolutely elated by the marriage, the Marcher border lords with Welsh holdings. One by one they sought Joanna out, to wish her well, to express the hope that she'd soon bear Llewelyn a son, to praise her father's wisdom and foresight in making of Llewelyn an ally. She was surrounded now by a group of these men, one of whom was, to her delight, none other than Aubrey de Mara. He had fallen into Prince Llewelyn's hands when Llewelyn took Castle Mold some years back, he explained, and whilst waiting for his ransom to be paid, a mutual regard had developed. He did indeed think of the Prince as a friend, would never have missed his wedding to a girl he remembered with such fondness.

Joanna had no interest, however, in reminiscing of Mirebeau. Her concern was more immediate, was in learning all she could of the man to whom she was now wed. She was most interested, therefore, in what Llewelyn's Corbet kin had to say, listened attentively as Hugh Corbet obligingly related anecdotes of Llewelyn's Shropshire boyhood. Hugh gave her more comfort than even he knew; the mere fact that he'd remained on such friendly terms with Llewelyn, although his wife, Llewelyn's mother, was five years dead, was to Joanna reason for reassurance.

But she did not like Hugh's nephew, Thomas Corbet, not at all; she'd been greatly offended by several snide remarks he'd made, revealing a deep-seated dislike for Llewelyn. To make such remarks in her hearing was in the worst of taste, was to imply that she was ignorant of the most basic loyalties a wife owed her husband, and she soon made an excuse to escape the Corbet company.

A man lurched toward her, so unsteady on his feet that he could not stop in time, shoved Joanna back against the wall. She'd been introduced to him earlier in the evening, remembered him only because he was surely one of the last men she'd have expected to find at her wedding, Fulk Fitz Warin, the Shropshire baron who'd led an abortive rebellion against her father. He'd eventually capitulated, sued for John's pardon and, to the surprise of many, had gotten it. That seemed to be what was on his mind; he launched into a rather incoherent speech of gratitude, although she could not be sure whether he was praising her father for pardoning him or Llewelyn for giving him refuge.

Joanna was more amused than affronted; the man was so obviously besotted. She was glad, nonetheless, when several of his companions, slightly more sober, came to her rescue. They, too, had earlier introduced themselves as friends of her husband, Stephen and Baldwin de Hodnet; with extravagantly elaborate apologies, they sought now to distract Fitz Warin. But he, with the peculiar obstinacy of the inebriated, was determined to continue his disjointed conversation with Joanna, assuring her solemnly that he wished only the best for her, that Prince Llewelyn was indeed a lucky man, and then, to Joanna's horror, that it was surely time to escort her and her lord husband to the bridal chamber.

Joanna stared at him in dismay. His voice was overly loud, carried. At any moment others might hear, pick up the chant, and she was not ready yet, needed more time. Her fear of the marriage bed was not a fear of Llewelyn himself, for he had given her no reason to think he'd be brutal or abusive. Her fear was rather of the unknown. She could not imagine what it would be like, other than that there would be pain, and she shrank from the thought of being used so intimately by a man who was, in all respects, a stranger to her.

But if her aversion to the bedding itself was rooted in ignorance, her fear of the bedding revels was grounded in experience.

She'd been to countless weddings, knew all too well what to expect. The women would take her up to the bridal chamber, where she would be undressed and made ready for her husband. The men would then follow with Llewelyn, would see that he was stripped and put into bed with her. Even under ideal circumstances, the bedding ceremony was an open invitation to unseemly and bawdy behavior, to raunchy, crude humor; at worst, it could degenerate into a drunken brawl. Joanna dreaded the bedding revels even more than she did the actual consummation of her marriage, and she pleaded now with Fitz Warin, "Do hush, please! Not so loud!"

He merely blinked at her in bleary incomprehension, but at that moment, much to Joanna's relief, Llewelyn sauntered over and not only managed to quiet Fitz Warin, but was able to send the man reeling off in search of the Earl of Chester.

"Thank you," Joanna said, as soon as the de Hodnets went weaving off after Fitz Warin, vowing to keep him out of trouble. Thanking Llewelyn was, she thought, getting to be a habit. But he did have a most convenient sense of timing, in truth.

It occurred to her suddenly to wonder if he could possibly be keeping an eye on her, but she had no time to ponder the unlikelihood of that, forgot all else when he said, "I could not help hearing. I gather you'd as soon shun the bedding revels?"

Joanna gave him a startled look, quickly averted her eyes. She was not accustomed to having her face read as easily as this, did not like it in the least. But she was too dispirited to lie. "Yes, I would," she admitted, offering no further explanation. She was so tired of struggling to camouflage her reluctance, to play her part. Let him think what he would.

Llewelyn was pleased, for she'd touched in him a protective chord from their first moments together in the window seat. He welcomed this opportunity, wanting to ease her qualms if he could, to see the fear fade from her eyes. Nor would he deny that the challenge of seeking to outwit an entire hall full of people had in itself an almost irresistible appeal.

"In a few moments, Joanna, I want you to make your way toward the south end of the hall . . . without attracting attention. Once you reach the door, just wait there for me. Can you do that?"

"Yes, but . . . but why?"

"Did you not say you had no taste for the bedding revels?"

"I do not understand," Joanna said slowly. "We could never

hope to escape the hall unseen. Nor could you forbid the revelries. Too many men are drunk, beyond reason.''

''I can see your father never told you much of his campaigns, did he? You're woefully ignorant of battle tactics,'' Llewelyn said and grinned. ''No more questions. You must take me on trust, love, or not at all!''

The unexpected endearment so flustered Joanna that she abandoned further argument, did as he bade. By the time she'd taken up her position near the door, she'd managed to guess what he had in mind; a quick glance back over her shoulder caught him in whispered collusion with two of his men. But even though she was expecting what happened next, the realism of the brawl took her by surprise. A shove, a snarl, and suddenly they were rolling about on the floor, pummeling one another with enough verve to draw all eyes. Joanna, too, found herself straining to see, did not even notice Llewelyn's approach until he grabbed her hand, pulled her through the doorway.

''Make haste,'' he warned, ''ere we be missed,'' hurrying her across the solar, toward the corner stairwell. They were only halfway up when they heard the sudden noise rising from the hall. Llewelyn swore, quickened his pace, all but dragging a breathless Joanna after him. By the time they reached the top of the stairs, they could hear a hue and cry below, but by then Llewelyn had the door open, shoved Joanna inside. He was laughing so hard that he could hardly get the bolt into place, managed it only moments before the first of their pursuers lurched against the door.

Joanna sank down, panting, upon a coffer. ''My lord, that was wonderful!'' she exclaimed, looking at Llewelyn with shining eyes.

Still laughing, Llewelyn moved to the table, reached for a wine flagon. ''Do you not think it time you began to make use of my given name?'' he asked, and with that, Joanna's excitement congealed into ice.

''Do you want wine?''

Joanna shook her head, at once regretted her refusal. Mayhap wine would have warmed, have thawed this frozen feeling that seemed centered in the pit of her stomach. Unable to meet Llewelyn's eyes, she glanced nervously about the chamber. Isabelle and the other ladies had done their work well. There were fresh rushes for the floor, a plenitude of candles, wine, and wafers, a well-stoked fire, for May nights could be chill in Cheshire. The enormous bed was one of Chester's best, curtained and piled high with coverlets; there were even flower petals strewn over the turned-back sheets.

"Oh, no!" Joanna was on her feet, staring at the bed. "My lo—Llewelyn, the blessing! I did not think of it before, but in shunning the revels, we'll forfeit, as well, the priest's blessing of our marriage bed!"

"Well, that can be remedied easily enough. We need only open the door."

Joanna's hesitation was brief. From the noise in the stairwell, it sounded as if half of the wedding party were congregating outside the door. No longer pounding for admittance, they'd begun to serenade the bridal couple with ribald good humor, interspersing the song with rather explicit encouragements and instructions.

"No, let's make do without the blessing," she said hastily, and Llewelyn bit back a smile. Setting the wine cup down, he said, "Joanna, come here."

She did, slanting one swift look up at him through her lashes, a look of involuntary entreaty.

"Your veil is askew." Tossing it onto the table, he let his hand linger upon her hair. Her lashes now shadowed her cheeks. She scarcely seemed to be breathing, so still was she, but her body was rigid under his touch; sliding his fingers along her throat, he could feel the wild throbbing of her pulse.

When had he first realized he could not take this little girl to bed? When she'd fled the window seat, leaving behind a rose-colored veil? Or was it when she'd begged him to let her keep her dog, sounding for all the world like one of his own daughters? He leaned down, brushed his lips against her forehead. He could find in himself no desire to bed a child. Mayhap if she were naked under him in bed . . . but why should he force himself to a coupling that would give him little pleasure and her none at all? It had been only two days, after all, since he'd lain with Cristyn. He felt no particular need for a woman tonight, would as soon sleep; in truth, it had been no small strain, seeking to keep his men and Chester's from each other's throats. But how best to explain it to the lass, to keep her from seeing his restraint as rejection?

"I would not have you fear me, Joanna. I would not ever hurt you, God's truth, I would not."

"I shall do my best to be a good wife," Joanna said, almost inaudibly, sounding so young that Llewelyn felt a sharp pang of pity.

"Joanna, listen. You need not deny your fears, not to me. It is only natural that you should have such qualms. I think, though, that I can ease your mind. We have time enough and more, need not consummate our marriage this first night. There is no reason why we cannot wait until I am not such a stranger to you."

Joanna stared at him, openmouthed. She did not know what to say, almost thanked him, realizing just in time how insulting that would sound. He'd turned away, moving to extinguish the candles. She watched until he began to undress, then she retreated to the other side of the bed, fumbling with the lacings of her bliaut. Unlike Llewelyn, who stripped with casual haste, letting his clothes drop where they lay, she took her time, carefully folding each garment in turn, not approaching the bed until he was already settled under the coverlets. Sliding in on her side of the bed, she tensed as Llewelyn leaned toward her, but he merely kissed her lightly on the cheek, murmured, "Sleep well, Siwan."

Only then did Joanna relax, stretch out on the sheets. She lay very still for a time, listening to Llewelyn's even breathing beside her in the dark, utterly bewildered by the perversity of her own emotions. She should be so thankful, so grateful for this reprieve . . . and she was. So why, then, was there this strange sense of . . . almost of letdown? Why was there such a flat, empty feeling? It was not at all uncommon for a man to wed a very young girl, not laying with her until she was of age. But she was not a child. She was fourteen, fully two years older than Isabelle when Papa had bedded her. No man would ever have abstained from Isabelle's bed, that she knew for certes. How little to Llewelyn's liking she must be.

Without warning, tears filled her eyes. She blinked them back angrily, wiped her face on the corner of the sheet. She'd not give in to self-pity. She had no cause to feel sorry for herself. Llewelyn could have been so different, could have been arrogant, crude, even cruel. But he was none of those things. Had he not been Welsh, had he only been a Norman lord, she would have been thanking God for her good fortune. And the worst was now over, their first meeting, the wedding, the bedding revels, the—

"Oh, Jesus God!"

Sitting upright in the bed, she reached over, shook Llewelyn's shoulder. "Llewelyn, Llewelyn, wake up . . . please!" He awakened at her touch, but looked at her so blankly that she realized he did not at once remember who she was. "The sheets! Come morning, the wedding party will enter our chamber, will examine the sheets to see if they be bloodied, to see if I came to my marriage bed a virgin. But the sheets will be clean! They'll be clean, and I . . . I'll be shamed, shamed before all . . .''

Llewelyn swore under his breath; the words were Welsh, but his tone needed no translation. Joanna shrank back. For a long moment, his eyes rested upon her face; even in the firelight, her pallor showed all too clearly. And then he threw the covers back, rose from the bed. Joanna heard him bump into the table, curse again, and she pulled the sheet up under her chin, having no idea what he was searching for in the dark.

There was a sudden flare of light; Llewelyn had at last found flint and tinder. He lingered by the table long enough to drink what remained in his wine cup. Now that he was fully awake, his sense of humor was beginning to reassert itself, and he was laughing quietly to himself by the time he returned to the bed; this was, after all, hardly the way he'd expected to pass his wedding night.

"Hold this," he said, thrusting a candle toward Joanna. Her eyes widened at sight of the slender dagger blade, and he could not help laughing again. What in God's name did she think he meant to do with it? "I hope you do not mind, love, if you lose your maidenhead with only modest bleeding? I've been fighting for nigh on twenty years, and have had my share of hurts, but I can say for certes that never will I get a stranger scar!"

Joanna said nothing, watched as he drew the blade against the underside of his forearm, stanched the bleeding with the sheets. She was very close at that moment to hating him; what was to him such a source of obvious amusement was to her an acute humiliation. How could he laugh at her like this, be so cruel? Did he not realize how it shamed her, that she must fake the loss of her virginity, when other wives, no matter how plain, were wanted, bedded, even cherished?

Llewelyn was leaning over, concealing the knife under the bed, and she breathed upon the candle. When he would have kissed her cheek, she averted her face, and he gave her a sudden thoughtful look, but he said only, "You'd best sleep now, Siwan. We do depart for Wales on the morrow."

"You did call me that before . . . *She*-one. What does it mean?"

"Siwan?" Llewelyn yawned. "It is Welsh for Joan or Joanna."

"I am Joanna! Not Siwan, Joanna! I'll not lose my name, too!" No sooner were the words out of her mouth than Joanna froze, appalled by what she'd done. A wife had no right to speak so to her husband. Women were beaten for much less. Llewelyn had raised himself up on his elbow, was staring at her, his face unreadable in the shadowy light. She swallowed, whispered, "I am sorry, my lord, so sorry—"

"No, Joanna, you owe me no apology," he interrupted, and then added something utterly incomprehensible to her. "You see," he said softly, "my mother's name was Marared . . . not Margaret." There was a pause, and then he rolled over, reached for his pillow. "Joanna it shall be. But I ought to warn you; I do not know what my people will make of it. Most of them speak no French . . . and there is no letter *J* in the Welsh alphabet."

The chamber was quiet. Feeling somehow as if she'd won the battle but lost the war, Joanna slid over, until the width of the bed was between them. It was only then that the full impact of his words registered with her. On the morrow, he'd said, they would depart for Wales. She'd been wrong, so very wrong. The worst was not over.

16

ABER, NORTH WALES

May 1206

Wales, Llewelyn explained to Joanna, was divided into cantrefs and commotes, similar in nature to the English shires. His favorite palace was at Aber, the royal seat of the commote of Arllechwedd Uchaf, fifty-three miles west of Chester. It was a journey of two days; they rode into Aber at dusk on Saturday.

"We're home, Joanna." Reining in beside her, Llewelyn smiled. "Aber Gwyngregyn—Mouth of the White Shell River."

"A beautiful name," Joanna said faintly. Only now were her breathing and heartbeat getting back to normal. She'd never been so frightened as in the past few hours, clinging dizzily to her mare's saddle pommel as the horse picked its way along an alpine trail of truly treacherous dimensions. So narrow that two horses could not ride abreast, so close to the cliff that Joanna could hear the pounding of surf against the rocks below. The pass of Penmaenmawr, Llewelyn called it, Welsh for "End of the Large Stone." By then, alerted by Joanna's chalk-white pallor, he'd taken the mare's reins himself, and as the trail wound ever upward, Joanna had at last simply closed her eyes, sought to concentrate only upon the reassuring murmur of Llewelyn's voice. She was embarrassed at showing her fear so nakedly, although at least she'd retained more dignity than Blanche, who, when not whimpering, was sobbing prayers to every saint on the Church calendar. Joanna belatedly understood why Llewelyn had declined the Earl of Chester's offer of a baggage cart. She could only marvel at the nonchalance of the Welsh, who braved these heights with the ease of eagles, and she was grateful when Llewelyn, after assuring her that Aber was not perched upon a mountain peak, confessed that he had no liking himself for the sea, never set foot on shipboard without feeling his stomach lurch, sink like a stone.

She was indeed lucky, Joanna reminded herself now, had no cause for complaint in the husband God and her father had given her. And she would do her best somehow to make his world her own. With that resolution, she drew rein for her first look upon Aber.

Llewelyn's palace was encircled by a deep, man-made ditch, fortified by wooden palisades, much like John's favorite hunting lodges at Freemantle and Clipstone. Passing through the gatehouse into a bailey packed with people, Joanna saw wooden buildings such as she'd expect in any Norman lord's manor: stables and barn, a kiln and kitchens, privy chambers, kennels for Llewelyn's hunting dogs, quarters for those not bedding down in the great hall. Joanna was not sure what she'd thought to find, but she felt relief, nonetheless, that her surroundings were so familiar, were neither alien nor exotic.

Llewelyn had no sooner dismounted than he was engulfed by well-wishers. For the moment forgotten, Joanna watched as a young boy and several small girls ran forward, flung themselves into Llewelyn's arms. Joanna was taken aback by the exuberance of their welcome; she would never have given her father so uninhibited a public greeting. But she was not as startled as she might have been twenty-four hours earlier. In that brief span, she'd seen ample evidence to document the Norman aphorism that there was not a Welshman born who did know his proper place. For certes, she thought, none of her father's subjects would have dared approach him as these Welsh men and women were crowding around Llewelyn.

Llewelyn had remembered he was bringing back a bride, and moving toward Joanna, he reached up to lift her from the saddle. Acutely aware of all eyes upon her, she slid to the ground, smiled at her husband's children. They were attractive youngsters, but solemn, unsmiling, and remembering her own nervous unease about meeting Isabelle, Joanna's heart went out to them.

Seated beside Llewelyn upon the dais in the great hall, Joanna received the acknowledgments of her husband's subjects, now hers, too. While the chief officers of Llewelyn's court spoke French of necessity, few of their wives did, and relieved of the need to make polite conversation, Joanna felt free to let her thoughts wander as they would. The gowns of the women were much like those at her father's court. But on their hair they wore only thin veils. Would Llewelyn want her to put aside her wimples? The men looked rather like Papa's nobles, too, though not so finely garbed. She slanted a sideways look toward Llewelyn. His tunic was shorter than the gown in which he'd been wed, the long, lavishly furred robe of a highborn Norman lord; both tunic and chausses were a subdued shade of green, his boots higher than was fashionable at her father's court, reaching to the knee. She was glad he'd dressed so richly for their wedding, would not have wanted Chester and the other lords to scorn him for the strangeness of his Welsh ways.

Mayhap life would not be as harsh and austere as she'd first feared. Looking about the great hall, she might well have been at Windsor or Winchester. And her bedchamber was in no way inferior to the royal apartments set aside for Isabelle's use. The rushes were sweet-smelling, the walls whitewashed, the bed hung with curtains, and the mattress filled with down, not straw. She'd not dared to ask Llewelyn if she would have her own quarters, like her stepmother and the queens on the Continent, and her relief had been intense and overwhelming upon finding it was so. But mingled with that relief was a reluctant sense of shame. No matter how often she told herself she had no reason for self-reproach, she flushed every time she thought of what she'd done at Rhuddlan Castle.

Llewelyn had taken Rhuddlan some ten years ago, and there they'd passed the second night of their marriage. They'd covered thirty-six miles, and Joanna was very tired. She was also utterly wretched, longing for what she'd left behind and dreading what lay ahead. Excusing herself soon after supper, she retired to their bedchamber, and when Llewelyn came to bed, she lay very still, pretended to sleep. Remembering that now, Joanna bit her lip, twisted her wedding ring until it chafed her finger. For a wife to deny her husband his marital rights was a sin of no small proportions. Not that she'd actually refused him, of course. But she could not stifle an uneasy suspicion that she'd violated the spirit, if not the letter, of her marriage vows.

Across the hall, her stepchildren had withdrawn into one of the window recesses. Joanna had been awaiting just such an opportunity to speak to them alone, and picking up Sugar, she made her way toward them. They rose at her approach, the girls staring more at Sugar than at Joanna, for such small dogs were a rarity in Wales. Gruffydd, however, kept his eyes focused upon Joanna's face; they were a vivid sea green, fringed with thick golden lashes. He was a handsome lad, Joanna thought, if very unlike his father. His sister Gwenllian shared his coloring, had pale skin and auburn hair, burnished curls spilling down her back in a cascade of copper, while Gwladys and Marared were as dark as Gruffydd and Gwenllian were fair. They were a striking quartet, but as wary as fawns, would need gentle handling. Joanna smiled, held out the dog toward Gwenllian, the youngest.

"Would you like to pet her?" The child reached out, her fingers brushing Sugar's long, silky fur, but Gwladys hissed something in Welsh, and Gwenllian jerked her hand back.

"You need not fear; she'll not bite," Joanna said reassuringly. Getting no response, she tried another approach. "As I do not speak Welsh, I should like to make sure that I am saying your names correctly. *Griff*-ith, is it not? And *Glad*-is? Your lord father told me that is Welsh for Claudia . . ." Her voice trailed off, for a disconcerting thought had just come to her. "You do speak French?"

The little girls were now looking not at Joanna, but at their brother. Gruffydd drew an audible breath. Joanna caught but one word of the outburst that followed: *Saeson*. As ignorant as she was of Welsh, she knew *Saeson* to be a contemptuous term for the English. But even had she not known its meaning, she would have needed no translation. It was there for all to read in the defiant jutting of Gruffydd's jaw, in Gwladys's black eyes, in Gwenllian and Marared's shocked giggles.

"Gruffydd!" The voice was angry, was so like Llewelyn's that Joanna was startled to see a stranger. No, not a stranger, she amended, for this man's kinship to her husband was emblazoned upon his face for all to see. He had Llewelyn's coloring, the same finely chiseled bone structure, the same deepset dark eyes. But his mouth was not Llewelyn's; thin and rigid, it spoke not of laughter, but of pain denied, of secrets never to be shared. He snapped a command in Welsh, and Gruffydd's color faded. Not looking at Joanna, he mumbled,

"I ask your forgiveness, Lady, for my bad manners."

"Of course," Joanna said automatically. The boy's French was flawless. She watched as he fled the hall, his sisters in flustered pursuit, and all she could think of was her own first meeting with Isabelle, of how little it had taken to win her heart.

"You must pay my nephew no mind, Madame. Ten is a troublesome age."

"You must be Lord Adda, Llewelyn's brother." Joanna ventured a smile, and he nodded gravely, shifted his crutch so he

could bow over her hand. Joanna almost implored him not to
make the effort, checked herself just in time.

"Do call me Joanna." She hesitated, but who else was there to
ask? "My lord . . . Adda, will you tell me the truth? There was
not much sentiment amongst your people for this marriage, was
there?"

He did not reply at once, but she got the impression not that he
was weighing his words, rather that he was weighing her, assessing her ability to accept honesty. "No," he said at last. "Most of
Llewelyn's subjects would rather he'd wed a Cymraes . . . a
woman of our blood. But a Welsh wife would bring few political
gains, so they'd reconciled themselves to a foreign marriage. It
was thought Llewelyn would wed the daughter of the Manx
King, but then your father did offer you in her stead. Llewelyn
would have had to be utterly mad, of course, to refuse. But not
all are as clear-sighted as he, and some were affronted that he
would take an English wife. I do not mean to offend you, but the
Welsh have been given little reason to love the English."

Joanna had never thought of herself as English; in fact, to one
of Norman-French descent, that qualified as an insult. She did
not quibble at Adda's inaccuracy, however, realizing that to the
Welsh, the distinction drawn between Norman and Saxon was
irrelevant. But that understanding only intensified her sense of
isolation, her awareness that she was a political pledge, a hostage
for England's amity.

"I thank you for your honesty, Adda. Be honest with me now,
too. Tell me if you believe Gruffydd will come to accept me as
his father's wife."

Adda was silent for some moments. "He's a headstrong boy,
thinks the world of Llewelyn . . . and for five years he has not
had to share his father's love. It is only natural that he should
resent you, see you as a rival, an intruder . . ." But Joanna was,
after all, very young herself, and Adda compromised his candor
with a half-truth, adding, "Mayhap with time . . ."

"Yes, with time," Joanna echoed, lowering her lashes to hide
her hurt.

Joanna's life as Princess of Gwynedd was not utterly devoid of
compensations or satisfactions. Never before had she her own
private bedchamber. Never before had she money of her own.
All her life she'd been dependent upon the generosities of others.
But as Llewelyn's consort, she had her own privy purse, was
entitled to one-third of his private incomes. As far as she knew,

English law made no like provision for English queens. Nor had she ever before experienced the sweetness of giving commands, of having them obeyed at once. She'd been greatly pleased when her father had engaged Blanche for her. Now she had her own household: chaplain, seneschal, chief groom, handmaiden, candle bearer, doorkeeper, page, even her own cook and food taster. If she wanted to write to her Aunt Ela, she need only dictate to her chaplain, and within the hour a courier would be dispatched to Salisbury Castle. Bread, a staple of the Norman diet, was not as often found upon Welsh tables; they were herdsmen, not farmers. Joanna had casually confessed to a longing for wheaten bread, making but idle conversation with Blanche and Enid, her Welsh maid. The next day a freshly baked loaf was laid out by her trencher, and at every meal thereafter.

For the first time in her life, Joanna understood what a potent drink power could be. And she realized, too, that she'd not known herself as well as she once thought, that she was not so lacking in ambition, after all. It seemed that she was Eleanor of Aquitaine's granddaughter in more ways than one, a thought that gave her amusement and astonishment in equal measure.

But these pleasures were of fleeting moment, fireflies in the dark. The summer that followed her marriage was the most miserable of her life. Unable to speak Llewelyn's language, she felt herself an isolated island in a sea of Welsh. Since she had no duties to perform, her days were unstructured, endless. She was not blind to the beauty around her. Aber fronted on the sea, offering spectacular views of the Eryri Mountains. But at night she lay awake, longing for the sounds of the city, shivering at the distant howling of a wolf pack on the prowl. London, York, and Winchester seemed as far away as Jerusalem. Her husband's domain held neither towns nor cities. No fairs or markets. It was, to Joanna, a wild and awesome land, and she knew that Gruffydd was not alone in thinking her an intruder.

She was desperately homesick in those first weeks. Her yearning for her loved ones, for what was known and familiar to her, was a constant, unrelenting ache. She so wanted to go home, and knew that what she most wanted was now forever denied her.

The worst of her loneliness was that she did not feel connected to any other living soul. Her father and Isabelle were in Gascony. So, too, were Richard and her Uncle Will. Blanche, never a comfort even in the best of times, had become all but insufferable; she hated Wales, looked askance at the Welsh, drove Joanna to distraction with her whining, her constant complaints.

Enid's French was inadequate for more than the most rudimentary conversation. Most of the women at Llewelyn's court spoke
no French at all. One of the few who did was the Lady Gwenllian,
wife to Llewelyn's friend Ednyved ap Cynwrig. But Gwenllian
offered no friendship; even her courtesy seemed grudgingly given.

Nor did Joanna have any better luck with the men. For a time
she'd hoped to find an ally in her husband's brother. But Adda
did not encourage her overtures. Aloof and reserved, he went his
own way; only with Llewelyn did he thaw, let his defenses
down. Ednyved, Joanna avoided if possible. She realized his
sarcasm was not meant to be spiteful, but all her life she'd been
wary of sardonic tongues. Rhys ap Cadell, her husband's other
intimate friend, was rarely at court that summer; his wife was in
the last stages of a troublesome pregnancy, and Rhys stayed upon
his own estates, awaiting Catrin's time. Men like Morgan ap
Bleddyn, Llewelyn's chaplain, and Gwyn ab Ednywain, his Seneschal, were well into their forties, had little in common with a
girl of fourteen.

As for her stepchildren, all of Joanna's fears had come to pass.
Gruffydd was not to be won over. Every smile Llewelyn bestowed upon her, Gruffydd begrudged. Each time he heard her
addressed as "Madame" or "Your Grace," his face shadowed.
Gwladys, the most devoted of disciples, loyally followed her
brother's lead, and between them they effectively curbed any
conciliatory inclinations that Marared or Gwenllian might have
harbored. To Joanna, this was the most bitter disappointment of
all.

Perversely enough, that which she had most reason to be
thankful for—Llewelyn's solicitude—was yet another source of
anxiety. Because he was so very good to her, she despised
herself all the more for her discontent. Each time she thought of
the French Queen Ingeborg, thought of the wives who'd have
bartered their very souls for a husband like hers, she felt an utter
ingrate. When compared to women who were beaten for trifles,
treated as chattels, used only as brood mares, what had she to
complain of, in truth? Isabelle had been right; many women
would indeed envy her.

Not that Llewelyn was without flaws. In fact, the qualities she
most admired in him, his easy self-assurance and his intelligence,
were virtues with the potential to become vices. His self-assurance
was occasionally flavored with arrogance, and like many quick-
witted people, he was often impatient when others were slow to
follow the swiftness of his thoughts. He had a tendency to lose

sight of the immediate in pursuit of the long-range goal. And his
ambition was frightening to Joanna. For if her father aimed to
prevent a Welsh-French alliance, Llewelyn had aims of his own.
He saw their marriage as a way to keep John out of Wales,
enabling him to deal with his old enemy, Gwenwynwyn of
Powys. But Joanna did not think her father would give Llewelyn
the free hand in Wales that he seemed to expect. She remembered all too well her father's remark upon the day of her
betrothal, that Llewelyn needed to be "reined in." She could
imagine nothing worse than conflict between the two, to find
herself torn between her husband, to whom she owed her loyalty,
and her father, to whom she owed her love.

But Llewelyn's faults seemed of little consequence when she
thought back to Chester's aloof moodiness or William de Braose's
suave brutality. And in the three months of her marriage, Joanna
had found much in him to admire. For all that he expected—and
got—prompt obedience, he was not arbitrary, and he was rarely
unfair. Once, when he'd flared up at his clerk, Hwfa ap Pilthe, in
an unjustified public rebuke, he'd later sought Hwfa out and
offered apology; Joanna could not remember her father ever
apologizing to anyone for anything. But Llewelyn was much
more easygoing than her father. He was quick to laugh, even at
himself, had been amused, not affronted, when Joanna could not
resist teasing that she wished she could be as sure of one thing as
he was of all things. And he was unfailingly kind to her.

It was true that he did not treat her like a wife. His was more
the casual, affectionate playfulness of an older brother for a much
younger sister. But he never failed to smile at sight of her, saw
that she was accorded all due respect as his Princess, just as he'd
done on their wedding day, when he'd backed her up before
Maude de Braose; she was convinced now that there was nothing
coincidental in his providential appearances that night. And since
their marriage, he had always been there when she most needed
him, as on that dreadful day when her dog chased a squirrel onto
the wooded slopes of Maes y Gaer, and she'd come running to
him in a panic, for Sugar was all she had of home. He had
soothed her, sent men out to search for the dog, had even
forborne to tease, at least until after the animal was found.

Above all, Joanna appreciated Llewelyn's kindness in not
flaunting his concubines at court. Even had she been sharing his
bed, she would not have expected him to be faithful; fidelity was
a marriage vow for women. She did not doubt that Llewelyn had
a mistress. But he did not do as so many Norman lords did,

parade his conquests before one and all, heedless of his wife's discomfort. Not all men did swagger over their sins, of course. Her father had amazed many with his unexpected discretion after taking Isabelle as his bride. He was not faithful to Isabelle, but for a man notorious for his wenching, he showed a surprising sensitivity to Isabelle's pride. Joanna alone had not been surprised, for she knew that, in his way, her father loved Isabelle. But Llewelyn did not love Joanna, and that made his consideration all the more remarkable to her, made her all the more grateful for it.

Llewelyn was her one comfort in a world that frightened her, and she regretted deeply that he was so often gone from Aber. He was a man ever in search of additional hours in the day, juggling innumerable interests like so many colored balls, presiding over the Uchel Lys, his High Court, fortifying his various mountain strongholds, consulting with vassal lords, with his rhaglaws and rhingylls—bailiffs and court officials. Like John, he traveled extensively about his realm. But John always took Isabelle with him, and Llewelyn never offered to take her.

The great hall was lit by rushlight; torches were used sparingly in Wales, pine and fir trees being less common there than in England. It was a cool night for August, and a fire blazed in the center hearth. Of all that Joanna found foreign in Wales, the altered dinner hour had been hardest for her to accept. In England, dinner, the main meal of the day, was served between ten and eleven in the forenoon, followed by a light supper at five. But the Welsh ate just one meal a day, and that in the evening.

The food and the trestle tables had been cleared away. Llewelyn was sitting by the hearth, picking out a plaintive melody on a finely tuned harp. Joanna knew no people who loved music as the Welsh did. Every house, no matter how poor, had a harp; it passed by law to the youngest son, could never be seized for debt. Remembering how her father's lords had sneered at the Welsh passion for music, claiming that every pigsty did hold a harp, Joanna frowned. The unfairness of that gibe rankled. Whatever their faults, the Welsh were not at all as Normans saw them; that she could say with certainty after three months in their midst.

Llewelyn was the focal point of all eyes. While that was normally the case, there was an emotional intensity in the looks he was getting tonight, for he had given them all a bad scare. Five days ago, he and a few friends had gone off for a day's hunting. Because it was not an official circuit or *clych*, had no purpose but pleasure, he had been accompanied by only a token escort, and when the second day passed without word from him, a sense of unease began to spread. By the third day, all pretense was gone, and people were openly voicing their concern. Joanna found her sleep haunted by visions of twisting mountain trails; she could not stop thinking of the wolves that roamed the lower slopes of the Eryri Mountains, nor of the tusked wild boars that could disembowel a horse, rip apart a man with such murderous ease. But it was not until she talked to Enid that she became aware of a more sinister undertone to their fears. Fumbling for words, Enid drew upon enough broken French to convey Llewelyn's true danger, that he might have strayed too close to the Powys border. She needed to say no more; Joanna understood all too well. Gwenwynwyn would gladly risk war for a chance to catch Llewelyn off guard, for with Llewelyn's death, Gwenwynwyn would stand alone as the unchallenged power in North Wales.

On the fourth day, Rhys had ridden in from his own estates on the isle of Môn, at once ordered out search parties. That night Joanna could not bear to withdraw to her own chambers, remained in the great hall, where word would first come. Ednyved's wife, Gwenllian, was there, too, and she made Joanna feel as if she were somehow intruding where she had no right to be. But for all the resentment smoldering in Gwenllian's eyes, Joanna was utterly unprepared to hear her remark, "I marvel that she does pretend to such concern. Who does not know, after all, that Llewelyn's death would give her what she most craves—widowhood." Joanna had been too shocked for anger, and thinking back upon it later, she'd sought to find excuses for the other woman, reminding herself that Gwenllian's husband was missing, too. Yet no matter how she tried to mitigate Gwenllian's malice, she knew the woman had meant for her to overhear; she'd spoken in French.

Soon after midnight, a courier from Llewelyn had ridden in. After that first surge of relief, Joanna blessed her husband's good manners, for he'd addressed the message to her, and she had the satisfaction of telling Gwenllian and the others that he was safe. There'd been a mishap, as feared, but the trouble had befallen one of Llewelyn's men; he'd taken a fall, broken a leg, had to be carried on a makeshift horse litter to the nearest shelter, the mountain priory at Beddgelert.

Remembering that now, Joanna was remembering, too, how she'd once hoped most fervently for Llewelyn's death. Not that she'd actually prayed for it; such sinful prayers were all too likely to rebound upon the one seeking them. But she had wished for his death, would willingly have bought her freedom with his blood. Yet during the past four days, she had felt only anxiety. Not once had it even crossed her mind that with Llewelyn's death, she would be a widow, free to return to her world, her people. Why had it not? She found herself watching Llewelyn's fingers move nimbly over the harp strings; he did, as Isabelle noted, have beautiful hands. Was the answer truly so difficult? She had not known Llewelyn before; it was easy enough to wish for the death of a stranger. But now . . . now he was very real to her, a flesh-and-blood man with a passionate love for life, a man who'd shown her only kindness, a man she liked, liked very much.

No, she did not want Llewelyn to die, most assuredly not. She was not even sure she wanted to end their marriage. This alliance was no less important to Papa now than it had been nigh on two years ago. Nor was it likely that she'd be so fortunate in her father's selection of a second husband. Moreover, in the eyes of Holy Church, she was Llewelyn's wife, for better or worse. Mayhap if she were not wife in name only . . . mayhap then she would not be so unhappy, would not feel so utterly alone. It was not the first time this thought had occurred to her. And why not? She was old enough to be a wife, in just a month would be fifteen. Nor had she any reason to shun Llewelyn's bed. Isabelle said a woman's pleasure depended upon the man. Watching her husband, Joanna felt color creeping into her cheeks. Llewelyn was not a man to abuse a woman, in bed or not. She had nothing to fear from him, was sure he'd be gentle, tender even.

But what did it matter that she was now willing to be a true wife to Llewelyn, when he showed no desire to take her to his bed? She could scarcely go to him, after all. She could only wait, until his need for an heir would bring him to her bed. For now she did remain in limbo, a wife and yet not a wife. Just as at her father's court. The King's bastard daughter, not truly belonging there, either.

Llewelyn put aside the harp, studied his friends with exasperated amusement. "Jesú, to hear you all talk, I'm in need of a keeper! What did you think, that I'd go blundering into Powys like some green stripling? You should only see the day dawn, Rhys, when I do get lost in Gwynedd!"

"Not lost," Morgan interjected dryly. "It did cross our minds that you might have deliberately sought to lure Gwenwynwyn into breaking the truce."

"Well, what better bait? That is a thought well worth exploring. But you should have known I'd not have been such a fool as to try it with only ten men."

"How many have you in mind?" Adda asked laconically, and Llewelyn laughed.

"It'll not take as many as I once thought . . . thanks to my father-in-law, the English King. If Gwenwynwyn expects John to pull his chestnuts from the fire, they'll be well roasted, in truth."

Rhys's eyes kindled with sudden interest. He knew that Llewelyn's dislike of the Powys Prince was as much personal as political; Gwenwynwyn was responsible for the murder of Llewelyn's uncle Owain at Carreghova, and a blood debt demanded blood payment. "Are you sure that John will not interfere?"

"As sure as any man can be when dealing with a snake. John and I came to an understanding at Worcester; it was that which he used to sweeten his offer of marriage. He gets what he wants, me as ally . . . expecting, I daresay, that a son-in-law will be easier to keep on a short leash. I get what I want—Powys. And Gwenwynwyn gets . . . trouble."

They all laughed at that, but Ednyved could not help cautioning, "Assuming, of course, that John can be trusted."

Llewelyn grinned. "I know what you're thinking, that it's risky indeed to sup with the Devil. But rest assured, I do plan to use a very long spoon!"

Glancing across the hall, Llewelyn's gaze was drawn to his girl-wife. Such an innocent-looking lass, a sweet bird in the hand, so unlikely an instrument of Gwenwynwyn's downfall. But there was a sadness about her that he'd never before noticed; how forlorn she seemed, a flower put down in alien soil. Rising, he crossed to her, leaned over to murmur, "It occurs to me, lass, that you've yet to see much of my homeland. What say you we remedy that? On the morrow, should you like me to take you into the Eryri Mountains, to show you those sights closest to my heart?" He'd spoken on impulse, and it was an offer that would cause him no small inconvenience, would result in the utter disruption of his plans for the week, but he thought himself more than repaid now by the delighted smile that lit up Joanna's face.

It was to be one of the happiest days Joanna had known in months. Although both Ednyved and Rhys opted to accompany them, Llewelyn rode at her side, devoted his attentions to her alone, speaking with animation and at length of that which men rarely discussed with women.

He explained why he thought the bishopric of St David's should be independent of Canterbury, why he wanted a Welsh-born bishop for the See of Bangor. He was in the process now, he confided, of codifying Welsh law, that which had been passed down from the tenth-century Prince of blessed memory, Hywel the Good. Not that he thought Hywel's code to be sacrosanct, come down from Mount Sinai carved in stone. Laws needed to be flexible, to reflect the changing needs of changing times. For example, under the old laws, an act of violence was a crime against only the victim. If the offender made proper restitution to the victim's kin, he was absolved of further liabilities. That was no longer enough; Llewelyn would have the man held account-able to his Prince, too. In that way, society could be better served, made safer for those dwelling under the law. But he was encountering some resistance. There were those who clung mind-lessly to the old ways. As it was once done, so must it always be done, till the memory of man runneth not to the contrary, he said, and laughed ruefully.

Joanna listened intently, awed by the realization that Llewelyn was even more ambitious than she had first thought. But his ambition went well beyond what most men sought, power and land, entailed no less than a transformation of Welsh society. She'd never before met anyone who dared to dream so big, and she found herself hoping that he'd not be disappointed, that his dreams would indeed come to pass.

She was no less interested in personal than in political revela-tions, listened with fascination as he talked of his mother, with such obvious affection that she felt a rush of empathy, thinking that his abiding love for Marared was very like her own love for her father. He spoke but briefly of Marared's death, saying only that he thanked God she'd lived to see him in sovereign control of all of Gwynedd, and then he gave Joanna a deliberately lighthearted account of the rebellion begun at fourteen—''just your age, lass.'' It seemed perfectly natural to Joanna to tell him, in turn, of her own life, to tell him what she'd never before told anyone but John, of her mother's despairing last days, even of that brutal rejection in the solar at Middleham Castle. Llewelyn reined in abruptly at that, with an exclamation of incredulous outrage.

''Christ of the Cross! He turned his back upon a child, his own sister's flesh and blood, not knowing or caring what evil might befall you?'' He shook his head. "These d'Arcys, where are their lands? Are they near the Welsh border?''

"No, in Derbyshire, I think.''

"A pity," he said, flashed her a sudden smile. "If ever there were people who do deserve a little trouble in their lives . . .''

"Almost, you sound as if you do mean that!'' Actually, it mattered little to Joanna whether he meant it or not. It was enough for her that he'd said it, that his first impulse had been to avenge her wrong, to inflict punishment for her pain. It was, she thought, as great a gift as anyone had ever offered her.

"Know you what Eryri does mean? 'The Haunt of Eagles.' Apt, is it not? Tell me, Joanna, what think you so far of Wales?''

Joanna hesitated. It was indeed a beautiful country, but awesome, foreboding, not a land to submit tamely to man's control. Stark grandeur it had, but Joanna yearned for a softer harmony. "Everywhere I look, I see a sight to take my breath, see mountains that might in truth serve as stepping stones to Heaven. But . . . but it makes me feel very small, Llewelyn, as if I do count for naught.''

Llewelyn nodded. "Yes," he said approvingly. "But in time you'll come to see the splendor of it, too.'' Glancing back over his shoulder, he gave the signal to halt. "Rhys, hold the men here. I want to show Joanna Rhaeadr Ewynol.''

The sudden coolness of the air took Joanna by surprise. The woods were shaded with summer green, suddenly hushed and still as Llewelyn led her forward. She could hear the river now, glimpsed the fall of white water through the trees. But she hung back, no longer following as Llewelyn moved toward the edge of the cliff.

"I . . . I have an unease of heights,'' she said apologetically.

"So I've noticed," Llewelyn said and smiled at her. "But I'll not let you fall, do assure you that not one princess of Gwynedd has ever drowned in Rhaeadr Ewynol. That's it . . . lean back against me. See how much better the view is from here? This has ever been my favorite place. And Dolwyddelan is but nine miles to the south; we'll pass the night there and return to Aber on the morrow.''

Joanna was no longer listening. She felt no fear, for she was oblivious to the surging cataract, the wind-driven spray. Llewelyn was holding her back against his body; she could feel his encircling arms pressing against the undersides of her breasts, feel his breath upon her cheek, the soft tickle of his mustache against her temple, his hand warm on her wrist.

"You can let me go, Llewelyn. I am all right now," she said, but her voice was so muffled that he at once drew her back from the cliff.

"You're trembling, Joanna; were you as fearful as that? Your face is flushed, too . . ." He put his hand to her cheek, and Joanna gasped, wrenched free of his embrace, stumbling in her haste to put space between them.

Backing away, she leaned against the nearest tree. "I . . . I'm sorry, but I . . . I was afraid . . ."

"Yes, so I see," he said, and the coldness in his voice brought her eyes up to his face in utter dismay. As flustered as she'd been by his touch, that was as nothing to the way she felt now, with the wretched realization that he'd read fear into her confused recoil. She opened her mouth, but the words would not come. It was not that she'd liked his embrace too little; it was that she'd liked it too much. But how could she ever tell him that?

Ednyved crossed the great hall, sloshed a dripping cup into Llewelyn's hand. "Here. Whenever I am wroth with Gwenllian, I find mead to be a great restorative."

"Why should you think I'm wroth with Joanna?"

"Why, indeed? The lass spoke not three words at dinner, fled ere the tables could be cleared away, and now you keep to the hall like a man in search of sanctuary. But you have not quarreled—not you."

"I did not say that. I said I was not angry with Joanna. Well . . . I admit I did lose my temper this afternoon. I should not have, but I do keep forgetting how very young she is. It is for that reason that I've kept to the hall, my way of making amends. You see, Joanna did not realize there is no lady chamber here at Dolwyddelan. She took one look at our bed, and her face took on all the colors of sunset. So . . . I thought to give her time to get to sleep first . . . my good deed for the day!"

"She's nigh on fifteen, is she not?" Ednyved asked, his voice noncommittal.

"But she still has the emotions of a child, Ednyved, is not yet ready to be a wife."

"You know her better than I. But there are women who shrink from the marriage bed, from a man's touch. Are you sure that your Joanna is not one such?"

"As to that, I cannot be sure till I bed her. But I think not, think she merely needs time."

Ednyved looked at the other man, startled by a sudden surge of envy. It was obvious it had not even occurred to Llewelyn that Joanna simply might not find him to her liking. Just as it had not occurred to Rhys to worry whether Catrin would want him, would share his sudden passion. Ednyved reclaimed the cup of mead, wondering what it would be like to be so free of self-doubt. With only one woman had he felt it, with his first wife. Tangwystl, daughter of Lord Llywarch of Bran; he and Llewelyn had often joked about it, the confusion that resulted from their women sharing a Christian name. In the early years of their marriage, she'd come quite eagerly to his bed. But then the pregnancies began. Six sons she'd given him in less than nine years, had died giving birth to their last-born. Four years ago he'd married Gwenllian, heiress of Dyffryn Clwyd, daughter of Lord Rhys, Prince of South Wales. It was a brilliant match, but a loveless marriage. Most of the time he did not feel the lack. But there were nights, like this one, when he remembered the gentle, dark-eyed Tangwystl, felt the dull throb of an old grief.

"So what mean you to do, Llewelyn . . . wait for Joanna to grow up?"

"Why not? If a wife is not worth taking some trouble with, who is? Besides, I like the lass, would rather she be content than not." Llewelyn half rose, beckoned to a cupbearer. "Nor is my forbearance all that unselfish. What man would choose an indifferent bedmate over an ardent one? If Joanna needs time to reach womanhood, I'm willing to give her that time. It's not as if I need her now to warm my bed, after all." Llewelyn smiled at that, thinking of Cristyn.

"Indeed, I'd say not," Ednyved agreed, so emphatically that Llewelyn knew he, too, was thinking of Cristyn.

Dawn light was spilling through the open shutters. For a confused moment, Joanna did not remember where she was—not until she saw Llewelyn lying next to her in the bed. At that, she remembered all too well. She'd lain awake for hours, waiting for Llewelyn, desperately trying to decide what she could say to him. But when he'd finally come to bed, her courage had failed her again, and as on that night at Rhuddlan Castle, she'd taken refuge in feigned sleep.

Llewelyn was sprawled on his back; even in sleep, he sought space. He was only partially covered with the sheet, and Joanna saw now what he'd meant when he'd spoken of his "share of hurts." A knotted, faded scar seared the skin across his ribcage; another, more recent, zigzagged from armpit to collarbone.

Reaching for the sheet, she took care in tucking it about him. He had a third scar, almost invisible, a faint white mark just under his right eyebrow; she'd never noticed it before. Her eyes lingered upon his face, traced the sleep-softened curve of his mouth. Was it so much to have asked for? A husband she could respect, a marriage of mutual affection. She could have been well content with that. But this . . . she could take no joy now in what she was feeling for the man asleep beside her. All her life, she'd had a horror of making a fool of herself; what could come of this passionate yearning except hurt? And humiliation. Again she reached out; her fingers stopped just short of Llewelyn's cheek. In her innocence, she'd once thought the worst that could befall a woman was to find herself wed to a husband she did not want. But what of the wife wed to a man who did not want her?

17

ABER, NORTH WALES

September 1206

The air was cool and crisp. Like cider, Joanna thought; it carried
a snap. A fleet of rain-swollen clouds sailed across the sun,
casting sudden shadows upon the sand. Even the sea seemed to
lose color, to take on the chilled grey of darkest December.
Joanna shivered, pulled her mantle closer. And then the sun
broke through again, resurrecting all the glories of an afternoon
in early autumn.

The unexpected resurgence of warmth and light took Joanna
by surprise. It was almost, she acknowledged wryly, as if she
wanted leaden skies and biting winds, wanted a world that mirrored her mood. Snapping her fingers for Sugar, she walked
closer to the water's edge. Yr Afon Fenai, the Welsh called it,
the narrow strait that cut off the island of Môn from the mainland. It was, Llewelyn had told her, a deceptively dangerous
stretch of water, for the currents ran very swift, forming sudden
eddies and undertows; and where the tides came together, a lethal
whirlpool, Pwll Ceris, had taken more than a few men to a death
by drowning. Llewelyn had palaces on Môn, at Aberffraw and
Rhosyr. But she'd yet to see them; like so much of his life, that,
too, was closed to her.

A piece of driftwood lay at her feet. On impulse she knelt,
patted the sand smooth, and scrawled her name in the path of the
incoming tide. Beneath it she wrote LLEWELYN, and then watched
as the waves washed their names away. A dim memory stirred,
took on substance. So had she passed the time on another birthday, ten years past, lying in the heather before Middleham Castle
and laboriously tracing CLEMENCE and JOANNA in the dirt.

Birthdays had never been joyous occasions for her. Beneath

the surface celebration lurked a lingering unease, a vague fore-boding that she could neither identify nor yet ignore. She wondered suddenly if her aversion might not be rooted in that long-ago Yorkshire birthday. How vivid it still was: her desperate desire to please her mother, her futile yearning for a dog, the water stains upon her skirt, that closed bedchamber door. Two days later her mother was dead, leaving her with only the memory of a tear-splotched, swollen face, ghostly white in the moonlight.

Getting to her feet, Joanna tossed the stick out to sea, began to brush the sand from her mantle. Foolish to dwell upon a birthday ten years gone, to prod and prick at old hurts until they bled. Of all she least liked about herself, her weakness for self-pity must, for certes, lead the list. Nor was she going to squander what remained of this, her fifteenth birthday, in feeling sorry for herself. If truth be told, she was to blame, too. Why had she not told Llewelyn plain out that her birthday fell in mid-September? He would surely have marked the day in some way, might even have taken her with him to Cricieth Castle. But no, she'd had to be clever, had to test him, making just one deliberately casual mention over a fortnight ago. Had her words even registered with him? Or was it that he had not thought her birthday important enough to remember?

How right she'd been to be afraid, that night at Dolwyddelan Castle. She did not want to love Llewelyn. But she did not know how to stop. He had only to appear, and all others ceased to exist for her. So far she'd managed to cling to the shreds of her pride, but how long ere she well and truly singed her wings? She was so . . . so obvious, after all. Seeking him out on the slightest pretext, contriving reed-thin excuses to keep him in her company—only to freeze as soon as their eyes met, to find herself flustered, hopelessly tongue-tied. Joanna did not know which she feared more, that he should now think her an utter fool, or that he had not even noticed her peculiar behavior. She did know that she'd have given anything in her power to have him with her this day, that she missed him as she'd never missed anyone in all her life before.

Alerted by Sugar's barking, Joanna turned, saw her husband's two youngest daughters standing a short distance away, watching her with grave, wary eyes. Joanna started to speak, stopped; that road led nowhere. Instead she knelt and, using a shell as a shovel, began to scoop up handfuls of damp sand. Within mo-ments she had a castle motte, ready to receive the keep. She dug in silence, as if utterly intent upon her handiwork, not looking up until a small voice said, "Is that a Welsh or an English castle?"

Marared and Gwenllian were now close enough to touch. Joanna felt much the same pleasure she would have had a wild bird suddenly alighted upon her hand. "I do not know yet," she said thoughtfully. "What do you think it should be?"

"Welsh," Marared said, coming closer still, and when Joanna offered her the clam shell, she took it without hesitation. With four small hands to help, the castle was not long in taking on impressive dimensions: an inner and outer bailey, a thick curtain wall, a lopsided gatehouse that Gwenllian insisted she alone should build. Joanna deferred to their decisions, let them place the towers where they would. Nor did she try to draw them out in conversation, as she had in the past. And within the hour she had her reward.

Marared had settled back on her haunches to inspect their creation. She drew so sharp a breath that Joanna at once looked up, saw on the child's face an expression of sudden dismay. Turning, she saw Gruffydd moving toward them. He stopped abruptly, all but stumbled over his dog. Since Adda's reprimand on the day of her arrival, he'd not let his hostility blaze forth again. But it smoldered in his eyes, showed now in the rigidness of his stance, the set of his shoulders.

Always before, he had only to appear for his sisters to shun Joanna as if she were a leper. But Gwenllian and Marared so far showed no sign of flight, and Joanna took heart. "If we dig a moat," she suggested, "we can fill it with sea water," and saw at once that she'd said just the right thing.

From time to time, Marared cast nervous glances over her shoulder, but she stayed put; Gwenllian seemed to have forgotten Gruffydd altogether, so absorbed was she in deepening the moat. At last it was ready to be filled, and the little girls grabbed their clamshells, ran toward the water, Joanna following. She allowed herself one look back at Gruffydd. He was still standing some yards away, watching.

"Should you like to help us?" Joanna asked, knowing she did but waste her breath. When he did not reply, she turned back toward the water. It was then that she heard Gwenllian cry out. Joanna spun around in time to see Gruffydd's alaunt hound smash into the castle. Within seconds the big dog had wreaked utter havoc, flattened walls and towers, sprayed sand in all directions. Grabbing for the driftwood, he tossed it playfully up

into the air, caught it deftly again, and carried it triumphantly
back to his young master.

Gwenllian had begun to sob. Marared flung down her clam-
shell as if it were something suddenly shameful. Joanna did not
move, watched as Gruffydd whistled to his dog, slowly sauntered
away. She was as angry as she'd ever been in her life, and it
helped not at all to remind herself that he was only a child. She
saw nothing childlike in what he had done; it was both deliberate
and malicious, not to mention clever. How to prove, after all,
that he had not simply misjudged his throw? She could not, of
course, as he'd well known.

"We can rebuild the castle, Gwenllian," she said, as evenly as
her anger would allow. But their fragile camaraderie had collapsed with the sand castle. Gwenllian sniffed, shook her head.
Marared was already edging away.

Joanna made no move to keep them. It would, she knew, have
served for naught. But as she stared down at the wreckage of
their rapprochement, her rage hardened into resolve. She would
not let that wretched boy win. For four months now, she had
been seeking to gain his friendship. No more. Let him hate her;
she no longer cared. But she would not give up on his sisters.
Today she had made the first breach in their defenses. If a direct
assault would not work, mayhap infiltration would.

Walking up the slope to Aber, she paused to watch as a small
flock of bleating ewes and lambs were herded into a pen. Shear-
ing had already been done early in the summer; today the clip-
ping would be confined to the greasy wool at each ewe's neck
and udder. This wool, Joanna knew, would be washed in cold
water and then boiled. As the grease rose to the surface, it would
be skimmed off the water, reheated, and then strained through
linen. Once it was cool, vegetable oil and scent would be added,
the resulting concoction being a highly effective ointment.

Joanna was rather pleased that she now knew something of the
process. In fact, she'd learned much in these months in Wales,
had watched with interest as goatskins were stretched taut on
square frames, scraped with strickle knives, the first step in the
making of parchment; watched as hides were soaked in lime vats
to remove hair, preparatory to tanning; as mutton fat was boiled
with wood ash and caustic soda to make soft soap, and whitethorn bark was soaked in water, boiled, and left to thicken into
ink. At her father's court, such activities were done behind the
scenes; at Llewelyn's court, Joanna found herself closer to na-

ture, living a less insulated life, much like the vast majority of her father's subjects.

She watched until the sheep were penned, then moved indecisively away. She did not want to return to her chambers, was in no mood to put up with Blanche's carping. She hesitated, and then remembered what Llewelyn had told her, that there was an impressive cataract at the end of the glen. It was, he said, a sight well worth the seeing, for the River Coch cascaded over a hundred feet down a sheer cliff.

It proved to be a very pleasant walk. On her left rose the heights of Maes y Gaer, on her right thickly wooded hills. As the path wound upward, she could look back and glimpse the sea. She'd been walking for about half an hour when she saw a glimmer of light through the trees. She quickened her step, some fifteen minutes later came to a sudden halt. Llewelyn had been right; Rhaeadr Fawr was well worth the walk. It had none of the wild, surging power of Rhaeadr Ewynol, but there was a stark elegance nonetheless in that narrow ribbon of white water. The stream was wider here, so clear she could count the mossy rocks lining the river bed, and wherever she looked she saw wildflowers: golden rockroses, purple bell heather, snowy blackthorn blossoms, marsh marigold, others she could not name.

Joanna had turned aside to gather honeysuckle when she saw the man standing at the base of the falls. He turned a startled face toward her, then began to climb nimbly up the rocks. By the time he reached her, Joanna had recognized him as her husband's friend, and she said with a smile, "Lord Rhys, you did take me aback! I'd not expected to see another soul here but a stray sheep or two."

Rhys was frowning. "Madame, you should not be wandering about on your own. What if you'd slipped, fallen upon the rocks? May I escort you back to Aber?"

It was phrased as a question, but given as a command. Joanna bridled a bit, but curiosity won out, and she fell docilely in step beside him. She knew this man hardly at all, had spoken to him so rarely that for a long time she'd thought he knew no French. He put a hand firmly on her elbow, but made no attempt at small talk, seemed to be one of those rare individuals not in the least disconcerted by lengthy silences. Joanna studied him covertly through her lashes. He was, she decided, surely the most handsome man she'd ever seen. So why, then, did she find Llewelyn more attractive, why was it Llewelyn whose touch caused her pulse to race, her imagination to take fire? Mayhap because she'd never known a man who derived so much joy from life, a man so at one with his world, doing exactly what he most wanted to do, doing it very well, and taking such abiding pleasure in it all. But why seek out hurt like this? Must her every thought be of Llewelyn, when he had nary a thought for her?

"I understand Llewelyn does return from Cricieth in a fortnight, and then the court moves to Môn?"

Joanna nodded. "He has a . . . a *plas* at Aberffraw, does he not?"

"Aye, but he'll go to Rhosyr. He has no liking for Aberffraw, not anymore." Joanna had not realized her curiosity showed so nakedly until Rhys added matter-of-factly, "The Lady Tangwystl died at Aberffraw." He did not pause for her response. "The Lady Catrin, my wife, did give birth just a month ago, was stricken after with the milk fever. She is better now, God be thanked, but she's not yet able to travel. She is very eager, though, to meet you, and I would ask a favor of you." He stopped, turned to face her, and Joanna realized he had not been making idle conversation, after all.

"When the court moves to Rhosyr, would you come to my manor at Tregarnedd? It would mean much to my Catrin, Madame, in truth it would."

Joanna could find in herself no enthusiasm for meeting the Lady Catrin, not after making the acquaintance of Ednyved's wife. But she could think of no graceful way to decline, and she said, "Yes, of course."

They walked the rest of the way in silence. As they approached the gateway, they saw Blanche pacing back and forth distractedly. She gave a glad cry at sight of Joanna, ran to meet her.

"Madame, thank God you've come! Sir Hugh Corbet has just ridden in, is awaiting you in the great hall!!"

"Oh, sweet Lady Mary!" Joanna tried to collect her thoughts, tried to remember all she must do for an honored guest. Give orders for a special meal, one of several courses, ask Llywarch to sing for Hugh. See that a chamber was prepared for his stay, that his men were bedded down, too. What else? Jesú, what of a bath?

Joanna came to a sudden stop. It was customary, of course, to offer a bath to any guest planning to pass the night. If the guest was of high rank, it was expected that the lady of the manor herself would assist him in bathing. To neglect so basic a courtesy would be no small insult. But Isabelle had never performed

such tasks; was a Princess, too, exempt? Nor did she even know
if this ancient Norman custom was followed amongst the Welsh.
It would be dreadful to slight her husband's stepfather. But
neither did she want to embarrass Llewelyn by turning her hand
to a task better left to her maids. If only she knew what was
expected of her, if only there was a woman she could ask.

Well, she must blunder through as best she could. Mayhap
Hugh would give her some hint as to what he expected. Why was
it that, the first time she had to act on Llewelyn's behalf, the
guest must be one so important, must be her husband's kin?

Hugh resolved her dilemma, however, in a way she'd not
anticipated. He could not pass the night, he explained regretfully,
for it was urgent that he reach Llewelyn as soon as possible.

"I fear Llewelyn is some miles to the south, in the commote of
Eifionydd. He is building a seacoast castle at Cricieth, wanted to
judge the progress for himself. If you are set upon departing in
such haste, we will gladly provide you with an escort and fresh
mounts." Trying to hide her relief, Joanna racked her brains to
recall what little she knew of Welsh geography. "You could pass
the night at Dolwyddelan, or at Beddgelert Priory, should you get
that far." She hesitated, for the first time seeing the fatigue
already well etched into Hugh's face.

"Sir Hugh, may I ask why you are in such a rush to see my
husband? Is there trouble?"

"Of a sort." He drew her toward the privacy of the window
seat, said in a low voice, "Prince Gwenwynwyn of Powys has
been a widower since the spring. Two days ago he was wed to
my niece Margaret Corbet, my brother Robert's daughter. I want
to get to Llewelyn ere he hears of it from anyone else."

Joanna needed to hear no more; after four months as Llewelyn's
wife, she had no doubts whatsoever as to what his reaction would
be. "It sounds rather as if it were something of a hole-and-corner
marriage," she said coolly. "Why? To keep Llewelyn from
finding out beforehand?"

"Exactly." Hugh grimaced. "My brother can be a fool at
times. Had I only been consulted, I'd have told him Llewelyn
would be sure to take such a marriage as a personal insult. But he
pays too much heed these days to my nephew Tom, and Tom is
no great thinker. Neither he nor Rob seems to realize that times
have changed. It did work well once to play off the Welsh
princes, one against the other. Fifteen years ago, such a marriage
would have been a shrewd maneuver. But those days are gone.

Gwenwynwyn's goodwill counts for little against Llewelyn's. I
only hope they do not have to learn that to their cost.''

"What will Llewelyn do?''

"For the moment, nothing. It's done and beyond changing.
But he's not likely to forget, even less likely to forgive. Stupid
and shortsighted, the both of them. They have yet to get it into
their heads that Llewelyn is not just another Welsh prince, to be
bought off or duped as their need dictates. I've told them that the
day may well come when he'll hold all of Wales, but they laugh.
Fools. I only do hope I'm wrong, for Llewelyn's sake as much as
ours. No English king could ever permit a Welsh prince to wield
so much power; John would have no choice but to break him. I,
for one, would not want—'' He stopped suddenly, having remembered too late to whom he was speaking.

Joanna had gone very white; her eyes suddenly seemed enormous, so dark they were almost black. "Do not say that," she
pleaded. "That must never happen.''

Cursing himself for his clumsiness, Hugh made haste to repair
the damage done. "Indeed it will not, Lady Joanna," he said
soothingly. "When I am tired, my tongue tends to outrun my
brain; such talk means nothing. Your husband and father are
more than allies of the moment; you are the living link that binds
them together.''

Joanna nodded; color slowly began to come back into her face.
Hugh gave her shoulder a reassuring pat, wondering for whom
she feared, John or Llewelyn.

As eagerly as she awaited Llewelyn's return, Joanna felt some
anxiety, too, remembering her father's rages, his dark, moody
silences. But however violent Llewelyn's initial reaction might
have been, he had his temper well in hand by the time he got
back to Aber, made no mention whatsoever of his Corbet kin.
Joanna began to wonder if she had misjudged him; she'd been so
sure he would take the marriage as a mortal affront. She had to
know, at last asked him point-blank how he felt about it.

He looked at her with a faint smile. "My cousin Tom has ever
been one for grazing on both sides of the hedge. That is his
misfortune." And Joanna saw that she had not misjudged him at
all.

It was a mild October afternoon four days after their arrival at
Rhosyr. Joanna was in no hurry to reach Tregarnedd, had covered the eight miles at a leisurely pace. She only hoped the Lady

Catrin spoke some French. On the other hand, if she did not, that would be as good an excuse as any to cut the visit short. At least it was a delightful day for a ride. And she would confess to some curiosity about the woman Rhys had married, wondered if Catrin would be a mirror image of her handsome husband.

Tregarnedd was an agreeable surprise; it was much like a village, for Ednyved had a manor here, too, and, as in England, there were people who preferred to dwell, for safety's sake, in the shadow of a lord. But the real surprise waited within, a smile of welcome upon her face.

"I am Lady Catherine, Madame. How good of you to come to me like this; in truth, you honor our house. I've so longed to meet you. For the first time in my life, I did regret that I know not how to write. Of course, I could have dictated a letter to our chaplain, but . . ."

Joanna stared at the other woman, astonished. It was not Catherine's appearance that so startled her, although she was not the ravishing beauty Joanna had been expecting. She was a buxom, pretty woman with fair, creamy skin, thick golden lashes, and hair so blonde it was almost white. It was her speech, however, that riveted Joanna's eyes upon her; her French was not only fluent, it was colloquial.

"You are Norman!" Joanna blurted out, and then blushed. But Catherine merely laughed.

"Indeed. Did Rhys not tell you? Ah, that man!"

On reflection, Joanna realized there was no reason for such surprise. Intermarriages were not that uncommon, after all; the Corbets were not the only Marcher border lords to see the advantages in a Welsh connection. It was just that Rhys, so proudly, defiantly Welsh, seemed the last man to choose a Norman wife.

As if reading her thoughts, Catherine said, "I know no people who value bloodlines as do the Welsh. But they have never balked at accepting foreign wives, for a woman takes on her husband's nationality, and any children of such a union have full rights under Welsh law. It becomes rather more complicated when a Welshwoman does wed with an *alltud* . . . a man of foreign blood. But I expect Llewelyn has explained all this to you . . ."

Ushering Joanna into the great hall, she at once sent for wine and wafers, settled Joanna in the seat of honor by the hearth, and beckoned a nurse forward to show Joanna a small, dark-haired infant swaddled in folds of soft linen.

"My daughter Gwenifer. Rhys always does hope the girls will have my coloring, and always in vain. This is the fifth time I've been brought to childbed, and each one has hair black as sin."

Joanna laughed. She'd all but forgotten how wonderful it was just to sit and talk, to make inconsequential, easy conversation. She had, of necessity, learned to tune out the disgruntled Blanche's litany of complaints, and her encounters with Llewelyn were so fraught with sexual tension that she could take little pleasure in them.

"Now . . . do tell me how you like Wales. Llewelyn is well? I must confess that I'm half in love with him, do not know a woman who is not, in truth! My husband may turn all female heads, but yours is the one they'd run off with if . . ." Her words trailed off, for Joanna's color had deepened, dark patches showing high on her cheekbones. Catherine realized she had trod amiss, but she was puzzled as to how. Surely the girl knew she was but joking? Unless . . . unless she knew about Cristyn? Catherine was now the one to be embarrassed, sought hastily for safer subject matter.

"Should you like, my lady, to hold Gwenifer? You do know, I'm sure, that you have all our heartfelt prayers that you may soon have a babe of your own. It must weary you, in truth, to have the women ever measuring your waistline, whispering if you so much as miss a meal! But it is always so with newly wedded wives, and when your husband is our lord Prince . . ."

Joanna came to her feet so abruptly that she knocked her wine cup onto the floor. Would she never learn? This woman was even more malicious than Maude de Braose and Gwenllian, for they at least had pretended no friendliness. But Catherine drew blood with a smile, and for that, Joanna would never forgive her. "Your jest is little to my liking," she said, all the more furious that her voice was not as steady as she would have wished.

"But Madame . . . what have I said? How have I offended you?" Catherine, too, was on her feet now. Her distress seemed so genuine that Joanna felt the first glimmer of doubt.

"The entire court does know. Surely your husband would have told you . . ."

"Rhys never gossips," Catherine said simply. "I do not know of what you speak, my lady, I swear I do not."

For a long moment, Joanna stared at her, and then sat down again. "If I did missay you, I am indeed sorry. You see, I thought you were mocking me. Llewelyn and I . . . we do not share a bed, and there is not a soul at Aber or Rhosyr who does not know that . . .''

"I did not know, Madame," Catherine said, after some moments of silence. "That is not something Rhys would think to mention. It is not that unusual, after all, when the wife is quite young and her husband some years older than she."

Some of Joanna's shame gave way to gratitude. Whether Catherine believed that or not, it was kind of her to say so, and she was very much relieved when Catherine began tactfully to talk of other matters.

Joanna was never able to pinpoint the exact moment when she let her defenses down. For the first time in five months she had a sympathetic ear, and it was perhaps inevitable that she would find herself confiding in Catherine, Catherine who spoke her own tongue, who knew what it was like to be a bride in a foreign land, Catherine who offered friendship. She did not lower all of the barriers, spoke of Llewelyn in only the most conventional, cautious banalities. But she did speak of her loneliness, her homesickness, spoke of the utter isolation and the cries of wolves on the wind and a forgotten fifteenth birthday.

There was a great relief in sharing; hers were secret sores much in need of healing balm. But there was unease, too, once she realized just how much she'd revealed. Isabelle was the only confidante she'd ever had, and entrusting a secret to Isabelle was rather like toting water in a sieve. Very thankful that her tongue had not completely run away with her, that she had not betrayed the one secret that truly mattered, Joanna watched as Catherine bathed Gwenifer, then turned the child over to the wet nurse for suckling. She'd always nursed her own, Catherine admitted, although the Lady Gwenllian and others mocked her for it, would have suckled Gwenifer, too, had her fever not dried up her milk.

Catherine was emerging as more and more of an enigma to Joanna. She was, by her own admission, not educated. She'd made a self-disparaging remark about marriage portions when their conversation had turned to Margaret Corbet and Gwenwynwyn, laughing and saying she'd brought Rhys naught but headaches. Joanna had been distinctly taken aback; it was almost unheard of for a Norman lord to take an undowered wife. And if she was, in truth, no heiress, how in the name of Heaven had they even met, much less married?

"Catherine . . . would you think me rude if I asked how you came to marry Rhys?"

Catherine smiled. "I'd not mind in the least, Joanna. That is a story I never tire of telling. My first meeting with Rhys goes back some thirteen years, to the autumn of the year after King Richard was taken captive on his way home from the Holy Land. My father was bailiff on Lord Fitz Alan's manor of Middleton, in Shropshire. I was the youngest of six, the only girl. My mother died when I was four, and my father made rather a pet of me; so, too, did my brothers. That spring I did turn fifteen, and it was more or less understood that, come winter, I'd be wed to a neighboring knight, Sir Bernard de Nevill. He and my father were talking of a betrothal at Martinmas, a wedding after Advent."

"Were you willing, Catherine?"

"I was not offered a choice, Joanna. I felt it was my duty to do as my father bade me. And it was indeed an advantageous match. Sir Bernard held his own manor of Lord Fitz Alan; I'd be lady of the manor, with my own household and servants. And since Sir Bernard had no children by his first marriage, a son of mine might one day inherit the fief; not many second wives could say as much. Moreover, he seemed to be a good man, a devout Christian, well thought of by all. But . . . he was also nigh on fifty, and balding, with breath rank enough to stop a mule in its tracks. So I'd not say I was counting the days till the marriage!"

"What prevented the marriage?"

"A sunlit September day," Catherine said and laughed. "My brother Adam was taking an oxwain into Blanc Minster, had a load of wool skeins to deliver to Will the weaver. Blanc Minster was only three miles away, but I was never allowed into town without one of my brothers. On that particular day Adam agreed to take me along, and so it happened that I was sitting out in the oxwain at noon as Rhys rode by. The Welsh often came into Blanc Minster to trade for goods, and even in war I never saw a merchant turn down their money. I did not know then, of course, that Rhys was Welsh. I knew only that he was the handsomest man I'd ever hoped to see in this life!"

"He is that," Joanna agreed generously. "What happened then?"

"He drew rein right there in the street, stared at me, and when he smiled, I . . . I fell in love. But then he dismounted, and I realized he meant to speak to me. At that I panicked. If Adam had ever seen me talking with a stranger, I'd have been beaten black and blue. As for Rhys, Adam would have run him through . . . or tried to. You can always tell if a man be handy with weapons, and Rhys had that look about him. So when he started toward me, I scrambled off the oxwain, fled into the weaver's. I was terrified that he might follow me in. He did not, but he was still there when Adam and I came out. Fortunately, he did not say anything; he just looked at me. I could feel his eyes on me all the while Adam was joking with Will, was never so aware of anyone in all my life as I suddenly was of Rhys."

"Yes," Joanna said softly. "I do know the feeling. When did you see him next?"

"Adam had to return the following day, and I coaxed him into letting me go with him. I did not truly expect Rhys to be there again, but he was—almost as if he was waiting for me. Much later I learned he was; Will had told him Adam would be coming back that afternoon. What followed was the most unnerving, exciting hour of my life. I knew what a dangerous game we were playing, for at any moment Adam might take notice. But I could not help myself. I sat there on the cart, and each time our eyes met, it became harder and harder to look away. And then Adam's business was done, we were on our way home, and I knew I'd never see him again. I did not even know his name, had never exchanged a single word with him, but I cried half the night. Does that sound foolish to you?"

Joanna shook her head.

"I thought of him every waking moment in the days that followed. What I did not know was that he was keeping a close watch all the while on Middleton, waiting for the chance to find me alone. He later confessed he'd even thought of riding up to the manor house, asking my father for me. Thank Jesus he did not, for there'd have been a killing for certes.

"I gave him his opportunity at week's end. It was a Saturday, just at dusk, as hot as Hades, and I decided that, whilst the light held, I'd walk to the spring, wash my hair. I brought my towel, hairbrush, and a sliver of soap, sat down in the grass to unbraid my hair. I never heard a sound, not even a twig snap, not until he was behind me, put his hand over my mouth. I've ever been an utter coward, Joanna; I made it very easy for him, fainted dead away!

"When I came to, I was all trussed up in a blanket, being held before him on his saddle." Catherine's smile faded; she said quietly, "I was terrified, and with reason. It is common enough to abduct an heiress, to force her into an unwanted marriage. What woman does not know that?"

Joanna nodded. "Even so great a lady as my grandmother, Queen Eleanor, was held to be fair game. Two such attempts were made upon her after she divorced the French King."

"But you see, Joanna, I was no heiress. I was a bailiff's daughter, had nothing to offer a man except my body. And yet, if he had rape in mind, why did he not just take me there by the spring? The more I tried to make sense of it, the more fearful I became. I must have made some sound, whimpered or sobbed, for he realized I'd recovered my senses, at once sought to comfort me. He knew my name, called me Catrin, swore he'd not hurt me, that I had no cause for fear. That might have helped some, had it not been for 'Catrin.' For as soon as I knew he was Welsh, I was even more terrified; all knew the Welsh were half-wild, capable of any madness.

"It was full dark by then. Not that I could see a blessed thing; I could barely breathe, wrapped in that blanket like a cocoon. I've no idea how long we rode; after a time we stopped and he lifted me from the saddle. Know you what a *hafod* is? It is a summer hut, used by the Welsh herdsmen when they move their flocks to higher ground for pasturing. It was to a *hafod* that he took me, empty now since it was September, a most convenient place for a . . . a tryst. It was too dark inside to see much; I just lay there shivering on the blanket. He'd already laid in firewood, and it took but a moment to get a fire going. He lit a candle from the flames, carried it back to me, and for the first time, I saw his face."

"You had not known it was Rhys?" Joanna interrupted, startled, and Catherine shook her head.

"No, not till he lit the candle; how could I? He sat beside me on the blankets—you'll find no proper bed in a *hafod*—and touched my hair, very gently. Then he began to talk. He told me he'd known from that first moment in Blanc Minster that I was his and only his, but I must not fear, for he did not mean to dishonor me, would have me for his wife, had taken me by force only because he'd known no other way."

Catherine's voice had softened. Her eyes were no longer acknowledging Joanna, were gazing into a private vista of her own. Joanna suddenly had the fanciful thought that, if she but leaned forward, she could see captured in the pupils of Catherine's eyes the firelit image of a fifteen-year-old girl and a nineteen-year-old boy upon a pile of blankets in a summer *hafod*.

She hesitated; as candid as Catherine had been, it somehow seemed wrong to question her now, an unwelcome intrusion into a past not for sharing. At last she said shyly, "Catherine . . . when did you stop being afraid? Do you remember?"

Catherine's eyes shifted to her face, no longer clouded, remote. "Oh, yes, I remember—when Rhys first struck that candle."

She glanced down at her wedding ring; it was of an unusual, almost primitive design, a heavy gold studded with gemstones. "We sent the priest who married us to my family. My father swore he'd never forgive me. But within a year Llewelyn had won that brilliant, bloody victory at the mouth of the Conwy, had laid claim to half of Gwynedd, and Rhys was ever at his right hand—*was* his right hand. My father died nigh on ten years ago, but he lived to see his first grandson. And my brothers come often to Tregarnedd."

"You've been very lucky," Joanna said slowly.

Catherine's smile was radiant, innocent. "I know," she said.

Joanna found herself looking, too, at Catherine's wedding band. It did not surprise her in the least that Catherine should have been so easily seduced. What girl would have chosen an aging, ungainly neighbor over a reckless, lovestruck youth with the nerve of a highwayman and the face of a dark angel? But beneath the undeniably romantic appeal of Catherine's tale, Joanna felt the tug of common sense. What if Catherine had, indeed, cared for her greying knight? If she had resented being carried off as a prize of war? What might have happened then?

No, for all that Catherine had obviously found all she'd ever wanted in that deserted *hafod*, Joanna could not but think Catherine's luck had been stretched to the very limit and then some. And yet she was aware of an undercurrent of envy. For Catherine had one treasure beyond value, had what she'd have given anything in the world to have herself—the rare and precious certainty that her husband loved her, not for what she could bring to his coffers, not for castles or bloodlines or connections, but for herself alone.

18

RHOSYR, NORTH WALES

November 1206

"Catrin, my love!"

Llewelyn turned, swept Catherine up in a lover's embrace, then gave her a chaste kiss on the forehead. Laughing, she hugged him back.

"Have you some moments to spare? I need to talk, Llewelyn."

"For you, always . . . day or night." As he led her toward the window seat, it occurred to Catherine that her relationship with Llewelyn—teasing, affectionate, mildly flirtatious—was one an insecure, jealous young wife might possibly misconstrue. She would, she thought regretfully, have to strive for greater decorum. A pity, for as much as she liked to flirt, that was a game she dared play with Llewelyn alone. Having led an all but cloistered life prior to her marriage, she'd then made the belated discovery that it could be fun to talk and tease and coquet—a little—with other men, to her an innocent diversion that did not in the least diminish her love for Rhys. But she'd also discovered that her husband was intensely possessive, begrudged her any and all male companionship, no matter how innocent . . . save only for Ednyved and Llewelyn. Ednyved was little inclined to flattery, even less so to gallantry, but in Llewelyn, Catherine had found a kindred spirit, and they'd established a rapport from their first meeting. In the beginning, an unsettling misgiving had imperiled Catherine's peace, the suspicion that if her husband tolerated Llewelyn's banter and familiarity while bristling if another man so much as glanced in her direction, it must be that Rhys trusted Llewelyn but did not truly trust her. That was so disturbing a thought, however, that Catherine had swiftly buried it deep; hers was not a nature to probe for that which she'd rather not know.

"How is my godson and namesake?"

"As much of a hellion as you were at his age . . . and still are."

"Do not be cruel, Catrin," Llewelyn said and grinned. "It is good to have you back at court. Joanna tells me your newest babe is as beautiful as her mother; how does she?"

"Gwenifer is fine." Catherine paused. "I just wish I could say as much for Joanna."

"What do you mean?"

Catherine did not reply at once. Having already plunged into the water, it was no time now to be worrying if she'd gotten in over her head. But she could not suppress a nervous qualm or two. As fond as Llewelyn was of her, he was not likely to thank her for pointing out all his shortcomings as a husband.

"We've been friends for nigh on thirteen years. I must hope that our friendship does give me the right to speak plainly . . . about Joanna and you. You've not done right by her, Llewelyn; I know no other way to say it than that."

"Indeed?" Llewelyn was both surprised and annoyed. Leaning back in the seat, he gave her a distinctly cool look. "I do not know to whom you've been listening, Catrin, but you are wrong. I think I've been very good to Joanna. Even ere we were married, I spared no expense in having her chamber made ready for her. Nor have I denied her anything since we've been wed, have given her whatever she asks for, have made sure that none do speak disparagingly of her father in her hearing, that she's accorded the respect due her as my wife. I've been patient, too, keeping in mind her youth, have not forced her against her will, and I've taken care that my liaison with Cristyn should not cause her hurt. Now if that is not doing right by her, what more would you have me do?"

Catherine bit her lip. Rhys had an unfortunate and infuriating tendency to stalk out whenever he was irked with her; she felt sure that even if he refused to act upon her advice, Llewelyn would at least hear her out. But she was not getting off to the best of starts; the last thing she'd wanted was to put him on the defensive.

"I did not mean you've been unkind," she said hastily. "I was speaking rather of sins of omission. I do not deny what you've done for her, but Llewelyn, do you ever think of Joanna, truly think of her as a woman, as your wife? Do you know how unhappy she is? How homesick? Do you know that she has been trying for months now to befriend your children, but to no avail? Or that she did turn fifteen more than two months ago?"

Llewelyn was listening intently, his face thoughtful now rather than irritated, and Catherine gathered up her courage, concluded bluntly, "I suspect . . . and please do not take this amiss; I do not mean it as a criticism, for I know how heavy your burdens be. But I suspect you forget about Joanna altogether when she's not right there in front of you." And then she held her breath, waiting.

"Yes," he said at last, "I suppose there is some truth in what you say. I am fond of the lass, Catrin, but she's not all that often on my mind, I admit. Is she truly as unhappy as that? I thought she'd adjust in time . . ."

"She tries, wants so much to do what is expected of her. But she's very young, and very alone. She speaks no Welsh, and how many at your court do speak French? She cannot even communicate with her maid, and with you so often away, there are days when she has no one at all to talk to. She's lonely and homesick, finds herself an alien in a land not her own. Can you not imagine how that would be?"

Llewelyn drew an audible breath. "Yes," he said slowly. "I can imagine quite well; I've been there."

Catherine leaned over, kissed him on the cheek. "Joanna is a lucky girl, and someday I shall tell her so," she said, smiled at him. The puzzle lacked but one piece now, and since he'd been the first to make mention of it, she felt no compunctions in saying, "You said you were being patient with Joanna, because of her youth. Then that is why you've not yet bedded her?"

Llewelyn nodded. "Why else? I knew, of course, that she was fourteen. But to tell you true, Catrin, it came as rather a shock to find out just how very young a fourteen she was." He gave a rueful laugh, thinking back upon his wedding night. "Not having a taste for rape, I thought it best to give her time—" He broke off abruptly. "Surely you do not think I was wrong?"

"Indeed not! I think your forbearance was much for the best, was as clever as it was kind. But as fearful and reluctant as Joanna may have been on her wedding night, Llewelyn, that was over six months ago. How long do you mean to wait?"

She saw amusement in his eyes, saw sudden interest, too. "Did Joanna speak to you of—"

"No!" she interrupted, quite indignantly. "Do you truly think I'd betray her confidence if she had? I would never tell you what she'd confided to me in trust; you ought to know that. It is because she did not that I felt free to come to you like this, to tell you what I think."

"Which is?"

"That Joanna is not the child you think her to be. And I'd venture to guess that if you were to stop neglecting the girl and pay her some long-overdue attention, you might be pleasantly surprised!"

Putting down Richard's letter, Joanna began to reread her father's. These were the first letters she'd had since their departure for La Rochelle in late May. She'd expected such a silence, for John would have little time for letter-writing in the midst of a campaign, Isabelle was a notoriously poor correspondent, and Richard had not the funds to engage a courier of his own. It had been a long, lonely wait, but the news was good, was all she could have hoped to hear. Her father was coming home.

Reaching for her mantle, Joanna hastened from her chambers, out into the bailey. She knew Llewelyn was conferring that morning with Iorwerth ap Madog, the lawyer he'd chosen to compile the ancient law code of Hywel the Good, and she headed for the great hall. Catching sight of her husband in the window seat, she started toward him.

"Llewelyn, I've had a letter from my father! He—" Coming to an abrupt halt, staring at Catherine.

The window was covered with oiled linen, casting the seat into sun and shadow. Llewelyn positioned a cushion behind Joanna's back, sat down beside her. He was so close that she felt his breath upon her cheek as he leaned over to unfasten her mantle, so close that she could think of nothing else, sitting in silence until he prompted, "Are you not going to tell me what your father wrote, Joanna?"

"He . . . he has won signal victories against the French, did take Montauban Castle in just fifteen days." Joanna raised her eyes to Llewelyn's, found she could not look away. "He writes that he has secured his hold upon Poitou, that he and Philip have agreed to a two-year truce."

"It does sound as if his campaign was indeed a success," Llewelyn agreed politely, forbearing to tarnish John's triumph by pointing out that he may have regained Poitou, but Normandy was still lost to Philip.

Joanna nodded. "Not even Charlemagne could take Montauban, but Papa did," she said proudly. "He took Angers, too." She hesitated then, before saying with studied casualness, "What were you and Catherine talking about?"

Llewelyn had, however, caught her inadvertent look of dismay at sight of them together. Having long ago learned that a half-truth was often far more effective than an outright denial in allaying suspicions, he said, with equal nonchalance, "As it

happens, we were talking of you. Catrin was taking me to task
for having forgotten your birthday.''

"Oh,'' Joanna said, much relieved. She was not sure what
she'd feared, for even had Catherine repeated verbatim every one
of their conversations this month past, would that have been so
dreadful, after all? Actually, she was glad that Catherine had told
him about the missed birthday; she wanted him to know.

"I expect it's best that you find out the truth about me early
on.'' Llewelyn's smile was wry. "You see, love, I do have an
appalling memory for dates, be they birthdays, name days, saints'
days, whatever. Tangwystl finally resorted to laying out tally
sticks in our bedchamber, to remind me of the days remaining
until her birthday. And my children do take no chances, talk of
nothing else for fully a month beforehand.''

"Alas, and I thought you were without flaw,'' Joanna said
lightly. She was suddenly very happy. They'd often sat and
talked, but this conversation was somehow different; Llewelyn
was somehow different. She could not have articulated the change,
knew only that there was an intimacy between them that she'd
never felt before.

"I take it I'm forgiven? I should like to make amends, though,
so you may ask of me what you will.''

"Anything? Anything at all?''

"Well, anything within reason,'' Llewelyn hedged, but then
laughed, realizing she was teasing.

Joanna laughed, too. "I shall have to give it some thought. An
opportunity such as this is not to be wasted, must be . . .'' And
then her eyes fell upon the letter in her lap. Very much in earnest
now, she put a hand imploringly upon his arm. "Did you truly
mean it, Llewelyn? For there is something I do want, more than
you could ever know. My father wrote that he expects to land at
Portsmouth within the fortnight. I've not seen him for nigh on
seven months, and . . . and it would mean so much to me to be
there on the docks, waiting for him. May I, Llewelyn? May I go
home for a visit?''

She did not, Llewelyn saw, even catch her slip of the tongue,
the use of "home.'' Catrin had been right; he'd not done all he
could for the lass. "Of course you may go to Portsmouth,
Joanna, if that be your wish.''

"Thank you, oh, thank you!'' For a moment he thought she
was about to fling her arms around him; she made an indecisive
movement, and then jumped to her feet. "May I go now? Today?
It'll take a week to reach London, after all, and I know not when

he's sailing. I could stay with my Aunt Ela, and we could travel together to Portsmouth. And . . . and if you'd not mind, I could remain for Papa's Christmas court?''

"I'd not mind in the least. What could be more natural than that you'd miss your father, your family? Now, if you truly want to depart this noon, you'd best set your maids to packing. Meanwhile, I'll see about getting you a proper escort.''

Joanna had begun to thank him again, and he rose, put his arm around her waist. "Why do you not," he suggested, "ask Catrin to help you pack? You did look rather . . . taken aback at sight of her earlier, and I'm sure you'd not want her to think she'd somehow displeased you. She's a good friend, Joanna; they do come no better. You need never fear that she'd betray a confidence, share your secrets.''

"Was I so obvious as that?" Joanna asked softly, and Llewelyn nodded, gave her waist a gentle squeeze.

"So you admit, then, that you have secrets from me?" he murmured, and Joanna's eyes widened. On the surface, it could have passed for his usual banter, but the undercurrent carried an altogether different message. He was, she thought in utterly amazed delight, flirting with her.

"That," she said impishly, "is for me to know and you to find out.''

Llewelyn burst out laughing, more than a little intrigued. It was a child's answer, the sort of flippancy that any of his daughters might have uttered, but there was nothing at all child-like in the look she gave him, a look impossible to misread, for he'd had it from too many women in the past not to recognize it on sight for what it was—an invitation to further intimacies.

Blanche was even more excited than Joanna at the prospect of returning to England, and she completed the packing in record if disordered haste. Within the hour, Joanna found herself out in the bailey, watching as her coffers were loaded onto pack horses. Enid came forward, made a quick curtsy, and retreated as if she feared Joanna might change her mind, make her accompany them to the English King's court, after all. But Joanna merely smiled, and then startled Enid by giving her an utterly inappropriate hug. Embracing Catherine next, she waited until Sugar was safely settled into her traveling basket, and then moved toward Llewelyn.

He was standing with her seneschal, turned at her approach. "Dylan and I have just been determining your route. You'll be ferried across the strait at Abermenai; Dylan will swim the horses

across. Ordinarily, I'd have you pass the night with the monks at
Aberconwy, but you're getting a late start, and I'd as soon you crossed
Penmaenmawr in full light. So you'd best halt at Aber tonight."

He drew her away from the others then, put something into her
hand. "Here, this is a gift for your father. I had it looped upon a
chain so you could wear it around your neck, for safety's sake."

It was, Joanna saw, a square-cut ruby ring, set in heavy gold.
"I shall present it to Papa with your compliments," she promised, and Llewelyn shook his head.

"No, Joanna. I've arranged for a falcon from Ramsey Island
as my New Year's gift. This will be from you, and you alone."
He smiled, for the ring had been taken in one of his grandfather's
wars with the English, and it amused him to think of the English
King wearing booty from a border raid.

Joanna was staring down at the ring. Her father had a passion
for jewels, but she had never before been able to indulge that
passion, to give him a gift so sure to please. "How generous you
are, how good to me," she said, and reached up, kissed him
quickly upon the cheek.

On impulse, Llewelyn stepped closer, took her in his arms.
Curious as to what her response would be, he bent his head,
touched his lips to hers. He was half expecting her to recoil, as
she had at Rhaeadr Ewynol, but he was, just as Catherine had
predicted, very agreeably surprised. Far from shrinking back,
Joanna at once put her arms around his neck. He tightened his
hold; there was a fluid feel to her body, as if she'd flowed into
his embrace, so yielding was she, so softly supple and pliant, so
utterly unlike the girl who'd once gone rigid at his lightest touch.
Her breath was sweet, her mouth opening under his like a flower.
When he probed it with his tongue, she clung all the closer, showed
herself to be a quick study, responding with timid tongue-flickerings
of her own. It was, for a kiss born of curiosity, one that offered
infinite and unexpected promise for the future, and it was with
genuine regret that Llewelyn released her, ended their embrace.

He'd noted before that Joanna had unusually beautiful eyes;
they changed with the light, her mood, reflected color like crystal, hazel brown to gold-flecked emerald within the span of
seconds. They were very green now, a misty, glowing green,
wide with wonderment. She was quite flushed, was running the
tip of her tongue over her lips, as if she were still savoring his
kiss, and Llewelyn suddenly laughed. Was this how Eve had
looked upon first tasting the forbidden fruit?

"Do not," he said, "be gone too long."

19

PORTSMOUTH, ENGLAND

December 1206

"How long must we wait, my lady? I'm so cold, am like to catch
my death if we . . ."

But Joanna was not listening to Blanche, for she'd caught sight
of her father. He had emerged from the sheltering tent, was
watching as sailors secured their moorings. Beside him, Joanna
recognized Peter des Roches, Bishop of Winchester, one of the
few churchmen her father seemed inclined to trust. Isabelle was
now out on deck, too, looking improbably beautiful in a hooded
mantle of silvery fox fur, cuddling a small dog that might have
been Sugar's twin. Joanna could wait no longer, pushed her way
to the forefront of the small crowd assembled upon the dock.

John was halfway down the gangplank when he saw Joanna.
He paused, then smiled, kept his eyes upon her all the while the
city fathers bade him welcome. As the wind was biting enough to
curb even the most effusive of tongues, the official greetings
were mercifully brief, and within moments Joanna was curtsying
before her father. He raised her up, then drew her to him in a
warm, enveloping hug.

"I could ask for no more agreeable surprise than this. But how
did you manage it, lass? You are not a runaway wife, are you?"

His banter did not ring altogether true; for all that it was
playfully posed, the question articulated a genuine concern. What
did Papa fear—that she was unhappy as Llewelyn's wife? Or that
her unhappiness might jeopardize his alliance with Llewelyn?
Probably both, Joanna acknowledged, but without resentment.
Papa would be counting up political gains and losses even upon
his deathbed. So, she suspected, would Llewelyn.

"You need not worry, Papa," she said, and smiled at him. "I have a very indulgent husband."

"Will you be coming to me tonight, John?"

Isabelle's ladies were preparing her for bed, and she was clad only in her chemise, her hair loose and flowing down her back. A lovely child, she was maturing into a breathtaking woman; John never tired of looking at her, had yet to tire of sleeping with her. Crossing the chamber, he drew her to him, into a possessive embrace. "Does that answer your question? But it'll not be till late, so you need not wait up for me. I'll wake you." He kissed her again, then turned toward Joanna.

"How about a kiss from you, too, sweetheart?" he said, and Joanna smiled, came quickly into his arms. Stepping back, he looked for a long moment into her face, and she thought he meant to ask for assurance. But he did not, and she wondered why; was it that since he could not change what was writ, he'd rather not know if the price had been too high?

Isabelle was dismissing her ladies. "That will be all. The Lady Joanna can see to my needs." As soon as they were alone, she beckoned Joanna toward the bed. "Well? Are you not going to tell me about Llewelyn?"

Joanna nodded. "Yes," she said slowly, "I am." She'd given it a great deal of thought in the last fortnight, had concluded that she had no choice but to confide in Isabelle. She was not blind to the risk; Isabelle was not the most reliable of confidants. Yet there was no one else. For a time she'd considered her Aunt Ela, for Ela was a pious, earnest woman who'd go to her grave before she'd betray a trust. And like Joanna and Isabelle, Ela had been married very young, to a man much older than she. But there'd never been true intimacy between them; no matter how she tried, Joanna could not envision herself discussing so sensitive a subject with Ela. Nor did she think Ela was a likely source for the sort of advice she needed; Ela was too passive, too docile, too . . . good. Ela would not understand. But Isabelle would. That Joanna never doubted.

"I do need your counsel, Isabelle. Things are not right between Llewelyn and me, not as they should be. But ere I say one blessed word, you must swear to keep secret whatever I do tell you, swear upon your very soul."

"That is insulting, Joanna. Think you that I cannot keep a secret?" Joanna merely looked at her in significant silence, and Isabelle yielded, said reluctantly, "Very well, I do so swear.

You surprise me, though. I was so sure you'd take to Llewelyn . . ."

"I did that, in truth," Joanna said ruefully. "I love him, Isabelle. I did not want to, but I do. And now I'm frightened . . . because for the first time I think he's starting to see me as a woman. I want so much to believe that, but if I'm wrong . . . I do not think I could bear it. I'm afraid to go back, afraid to find out. And I'm afraid, too, that when I do, I'll say or do the wrong thing, that I'll—"

"Joanna, I want to help, I truly do. But I know not what you're talking about. If you love him, what then, is the problem?"

"That he's not yet taken me to bed," Joanna said, before she could lose her nerve.

Isabelle's brows rose. "Why not?"

"I think . . . think I'm not to his liking, not the way a man wants a woman."

Isabelle did not make the conventional polite denial. For several moments, she said nothing, and then she shook her head. "That's not likely, Joanna. I grant you your coloring is unfortunate. But no man thinks of such matters in bed. Now if you were rail-slat thin or partridge plump . . . but you're not, have high breasts, a waist a man could span with his hands—" She broke off, began to laugh. "I sound as if I'm tallying up the finer points of a filly I hope to sell—fifteen hands high, with a gait smooth as silk!"

Joanna laughed, too. Isabelle was unpredictable and irreverent, but she could be perversely comforting, too, and Joanna very much wanted to believe her. "Why, then, Isabelle?"

"Well . . . sometimes a man can be so besotted with one woman that he has no desire to be bed with any others," Isabelle said, rather dubiously, and at once wished she had not, for Joanna looked stricken. "But such men are as rare as unicorns. And you'd know if he were so smitten with a mistress; all the court would know, as when old King Henry doted so shamelessly upon Rosamond Clifford." She signaled for Joanna to pour them wine, added thoughtfully, "Of course, it may just be that he thinks you're too young for bedding . . . or unwilling. Have you given him cause for that, Joanna?"

"Yes . . . I suppose I have," Joanna admitted, startled. "He did not seem to want me, you see, so I . . . ."

"So you returned the favor. Foolish . . . but not fatal. I daresay you can mend the damage easily enough. You need only let him know, Joanna, that you want him in your bed; what could be simpler?"

"But how do I do that? I cannot very well tell him, can I?"

"Why not? I assure you, no man ever took a woman's admission of desire as an insult. But there are any number of ways to let a man know you want him. Make an excuse to seek him out in his bedchamber, invite him into yours, look upon him with loving eyes, talk softly, tease . . . Dearest, it is so easy, in truth!"

"For you, yes, but not for me!"

"You may be an innocent, Joanna, but your husband is not. He'll take your meaning quickly enough. In the morning we'll go through my coffers, pick out colors that become you. Now I want to show you what John gave me for my name day, a necklet of sapphires and silver . . ."

Joanna lay back against the pillows, only half listening to this accounting of Isabelle's newest acquisition; Isabelle already had, she knew, jewels enough to bedazzle any queen in Christendom. But where men were concerned, Isabelle's instincts were sound. She must somehow dispel Llewelyn's doubts, let him know she was now most willing to be his wife . . . if, in truth, she had not already done so, out in the November sunlight before half his court. And closing her eyes, she gave herself up to remembering the feel of Llewelyn's mouth upon hers, that kiss so sweet, so hot, and so surprising.

John had returned to England in good spirits, pleased with the fruits of his summer campaign. His sense of satisfaction had done nothing to curb his innate restlessness, however, and he let neither heavy snows nor the grumbling of his courtiers slow his pace. Landing at Portsmouth on December 12, he held court in the fortnight that followed at Beer-Regis, Clarendon, Lugershall, Marlborough, Winchester, and Farnham.

This constant, almost compulsive movement set most tempers on edge, for roads were bad, the weather was worse, and accommodations hard to come by for those dragged along in John's wake. Joanna was one of the few to accept the chaos and inconvenience in good humor. For the first time in her life she had money to spend, and she did so with abandon, purchasing bolts of the finest Lincoln wool for Catherine, a magpie and a wicker cage for Gwladys, dolls with dyed hempen wigs for Marared and Gwenllian, wooden tops for Tegwared and Anghared, the twins she'd yet to meet, a sachet of orris root and anise for Enid. She'd even selected an ivory-handled eating knife for Gruffydd, although she felt herself a hypocrite for doing so, knowing she had bought the knife not for the boy, but because she did not want Llewelyn to know she disliked his son. But her greatest joy was in choosing gifts for Llewelyn: a chess set of jasper and crystal, ivory dice, a pellison of soft vair to wear over his tunic. She had even, with some misgivings, purchased two pairs of chamois-skin gloves; gloves were still something of a novelty, were worn only by men of the very highest rank, and she was not altogether sure that Llewelyn would be willing to adopt this new Norman fashion.

The Thursday after Christmas found the court settled at Guildford in Surrey, some thirty miles south of London. Joanna was delighted, for Guildford was a noted center for the cloth trade. With Richard in patient attendance, she'd lingered over the wares so eagerly spread out for her inspection, eventually selecting a ruinously expensive length of Spanish cotton, a deep russet velvet, sindon linen fine enough to see through, and, despite his token protest, a rich Coventry blue for Richard.

Richard watched in amusement as the merchants all but fell over themselves in their zeal to please his sister. "You shall have to buy additional pack horses to get all your purchases back to Wales, you know," he gibed, moving forward to help her mount her mare. "But are you still set upon departing on the morrow, Joanna? We thought sure you'd stay through Epiphany, and I do not doubt Llewelyn did, too."

"Wales is not at the back of beyond, Richard. I'll come again."

"I just do not understand your haste. Nor does Papa, I'd wager."

"No, he does not. And I confess I am surprised, Richard. I'd have thought Papa would be pleased that I do miss the husband he chose for me. But when I told him I was leaving, he did give me the strangest look. As foolish as this is going to sound, I suddenly felt guilty, although why I do not know."

A light snowfall was powdering the ground by the time they reached the King's manor. Hastening into the great hall, Joanna came to an uncertain halt. Something was amiss; she sensed it at once. So, too, did Richard. He took her arm, followed her toward the dais. Isabelle was standing at John's side, her face turned imploringly up to his, speaking softly, placatingly. He did not seem to be listening, but as she persevered, he shook her hand off his arm, snapped, "Be still, Isabelle. I'd not have you meddle in that which you do not understand."

Isabelle recoiled. "I did only mean to comfort you," she said, sounding hurt. But John had already turned upon his heel; men hastily moved aside to let him pass.

"Isabelle, what has happened?"

"I've never seen him so angry, Joanna. When he first read the Pope's letter, he went so red I truly feared he might be stricken with a palsy. And then he blistered the air itself with his oaths. I'd have begged him not to blaspheme, but I had not the courage. And when I did say—"

"The Pope has given his decision, then?" Richard interrupted, with such urgency that Isabelle forgave his rudeness, nodded bleakly.

"I cannot believe what he has done, Richard. He declared Reginald's election invalid, just as he earlier repudiated Bishop de Grey's election. But then he instructed the monks to elect a man of his choosing, Stephen Langton, cardinal priest of St Chrysogonus, a member of the papal court. They did as he bade, of course, and he now writes that John must recognize Langton as Archbishop of Canterbury, says that since the election was held in Rome, there is no need for John to give his assent!"

Richard was stunned. "Christ Jesus help us all," he breathed, and turned away. Joanna followed, clutched at his arm.

"Richard, I do not understand. What does this mean?"

"You truly do not know?" He stared at her in such surprise that Joanna blushed.

"No," she confessed, "I do not. I knew, of course, that the Archbishop of Canterbury had died, but to be truthful, Richard, I thought of little last year except my own troubles. I was, after all, facing a marriage I dreaded. And I've been in Wales since May. Will you tell me what has happened?"

"The trouble began last year, with Archbishop Walter's death. A faction of the Christchurch monks held a clandestine midnight meeting, elected Reginald, their subprior, as Archbishop, sent him secretly to Rome to secure the Pope's confirmation. When Papa got word of this, he was understandably wroth. The King has ever had the right to have his own man as Archbishop; for more than a hundred years, so has it been. Papa confronted the monks at Canterbury, and they repented their folly, disavowed Reginald's election. Last December they did choose an Archbishop more to Papa's liking, John de Grey, Bishop of Norwich."

Richard frowned. "This past March the Pope declared Bishop de Grey's election invalid, ordered the monks to send a new delegation to Rome. And now he has dared to handpick his own man as Archbishop of Canterbury! Papa can never ratify Langton's election, never. No English king would.''

''Oh, dear God!'' Joanna sat down suddenly in the window seat, staring up at her brother in dismay. ''The Pope will not back down, either, Richard. If Papa will not recognize Langton as Archbishop of Canterbury, he may well lay England under Interdict!''

Joanna bit her lip, remembering how the innocent had suffered when the Pope laid France under Interdict six years ago. Few papal weapons were as effective, and few were as unfair, inflicting pain upon the many to punish the few, denying to the faithful all Sacraments save the Last Rites, denying them Mass, confession, burial in consecrated ground. Philip was a monarch noted for his inflexible nature, his unimaginative obstinacy. He had capitulated in seven months. But Papa will not, Joanna thought with sudden certainty. Even if the Pope does lay all England under Interdict, he'll not yield. And then the Pope will have no choice. To compel earthly obedience, he will sacrifice Papa's immortal soul, will lay upon him the anathema of excommunication.

Joanna had been present when the Bishop of Lincoln excommunicated a baron who'd run afoul of Church law. She'd never forgotten it. The church had been hung with black tapestry. Moving with a slow, measured step, the Bishop and priests had entered the chancel, each holding aloft a flaming candle. And then the Bishop had cried out in a truly terrible voice, a voice that carried to Joanna the shiver of thunderbolts and the smell of sulphur, ''Gilbert de Remy! Let him be cursed in the city and cursed in the field; cursed in his granary, his harvest, and his children; as Dathan and Abiram were swallowed up by the gaping earth, so may Hell swallow him; and even as today we quench the torches in our hands, so may the light of his life be quenched for all eternity, unless he do repent!'' An appalled silence had fallen over those watching, and then they had flung their candles to the ground, casting the church into darkness.

''Papa will not yield, Richard. You know he will not. And if he does not . . .''

''If he does not,'' Richard said bleakly, ''God pity England.''

ABER, NORTH WALES

January 1207

"Is Aber much farther, Madame?" Alison's face was hooded by her mantle, but her voice was slurred with fatigue. Joanna felt a prick of remorse, for she was responsible for their punishing pace, having overruled Dylan and insisted that they push on for Aber instead of passing the night in comfort at Aberconwy Abbey. She knew she was being unfair to the others, especially to Alison. But she'd had six weeks to nurture her hopes, to hone her expectations to a fine edge.

Moreover, there was an element of calculation in her insistence; she wanted to arrive at Aber after dark. It was well and good for Isabelle blithely to advise her to lure Llewelyn to her bedchamber, for Isabelle's shyness had not survived her first glance into a mirror. But Joanna did not think she had either the experience or the self-assurance to carry off an amorous ambush, to play the coquette with such obvious intent. If she were to reach Aber at night, however, what would be more natural than that she'd go to Llewelyn's chambers to let him know of her arrival? If he responded as she hoped, her journey would end in his bed; if not, she could at least protect her pride, would be able to make a dignified departure for her own chambers. The more Joanna thought on it, the more foolproof it seemed—and the more appealing, a private reunion in soft firelight, with a bed so invitingly available for more intimate conversation.

Winter travel was always a dubious proposition; men who might easily cover thirty miles of a summer's day in June would find themselves lucky to make half that distance come January. But Joanna had allowed for that, felt sure they would still reach Aber soon after dark. What she had not allowed for was the snowstorm. It slowed them to a walk, for a time halted them altogether, and when at last they rode into Aber, it was well past midnight.

Joanna's disappointment was not as acute as it might otherwise have been; by then she was so tired and so cold that she yearned only for sleep, and as soon as a fire was lit in her chamber, she and Alison fell, shivering, into bed. She awoke just before dawn, to find Alison already up and dressed; when she offered apologies for the harshness of Alison's introduction to Wales, the other girl said with a grin, "If those mountains are as fearsome as you said, Madame, I think it was probably a mercy that I was spared the sight of them!"

Joanna grinned, too, remembering her first glimpse of Penmaenmawr Pass. "I daresay you're right!" Alison was a genuine jewel, she thought fondly, blessing her luck in having thought to mention Blanche's sulks to Isabelle. In one brief afternoon Isabelle had resolved the problem, finding Blanche a position with the Countess of Surrey and finding Alison for Joanna. A Yorkshire knight's younger daughter, Alison was ambitious enough to jump at the chance to serve in a royal household, and plucky enough to look upon a sojourn in Wales as an adventure. She was, Joanna now saw, holding out the most becoming of Joanna's new gowns. Joanna had been dubious of the color, a dark wine red, but Isabelle had brushed aside her qualms, and as always, her fashion sense was flawless; when worn with a rose-colored bliaut, the effect was pleasing even to Joanna's hypercritical eye.

"You seemed so eager to be back with your lord husband, my lady, that I thought you would wish to go to him upon waking."

Suddenly Joanna was wide awake. She stared at the gown; it glowed with soft, seductive color, and her pulse began to quicken. "Yes," she said, "I do."

Dressing with nervous haste, she fidgeted as Alison combed out her long, dark hair; she'd made the daring decision to leave it unbound, flowing free down her back. And then Alison was holding out her mantle, saying with a smile, "How pleased Lord Llewelyn shall be to see you, Madame."

The snow had ended in the night, but the bailey was blanketed in drifts and a chill, damp wind was sweeping off the sea. Clutching the most elegant pair of Llewelyn's new gloves, Joanna cautiously made her way toward her husband's quarters; never had the Welsh partiality for separate buildings seemed so ill advised. The sky was just beginning to lighten, but the mountain peaks were crowned with clouds, warning that the sun's sovereignty was likely to be brief.

She knew Llewelyn was an even earlier riser than most, but this morning he seemed to be lingering abed, for his squires were still asleep, bundled under blankets in the outer chamber. The guard, too, was dozing, but he jerked upright as Joanna closed the door, blinking at her as if she were an apparition. "Holy Jesus, Madame, where did you come from?" he blurted out, with such a guileless disregard for protocol that Joanna had to laugh.

"You're dreaming; I'm still in London," she said teasingly, and moved past him into her husband's bedchamber. The room was in semidarkness, shutters drawn and candles as yet unlit, and she paused in the doorway, hesitant until she heard Llewelyn's voice. There was a smoky sound to it, a lazy languor that warmed her like a physical touch. She'd never before realized how musical a language Welsh was; it had a lilt and cadence all its own. The bed curtains were partially pulled back; she took a step forward, saw the woman first. She was propped up on an elbow, her face in shadows, but as Joanna watched, she leaned over, spilling dark-honey hair onto Llewelyn as their mouths met. He said something that made her laugh, kissed her again, and started to sit up. As he did, he turned his head, saw Joanna standing frozen in the doorway.

"Joanna?" He sounded utterly incredulous, as if doubting his own senses, and that broke the spell. Joanna spun around, fled into the antechamber, out into the snow. She fell twice; the second time her ankle twisted under her and she lost Llewelyn's gloves, but she regained her feet before any of the startled spectators could come to her aid, at last reached the refuge of her bedchamber.

"My God, Madame, what happened?"

Joanna pulled the bolt into place, stumbled toward the nearest coffer. Her ankle had begun to throb. Raising her hand to her hair, she found it wet with snow; so, too, were the skirts of her wine-red gown.

"Madame, you're trembling so! Can you not tell me what be wrong?"

"No," Joanna said. "No."

At a loss, Alison did what she could, cleaned the snow from Joanna's gown, removed her mantle, poured her a cup of wine. Joanna set it down untouched. She seemed oblivious to Alison's awkward attempts at consolation, but she jumped to her feet at the sound of footsteps in the antechamber.

"Joanna, we do need to talk."

Alison was reaching for the bolt when Joanna shook her head vehemently. "But Madame, he is your husband!"

"Joanna, open the door."

Alison looked helplessly to Joanna for guidance. Joanna said nothing, staring at the door.

In the outer chamber, Llewelyn, too, was staring at the door. His demands for admittance were accomplishing nothing except to attract an audience. Turning, he slammed the antechamber door in their faces, again tried the latch in vain. He was not accustomed to being defied, nor to being made to feel foolish, and at this moment he felt very foolish indeed. It was almost a relief, therefore, to have Joanna present him with a legitimate grievance, to be able to ease his discomfiture in anger.

"Joanna, I'll not tell you again. If you do not open this door, I swear by Christ that I'll fetch an axe and force it!"

There was a long silence. Just when he'd begun to fear he might have to follow through on his threat, he heard the bolt slide back. The girl who opened the door was unfamiliar to him, obviously frightened. Joanna was standing by the trestle table. She took several backward steps as Llewelyn strode toward her, said, "Do not ever lock a door against me again."

She flinched, and he saw then that she was no less frightened than her maid. Norman men were, he knew, free with their fists, apt to follow up a verbal reprimand with physical reinforcement. That realization took some of the edge off his temper. So, too, did the tears glistening behind her lashes.

Llewelyn took a deep breath, remembered he was here to redress a wrong, not to inflict new ones. "I did not want to hurt you, lass, in truth I did not."

But when he put his hand on her arm, she said stonily, "Go away. Just go away and leave me be."

She was, Llewelyn thought, making this needlessly difficult. "Joanna, I am sorry," he said, to Joanna not sounding sorry at all. "But this was not all my fault. I did not expect you back for a fortnight, at least. How was I to know you'd return so suddenly, or that you'd make a dawn appearance in my bedchamber? For most of our marriage, you've acted as if that was the last place you'd ever want to be!"

Joanna crimsoned. Her humiliation was, for the moment, even stronger than her hurt; she could think only of what a fool she'd made of herself. If only she had it to do over, if only God would give her back those shaming moments before his bed. "You need

not worry," she said, much chagrined by the sudden tremor in
her voice, "I'll not intrude upon you again. You can go back to
your bed, back to your slut, finish what I so rudely interrupted."

"Cristyn is no slut," he said coldly. "She is Tegwared and
Anghared's mother."

Cristyn. Did he call her "beloved" and "darling"? Did he
murmur Welsh words of endearment whilst making love? "Forgive my innocence, my lord husband, but even amongst the
Welsh I'd not think bearing two bastard children would be a
testament to a woman's virtue!"

Llewelyn looked at her without speaking for an unbearably
long moment. " 'Even amongst the Welsh,' we do honor those
who gave us life. The slurs you cast upon Cristyn can as easily
be turned against your own mother, can they not?" He did not
wait for her response, but turned and walked out.

Joanna's anger ebbed away, to be replaced by desolation. She
sank down, trembling, upon the nearest stool. Llewelyn was
right. In seeking to belittle Cristyn, she had indeed besmirched
Clemence, too. Far worse, she had affronted Llewelyn beyond
forgiving. He would hate her now, would never want her as his
wife.

So caught up was she in her own misery that it was some time
before she became aware of Alison. The girl was kneeling by her
stool, looking up at her with eyes full of fear.

"Ah, Madame, what have you done?" she whispered. "Go
after him, beg his forgiveness ere it be too late!"

"It is already too late," Joanna said wretchedly, but Alison
shook her head.

"He is angry, yes, but his heart has not had time to harden
against you. You must seek him out ere it does. Madame, listen
to me. I do know what it is like to live in a house without love.
My mother had too sharp a tongue, and then, too, my father
blamed her for failing to give him a son . . . Well, the reasons
count for naught. What does is that he did not use her well,
Madame, made of her life a Hell on earth. A man can do that,
my lady, can treat his wife no better than the meanest serf, and
who is to gainsay him? She is his, after all, to be lessoned as he
chooses. And in this we all are sisters. High birth did not spare
Philip's Danish-born Queen. Nor your grandmother, Queen Eleanor of blessed memory. And your husband is a Prince, is a man
to expect obedience above all else. I was astonished, in truth,
that he did not take his hand to you, but you're not likely to be so

lucky a second time. Go to him, tell him you're sorry. Would
you have him hate you for all your married life?''

"No," Joanna said. "Oh, no!" And before she could repent
of her resolve, she snatched up her mantle, ran from the chamber.

The bailey was now astir with people; they turned to stare as
Joanna passed. There was no one at all, however, in Llewelyn's
outer chamber. Joanna leaned for a moment against the door,
sought to catch her breath. She'd not yet thought what she was
going to say to him, knew that if she dwelt upon it, she'd lose
her nerve. Tapping lightly on the door, she said, "Llewelyn, it's
Joanna. May we talk?"

She heard footsteps, and then the door swung open. Joanna
stiffened at sight of Cristyn. She'd not dreamed Cristyn would
still be there; surely, if the woman had any decency at all, she'd
have withdrawn at once. Yet Cristyn had not even bothered to
dress, was clad only in a linen chemise. This was the first real
look Joanna had gotten at her husband's mistress. She saw before
her a tall, poised woman in her mid-twenties, with rather unusual
and striking coloring. Cristyn had very white skin, masses of
dark gold hair, and brown eyes. She was not beautiful; her mouth
was too large, her nose too tip-tilted, but there was about her an
unstudied sensuality, a provocative earthiness more alluring than
mere prettiness. Joanna could understand all too well the appeal
Cristyn might have for a man, for Llewelyn.

For a heartbeat they stared at each other, and then Cristyn said,
in passable French, "Llewelyn is not here. He was to meet this
morn in Bangor with Bishop Robert and the Bishop of St
Asaph, rode out directly after he did talk to you."

Turning away, she moved back toward the bed. "You will
excuse me whilst I finish dressing?" she said, reaching for her
stockings.

"I do not recall giving you leave to sit in my presence,"
Joanna snapped, saw a resentful flush rise in Cristyn's face and
throat. She came reluctantly to her feet, making it quite clear that
she thought Joanna was not playing fair. Joanna did not care;
fairness was the furthest concern from her mind. If she'd thought
her command would have been obeyed, she'd have banished
Cristyn then and there into English exile, even unto Ireland if she
could.

Cristyn was waiting, brown eyes suddenly wary. "Madame?"
she said icily, and Joanna felt so much hatred that it frightened
her. She stared past Cristyn at the bed; it was still unmade,
rumpled and warm where they had lain, Llewelyn and Cristyn,

making leisurely love through the night. Whirling about, Joanna crossed the threshold, beckoned to one of the men loitering without.

"Madame?"

"Take that bed out into the bailey, and there burn it," she said, saw the man's jaw drop.

"Jesú, Madame, I cannot do that! It is my lord's bed, is worth—"

"And I am your lord's wife, am I not? I have just given you a command, so see to it—now."

Cristyn had followed Joanna to the doorway of the antechamber; she, too, looked dumbfounded. The man's eyes flicked from her to Joanna, and then he nodded. It took four men to wrestle the mattress out into the bailey; cursing and panting, they dragged it a safe distance from the building. By now a large, curious crowd had gathered. Someone brought forth a torch; there were loud murmurings among the onlookers as the bed coverings ignited, burst into flame.

Joanna stood motionless, watching as the bed burned. After a time the wind shifted, blew smoke into her face, and she coughed, turned away.

"What of the bedframe, my lady? Shall we torch that, too?" The voice was young, the face friendly, lit by an engaging grin.

"No," Joanna said, startled to see that most of the other faces were friendly, too. She'd not expected that. They were watching her with amused interest, even approval, seemed to take her action as a great joke. To Joanna, it was anything but that. She was just beginning to realize what she'd done. She must have been mad, in truth, for Llewelyn would never forgive her now, never.

Although Alison had managed to infect Joanna for a time with her panic, it soon passed. Llewelyn wanted an alliance with her father, would do nothing to jeopardize it. He'd not send her back to England in disgrace. Nor would he ever abuse her as Philip abused Ingeborg. She felt sure that was not Llewelyn's way.

He might well beat her for burning the bed, though. Even the most indulgent husband was likely to react with rage to folly of that sort. Each time Joanna thought of facing him with such a sin on her conscience, she shivered. She'd once seen a knight strike his wife in the great hall at Westminster, before a score of wellborn witnesses; blood had gushed from the woman's nose, stained her gown and wimple. And while the man's action had been greeted with almost universal disapproval, it was not his brutality that earned him such scorn, but rather that he'd been so ill-mannered as to punish her in public. Even men who never hit their wives would still, Joanna knew, defend in principle their right to do so. Women were the lesser sex, after all, and even Holy Church said they were born to be ruled by man. Alison was right; she had indeed been lucky that morning.

But what she feared far more than a beating was the loss of Llewelyn's friendship. How could she bear to have him look upon her with distaste, to shun her company, treat her with chill politeness? And how could it be otherwise now? Even when he finally took her to his bed, it would be without affection or tenderness; he'd not make love to her, would make use of her to beget an heir. He might even install Cristyn openly in his bed, at his table. And it was her fault. She had allowed her jealousy to rob her of that which she most wanted.

The six-mile ride from Aber to Bangor Fawr yn Arfon had done much to cool Llewelyn's anger, as he'd known it would. He'd always had a happy faculty for concentrating upon one problem at a time, and by the time he arrived at the great cathedral church of St Deiniol, he had as his primary concern the upcoming meeting with the Bishops of Bangor and St Asaph. He was never able to put his quarrel with Joanna completely from his mind, but he did succeed in focusing his attention upon the matters at hand, and by day's end he was satisfied with what he had accomplished.

It was dusk as he made ready to return to Aber. His escort was augmented by Ednyved's force, for the latter had been a guest of Bishop Robert's, and was now planning to move on to his own manor at Llys Euryn in Creuddyn.

"I assume you can find me a comfortable bed for the night at Aber?" Giving Llewelyn a mischievous, sidelong glance, Ednyved added, "Or should I be offering you a safe bed at Llys Euryn?"

Llewelyn could not hide his surprise. "What have you—second sight?"

Ednyved grinned. "Just an ear for choice gossip. One of your men—who shall remain mercifully nameless—was kind enough to tell me about all I missed this morn. Did your girl-wife truly walk in on you and Cristyn? Jesus wept! What did you do? Mind you, this is not mere morbid curiosity, but in case I ever find myself in a like predicament!''

"I did what any man would do when he's caught in the wrong. I lost my temper."

Ednyved laughed, then nudged his mount closer to Llewelyn's. "Does Joanna know, Llewelyn, that you've given her grounds for ending the marriage? Is there any chance she's on her way home to England even as we talk?''

Llewelyn shook his head. "Joanna knows naught of Welsh ways, even after some months in our midst. Moreover, Joanna knows that John wants me as ally, and as hard as it may be to fathom, she has found in him much to love.''

Llewelyn was aware that he was a magnet for all eyes, but it did not bother him unduly; he'd lived most of his thirty-three years at center stage. He was bothered, however, by Joanna's failure to appear for the meal. Each time he glanced at her empty seat, he felt a twinge of guilt; nor was his conscience eased to be told she'd eaten nothing all day, had not ventured from her chambers since the morning. He sent a servant to the kitchen, and by the time dinner was done, a platter was waiting, mead and wafers and venison pasty. Ednyved sauntered over, drawled, "As peace offerings go, you'd get better results with moonstones and amethyst," accompanying Llewelyn as he departed the hall, stepped out into the icy dark of the bailey.

"My lord . . .'' A man emerged so unexpectedly from the shadows that they both started, instinctively dropped hands to sword hilts. But as he stepped closer, Llewelyn recognized Aldwyn, his silentiary.

"My lord . . . after you rode out this morn, your wife did go to your chambers in search of you. The Lady Cristyn was there and they had words.'' He paused, said unhappily, "My lord, I know not how to tell you, but . . .''

"But what?'' Llewelyn said sharply.

"Princess Joanna . . . she ordered us to burn your bed.''

"She did what?'' Turning, Llewelyn looked at Ednyved, and then, of one accord and to Aldwyn's indescribable relief, they were shouting with laughter.

"Lord Jesus,'' Ednyved gasped, wiping his eyes. "Just count yourself lucky you were not in it at the time, my lad!'' Sobering somewhat, he said, "I've a confession, one that'll make me sound an utter ass. But when Aldwyn gave that pregnant pause, the damnedest thought crossed my mind, that Joanna knew more of Welsh law than you thought, knew that, catching Cristyn in your bed, she had the right to claim Cristyn's life without paying a blood-fine!''

"Ah, but only if she did it with her own hand. Can you truly imagine Joanna stabbing Cristyn . . . or anyone else?'' After a moment, Llewelyn began to laugh again. "But then, I never thought her capable of burning my bed, either!''

Llewelyn found himself hesitating before the door of Joanna's bedchamber. He was perfectly willing to placate his young wife, to offer her the balm of smiles and soft, soothing words. He was not so willing to humble his pride, to play a role for which he'd had so little practice, that of penitent, and it was with an unexpected sense of unease that he beckoned to his servant, reached for the door latch.

He forgot his reluctance, however, with his first sight of Joanna. Her face was pinched and drawn, a mirror for such misery that he no longer begrudged her an apology, would give it gladly if that would but heal her hurt.

He gestured for the servant to put down his burden, waiting until they were alone to say, "I was told you'd eaten nothing all day, Joanna.''

Joanna was staring at the platter in disbelief. "You . . . you are not angry with me?''

"Ah, Joanna . . . I'm sorry, love, I swear I am.''

To be offered absolution when she'd been expecting damnation was, to Joanna, nothing less than miraculous, and when Llewelyn took a step toward her, she more than met him halfway, flung herself into his arms with a choked cry.

"I thought you'd never forgive me, never. Llewelyn, I am so sorry. I had not the right to speak to you as I did, no right to reproach you. It is not a wife's place to question her husband's actions. I know that. But I . . . I was so jealous, so very jealous . . .''

Llewelyn stroked her hair, tightened his arms around her. "Joanna, you had every right. Let's sit on the settle and talk about it.''

Joanna accepted a cupful of mead and, when urged by Llewelyn, even took a few bites of a cheese-filled wafer, but she tasted none of it. She still could not quite believe Llewelyn was here, sitting beside her on the settle, sharing her mead cup, for the first time calling her "love" as if he meant it.

"I think you need to know how we look upon women. It is

true, lass, that a Welshwoman cannot inherit her father's lands, whereas she would have a right of inheritance in England. But that is for the same reason that our laws do exclude men maimed, deaf, crippled, or stricken with leprosy. It was feared, you see, that women and such men could not hold their lands against attack. But we do not claim that womanly weakness on the battlefield should make her subordinate in all else, too, as you Normans do. Our women cannot be wed against their will, and a Welsh wife has no less right to walk away from an unhappy marriage than does her husband.''

"But Llewelyn . . . the Church does recognize only three grounds for voiding a marriage: a previous plight troth, kinship within the seventh degree, or spiritual affinity such as acting as godparent.''

"Well, to tell you true, Joanna, when the Church's teachings conflict with the old customs, we tend to go our own way. As in our preference for marrying cousins. We have a saying, love: 'Marry in the kin and fight the feud with the stranger.' So when it comes to interpreting the marriage bond, we follow Hywel the Good rather than the Pope.''

Llewelyn laughed suddenly. "I've been told that some Norman churchmen see my success as divine proof of the power of legitimacy. My father Iorwerth was a child of Owain Fawr's first marriage; when Owain later married his cousin Crisiant, the Church refused to recognize the union, and when he would not abjure Crisiant, Thomas à Becket excommunicated him. So they see my triumph over my uncles Davydd and Rhodri as ordained, they being sons of the so-called incestuous marriage. The only flaw in that theology is that my mother and father were themselves first cousins!''

He handed Joanna back the mead cup, said, "But we were talking of how we end a marriage. It may always be done by mutual consent. And then, a husband may disavow his wife if she claims to be a virgin and he discovers on their wedding night that she was not, or if he finds her in compromising circumstances with another man, of course, or if her marriage portion fell short of what was promised.''

Llewelyn had been, for some moments now, playing with her hair; the feel of his fingers on her throat was so delightfully distracting to Joanna that she was not fully concentrating upon what he was saying. But at that, she smiled up at him, murmuring, "Then you do have me for better or worse, since my father handed Ellesmere Castle over to you months ago, I would never be unfaithful, and I am indeed a virgin.''

"For much too long, I think," he said softly, dark eyes promising enough to bring a blush to Joanna's face. "But do you not want to know how a wife may shed an unwanted husband? There are four grievances that will gain her freedom: if the man contracts leprosy, if he has foul breath, if he is incapable in bed . . . or if he does three times dishonor their marriage vows.''

Joanna all but choked on her mead. "Now you are teasing me!''

"No," he said, "I am not, love. The first two times that a Welsh wife discovers her husband has bedded with another woman, she has the right to demand from him payment of a *gowyn*—a fine, if you will—for his adultery. With his third fall from grace, she may leave him, although if she does not, she then has no further cause for complaint."

Llewelyn paused. "There is one more reason for ending a marriage, Joanna—if a husband does ever bring another woman under his wife's roof.''

"As you did with Cristyn?" Joanna whispered, and he nodded.

"Yes, as I did with Cristyn. Amongst our people, that is one of the three great scandals, and the wife may at once disavow the marriage, disavow the husband who has so wronged her.''

"I . . . I would never do that, Llewelyn." Joanna was stunned; in her world, laws such as these were more than radical, they were revolutionary. She was silent for a time, trying to take in this astonishing new insight, that Llewelyn, not she, had been in the wrong.

"I thank you for telling me. You did not have to, you know . . .'' It came to her then, the reason for Llewelyn's remarkable restraint, and she cried, "Now I do understand why, as angry as you were this morn, you did not touch me! It was because I was in the right, was it not?''

"Joanna, I've never hit a woman in my life. You've not been listening to me, love. Did I not tell you we do not treat our women as the Normans do? Amongst my people, we do not take out our bad tempers upon our wives just because they happen to be handy. Welsh law does allow a husband the right to discipline his wife for three offenses only: if she is unfaithful, if she gambles away the family goods, or if she casts slurs upon his manhood. Should he strike her for any other reason, he is then obligated to pay her a *sarhaed* or honor-price.''

Joanna had been listening in astonishment. " 'A woman, a

serf, and a willow tree, the more you beat them, the better they be,' " she quoted, and shook her head. "But do men truly abide by these laws, Llewelyn?"

"Not all men, love. More do than not, however. You see, an abused wife has the right to appeal to her male kinsmen for succor, and if they fail to protect her, the shame then falls upon them. Knowing a careless slap will bring down upon his head the wrath of his wife's kin, and might even give rise to a blood feud . . . well, that does act to curb all but the most heedless of men."

Llewelyn drew her still closer, and Joanna shifted so that she could pillow her head against his chest. "I begin to think the greatest gift the Almighty could give any woman would be for her to be born Welsh!"

"Or to marry a Welshman," Llewelyn suggested, and kissed her. For Joanna, it was as it had been on that November noon at Rhosyr; she experienced again sensations exciting and unfamiliar, found her body responding to his touch like a flower starved for sun. All her senses seemed suddenly to have intensified, and when he slid his hand into the bodice of her gown, began to caress her breast, she gave a gasp, sought his mouth with hers.

Llewelyn was delighted. Brushing aside her fall of thick ebony hair, he put his lips to the pulse in her throat, with his free hand unfastening the side lacings of her bliaut. "Sweet . . . very sweet. I must have been well and truly out of my mind not to take you to my bed ere this," he murmured, utterly taken aback when Joanna abruptly went rigid in his embrace, then recoiled as violently as on that day at Rhaeadr Ewynol.

For a startled moment, Llewelyn did not move, staring up at her in amazement. He could not have mistaken her willingness, the way her body warmed under his caresses. She was not merely acquiescent, she was eager. That had been no pretense, he'd wager his life on it. Yet there was no pretense, either, in the stricken look on her face, no denying her sudden fear. He could only assume he'd gone too fast, fondled her too intimately, too soon. Coming to his feet, he said, "What is it, love? You've no cause for fear, Joanna, not with me."

"But you do not know what I've done!"

"What you've done?" Whatever Llewelyn might have been expecting to hear, that was not it.

On the verge of tears, Joanna nodded. "I did go to your chambers this morning to ask your forgiveness. She . . . Cristyn was there, and I . . . oh, Llewelyn, I burned your bed!"

Llewelyn bit down on his lower lip, pulled her back into his arms. "Yes, love, I know."

"You know?" she said incredulously. "And you're not angry?"

"Well, I'd rather you not make a habit of it." But with that, Llewelyn's gravity shattered into a multitude of mirthful splinters, and he laughed until he, too, was on the verge of tears.

Giddy with relief, Joanna began to laugh, too, until Llewelyn kissed her again. "Now," he said, with a grin that caught at her heart, "ere I take you to bed, have you any other sins to confess?"

Joanna found herself longing to admit how much she loved him. But she did not, for it was not fair to burden him with a love he might never be able to return. She shook her head, looking up at him with eyes so soft and glowing, such utterly trusting eyes, that Llewelyn caught his breath.

"It will be good for you, Joanna," he promised. "I'll give you as much time as you need; we do have all night."

"Do you know what Isabelle told me? That a woman will find the greatest pleasure in an older man's bed. She says a youth of twenty or so will pounce upon a girl like a dog on a bone, will be done and dying away almost ere he begins. But a man of a more seasoned age knows well how to—in her words, not mine—mount a mare and prolong the ride!"

"I'm almost afraid to ask, but how did Isabelle come to be so worldly, so knowing in carnal matters? John gave her a crown; did she give him horns?"

"Of course not! She knows that older men make better lovers because Papa did tell her so. Llewelyn . . . why are you laughing at me?"

"Because I suspect, my darling, that you're three swallows short of tipsy."

Joanna peered into her half-empty cup of mead, trying to remember whether this was her second or third. "I believe," she said thoughtfully, "that you might well be right. I do feel . . . strange."

Llewelyn moved his hand caressingly up her thigh. "How, Joanna?"

"Feather-light, as if all the bone and marrow in my body weighed no more than gossamer, as if your arms alone did anchor me to the earth." She shivered as Llewelyn tugged at the bodice of her chemise, freeing her breasts. His breath was hot on her skin, and she watched with fascination as her nipples swelled, became hard and taut. "Oh, Llewelyn, love, you're right, I am tipsy! What I do not know is whether it is the mead, or whether it is you."

"Let's find out," he said, and when she put her arms around his neck, he lifted her from the settle, carried her across the chamber to the bed.

Llewelyn had never before understood the appeal virgins had for other men, had always looked upon a woman's maidenhead as more of an impediment to pleasure than a proof of purity. But now, with Joanna, he found that virginity need not be embarrassing or inhibiting, that it could even be enhancing. There was something very exciting in Joanna's wonderment, in her surprise and her satisfaction. As she sighed, twisted against him, he knew she was experiencing sensations utterly new to her, experiencing all the urgency and pleasure that the body could give—for the very first time. To diminish her pain and prolong their enjoyment, he sought to keep physical needs under mental thrall, making use of all the tricks he'd learned in the twenty years since he had, as an awed fourteen-year-old, discovered how sweet the fruits of the flesh could be, drawing out their lovemaking until he dared delay no longer. She stiffened under him, but did not cry out, and he felt the barrier give way with his second thrust. Joanna was gasping his name. He covered her mouth with his own, and she clung tightly, then turned her head from side to side on the pillow, shuddering, all but blinding them both with the wild tossing of her hair. Yielding to his own need, he let it take him toward satisfaction, toward that ephemeral moment of release, so fleeting and yet so overwhelming in its intensity, in its peculiar union of pleasure and pain.

Joanna awoke with an enormous thirst, a dull headache, and a profound sense of wonder. Alison at once approached the bed, offering a cup of watered-down wine. Reaching for it eagerly, Joanna drank in grateful gulps. "What time is it?" she yawned, and winced, for she'd suddenly discovered that her thigh muscles were stiff and sore.

"Nigh on noon, Madame. My lord Prince said we were to let you sleep, and to give you this." Holding out an unsealed parchment.

This speaker was a stranger to Joanna, was a slender young woman with a delicate heart-shaped face and thick chestnut braids. "Who," Joanna asked, "are you?"

The girl made a shy curtsy. "I am Branwen, Madame. Lord

Llewelyn wanted you to have a handmaiden who spoke French, thought I might suit you better than Enid. I would have been here yesterday to welcome you back, but we did not expect you for nigh on a fortnight. That will not happen again, I promise.''

"That is all right, Branwen," Joanna said absently. Llewelyn's message was a letdown, a brief two lines: "*Cariad,* I do have to meet again with the Bishops in Bangor, will be back by dark." No more than that, unsigned but for a large scrawling double 1.

"Branwen . . . what does *cariad* mean?"

"*Cariad?* Why, that is Welsh for 'beloved,' Madame," she said, and Joanna sank back, smiling, upon the pillow.

Never had an afternoon passed with such excruciating slowness. Never had Joanna so begrudged daylight its domain. But with the coming of dusk had come, too, the snow. Joanna's spirits plummeted. When it was evident even to her that Llewelyn was not going to return in time for dinner, if he returned at all, she went off to preside over a glum meal in the great hall. The snow slackened somewhat as the evening dragged on, and twice the arrival of latecomers sent her flying to the window, watching hopefully as they dismounted in the bailey. The third time horsemen rode in, she did not even bother to look, having at last accepted the obvious, that Llewelyn had decided to pass the night in Bangor. But then Alison exclaimed, "Madame, I see lights in your lord's chambers!"

Joanna's excitement was contagious, and Alison and Branwen enthusiastically set about making her ready for Llewelyn, brushing out her hair, applying strategic daubs of perfume. Looking into the mirror Alison held up, Joanna was, for once, pleased with what she saw. Her eyes reflected the color of her moss-green gown, and she was becomingly flushed, a flush that seemed to be spreading through her entire body, the throbbing, languid warmth that claimed her each time she let herself think upon their lovemaking.

"My lady . . ." Alison turned slowly from the window. Not looking at Joanna's face, she said, "The lights . . . they've gone out."

Joanna put the mirror down. "Of course," she said steadily. "I did not stop to think; after a ride in such foul weather, my lord husband would be exhausted, in truth." But the reasonableness of that did little to ease her hurt. Could he not at least have come in to bid her good night?

Once in bed, she found it difficult to sleep. The memories of

what she and Llewelyn had done last night in this bed were too
vivid, too real. At last she dozed, only to be awakened with a
shock, with the feel of an icy breath against her cheek. Llewelyn
was sitting on the bed, shook snow onto them both as he leaned
over to embrace her.

"Not even a lantern left in the window for me, and sound
asleep in the bargain," he complained, caressing her all the while
with his eyes, and Joanna, fully awake now, threw herself into
his arms.

"I thought you came back hours ago, had gone to bed!"

Llewelyn grinned, started to remind her of the burned bed, but
something eager and innocent in her face stopped him, and he
said instead, "Now why ever would I want to sleep alone when I
could sleep with you?"

Alison and Branwen had discreetly disappeared. Joanna sat up,
reached for her bedrobe. "Where are your squires?"

"I sent them off to bed, thought I might persuade you to offer
a hand."

Joanna was as compulsively neat as Llewelyn was not, and she
snatched up his mantle and tunic almost before they hit the floor,
folded them conscientiously across a coffer chest. By now he was
pulling off his shirt, and she gave a concerned cry. "No! Over by
the fire, or you'll catch your death of cold."

"I do not recall you caring where I undressed last night," he
said, and Joanna blushed and then laughed.

"To tell you true, I do not even remember undressing last
night," she confessed, kneeling before him to help unfasten the
cords binding his chausses to his braies. "It just seemed to . . .
happen." He smiled down at her, and marveling how her body's
needs suddenly seemed to exist independently of her conscious
control, she reached for the nearest cord, saw that Llewelyn's
passions were kindled as quickly as her own. Her touch had been
light, inadvertent, but as her fingers brushed his upper thigh, his
reaction was immediate, pronounced.

"Women are lucky," she teased shyly, "for they can hide
their desire so much more easily than can men," and Llewelyn
laughed.

"Who wants to hide it?" he said, and stripped off his chausses
and braies. Joanna had often seen naked men, as a child had
occasionally entered John's bedchamber as he was dressing, had
assisted Ela in bathing more than one highborn guest at Salisbury
Castle, had passed serfs bathing in the river in summer. She'd
long ago mastered that which was essential in a society so

lacking in privacy: the elusive art of seeing and yet not seeing. Now, however, she let her eyes linger upon her husband's body. He was taller than most Welshmen, his the lean, wiry strength of stamina rather than of muscle and sinew. He had an insignificant amount of chest hair, his skin dark and smooth, marred only by the scars of old wounds, scars that now took on a new and sinister significance to Joanna, one tracking across his ribcage, another angled toward his collar bone, a third slanting in a thin white line from his pubic hair down his thigh. Joanna reached out, traced its path with gentle fingers.

"That must have been a frightening injury."

"That, my darling, was not the half of it!" he said wryly. "There is nothing like a groin wound to make a man repent his sinful past." He did then what Joanna had wanted him to do all along, put his hand on hers, showed her how best to give a man pleasure.

It was to Joanna enormously gratifying, to find that Llewelyn wanted her caresses and kisses even as much as she wanted his. "It is easy to understand how people came to use the term 'manhood,'" she said, rather breathlessly, "but how explain 'privy member'?"

"How explain any of them, Joanna: cock, shaft, codpiece, pizzle, sword? And in Welsh: *bonllost, gwialen, cal* . . . and those are just the polite terms."

"*Bonllost*," she echoed, amused by the unfamiliar phrasing, and then began to giggle. "I do hope none of our children ever ask me which Welsh word I did learn first!" Llewelyn had taken her into a closer embrace; she could feel his hands under her bedrobe, and she sighed, said softly, "I think, though, that I shall call it Merlin, in honor of the miracles it did work last night."

Llewelyn laughed, and drew her toward the bed. "And I begin to think," he said, "that I do owe the English King a far greater debt than I first realized."

"Llewelyn . . . whilst we were making love, you did call me *breila*. What does that mean?"

"A *breila* is a dusky wild rose. It does suit you, I think."

Joanna was touched almost to tears. "*Breila* . . . that's lovely." She lay back against him, cradled her head in the crook of his shoulder. "I know I was a disappointment to you at first, but . . ."

"Disappointment?" Llewelyn raised himself up on one elbow, saw with surprise that she was neither teasing nor fishing for flattery. "Has no one ever told you, Joanna, that you're beautiful?"

Now it was Joanna's turn to doubt him. "No," she said at last, "but when I was about twelve, I do remember hearing Maude de Braose say I looked verily like a Saracen."

"Who in Christ cares what Maude de Braose thinks?" Llewelyn reached for a long strand of Joanna's hair, pulled it across his throat. "If Saracen women do indeed have hair like black silk, eyes like emeralds, and blood hotter than Greek fire, little wonder men are so eager to take the cross, to reach the Holy Land."

"Oh, love . . ." Leaning over, Joanna gave him a lingering kiss. "That is blasphemous," she said huskily, "and the most memorable compliment any woman ever got."

In reply, Llewelyn dropped a kiss on the tip of her nose, then yawned. Joanna chose to disregard the hint, not yet willing to relinquish the utter euphoria of the moment. "Llewelyn . . . will you tell me of Tangwystl? Did you love her?"

"Yes, I did." Llewelyn did not open his eyes, but the corner of his mouth curved in a smile. "Tangwystl was a flaming redhead, and she did fret over her coloring fully as much as you do over yours, red hair being thought accursed since the days of Judas. But like you, she was fair to look upon . . . very fair."

Joanna did not begrudge Tangwystl that echo of past passion. She felt no jealousy for a dead woman; all her anxieties were for a rival very much alive, for Cristyn. Did he love Cristyn? That was the question she dared not ask.

"Did you never think to wed Tangwystl, Llewelyn?"

"I had not the right, had to make a marriage that would be to Gwynedd's good."

Joanna wondered why she'd asked a question with so obvious an answer. However lovely Isabelle was, she knew her father would not have married her had she not also been heiress to Angoulême, and Llewelyn was no less ambitious. "Llewelyn . . ."

He yawned again. "Joanna, had I known you were one for talking all night, I might have thought twice ere I told Aldwyn to move this bed and all your belongings into my chamber."

Joanna stared at him, momentarily rendered mute. He was so nonchalant, as if unaware of what he was offering her. Sleeping every night in his bed, she'd be a true wife in every sense of the word, not just a consort, a political pawn. And, Lady Mary, what it would mean, to be able to fall asleep in his arms, to reach out and touch him in the night, and, most blessed mercy of all, never to have to lie awake wondering if he was in Cristyn's bed.

"I thought we'd use this chamber for wellborn guests . . ."

Llewelyn paused, belatedly remembering that a private chamber was no small luxury. "Or would you rather keep it for your own, Joanna?"

"Oh, Llewelyn, beloved, need you ask? I'd rather sleep with you in a hut than alone in a palace!"

Llewelyn could not help laughing at the extravagant innocence of that avowal, at once regretted it, for he felt Joanna tense. She'd turned her head aside on the pillow, and he leaned over, touched her cheek. Her lashes lifted, their eyes met, and then she said, "You knew?"

"Let's say I hoped," he said with a smile, and Joanna flushed.

"That is why I did not want to tell you, so you'd not feel you had to . . . to be gallant. It's not fair to you." She bit her lip, all too aware that she was floundering. "What I'm trying to say, Llewelyn, is that I . . . I'm willing to settle for what you can give."

Llewelyn did not answer at once. He'd been rather bemused by her obvious affection for John, had finally conceded that, whatever his other failings, John had at least done right by Joanna. Now he found himself thinking that however much John had done for her, it was not enough. Not nearly enough.

"You hold yourself too cheaply, *breila*," he said gently. "It is true that when I came to Chester last spring, it was to wed with the English King's daughter. But I did ride back through a snowstorm tonight for Joanna."

21

TEWKESBURY, ENGLAND

November 1207

John leaned over the cradle, gazed down at his sleeping son. He felt no particular tenderness for the child, not yet; he'd never had any interest in infants. But he did feel a deep sense of wonder.

"Wherever did he get such red hair? I'm right glad that you are not a suspicious husband, love!"

"My father had reddish hair," John said absently, only half listening to his wife. But then he caught the scent of rosemary, felt her arms slip around his waist. For more than six years she'd been unable to conceive, to give him the heir a King must have. Had she ever despaired? Had she feared that he might put her aside, find grounds to disavow the marriage? He did not know, for they had never discussed it. He'd shrunk from ever saying it aloud, gripped by an irrational belief that to admit his fear would be to make it fact. Turning now, he looked at the lovely face upturned to his. How fair she was. But that had only served to feed his fear. For as the years had passed and her womb failed to quicken, he'd begun to suspect that God had played a macabre and sardonic jest upon him, giving him as wife and Queen the most beautiful woman he'd ever seen, the most desirable bedmate he'd ever had—only then to make her barren.

When she'd suddenly announced that she was pregnant, he'd been stunned, and then wary, not letting himself hope. She could still miscarry, could give birth to a daughter; God might well see that as the ultimate ironic jest. But her pregnancy had been utterly uneventful, and on the morning of October 1, she had given birth to a healthy son.

"Geoffrey, Richard, Osbert, Oliver, Henry . . . and now Henry again, for our babe. Why have you not named any of your sons after yourself, John?"

John shrugged, glanced across the chamber at the monk hovering in the doorway. "What is it?"

"Your son has returned from Wales, my liege. May he enter?"

John nodded, and a moment later Richard strode swiftly into the chamber. "You've given me a devil of a chase, Papa. I reached Winchcombe this morn, only to be told you'd departed for St Mary's Abbey, was not at all sure I'd be able to overtake you."

"Never mind that. What news of Joanna?"

Richard grinned. "The best news, Papa. On All Saints' Day, Joanna did give birth to a black-haired baby daughter."

"Did she now?" John smiled. "She and the babe, they are all right?"

"Indeed, Papa," Richard said without hesitation. In truth, Joanna had not had an easy time; the birth had been a difficult one. But Joanna was now convalescing, was rapidly regaining her strength, and Richard, ever a pragmatist, saw no need for his father and Isabelle to know.

"A girl . . ." Isabelle was staring at Richard in dismay. "Was Joanna very disappointed?"

"She was not disappointed at all."

There was a pause, and then Isabelle said, "I'm so glad," but without any conviction. She knew that had she herself given birth to a daughter, not all the balm in Gilead could have healed so grievous a hurt. Linking her arm in John's, she murmured, "A January return, a November birth—our Joanna did not waste any time putting my advice into practice, did she?" John looked at her so blankly that she prompted, "Do you not remember, love? What I told you about Joanna and Llewelyn?"

John gave a noncommittal grunt, and she fought an urge to laugh. One of the traits she most liked in John was their shared love of gossip. He was no less interested than she in court scandal, enjoyed regaling her with bawdy stories and ribald jests, with invariably accurate accounts of who was sinning with whom. But not once had she ever heard him mention the most scandalous stories of all, those lurid rumors of his mother's youthful indiscretions. And he was, of a sudden, showing the same reticence about his daughter's love life. It amused Isabelle in no small measure, but the lesson was not lost upon her. Seeing now that Richard was regarding her with uncomprehending curiosity, she gave him a meaningless smile, having no intention of enlightening him, for by her lights, secrets shared in bed did not count and her faith still remained unbroken.

John moved away from the cradle, settled himself comfortably in a cushioned window seat. "Do not keep me in suspense, Richard. What unpronounceable Welsh name did Llewelyn inflict upon that innocent babe?"

"Elen, which is Welsh for Helen."

John pondered that for a moment and then conceded, "Well, I grant you it could be worse. But is it true that Llewelyn is making Joanna learn that lunatic language of his?"

Richard laughed, before realizing that his father was not joking. "I do believe it was Joanna's idea, Papa," he said mildly, and John frowned.

"Indeed? It's well and good to be a dutiful wife, but . . ."

"Dutiful wife?" Richard echoed, much amused. "Papa, Joanna does—"

"John, love, did you not say you'd promised to spare some moments for Abbot Walter ere we sup?" Isabelle's intercession was adroitly done, her query conveying no more than a commendable wifely concern. But Richard was not slow; he gave his stepmother a probing look, then wandered over to the cradle to study his baby brother.

John was in no hurry to depart; it was some moments before he reluctantly went off in search of the Abbot. As soon as the door closed behind him, Richard demanded, "Why did you cut me short like that, Isabelle?"

"Because, my dearest, you were about to say that Joanna is hopelessly besotted with her husband . . . or words to that effect, were you not?"

"And if I was? It is true enough, after all."

"Of course it is true. But to say so would have done neither John nor Joanna a kindness, and least of all Llewelyn."

Richard started to protest, stopped, and reflected upon what she seemed to be saying. Isabelle was only a year older than he, and when he'd first begun to feel the sexual stirrings of manhood, he had, for a time of brief and exquisite torment, believed himself to be in love with his father's beautiful wife. So shamed had he been by these wayward yearnings that he'd fought them the only way he knew how, by scorning the object of his sinful lust, by convincing himself that Isabelle was a frivolous little fool, vain and flighty. As an amputation of the soul, it proved to be an effective if drastic cure, and in time he'd outgrown both the desire and the disdain. Within the past year or so, he'd found his sense of perspective returning, and he was once again able to look upon his stepmother without distortion, to see her for what she was and what she was not.

It would never occur to him to discuss with Isabelle the ramifications of John's ongoing quarrel with the Pope. Richard well knew that Isabelle gave little thought to the threat of Interdict and excommunication. But Isabelle knew his father as no one else did, was the first woman to hold his affections, in and out of bed. That was no small feat; it earned her the right to be heard, and he said, "Why do you say that, Isabelle? Papa wants Joanna to be happy; surely you do not doubt that?"

"Yes, he does," she agreed indulgently. "He wants her to be safe and cared for and content. He does not want her to be utterly and passionately in love with Llewelyn ab Iorwerth. Ah, Richard, do you know your father as little as that? Do you not know that John needs ever to come first with those who love him? Is that so surprising? Why do you think John did not attend Joanna's wedding? Oh, I know the reasons he gave why he could not. But if he'd truly wanted to be there, he would have been. He did not, and so he was not."

Joining Richard by the cradle, she began to rock it gently back and forth. "Trust me, Richard, in this. Do not speak to John of Joanna's abiding love for Llewelyn; he does not want to hear it. I think Joanna must sense that, for her letters to him are unlike those to me. To me alone does she go on at length about the unlikely perfections of her Welsh Prince." She laughed suddenly, giving Richard a look that was amused and affectionate and faintly flirtatious. "If he is half as good as she thinks, she's found herself a rare man indeed, one well worth the keeping! Now tell me . . . we know Joanna's heart. But what of Llewelyn? You've seen them together, Richard; does he love her?"

"That is a woman's question if ever I heard one! How would I be likely to know that, Isabelle? I can only tell you that he seems fond enough of her." Richard paused, considering. "He has a hunting lodge at Trefriw in the River Conwy valley. The nearest church is at Rhychwyn, about a two-mile walk up a mountain path too steep for horses, and when Llewelyn learned Joanna was with child, he ordered a church built at Trefriw to spare her that walk."

"He loves her, then," Isabelle declared with satisfaction, and Richard hid a smile, for he'd known she would be quickest to comprehend tangible expressions of caring.

"Madame?" One of Isabelle's ladies stood in the doorway. "Madame, the Lady Margaret de Lacy is without, seeks some moments with you."

Isabelle's face was suddenly still, remote. "No," she said. "I do not wish to see her."

As the woman withdrew, Richard gave Isabelle a pensive look. Like most people at John's court, he had been shocked by William de Braose's abrupt and unexpected fall from favor. The purported reason for the estrangement between John and de Braose was money; de Braose owed the crown a considerable sum, for in 1201 John had allowed de Braose to purchase the Irish honour of Limerick for five thousand marks, yet de Braose had unaccountably ignored the set schedule for payment, paying only a meagre hundred marks to date upon the debt. John had suddenly demanded payment in full, and when de Braose was unable or unwilling to comply, he found himself in political limbo, no longer welcome at John's court.

Richard did not doubt that Margaret de Lacy was here on her father's behalf, but what interested him now was the finality in Isabelle's refusal. Although she rarely interceded with John on behalf of petitioners, she generally accorded them a careless courtesy, was willing to hear them out. That she would deny Margaret de Lacy even the briefest audience was in itself significant to Richard, told him that de Braose was in much deeper disgrace than he'd realized.

There could be only one logical explanation for this surprising rupture of a relationship that had endured for fully half of Richard's lifetime, an explanation to be found within the shadowed silence of Rouen Castle. Richard was sure that Arthur was the key to the mystery of de Braose's downfall. Just as de Braose was the key to Arthur's disappearance.

Richard was, even at eighteen, a realist. He loved his father, but it had been more than four years since any man had laid eyes upon Arthur. Now he hesitated, but the temptation was irresistible. "Isabelle, have you never asked Papa about Arthur?"

"Jesú, no!" She was looking at him as if he were mad. "Indeed I have not!"

"But are you not curious? Do you never wonder, never want to know the truth of it?"

"No," she said flatly. "I do not wonder. I do not ask." The blue eyes were guarded, almost hostile. "I do not want to know."

22

ABER, NORTH WALES

March 1208

In Llewelyn's absence, Joanna had presided over the evening meal in the great hall. Now servants had dismantled the trestle tables, and she'd seated herself upon the dais, was making a request that Llywarch sing for them. Her halting Welsh grated unbearably against Gruffydd's ear. He hated how she mangled his language, hated her alien French accent, hated the way her clumsy efforts won his father's uncritical praise.

Feeling a tug at his sleeve, Gruffydd looked down, saw his little sister Marared holding out a thick strip of leather. "My dog's collar," she explained. "Make it fit tighter, Gruffydd." He obligingly cut another hole with his eating knife, and she went off, content. Gruffydd waited a few moments, and then moved casually in the direction of the hearth, stopping before the cradle. Seeing that no one was watching him, he leaned over, stared down at his baby sister.

He'd expected to hate her as he hated her mother. But each time he looked at her, he felt only relief, only an intense, abiding thankfulness that Joanna had not given birth to a son. For nine years he had been Llewelyn's only son and heir; the birth, three years ago, of his brother Tegwared had been a severe shock to Gruffydd. But Tegwared did not live at Llewelyn's court, was born of a concubine, and Gruffydd had gradually come around to a grudging acceptance of Cristyn's son. Joanna's son would be a far greater threat, a far more dangerous rival; although Welsh law did not distinguish between legitimate and illegitimate offspring, Holy Church did, would have to favor a child born in wedlock. If that woman ever bore Papa a son, he might lose all, even Papa's love.

Gruffydd drew an uneven breath, tried to fight back his fear.
He knew she would poison Papa's mind against him if she could.
But he had to have more faith in Papa. He had to— Suddenly
warned by a sixth-sense awareness, he raised his head. For the
span of several hostile heartbeats, his eyes held Joanna's, and
then she looked away. Hot color flooded Gruffydd's face. He'd
seen her look at him that way before—every time he came within
two feet of Elen. Damn her, did she think he'd ever hurt a baby?
He reached defiantly for the rattle, held it within Elen's range of
vision. Elen was his sister, was not to blame for her Norman
blood, and he would somehow see that she was raised right,
raised Welsh. He'd not let that foreign woman win.

"Take care, Gruffydd. Yours is too easy a face to read," a
voice cautioned behind him, and he spun around to face two of
Ednyved's sons, Hywel and Tudur. Tudur was the same age as
Gruffydd; they'd both celebrated their twelfth birthdays within the
past week. Hywel was two years older, was the one who'd spoken.

"So? As long as I am not rude to her, what right has she to
complain? She cannot fault me for what I'm thinking . . . at least
not yet." Across the hall, Joanna was thanking Llywarch, and as
Gruffydd listened, his mouth twisted scornfully. "Did you ever
hear anyone sound so peculiar? She makes a mockery of our
tongue every time she opens her mouth!"

Tudur gave a sympathetic nod, but Hywel shrugged. "I seem
to remember you blaming her last year because she insisted upon
speaking only French."

Gruffydd's eyes narrowed. "Elen was named after one of the
most celebrated of Welsh heroines, the Elen of the Hosts ac-
claimed in the Triads. But do you think she knows that? That she
even knows what the Triads are? She asked Papa one question
only, what Elen meant in Norman-French!"

"I do not deny that she is ignorant of our history, of our
ways," Hywel conceded, then jerked his head in the direction of
the Lady Gwenllian. "But I'd still trade our stepmother for yours
any day!"

"That shows how little you know, does it not?" Gruffydd
snapped, and Hywel's good humor vanished. For a moment the
two boys glared at one another; although Hywel had the advantage in years, Gruffydd was only an inch shorter than he, and in
their one brawl a few months back, they'd fought to a bloody
draw. Now Hywel was the first to look away.

"Have it your own way. Why should I care?"

He turned on his heel, but his brother caught up with him after a few steps, said placatingly, "Do not be angry, Hywel. Gruffydd's been in a bad mood these past days. Lord Llewelyn did forget his birthday, you see."

Hywel paused, willing to be mollified, and Tudur lowered his voice, said in confidential tones, "All Friday Gruffydd did expect a courier to come, and when none did, he was sorely hurt. He sought to hide it, but all could see it plain in his face, and the Lady Joanna . . . well, she just made things worse. She tried to make excuses for Lord Llewelyn, told Gruffydd how busy his father was, how preoccupied with Gwenwynwyn's border raids. Gruffydd was wild, as wroth as I've ever seen him. But he dared not say anything to her, not after Lord Llewelyn warned him to mend his manners, to show her respect. So you did touch a raw spot with him, and that's why he flared up."

"But why did her remarks anger Gruffydd so? It sounds as if she meant well."

"Mayhap she did. But there were others around, and Gruffydd thought she was deliberately calling it to our attention, that his father had forgotten him. And I know he much resented her offering apologies in Lord Llewelyn's name, saying she had no right, that his father did not need her to make amends for him. I can understand that, Hywel, in truth I can. Would you want our lady stepmother to make excuses to us for Papa?"

"No," Hywel admitted. "I would not. If Gruffydd— Tudur? You hear the dogs?"

Tudur nodded, and turning, he yelled, "Gruffydd! I think your lord father has ridden in."

Gruffydd was already moving eagerly toward the door. But Joanna was closer and, as Llewelyn strode into the hall, she reached him first, flung herself into his arms. Gruffydd stopped abruptly, watched as Llewelyn and Joanna embraced, watched as Joanna then took Llewelyn's arm, pulled him toward the cradle. As if he had no other children, Gruffydd thought bitterly. Joanna was claiming most of Llewelyn's attention, holding up their baby for his inspection, and Gruffydd's sisters, Marared and Gwladys and Gwenllian, were clamoring, too, for notice. It was some moments, therefore, before Llewelyn missed his son.

He found Gruffydd leaning against one of the wooden screens that blocked off the side aisle, moved toward the boy with a smile. "Have you no greeting for me, lad?"

"Indeed, Papa. Welcome home," Gruffydd said, quite coolly. But when he saw his father's smile fade, he was caught up in a welter of painful and confusing emotions, no longer sure why he'd wanted to punish Llewelyn, for having forgotten his birthday or for loving King John's daughter.

"Are you angry with me, Gruffydd?" Llewelyn studied his son, and then grinned. "I see. You think I did forget your birthday again. Not this time, lad. Come, see for yourself."

Men with torches stood outside in the bailey, and when Gruffydd saw what was evoking their admiring murmurs, his breath caught in his throat. The stallion was young, a pure milky white, the luckiest of colors, and bred for speed. Gruffydd whirled to face his father, entreating, "Say he's mine, Papa!"

"You surely do not think he's for Elen, do you? But he's newly broken to the saddle, so take it slow . . ." Llewelyn's cautionary words were lost; Gruffydd was already reaching for the reins. The stallion bucked halfheartedly under his weight, and Gruffydd guided him in a semicircle, grinned back over his shoulder at Llewelyn.

"He's begging to run, Papa!"

"Do not give him his head till you reach the shore. And remember . . . I paid a fortune for him, so if you have to break a neck, better yours than his!" Llewelyn laughed, and the wind carried back to him the answering echoes of his son's laughter.

Still laughing, Llewelyn reentered the hall, looked around for his wife. "Where did Joanna go?"

"To put your little Elen to bed." Ednyved pulled a chair closer to the hearth, and Llewelyn sank down gratefully in it, pushed away the more importunate of his dogs.

He'd been gone for a fortnight, a guest of his cousin Madog ap Gruffydd, Prince of Upper Powys, and because Powys shared a border with Cheshire, Llewelyn was at once bombarded with questions about the two topics currently dominating English conversations: the threat of a papal Interdict and William de Braose's fall from favor.

"I heard nothing new about John's quarrel with the Pope. It does seem to be a standoff; the Pope's man wears the mitre of Canterbury, but dares not set foot in England." Llewelyn accepted a cup of mead, drank, and said, "But I did hear something interesting about de Braose. His friends and family have prevailed upon John to grant him an audience; they are to meet at Hereford on the twenty-fifth of April. Not that I think it'll do him much good. There are few ruptures so bitter as a falling-out amongst thieves."

"What do you think be behind it, Llewelyn? It cannot truly be the money; de Braose has owed that for years."

"This is just a guess, Rhys. But I think de Braose pushed his luck once too often. The more John gave him, the more he wanted. I heard he'd been pressuring John for an earldom, and I think John finally ran out of patience. Either that or de Braose went too far, moved from implied to explicit extortion, mayhap made an out-and-out threat about what he knew of Arthur's death."

"I've never been able to understand why they did not give Arthur even a sham trial," Adda confessed. "Men might not have liked it much, but John had the law on his side. By resorting to a secret killing, he played right into Philip's hands. John's silence just gives credence to the more lurid rumors put about by the French: that Arthur was tortured, blinded, even slain by John's own hand. It was a stupid way to rid himself of a rival, since none can be utterly sure the boy be dead, and I do not see John to be a stupid man."

"He may not be stupid, but he has no liking for the light, has a natural affinity for shadows and silence and deeds done in the dark," Ednyved said dryly.

"Do you want to know what I've always suspected?" Llewelyn set down his mead cup, pausing instinctively for dramatic interest. "That Arthur's murder was an act of impulse, was not premeditated. I think John confronted the boy, and they quarreled; we know they'd done so in the past, that confinement had not broken Arthur's spirit. It is my belief that Arthur said or did something which so enraged John that he gave the command without fully thinking it through."

Ednyved looked skeptical. "Why unpremeditated, Llewelyn?"

"Because if Arthur's murder had been planned out in advance, John would never have been within a hundred miles of Rouen that night, would have put as much distance between himself and the crime as possible—" Llewelyn stopped abruptly, and an uncomfortable silence fell as Joanna came toward them. Not sure whether she'd overheard, Llewelyn rose, moved to meet her.

To his relief, she smiled. "Elen's begun teething, and I do not know how well she'll sleep, but she's abed now."

"That," he said, "sounds like a right appealing idea."

"What . . . sleep?" Joanna murmured, and laughed softly when he answered as she'd known he would.

"No . . . bed."

Joanna stretched, gave a small sigh of utter contentment, and Llewelyn leaned over, kissed her softly on the mouth. "You're purring like a cat, you know that?"

"Little wonder. That was a very satisfactory homecoming, my lord." She smiled at him. "I missed you so much. And I love you so much."

"I love you, too." He kissed her again, gently, tenderly. "But my darling, I'd love you so much more if you were to fetch me some wine."

Joanna gave a splutter of indignant laughter, hastily culling her meagre Welsh vocabulary for the proper putdown. *"Digrin,"* she chided, gratified to see Llewelyn's eyes open wide.

"Joanna . . . what did you want to call me?"

"A sluggard." She saw him bite down on his lower lip, said uncertainly, "Why? *Digrin,* it is not . . . ?"

"Diogyn means 'sluggard,' love." Llewelyn was openly laughing now. *"Digrin . . . digrin* means 'unwithered'!"

Joanna's first reaction was one of mild embarrassment and frustration. She was coming to envision Welsh as a tide beyond her control; it was always sweeping in, inundating her in alien sound, and just when she thought she was getting her head above water, it went roaring out again, stranding her high and dry. But after a moment or so, she began to see the humor in it, and joined ruefully in Llewelyn's laughter.

"Sometimes I despair of ever learning your language," she confessed, and he slid his arm around her shoulders, drew her closer.

"You'd learn it faster, Joanna, if we were to speak Welsh, not French."

"But as tongue-tied as I am, we'd never be able to communicate at all then. Except in bed!" She settled back in his arms, and then, before she could lose her nerve, she said, "You were talking about Arthur before, were you not?"

Llewelyn did not answer at once. "How much did you understand?"

"You were all talking so fast . . . just Arthur's name and Papa's. It was not hard to guess the rest. Llewelyn . . . do you think Arthur is dead?"

"Yes, love, I do," he said quietly, and after a moment, she sighed.

"So do I," she admitted. "It's been nigh on five years. Logically, he . . . he must be dead. But Llewelyn, could he not have sickened, died through mishap? Papa might well have feared to make it known, after the way his enemies have lied about him in the past. And if Arthur tried to escape . . ."

She looked at Llewelyn in mute appeal, and he said, with all the conviction he could muster, "It may well be, Joanna." But the day would come, he knew, when she would not be so readily reassured, when her faith might not be strong enough to prevail over fact. He smoothed her hair away from her face, said, "I'd rather not talk of John's nephew, *breila*. But I never tire of talking of his daughter."

That coaxed a smile from Joanna. "You did just earn yourself that drink of wine," she said, and reached for her bedrobe. The first time Llewelyn had said he loved her, soon after Elen's birth, she'd been convinced that was the happiest, most fulfilling moment of her life. But later, doubt had crept in. Llewelyn had been known to handle the truth with less than scrupulous care; how could she be sure he was speaking from the heart, not merely saying what he knew she needed to hear? Bringing the wine cup back to the bed, she watched as he drank, and then, as he leaned over to put the cup on the floor, the words seemed to come of their own accord. "Llewelyn . . . why do you love me?"

"Why? Because, in appearance and demeanor, you seem the perfect Norman lady—modest, reticent, aloof even. And then I get you in my bed, and you all but scorch the sheets!" He laughed, ran his hand caressingly along her back, down her thigh. "Not to mention your admirable good taste in loving me beyond all reason!"

Joanna could not help herself, felt a throb of disappointment. But she should have known better, in truth, should have known he'd not take such a question seriously.

Llewelyn reached up, drew her down beside him again. "No, you are not at all as you seem to be, *breila*. You are a constant surprise to me, and not just in bed. When I was a lad, my mother would oft tell me the legend of the bird with the resplendent plumage; shall I tell it to you now? When it nests in the grass, it is not easily seen, for it takes on the drab protective coloring of the earth that gives it refuge. But when it takes flight, soars up into the sky, its wings burst into flame, reflect all the glories of Heaven itself. As a boy, I spent hours searching for that bird . . . in vain, of course. Passing strange, that I should find it after all these years . . . and in my own bed."

Joanna had listened, mesmerized. "Me?"

"You're like that mythical bird, love. You cloak yourself in the muted colors of a wellborn Norman lady, seem soft-spoken, shy, and obedient. But that is not you, Joanna, not truly, and when I least expect it, your spirit takes flight like the bird with the sun-bright plumage, as when you did defy Maude de Braose on our wedding day . . . or when you burned my bed.''

''You'll never let me forget that, will you?'' Joanna laughed. ''But I need never explain why I do love you. How could I not, after hearing you say that? You are a man of many parts, in truth, Llewelyn, my love—Prince, warlord . . . and poet.''

''That is merely to be Welsh, *breila*.'' But she was not deceived by the playfulness of his reply, knew how deeply she'd pleased him, for she'd learned by now how highly eloquence was valued in his world. He'd begun to caress her again, and she wrapped her arms around him, soon forgot all else but the here and now, the feel of his hands upon her body and his mouth upon hers.

The sensual spell was a powerful one; only belatedly did they become aware of the noise in the antechamber, of the pounding on the door. Llewelyn jerked upright, swore. But then he pulled the sheet up over Joanna, said curtly, ''Enter.''

Joanna's reflexes were slower; she reoriented herself with greater difficulty, lay back against the pillow as Ednyved, Morgan, and Gwyn ab Ednywain hastened into the chamber.

They wasted no time with apologies for the intrusion, knowing none were needed. ''Llewelyn, a messenger has just ridden in from the Bishop of St Asaph. The Bishop would have you know that on Passion Sunday a proclamation is to be read in churches throughout England and Wales, laying both realms under Interdict until John agrees to yield to the Pope.''

The news was not unexpected. Llewelyn felt no surprise, only rage. He cared little whether John or the Pope prevailed in their war of wills; their quarrel was nothing to him. But the pain of his people was, and he was deeply resentful that the Welsh must suffer with the English, that the papal punishment should fall equally upon both lands.

''Damn them both to Hell,'' he said, with bitter blasphemy. ''Why should the Welsh have to suffer because a Norman King and a Roman Pope disagree over an English diocese?''

Morgan felt compelled at that to say, ''His Holiness had no choice but to do what he did.'' But his heart was not in his defense, not when he thought of how long the churches might stand silent and dark, or of how long the devout might be denied the Sacraments.

''Philip held out for seven months. But John . . . John could hold out for years,'' Ednyved said grimly. ''It's nothing to him whether he can attend Mass or not. He's not like to care even if the bodies of the dead are stacked up like kindling in the church-yards. Not when he's found a way to turn the Interdict to his profit. Bishop Reiner says he has ordered the confiscation of all church property in retaliation, is using the Interdict as a license to loot!''

"Llewelyn . . ." The sound of his wife's voice startled Llewelyn; he had, for the moment, forgotten she was there. Turning toward her, he saw that she'd paled noticeably, and the hand she put upon his arm was cold as ice.

"Llewelyn, you keep saying *gwaharriad*. That means 'Inter-dict,' does it not?" And when he nodded, she drew a sudden sharp breath. "Oh, no!"

"Joanna? Surely you knew it was likely to come to this . . ."

But she was not listening. "Morgan, Morgan, I know an Interdict means there can be no Masses said, no burials in consecrated ground, no confessions. But what of christenings, Morgan? May a newborn child still be christened?"

"Yes, my lady, you may rest easy on that. Holy Church would not damn an innocent soul if it could be saved."

"Thank God!"

"Joanna . . ." Llewelyn was staring at her. He started to speak, stopped, and glanced back toward the men. "We'll dis-cuss this on the morrow," he said, but they were already retreating.

As the door closed, Llewelyn tilted Joanna's chin up, looked intently into her face. "Joanna, are you with child?"

"I think so," she whispered. "My flux did not come this month. But it is too early to know for certes, and I did not want to tell you till I could be sure . . ." She averted her eyes at that, lest he guess the truth, that she'd been hoping she was wrong, that she was not pregnant. She wanted his children, wanted to give him a son. But not so soon. Elen was not yet five months old, and her memories had not had time to fade. Whenever she found herself remembering the pain-filled day of Elen's birth, she remembered, too, her fear. But she was ashamed that she could take so little pleasure in this pregnancy, and she forced a smile. "If I am right, I may well give you a son ere the year be out. Would that not please you, Llewelyn?"

"Yes, of course." He took her in his arms, rested his hand against her belly, so deceptively taut and flat, caressed the slen-der body that seemed such a fragile receptacle for a new life, repeated, "Indeed, Joanna, I am well pleased." But as she raised her eyes to his, she saw in them no pleasure, saw only the reflection of her own anxiety.

23

HEREFORD, ENGLAND

April 1208

William de Braose was surprised and disconcerted to find himself
hesitating before John's solar door. He'd spent a lifetime facing
down lesser men, men who lacked his cold-blooded courage, his
utter indifference to the rules of fair play, his intoxication with
high-stakes gambles. Never before had he shrunk from confrontation. But never before had he so much to lose.

A moment passed, and then another. De Braose stared at the
oaken door. And then he reached for the latch, shoved inward,
and strode into the chamber, his the assured, loose-limbered gait
of a man equally at home in the saddle or on shipboard, a man
with nothing to fear. But he broke stride abruptly at sight of the
others: the Earls of Salisbury and Pembroke, the Bishop of
Winchester, a shadowy fourth figure beyond the range of hearthfire.

De Braose was genuinely shocked, too shocked to hide his
dismay. He knew John as few men did, had never made the
mistake of underestimating him. But even he had never imagined
John would take such a chance, that he would risk witnesses to
their war of wills.

He had no conscious awareness of coming forward, kneeling
before John; the action was automatic. "Your Grace, I think it
best that we speak alone," he said warningly, never taking his
eyes from the man who was his sovereign, onetime carousing
companion, friend, and benefactor. "What I have to say be for
your ears alone."

"Indeed? I can think of nothing you could say that would
warrant a private audience. Be thankful, rather, that I was willing
to grant you any audience at all." John's voice was cool, impersonal, utterly at variance with what de Braose read in his eyes.
"What would you say to me?"

And in that moment de Braose understood. He had underestimated John after all. They might indeed share a bloody secret, but they were not—and this was his fatal mistake—partners in crime. He'd not thought John had the courage to call his bluff, and in this he had been wrong, too. The twisted, dark road they'd traveled together since that Eastertide at Rouen had come to an abrupt end here in the shadow-filled solar of Hereford Castle. John had thrown down the gauntlet in irrevocable and unmistakable fashion, before a roomful of witnesses. Now the choice was his. He could subject himself to his King, make a total and humiliating and costly surrender to a man not noted for generosity toward fallen enemies. Or he could make use of what he knew, could damn John and doom himself.

John showed no emotion, but his son Richard drew a sharp, audible breath, stepped from the shadows as if to forestall de Braose. For Richard, too, understood what was occurring. When he'd first realized what his father was doing, daring de Braose to speak of Arthur, to make a public accusation, Richard was appalled; until that moment, he'd not recognized how much he preferred not to know Arthur's fate. Now he stared not at de Braose, but at his father, awed by the risk John was willing to take.

But . . . but was the risk, in truth, all that great? As the silence spun out, Richard's eyes flicked rapidly to the faces of the other men, to his uncle Will, to the aging Pembroke, to the elegant Peter des Roches, one of the only two Bishops not to follow their brethren into French exile in the wake of the Pope's Interdict, and some of his anxiety began to ease. No, not so great a risk after all. His uncle would be loyal to the grave and beyond. Like Will, Pembroke was a man of rock-ribbed integrity, little imagination, and moderate ambitions, a man who had devoted the whole of his life to the fortunes of the House of Plantagenet. Whatever personal repugnance he might feel at hearing a confession of royal murder, it would not shake his loyalty, for his loyalty was to the crown, to the man anointed by God to reign . . . even if that man be revealed as Cain. And Peter des Roches was no rebel priest, was a worldly, accommodating, and ambitious Prince of the Church, not one to be shocked by the dark underside of men's souls. Even if the worst came to pass, and de Braose blurted out an admission of conspiracy and murder, none of the men in this room would ever act upon it; instead, they'd do their best to bury their unwelcome knowledge beyond recall.

But even as Richard realized that his father had shrewdly acted to minimize his political risks, he realized, too, that the personal risk John was willing to take was considerable. He could be sure that his brother and son would never betray him, no matter what they heard in this solar at Hereford Castle. But how could he be sure that they would forgive him?

"Well?" John demanded. "Have you nothing to say to me?" There was defiance in the query, but there was triumph, too, for he'd correctly interpreted de Braose's continuing silence as surrender.

De Braose did not answer. Once the initial shock had ebbed, he'd seen what Richard had, that John had picked his audience with a sure hand, an artful understanding of the men he'd chosen as witnesses. But if John was bluffing, so was he. He would never have made a public accusation of any kind. The day that he accused a reigning King of murder was the day he signed his own death warrant, and he knew it. But knowing what he had to do did not make it any easier.

"I do owe Your Grace five thousand marks. I am here to promise payment."

"Promises are cheap. You've made them before. And there are other considerations now. In the past year you've given me reasons enough to doubt your loyalty. As you know, a fortnight ago I dispatched the sheriffs of Gloucestershire and Shropshire and five hundred men-at-arms into the West Country. I thought their presence there might serve to prod your memory, to remind you where your interests lie. It would seem they did. But men-at-arms need to eat, expect their two pence a day. So, in addition to the five thousand marks you do owe me for the honour of Limerick, you now owe me another thousand marks for the cost of that campaign."

De Braose was truly taken aback by the utterly outrageous gall of that demand, that he should be assessed for the expenses of an army sent to ravage his own lands. "I serve the King's pleasure," he said at last, with such bitter irony that John smiled.

"Just so," he said softly. It was a warning as oblique as it was economical, but there was no need to say more. De Braose understood.

Of all his grandfather's castles, Will de Braose liked Abergavenny the best. He'd been born there, and had recently celebrated his twelfth birthday within Abergavenny's massive stone walls. On this Tuesday in late April, he was alone in the uppermost chamber of the polygonal tower. The chamber housed the de Braose family chapel, but Will was not there to pray; he was leaning recklessly out of the unshuttered window, watching the road that wound off toward the north, toward Hereford, where his grandfather was meeting with the King. He'd sent word that he would be returning this Tuesday noon, and Will had been keeping an impatient vigil as the day dragged on.

Down in the bailey he saw his father, Reginald de Braose, conferring with his uncle, William de Braose the younger. His young cousins were playing a rough-and-tumble game of ball with an inflated pig's bladder, under the watchful eye of their mother, Matilda. There'd been a full gathering of the de Braose clan at Abergavenny; only Will's Aunt Margaret and his Uncle Giles, Bishop of Hereford, were absent, Margaret having sailed for Ireland to rejoin her husband Walter, Lord of Meath, and Giles having gone into foreign exile in obedience to the Pope's Interdict. All were waiting anxiously for word from Hereford.

Will did not share their concern; he could not imagine any man getting the better of his grandfather. Moreover, he knew that his grandmother fully expected the King to restore her husband to favor, and Will needed no greater guarantee than that. As far back as he could remember, his grandmother had been the family linchpin. Imperious and earthy and blazingly outspoken, she'd always utterly eclipsed the Lady Gracia, Will's mother, a timid, passive personality who was reduced to wraithlike incompetence in the presence of her formidable mother-in-law.

Now Will decided to seek her out, to renew his faith in Maude's reassuring certainty that the bad times were over. The disgrace that had so suddenly come upon their family had been hard on Will. Since the age of seven, he'd been serving as a page in the household of Lord Fitz Alan, and when he was taunted by the other pages about his grandfather's fall from favor, Will had responded with hot, heedless rage, had gotten into so many bloody brawls that his training at Clun Castle came to an abrupt end. His father had been predictably furious; Will could not recall a time when he and his father had not been at odds. But his grandmother once again came through when it counted, saying cuttingly, "Christ Jesus, Reg, let the boy be. Just be thankful he has the pluck to stand up for himself, that he has the backbone you too often lack!" Her acerbic intervention had spared Will a beating, but added yet one more drop of poison to a relationship already soured beyond salvaging.

Will was remembering that as he entered the great hall, saw Maude sitting upon the dais, attended by the submissive daughters-in-law who never dared stray out of beckoning range. She frowned at sight of him, gestured for him to approach.

"I saw your cousin Jack's eye; your handiwork?"

Will was not fazed by the scowl. "He ran into my fist," he said, saw her mouth twitch.

"Do not make a habit of it," she said, but when Will grinned, she grinned back.

Settling down on the steps of the dais, Will began to occupy himself in carving a whistle. Within moments he'd attracted an admiring audience, his little cousin Philip. Will was quite contemptuous of his cousin Jack, whom he considered a weakling and a tattletale, but he liked Philip, who was only seven. Now he made room on the steps for the youngster, and turned obligingly so Philip could watch him whittle.

"Will . . . was it truly in this very hall that Grandpapa killed that Welsh lord and his men?"

Will nodded, cast Philip a sideways, searching look. Philip's eyes were wide; he was looking about him as if still expecting to see the floor rushes soaked in blood, the walls splattered with gore. Will understood, for he remembered his own confusion when he'd first been told of the Abergavenny massacre. Will had given to his grandfather all the love and respect he did not give to his father, and he'd been shocked to discover that his grandfather had so violated every tenet of the chivalric code. There was no way he could reconcile what his grandfather had done on that December day in 1175 with the accepted standards of knightly conduct, with the tales told by minstrels and bards of Roland and Arthur and the Knights of the Table Round, for his grandfather had lured his enemies to Abergavenny under the guise of friendship, murdered them while they ate and drank at his table, then abducted Seisyll's wife and put her young son to death before her eyes.

Will had been troubled enough to go to his father with his qualms, but his father had laughed at him. Apparently the Welsh were not covered by the chivalric code. That was not good enough for Will. He'd often heard his family jeer at the strange ways of the Welsh, heard them called "reckless" and "untamed" and "half mad." By Norman standards he supposed they were, but those were the very qualities that most appealed to him. Wales was to Will a wild, mystical land of legend and blood feuds and stark grandeur, and he loved it as if it were his own. Most of his twelve years had been spent within its borders; he spoke fluent Welsh, had friends named Rhys and Ifor and

Garwyn. He needed a better explanation for the killings at Abergavenny than merely that the victims were Welsh.

He'd gotten that explanation from his grandmother. "Those men were your grandfather's enemies, Will. The enemies of our House. We do not forgive a wrong done us, not ever. You are old enough to understand that, lad, to learn that in this world we have to look after our own, to do whatever be necessary to safeguard what is ours. Learn that if you learn nothing else, and never forget it."

Now Will gave his young cousin the same bleak, uncompromising answer his grandmother had once given him, saying tersely, "They were the enemies of our House, Philip." An answer that said all that needed to be said, that he had long since taken to heart.

He handed the completed whistle to the boy. "You can have this if you like." And then, because Philip was so young, because there was time yet before he had to learn the lessons of being a de Braose, Will drew Philip's thoughts away from that long-ago and bloody December day. "Life must have been right lively back then, Philip. Seisyll's surviving sons besieged Abergavenny seven years later and burned all but the keep; luckily for Grandpapa, he was elsewhere at the time of the attack! And then, some years after, Gwenwynwyn attacked our castle in the Machawy River valley, the one the Welsh call Castell Paen. Our grandmother put up so successful a defense that people started calling it Castle Maude!"

Philip laughed. "Which Welsh Prince is Gwenwynwyn, Will? I can never keep them straight."

"You'll have to learn; you're old enough now. Gwenwynwyn is Prince of Lower Powys; he's the whoreson who's been making raids upon our manors. South Wales is divided now between the sons of the Lord Rhys—Maelgwn and Rhys Gryg. And the North is ruled by the man Grandpapa says is the most dangerous one of the lot, Llewelyn ab Iorwerth, who is married to a bastard daughter of King John."

As soon as John's name had crossed Will's lips, he swallowed, grimaced as if he'd tasted something sour. In the past year he'd come to nurture a deep and abiding hatred for the English King who was giving his family such grief. He started to speak, and then stopped, head cocked expectantly to the side. "Philip, you hear? Grandpapa has just ridden in!"

Will's excitement congealed at first sight of the men accompanying his grandfather: Thomas Erdington, Sheriff of Shropshire,

Gerard d'Athie, Sheriff of Gloucestershire, and Falkes de Breauté, to whom William de Braose had been forced by John to yield up Glamorgan and Gwyllwg. The first two had, in the past fortnight, led an army onto de Braose lands; the third was a bitter and open enemy of their House. Will knew his grandfather would never have chosen their company of his own accord. He ran for the nearest window, looked out to find the bailey filled with men-at-arms, men who wore the red and white colors of the King.

Maude had risen, was staring at her husband in dismay. "Will? Will, why are they here?"

Will knew his grandfather was no longer young, was in his sixties, but he was so energetic, so fit that Will never gave his age any thought. He was shocked now to see how haggard his grandfather suddenly looked, exhaustion etched into the smudged hollows under his eyes, impotent and embittered fury in the rigid set of his mouth.

"Not now," he snapped, giving his wife a look that would have daunted all but the most intrepid or reckless, a look that made no impression whatsoever upon Maude.

"Name of God, Will, what has happened? Did you not see the King?"

"I said not now!"

But his unlikely escorts were not so reticent. It was Falkes de Breauté who told Maude what her husband would not, saying with conspicuous relish, "Ah, indeed he saw the King, Madame, and made many and varied promises to the King's Grace, amongst them to make payment of six thousand marks."

"Six thousand!" Maude's eyes narrowed, cut sharply toward her husband. "We do not have it," she said flatly, defiantly, and de Breauté grinned.

"You'll be relieved, then, Madame, to know you need not pay it all at once. A thousand marks are due today, but the balance may be paid in installments. Of course, you will have to surrender to the King's Grace your castles at Hay, Brecknock, and Radnor as a pledge for payment—"

"Jesus God!" Maude whirled around to confront her husband. "What have you done, Will?"

"What I had to do!" he snarled. "But we're damned well not going to talk about it here . . . or now!"

"Hay Castle is mine, to me! I'll not give it up!"

"Your husband has already done that, Madame." Gerard d'Athie spoke up for the first time. Sounding as if he was enjoying himself no less than de Breauté, he said cheerfully, "He gave the order two days ago to turn them over to the King's constables. We are here only to collect the thousand marks . . . and the hostages, of course. Not surprisingly, the King feels that your husband will be more likely to keep faith if he is keeping your grandsons!''

Maude gasped, and her husband took two swift steps forward. But even as he warned, ''Maude, no!'' she was swinging back toward Gerard d'Athie, her face flushed, mouth contorted.

''Are you mad? Do you truly think I'd ever agree to that? Give my grandsons up to the man who murdered his own nephew? Never in this lifetime!''

Will's throat had closed up, cutting off an involuntary cry of protest. But his fear lasted only until Maude began to speak. He found himself blinking back hot tears; never had he loved anyone as much as he loved his grandmother at that moment, his grandmother who would dare to defy the King of England for his sake.

And then he became aware of the utter and absolute silence, then he saw the looks of horror on the faces of the adults. His grandfather had gone grey under his tan; even his lips were bloodless. His grandmother was standing very still. Will could not see her face. But he could see the faces of Falkes de Breauté and Gerard d'Athie. Astonishment had given way to exhilaration; they both wore the jubilant grins of men unable to believe how fortune had favored them.

William de Braose at last turned away from his wife, turned fathomless grey eyes upon Erdington, d'Athie, and de Breauté. All three men reacted as one, dropped hands to sword hilts. Falkes de Breauté said coolly, ''We'll be rejoining our men. You do remember the men-at-arms awaiting us in the bailey? You need not offer us your hospitality for the night, after all.''

De Braose said nothing. They departed the hall with enough haste to compromise their dignity, hands still on sword hilts. Only then did William de Braose move. Crossing the space that separated him from his wife, he struck her across the face.

Maude's head rocked back; she stumbled, put up a hand to stanch the sudden gush of blood. No one spoke. Her sons looked away. Will alone took a shocked step toward her.

''You stupid bitch.'' William de Braose's voice was low, raw with rage, but it carried clearly to all in the hall. ''Know you what you've done? You and your accursed unbridled tongue, you've destroyed us all!''

24

SHREWSBURY, ENGLAND

October 1208

Soon after Maude de Braose publicly accused John of murder,
William de Braose and his sons made a desperate attempt to
regain possession of the castles de Braose had surrendered to
John. Failing in these assaults, they plundered and burned the
market town of Leominster. John proclaimed de Braose a traitor
to the crown, and on September 29 he freed de Braose's vassals
from all allegiance to their fugitive lord.

Gwenwynwyn, Prince of Lower Powys, at once sought to take
advantage of the resulting chaos by launching raids upon the de
Braose lands and those of neighboring Norman lords. John responded with more force than the Welsh Prince could hope to
equal. The two agreed to meet at Shrewsbury to discuss peace
terms.

Shrewsbury Castle had been held by the crown for more than two
hundred years, and the great hall had been rebuilt in stone by
John's father. John's son was thinking of that as they awaited the
arrival of the Welsh Prince, wondering if his grandfather would
have done what John meant to do. Probably so, Richard decided;
his father's lessons in cynical statecraft had been learned under
Henry's tutelage.

Now he glanced about the hall, at the other men: Ranulf de
Blundeville, Earl of Chester; Thomas Erdington, Sheriff of Shropshire; Lord Robert Corbet and his son Thomas; Robert de Montalt.
There was no one else in the hall; Chester had cleared it of
retainers, servants, and men-at-arms. Richard knew why, knew
Chester was seeking to make Gwenwynwyn's capitulation as
painless as possible. No easy task, given the surprise they were

about to spring upon him. But he gave Chester credit for trying; tact was an attribute Richard appreciated.

Richard had only recently joined the knights of Chester's household, but the past weeks had caused him to revise his earlier unfavorable opinion of the Earl. He was not a particularly likable man, was of a reserved and taciturn nature, but he was an astute judge of character, shrewd and surprisingly subtle, and he had soon won Richard's respect. Richard knew this coming confrontation with Gwenwynwyn had to be awkward for Chester; the two men had once been allies. But nothing showed in Chester's face or demeanor. There was in his manner only the dispassionate resolve of a man set upon doing his duty, upon carrying out the King's command . . . however little he might like it.

Richard wondered if the Corbets shared Chester's reluctance to do what John wanted done. Theirs was an even more awkward position, for Gwenwynwyn had taken Robert Corbet's daughter to wife. But they'd voiced no protests, raised no objections. With the fate of William de Braose still uppermost in all their minds, few of John's barons were eager to incur his displeasure in this, the tenth year of his reign.

"Richard?" Thomas Corbet was looming over him. Without waiting to be asked, he sprawled down beside Richard in the window seat. Richard retreated as far as he was able, but not in time to avoid Thomas's elbow in his ribs. He was not comfortable with such close physical proximity, even with those he liked, and he did not like Thomas Corbet. For all his self-professed contempt for Llewelyn, Thomas was showing himself quite willing to trade upon Llewelyn's marital connection with the crown and his own tenuous connection with the Welsh Prince to establish an unwelcome familiarity with Llewelyn's brother-in-law, and his sensitivity was such that he was utterly oblivious to Richard's measured recoil.

"Have you had further word on de Braose's whereabouts?"

Richard was tempted to deny Thomas the pleasure of being one of the first to know. But all would know soon enough, and he said grudgingly, "De Braose and his family fled to Ireland on Thursday last, are seeking refuge with his son-in-law, the Lord of Meath."

"Indeed? And will your lord father the King now . . ." But Richard was spared further conversation by the arrival of Gwenwynwyn. Richard had never met the Prince of Powys, but he was quite curious about this man who was Llewelyn's avowed and embittered rival, and he watched with considerable interest

as Gwenwynwyn was escorted into the hall. He was a good ten
years older than Llewelyn, appeared to be in his middle to late
forties; a short, dark-complexioned man, stocky and sinewy, he
bore a surprising resemblance to the swarthy, thickset Earl of
Chester. And like Chester, Gwenwynwyn had black eyes ablaze
with keen intelligence, sharp with suspicion.

Chester was advancing to greet him. Gwenwynwyn's eyes
flicked past the Earl, encompassed the hall. "I was summoned to
meet with King John," he said, in fluent Norman-French. "Why
is he not here?"

"The King's Grace has instructed me to act on his behalf."
Chester's voice was neutral, matter-of-fact. "He has been griev-
ously affronted by your recent incursions into Norman lands in
South Wales. No man, be he Welsh or Norman, may violate the
King's Peace with impunity. The King has therefore directed me
to take you into the custody of the crown, to detain you here in
Shrewsbury Castle."

Richard saw the looks of incredulous outrage upon the faces of
Gwenwynwyn's Welsh followers, saw hands drop to sword hilts.
Gwenwynwyn looked no less outraged, but he showed now that
he resembled Chester in more than coloring, showed himself to
be the same sort of hardheaded realist. Having walked trustingly
into John's trap, he could accept defeat with as much dignity as
he could muster, or he could cast his life away in a gesture of
grand defiance. He chose the former, snapped a command to his
men, and then turned back to face Chester.

"I came here in good faith," he said, with such scalding
contempt that suddenly none of the Normans could meet his eyes;
even Thomas Corbet looked somewhat discomfited.

"You came here to answer charges brought against you by
Marcher lords like Peter Fitz Herbert, that you've been raiding
Norman manors, running off livestock, and burning crops,"
Chester said, quite flatly, and Gwenwynwyn's lip curled.

"Y ci a fyner ei grogi dywedir ei fod yn lladd defaid," he said
scornfully.

Even Marcher border lords like the Corbets had never bothered
to learn Welsh; Chester alone spoke the language. It was he who
translated for the benefit of his companions. " 'The dog we
would hang is said to devour sheep.' If, by that, you mean the
King has contrived an excuse to seize your lands . . . ."

"What else would I think? I would like to know, though,
where this pretty plot was first hatched . . . Westminster? Or
Aber?"

"Aber? You think the King is obliging Llewelyn ab Iorwerth in this?" Chester shook his head, even smiled faintly, as though at Gwenwynwyn's naïve misreading of English aims. "Your suspicions are understandable, but unwarranted. I assure you the King has no desire to see Powys fall under Llewelyn's control. Royal couriers are even now on their way to Gwynedd and to the courts of Prince Maelgwn and Prince Rhys Gryg in South Wales, forbidding them to take advantage of your troubles with the King, telling them to keep out of Powys."

"And you truly think Llewelyn will heed such a command?" Gwenwynwyn was staring at them in bitter disbelief. "You fools. You poor bloody fools. It would be laughable, in truth—if I were not to be the one to pay the price for your stupidity!"

No one answered him. Chester gestured abruptly and men-at-arms emerged from behind the screen, moved to escort the captive Welsh Prince to his confinement. In the silence that followed, Thomas Corbet stepped toward Chester, began to assure the Earl that he knew Llewelyn well, that he would not dare to defy the King's command. No one asked Richard for his opinion, and he did not volunteer it. He admittedly did not know Llewelyn as Thomas Corbet did, had only met him twice. But he suspected that Gwenwynwyn knew Llewelyn better than any of them, and if Gwenwynwyn was right, he thought uneasily, there would be Hell to pay. For his sister's sake, he could only hope that Thomas was right and the Welshman wrong.

Greying dawn light was illuminating the snow-drifted peaks of Eryri, turning the crystalline lakes of the high mountain reaches to glistening blue ice, bringing day to the River Lledr valley and the castle standing stark sentinel in the shadow of Moel Siabod.

Joanna stood by the hearth in their bedchamber, watching her husband dress. As always when he was in a rush, Llewelyn lacked patience, preferring not to summon his squires to do what he could more quickly do himself. It was cold and Joanna pulled her bedrobe close, sought with chilled fingers to fasten the belt over her swollen abdomen.

"I still cannot believe it," she said when she could keep silent no longer. "I cannot believe you'd do this, leave me when my time is nigh. The babe is due in six weeks, Llewelyn. You would truly leave me when I do need you the most . . . and for what? A bloody border raid!"

"Joanna, you are not hearing me, not listening to what I say. I know you are distraught, and I am sorry for that, love. But a

chance like this will not come again. With Gwenwynwyn caged
in Shrewsbury, all of Powys lies open for the taking. You think
Maelgwn and Rhys Gryg are not planning to carve it up between
them even as we talk? You know what I want for Wales, know
what it would mean to hold both Gwynedd and Powys. Can you
truly expect me to forfeit such an opportunity? I cannot do that,
Joanna, not even for you.''

"My father will not forgive you,'' she said, saw him shrug.

"I expect I can live with that,'' he said, and his indifference
only served to fan Joanna's fury all the higher. In the night she'd
clung to him, put aside her pride and confessed her fear, her need
to have him with her when the babe was born. And he'd been
very tender, very loving. But he'd not weakened in his resolve to
depart on the morrow, to lead an army into Powys, and when she
said her father would not forgive him, she was in fact warning
that she might not be able to forgive him either.

Llewelyn buckled his scabbard, felt the familiar weight of a
sword at his left hip, sheathed a razor-edged dagger, and then
crossed the chamber, put his hands on Joanna's shoulders.

"You say the babe is not due for six weeks, breila. That
means there still will be time enough. Once I'm entrenched in
Powys, neither Maelgwn nor Rhys Gryg is likely to mount any
sort of challenge to my suzerainty. If all goes as I expect, I'll
leave Ednyved in temporary command and come back for the
birth.'' He smiled at her, a smile to break her heart, said,
"I promise, love, promise to be back in time,'' and she wrenched
free.

"Think you that I'm a child to be mollified with sugared
words, placated with promises? You're not God, cannot give me
an assurance like that. How can you be sure the babe will not
come early, before its time? That you'd not be delayed by foul
weather, reversals of the campaign? Or that you'd not get so
caught up in that campaign, in the killing and the conquest and
whatever it is that makes men lust so after war that you'll forget
all else? Who is going to remind you that you've a wife in need
of you, a wife about to bear your child?''

"Joanna, I have to do this.''

"Was that what you told Tangwystl, too?''

Joanna at once regretted it; there were taunts that not even the
most justifiable anger could excuse. She knew Llewelyn's grieving had been all the greater for not having been with Tangwystl
when she died, and she said hastily, "I am sorry.''

"You damned well should be!'' He turned away from her,

strode toward the door, only to stop with his hand on the latch. Wheeling about, he came back, reached out, and jerked her toward him. He was not gentle, pulled her into an angry, ungainly embrace, made awkward by the unwieldy burden of her pregnancy. "I will be back, Joanna."

She wanted to fling his grudging promise in his face, to say she'd see him damned and in Hell ere she'd beg him again to stay. Instead she wrapped her arms tightly around his neck, for a moment buried her face in his shoulder. But there was no healing in their embrace. Llewelyn stepped back, again turned toward the door.

"Llewelyn."

He paused, but she saw he was impatient to be gone, his mind already upon Powys and plans of conquest. "Take care of yourself," she said, and even to her own ears, her voice sounded strange, made flat and toneless by her fear. "Take care," she repeated bleakly. "I would look dreadful in black."

Upon arriving at Aber, Richard was disheartened to be told that his sister was awaiting her confinement at Dolwyddelan Castle, more than a day's journey to the south. But the winter was so far proving to be a mild one, and the passes were still clear of snow. With Welsh guides who knew every rock and crevice of the Eryri heights, they encountered no difficulties, rode into the bailey of Dolwyddelan soon after dark on November 18.

This was his first visit to Dolwyddelan, and Richard was looking about with interest as he followed Dylan, Joanna's seneschal, up the stone outer stairs into the keep. But as soon as he stepped across the threshold, he sensed that something was very wrong. Morgan ap Bleddyn, Branwen, and Alison were clustered awkwardly to one side, and barely glanced his way. In the center of the chamber Joanna and Gruffydd were standing. At sight of his sister, Richard felt a throb of alarm; she looked ill, eyes hollowed and swollen, skin showing a greyish pallor even in the warming, reddish glow of hearth fire. She had yet to notice him, had all her attention focused upon her stepson. Richard spoke no Welsh, but it was obvious that the conversation was a strained, labored one. Joanna paused frequently, fumbled for words, and at last switched into French, saying in a very low voice, "What more can I say than that I am sorry?"

Gruffydd had been staring past her into the hearth. At that, he raised his head, and Richard took an instinctive step forward. He did not dismiss the passions of the very young with indulgent amusement. At nineteen, he was still young enough himself to remember; he knew that a child's hatred might be even more intense than that of a man grown, for the man's emotions were likely to be tempered with painful adult experiences in the arts of compromise and conciliation. The child's passions were purer and more primitive, and the hatred of a child could easily get away from him, take on dimensions and depths he could not hope to control. Such a hatred was now naked upon Gruffydd's face, a helpless, soul-scarring hatred for his father's wife.

Gruffydd somehow fought back the words rising up to choke him, whirled and bolted for the door. Joanna signaled to Morgan, and the priest swiftly followed the boy from the chamber. It was only then that she saw Richard. "Oh, Richard, thank God!" she cried, with such an intensity of emotion that what was meant as a welcome became an involuntary confession of despair.

Richard was not normally demonstrative, but he came forward quickly, gave her a prolonged hug. Waiting until they were together in the window seat nearest the bed, he watched her fidget with the lap robe Branwen had tucked around her, and finally said quietly, "Are you not going to tell me what that was about?"

She did not want to tell him; that was evident. She fidgeted a while longer, lavishing undue attention upon the small dog curled up beside them. "Poor Sugar, she cannot comprehend why I no longer have a lap for her to sit in." She sighed, then said with obvious reluctance, "I'll tell you. But you must understand how it has been. My nerves are so on the raw these days that I find myself always on the edge of anger, much too quick to flare up, to take offense. But I cannot seem to help it. In truth, I have been feeling wretched for months with this babe, even before Llewelyn left me, and these five weeks that he's been gone . . . well, I'd not ever want to relive them, Richard, not even for the surety of my soul!"

He waited without prompting, for he was that rarity, a Plantagenet with patience to spare, and Joanna sighed again. "This morn Sugar ran off, disappeared without a trace. I was so fearful for her, sent servants out to search, to no avail. Then . . . then the child of one of the grooms told me that he'd seen Sugar down by the riverbank, ere he knew she was missing. And he said she was with Gruffydd."

"Ah, Joanna, surely you did not?"

Joanna flushed, "Yes, I did," she admitted, with a trace of defiance. "I accused Gruffydd of chasing Sugar away." From the way she averted her eyes, Richard suspected she'd accused Gruffydd of even worse. He said nothing, and she stroked the dog until the heat had faded from her face. "I was in the wrong, I know that. I had no proof, should not have . . . but I did, and within the hour, Sugar came back of her own accord, muddy and matted and unhurt. I apologized to Gruffydd, but as you saw, he will not forgive me. I knew he would not, not the way he cherishes a grudge!"

"Joanna, you can hardly blame him for being hurt and resentful. How old is he now, not thirteen till the spring, no? Well, you have to—"

"Richard, you do not understand. I should not have said what I did, would to God I had not. But you do not know what a wretched, hateful boy he is. Believe me, he's quite capable of harming a dog out of spite!"

"Have you ever talked to Llewelyn about him?"

"No. At first I thought I should be capable of handling him myself. As Llewelyn's wife, I owed it to him to make peace with his children; a man should not be burdened with problems of the hearth. And . . . and it would serve for naught, would only cause Llewelyn hurt. With the girls, I think I've finally managed to gain their trust. Even Gwladys. I asked her to stand as Elen's godmother, and since then she's been slowly—ever so slowly— warming toward me. But Gruffydd has given me naught but grief from the moment of my arrival at Aber. I detest him, Richard, I truly do. He's wild and perverse and dangerously unpredictable, has none of Llewelyn's strengths and every damned one of his failings!"

Richard glanced up sharply. "Do you want to talk about that—about Llewelyn's failings?"

Joanna hesitated, and then confessed, "Yes, I think I do. We had a truly dreadful quarrel when he left, by far the worst of our marriage. I was so angry with him, Richard; I still am. He knows how fearful I've been about this baby, he knows, but it was not enough to keep him with me. That's hard for me to understand, harder still to forgive."

"We heard he was encountering little resistance, found Powys was his for the taking. Is that true?"

Joanna nodded. "Llewelyn has few peers on the battlefield," she said, with perverse pride in that which gave her so much anxiety. "Men say he is a brilliant commander."

That, Richard thought grimly, was precisely the trouble. "Think you that he'll stop at the borders of Powys?"

"You have not heard, then? He has crossed into Ceredigion, into the lands of Maelgwn ap Rhys, has pushed as far south as the River Ystwyth."

"Jesú! But how can he hope to hold it? Maelgwn is no man to yield up what is his. I know the man, Joanna, met him often when I served in South Wales with William de Braose's son. His past is a bloody one, includes the murder of a brother and the imprisonment of his own father. He makes a bad enemy."

"I know. Ednyved's wife Gwenllian is sister to Maelgwn and Rhys Gryg; they paid a visit to our court last year. After meeting them, I found it easier to understand why Gwenllian is such a bitch! But to answer your question, Llewelyn does not mean to hold Ceredigion for himself. He means to turn most of it over to Maelgwn's nephews. They've been feuding with their uncles for years, are more than willing to acknowledge Llewelyn as their overlord in return for his backing against Maelgwn."

"Yes," Richard said slowly, "I expect they would be." Joanna could not have given him a more disquieting answer. Had Llewelyn merely acted to seize what lands he could for himself, it would be much easier to dismiss him as just another of the power-hungry princes and lords of the Welsh Marches, a region that seemed to spawn more than its share of renegades, outlaws, and rebel barons. They could be troublesome, the de Braoses and Maelgwns and Fulk Fitz Warins, but their aims were understandable, their vision was limited, and sooner or later they overreached themselves, were undone by their own greed. But a man who would voluntarily yield to others land he had himself won at swordpoint, such a man had ambitions above and beyond filling his coffers, plundering his weaker neighbors. Such a man posed a genuine danger to England's interests, would have to be dealt with.

"Joanna . . . what does Llewelyn want for himself, for Wales?"

She surprised him then, said, "Are you asking for yourself, Richard? Or for Papa?"

"For myself," he said, and she smiled, reached out to brush the hair back from his temples. But she did not answer his question.

Branwen approached with mulled wine, retreated discreetly out of hearing range. Richard drank, studying his sister. Despite the fact that John's mother'd had one of the best political brains in Christendom, or perhaps because of it, he had never encouraged Joanna to take an interest in statecraft. He'd pampered her and protected her, indulged her and lavished love upon her, but he'd never asked her what she thought, never shown any curiosity in the workings of her brain. Her political education had come from her grandmother, during those months she'd spent with Eleanor in Poitiers. And, it was becoming disturbingly apparent to Richard, from Llewelyn ab Iorwerth.

Richard drank again, spat out sediment that had not settled to the bottom of the cup. He found himself wishing that Joanna were not becoming so quick to comprehend the subtleties and consequences of power, to grasp that which women need not know. Far better for her if she were like Isabelle, if she cared only for womanly whims and the joys of the moment, if she were not aware of the gathering clouds.

Suddenly he felt very dispirited, felt caught up in currents beyond his control. He knew his father had no liking at all for Joanna's husband, that he distrusted the Prince and disliked the man. But Richard did like Llewelyn, for he could not help but see the changes marriage had wrought in Joanna. Neither he nor his father had been able to give Joanna what she most needed, a sense of belonging. Llewelyn had somehow succeeded where they had not, and Richard was grateful to him for it. He knew Joanna had found more than contentment in her marriage, that she'd found a rare and real passion. He knew how deeply she loved Llewelyn, and he wished that she'd never laid eyes upon the Welsh Prince, wished that he had the power to blot the past thirty-one months from her mind and memory, for he did not think her present happiness was worth the suffering that was sure to come.

She had refused to answer his question, but he knew what her answer would have been, knew all too well what Llewelyn ab Iorwerth wanted. He wanted a Wales free of all English influence, wanted a united country under his own rule, a sovereign, independent kingdom like Scotland. And Richard knew his father would never allow it to be. No English King could.

"Richard . . . was Papa very wroth with Llewelyn for laying claim to Powys?"

"Yes, I fear so," he said reluctantly, hoping she would not interrogate him further, not wanting her to know the true extent of John's rage when he was told that Llewelyn's red-and-gold lions were flying over much of mid-Wales.

"I knew he—" Joanna gave an audible gasp; her wine cup splashed its contents onto the window-seat cushions.

"My God, Joanna, is it the babe? Do not move, I'll fetch your women . . ."

Joanna's breath was coming back. "You need not panic," she

said, sounding faintly amused. "It was just a stray pain. They
come and go in the last days, mean only that my time is growing
nigh."

Richard's relief was considerable. Like most men, he knew
next to nothing about the birthing process, was quite content to
keep it that way. "You'll have a midwife, of course, and women
to help, to do whatever . . . whatever must be done?" he asked
awkwardly.

"Two midwives, Dame Rhagnell and Dame Meryl. And
Branwen and Alison, of course. I should have liked Catherine to
be with me, but her youngest has been ailing." Joanna frowned;
having Catherine with her would have gone far to allay some of
her anxieties. "I wish I were not so fearful, Richard, wish I did
not dread it so, for when a woman is tense and fearful, the pain is
worse. If I did not remember Elen's birth so vividly . . . But I
will not be so afraid if I know Llewelyn is here. As long as he is
close at hand . . ."

Joanna's voice trailed off; after a moment, she looked up, gave
Richard a shy smile. "I never knew it was possible to be so
angry with a man and yet want him so much, too. But right now
I think I'd gladly forgive him any sin on God's earth if only he'd
walk through that door, if only he comes back for the baby's
birth . . ."

Richard would never have admitted his doubts to Joanna, but he
thought it very unlikely that Llewelyn would return in time.
Richard had known few husbands all that eager to endure long
hours of waiting outside the birthing chamber, and he found it
hard to believe a man would interrupt a military campaign because of a young wife's fears. Mayhap for a first child, but
Llewelyn already had seven children, already had a son. He said
nothing, however, did what he could to raise his sister's flagging
spirits, and was never so pleased to be proven wrong as when
Llewelyn rode into the castle bailey just before Vespers on
November 20.

Richard awoke with a start, a sleepy sense of disorientation.
After a moment or so, he remembered where he was, in the great
hall at Dolwyddelan, and glanced over at the pallet where his
brother-in-law had been sleeping. But Llewelyn's pallet was
empty. Despite the hour, Richard felt no surprise; several times
in the night he had heard Llewelyn rise, go out into the rain, and

each time he returned, wet and shivering, he had answered
Richard's low-voiced queries with a shrug, a shake of his head.

Pulling on his boots, Richard moved to the heavy oaken door,
opened it a crack. It was just before dawn, a blustery, cold
Monday; the wind was still gusting, and after a night of unrelenting rain, the bailey was ankle-deep in mud. Llewelyn was mounting the stairs up into the keep. He'd not be given entry, Richard
knew; men were strictly barred from the birthing chamber. But
Branwen or Alison would join him on the drawbridge in the
forebuilding, would give him word on Joanna's progress.

Richard retreated back into the hall, sent his squire for a
chamber pot and then a cupful of ale. It was a quarter hour before
Llewelyn returned. Moving at once to the center open hearth, he
stood as near the flames as he could, blew on his hands to
combat the crippling cold, and rejected an offer of bread and
cheese to break his fast. In the harsh morning light, he looked to
be a different man from the one who'd come back in such
triumph just three days ago, jubilant after six weeks of successive
victories. He suddenly seemed a stranger to laughter; lack of
sleep and a failure to shave gave him a haggard, unkempt look.
And remembering how he'd doubted that Llewelyn would return
for Joanna's travail, Richard wondered how he could ever have
been so stupid.

"How does she?" he asked, again got a weary shake of the
head in reply.

"No change, or so they claim." Llewelyn accepted a cupful of
ale, swallowed without tasting. "Eighteen hours it's been," he
said, and Richard realized he did not even know if that was an
excessive length of time.

"Is that overly long?"

"Not if the pains are light, feeble. But Branwen says Joanna's
pains are right sharp, and coming close together. She got no rest
at all last night. If the birth drags on . . . So much can go wrong,
Richard, so much. If the babe is lying in the wrong position, the
midwife has to reach up into the womb and try to correct it. If
she cannot, both mother and child are like to die. Or the babe can
be too big. Or the pains can go on so long that the woman's
strength gives out. There's always the danger that she'll lose
heart, the danger of sudden bleeding. And afterward, the danger
that she'll not expel the afterbirth."

Richard looked utterly blank, and Llewelyn said impatiently,
"That is the skin that held the babe when it was in the womb. If
it does not come out of its own accord, and the midwives cannot

pull it out, the woman will sicken and die. And even if she gives
birth safely and then expels the afterbirth, there is still the risk of
milk fever. They say as many women die from that as from the
birthing itself.''

Richard had already been told more than he'd ever wanted to
know about childbirth. "How in God's name do you know so
much about it? The midwives I've met have been as close-
mouthed as clams.''

"I asked Catrin to tell me." Llewelyn was staring into the fire,
caught up in memories of a woman with hair the color of the
flames, in memories of a summer seven years past. After a long
silence, he said, "I wanted to know why Tangwystl died."

For Llewelyn, those hours just before a battle always passed with
excruciating slowness. But nothing in his past had prepared him
for the way time fragmented and froze as he waited for Joanna to
give birth to their child. When it had become clear that Joanna's
delivery would be neither quick nor easy, he'd sent for Catherine, hoping that her presence might give Joanna comfort. But
although she was only twelve miles away at Trefriw, she had yet
to arrive, and he did not know whether to attribute the delay to
the rain-swamped roads or to the continued illness of her child.
Each time he made that grim trek across the bailey, sought scraps
of information from an increasingly evasive Branwen, he was
aware of a new and frightening feeling, a sense of utter impotence.

The rain fell intermittently all morning. Just before noon, the
cloud cover began to break over the mountains; patches of sky
became visible. Llewelyn at last humored his ten-year-old daughter, agreed to Gwladys's pleas that he allow the cooks to prepare
a meal for him. He was making desultory conversation with
Adda and Richard, relating how Maelgwn razed three of his own
castles in Ceredigion rather than have them fall into hostile
hands, when Branwen appeared without warning in the doorway
of the hall.

Her hair was falling about her face in wind-whipped disarray,
her gown mud-stained to the knees, and when Llewelyn reached
her, he saw that her eyes were filling with tears.

"The baby will not come," she whispered. "We do not know
what else to do, my lord. We've massaged her belly and anointed
her private parts with hot thyme oil, laid agrimony root across
her womb, given her bark of cassia fistula in wine, even given her
pepper to make her sneeze. The pains are coming very quick
now, very sharp, but the babe is no nearer to delivery than it was

three hours ago. My lord . . . she cannot go on like this much longer. Her strength is all but gone and she has begun to bleed.''

To Llewelyn, that was a death knell. It showed on his face, and she said quickly, "No, my lord, bleeding need not be fatal, God's truth! She's lost mayhap a cupful, no more. But she's losing, too, her will to endure, losing all hope. And once she begins to believe she and the babe will die . . .''

She was weeping openly by now. "My lord, Dame Rhagnell did send me to tell you that we do need a vial of holy water. Will your chaplain—"

"Holy water? No! No, I forbid it!''

"But my lord, you do not understand! It is for the babe. By pouring holy water onto a baptismal sponge, we can insert it up into Lady Joanna's womb, baptise the babe whilst it still lives!''

"Are you mad? You've just admitted that Joanna now despairs of delivering this child. You tell her you want to baptise the child whilst in her womb and you'll be passing a death sentence upon her!''

"I know," she said, and sobbed. "But if we do not, if the babe dies unbaptised, its soul will be lost to God! What choice have we, my lord, what choice?''

"Llewelyn, she is right." Morgan, Richard, and Adda had come up behind them. "She is right, lad," the priest repeated softly. "If a child is not baptised, it is forever denied Paradise, may never look upon the face of God. Your child, Llewelyn. Can you risk that?''

When Llewelyn did not answer, Morgan reached out, put his rosary into the younger man's hand. Llewelyn's fingers closed tightly around it; he could feel the beads digging into his palm. He brought them up, touched them to his lips, and then handed them back to the priest. "If I must choose between Joanna and the child," he said huskily, "I choose Joanna.''

Alison opened the door just wide enough to allow her to slip through to join Llewelyn out on the drawbridge. When he grabbed the latch, pushed past her into the bedchamber, she cried out in shock, "My lord, no!" but made no move to stop him. Nor did Branwen, a mute, miserable ghost trailing him across the bailey and up the stairs. Both midwives, however, reacted with outrage.

"My lord, you cannot enter the birthing chamber! You must go from here at once!''

Llewelyn did not even hear them. He stood immobile for a moment, staring at Joanna. Although the chamber was chill, she was clad only in a chemise. It was linen, not a clinging material, but it had molded to her body like a second skin, so drenched was she in perspiration. Her head was thrown back so far that her hair was sweeping the floor rushes, and the taut, corded muscles in her throat told Llewelyn more of her pain than any scream could have done.

Dame Rhagnell had stepped in front of him, barring his way. He thrust her aside, knelt by Joanna. The contraction was easing; she was no longer writhing upon the birthing stool, no longer gasping for breath. He murmured her name, and she turned her head toward him. Sweat ran down her face like rain, soaked the bodice of her chemise; he was close enough now to see that her skirt was filthy, soiled with mucus and urine, stained with blood. But what appalled him was the expression in her eyes, the hopeless, despairing look of an animal caught in a trap.

"Llewelyn . . . ." He'd never heard so much gladness compressed into one word, had never before heard his name invoked as a prayer. Her lips were cracked and bleeding; he touched them with his fingers, and she reached for his hand, clung tightly, desperately.

"I've sent for Catrin. She'll be here soon, love," he said, saw her try to smile, and found himself blinking back tears. He'd long ago learned to freeze feelings until he could deal with them. If he had not, he'd not have been able to survive twenty years of border warfare, to see death claim men who mattered to him, and not mourn them until the battle was won. But the lessons of a lifetime now served for naught; he could not dissociate himself from Joanna's pain. He watched the red stain widening over her skirt, and could think only of Tangwystl, bleeding her life away in the bed they'd so often shared.

The midwives were by no means reconciled to Llewelyn's alien presence in a female sanctum. But they temporarily abandoned their protests, turning all their attention to Joanna as her pain began anew. Dame Rhagnell knelt before the birthing stool, poured oil onto her hands, and began to probe under Joanna's skirt. She withdrew her hand only when the pain subsided, beckoned the other midwife aside.

When Dame Meryl continued to shake her head, Dame Rhagnell turned away from her, said abruptly, "From what I could feel, the mouth of the womb is fully open. But her waters have not broken and the membranes of the water bag are blocking the babe's passage from the womb." She'd not even glanced at

Joanna or the other women, was speaking to Llewelyn and Llewelyn alone.

"Do you understand?" Challengingly.

He nodded. "Yes. You're saying this water bag should have broken of its own accord by now, but has not. Can you break it?"

"Yes. But there are risks in doing so. Ofttimes a woman's delivery will be hastened by breaking her waters. But once the bag is broken, the pains become more severe, and if the birthing is prolonged, she'll suffer more. Dame Meryl thinks we should wait for the bag to break on its own. I would rupture it myself. The mouth of her womb has been open for hours; the babe should have come by now. So . . . you tell me, my lord. Since you are here, you decide. What would you have us do?"

Llewelyn knew what she was doing, acting to protect herself should the wrong choice be made, should Joanna die. He knew, too, that she was also taking vengeance the only way she could, trying to punish him for his intrusion into her domain. What he did not know was which choice was the right one. How could he know? If he guessed wrong . . .

He looked at Joanna in an agony of indecision. She was already exhausted, could not survive many more hours of this, that he did not doubt. Still he hesitated, but with him the need to act would always prevail in the end. He swallowed, opened his mouth to tell her to go ahead, when Joanna forestalled him. She'd not grasped all of what was said, but she did understand that the midwife was forcing upon Llewelyn a choice no man should have to live with.

"It is my decision to make," she said, speaking slowly and very carefully in her faulty Welsh. "I want you to break the water bag, Dame Rhagnell."

The midwife studied her for a long moment, and then nodded. "It is the right choice, Madame, I am sure of it."

They all watched tensely as she anointed her hands again in oil, seized a goose quill, and lowered herself onto her knees before Joanna. "My lord, sit behind her on the stool and put your arms around her, high over her belly. We must wait for the next pain."

Llewelyn did as she instructed, straddled the wooden plank protruding from the end of the stool, and braced Joanna back against his own body. She had closed her eyes tightly, was whispering rapidly, "Mary, Holy Mother of our Lord Jesus Christ, into thy hands and those of thy blessed Son now and

forever I commit myself, body, soul, and spirit.'' Llewelyn
stroked her hair until he felt her stiffen, twist against him.

The midwife at once jerked up Joanna's skirt, leaned forward.
Joanna continued to writhe in Llewelyn's embrace. And then the
midwife was pulling back, and suddenly there was liquid gushing
onto Joanna's skirt, onto the floor rushes, even splashing over
Llewelyn's mud-caked boots.

Llewelyn could tell almost immediately that Joanna's discomfort had been eased somewhat; her breathing was no longer so
rapid and shallow, and when Branwen put a wine cup to her lips,
she drank in gulps.

Dame Rhagnell let Joanna's skirt drop. ''The bleeding has
ceased,'' she said triumphantly, and Llewelyn forgave her all.

''So, too, has the pain.'' There was wonder in Joanna's voice
at first, and then, returning fear. ''What does that mean, Dame
Rhagnell? Why have the pains stopped?''

''It ofttimes happens after the water breaks, my lady.'' The
midwife had regained her professional poise, said now with
calming certainty, ''Soon the pangs will begin again, and when
they do, the child will come quickly, and with surprising ease.''

Whether she was lying or not, Llewelyn had no way of knowing. But Joanna was free of pain for the first time in many hours.
Her queasiness had mercifully abated, too, and with Branwen's
help, she was even able to walk the few steps into the privy
chamber. When she emerged, Llewelyn put his arm around her,
slowly steered her toward a chair. She leaned so heavily upon
him that his fears came rushing back; as weak as she was, how
much more could she endure?

''Llewelyn, I'm afraid . . .''

''I know, love, I know.''

''. . . afraid you shall be disappointed. You see, I think the
babe may be a girl. Dame Meryl said sons are more easily
birthed than this.''

He could not answer her at once, made mute by the utter
intensity of his relief. His greatest fear was that she would lose
heart, would begin to look upon death as a release; he'd watched
too many men die because dying was easier than suffering. But if
Joanna had indeed been teetering upon that precipice, she had
pulled back in time, had found new reserves of courage to draw
upon, to see her child born.

''I expect we can make do with a daughter if we must,'' he
said, tenderly teasing, and kissed her swollen eyelids, the corner
of her mouth.

The respite was brief; as Dame Rhagnell had predicted, Joanna's pains soon resumed. As the contractions increased in frequency and intensity, Dame Meryl stripped off Joanna's bloodied chemise, began to massage her abdomen. Joanna was groaning, taking deep gulping breaths, but she was not fighting the pain, was going with it, so intent upon her body's inner directives that she no longer seemed aware of Llewelyn and the midwives. She gasped, digging her nails into Llewelyn's wrist, and suddenly he could see the child's head. Joanna's body convulsed again, and the baby's shoulders appeared; it slid between her thighs into the eager waiting hands of the midwife.

It happened so quickly that Llewelyn was taken almost by surprise. He had only a fleeting glimpse of a small dark shape, skin puckered and covered with what looked like slime, bloodied and bruised, and he felt a sick horror that Joanna should have suffered so, only to give birth to a dead child. But then the infant made a mewing sound, and the midwife held it up with a cry of triumph.

"A man-child," she exulted. "You've a son, my lord, a son!"

Llewelyn reached out, touched one of the tiny waving fists, and laughed. The midwives did, too, for the birth of a male child called up instinctive and ancient loyalties, and they rejoiced in being able to present a son to the man who was their Prince. Joanna was all but forgotten until she demanded weakly, "Give me my son."

Dame Meryl started to do so, instead handed the wet, squirming infant to Llewelyn, and it was he who laid the baby against Joanna's breast.

Joanna had never before felt for anyone, not even Elen, what she now felt as she held her son for the first time, a fierce, passionate tenderness, love immediate and overwhelming. "He's so beautiful," she whispered, and Llewelyn laughed again, for he thought the baby could not have been uglier, splotched and red and smeared with his own feces, with his mother's blood. Joanna looked up as he laughed, and smiled at him, a smile he would remember for the rest of his life. But then she jerked spasmodically, groaned.

One of the midwives grabbed for the baby, at once tied and cut through the navel cord, while the other pressed down upon Joanna's belly. Blood was spurting down Joanna's thighs, clotting on the floor. But Branwen was already at Llewelyn's side, Branwen who knew Tangwystl had bled to death, saying hastily,

"It is not what you fear, my lord. The afterbirth does come, that be all."

He saw she was right, soon saw a soft, spongy mass expelled into Dame Meryl's outstretched hands. She caught it deftly, scooped it into a waiting blanket. "It must be kept, must be properly buried," she explained, "lest it attract demons." Then she added, with more mischief than malice, "Should you like to look at it, my lord?"

"Not really," Llewelyn said, and when he grinned, she grinned back.

Dame Rhagnell now laid the baby back in Joanna's arms. "You may hold him for a few moments, Madame, but then he must be cleaned and rubbed with salt, must have his gums rubbed with honey."

Llewelyn stood watching his wife and son, not aware of Branwen until she had twice touched his arm. "Here, my lord," she said, handing him a goblet full of mead. "Is it not a wondrous thing, to see your child born?"

He nodded. "Indeed. But I'll tell you what is no less wondrous to me right now. That after a woman endures all this, why she is then willing to let any man ever again get within ten feet of her bed!" Although he spoke partly in jest, he was partly in earnest, too, and the women recognized it, legitimized with lusty, approving laughter his brief incursion into a secret inner realm, the world within a world of women.

When Joanna awoke, the chamber was deep in shadows. She started to sit up, grimaced, and sank back weakly against the pillow. At once Llewelyn was beside her, leaning over the bed.

"How do you feel, love?"

"I ache all over." To her dismay, she was suddenly shy with him, suddenly fearful that he might feel differently toward her now. "I wanted you so much," she confessed, "even begged the midwives to send for you when the pains got too bad. They said they could not, that it was not seemly, that a man would be sickened by the birthing . . ."

"Joanna, I was fifteen the first time I killed a man. In the years since, I've seen men gutted, beheaded, hacked to pieces. I rather think there is more blood on the battlefield than in the birthing chamber," he said wryly, and when she raised herself up awkwardly on her elbows, he gathered her gently into his arms.

"The baby . . . where is he? Has he been fed?"

"He is fine, *breila*." Seeing the doubt in her eyes, he beckoned, and a wet nurse approached the bed, gave Joanna her sleeping son.

"You've arranged for the christening, Llewelyn?" she asked anxiously, not wanting to wait a moment longer than necessary to put her child under God's protection, and he nodded.

"This evening in the chapel; I'll tell you about it after. Catrin has come; she rode in just after you fell asleep. I've asked her to stand as godmother, and as godfathers, Adda and Richard. Does that please you?"

"Very much." Joanna cradled the baby, touched a finger to his cap of dark, feathery hair. "But ere he can be christened, we must pick a name for him. Have you one in mind?"

"If you like, we could call him Sion."

Joanna drew a sharp breath. "Ah, love, you'd truly do that for me? Let me name him after my father?" She reached for his hand, saw the scratches she'd inflicted, sought feverishly to think, to give him a gift of equal generosity. What name would be most likely to please him? It was not a common custom amongst the Welsh to name a son after the father. Iowerth? Morgan?

And then she knew, and she smiled at him, said softly, "I do thank you, beloved. But there can be but one name for our son, for a Welsh Prince. We must name him after the most cherished of your saints, we must name him Davydd."

Beyond the castle, the world was utter blackness, the sky a vast, starless void. Gruffydd was blinded by the night, kept stumbling, and his face and the palms of his hands were soon scratched from sprawling falls into the tangled underbrush. But he did not slow, did not halt his headlong flight into the dark.

He ran until his body could absorb no more abuse, and he staggered, fell to his knees, struggling to fill his lungs with the ice-edged November air. A sharp, pulsing pain was pressing against his ribs, and he dropped down upon the ground, lay panting, his face pressed into the earth. The ground was damp, cold, scattered with dead and decaying leaves. He could feel sweat trickling down his neck, and then tears, seeping through his lashes and searing his skin. He beat his fist against the hard, unyielding earth until his knuckles were raw and bleeding, until he wept.

25

WOODSTOCK, ENGLAND

October 1209

"Harri, throw the ball to me. *Brysiwch*, Harri!"

Joanna, listening to her children play with Isabelle's two sons, found herself smiling, amused both by her small daughter's queenly commands and by the way she switched back and forth from French to Welsh. Henry was, at two, the oldest of the quartet, but he did Elen's bidding no less promptly than her brother. Davydd was normally Elen's favorite playmate, but he showed no resentment at being supplanted by Henry, played with his own ball until Richard crawled over, made an awkward grab for it.

Isabelle sighed, bracing herself for the inevitable squabble, to be followed by tantrums and tears, but Joanna knew better; she felt no surprise when Davydd good-naturedly rolled the ball toward the younger boy. "He has ever been like that," she said proudly, "ever been willing to share. Unlike Elen, whose first word was 'mine'!"

"She is rather an imp, is she not? Not like you at her age, I'll wager!"

Joanna laughed ruefully, gave her dark-haired little daughter a look of bemused affection. "Lord, no. She must take after her father, for she surely does not take after me. You'd not believe the trouble she gets into, and still a fortnight from her second birthday. But she is clever, Isabelle, so clever; do you know she talks to me in French and Llewelyn in Welsh?"

The children's wet nurses had now entered Isabelle's chamber, and the game was forgotten; all four were still suckling, and would be until past their second birthdays. Joanna watched as they were ushered toward the far end of the chamber, said, "This has been such a good year, the best I can remember: Llewelyn agreeing to pass Easter with Papa at Northampton; getting to see

326

you and Papa again just six months later; above all, Papa forgiving Llewelyn for going into Powys as he did. As much as I dread to see Llewelyn ride off to war, I was almost pleased when Papa wanted him to join the campaign against the Scots. I felt that might well mend the rift between them. And it did, showed Papa that Llewelyn does mean to hold to his oath of allegiance.''

"That was a marvelous war, was it not? The best kind, brief and bloodless and oh, so profitable! John was right pleased, says those who call the Scots King 'William the Lion' ought better to call him 'the Lamb'!''

"What shall be done with William's daughters, Isabelle? The ones he was forced to yield up to Papa as hostages?''

"They shall be well treated, kept at court. John never maltreats women; look how he provides for his niece, Eleanor of Brittany, sees that she has whatever she wants.''

"All save freedom," Joanna said sadly. "She was about seven years older than I, which would now make her twenty-five or so. By that age, most women have husbands, children . . .'' She did not go on. She did not blame her father, understood he had no choice. But it hurt, nonetheless, to think of her cousin's gilded confinement at Bristol Castle, and she sought hastily for another topic of conversation. She'd been somewhat taken aback by the luxury of Isabelle's chamber. She and John were not at Woodstock all that frequently, yet the walls had been wainscoted with fir shipped from Norway, painted a brilliant green and gold, and the windows were glazed, set with costly white glass panes. "Your chamber is a marvel, Isabelle. Papa does right by you, in truth.''

"Dearest, nothing comes to a woman unless she asks. You ought to coax Llewelyn into having your chambers done over. If you're clever, he'll not refuse, will even come in time to think it was his own idea.''

Joanna laughed. "How little you know of Wales. Llewelyn could never hope to raise the revenues that Papa does; his country is so much smaller, so much poorer. In fact, I wonder that Papa could afford all this either. From the way he talks, he is ever hard pressed for money.''

"John refuses me nothing these days," Isabelle said, backed up her boast by opening an iron casket, lifting out a magnificent ruby necklet. "What will it avail him to have peace with the Scots if he has no peace at home?''

Joanna opened her mouth, shut it abruptly. She'd only been at Woodstock for two days, but it was time enough to become conscious of the whispers, the knowing smiles, the way her father's eyes followed the young, pretty, blonde wife of one of his household knights. Joanna was sympathetically sure that Isabelle was aware of what was occurring; Isabelle, of all women, would never have missed the subtle yet significant indications of infidelity. Joanna knew a blithe, worldly spirit like Isabelle's was not likely to be lacerated by a husband's adultery, but she had not expected her stepmother to react with such nonchalant sangfroid.

"It . . . it does not grieve you any?"

"Ah, Joanna, you are such an innocent. Would it matter if it did? Would John then repent, forsake all other women? What cannot be changed must be accepted, no?" Isabelle held the ruby necklet up to the light, looped it over her fingers. "If we are supposed to profit from our own mistakes, why should we not, as well, profit from the mistakes of others, from the indiscretions of erring husbands?" She reached over, draped the necklet around Joanna's throat. "You may wear it at dinner if you like. Surely I have not shocked you, darling? You do not truly think your Llewelyn is faithful, do you?"

"Yes," Joanna said, and then, seeing Isabelle's smile of pitying disbelief, she added hastily, "Oh, I am not so naïve as to believe he has never strayed. I do not doubt he finds women to warm his bed when we are apart, as when he was away in Scotland and England for two full months this summer. Whatever the Welsh laws may hold on fidelity, Llewelyn is no man to live like a monk. But I know how little such encounters mean to him, and I know that he does not lay with another woman when he can lay with me."

"No mistresses, no concubines? Not even that woman who bore his twins?"

"No," Joanna insisted, so resolutely that Isabelle said indulgently, if still skeptically:

"It's glad I am for you, then." She removed the circlet anchoring her veil and wimple, handed Joanna a brush, confiding, "I had a scare this spring, thought I might be with child again. I do not mind having more, think I'd like a daughter. But I've borne John two sons in fifteen months, have no desire to drop a litter a year! So . . . to give myself some breathing space, I've been taking brake-root in wine."

"But Isabelle, that is a sin. You know what the Church does say, that nothing must be done to prevent a child's conception."

Isabelle shrugged. "I know, too, who gets to bear that child— not His Holiness the Pope. But you cannot be all that eager yourself to face the birthing chamber again, Joanna. At the least, you should put a jasper stone under your pillow when you lay with Llewelyn. Ask him to get you one; you need not tell him what it is for."

"Of course I would tell him! Think you I'd do that without his consent?"

"And what if he balks? If he is one of those men who judges his manhood by his wife's protruding belly?"

"Not Llewelyn," Joanna said and smiled. "The midwives think it unlikely that I'll be able to carry a child again to full term, think I might not even conceive again. When I told Llewelyn that, he said, 'Thank the Lord God!' He has ever—" Breaking off in mid-sentence, she jumped to her feet, ran to console her son. Davydd had begun an unsteady trek across the chamber toward his mother, only to lose a precarious balance and fall upon his face. Picking him up, Joanna soothed and teased until his sobs ceased, until he settled contentedly in her lap, began to suck upon a sticky little thumb.

"Joanna, I confess I still do not understand Welsh laws of succession. John says illegitimacy is no bar, that Gruffydd has the same rights as your son. Is that true? Does that make him Llewelyn's heir, as the firstborn?"

"Under Welsh law, all sons share equally in the father's estates. It is a fair system for the common people, fairer for younger sons than Norman primogeniture, which gives all to the eldest son. But it has one dreadful drawback, Isabelle; how do you divide a kingdom? What inevitably happens when a prince dies is that his sons fight amongst themselves, winner-take-all to the survivor."

"You're saying that when Llewelyn dies, Gwynedd would be partitioned between his two bastard-born Welsh sons and your Davydd?"

Joanna nodded grimly. "And the very thought does terrify me. It is not just a question of preserving Davydd's rightful inheritance. Should evil befall Llewelyn ere Davydd reaches manhood, it would become a question of Davydd's very life."

"Is there nothing you can do, Joanna?"

"There must be." Joanna brushed her lips to her son's pitch-black hair. "Blessed Mary, but there must be."

"I think not, have no desire for an English knife at my throat."

"Do not be insulting; I am Norman, not English. And you let me cut your hair, do you not? So why should I not shave you? Unless you truly want to trust your throat to a barber so greensick from wine that he seems stricken with palsy? Now lie down. I'll be right careful, have no wish to get blood all over the bed!"

"Why am I so sure I am going to regret this?" But Llewelyn did as Joanna bade, lay back and rested his head in her lap.

"There now," Joanna said with satisfaction some minutes later. "Almost done and I've yet to draw blood." She cocked her head to the side in playful appraisal. "Have you never wondered how you'd look without your mustache?"

Llewelyn's eyes snapped open. "You would not dare!"

"Ah, Llewelyn, how I wish you had not said that. Now I feel obliged to prove to you that I would!" She let the razor hover tantalizingly close to its target, laughing, and when he grabbed her wrist, sought to pull her down beside him, she wriggled free, defended herself with the pillow. Neither realized how close they'd rolled toward the edge of the bed, not until it was too late, until their struggle carried them over the side, tumbling down onto the floor rushes.

Joanna was breathless but unhurt; in falling, Llewelyn had managed to twist away, to keep from landing on top of her. She rose to her knees, pulled her skirt down. "Are you all right?" she asked, stopped laughing when he admitted reluctantly:

"No, I think not . . ."

"Oh, love, you did not hurt your back again?" She leaned toward him solicitously, then gave a muffled scream when he pounced, rolling over and pinning her under the weight of his body.

Joanna found herself utterly helpless, unable to move. "I should have known; you're so untrustworthy," she scolded, smothering her laughter against his shoulder. "Now let me up. Papa is awaiting us in the great hall."

"Make it worth my while and I might."

"If I were to say I was sorry, that I do love your mustache?" He considered gravely, shook his head. "Not good enough."

"Well, that was my best offer." Squirming under him, she made an intriguing discovery. "When Gwenwynwyn and Maelgwn call you hard, they do not know the half of it, do they? So it's not true, then, that when a man gets to be your age, his powers begin to wane?"

"My age?" he echoed, with mock indignation. "I'm but six and thirty!"

"That is, after all, twice as old as I am," she pointed out gleefully, and deliberately shifted her hips to make the most of his erection.

"Wanton," he murmured, his mouth against her throat. "If you do not stop tempting me, we are going to bypass the great hall altogether, are going to continue this conversation in bed. So do not say you were not warned."

"Love, you know we have to be there." Joanna sighed, with real regret. "Otherwise, I'd like nothing better than . . . conversing with you. You're such a deep, penetrating conversationalist, after all," she said, all but choked in trying not to laugh at her own weak pun.

She'd never yet bested him at wordplay, and she waited expectantly to see how he would improve upon her effort. Instead he said, "Do come in, John."

"You'll have to do better than that," Joanna scoffed. "You played that trick upon me once before, remember? Looking up and saying, 'Yes, Morgan?' at a moment when we most definitely had no need of witnesses!" The memory made her laugh; Llewelyn did, too. But then he sat up.

"I was not jesting, Joanna," he said, and Joanna turned her head, saw her father standing in the doorway of the bedchamber.

John's face was impassive, showed absolutely nothing of what he was thinking. "I trust I'm not interrupting anything of urgency?"

Llewelyn grinned, but he could see the embarrassed blush rising in Joanna's face and throat; taking pity on her, he held his tongue, showed his amusement only in the exaggerated gallantry with which he helped her to her feet. Privacy was an unknown luxury, and Joanna had long since become accustomed to people intruding into their bedchamber at inopportune moments, surprising her on Llewelyn's lap, in his arms, once in the midst of a soapily erotic shared bath. But never before had she felt as she did now, flustered and thoroughly discomfited.

"The last of the Welsh Princes have arrived, and they are awaiting us now in the hall." For the first time John looked directly at Joanna, his eyes opaque, utterly unreadable. "I thought we would enter together."

"We would be honored, Papa." Joanna hastily snatched up her veil, crossed to her father. Laying a hand upon his arm, she looked searchingly into his face. She still thought him to be a handsome man, but she thought, too, that time was not treating him kindly. She knew he would not be forty-two until December, yet the ink-black hair was liberally flecked with grey; his eyes were bloodshot, shadowed by suspicions beyond satisfying, the mouth thinned, inflexible, not as open to laughter as Joanna remembered.

What could she say, that she ached for him, grieved that he had so much and so little? "I love you, Papa," she said, saw his mouth soften, and put her arms around his neck.

"I love you, too, sweetheart," John said gently, for a moment held her in a close, comforting embrace. But he was not looking at his daughter, was gazing over her shoulder at the man she'd married.

Joanna watched as Llewelyn knelt before her father, did homage to John as his King and liege lord. The hall was quiet; Llewelyn's voice carried clearly to all, his matter-of-fact tones revealing none of the distaste Joanna knew he must feel.

John was now making the obligatory response, promising to do all in his power to guarantee Llewelyn's peaceful possession of Gwynedd, raising his son-in-law up to give him the ritual kiss of peace. Llewelyn then declared, "In the name of the Holy Trinity and in reverence of these sacred relics, I swear that I will truly keep the oath which I have given, and will always remain faithful to you, my King and seigneur," and then it was over, and Joanna took more comfort from the ceremony than she knew it warranted, tried to convince herself that there could indeed be a true and abiding harmony between the two men she loved.

Gwenwynwyn alone was absent, a prisoner of the crown for the past twelvemonth. But Madog ap Gruffydd was there, Prince of Upper Powys, Llewelyn's first cousin and ally. So, too, were the Princes of Deheubarth, of South Wales, Maelgwn and his brother, Rhys Gryg, and one by one they followed Llewelyn to the dais, knelt to do homage to the English King. After them came the younger Welsh lords, Llewelyn's cousin Hywel and Maelgwn's estranged nephews, Owain and Rhys Ieuanc; all three were in their mid-twenties, and all three were Llewelyn's sworn men. It was Hywel who was to give a deliberate and dramatic demonstration of where his loyalties lay. No sooner had he done homage to John than he crossed the hall, knelt before Llewelyn, and swore oaths of homage and fidelity for the lordship of Meirionydd.

The Welsh system of inheritance did not promote family unity; all too often it fostered fratricide, set brother against brother in a bitter battle for supremacy. So it had been with Llewelyn's father and uncles. So, too, it had been in the South, where Maelgwn and Rhys Gryg were the survivors of a long and bloody war of succession. Owain and Rhys Ieuanc were a rarity, therefore, brothers who were not rivals, who acted as one. In the silence that settled over the hall after Hywel's acknowledgment of allegiance, Owain and Rhys exchanged wordless looks of perfect understanding. Then they, too, crossed the hall, did homage to Llewelyn for Ceredigion.

A man could, and very often did, owe allegiance to two or more liege lords. In choosing to do homage to Llewelyn, the

Welshmen were well within their legal rights. But Joanna wished
fervently that they had not done so, had not acted to tarnish her
father's moment of triumph. Maelgwn was standing just to her
right, close enough to touch. He was a striking-looking man in
his early forties, no taller than John, with a thick head of tawny
hair and the blue eyes of the true Celt; those eyes were the
coldest Joanna had ever seen. She watched his face as his nephews did homage to Llewelyn for lands once his, and shivered,
suddenly and uncontrollably.

"Did Llewelyn plan that?" a voice murmured at her ear.
When she shook her head, Richard swore under his breath.
"Papa will not ever believe he did not, Joanna," he said somberly.

Richard took a seat as inconspicuously as possible, not entirely
comfortable to be in the company of these men, the most powerful lords of his father's realm. As he glanced about the table, it
was with a distinct shock that he realized how few of them bore
his father no grievances, how few were not in some sort of disfavor.

Chester seemed to have weathered John's earlier suspicions.
And his Uncle Will, of course, still stood high in John's favor.
So, too, did John's mercenary captains, Falkes de Breauté and
Robert de Vieuxpont. Richard thought them to be men without
honor, men who whored for the lord who'd pay the most, but
their very practicality would keep them loyal; none could pay
better than the King. Peter des Roches had proved his loyalty
even to John's exacting satisfaction, remaining in England despite the Pope's Interdict. The same could not be said, though,
for the others.

William de Ferrers, Earl of Derby, had the bad luck to be a
nephew to William de Braose. The northern baron Eustace de
Vesci was suspect because of his links to the Scottish crown; he
was wed to a bastard daughter of King William. The Earl of
Huntingdon's predicament was even more acute; he was the
Scots King's brother. Richard de Clare, Earl of Hertford, was
twice damned in John's judgment; he had welcomed John's
accession to the throne with less than wholehearted enthusiasm,
and his daughter was wife to William de Braose's eldest son.

William de Braose was casting a long shadow indeed, Richard
thought bleakly. Even the faithful, upright Earl of Pembroke had
stumbled over it, had foolishly taken pity on the fugitive de
Braose family, had briefly given them shelter on his Irish estates,
for which John had yet to forgive him. The truth his father did
not want to face was unpleasantly clear to Richard, that there was

a growing groundswell of sympathy for de Braose among his fellow barons, not because he'd been liked, but because he'd been so powerful, so apparently invulnerable. There was not a man in this chamber, Richard knew, who had not thought to himself: The same thing could happen to me, to mine, should the King ever turn against me as he did de Braose.

This was the first council meeting since they'd departed Woodstock for John's hunting lodge at Silverston. Richard knew what his father wanted to discuss: his coming campaign in Ireland, with its dual purpose of capturing the de Braoses and punishing those lords who'd dared to harbor them, an expedition he meant to finance with the fifteen thousand marks he'd extorted from the King of Scotland.

The council meeting began on an entirely different and discordant note, however. Eustace de Vesci leaned across the table, said with poorly concealed relish, "I've news Your Grace should know. The Pope has given the order for your excommunication."

Suddenly the chamber was very quiet. The Interdict was causing no small degree of suffering for John's subjects, but so far it had not had the effect the Pope desired, had not undermined the allegiance of the English. A large majority still supported John's position, that it was the King's right to choose an Archbishop of Canterbury, and not for the Pope to force his own man upon them. It was only to be expected, therefore, that the Pope would resort to excommunication, which made of John an outcast among all men of faith. No Christian was to break bread with an excommunicate; he was to be shunned as a moral leper, as a man doomed to eternal damnation.

John looked at de Vesci for a long moment, then smiled coldly. " 'When I was a child, I spake as a child, I understood as a child, I thought as a child, but when I became a man, I put away childish things.' "

Richard heard more than one indrawn breath, and looking around, he saw that his father had profoundly shocked most of the men. Even the cynical de Vesci seemed taken aback.

How much bravado was there in John's blasphemy? Richard did not know. The sentence of excommunication had come as no surprise to John; he'd been privately warned days ago by Peter des Roches that the decree was imminent, had time enough to come to terms with it. Richard knew, of course, that his father was not the most pious of men, but what man could contemplate damnation forever and aye without recoil, without an inner shudder of the soul?

It was the pragmatic Chester who at last ended an acutely
uncomfortable silence, saying calmly, "Have you thought, my
liege, of the problems this will pose for you . . . for us? How the
common people will react?"

"The common people are not likely even to know. Let the
Pope proclaim it from now till Judgment Day—in France, Brittany,
Normandy. But who's to proclaim it for him in England? My
lord Bishop of Winchester is the only prelate still on English
soil."

Peter des Roches smiled imperturbably, confirming what all
already knew, that he'd chosen his King over his Pope, ambition
over obedience. "Your Grace is, as ever, quite right," he said
blandly. "Shall we speak now of Your Grace's Irish expedition?"

"Not yet." John signaled for wine, said, "I've had word from
Shrewsbury. Gwenwynwyn is offering no less than twenty hostages for his freedom, as a pledge of future loyalties."

That was of little interest to de Vesci and the Earl of Derby;
theirs were not Marcher lands. It was of enormous interest,
though, to border lords like Chester and de Clare. And to Richard, for altogether different reasons.

"Do you intend to release him, Your Grace?"

"I expect so . . . sooner or later."

"You do know that will mean war?" Chester's eyes were
suddenly speculative. "Once Gwenwynwyn is free, he'll seek to
regain what was his."

"You think he can?" John asked, and Chester considered,
shook his head.

"Against Llewelyn? No, Your Grace, probably not. Not unless he does get help."

"I agree with you," John said, no more than that, but Chester
was sensitive to nuance, to the unspoken.

"You would aid Gwenwynwyn, my liege?" he asked, and
John acknowledged his percipience with a faint smile.

But it was Will who answered him, saying with some indignation, "No, he would not! Llewelyn is his daughter's husband,
my lord Chester. Moreover, he has proven his loyalty in answering my brother's summons for war against the Scots. I grant you
he erred in disobeying John, in attacking Powys, but what's past
is past, forgiven and forgotten, and he—"

"Whatever makes you think I've forgiven him, Will?"

"Why, because . . . because you made him welcome at court,
John, showed no sign that you bore him any ill will—"

"I do not ever forget a wrong done me, Will. Not ever," John

repeated softly, and again Richard heard someone catch his
breath. Only the men whose swords were sold to the highest
bidder, Falkes de Breauté and Robert de Vieuxpont, appeared
unaffected by the threat. Every other man in the room seemed to
have taken John's ominous admission to heart. Will looked troubled, Chester inscrutable, de Vesci grim, expressions of unease
flickering from face to face, the awareness that John's warning
was meant as much for them as for his Welsh son-in-law.

"You were all at Woodstock, saw what happened, saw what
he dared to do." John's color had deepened; there was in the
low, precise voice echoes of remembered rage. "For those of
you who are not that well acquainted with Llewelyn ab Iorwerth's
predatory past, he seized power from his uncle at twenty-one,
and in the intervening fifteen years has steadily increased his
holdings—always at someone else's expense. He'll eventually
swallow up all of Wales . . . if left to his own devices."

Richard bit his lip, much disquieted. He knew Joanna had
spoken privately to their father, had left for Wales confident she
had convinced John that Llewelyn had not known what his young
allies meant to do. It bothered Richard that John had not been
honest with Joanna, bothered him that John had been nursing a
grudge for more than a year, bothered him that the other men
were so quick to nod agreement. He knew he owed it to Joanna
to object, to defend her husband. But he knew, too, that he was
there only on John's sufferance, that there was no voice in
council for the King's twenty-year-old bastard son, and that
silenced him, that and an instinctive reluctance to move from the
sidelines to center stage, to abandon the protective coloring
developed during a solitary, introspective childhood, the unquestioning, fatalistic acceptance that had enabled him to look upon
his father's darker side and neither approve nor condemn.

It was Chester who unexectedly did what Richard felt he could
not—offer a measured, unimpassioned protest. "You understand
the Welsh quite well, my liege, better than your brother ever did.
And making use of one Welsh prince to checkmate another is
indeed a shrewd and proven strategy for dealing with Wales."

John, too, was responsive to insinuation. He frowned, said
challengingly, "But not this time?"

"Llewelyn ab Iowerth is an unusual man, Your Grace. He is
exceedingly ambitious, just as you say, but he is intelligent, too.
I think he understands the limitations of power . . . of Welsh
power. And because he does, I would prefer to keep him as an

ally, even if it means giving him a free hand in Wales. I fear that if we do not, we risk pushing him into open rebellion."

"And what if we do? Are you saying a Welsh rebel could prevail against the English crown?" John's voice was scornful, but Chester refused the bait.

"No, Your Grace, of course I am not. He could not hope to defeat you. But I am not sure you fully realize what victory might cost. It is too late, you see, to use a Gwenwynwyn or a Maelgwn to rein him in; the balance of power has already shifted too far in his favor. If you do not come to terms with him, it would not be enough to defeat him. You'd have to destroy him."

Chester paused, waiting. But John made no response.

"As I said, Your Grace, I do not doubt the eventual outcome. But it would be a drawn-out, bloody, and brutal war. Wars with the Welsh always are. They disappear into inaccessible mountain retreats, phantom foes we cannot find. But they have no trouble finding us, my liege; they excel at ambush, at surprise attack and counterattack upon the morrow. There is no glory in wars against the Welsh, only blood-spattered rocks and shallow graves, and once you win, you find precious little for the plundering. I would not undertake such a war merely to rid myself of a man I could more easily befriend, Your Grace."

"Would you not? And if I were to order you to do just that, order you to lead an army into Gwynedd, what then? Would you balk, beg off from a duty you find so distasteful?"

The sarcasm was savage, utterly undeserved, and Richard winced. Chester had gone rigid in his chair; Richard was close enough to see how the muscles clenched along his jawline, how the tendons tightened in his throat. "I serve the King's pleasure," he said, quite tonelessly. "When Your Grace commands, I obey."

"How very reassuring," John said dryly. His gaze shifted from Chester, moved slowly from face to face. The other men averted their eyes, guarded their thoughts. All save Will, who leaned across the table, put his hand upon John's sleeve, and asked what Richard so needed to know.

"John, Llewelyn is wed to your daughter. What of her? What of Joanna? I cannot believe you'd want to see her hurt."

John exhaled a deep, drawn-out breath, stared down at his clenched fist, at the imprints his nails had left in the palm of his hand. "No, I would never want that," he said. "Never." He looked up then, raised troubled hazel eyes to his brother's face. "But I fear that marriage was a mistake, Will, a great mistake."

26

CRICIETH CASTLE, NORTH WALES

August 1210

William de Braose turned from the window, from the shimmering blue expanse of the bay. "It is good of you, my lord, to make my grandson and me welcome at your castle of Cricieth."

"To the Welsh, hospitality is a binding obligation. We never turn away a man in need of shelter, offer him food and a bed, guarantee his safety as long as he remains a guest at our hearth. I understand the Normans do have different customs," Llewelyn said, very dryly, saw the older man's face mottle with color, saw his barb bury itself in the scar tissue of an old shame. He was not surprised when de Braose made no effort to defend himself; to de Braose, the Abergavenny massacre required neither explanation nor expiation. Nor was he surprised when de Braose forbore to take offense, for he knew how much the Norman lord needed his help.

"I hear John has been laying waste to half of Ireland. Have you no fears for your wife, your family?"

"There is no need. As soon as John moved into Ulster, my wife and sons took ship for Scotland."

"A wise decision," Llewelyn conceded. "John makes a bad enemy."

"You should know."

"Should I?"

De Braose closed the space between them, stopped before Llewelyn's chair. "Can you not feel the noose tightening about your neck? John had to delay his Irish expedition to deal with the Scots King, and he now delays your destruction whilst he settles a grudge against me and mine. But your turn is coming, my lord. Can you, in truth, doubt it? After John did take Ellesmere Castle from you?"

338

Llewelyn tensed. It was months since John had abruptly re-claimed the castle he'd yielded to Llewelyn as Joanna's marriage portion, but the mere mention of Ellesmere was enough to ignite a still-smoldering anger, anger that gave the lie to his affectation of indifference. De Braose saw, and smiled.

"I have friends still in Wales, in England, am kin by blood or marriage to Derby, de Clare, Mortimer. To a man, they hate John, and with cause. They'd heed a call to rebellion. So, too, would Maelgwn and Rhys Gryg, especially if you came in with us, my lord. With John occupied in Ireland, this is a God-given opportunity; we'd be fools not to take advantage of it. At the least, we could then treat with him from strength, pressure him into buying peace on our terms. And with luck, we might be able to do more than maim, we might even be able to bring him down. You do not fear him as most men do, so you do not realize the extent of their hatred. Let them scent blood, and they'll react like a pack of hounds with a live hare in their midst. Think what it would mean, my lord. With John shackled, one way or the other, Wales would be yours for the taking. And of course you'd have my full support, that of my kindred."

"Of course," Llewelyn echoed cynically. But the thrust of de Braose's argument could not be dismissed as easily as his self-serving promises. Llewelyn was quiet for some moments, at last shook his head. "I'll not deny there is truth in what you say. And if I truly thought we had a chance to succeed . . . But the risk is too great. I've never been so hungry that I was willing to lick honey off thorns."

"If rashness is a flaw, so, too, is an excess of caution. Sooner or later a day of reckoning is coming between you and John. Better that you should be the one to pick when and where. Think on what I've said, that is all I ask. Think on it."

The sun was sliding into the sea by the time Joanna returned to the castle. So great was her sense of outrage that she'd been unable to remain under the same roof with William de Braose, and had gathered up her children and taken them down to the beach for a day in the sun, out of sight and sound of the man who was her father's avowed enemy.

Davydd and Elen had been thrilled with this break in their daily routine, splashed in the shallows and dug in the sand. But Joanna was utterly miserable. How could Llewelyn do it, how could he make welcome a man outlawed, a traitor to the crown? Did he not realize—or care—what her father would make of that?

Alys, Davydd's wet nurse, had packed a basket full of food, but
Joanna could swallow no more than a mouthful of cheese. In the
months since Woodstock, she'd watched helplessly as her life
careened out of control, as her father and husband moved closer
and closer to an irrevocable break. She'd been deeply hurt by her
father's seizure of Ellesmere, saw the revoking of her marriage
portion as a denial of her marriage, felt that her father had
somehow betrayed her. That Llewelyn would receive William de
Braose was, in a different way, no less a betrayal.

Once they were within sight of the castle, Joanna felt free to
dismiss Alys and the three men she'd taken along as an escort,
knowing Llewelyn would have been furious with her if she'd
gone off without them. She was in no hurry to climb the slope up
to the castle, not when William de Braose might still be within,
and she loitered for a time by the water's edge, watching gulls
squabble over the last of her bread. When Elen came running up,
brandishing a dead crab, Joanna made the obligatory response,
delighted her daughter by shrinking back in mock horror, not
confiscating the crab until Elen tried to stuff it down the front of
Davydd's tunic.

Elen burst into thwarted tears, sobbing pitifully and resisting
with all the strength in her small body as Joanna pulled her away
from the water, in the direction of the castle. Just when Joanna's
frayed patience was about to give way, Elen wriggled loose,
sprinted forward with a glad cry of "Gruffydd!"

A short distance away, three boys were sitting upon a log,
throwing knives at a small piece of driftwood. Joanna was now
close enough to make a grudging recognition of her stepson and
Ednyved's son Tudur. The third youngster had sun-streaked blond
hair and a deep tan; she only belatedly recognized him as William de Braose's grandson and namesake.

He rose politely, if briefly, to his feet at sight of her; so did
Tudur. But Gruffydd did not move, managed to make of his
slouching pose a deliberate provocation. In the five months since
he'd attained his fourteenth birthday and his legal majority,
Gruffydd's relationship with Joanna had deteriorated rapidly. No
longer sullenly mute, he was becoming openly antagonistic, almost as if defying Joanna to fall back upon her weapon of last
resort, to complain of his rudeness to Llewelyn. Joanna did not
know whether he was testing his newfound manhood or testing
her, knew only that they were racing headlong toward a confrontation, and she watched grimly as Elen flung herself onto her

brother's lap, wrapped her arms around his neck, and entreated, "Make me fly, Gruffydd!"

Coming to his feet, Gruffydd obligingly swung the little girl up into the air, high over his head, making her shriek with laughter, as Davydd watched wistfully. But while envying his sister's swooping flight, he stayed where he was, for he was somewhat afraid of Gruffydd. His every overture had been rebuffed so brutally that he now avoided Gruffydd whenever possible; although his awareness was still only on an unconscious level, he'd begun to sense that when his brother Gruffydd looked at him, it was with loathing.

Setting Elen down upon the sand, Gruffydd sprawled back upon the log. "I hope you have an explanation for your disappearance. My father is less than pleased with you for running off as you did."

"That is hardly your concern."

As always, their conversation sounded discordant, somehow off-key, for Gruffydd refused to address Joanna in Welsh, and she just as stubbornly renounced French. Will was beginning to look amused, and it was to him that Gruffydd said, "A Welsh-born wife would rise even from a sickbed to make welcome a guest in her husband's house. There was a time, in fact, when women did not come and go just as they pleased. In the reign of Hywel the Good, a prince's wife shunned the great hall in his absence, kept to the women's quarters until her lord returned. But then you Normans invaded England, brought queer and outlandish customs with you like some noxious foreign pox."

"I find it passing strange that you would choose to boast of the more backward aspects of your heritage," Joanna snapped, and Will laughed aloud.

"Check and mate," he pronounced, with a mocking grin that endeared him neither to Joanna nor to Gruffydd.

"Sugar!" Joanna whistled for her dog. With Davydd holding onto her skirt and Elen dawdling behind, she started toward the castle. She'd taken only a few steps, was still within earshot when Will laughed again.

"So that is your father's wife."

"That," Gruffydd said, quite clearly and distinctly, "is my father's whore."

Joanna froze, disbelieving, and then spun around.

"I want an apology from you, and I want it now. If not, I shall go to Llewelyn, tell him the way you dare to speak about his wife."

Gruffydd's eyes narrowed. "Go ahead. I'd deny it."

"Do you truly think he'd believe you over me?" Joanna said, and he rose, took a sudden step toward her. He was taller than she, as tall already as Llewelyn, and for the first time she was aware of a physical menace, aware that a boy's raw, raging passion was now contained within a man's body.

Will moved to Joanna's side. " 'My father's whore,' " he drawled. "Did you forget, Gruffydd, that I heard you, too?"

Gruffydd was taken aback, but not for long. "You keep out of this!"

Will smiled. "Make me," he said.

"Stop it," Joanna said sharply. Will had shifted his weight, bracing himself; a hand had dropped to the dagger at his belt. Gruffydd, too, wore a dagger, and he was, Joanna knew, utterly fearless. They were, the both of them, too old for boyhood squabbles that left only scratches and bruises, but not old enough to judge what was worth fighting or dying for, and Joanna was suddenly frightened. "Stop this foolishness," she repeated, knowing even as she spoke that they were not likely to heed her.

It was Elen who stopped it, Elen who was tired of being ignored and sought to call attention back to herself by quoting parrotlike, " 'Father's whore.' Is that you, Mama?"

Gruffydd drew a quick breath, looked down at the little girl, and Joanna saw in his eyes a sudden shame. His hand unclenched from his dagger hilt; he flexed his fingers, rubbed his palm against his tunic. He obviously did not know what to say to Elen, at last mumbled, "You must forget that, lass, must not say it for others to hear—"

Joanna interrupted hastily, knowing nothing would be more likely to brand the word into Elen's brain. "It is just another word for . . . for Norman, Elen."

As Elen wandered away, satisfied, Gruffydd looked at Joanna. "I was wrong to say that," he said, very low. "I never meant for my sister to hear. It will not happen again." The apology cost him dearly, but in making it, he unexpectedly achieved a certain bleak dignity, which not even Joanna could deny.

Gruffydd's eyes flicked briefly to Will, back to Joanna. "I owe my lord father better than that," he said, turned and walked away.

Joanna paused on the wooden stairs leading up to her chamber in the Great Tower, looked thoughtfully down at Will. "Thank you for escorting us back to the castle. But tell me, why did you take my side against Gruffydd?''

''I'm naturally gallant,'' he said, and laughed, then shrugged. ''Mayhap because you're Norman, a woman. Or mayhap because I was not much taken with your stepson.''

''I was surprised, in truth, to see the two of you together. I'd have thought Gruffydd would sooner befriend a *caeth*, a bond servant, than one of Norman blood.''

''Well, I expect it helped that I speak so much better Welsh than you! And we did discover a common bond, a shared loathing for the King of England.''

''I see,'' Joanna said slowly. She knew his candor was a deliberate challenge, but how could the boy not blame her father for the downfall of his House? ''You know, of course, that I am King John's daughter. I take it you do not believe, then, in blood guilt?''

''Now you are mocking me,'' he said composedly. ''But yes, I do believe in blood guilt . . . for men, for sons. Not for a woman, though, at least not a woman who looks like you do!'' There was in his grin both impudence and a certain cocky charm, and Joanna had to laugh.

''For your sake, Will de Braose, I hope you do learn to curb your tongue; you cannot trade upon being fourteen forever!'' She turned to go, paused again. ''You remind me of someone, and I've just realized who. I think my husband must have been much like you at fourteen.''

Will looked pleased. ''If I can win as much with my sword as Llewelyn ab Iorwerth has won with his, I'd be well content.'' He backed away from the stairs, stood looking up at Joanna. ''I shall remember you, my lady. And to prove I am generous as well as gallant, I do have some free advice for you. Talk to your lord husband about his son.''

Joanna knew Will was right, but she knew, too, that now was not the time. Her relationship with Llewelyn was strained enough this summer, needed no more pressures brought to bear upon it.

Pushing open the door of her chamber, she came to an abrupt halt at sight of William de Braose. That Llewelyn should have brought de Braose here, to their private chamber, was more than she could forgive, and when de Braose moved toward her, kissed her hand, she was hard put not to snatch it from his grasp. She managed a grudging nod, but no more.

As soon as they were alone, Llewelyn said curtly, ''When I

make a man welcome at my hearth, I expect my wife to treat him with courtesy. Is that clear, Joanna?''

''Yes.'' But the mutinous set of her mouth belied the dutiful submission. Crossing to her clothes coffer, she jerked the lid up, let it drop with a slam. ''How can you allow that man at your table? You know what he is, a traitor, a fugitive from the King's justice. Why must you do this? Why must you antagonize my father to no purpose?''

''Joanna, I cannot shape my life around what will or will not please your father. Even if I were willing to do that, to turn myself into his puppet, it would avail me naught. For some months now, John has been looking for excuses to find fault, to curtail my authority in Gwynedd.''

''That is not fair! Nor is it true!'' Branwen had hung a gown on the wooden wall pole; Joanna pulled it down, began to fumble with the lacings of her bliaut. The knots defied her fingers, and she was finally forced to ask Llewelyn's help. He had no more luck with the ties than she, jerked impatiently until one of the laces broke off in his hand.

''Thank you so much, that I could have done myself!'' Joanna managed to get the bliaut over her head, flung it to the floor. She started to remove the gown, but then she paused, glared at him, and retreated around the curtained bed to strip off the dress.

''Joanna, just what secrets do you think you could have from me after nigh on four years of sharing my bed?'' Llewelyn sounded both amused and exasperated. But when she reemerged, he said, quite seriously, ''I am bone-weary of these constant quarrels, bone-weary of having to defend to you every decision I make. You are my wife as well as John's daughter, but there are times when you seem to forget that.''

''That is so unjust, Llewelyn! You know I do love you. But I love my father, too. What would you have me do, choose between you?''

He did not give her the reassurance she expected. ''I would hope it will never come to that, Joanna,'' he said quietly, and she stared at him in dismay, at a loss for words.

There was a sharp rapping on the door and Ednyved entered. ''Llewelyn, a messenger has just ridden in from the south. John landed at Fishguard, in South Wales, three days ago. And he brought with him Maude de Braose.''

Will swallowed. ''My parents?'' he said. ''My little sister? Were they taken, too?''

William de Braose seemed not to hear. It was Llewelyn who reassured the boy, said, "No, lad, they were not."

"How . . . how was my grandmother taken? I thought they'd gotten safely into Scotland."

"They did, but at Galloway a Scots lord took them prisoner, held them for John. Your parents escaped; so did your Aunt Margaret and her husband, de Lacy. But Maude was taken, and so was her daughter Annora, her son Will, and his four young sons. They were sent under guard back to Ireland, to John at Carrickfergus." Llewelyn looked from the boy to the still silent de Braose. "What will you do?" he asked, and de Braose bestirred himself with an obvious effort, shrugged.

"What can I do? You said John is heading for Bristol. I shall have to go to Bristol, too, try to come to terms with him."

The Welsh murmured among themselves at that, looked at the Norman lord with the first glimmerings of respect. Even Llewelyn was somewhat impressed. "I wish you well," he said, and meant it, thankful that he would never be facing de Braose's dilemma, that his own wife had nothing whatsoever to fear from John.

De Braose seemed to have aged years in a matter of hours. He ran a hand roughly through greying blond hair, said heavily, "My lord Llewelyn, I do have a favor to ask of you. I know we are not far from the port of Pwllheli. Can you provide a guide for my grandson, get the lad safely there?" And when Llewelyn nodded, he turned to Will, said, "At Pwllheli, you can take ship for one of the southern ports, Tenby or Swansea, and from there, sail with the tide for France."

Will had lost most of his youthful bravado; he looked shaken and, although he tried to hide it, fearful. Joanna had so far listened in silence, but with that, she came forward, said, "That would be a dangerous voyage for a boy of Will's years to undertake alone. Would it not be safer to leave him here, at my husband's court?"

"No, Madame, I think not." William de Braose shook his head, said very evenly, "Whilst that is a kind offer, I would not rest easy as long as there was any chance my grandson might fall into the King's hands."

Joanna felt as if she'd been slapped. "My father would never harm a fourteen-year-old boy!"

De Braose did not dispute her. But neither did he believe her, and it showed. Far worse, she could read the same skepticism on her husband's face, on the faces of the others in the hall. She looked about her, saw only disbelief, derision, and pity, and she whirled, fled the hall.

When Llewelyn followed, he found her in their bedchamber, standing by a window opening onto the sea. "Joanna," he said, and as she turned, he saw tears streaking her face.

"My father is not a monster. He's not!"

"Ah, lass, I never said he was."

"But you do think he would hurt Will, do you not?"

"I do not know, Joanna. I can only tell you that if it were my son, I'd not be willing to gamble his life on John's sense of justice."

"Llewelyn, listen to me. For once, please hear what I am saying. I know my father has flaws; what man does not? You've your share, too. But Papa has never been anything but kind to me, and to my brothers. He treats his wife far better than most men do. And he is a good King. When he travels, he is ever willing to halt by the roadside, to let the common people petition him for redress of grievances, and no king within memory has labored so to provide all free men with access to his courts. He even sits himself when cases are tried. When poor crops caused the price of bread to rise beyond the ability of many to pay for it, he ordered that large quantities be bought, be offered to the people for a pittance, and he oft gives money for alms, for—"

"Joanna, there is no need for this, love." There was in Joanna's frenzied recital of her father's benevolences a desperation that told Llewelyn she was not as free of doubts as she would have him believe. "Joanna, what you say is true; I know that. John can indeed be very generous, can be merciful and just . . . but only to the poor, the powerless. To those whom he does see as a threat, he is utterly without mercy."

"You are wrong, Llewelyn, so very wrong." Joanna brushed away tears with the back of her hand. "You do not know him as I do. Why will you not believe me? Why will you not at least try to allay my father's fears? You know he is of a mistrustful nature, know how quick he is to suspect the worst. He has never truly trusted you after you defied him and seized Powys, we both know that. And now, when he learns that you gave shelter to an enemy like William de Braose—"

"You do not understand at all, do you, Joanna? You still do not see. This is my land, the land of my father and his father before him and his father before him. I am of the House of Cunedda, who ruled in Gwynedd in the fifth century after the birth of the Lord Jesus Christ. Can your Norman kings trace their ancestry back seven hundred years? I think not, yet they dare to sneer at our customs, to mock our heritage and our language.

"I am Welsh, Joanna, and even now you cannot comprehend what that means. Normandy, Anjou, England—it is all the same to you of Norman birth. Your people have dwelt in England for over a hundred years, yet you do not think of yourselves as English. You do not sicken when uprooted or exiled, you do not recognize the kinship of the tribe, which goes beyond the *cenedl*, the kinship of blood. You know nothing of *hiraeth*. And you will never understand what I feel when I see Norman castles guarding Welsh mountain passes, when I hear French spoken instead of Welsh in the valley of the Rhondda, knowing French might one day be heard in the valleys of Gwynedd, too."

Joanna had listened in stricken silence. Their most heated quarrels had not frightened her so much. Not since the first days of her marriage had she felt as she did now, as an alien in a world that would never make her welcome, that she could never understand.

"You are right, Llewelyn," she said softly, wretchedly. "I do not understand. I would to God I could, but I do not. I love you, though. Does that count for nothing?"

"I know you love me, Joanna. But you believe your father is in the right and I am in the wrong, believe all would be well if only I'd act as a proper vassal, submit myself unto the King's will."

She could not deny it, and that frightened her all the more. How much strain could a marriage absorb, how many quarrels before the foundation cracked, split beyond repair?

"I know that of a sudden we seem to be arguing all the time, and I hate it, I do. I will not lie to you. There have been times this summer when I have not liked you very much. But I never stop loving you, Llewelyn, no matter how angry I get. You must believe that." She paused for breath, forced herself to ask, "You . . . you do still love me?"

"Ah, Joanna, how young you still are . . ." He crossed the chamber, stopped before her. "When I married you, you were an appealing, courageous child. You've grown into a beautiful, courageous woman, and I have learned to love you, *breila*. But—"

"No," she entreated, reaching up and laying her fingers against his mouth. "You say you do love me. Let's stop with that, let's not talk any more . . . please. Love me, Llewelyn. Make me forget all but you."

He tilted her face up, kissed her, gently at first, and then he lifted her in his arms, carried her to the bed, where he did make her forget . . . for a time.

When William de Braose, under escort, entered the solar of the King's castle at Bristol, he felt no surprise at sight of so many highborn witnesses: the Earls of Salisbury, Derby, Surrey, and Chester, Eustace de Vesci and Geoffrey Fitz Peter, John's Justiciar. De Braose understood all too well. There was no longer need for caution, no longer need to fear betrayal, not with de Braose's wife, son, and grandsons under close guard in this very castle.

De Braose was actually glad of an audience. Derby and Chester had intervened on his behalf, had persuaded John to issue a safe-conduct, and de Braose thought John would be more likely to honor it in the blaze of full noon. He knelt, said, "I have come to beg my King's pardon, to ask what I must do to make amends, to regain your trust."

"Indeed? Shall I tell you how to mend a broken trust? Pluck the feathers from a goose, scatter them to the four winds. Then gather them all up, each and every one, and put them back on the goose. It is as easy as that."

John had won triumph after triumph during his two months in Ireland, had scattered his enemies, brought the ever-rebellious Irish barons to heel, had Maude in his hands and her husband on his knees. But he did not look like a man savoring his victories; he looked drawn and tired, almost haggard, and de Braose could take no comfort from what he read in those narrowed hazel eyes.

"I have offended you, and for that I am well and truly sorry. But I am loyal to you, my liege, would never betray you. Let me prove myself. Set for me a task, I'll not fail you." De Braose sought to slow his breathing, added very softly, "Christ, John, it never had to come to this, I swear it."

John's favorite falcon was perched upon his left arm, talons digging into the padded leather wrist-guard. It was unhooded, made harsh, guttural sounds low in its throat, and John stroked the sleek feathers with a gloved hand, spoke softly and soothingly until it quieted. "My lords of Chester and Derby, amongst others, have urged me to show mercy. I would not want it said that I was arbitrary, unjust. Mayhap we can yet reach an accord. If you were to pay a fine, one large enough to discharge your indebtedness to the crown, and to cover the costs I have incurred because of your rebellion, I would be willing to overlook your past offenses, to give you and your sons full pardons.''

De Braose was stunned. ''And my wife? What of her?'' he demanded, even as he sought feverishly to detect where the snare lay.

John smiled mirthlessly. ''I've no wish to have her on my hands for life, that I assure you. She would be released into your custody.''

De Braose was still struggling with disbelief; he might have found it easier to believe John if he had not shared John's summary way with enemies. ''I do accept your terms, Your Grace, am speechless, in truth,'' he said, without irony. ''Have you an amount in mind?''

''I think forty thousand marks to be a fair sum,'' John said, and then de Braose understood.

''Indeed,'' he said tonelessly. ''When do you want payment, my lord?''

There was no surprise whatsoever when John said, ''You do have a fortnight to raise the money. Will that be acceptable?''

''Quite acceptable.'' At John's gesture, he rose to his feet, took the wine cup John was offering, his own. Their eyes held as he drank, as he drained the cup. And then John gestured again, this time in dismissal.

Maude kept squeezing her husband's arm, as if to reassure herself of the reality of his presence. ''When they told me you were here, I could scarce believe it!''

''What of Will, Annora, the lads? Are they all right?''

She nodded. ''Fearful, but unhurt. I'll confess, Will, that I've been none too easy myself.'' And even that understated admission surprised him; hers was a haughty spirit that made no allowances for frailties, that would never acknowledge weaknesses in herself. ''Well? For the love of God, Will, tell me! What did John say?''

''That we can buy absolution . . . for forty thousand marks.''

''Forty thousand! You must be joking! We could never raise that, no one could. Did you not tell him so?''

''He already knows.''

She stared at him, then sat down suddenly on the nearest coffer. ''We . . . we could raise four, mayhap even five thousand. You could borrow from Derby and de Clare. Pembroke might even—''

''Maude, it would not matter. Even if, by some miracle, we

begged and borrowed the entire amount, it would not matter. Can you not see that? He deliberately demanded a sum he knows we can never pay. He is not going to give any pardons, and he is not going to let you go, not for forty thousand marks, not for twice that amount.''

Her face did not at once show full comprehension; it came only in degrees, as if she were clinging as long as she could to the illusory security of denial. ''Christ have mercy,'' she whispered. ''He'll keep me caged till I rot.'' She rose, began to pace. ''God in Heaven, how I hate that man! May his misbegotten, cankered soul rot for aye in Hell everlasting!''

She raved on like that for some moments, abusing John in language even her husband could not have improved upon, at last turned back to face him, said tautly, ''What mean you to do now, Will?''

De Braose looked away, stared into space over her head. ''There is a ship sailing at dawn for Barfleur. For the right sum, the captain will smuggle me on board.''

''You mean to flee to France? To abandon me and your children to John? Jesus wept, Will!'' There was so much shock in her voice that he flushed, lashed out savagely.

''I did what I could for you, more than you deserve, for none of this would have happened if not for you! What would it serve to share the same dungeon? I cannot help you, Maude, can only save myself now. And I'm damned if I'll feel guilty about it!''

Her mouth twisted. ''Do you want to tell our grandsons that, or shall I?'' she jeered, and he almost hit her. Unclenching his fist, he swung away from her, toward the door.

''I suppose I should wish you luck! It will not be easy, you know; I daresay John has you under close surveillance. It'll be a miracle if you even make it to the wharves.''

He paused, hand on the door latch. ''You still do not see, do you, Maude? It was not me John wanted. It was you. It has been you from the beginning, from the day you opened your damned fool mouth and doomed us all.''

27

ABER, NORTH WALES

May 1211

Catherine was being escorted across the bailey toward Joanna's chamber when she heard the screams, screams of such total terror that she gathered up her skirts, began to run. In the antechamber Branwen was retching into a water bucket, with Alison hovering helplessly nearby. The screams were abruptly choked off as Catherine reached for the door latch. Within the chamber, Llewelyn was braced against a high-backed chair, while Joanna knelt beside him, trying frantically to comfort the screaming child he held upon his lap. As Catherine watched, sickened, Llewelyn's barber straightened up, holding a pair of pincers and a small bloody tooth.

Elen writhed against Llewelyn's restraining hold, let out a high, keening wail of pain, fright, and outrage. Almost from the time she could walk, she'd shown a decided preference for her father, but now it was for Mama that she sobbed, and Joanna gathered her into a close embrace.

Elen's face was beet-red, her eyes swollen, her bodice stained with saliva and blood and vomit, but her parents looked no less stricken. As Joanna crooned to the weeping child, oblivious to the blood smearing her own clothing, Llewelyn rose, poured himself a full cup of mead with a hand that shook.

"Christ, Catrin," he said softly, "I do not think I could go through that again for the very surety of my soul."

Catherine understood exactly how he felt; a child of hers had once been subjected to the same ordeal. "You tried cloves, bettony?" she asked, and he nodded wearily.

"Every remedy we could think of, and then Joanna lit candles to St Apollonia, but to no avail." Elen's screams had yet to

351

abate; he reached out, stroked the heaving little shoulder, and then retreated, leaving Joanna to minister to their daughter's pain.

It was a long time before Elen quieted, even longer before she slept. Joanna slumped down upon a coffer, already dreading the moment when Elen would awake, when her suffering would begin again. "I do not know when I've ever been so tired, Catherine . . ."

She did look utterly exhausted, and Catherine felt a throb of pity, for she knew how bad a year it had been for Joanna. A bad year for them all, but above all for Joanna, who loved both John and Llewelyn, who was caught between anguished, irreconcilable loyalties.

Soon after William de Braose's flight to France, the Earl of Chester and the Bishop of Winchester had led an army into Gwynedd, advancing as far as the east bank of the River Conwy, where Chester rebuilt Deganwy Castle, which Llewelyn had razed in a futile attempt to keep it out of Norman control. At about the same time, John released Gwenwynwyn from his two-year confinement, giving him money and men-at-arms to mount a challenge to Llewelyn's hold upon his domains. Llewelyn thus found himself fighting a war on two fronts, and by December he'd been forced to withdraw from most of southern Powys. But he struck back hard at Chester, making raids of reprisal into Cheshire, burning the Earl's manors and running off his livestock. Christmas that year had seen smoke-filled skies on both sides of the border, and Joanna, then in the second month of a stressful pregnancy, had miscarried on Epiphany Eve.

With Easter, a fragile, false peace settled over the Marches. All knew it would not last. Chester's men were still entrenched in Deganwy, and Llewelyn would never accept an alien presence on Welsh soil. Gwenwynwyn was now back in power in Powys, with a blood score to settle. And John had spent the spring forging alliances of expediency with Maelgwn and Rhys Gryg. What should have been a season of rebirth and renewal was now no more than a time of uneasy waiting, was to be but a brief prelude to a summer of war.

"Joanna . . . how is it between Llewelyn and you these days? Are you getting on better?"

"Yes, we are," Joanna said, then gave Catherine a sad smile. "But that is because he has been so often gone from Aber this spring."

"You argue about John, about your father?" Catherine asked tentatively, and Joanna nodded.

In the past year her life with Llewelyn had fallen into a disquieting pattern: sudden, sharp quarrels during the daylight hours, later reconciled in bed. "I love him, Catherine, and I believe he still loves me. But . . . but we find little to laugh about these days, and I remember how we used to laugh together all the time . . ."

She rose, reassured herself that Elen still slept, and then turned back to Catherine. "When all began to go sour between my father and Llewelyn, I blamed Llewelyn for much of it, Catherine. I kept thinking if only he'd try harder to earn Papa's trust, if only he were not so set upon having his own way, so prideful . . . But then my father sent the Earl of Chester into Gwynedd, gave Gwenwynwyn the means of making war upon Llewelyn. Oh, God, Catherine, how could he? However angry he was with Llewelyn, did he never think of me? For my sake, could he not have found another way?"

Joanna was alone in their bedchamber, waiting for Llewelyn. Branwen had unbraided her hair, and she reached for the silver-backed brush Llewelyn had given her just four days ago, on their fifth wedding anniversary. As she did, her eyes fell upon a small crystalline stone, mottled with bronze streaks. Picking up the jasper pebble, she fingered it pensively. The stone was no talisman, was a goad to memories she'd rather not recall, memories of her January miscarriage.

But brake-root was not any more effective than jasper as a contraceptive. Isabelle had become pregnant within days of their confidential conversation at Woodstock, had given birth to a daughter while John was pursuing Maude de Braose in Ireland. That, too, was a memory Joanna preferred not to dwell upon, for she'd had an utterly unexpected reaction to the birth of her half-sister. She'd never realized how much it mattered to her—being John's only daughter amongst eight sons—not until it was no longer true, until Isabelle had given John a fair-haired baby girl and he'd given her Joanna's own name.

It was a common if confusing Norman custom to have legitimate and baseborn children share the same name; John had twice christened sons Henry and Richard. But Joanna could not keep from reading a superstitious significance into John's choice of names, could not keep from being hurt by that choice.

She'd had ten months to accustom herself to the loss of her privileged status, no longer felt jealous of the baby sister she'd yet to see. But she had not heard from her father for months, not since that past autumn, and on this warm night in mid-May, she felt forlorn and forgotten and very much afraid of what the future might hold.

Suddenly sensing she was no longer alone, she looked up, saw Llewelyn standing in the doorway. "I did not hear you come in. Have you been there long?" She gave him a self-conscious smile, for she did not like to be watched unaware. "I finally had to give Elen a mild sleeping draught, the pain was so— Llewelyn? Llewelyn, what is wrong? What has happened?"

"What was bound to happen. Your father is gathering a large army at Chester."

She came to her feet with a choked cry, and he said bitterly, "You cannot be all that surprised. It has been obvious for months that John wanted war." But even as he spoke, he saw that her shock was unfeigned, that she'd somehow managed to convince herself the inevitable could be defeated merely by refusing to acknowledge it.

"No, it must not come to that, it must not! Llewelyn, please, you must act whilst there still be time. Go to my father, seek his pardon. Oh, please, I beg you!"

"Seek his pardon?" he echoed, incredulous. "For what, putting him to the inconvenience of an invasion?" He swung about, too angry to risk remaining, but she was already at his side, clutching frantically at his arm.

"No, you do not understand! I'm not saying Papa is right. He's not, he's not! But there cannot be war between you. When I think of you and Papa facing one another across a battlefield, I— Llewelyn, please, please do not let it come to that!"

"Joanna . . . Joanna, I cannot lie to you, cannot pretend this is just one more border skirmish. John wants as much of Gwynedd as he can conquer, wants my head on a pike."

"No, Llewelyn, no. He'd not go as far as that, not if he loves me. And he does, he—"

"I know you love him, Joanna, but do not defend him. Not tonight, not to me."

She stared at him, her eyes slowly filling with tears. "My God, Llewelyn, what are we going to do?"

He reached out, traced a tear's path with his thumb, brushing it away before it could reach her mouth. "I do not know if it will comfort you any, Joanna, but you need not fear a battlefield confrontation. I have no intention of taking the field against John."

She drew an audible breath, and her hand tightened upon his arm. "Oh, my love, my love, thank you!"

Although the temptation to lie to her was overwhelming, he shook his head. "I do not do it for you, Joanna. John can call upon all the resources of the English crown, has the support, as well, of most of the Welsh Princes. He can put ten, twenty times as many men under arms as I ever could. I'd have to be out of my wits to engage him on the field in open battle." Llewelyn paused. "And if he thinks I'm that big a fool, thinks my pride will utterly vanquish my common sense, he's made the greatest mistake of his life."

The night was so unseasonably warm that no fire had been lit in the hearth. But Joanna had begun to tremble. "I'm so cold . . ." she said, and when Llewelyn turned toward the table, thrust a wine cup into her hands, she had to lock her fingers around the stem to hold it steady. "What . . . what mean you to do, Llewelyn?"

"I mean to instruct John how wars are waged in my country." He reclaimed the wine cup, took several swallows. "In England and France an army is expected to live off the land, off the spoils of war. But Wales . . . Wales has no towns lying open and easy for the taking. Aside from the few settlements that have grown up around the church in Bangor or my palaces at Aber and Rhosyr, my people live scattered about the hills. They're herdsmen, hunters, not farmers, Joanna. Much of Gwynedd is virgin soil, has never felt a plow. John's men will find no crops in the fields, no villages ripe for the plundering, no women for the taking, and nothing to fill their bellies. I'd wager that within a fortnight they'll be eating their own horses," he said, with such savage satisfaction that Joanna shuddered.

He saw, and put an arm around her shoulders, drew her to him. But he offered her no words of comfort, no assurances that all would be well, no lies.

Most of the Welsh lived in circular, timber-framed houses with earthen floors, wattle-and-daub walls, and thatched roofs, simple structures that could be abandoned without regrets. In hasty obedience to Llewelyn's command, they gathered up their bedding, their kitchen utensils, their chickens, drove their livestock ahead of them as they fled into the deeply wooded hills, lost themselves in the formidable heights of Eryri.

On May 18, the English army moved out of Cheshire, crossed the border into a ghost country, exceedingly beautiful and eerily still. The few huts their scouts found were deserted, stripped bare. The only signs of life were distant spirals of smoke high up in the hills. They advanced warily along the coast road, advanced farther and farther into an alien land of ominous silence and unseen eyes.

By the time they reached the east bank of the River Conwy, morale was at a dangerously low ebb. Soon their supplies were, too. As rations were cut and cut again, men began to appraise their neighbors' shares, began to dice for larger portions, and then to fight for them. While John and his captains argued whether to attempt a crossing of the Conwy, word spread through the ranks that scouting parties sent to search for the Welsh had not returned. Men began to sicken. Others riding out to hunt for game disappeared without a trace into the dark, foreboding forests that rose up on both banks of the river. John consulted urgently with Chester and Pembroke, calmed the camp by announcing that men were being dispatched back to England for wagons of flour, bacon, and cheese.

The supply party set out the next day at dawn. At noon the few survivors staggered, bleeding, back into camp. With the realization that the man they were hunting had become the hunter, that Llewelyn had swung around behind them and cut off access to England, John's captains were hard put to maintain order. By month's end, Llewelyn's grim prediction had come to pass; they'd begun to butcher their horses.

Richard was standing by an open window in the keep of Deganwy Castle, gazing down at their encampment spread out upon the slopes below. To his right flowed the fluid barrier of the Conwy, and beyond, the whitewashed buildings of Aberconwy Abbey. Richard knew the white-robed monks would be moving about their daily chores, as if oblivious of the fact that only the width of the river lay between them and an enemy army. He wondered if the monks realized just how lucky they were. The abbey had flourished under Llewelyn's patronage, reason enough in his father's eyes to have treated the monastery as spoils of war.

The silence in the chamber was oppressive, utterly disheartened. His Uncle Will and the Earl of Pembroke had unrolled a crude map of North Wales. No one else was making even a pretense of productive activity. Richard's older half-brother Oliver was sprawled in a far corner, trying to sleep. So, too, was Oliver's uncle, Fulk Fitz Warin. John's mysterious magnanimity in pardoning Fitz Warin's treason had been resolved for Richard upon learning that Oliver's mother was Fitz Warin's sister. He could not help thinking upon that now, wondering at the perverse inconsistencies in his father's nature, that the same man who'd forgive a rebel for the sake of a onetime bedmate would also undertake the destruction of a loved daughter's husband.

The door opened and Eustace de Vesci entered, followed by Robert Fitz Walter and Henry de Bohun, Earl of Hereford. They squatted down in the rushes, began to pass a wineskin back and forth. But they kept their eyes upon John all the while; Richard could not help noticing how many of his father's barons did that, watched John whenever he was not looking.

De Vesci had left the door ajar. It was jerked back now with a violence that spun all heads around. Ranulf de Blundeville, Earl of Chester, strode into the solar. Ignoring the others, he addressed himself to John, with a complete disregard for preamble or protocol.

"There've been three more stabbings today."

John got to his feet. "What of it? Soldiers are bound to brawl amongst themselves."

"Indeed, that's so. But in the past when my men fought, it was over a wench—not over bread!"

"I hardly need to hear again about the shortages!"

"I think you do. We're running out of more than food, we're running out of time. Do you know a man with an egg can sell it for a penny and a half? That'd buy him an entire chicken back in England! There's not a dog or a hen left alive in the castle, and the pantry, larder, and buttery have been emptied to feed your men, supplies that were to maintain my garrison for months. It took me two months to fortify Deganwy, fighting off the Welsh almost daily. How in Christ do you expect me to hold this castle now?"

John did not reply, and Chester took a step closer. "How much longer do you mean to deny the truth, that this is a war we cannot win? You need proof? Just go out and take a walk through the camp! So many have taken sick that you cannot get within ten feet of the latrine pits, the stink be so vile! What are you waiting for, until the bloody flux kills off those who do not starve?"

The chamber was utterly still. It had been years since any man had dared to defy John like this. Both Will and Pembroke had come to their feet. Richard took one look at his father's face and he, too, moved forward. But Chester was beyond discretion or prudence.

"You cannot say you were not warned, my liege, because I

told you it would likely come to this! I told you this man would be no easy fox to snare, that he'd be too shrewd to take the field against you, that you'd find your quick, clean war of conquest being fought on his terms. Now do you believe me? Now are you ready to admit defeat, to cut our losses whilst we still can?"

"You've said enough, more than enough! I'm beginning to wonder just where your loyalties lie. You've never had any stomach for fighting this man. Why? It could not be that the two of you have reached a private accommodation, could it?"

Chester's eyes glittered, black pools of utter outrage. "I do not deserve that, have served you faithfully. If you call me disloyal for daring to speak my mind, to be honest with you, so be it then. But answer me one question, my lord. Have you so many men whom you can trust to tell you the truth that you can afford to spare even one?"

"Ah, yes, and Scriptures tell us to 'rejoice in the truth,' do they not?" John said mockingly. But it was a surprisingly restrained response, showed Richard that Chester had unexpectedly hit a nerve. Chester sensed it, too, was quick to press his advantage.

"I'm not saying Llewelyn ab Iorwerth could not eventually be run to earth, though I still think it'd be a Pyrrhic victory. But there'll be no victory at all this time. He's won, you have to face that. It is done, my liege, done."

John turned away, walked to the window. He stood there for some minutes in silence, staring out at Llewelyn's alpine citadel, the remote, cloud-crested peaks of Eryri. "No," he said. "Not yet."

The hill the Welsh called Mynydd y Dref rose some eight hundred feet above sea level, offering sweeping views of Conwy Bay, the river, and Deganwy Castle. Joanna moved cautiously toward the edge of the cliff, was grateful when Llewelyn slid a supportive arm around her waist.

A high wind was gusting, but the sea was a brilliant sapphire blue, and the light was resplendent upon the grey stone church below; the monastery looked prosperous and orderly and utterly at peace. But the encampment on the far side of the river was a scene of disorder and desolation. Some tents were still standing, flapping forlornly in the wind; the area was littered with debris, scarred by ditches and smoldering campfires; bones and rotting carcasses of dead horses were piled at the water's edge, and when the wind shifted toward the west, it brought to them a sickening stench of death and decay.

"My lord! It's true, they're gone!" Several horsemen were coming up the slope at a gallop. The lead rider was soaked from the river crossing, shivering and short of breath, but he was exultant, stammering with excitement.

"They've pulled out, all of them, even the castle garrison!" He glanced then toward Joanna, said in a lower voice, "You'd best not let your lady cross the river, my lord. The English King left his dead for you to bury."

"That much ground I'm willing to yield up to John," Llewelyn said, and the other men laughed, began to crowd around him, gesturing toward the deserted encampment, interrupting one another freely, making boisterous jests and sardonic puns, theirs the grim gallows humor of the suddenly reprieved. Joanna turned, walked away.

Finding a sheltering boulder some yards from the cliff, she stood gazing out to sea, watching as gulls skimmed the wind-crested waves of the bay, circled above her father's abandoned castle keep. She could still hear Llewelyn's laughter, as buoyant and soaring as the birds wheeling overhead; if sunlight were not silent, she thought, it would sound much like Llewelyn's laughter. It had been so long since she'd heard him laugh.

After a time, Llewelyn broke free from the encircling men, came to stand beside her. His hair was blowing about wildly, and she raised her hand, brushed it back from his eyes. As she did, he caught her hand in his.

"I understand that you cannot rejoice in my victory, Joanna, but I hoped you'd not begrudge me the joy I take in it."

"I do not, God's truth, I do not!"

"My poor Joanna; no matter who won, you had to lose. But it's over now, *breila*." He reached for her other hand, drew her toward him. "You can await me at the abbey whilst I cross over to the camp. Then we'll go home."

Joanna swallowed, rested her head for a moment against his chest. "It is not over, Llewelyn," she said, her voice so muffled it was all but inaudible.

His eyes had seemed full of light, showed golden glints in the sun. But as she looked up at him now, she saw that all the light had been completely quenched; his eyes were utterly opaque, bleak and chill.

"You think he'll come back," he said flatly, and she nodded.

"I know he will, Llewelyn." She moved back into his arms, whispered, "I know he will . . . ."

*   *   *

Llewelyn knew that Joanna's love for her father blinded her to what others saw in John. Yet for all that she was disbelieving of his darker impulses, she still knew better than most the intimate workings of his mind. Llewelyn accepted her anguished certainty as grim gospel. But neither one of them expected John to act with such ruthless, single-minded resolve, or with such stunning speed.

He at once set about making ready for a second Welsh campaign, and because he was both willing and able to subordinate all else to this aim, by early July a large army was assembling at the border town called Blanc Minster by the Normans and Croes Oswallt by the Welsh. This time he'd provided for pack horses heavily laden with salt, beans, cheese, flour, and sides of bacon and beef. He'd also summoned carpenters and craftsmen, brought along laborers as well as soldiers, packed spades, axes, picks, and nails.

On the second Friday in July they moved into Upper Powys. Llewelyn's cousin and ally, Madog ap Gruffydd, prudently offered no resistance, let the English army pass unmolested through his domain. At the same time, John's allies Maelgwn and Rhys Gryg began a well-coordinated plan of attack from the south.

Swinging up the Vale of Llangollen, John crossed into Gwynedd, pressed on toward the River Conwy. And as he pushed west, he began to build Norman castles on Welsh soil. They were hastily erected fortresses, constructed of Welsh timber by conscripted English carpenters. But they were also symbols of power, of the might of the English crown, and each one cast a foreboding shadow over the countryside it now controlled.

Llewelyn was hopelessly outmanned, was forced to fall back before the inexorable advance of the English army, to withdraw into the deepest reaches of Eryri as John swept all before him. First Rhuddlan Castle and then Deganwy were reclaimed, and in the fourth week of July, John's men crossed the River Conwy. It was the first time in well over a hundred years that an English invasion force had penetrated this far into Gwynedd.

After sacking the Cistercian monastery at Aberconwy, John encamped his army upon the west bank of the river, then dispatched a large raiding party up the coast. With Welsh guides provided by Gwenwynwyn, they made their way through the pass of Penmaenmawr, on to Llewelyn's deserted palace at Aber, which they put to the torch. From Aber they rode for Bangor Fawr yn Arfon, the episcopal see for the diocese of Bangor, where they dragged the Bishop from the High Altar, brought him back a prisoner to John's camp by the Conwy. But before they did, they set fire to the cathedral church, burned every house in Bangor to the ground.

At dusk, Llewelyn's young allies, Owain ap Gruffydd and his brother Rhys Ieunac, rode up from the south. Her private chamber having been appropriated for a council of war, Joanna was at a loss as to where to go, unwilling to subject herself to the stares in the great hall. She'd thought her husband's countrymen had long ago reconciled themselves to his alien English consort, but during the past weeks she'd come to realize how tenuous that acceptance was. As her father's army moved into the very heartland of Llewelyn's realm, there were many who looked upon Joanna and saw not Llewelyn's wife, Davydd and Elen's mother, saw only John's daughter.

Joanna finally climbed the stairwell up to the battlements that enclosed the gabled roof of Dolwyddelan's keep, her need to be alone prevailing over her dislike of heights. Even this refuge she had to share with several sentries, but they seemed to sense her mood, kept prudently to the other side of the walkway.

The keep towered more than forty feet up into the twilight sky. By daylight the view was breathtaking, affording panoramic vistas of the River Lledr below and the mountains beyond. But as darkness descended over the vale, Joanna's attention was riveted upon the horizon. A pale reddish glow lit the sky to the north. She knew what it was; Llewelyn had gotten word hours ago that Bangor was burning.

Joanna set her lantern on the embrasure, unable to take her eyes from that eerily streaking sky. By dawn, all of Bangor would be reduced to ashes and charred rubble. Aber still smoldered. How long, she wondered, ere Dolwyddelan, too, fell to her father's army?

By now it was full dark. So absorbed was Joanna in her own purgatory that she failed to hear approaching footsteps, started violently when Morgan touched her arm.

They stood in silence for some moments, Joanna studying him through her lashes. She knew he was in his middle fifties, although he looked much younger, for he had a magnificent head of silvered hair, and sculptured cheekbones that aging only enhanced. In every sense but the biological one, he was a father to Llewelyn, and Joanna had tried repeatedly over the years to break through that cool, disciplined exterior, to bypass the priest and befriend the man, but to no avail. He kept others at a distance no less effectively than did Adda. Only with Llewelyn did he permit himself the luxury of emotional intimacy, and Joanna often wondered if he'd acknowledged even to himself how deep the bond between them was, that Llewelyn was a son in all but blood.

"Owain ap Gruffydd brought news, Madame, that I think you should know. Lord Hywel of Meirionydd and Prince Madog have deserted Llewelyn, have gone over to your father."

"Jesú, no! But they are Llewelyn's cousins, his blood kin!"

"They are also frightened men trying to save what is theirs. They see Llewelyn as doomed, do not want to be dragged down with him."

Joanna stared at him in silence, trying desperately to get her fear under control, trying not to panic. Maelgwn and Rhys Gryg and Gwenwynwyn were already fighting for John. With Prince Madog's defection, Llewelyn would be utterly isolated, surrounded, facing enemies on every side.

"If what you're saying be true," she whispered, "then Llewelyn is trapped, trapped with no way out."

"Yes," he said dully, "I know. And so does Llewelyn."

Joanna could hear angry voices while still in the stairwell. But as she followed Morgan into the chamber, a sudden silence settled over the room. All eyes turned toward her, and in many of them she read a chilling suspicion, a doubt none would dare to voice in Llewelyn's hearing: Can we speak freely in front of her? Feeling like an intruder in her own bedchamber, Joanna settled down as inconspicuously as possible in the nearest window seat.

Llewelyn and Owain ap Gruffydd were standing by a trestle table partially covered by a crude map of Wales and the Marches. Joanna's unexpected entrance had thrown Owain momentarily off stride. Turning back to Llewelyn, he gestured toward the map.

"You need look no farther than this, my lord, no farther than Eryri. What better stronghold could you find? You know these mountains as few men do; they'd never be able to take you."

"What would you have me do, Owain, live like a rebel on the run?"

"There are worse fates, my lord," Owain said evenly, and Llewelyn shook his head.

"You look at the map, but you still do not see. How can you be so blind?" Unsheathing his dagger, Llewelyn made a slashing cut in the parchment. "John has erected a castle here." Again the blade flashed. "And there. There, too. At Bala, Treffynnon, Mathrafal, Deganwy, Rhuddlan. Fourteen at last count, Owain, fourteen! Given time, he'll refortify each and every one in stone and mortar, put down roots so deep we'll never be able to dislodge him. Christ, man, do you not understand? He means the complete conquest of North Wales, means to turn all of Gwynedd into a God-cursed English shire!''

None could deny it. Nor could they meet his eyes. Owain mumbled, ''I know, my lord, I know. But you've got to think of saving yourself now. It is too late to save Gwynedd.''

''No,'' Llewelyn said violently, ''no!'' He stared down at the map, and then, with a sudden, swift thrust, he plunged the dagger downward, impaling the map and burying the blade deep in the soft pine tableboard.

It was so quiet that Joanna could hear the slight scraping of Adda's crutch as he dragged it through the floor rushes, limped to Llewelyn's side. ''Llewelyn, I understand how you feel; how could I not? If I thought you had any chance at all, I'd say yes, go to the English King, seek to save what you can. But we're talking of John, Llewelyn, John who nurses a grievance till it festers. Not two months ago you made him look a right proper fool, cost him money, men, and no small loss of face. He's gone to a great deal of trouble to get you just where you are this night, and the only terms he's likely to offer will be a generous bounty to the man who can bring him your head.''

''He'd listen to me.'' Joanna stood up, found her knees suddenly weak; her heart was beating so rapidly that she felt slightly queasy. She had a blurred glimpse of faces, most expressing shock at the very thought of entrusting all to a woman, and then she'd crossed the chamber, had laid her hand on Llewelyn's arm.

''Let me go to him, Llewelyn,'' she pleaded. ''He cares for me, and I can make him listen. I know I can.''

His face was hard to read; she could not immediately tell what his reaction was. Nor was she given a chance to find out, for Gruffydd could keep silent no longer.

''Papa, do not listen to her! You cannot trust her to speak for you; she's his daughter, of his befouled blood. She'd betray you, I know it!'' The boy was too agitated to guard his tongue, pleaded with no less passion than Joanna, ''You cannot do this, cannot yield to him. Think how he'd humiliate you, make you grovel—''

''That will be enough, Gruffydd!''

''I'd die ere I'd do that, Papa! And if you go to him, shame yourself like that, you shame us all!''

Llewelyn took a swift step toward Gruffydd. Although he'd clenched his fist, he did not hit the boy. But Joanna saw him

draw a deep, unsteady breath, saw how close he'd come to it.
"Be thankful, Gruffydd," he said scathingly, "that I remember
I, too, was a fool at fifteen."

Gruffydd flushed to the roots of his hair, and Joanna suspected
he'd rather have been struck. "Papa . . ." he whispered, but
only Joanna was close enough to hear him. Llewelyn had turned
away, was already moving toward the door.

When Rhys would have followed after him, Morgan stepped
from the shadows, said, "No, let him be. He needs time to be
alone, to think. Whatever price is to be paid, he must be the one
to pay it. So the decision, too, must be his, his and his alone."

Even dulled by moonlight, the stallion's coat shone like bronze;
although white was the preferred color for horses, Llewelyn's
memories of Sul had given him an unfashionable fancy for
red-gold chestnuts. No longer grazing, the stallion had begun to
nuzzle his tunic, but now it jerked its head up, nickered softly.
Llewelyn reached for his sword, faded back into the shadows.

A black-clad figure emerged through the trees, and he lowered
the sword, watched as Morgan swung from the saddle. Morgan
was unsure of his welcome, said somewhat awkwardly, "Joanna
guessed you might be here. You've been gone so long we grew
worried. But I'll go if you'd rather be alone."

"I've not been alone. I've been keeping company with Arthur
of Brittany, Hugh de Lusignan, Walter de Lacy, William de
Braose, all of the men in the last twenty years who made the fatal
mistake of underestimating John Plantagenet."

Walking to the edge of the cliff, Llewelyn gazed down at the
cataract. Although rain had been scarce that summer, as if even
nature were favoring John's campaign, the river still surged
against its banks, plummeting over the jutting rocks and turning
the pool below into a seething cauldron of froth and spume, an
impersonal and awesome affirmation of infinity.

"We're our own worst enemies, Morgan, God's cursed truth
we are. The Gospels say every kingdom divided against itself
shall be made desolate; that could well serve as the epitaph for
Wales. Since the time of William the Conqueror, we've allowed
the English kings to play the same damnable, deadly game with
us, to set our princes one against the other. And we never learn.
Christ knows I did not, I fell into the same time-worn trap. If I'd
found a way to come to terms with Maelgwn and Rhys Gryg,
they'd be fighting the English now instead of collaborating with

them. If we'd banded together at the outset, all offered resistance, we could have stopped John dead at the Conwy."

"That is the great weakness of the Welsh, Llewelyn. We've never learned to act for the common good. I sometimes suspect that unity is not a word native to the Welsh tongue. It has ever been that way, ever will be."

"No, Morgan, you're wrong. The day must come when our people will unite around one man, around one prince." Llewelyn paused, then gave Morgan a twisted smile. "But I always thought it would be me."

Morgan made no facile disclaimers, offered no polite, empty assurances. But Llewelyn knew him far too well to expect any. Moving away from the cliff, he said, "You did not ride all this way without fetching me something to drink, I hope?"

Morgan managed a smile of his own. "Indeed not," he said, handed Llewelyn a flask. "I was watching you when Joanna offered to go to her father. You were the only man in the room who did not look surprised. Had it already occurred to you to have her intercede with John?"

"Of course. What could be more obvious?" But Llewelyn then lowered the flask, revealed his own ambivalence. "Why?" he challenged. "You see it as sheltering behind a woman's skirts?"

"I see it as the only action open to you. What matters it if she's a woman when she is also the only one in Christendom with any chance of swaying John? But can you trust John, Llewelyn? Even if Joanna can somehow persuade him to offer terms, can you be sure he'd honor them? That he'd not agree to a safe-conduct merely to get you into his hands?"

"He might well refuse Joanna's pleas, but I do not think he'd use her as a lure, as bait. Not even John would do that, not to his own daughter." He added dryly, "But then, I'd have to believe that, would I not?"

Llewelyn drank again, passed the flask back to Morgan. "I was at Norham Castle with John when the Scots King came to surrender, to buy peace on John's terms. John demanded far more than money, left him nothing, neither pride nor manhood."

He looked at the priest, suddenly dropped all defenses and said with anguished, unsparing honesty, "I do not know if I can face that, Morgan. There is a part of me that feels as Gruffydd does, that I'd rather die ere I let him do to me what I saw him do to the Scots King."

Morgan found himself blinking back tears. "I do not know what to say to you, lad, would to God I did."

"Do you remember what you once told me? You assured me
that accommodation to superior strength is no shame. That helped
ease a boy's hurt, taught me a truth I thought I'd taken to heart.
But . . . but it avails me little now, Morgan. Not when I think of
John, and what he will demand of me."

Joanna had finally fallen into a fitful doze. She awoke at once,
though, when Llewelyn closed the door, sat up as he approached
the bed.

"Did Morgan find you?"

"Yes. How did you know I'd go to Rhaeadr Ewynol?"

"I remembered you told me you'd gone there when Tangwystl
died."

He made no comment. She felt the bed shift as he lay down.
He was still fully clothed, had not even taken his boots off. As
she'd lain awake waiting for him, Joanna had decided to take her
cues from him. If he wanted her to comfort him with her body,
she would. If he wanted silence, she'd keep still. If he wanted to
talk, she'd listen. But now that he was here beside her, she found
herself so afraid of saying or doing the wrong thing that she
could do nothing at all.

His rage seemed to have burned itself out; she could see only
exhaustion in his face. Leaning over, she touched her lips to his
forehead. He opened his eyes, looked at her, and then reached
out, grasped a handful of her straight black hair. "You do, in
truth, look Welsh," he said, let her hair slip through his fingers.

"Llewelyn, please. Let me go to my father."

He raised himself up on his elbow, and then he nodded.
"Tomorrow," he said. "Tell him that he's won, that . . . You
know what to tell him."

She was no longer so sure of that. She'd prayed that he would
agree, but now that he had, she was suddenly terrified. He was
putting his life in her hands. What if she failed him, if Adda was
right, if her father would not listen to her?

"I'm frightened, Llewelyn," she said, and he put his arm
around her, held her close.

"I know, Joanna." After a long time, he said, very softly,
"So am I."

28

ABERCONWY, NORTH WALES

August 1211

Once she had ridden into the English camp, Joanna was separated from her small Welsh escort, taken into the outer parlour of the abbey. Too tense to sit for long, she paced the confines of the small chamber as if it were a cage, until she could endure the waiting no longer, escaped out into the west walkway of the cloisters.

The Cistercian monks had fled before John's army; more than a dozen soldiers now lounged on the grassy inner garth. Joanna's unexpected appearance momentarily stopped all conversation; heads jerked around. Of all the privations peculiar to campaigning in Wales, the one the soldiers found most difficult to accept was the utter lack of women. Theirs was the most uncommon of army encampments, one in which there were neither willing harlots nor unwilling captives.

They were watching Joanna with avid interest, but warily, too, for her gown was a finely woven wool, her veil a gossamer silk. She could hear them murmuring among themselves, speculating whether she was a "Crogin," a contemptuous slang term for the Welsh; that would, she realized, have made her fair game. At last one of the men rose, sauntered toward her. "What can I do for you?" he asked, and while the words themselves were innocent enough, both his smile and his tone were slyly suggestive.

"Nothing whatsoever," Joanna snapped. Although he was already backing away, warned off by the jeweled rings adorning her fingers, she added maliciously, "But I shall tell my father the King of your concern," and had the dubious satisfaction of seeing him blanch. The men could not have retreated any faster had she revealed herself to be a witch; within moments she was all alone on the walkway, filled with a rage as unfocused as it was impotent, that what should now matter most in Llewelyn's own realm was not that she was his wife, but that she was John's daughter.

A man was emerging from the monks' frater. He came to an abrupt halt at sight of Joanna, then limped toward her. She was no less surprised to see him. For several years, Hugh Corbet had been suffering from the disease known as the "joint evil," and his health was no longer up to the rigors of a military campaign.

"You've come on Llewelyn's behalf?" he asked, and she nodded.

"Yes. And you?"

"At the King's command."

Joanna felt a chill. How would she ever get her father to listen if he was as vengeful as that, enough to make Llewelyn's ailing stepfather an unwilling witness to his downfall?

"Joanna . . . when you see the King, weigh your words with care. He is in a foul temper this morn. He got word, you see, that William de Braose has been stricken with a mortal sickness. It's said he's sure to die."

Joanna's eyebrows rose. "I'd have thought my father would be gladdened by news like that!"

"I expect he was. But he was not so glad to hear that Stephen Langton was at de Braose's deathbed, that he means to officiate at de Braose's funeral."

"Good God, no wonder Papa was wroth!"

"With cause," Hugh conceded. "It is Langton's way of spiting the King, of course. For all that the Pope has anointed him as Archbishop of Canterbury, he dares not set foot on English soil. But de Braose was formally outlawed, declared a traitor to the crown. It's not fitting for Langton to pay such honor to a rebel."

"It may not be proper, but it certainly is political!" Joanna shook her head, bemused. "I wonder if my father will release Maude de Braose once her husband is dead. I'd think he— Hugh? Whatever ails you?"

"I thought you knew. Maude de Braose is dead." Hugh hesitated, no longer met Joanna's eyes. "She . . . died in prison."

"No, I did not know." Joanna frowned. "Strange that Llewelyn never mentioned it. Surely he must have heard." But then she forgot all about Maude de Braose and her dying husband, even forgot about Hugh, for a familiar figure was coming down the north walkway. Gathering up her skirts, she ran to meet her brother.

"Thank God, Richard! I prayed you'd be here. Papa . . . he will see me?"

"Did you ever doubt it?" Richard had his mother's pale blue eyes, often remote, not easily read; she saw in them now only pity. "He sent me to fetch you, awaits you in the small parlour next to the Chapter House."

"Richard . . . tell me the truth. Do you think he'll heed me?"

"Ah, Joanna . . ." But as reluctant as he was to answer, when he did, it was with uncompromising honesty. "No, I do not."

John did not say anything, merely held out his arms, and for a few brief moments Joanna tried to take refuge in memories, sought to find again in her father's embrace the protected peace of childhood.

"I've been so frightened, Papa," she confessed, finding it as easy as that to revert back to the role decreed for her so long ago at Rouen. John, too, seemed reluctant to let go of the past, speaking softly and soothingly as if hers were still childhood hurts, of no greater moment than scraped knees or a lost doll, hurts to be healed with smiles and the promises of sweets.

"I know, lass. But all will yet be well for you. I'll make it so, I swear. Come now, seat yourself at the table. I've food set out for you; you can eat as we talk."

Joanna did as he bade, watched as he acted as cupbearer for them both, but not for Richard or Will. She had no appetite, though, merely toyed with the bread and cheese put before her. John took a seat facing her, said, "You've been much on my mind, Joanna. I'd not have you suffer for sins not yours, think I have found a way to make certain you do not. Tell me of your son, of David. It's lucky, in truth, that he's too young to understand what's been happening."

"I would that were so, Papa. But Davydd now wakes in the night whimpering, has begun to talk about creatures lurking out in the dark, hiding under the bed. And Elen, too, senses something is amiss. She has—"

"When will he be three . . . November? And the age of majority amongst the Welsh is fourteen, no? Of course, he'd need guidance and counsel long after that, would need—"

"Papa, what are you saying?"

"I am saying, sweetheart, that you need not worry, that I mean to protect your son's inheritance. I shall have to take much of Gwynedd under the control of the crown, but I'll leave David a fair share, that I promise." He leaned across the table, with a

smile of familiar, fond charm, the smile that invariably heralded
the giving of a memorable gift. "And I see no reason, Joanna,
why you yourself should not act as regent until David comes of
age."

Joanna sat very still. She was aware of perspiration trickling
clammily down her throat, between her breasts, along her ribs,
rivulets of cold sweat that seared her skin like ice, set her to
trembling. Richard had moved behind John's chair, and when she
opened her mouth, he gave a swift, warning shake of his head.
She let her protest ebb away on an uneven, labored breath,
grabbed for a wine cup, and drank without tasting.

John had been watching her intently. "I see," he said at last,
quite coolly.

"No, Papa, I do not think you do." Joanna set the wine cup
down, reached at random for something she could not spill,
clutched at a thick slice of bread. "It would not work, you see.
The Welsh would never accept a woman as regent. It is true that
in most ways their women enjoy greater freedom than ours, but
those freedoms are personal, not political."

"Then we need only select a regent amenable to our wishes,
eager to cooperate with the crown. You'd still act as regent, in all
but name. Does that frighten you? It need not, for you'd not be
alone, lass. I'd see that you had advisers you could trust, men
who—"

"Your advisers, Papa? Men of Norman blood? How do you
think the Welsh would react to that? No, you still do not understand. It's not just that the Welsh would never accept me. They'd
not accept Davydd, either. He is a babe, half Norman—and your
grandson. Those would be liabilities to cost him the crown.
Should aught befall Llewelyn, his people would not look to
Davydd, they'd look to Llewelyn's other son, his Welsh son."

"Gruffydd?" he said, showing her he was all too familiar with
Llewelyn's court. "And if he were not available?"

"It . . . it would not matter. Llewelyn has another son,
Tegwared. He's still a child, but the Welsh would prefer him to
Davydd. They'd even prefer Llewelyn's cousin Hywel. Davydd
must earn the acceptance of his father's people, must prove to
them that his heart and soul are no less Welsh than Gruffydd's.
I've given this much thought, Papa, from the very day of his
birth. I do think he can eventually win their allegiance. But he'll
need time, time to grow to manhood. Until then, only his father
can safeguard his inheritance, only Llewelyn." Joanna had unwittingly been tearing at the bread as she spoke; the tablecloth

was littered with crumbs. She put the crust aside, said, "That is why I have come, Papa. To beg you to spare Llewelyn . . . for the sake of my son."

"You are saying, then, that all your concern is for David, none of it for Llewelyn?"

John sounded so skeptical that Joanna blushed, remembering the bedchamber scene he'd witnessed at Woodstock. "No, Papa," she said, as steadily as she could, "I am not saying that. I do care for Llewelyn. How could I not? He treats me quite well. I've been his wife for five years, have borne him two children, would not want to see him harmed."

She reached across the table, caught at John's sleeve. "If I owe Llewelyn a wife's loyalty and Davydd a mother's love, I owe you much, too. I told you at the time I agreed to wed Llewelyn that there was nothing I would not do for you. I meant it, Papa, proved it by making a marriage I dreaded. Did you know that, know how much I feared it? But I did it for you . . . and then found in that marriage an unexpected and abiding contentment."

John shifted in his seat, drew back out of reach. "Does it matter so much to you, Joanna, being Llewelyn's wife?"

"Not his wife, Papa . . . his consort."

That was an answer he was not expecting. He leaned back in his chair, subjected her to a troubled appraisal. "In truth, Joanna? At the time of your marriage, I seem to remember you counting a crown of little worth."

"At the time of my marriage, I was only fourteen. The truth is, Papa, that I'm pleading not just for Davydd, but for myself, too. Even now it often seems no less than a miracle to me, that I could be bastard-born and yet wear a crown. I do not think I could bear to give it up. You, of all men, should be able to understand that."

"Yes," he admitted, "I can. I only wish I'd known . . ." He rose abruptly, moved to the window. "I am sorry, lass, I swear I am. But you ask too much of me."

"Not if you love me." Joanna had risen, too, stumbled over her skirts in her haste to follow John to the window. "Papa . . . you do still love me?"

He swung around, stared at her. "Jesú, do you doubt it?"

"I . . . I do not know. God knows I do not want to! But you led an army into my husband's lands, my lands, too. Your men even burned Aber, and that was my home, Papa, mine no less than Llewelyn's. What if my children or I had still been there, if we'd not—''

"Ah, Joanna, do not! This is between Llewelyn and me, has nothing to do with you. I'd not hurt you for the world. You have ever been my dearest child, do you not know that?''

"Help me, then, Papa. You're the only one who can. For Davydd and for me, I beg you . . . please!'' Joanna's voice broke; she started to kneel, and John stopped her, pulled her almost roughly to her feet.

"Do not, lass. There's no need.''

Joanna caught her breath. "Does that mean you'll do it, Papa? You'll pardon Llewelyn?''

There was a long pause, and then he nodded. "It seems I have no choice.''

Joanna had often heard Llewelyn quote a caustic Welsh proverb, one that spoke of a borrowed smile. She could feel just such a smile twisting her mouth, a counterfeit coin to pay a debt of dishonor. She could take no pride in what she had accomplished. Gratitude, too, was an alien emotion to her at that moment. Even her sense of relief was curiously muted. She was aware only of her utter exhaustion, and when John led her toward a bench, she sank down upon the hard wood as if it were a cushioned settle.

She'd once seen a swimmer collapse upon the beach after battling the sea back to shore; he'd lain panting in the shallows, digging his hands deep into the sand as if to anchor himself to the earth, too weak to do more than marvel at his reprieve. She felt much the same way now, wanted only to sit and be left in peace, if only for a little while.

But John had seated himself beside her on the bench, and he was saying grimly, "If Llewelyn comes to me here at Aberconwy, I will accept his surrender—for you, Joanna. But more than that I cannot do. He has much to answer for, and if he wants peace, it must be on my terms. You do understand that?''

She nodded, and John relaxed somewhat, sought then to swallow a noxious draught with grudging grace. "I expect you'll want to send word at once? How many hostages will he want as pledges for his safety? Five? Ten?''

"No, Papa. He wants but one . . . your brother Will.''

John stiffened. "Christ Jesus!''

"John, I do not mind, in truth I do not,'' Will interjected mildly, as Joanna had known he would; it was one of God's minor miracles that Will had somehow survived more than fifty years without compromising his faith, without forfeiting his innocence. "It is only a formality, after all. I'm glad to do it for you, and for the lass here."

Joanna could endure no more. Jumping to her feet, she kissed first her father and then her uncle. "I shall never forget what you're doing for me," she said huskily. "Never."

But once she emerged out into the cloisters, she faltered. The sun seemed hot enough to blind, to burn all it touched; even when she closed her eyes, she could not squeeze out the light. She leaned for a moment against one of the stone columns, and then felt Richard's supportive hand on her elbow.

"Come," he said, "there's a bench in the garth."

They were alone in the sunlight. Richard had a soldier's flask at his belt. He drank, then passed it to Joanna. "He was so set upon vengeance," he said wonderingly. "You need never again doubt that he loves you, Joanna."

"I know." Joanna drank from Richard's flask, found it filled with a pungent, spiced wine. She gasped, sputtered, and then blurted out, "I do not know how I can ever look Uncle Will in the face again."

"You were just acting as your husband's messenger. Uncle Will understands that."

"No . . . I was not. Llewelyn told me to insist upon hostages of high rank, men that Papa would be loath to lose. But he did not demand Uncle Will as one of the hostages. He would never have done that, for he knows how dear Uncle Will is to me." The blood rose in Joanna's cheeks so swiftly that her skin seemed on fire. "I do love Uncle Will, Richard. That's what is so unforgivable. For I never hesitated." Joanna's voice trailed off. After a long silence, she confessed, "But I suddenly knew that I was not willing to risk Llewelyn's life on my father's word alone."

Llewelyn drew rein on the crest of the hill, stared down at the English encampment. Seventeen years ago he'd won a decisive battle on this very site, had defeated his uncle and made himself ruler of half of Gwynedd at age twenty-one. All of Gwynedd had been his before he was thirty. But the banner now flying over the abbey was emblazoned with the royal arms of England.

The sun was hot, the hill infested with horseflies and mosquitoes, but none of the men complained. They waited in sympathetic silence for Llewelyn to nerve himself for the ride down the hill, for his surrender to the English King. When he finally moved, it was sudden, swift, took them by surprise. He gave the chestnut its head, and it plunged down the slope, mane and tail taking the wind like flame, blazing into the English camp as if it had somehow seen into its rider's heart, shared his fettered rage, his fear, and his defiant despair.

His men spurred their horses to overtake the chestnut, some of them shouting as if on the trail of wild boar, and the resulting entrance of the Welsh into the camp was a tumultuous one. But as they gazed about them, realized what John had in mind, they fell silent, lost much of their bravado. A few swore under their breaths, most tightened grips on sword hilts, and all looked toward Llewelyn.

The chestnut was fractious, fighting the bit, but Llewelyn scarcely noticed. For days now he'd been morbidly reliving the scene in the great hall at Norham Castle, putting himself in the place of the discomfited Scots King. But once again he'd under-estimated John's capacity for imaginative reprisal. For his was to be a very public humiliation, to be no less a spectacle than a bearbaiting or the hanging of a notorious highwayman. His sur-render was not to be made in the abbey hall, nor in one of the English command tents, but out in the open in the glare of high noon, witnessed by all of John's troops and those of his Welsh allies.

One of the Abbot's high-backed chairs had been brought out for John; to his right were gathered the lords of his court, to his left the Welsh Princes. Llewelyn could count his enemies like rosary beads: Gwenwynwyn, Maelgwn, Rhys Gryg, Thomas Corbet. Men who'd long hungered for this day, men who watched him with mocking eyes and smiles like unsheathed daggers. Even worse were the faces of his friends, his stepfather, Stephen and Baldwin de Hodnet, his conscience-stricken cousins Madog and Hywel. They averted their eyes, like men too polite to look upon another's nakedness, offering him the lacerating balm of their pity; and Llewelyn's resolve faltered. For several harrowing sec-onds he found himself overwhelmed by emotions he'd never before experienced—a physical fear of entrapment and a shatter-ing sense of his own helplessness.

Dismounting was an act of utter faith, the most difficult one of his life. With an intense effort of will, he blotted out the audi-ence, focused his thoughts solely upon the man in the Abbot's oaken chair. And then he walked forward, knelt, and handed John his sword.

"I submit myself unto the King's will," he said, and John smiled.

"Surely you can do better than that. Not even the Lord God will forgive a man unless he first confesses his sins and then repents of them."

Llewelyn had known John might demand this of him—had known, too, that he could never bring himself to do it. His mind raced, but he could think of no way to satisfy John while still salvaging his pride, and at last he said, with the candor born of desperation, "What would be the point? No matter how convincingly contrite I was, you'd not believe me, would know I did not speak from the heart. Would it not make more sense to speak of hard, irrefutable facts, of power? You've won. I admit your victory, acknowledge your authority as my King and liege lord. That I am here proves it beyond question, as does my willingness to do homage, to swear oath of allegiance as your vassal lord and liegeman."

John laughed. "To put it in your own words, what would be the point? Twice in the past seven years you've done homage to me, have you not? So all you've proven beyond question is that a Welshman's sworn oath is worthless."

Llewelyn was unnerved by the intensity of his rage, by the realization of how close he was to losing control of his temper, his tongue. He stared at John, his ears filled with the derisive laughter of John's soldiers, his heart filled with such hatred that he knew it must show on his face for all to see.

"Should I gather from your silence that you're loath to ask for absolution? Surely your pride is not as tender as all that. It did allow you, after all, to send a woman to plead for you!"

Llewelyn was livid. "And would your brother Richard have pardoned you at Lisieux if not for the intervention of your lady mother?"

This time the laughter came from behind Llewelyn, came from his own men. He saw John's face twitch, saw he'd drawn blood. John had gotten to his feet so abruptly that the chair tilted, and Llewelyn instinctively started to rise, too, only to freeze as John swung the sword up. The weapon was three feet long, honed to a razor edge, tapered for thrusting. It had been custom-made for Llewelyn, and he knew better than most its killing capabilities. Now, with that naked blade leveled at his throat, his mouth went dry, he dared not even blink. He heard a woman cry out; although it did not sound like her, he knew it could only be Joanna.

The sword's point was pressed against his windpipe, but Llewelyn's pulse was slowing, his breathing steadying, for he'd real-

ized that John did not mean to kill him. He would never know
what had stayed John's hand; Joanna's scream? Fear for Will? He
could not even be sure John had ever meant to follow through on
that first thrust. He knew only that John's eyes did not mirror the
passion of a man provoked beyond all reason; his was a rage
more glacial than volcanic, utterly implacable but controlled,
icily deliberate, the rage of a man willing to wait for his vengeance.

It was not the first time Llewelyn had seen his death foretold in
another man's eyes, but never had the threat carried so much
lethal conviction, all the more chilling in eyes eerily like Joanna's. He felt the pressure increase, felt a stinging sensation, knew
that John, too, had drawn blood. And then the sword was withdrawn and John stepped back, beckoned to one of the watching
men.

"Take this," he said, "and break it."

The man looked dubiously at the sword, uncomfortably aware
how much pressure the blade was meant to bear. But he made
haste to obey, grabbed the sword and withdrew, shouting for a
hammer and anvil.

Llewelyn was becoming aware again of their audience.
Gwenwynwyn looked like a man at peace with himself for the
first time in three years, a man who'd just received payment for a
long-overdue debt. Thomas Corbet, too, was gleefully jubilant,
Chester his usual impassive self, Hugh Corbet haggard, obviously ailing, while Eustace de Vesci ignored Llewelyn altogether,
watched John with unblinking intensity. Surprisingly, Maelgwn
had lost his smile; his eyes held Llewelyn's for several moments,
but his thoughts were masked, utterly his own. Joanna, however,
was not within Llewelyn's range of vision. He'd have given a
great deal had she only been back at Dolwyddelan, been anywhere but here, witness to his shame.

"Your Grace!" Grinning triumphantly, a man was hastening
toward John, holding out Llewelyn's sword. But it was no longer
a weapon, was no more now than two twisted pieces of jagged
metal.

John reached out, took the hilt in one hand, the sundered blade
in the other. "As easily as I broke this sword, so could I have
broken you . . . and would have, if it were not for my daughter.
But do not count upon her to save you a second time. From this
day forth, the Virgin Mary herself could speak for you and it
would avail you naught."

He flung the sword fragments to the ground. "Now you may

withdraw," he said contemptuously, "and wait until I have time to speak with you about the terms of your surrender."

Llewelyn got slowly to his feet. His pride was already in shreds; he knew that if he allowed John to dismiss him as if he were a serf, the memory would haunt him for the rest of his life. But he saw no way out of the trap. He stared down at his broken sword, and then looked up, saw his wife.

Joanna's face was ashen, wet with tears, but her eyes were a brilliant, blazing green, and her mouth was contorted with rage. Richard was beside her, was gripping her arm, but as her eyes met Llewelyn's, she jerked free of her brother's restraining hold.

Llewelyn stood very still, watched as she moved toward him. All were watching her now. John took an involuntary step forward, said her name. She seemed not to hear, never took her eyes from Llewelyn. Coming to a halt before him, she said loudly and very clearly, "My lord husband," sank down on the grass in a deep, submissive curtsy.

It was more than a clever face-saving stratagem, it was an avowal of loyalty, of love. Llewelyn raised her up, looked for a long moment into her face, and then kissed her, kissed her as if they were alone, as if nothing mattered but that moment and the woman he held in his arms. Even he could not have said which meant more, that he was kissing John's daughter or kissing his wife.

Joanna could hear the erratic hammering of his heart, could feel the tremor in his arms, and behind her closed eyelids she could still see the sun glinting on the blade of his sword. She touched her fingers to his throat; they came away bloodied, and she shuddered, raised up and kissed him again.

Llewelyn smiled at her; she'd never seen his dark eyes so soft, so tender. And then she saw his smile change, saw it twist with triumph. She turned slowly and, like Llewelyn, looked at her father.

John's face was burning with color, but his eyes were blank, utterly without emotion. Joanna could read nothing in them, not even recognition. Although she and her father were only some ten feet apart, it suddenly seemed to Joanna that the distance was widening with each silent second that passed. And then John had turned away, was walking rapidly toward the abbey, not looking back.

Joanna watched, and there was a part of her that wanted nothing so much as to run after him, to try to make things right. But she did not move; she could not.

She looked so desolate, so achingly vulnerable, that Llewelyn put his arm around her shoulders. She had, he thought, burned more than a bed this time; she had burned a bridge.

He said nothing, but Joanna knew it, too. "He'll never forgive me," she said softly, "never."

It was dusk before John summoned Llewelyn to the monks' frater. He watched as the Welsh entered the dining hall, waited until Llewelyn and Joanna approached the dais, and then said cuttingly, "A woman has no place in the council chamber. Have your wife await you outside."

Joanna flushed, and John discovered that hurting her did nothing to ease his own hurt. She curtsied, looked first at her father and then at her husband, and John was swept with rage when Llewelyn nodded, as if he had the right to confirm a royal command. He saw now that the younger man had not washed away the dried blood on his throat, knew that was no less deliberately done than his own refusal to see Llewelyn for more than six hours, and at that moment there was nothing he would not have given to revoke Llewelyn's reprieve—save only the life of his brother.

The hall was crowded. John was flanked by the Earls of Chester and Pembroke, was accepting a wine cup from his cousin, William de Warenne, Earl of Surrey. Llewelyn recognized most of the Normans gathered around the dais. Eustace de Vesci looked, as ever, like a man nursing a perpetual toothache. Beside him stood his cousin Robert Fitz Walter, whose friendship with de Vesci was mystifying to those who knew them best, for Fitz Walter was a swaggering, jovial prankster and braggart, utterly unlike the aloof, sardonic de Vesci. Fitz Walter, whose estates were primarily in Essex, looked no happier than de Vesci to be embroiled in John's vendetta against a Welsh Prince. But Llewelyn noted that even the Marcher lords, like the Earl of Hereford and Richard de Clare, did not appear to be savoring John's triumph. To Llewelyn, that was dramatic and intriguing evidence of the growing estrangement between John and his barons, that they could take no pleasure in any victory that strengthened the crown.

With a start, Llewelyn realized what he was doing, standing midst the burning embers of a charred ruin and envisioning it resurrected from the ashes and rubble, no less ambitious in design, far more impregnable to attack. It was heartening to discover that he had not yet lost all hope, even now as he braced himself for what was to come, for the price he would have to pay for John's truce. He knew, just as John did, that it was not a peace.

John wasted no time. "I expect to be compensated in full for the cost of this campaign. But I am not vindictive. Since I know what a poor, wretched country Wales is, how limited your resources are, I am willing to take payment in livestock. I shall want some of your best horses, hawks, and hunting dogs for my own use, will let you know how many. But you are to pay tribute to the English crown in cattle—twenty thousand head."

"Christ!" Llewelyn was staggered. "You do not understand how dependent we are on cattle. If you reduce our herds by twenty thousand, my people will starve!"

"You're the one who does not understand. You're not here to argue, to negotiate. You're here to listen whilst I tell you what I want from you. And what I want are cattle . . . and land. All of Gwynedd west of the River Conwy, the four cantrefs you call the Perfeddwlad."

With one stroke he'd just cut Gwynedd in two, gained half of North Wales for the English crown. Llewelyn stared at him, saying nothing, taking what meagre consolation he could from a grim resolve, that claiming the Perfeddwlad would be easier than holding onto it.

It was not difficult for John to guess the tenor of his thoughts, for he'd made no effort to dissemble, and everything about him, from his stance to the set of his mouth, spoke of silent defiance. More than ever, John regretted what he'd done for love of his daughter. But he had one great advantage over most men, a lesson learned at bitter cost during those years he'd dwelt in the shadow of a brother he hated, in the shadow of the crown. He knew how to wait.

"Whatever my other faults, naïveté is not amongst them. I know, of course, that you cannot be trusted out of my sight, that an oath of honor means no more to a Welshman than it would to an infidel Saracen. Therefore, I shall have to take measures to make sure you keep faith. I want thirty hostages as pledges for your fidelity to the crown. They are to be wellborn, the sons of your Welsh lords, scions of noble Houses."

Llewelyn knew it was a common Norman custom to take hostages, knew John had in custody not only the daughters of the Scottish King but the sons of those of his own lords who'd fallen into disfavor. Even the powerful and respected Earl of Pembroke had been forced to yield up two of his sons to allay John's feverish suspicions. But knowing that did nothing to ease Llewelyn's sense of outrage. "As you will," he said tersely, not trusting himself to say more.

"You are to select them, to take upon yourself the responsibility for their fate. But of the thirty, one must be your son Gruffydd."

Llewelyn's head came up sharply. "No!"

There was a sudden, tense silence. Chester glanced toward John, then took it upon himself to say, "Need I point out, my lord, that you're in no position to refuse anything the King might demand of you?"—making it a simple statement of fact when another man might have turned it into a mocking taunt.

"He's holding two sons of mine," a voice close at hand said in Welsh, and Llewelyn turned, stared for a startled moment into the ice-blue eyes of an old enemy. Maelgwn seemed surprised himself, as if his words had somehow come of their own volition. He shrugged, murmured coolly, *"Mae yn rhy hwyr edifaru ar ol i'r ffagl gyneu."*

It was an oft-quoted Welsh proverb, one Llewelyn knew well: It is too late to repent after the flame is kindled.

He looked from Maelgwn to Chester, realizing that these two men, the most unlikely of allies, were, nevertheless, trying to do him a good turn, to remind him of the wretched realities of defeat, the likely consequences of refusal. He realized, too, that they were right. But how in Christ's blessed name could he ever do what was being demanded? How could he give up his son to John, to John of all men?

John was smiling faintly. "The boy is in the camp; it would be easy enough to take him. But I've a question to put to you first, my lord Prince of Gwynedd. You speak with such passion of your concern for your people, speak as if you truly care whether they have meat to put in their bellies. Tell me, then, how you can agree to offer up other men's sons, whilst refusing to yield your own."

Llewelyn sucked in his breath. He no longer looked defiant, looked shaken, and John took some satisfaction from that, but it was not enough, not nearly enough.

He rose from his chair, and Llewelyn took a step toward the dais. "Will Your Grace spare me a few moments . . . alone?"

John frowned, but curiosity won out, and he nodded, waved the other men away from the dais. They retreated with obvious reluctance, no less curious than he. As soon as they were out of earshot, he demanded, "Well? What have you to say to me?"

of seconds. "Well, I do have something to say to you, and say it I shall!"

John was staring at her as if at a stranger, for it was the first time he'd ever seen Joanna truly angry. He hesitated, then made a gesture of dismissal. The other men in the tent withdrew, leaving him alone with his daughter.

"I did not betray you, Papa. Yes, I love my husband, but I am not going to feel guilty about that, not anymore." Joanna drew several unsteady breaths; regaining some of her composure, she said more calmly, "Ah, Papa, do you not see? The human heart is not like a loaf of bread; if I give a large portion to Llewelyn, it does not follow that I must then give you a smaller slice. I love you both, in different ways. If I stood with Llewelyn on Sunday, it's not that my love for him was greater, but rather that his need was greater."

John said nothing; she could not tell whether her words were reaching him or not. "Papa, you told me once that your mother and father had ever used you and your brothers as weapons against each other. You said you could not please the one without first damning the other. I'm asking you—no, I'm begging you. Do not do to me what they did to you."

"Joanna . . . that's not what I ever meant to do. Surely you know that?"

"What I know, Papa, is that I love you and I love Llewelyn, and the two of you are tearing me apart!"

John flinched. "I never wanted that, lass," he said softly, "I swear it."

Joanna moved around the trestle table, moved into his arms. He hugged her close, then stepped back and smiled at her. "I think it a good thing I had sons. Daughters are much too resourceful at getting their own way, are much harder on the heart!"

Joanna took her cue from him, did her best to echo his wry, teasing tone. "I do not know about that, Papa. I'd wager most daughters are more docile and biddable than a man's scapegrace sons."

"So would I, until this morn. In truth, Joanna, I never suspected you had such a temper!"

"I am your daughter, Eleanor of Aquitaine's granddaughter. Are you not the one always telling me that a pure-blood horse breeds true?"

John laughed, and it was as if their estrangement were forgotten, as if all were as it had been. But as much as Joanna wanted to believe that, she knew it was not so, for either of them.

As she followed John from the tent, Joanna discovered that the Welsh were waiting for her. Llewelyn was already astride his chestnut stallion. He watched as John escorted Joanna toward her mare, as they embraced and John helped her to mount. He raised his hand then, gave the signal to depart. But John still retained his hold on Joanna's reins.

"Be sure," he said, "that you take care of my daughter."

"Your Grace need not worry about my wife. You take care of my son."

Joanna saw the look that burned between them; the very air seemed charged with static. She had no illusions left, knew their truce would not last. There would be a reckoning. There would be another war, and there was nothing she could do, for both men wanted it so.

29

CAMBRIDGE, ENGLAND

March 1212

John rode into the riverside town known as Cantebrigge at dusk on Good Friday, settled himself and his court in the stone-and-timber castle built by William the Conqueror.

Cantebrigge was a sprawling, unwalled town of some two thousand inhabitants, like most of the English towns Gruffydd had seen in the past seven months in that it had a marketplace, a leper hospital, a disproportionate number of stone churches, a Jewish ghetto called the Jewry, and a gallows, stocks, and pillory. But Cantebrigge was also home to a university with a large, raucous student population, in consequence of which it had more than its share of alehouses and bordellos.

Passing through the town, Gruffydd's companions took enthused notice of the latter, began to make plans for a night of disreputable pleasures. As ever, it struck Gruffydd as strange indeed that in some ways he should have greater freedom as a hostage of the English King than as the son of Gwynedd's Prince. In Wales he'd been conscious at all times of his rank; as Llewelyn's firstborn son, he was accustomed to being the focal point of stares, the target of whispers. Unable to escape his identity, he could only do his best to live up to it, and his dread of being made to look ridiculous had imposed upon him an unwilling chastity. He'd known there were women of easy virtue, women of the brake and bush who'd lay with a man for money. But each time he was tempted, he would begin to fear that he might not know what to do, that the woman would laugh at his inexperience and, far worse, then tell everyone about his inept fumbling, his greenness.

But once in England, he discovered that for the first time in his life, he was not the center of attention, not known by sight to all.

The sudden anonymity was unsettling, but liberating, too. On a night in mid-November, he'd accompanied some of his fellow hostages to a Hereford bawdy house and had lost his virginity to a plump Saxon whore named Edwina, who smelled of sweat and garlic and charged him half a penny, but called him "love" and put to rest any lingering doubts about his manhood.

Now, when his friends Collen and Emlyn pressed him, he fell in with their plans willingly enough. He was beginning to want more than hurried couplings on fetid, scratchy straw, to want a bedmate he did not have to buy. But he did not see much likelihood of his forming an attachment of the heart at the English court, and if he could not ease his loneliness, his heart-sick yearning for Wales, he could at least relieve his body's needs.

It was dark by the time a fasting-day fish supper had been served, before Gruffydd and his companions were able to find beds for themselves in the side aisles of the great hall. Madoc ap Maelgwn sauntered past, nodded coolly. Gruffydd gave an equally cool greeting in return, was glad when Madoc moved on; he was not good at dissembling, found it awkward to be in such close proximity with the son of his father's enemy.

He knew Collen's father had not sent him any money for some weeks, and he was counting his own coins to make sure he could pay for them both, when a man clad in the red and white livery of the King stopped before his pallet.

"I've been sent to escort you to the King's Grace," he said brusquely, and Gruffydd's heart skipped a beat. He could think of very few reasons why John should be summoning him, none of them reassuring.

The room was circular, lit by smoking wall cressets, cluttered with open coffers and clothing. Gruffydd found it almost intolerable to be in John's presence, sometimes thought he might choke on his hatred, and it was with the greatest reluctance that he came forward, knelt.

But in the next moment the English King was forgotten. Gruffydd got abruptly to his feet, stared openmouthed at the woman standing next to John. He would never have believed he could be so glad to see one he so detested, but now he stepped toward her, said eagerly, "Do you bring a message from my father, Madame?"

Joanna shook her head, and he felt his throat close up with disappointment. But then he heard a familiar voice say, "Why should I give Joanna a message I can better deliver myself?" and he spun around, disbelieving.

"Papa?" He sounded stunned, and Llewelyn laughed, came swiftly across the chamber.

"I wanted to surprise you, lad, not send you into shock!"

Gruffydd still could not believe his father was here, on English soil, in John's private chamber, not even when he found himself gathered into an affectionate embrace. His sense of unreality went spinning wildly out of control when Llewelyn turned, said with the utmost nonchalance, "John, I'd like to take Gruffydd back to my own chamber now, so we can talk."

And when John replied composedly, "By all means; Joanna can stay and visit with me, giving you time alone," Gruffydd decided that the world had gone mad, and all in it.

He somehow managed to hold his peace as they crossed the bailey, entered the northwest tower, mounted the spiral stairway to the chamber allotted for Llewelyn and Joanna's use. But as soon as the door closed behind them, he blurted out, "Papa, what in God's name are you doing here?"

"Just what it looks like," Llewelyn said blandly. "I am celebrating Easter with my wife's family." And then he gave a sardonic laugh, added, "Of course, this reunion required a safe-conduct and an exchange of hostages!"

"Are you sure that you're safe here?"

"As safe as Salisbury's life can make me. John sent his brother again as a pledge of faith."

Gruffydd's anxiety abated somewhat, although not his bewilderment. "But if he did not lure you to England to imprison or murder you, what has he in mind? Why is he being so polite to you?"

Llewelyn laughed again. "He cannot very well do otherwise as long as I am a guest at his court. Ostensibly he summoned me so he can visit with Joanna, whilst magnanimously giving me the chance to see you. The reality, of course, is that John wants something from me. Sit, and we'll talk about it. Do you know what has been happening in Wales?"

"Not much," Gruffydd admitted. "Just what we manage to overhear. I do know that John sent Falkes de Breauté and Maelgwn into Ceredigion, that they defeated Owain and Rhys Ieunac, forced them to surrender, to come to London and make a public submission to John." That was a distasteful memory to Gruffydd. He grimaced, said, "They were thoroughly cowed, Papa, showed no spirit at all . . . not like you."

That was, Llewelyn realized, Gruffydd's oblique way of making amends for those earlier accusations of cowardice. He smiled at the boy, said, "But John then made a fatal blunder. Rather than turning Ceredigion back to Maelgwn, he claimed it for the crown, set Falkes de Breauté to building a castle at Aberystwyth.''

Gruffydd gave a low whistle. ''Maelgwn must have thrown an apoplectic fit!''

Llewelyn nodded. ''I cannot say John is his own worst enemy; the competition for that honor is too fierce! But he does have a decided tendency toward self-sabotage. He has always to push his advantage to the breaking point and then beyond. As a result, his victories, no matter how brilliant, are always ephemeral, of fleeting moment. Maelgwn and Rhys Gryg are no fools, soon realized that John means to claim as much of Wales as he can, their lands as well as mine. Whatever their other failings, they are not men to become puppets of the English crown. They besieged John's new castle at Aberystwyth, burned it to the ground. At the same time, John gave Robert de Vieuxpont a free hand in Lower Powys, so Gwenwynwyn, too, is growing restive. For months now, all of South Wales has been in turmoil, and I suspect John is worried lest I throw in with Maelgwn and Rhys Gryg. My guess is that he's sent for me to try to ferret out my intentions and, if need be, to use threats, even promises, to fetter me to the crown.''

''And will he, Papa? Will he fetter you to the crown?''

''What do you mean, Gruffydd?''

''You say Maelgwn and Rhys Gryg are in rebellion, that South Wales is ablaze. But not Gwynedd. It has been more than seven months since John took from you the Perfeddwlad. Passive acceptance is not like you, Papa. You have stayed your hand because of me, have you not?''

''Yes.''

''You cannot do that, Papa. The longer you allow John to hold the Perfeddwlad, the harder it will become to dislodge him. You cannot give him the time he needs to entrench himself—not without losing our lands forever.''

''That is what I want to talk with you about, Gruffydd.'' Llewelyn rose, began to pace. ''What we feared is coming to pass. John is refortifying in stone those timbered castles he erected last summer. His men patrol the roads, the passes, cross the Conwy into my domains at will, as if seeking to provoke a confrontation. And he is planning to bring in English merchants and their families, to charter towns as the Normans did in South Wales.'' He swung around to face Gruffydd, said with sudden passion, ''The Normans would never have been able to steal so much of Deheubarth if not for towns like Swansea, Pembroke,

Fishguard, Tenby. They are towns on Welsh soil, but no Welshman may become a citizen, or bear arms whilst in the town, or sit on a jury in any lawsuit between a Norman and one of Welsh blood. The Welsh in much of South Wales are intruders in their own land. But I'll not let that happen in Gwynedd. Christ forgive me, Gruffydd, I cannot!''

Gruffydd swallowed with some difficulty. In arguing that Llewelyn must try to reclaim the Perfeddwlad, he'd spoken from the heart; he truly believed every word he'd uttered. But it was no less true that he had not expected his father to agree with him. Now he found himself approving what Llewelyn meant to do, while at the same time feeling a shocked sense of betrayal that his father would put anything, even Gwynedd's sovereignty, above his own safety. He'd have been put on the rack, though, before he would have admitted it, and he made an enormous effort, said as calmly as he could, ''I suppose, then, that we should think upon what I might expect from John. I know he has not harmed Maelgwn's elder son; Madoc is still at court. What of the younger son? Was he made to suffer in any way for Maelgwn's rebellion?''

''No, the lad is quite safe in Shrewsbury.''

''Well, that is reassuring.'' Gruffydd managed a smile, but he had to ask. ''Papa . . . has John ever harmed a hostage?''

''No, Gruffydd, he has not. Not even when Hugh de Lusignan offered up hostages for his freedom after Mirebeau, only to betray John within days of his release.'' Llewelyn moved back to the settle, sat down beside the boy. ''John is utterly without mercy to those who have offended him, but he has never avenged himself upon the innocent. His quarrel is with me, and it is with me that he'll settle it, not you, lad.''

Gruffydd was showing more courage, more maturity than Llewelyn had dared hope for; he was making it almost too easy. Llewelyn had never been so proud of his son, or so aware of his own failings as a father.

''Gruffydd, I want only the best for you. But I'd not blame you if you did not believe me, lad.'' He hesitated, then said, ''I've done a great deal of thinking these months past, found out things about myself that I'd rather not have known. I wish I could say that nothing mattered to me but those I love. I cannot.''

Gruffydd was not sure what response was expected of him; he could not recall ever talking with his father about intangibles or imponderables, about emotions and doubts, secrets of the heart. ''I know you love me, Papa,'' he mumbled, and flushed.

"Yes, I do. I loved your mother, too, lad. I loved her very much. But I could not allow myself to marry her, for there'd be no political advantage to the marriage; Gwynedd would have gained nothing from such a match. I was willing to wed Joanna, though, to take her sight unseen, to yoke myself for life to a woman I might find both undesirable and unlikable, because she was the King of England's daughter, brought me what Tangwystl could not, a border castle and a political alliance with the English crown."

Gruffydd was silent for some moments. "You're saying, Papa, that you've always put Gwynedd first. I understand that, in truth I do. You see, that is the way I feel, too. There is nothing I would not do, nothing I would not give up if only you'd name me as your heir."

Gruffydd's words had come without calculation. His was an uncomplicated, elemental nature, one not attuned to subtleties, still less to subterfuge. But the expression on his father's face was a revelation to him. He suddenly realized that Llewelyn's decision to break faith with John could work to his advantage and Davydd's disadvantage, that he would have a powerful claim indeed upon his father's conscience, that his would be a wrong much in need of redress.

"No man could have a son with greater courage, Gruffydd," Llewelyn said softly.

"It means much to me that you think so, Papa. But what I need to know now means even more. Did you forget my birthday again?"

Llewelyn grinned. "Brace yourself, lad. This time I remembered!"

They both laughed. Neither mentioned what Llewelyn's decision could mean—years of confinement for Gruffydd—the boy because he did not fully comprehend the risks, and the man because he'd managed to rationalize those risks, to convince himself that John's past generosity toward the innocent and the unoffending was an adequate guarantee for his son's safety.

Joanna crossed the crowded hall, slipped her arm through Llewelyn's. "Papa wants to talk to you, love." She hesitated, then murmured, "He does seem to be trying, Llewelyn. It's not so impossible to believe, is it, that he might truly want peace?"

"John's peace is rather like the peace of God—in that it passeth all understanding." But there had been so little conviction in Joanna's voice, so much wistfulness, that Llewelyn added, "I will admit he's made this visit far more tolerable than I expected."

John beckoned them up onto the dais, gestured for a page to serve them wine. For several moments they made desultory conversation, bland in form and banal in substance. But then John directed his attention solely to Llewelyn.

"A strange rumor has reached my ears, that a papal nuncio has been traveling in Wales, that he was, in fact, received at your court. I should like you to tell me if this be true and, if so, the purpose of that visit."

So that was why he was in Cantebrigge this Easter Sunday! Llewelyn smiled, said with complete sincerity, "I should be right pleased to do so, Your Grace. I fear His Holiness the Pope is losing patience. You did spurn his last offer to compromise your differences, did you not? If I'm not mistaken, you even went so far as to promise to hang Stephen Langton should he set foot on English soil . . . or words to that effect."

"Those very words exactly," John said coldly. "But we were not talking of the Pope and myself. We were talking of you and the papal nuncio. What did he want from you?"

By now the hall was quieting; people were drifting toward the dais. Llewelyn pitched his voice for their growing audience, said, "The Pope has lifted the Interdict from Wales. He has also absolved all the Welsh Princes from their oaths of allegiance to you, my liege, and urges us to join together in a holy crusade to depose you, claiming you to be a man beyond God's grace, no longer deserving to wear the crown of a Christian King."

John's war of wills with the Pope had been dragging on for four years, but the Pope had just dramatically and dangerously raised the stakes. John caught his breath. He would not give Llewelyn or the others the satisfaction of seeing that he was shaken, though, and he summoned up a taut, derisive smile.

"Tell me," he challenged, "do you, as a good son of the Church, mean to follow the Pope's directive?"

Llewelyn was enjoying himself. "If I were truly such a good son of the Church, I would not be here at Cantebrigge, at your court. Your Grace is excommunicate, after all, and a man excommunicated is to be shunned by all Christians, to be treated as an Ishmael, as one facing eternal damnation."

There was a strained silence. Joanna gave Llewelyn a look that was half resentful, half reproachful, and leaned over John's chair, whispering something meant for his ears alone. Llewelyn glanced around the hall, saw on other faces confirmation of his own belief, that he'd taken the honors in that exchange.

With those whom he knew well, Llewelyn could sometimes

communicate without need of words, most often with Joanna, occasionally with Ednyved. But he experienced now just such a moment of shared, silent understanding with a virtual stranger. His eyes happened to catch Eustace de Vesci's; for several seconds the two men looked at one another, and in that brief span they reached an unspoken accord, one to be explored further at a more opportune time.

There was a sudden commotion at the end of the hall. Llewelyn turned, saw an extraordinary apparition stumbling through the doorway. He was uncommonly tall, so gaunt he looked almost skeletal, clad in a long, ragged gown of unbleached sacking, his feet grimy and bare, his hair drifting about his shoulders like dirty, windblown snow, his beard wild and unkempt. But although he'd obviously reached his biblical threescore years and ten, his face was curiously unlined, untouched by time, and his eyes, a startling shade of blue, were utterly without guile.

Joanna turned toward her father. "Whoever is that strange old man?"

"A crazed hermit who has been wandering about Yorkshire for some weeks, prophesying my death. When reports first reached me, I did not pay them any mind. If I concerned myself with every lunatic roaming about the countryside, I'd have time for little else. But this lunatic," John said dryly, "is beginning to attract crowds."

The old man seemed bewildered by his surroundings. He had to be shoved forward by his guards, and when he reached the dais, he stood there, blinking, until one of the men put a hand on his shoulder, directed him to kneel.

John leaned forward. "Are you the one they call Peter of Wakefield?"

"Yes, lord." He did not sound frightened, just confused. He squatted back on his heels, waited patiently for John's will to be revealed.

"I was told you've been preaching that I'm to lose my crown by Ascension Day. Is that true?"

"No, lord!" The astonishing blue eyes opened wide. "Not this Ascension Day, lord. The Ascension Day next to come."

John gave an abrupt, incredulous laugh, one that did not sound very amused. "God tells you this, I suppose?" he said sarcastically, and the hermit nodded.

"Yes, lord," he said, so calmly that John lost all patience.

"Who put you up to this, old man? Who's paying you?"

Peter blinked. "No one, lord. I am an instrument of the Almighty. He has given me second sight."

There was something unexpectedly compelling in the utter simplicity of that statement. People murmured among themselves; a few surreptitiously made the sign of the cross. Llewelyn had less than the normal amount of superstition in his makeup, but even he was affected by the old man's composure, by his eerie certainty, and he was suddenly glad that the hermit's prophecy was not directed at him. He glanced curiously over at John, but the latter looked more angry than uneasy.

"You try my patience, old man, in truth you do. Go back to Wakefield, keep your foolish babblings to yourself, and I'll overlook the trouble you've caused me. But you'd best not expect me to be so lenient a second time."

"I am sorry, lord; I do not mean to displease you. But I cannot do that. My visions are not my own. They come from Almighty God. He has chosen me to spread His word, and I cannot fail Him."

The hall was very still. John stared balefully at the elderly hermit, shabby and emaciated and perplexingly tranquil; he met John's eyes quite placidly, as if his own fate was a matter of utter indifference to him. He did not flinch, did not react at all as John said grimly, "As you will, old man." He gestured to the waiting guards. "Take this 'prophet of God' to Corfe Castle, confine him there until Ascension Day of next year."

They seized the hermit, dragged him to his feet. He offered no resistance. "I shall pray for you, lord, when your time is nigh."

John looked about the hall, saw he was suddenly the object of morbid speculation. He did not doubt that many among them would lay grisly wagers on this madman's prophecy, that they'd count the days till Ascensiontide, 1213, with unholy glee. Few faces showed any sympathy; far more showed covert, cautious amusement. His son-in-law alone was making no attempt to hide his mirth, was openly grinning. John stared at Llewelyn, and for a long moment his brother Will's life hung in the balance.

"He amuses you, this pitiful lunatic?"

"Actually," Llewelyn said coolly, "I found him to be surprisingly convincing, found myself wondering if he might, indeed, be one of God's chosen."

Joanna was close enough to hear her father's sharp inhalation of breath. She put her hand imploringly upon his arm, but he shook it off, keeping his eyes on Llewelyn.

"Sooner or later," he said, very softly, "you will make a misstep. And when you do, Christ Jesus Himself shall pity your fate."

*   *   *

Joanna knelt, hugged in turn her four-year-old half-brother Henry,
three-year-old Richard, and her namesake and half-sister Joanna,
who was not yet two. None of them had their father's dark
coloring; Henry and Richard were redheads like their grandfather, and little Joanna had inherited Isabelle's blondeness. They
accepted Joanna's kisses shyly, for she was a stranger to them,
then approached the bed to receive goodnight kisses from their
mother.

Isabelle smiled fondly, ruffled Henry's untidy, bright hair,
forbore to scold when her daughter left a dirty little handprint
upon the skirt of her gown. But after a few moments, she
signaled to the nurses, and the children were shepherded from the
chamber.

The sight of them, the feel and smell of their sturdy little
bodies, had stirred up Joanna's longing for her own children.
Never before had she been separated from Davydd and Elen for
more than a few days, and she did not understand how Isabelle
could be content to see her children so infrequently. Isabelle
seemed proud of them, bragged about them often enough, but she
reminded Joanna of Elen, who lavished much love upon her
dolls, but only when she wanted to play at being a mother.

As the children departed, Joanna rose, too. "I want to see
Papa tonight, think I'd best go ere it gets too late."

Isabelle, too, had been a witness to that scene in the great hall.
She gave Joanna a wryly sympathetic smile, shook her head.
" 'Blessed are the peacemakers, for they shall be called the
children of God.' That may be true in Heaven, but they get
precious little credit here on earth, darling."

"What would you have me do, Isabelle? Just stand by, watch
and do nothing? What would you do if you were in my place? If
you were the one being torn between husband and father?" But
even as she asked, Joanna realized the futility of expecting
Isabelle to experience another's pain. She was coming to see that
Isabelle's emotional landscape was an alien world to her, a world
in which flowers bloomed upon the surface in generous, dazzling
profusion, but nothing was rooted deep.

Isabelle was frowning; the blue eyes were soft with pity. At
last deciding that she could best serve Joanna by helping her to
face the realities of her predicament, she said candidly, "I would
be as loving a wife and daughter as I could. I would try not to let
their hatred for each other poison their love for me. I would try to
make each one see that I understood his grievances against the

other. Above all, Joanna, I would try to reconcile myself to a bitter truth—that there could be no happy ending."

"The hearth fire is almost out, Papa. Shall I fetch a servant to stoke it?"

"No, do not bother. But you can get me another cup of wine."

Joanna obeyed, although she suspected that he'd already had more than enough wine that night. As soon as she'd been given admittance into his chamber, found him sitting all alone in shadowed gloom, she'd abandoned her intention to talk to him about his latest clash with Llewelyn. This was not the time for it.

"Isabelle tells me that you mean to give Uncle Will custody of Cantebrigge Castle. That's most generous of you, Papa."

"I suppose," John agreed absently. He was gazing into the dying fire, so absorbed in his own thoughts that Joanna made no further attempts at conversation. When Llewelyn drank too much, he tended to get playful, laughing a lot and making atrociously bad puns and eventually becoming amorous. But John's drinking had a darker, more disturbing texture to it; she'd never seen him well and truly drunk, knew she did not want to.

"You do not think he could actually have second sight?"

"No," Joanna said hastily, if not entirely truthfully, "of course not! Why would the Almighty bestow so great a gift upon one so unworthy?"

"Why indeed?" he echoed. The only light came from a single wall cresset; she could not see his face. She rose from her seat, moved toward him. But he rose, too, began to wander aimlessly about the chamber, picking up and discarding items at random.

"Do you believe in God, Joanna?" he asked suddenly, so shocking her that she was momentarily rendered mute. In all her life she had never heard anyone ask such a question.

"Yes, I do. Surely you do, too, Papa?"

He shrugged, again said, "I suppose . . ."

Another silence fell. John stopped before the hearth, reached for the fire tongs, and tried to prod the embers back into life.

"Talk to me, Papa," Joanna entreated. "Tell me what you're thinking. I'm here, I want to help, if only you'll let me."

"What makes you think I need help?"

"Even a blind man could see that you're troubled! Is it the Pope? His meddling in Wales?"

John thrust the fire tongs aside, called the Pope an imaginatively obscene name. "You know what he'll do next, Joanna? He'll announce to all of Christendom that I am no longer fit to be

King of England, anoint that grasping hellspawn Philip to lead a
'holy crusade' to depose me. And as Philip's reward for acting as
the papal catspaw, he'll bestow upon him the crown of England,
if he can take it from me. Do you know what that would mean?
Every whoreson in England with half a grudge or half a brain
would flock to the French banners.''

"Then come to terms with him, Papa . . . ere it be too late.''

"No,'' he said. "No, I will not. I'll not yield, not when I'm in
the right.''

"It seems to me, Papa, that the relevant question is not who's
in the right, but whether this is a war you can win.'' Joanna
crossed to him, laid a hand on his sleeve. "I fear for you,'' she
confessed. "Not just for your crown, for your soul, too. If you
die excommunicate, you're damned to Hell for all eternity. What
could be worth so great a risk, Papa?''

"I'm damned whether the Pope absolves me or not. The things
I've done . . .''

Arthur, she thought numbly. She swallowed, said, "What things,
Papa?''

He looked at her, and for a moment she truly thought he was
going to answer. But he said only, "Things God could never
forgive.''

"That's not so, Papa. There is no sin so great that God cannot
forgive it.''

He took her hand in his, raised it to his lips, and then he
laughed, backed away. "Do not believe it, lass, not for a moment! There is no forgiveness, either in this world or the next.''

"You're wrong, Papa.'' Joanna drew a deep breath, said, "I
could forgive you any sin.''

John gave her an odd smile, shook his head. "No, lass,'' he
said. "You could not.''

He moved to the table, with an unsteady hand poured himself
another cupful of wine. "If that mad old man be right, I'll have
reigned for fourteen years. Passing strange, for it seems longer,
much longer.'' He turned back to face Joanna, still with that
strange smile. "There is but one lesson worth learning, one you
must teach your children, Joanna. That nothing in life turns out
as we thought it would, nothing . . .''

On a cloudy, cool day in late May, the Welsh Princes came to
Aber. Llewelyn greeted them in the great hall, but he then led
them into his own chamber for the privacy such a volatile gathering required. He had not been entirely sure that they all would

come. But he knew that if Maelgwn came, so, too, would his brother, Rhys Gryg. There was no love between them, but they had finally reached a grudging accord, more than a truce, less than an alliance. There was no question in his mind that his cousins Madog and Hywel would come, for he knew neither one was proud of the part he'd played in last summer's campaign. And Gwenwynwyn would come if the others did, for he had far too suspicious a nature to allow such a council to take place without him.

"I thought Aber was burned, compliments of your wife's father."

There was mockery in Gwenwynwyn's smile, but Llewelyn ignored it, said evenly, "I had it rebuilt . . . on a larger scale."

Maelgwn took a seat next to Ednyved, giving him a cool nod; they were brothers by marriage, but not friends. "What of my renegade nephews? Did you not invite them?"

"Owain and Rhys were unwilling to come," Llewelyn said regretfully. "Their defeat at John's hands seems to have left lasting scars upon their souls." He saw no reason not to come straight to the point. "I expect you've guessed why I asked you to Aber, to talk about forming a league of amity. I think it time we put aside our differences, band together against a common enemy, the English King."

"You expect us to forget years of bad blood, mistrust, betrayals?" Gwenwynwyn's voice was scornful. "Nor do I believe you've suddenly become such a bloody saint yourself, willing to overlook the part we played in your defeat at Aberconwy."

"I've no claims to sainthood, but I like to think I'm capable of learning from past mistakes. What about you, Gwenwynwyn? Can you say as much?"

"You think I could ever trust you? I'd sooner deal with the Devil!"

Llewelyn shrugged. "You think you could ever trust John?"

Madog had yet to take a seat. Now he moved toward Llewelyn, stopped in front of him. "Your mother and my father were sister and brother; that makes ours the most significant of bonds, one of blood. It gives me the right to speak plainly. You're making a great mistake, Cousin. John's hatred for you is mortal. You move into the Perfeddwlad, and you'll see an English army in Wales within a fortnight. He'll take all of Gwynedd this time, Llewelyn, and then he'll burn every hut, every tree if need be, in order to run you to earth. Need I tell you what befalls a man charged with treason? He's dragged behind a horse to the gal-

lows, hanged and cut down whilst he still breathes, gelded and
disemboweled ere he's finally—and mercifully—beheaded. And
there are even worse deaths. You need only remember Maude de
Braose's fate.''

Llewelyn had heard enough. ''You're overlooking something,
Madog. Whether I keep the truce or not, sooner or later John
would find an excuse to move against me. Besides . . . this time
I do not intend to lose.''

Madog shook his head; there was on his face an expression of
genuine regret. ''As you will. But I want no part in this. If I must
come to terms with the English King in order to hold on to my
lands, so be it. I know the limits of my power, would that you
did yours.'' He walked to the door, paused. ''I wish you luck,
Cousin. I very much fear you'll need it.''

With Madog's departure, a pall settled over the room. Llewelyn
sought to dispel it by saying defiantly, ''Of course we can do
nothing, can go on as we always have, fighting one another,
allowing the English kings to play their sport of divide and
conquer. Is that what you want, Maelgwn? You want to wait
until John has the time to deal with your rebellion, until you find
yourself facing an English army?''

''You made a mistake in taking Ceredigion,'' Maelgwn said
coolly. ''And then I made one in backing John. I expect that
makes us even . . . at least for now. You do not have to talk me
into an alliance. I might not like it any; for certes, I do not like
you. But it makes sense.''

Llewelyn grinned, looked toward the others. ''What say the
rest of you?''

Hywel nodded, grinned back. Rhys Gryg glanced over at his
brother, then rose to his feet. Maelgwn was by far the more
physically impressive of the two. Rhys was balding, freckled,
with bloodshot blue eyes and a harsh, rasping voice, the result of
a throat injury which had earned him the name Rhys Gryg, Rhys
the Hoarse. As Llewelyn thought him to be fully as capable as
his brother, although less trustworthy, he waited tensely for the
older man's verdict.

''It seems to me,'' Rhys Gryg said slowly, ''that you could act
verily as a magnet for disaster, could draw John's wrath down
upon us all. You did not have much luck against John last
summer. What makes you think this time it will be different?''

''I made it easy for John, let him cut me off from my natural
allies—other Welshmen. This time he will not be able to play us
off against each other. This time we're not acting as rebels, but at

the urging of the Pope. And this time we'll have allies. I've sent envoys to the French court; even now they are negotiating an alliance with Philip."

Rhys Gryg looked startled, then impressed. "That alone would sign your death warrant with John," he said. "I see you've been thinking about this for a long while."

"I've had nine months in which to think of little else. We seem to agree that the English kings have had great success in exploiting our weaknesses. But two can fish in those troubled waters, and John's enemies are beyond counting. When I was at the English court this Easter, I spoke with some of them. They're men who hate John even more than they fear him, men who want him dead. If he leads an army into Wales, that will give them the opportunity they've been waiting for. If he crosses into Gwynedd, he'll find that he has as much to fear from his own lords as he does from the Welsh." Llewelyn paused. "Need I say more?"

"No," Rhys Gryg said succinctly, and for the first time he smiled. By common accord, all eyes then turned toward Gwenwynwyn. He looked so perturbed that Llewelyn could not keep from laughing.

"It's rather like being asked to choose between dwelling in Sodom or moving to Gomorrah, is it not?" he gibed, and Gwenwynwyn scowled. But when the other men laughed, he, too, managed a very sour smile, a grudging nod.

Joanna's hair was unbraided, fell loose and free to her hips. Llewelyn entwined a long strand around his fingers, made of it a soft noose for his throat, entangling them both in its coil. "Your hair always smells of lemon," he murmured. "Did I ever tell you how much I like that?"

Joanna said nothing. She could feel his breath on her cheek, and then his mouth was on hers. It was an unhurried, easy kiss, strongly flavored with wine. He'd released her hair, and his hands were wandering at will over her body, his mouth tracking the curve of her throat. Joanna did not move, not even when he loosened the bodice of her gown, cupped and caressed her breast with a warm, knowing hand. He kissed her again, exploring her mouth as he was exploring her body, and then stepped back, abruptly ended the embrace.

"That kiss, Madame, could well give a man frostbite. What ails you, Joanna?"

"This afternoon I entered the antechamber, found that Madog had left our bedchamber door ajar. I listened at that door, Llewelyn, listened as you and the other Welsh Princes made plans for war.''

"I see. Just what did you hear?" When she did not reply, he said, "Joanna, tell me!"

"I heard you talking of Norman barons who mean to betray my father. I heard Rhys Gryg say these men wanted my father dead, and I heard him ask if you, too, sought Papa's death. You said you did."

"Not so, Joanna. I said that I would gladly see him dead, but I seek only to reclaim what is mine. I do not forget the vast and sovereign powers of the English King. Nor that you are of his blood. If he stays out of my lands, I shall be content. But if he leads an army into my realm, I will defend myself and mine as best I can, and make no apologies for it . . . not even to you."

"My father has given you cause to hate him; I find no fault with you for that. I do not want to quarrel with you, not with so much at stake. I know you so well, Llewelyn, know the secrets of your heart, your soul. You have ever been decisive, little given to self-doubts, but you are not impulsive. I must assume, then, that you have thought on this long and hard, that you are fully aware of what the consequences might be. And that is what I find so difficult to understand. You do realize what you are risking? Our son's inheritance. Our marriage. Your son Gruffydd's freedom. Above all, your life. You do know that?"

"Yes," he said, "I know."

She took a step toward him, held out her hands, palms up, in a gesture of despairing entreaty. "Why, Llewelyn? Sweet Jesus, why?"

"Joanna, I would that I had an answer for you, one you could accept. I do in truth understand the risks. There are nights when I lie awake, when I cannot keep my thoughts from dwelling upon disaster, upon all I have to lose. I think of my son as a prisoner of the English crown, and I think of you, a widow at the age of one and twenty."

"But still you mean to do this, still you are set upon war."

"Yes," he said bleakly.

After some moments of silence, he moved to her, pulled her into his arms. This time she did not stand rigid and unresponsive in his embrace; she clung tightly. "You are rushing headlong to your own destruction," she whispered, "and I know not how to save you."

NOTTINGHAM, ENGLAND

August 1212

Nottingham Castle was one of John's favorite residences, for it was all but impregnable against attack, situated on a cliff above the River Leen, with three baileys encircled by deep, dry moats. But Richard knew they would not be long at Nottingham; in just five days John was assembling an army at Chester.

John had gone at once into the great hall, but Richard was still loitering out in the middle bailey, watching as their baggage carts were unloaded. He was in no hurry to join his father, for John's temper was very much on the raw during this, the fourteenth—and if Peter the Hermit was to be believed, the last—summer of his reign.

His victories in Scotland, Ireland, and Wales had encouraged John to look Channelward. Time had not reconciled him to the loss of Normandy, and in the spring he'd begun making plans for an invasion of France. The summer of 1212, he assured Richard, was to be a season of retribution.

And indeed it was proving to be just that, Richard thought grimly, but not precisely as his father had anticipated. John was at the Scots border when word reached him of his son-in-law's rebellion. Llewelyn had chosen his time with care, and within a month he'd retaken all of the Perfeddwlad, save only Deganwy and Rhuddlan Castles.

Richard had never seen his father in such a violent rage, a rage that fed upon itself, gained ground with each passing day until John began to seem obsessed, so intent was he upon exacting vengeance. Philip was reprieved, the French invasion abandoned. There would be war, but the battlefield would be Wales. John gave orders for his vassals to gather at Chester, gave orders to recruit more than two thousand carpenters and six thousand laborers, men to follow in his army's wake and erect castles across the conquered land. None doubted that this was to be much more than a punitive campaign of retaliation. It was to be war with no quarter given, a war that would end only with Llewelyn's death and the conquest of his country.

Turning back toward the great hall, Richard saw his Uncle Will standing on the outer stairs; Will, too, had begun to avoid John whenever possible. They stood in silence for some moments, their thoughts tracking the same bleak trail.

"When your Uncle Richard was at war with Philip, they took to blinding each other's soldiers." Will grimaced. "I fear, lad, that this war shall be just as bitter, just as bloody. Know you that John is now offering a bounty for Welsh heads? He paid one man six shillings for six heads last week."

"Yes," Richard said, "I know," very much wishing that he did not.

"For a time I'd hoped that the London fire would turn John's mind from this war. Much of Southwark is but ashes and rubble, and I heard it said that more than a thousand people died. The homeless have to be sheltered, the injured tended, and John generally takes a personal interest in making sure that fire or flood victims are cared for. But not now. Now he can think of nothing except making his daughter a widow."

Just then, Richard's other uncle, William de Warenne, Earl of Surrey, appeared in the doorway behind them. "John wants you both," he said. "He's just learned that Llewelyn ab Iorwerth and the French King have entered into a treaty of alliance."

Richard and Will exchanged looks of dismay, for they both knew that had always been John's greatest fear, that his enemies should unite against him, that he should find himself fighting a war on two fronts.

John was striding up and down before the open hearth, clutching a crumpled parchment. He thrust it at Will, saying, "Read for yourself, see what that Welsh whoreson has dared to do!"

Richard, reading over Will's shoulder, saw that it was a letter from Llewelyn to Philip, one that spoke of a treaty "between the kingdom of the French and the principality of North Wales," that promised Llewelyn would be a friend to Philip's friends and an enemy to his enemies.

"How did you get this, John?" Will asked, and John gestured impatiently.

"How do you think? I've paid informants at the French court."

Snatching the letter back, he scanned it rapidly. "Listen to this. '. . . by God's grace, I and all the Princes of Wales unanimously leagued together have manfully resisted our—and your—enemies, and with God's help we have by force of arms recovered from the yoke of their tyranny a large part of the land and the strongly defended castles which they by fraud and deceit had occupied, and having recovered them, we hold them strongly in the might of the Lord.'"

The more John read, the angrier he became. "God rot his wretched soul for this," he spat. "But if he thinks Philip is going to save his skin, he's in for a bitter shock. What was it they said of the Romans, Will, that they made a desert and called it peace? That will be Wales, too, by Christ it will, and Llewelyn ab Iorwerth will go to his grave knowing that he brought destruction upon his people, he and he alone. Let him look out over the burning crops and smoldering woodlands, let him count the bodies and then say it was worth the price!"

He swung about, beckoned to the nearest man. "I want a gallows built in the bailey, and then I want to see Llewelyn's Welsh hostages hanging from it, each and every one. Maelgwn's, too. See to it . . . now."

His fury had dulled his perception, and it was several moments before he became aware of the utter silence. He turned, found they were all staring at him.

"My liege." The Earl of Chester stepped forward, said quietly, "My liege, I would advise against that. I do not deny Llewelyn has given you cause. But if you kill the hostages, your war will become a blood feud. You'll find yourself fighting the Welsh for the next twenty years." He lowered his voice still further, said, "Even more to the point, how are your own lords likely to react? If you hang these Welsh hostages, what do you think will happen the next time you ask a man to yield up his son? He might well prefer rebellion."

"Or do exactly what he's told, knowing now what will be at stake."

Chester was first and foremost a realist. He'd done what he could to dissuade John from committing an act that he saw as neither morally justifiable nor politically expedient. Having failed, his concern now was to dissociate himself from the killing to come, and he was quite willing to defer to the Earl of Pembroke.

If Chester's objections had been coolly rational, dispassionate, Pembroke's plea was unashamedly emotional. "My lord, listen

to me. When I was a little lad, my lord father rose up in rebellion
against King Stephen. My father had given me as a hostage, and
the King warned him that I'd be hanged if he failed to keep faith.
My father sent back word that he had the hammer and anvil with
which to forge other sons, and I was taken out to be hanged. I
was but six and I did not understand. I thought it was all a game,
and I laughed even as they put the noose about my neck. King
Stephen watched, and was moved to mercy. He stopped the
hanging, with his own hands removed the rope.''

He paused, but John said nothing. If he was moved, like
Stephen, by pity, it did not show in his face. Pembroke walked
toward him, said, ''Some of those Welsh hostages are just lads,
have not yet reached manhood. My lord, I ask you not to do this.
Do not take your vengeance upon the innocent.''

''You'd do better to tell that to Llewelyn ab Iorwerth,'' John
said coldly. ''He's the one who chose to gamble with the innocent, not I. If his son's life means so little to him, why should it
mean more to me? No, my lord Pembroke, he set the stakes for
this wager. I'm merely collecting what's due me.''

Will had been listening in appalled silence. He'd known this
war would be a brutal one, but the cold-blooded killing of
helpless hostages, many of them youngsters, far exceeded his
worst expectations.

''John, I beg you . . .''

''Do not, Will. Do not.''

Their eyes locked, held until Will could bear it no longer, had
to look away. ''At least,'' he mumbled, knowing how ineffectual
his protest was and despising himself for it, ''at least spare
Llewelyn's son . . . for Joanna's sake. If you murder the boy,
Llewelyn will be bound to blame her. Do not do that to her, John.''

''It matters little whether Llewelyn blames her or not. He'll be
dead ere the summer is out.''

Richard waited to see if Will would argue further. When Will
did not, shoulders slumping in demoralized defeat, eyes averted
from that which he'd fought a lifetime against acknowledging,
Richard realized that Will's moment of truth was his, too. His
every instinct told him to keep silent, to distance himself as he'd
always done, even as he moved toward his father.

''I think it could work to your advantage to spare Gruffydd,
Papa,'' he said softly. ''Llewelyn would be half crazed with fear
for the boy. You could make use of that fear, hold it over his
head like the sword of Damocles. To have leverage like that over
an enemy . . .''

He saw John's eyes narrow and he dared to hope he'd hit upon the one argument that might stay his father's hand.

"There is much in what you say, Richard," John conceded, "and I'd agree with you—but for one thing. Llewelyn ab Iorwerth is a dead man, and there is no need to seek leverage over the dead."

John glanced about the hall, saw that no one else meant to speak. "I want it done this forenoon," he said. "The sooner they die, the sooner word of their deaths will reach Llewelyn."

The first one to suffer from Llewelyn's rebellion had been his son. Gruffydd's status had been changed overnight from that of highborn hostage to prisoner of state. As yet, he was not being abused, and his confinement was in castle chambers, not the dark, airless dungeons that filled him with such fear. But his days and nights were passed under guard, and he was finding it harder and harder to keep at bay his most persistent enemies: boredom and loneliness.

Soon after their arrival at Nottingham, he had been escorted to the uppermost chamber in the Black Tower, and then left alone. The room was sparsely furnished, containing only a bed, trestle table, bench, and chamber pot. He wandered about rather aimlessly for several moments, indulging in the fantasy that occupied most of his waking hours, thoughts of escape. A pity the window was not large enough to squeeze through; mayhap he could have knotted the bedsheets, lowered himself down into the bailey once dark came. He never passed a church now without thinking of sanctuary, never picked up an eating knife without evaluating it as a weapon.

His meal had already been laid out for him; there was a glazed clay flagon brimming with ale, a round, flat loaf of bread marked with a cross, a chunk of goat's cheese, and a baked pigeon pie. Gruffydd would have liked to believe that his friends were eating as well as he, but he had no way of knowing. In these six weeks of his captivity, his isolation had been complete.

He was reaching for the clay flagon when the door opened. At sight of the three men, Gruffydd stiffened. It may have been the way they moved toward him, hands on sword hilts, saying nothing. It may have been the rope coiled from one man's belt. Or it may have been a more subtle indicator, an inborn sense of sudden danger. Gruffydd did not pause to puzzle it out; his reaction was as instinctive as it was immediate. He got to his feet, and as the first guard approached the table, he swung the flagon in a wide, deadly arc. It shattered against the man's face; he screamed and staggered backward.

They had not been expecting resistance, and that gave Gruffydd a momentary advantage. He overturned the table onto the second man, dived for the doorway. Had the third guard been slightly slower in his reflexes, he would have made it. But the man was cat-quick; slamming the door, he flung himself at Gruffydd.

He at once regretted it, for he could match neither Gruffydd's strength nor his desperation, and he found himself in a savage, no-holds-barred brawl in which he was getting much the worst of it. Unable to unsheath his sword, he soon stopped trying to keep Gruffydd from reaching the door and concerned himself only with keeping Gruffydd from killing him.

After what seemed a lifetime to him, his comrade untangled himself from the wreckage of the table, came to his aid. Even then, it took the two of them to subdue Gruffydd, and the struggle ended only when one managed to draw his sword, put the blade against Gruffydd's throat, and snarl, "Give me an excuse, go on, just blink!"

They forced Gruffydd to kneel, jerked his arms behind his back, began to bind his wrists tightly together, cuffing him about the head and shoulders when he resisted.

The third man had taken no part in the fight, was slumped, moaning, against the wall. But now he stumbled to his feet, and his companions swore in startled sympathy. His face was already swelling rapidly, bloated and bloodied, his mouth so distorted and puffy that it resembled nothing so much as the grotesque grimace of a scarecrow. He bent over, spat into his hand, stared incredulously at a bloody tooth. With that, he lurched toward Gruffydd.

For a moment he stood over the boy, looking down at him. And then he grabbed Gruffydd's tunic collar, struck him across the face. "You hear that hammering in the bailey? They're building a gallows for you and the other hostages. The King wants the lot of you to hang ere he dines. And you, you misbegotten Welsh bastard, you shall be the very first to die, I'll see to that!"

"No, my lord Salisbury said we're to wait with this one, that he's to be last."

The man swore, discovered another loose tooth, and hit Gruffydd again, this time in the stomach. "Mayhap that is even better. This way he'll have time to think on it, to imagine how that rope'll feel about his neck, how it'll feel to be choking for air, and not getting any!"

Gruffydd could not breathe; each breath was more constricted, more labored than the last. It was partly the blow he'd just taken, but mainly it was panic. Not only was hanging a dishonorable, shameful way to die, but it was, he knew, also a particularly painful death. Only if a man was hanged from horseback did the fall break his neck; otherwise he slowly strangled.

Never had Gruffydd known fear like this, terror made all the more intense by his utter helplessness. He strained against his bonds, tried frantically to free himself, while the men watched and laughed at his futile efforts. Out in the bailey, the hammering continued.

John stood at the window of the great hall, watching as the Welsh hostages were hanged. Some tried to fight, had to be dragged cursing and kicking up onto the gallows. Others, especially the younger ones, were too stunned to offer resistance. A few wept, a few pleaded. Richard had seen executions before, and had not thought he was particularly squeamish. But this had been too much for him; he'd turned away, unable to watch.

The hangings were still going on when dinner was served. The cooks had prepared one of John's favorite dishes, stewed lamprey eels in saffron sauce. It was a favorite of Richard's, too, but he found he could not swallow more than a mouthful. Some of the hostages being hanged were no older than the young pages serving the lamprey and roast peacock. He laid his knife down, did not pick it up again.

The pages were bringing in the subtlety, a spun-sugar creation sculptured to resemble a flame-breathing dragon. On their heels came the marshal of the hall. Kneeling before John, he said nervously, "I thought it best not to wait till the meal's end, Your Grace. A courier has just ridden in from Wales, bearing an urgent message from your daughter, the Princess Joanna. Shall I send him in?"

John nodded, and a moment later a young Welshman stumbled into the hall. He was unshaven, his clothing stained with sweat and the dust of the road, and at first Richard thought he was drunk; his eyes were glazed, slid blankly past John without seeing. But then he saw how the man's gaze kept coming back to the window, and he understood. Not drunk, in shock.

When prompted by the marshal, the Welshman knelt, held out a folded parchment. "My lady entrusted me with this. She said . . ." He swallowed, tried to remember, to blot out for a moment what was happening in the bailey. "She said I must give it into your hands and yours alone, that none but you must read it . . ."

John reached for the letter, made sure that the seal was indeed Joanna's and had not been tampered with. Only then did he break it open, begin to read. When he glanced up, he had paled noticeably.

"Someone give this man a shilling for his trouble. My lords of Chester and Pembroke, you stay. Will and Richard, you stay, too. The rest of you, out . . . now."

Men set down their wine cups, stared at him in astonishment, mouths full of unchewed food. But after taking one look at his face, they pushed resentfully away from the tables.

Within moments the hall was cleared. John rose, but he was suddenly reluctant to share the contents of Joanna's letter. He hesitated, and then said abruptly, "Joanna has written me that some of my own lords are plotting with Llewelyn and the other Welsh Princes. She says that they mean to rebel once we're in Wales, either to kill me or to turn me over to the Welsh."

As he spoke, his eyes moved intently from face to face, assessing the impact of his words. He did not truly suspect Chester or Pembroke, but he was relieved, nonetheless, to see that their surprise was unfeigned. At least these two could be eliminated as suspects. But that still left so many, half his court. How could he trust anyone? How could he ever be sure, ever be safe?

"John, what mean you to do?"

"I do not know, Will," John admitted. "I need time, time to think." He began to pace. "Christ, it could be any of them. De Vesci has always been a malcontent. De Clare never wanted me to be King; he thinks I've forgotten that, but I have not. Derby is de Braose's blood kin, and Huntingdon—"

The Earls of Huntingdon and Derby were Chester's brothers-in-law, and he interrupted hastily, "My liege, this serves for naught. We need more than suspicions. First of all, we must look to your safety. Thank Jesus for your daughter's warning."

John nodded. "My God," he said softly, "I'd have walked blindly into their trap. If not for Joanna . . ."

"She saved your life, Papa," Richard said, and again John nodded.

"Yes, lad, I think she did."

"Then give her a life in return, Papa—her stepson's life."

John frowned. "Joanna has reason to want Gruffydd dead," he said impatiently. "Good reason."

"But she does not want him to die, Papa. I know, for she asked me to protect him if I could."

John turned to stare at his son; his surprise was genuine. "You truly think she'd want me to spare him?"

"Yes, Papa, she would."

"I cannot for the life of me understand why! I do owe Joanna a debt, but . . ." He fell silent, began to reread his daughter's letter. He was remembering Llewelyn's surrender at Aberconwy, envisioning himself in Llewelyn's place, delivered into Llewelyn's hands by his own barons. It was a thought to make him flinch. Richard's words came back to him now: "To have leverage like that over an enemy . . ."

"Has Maelgwn's son been hanged yet?" he asked unexpectedly, and Richard gave a baffled nod.

"I think so, Papa. Why?"

"I was just wondering how the other Welsh Princes would react, if their sons were hanged and Llewelyn's alone was spared. I'd like to see him try to explain that to Maelgwn, in truth I would!" John said and laughed grimly. "Very well, Richard. Mayhap you're right, mayhap there's more to be gained by keeping the whelp alive. Tell the hangman this one fish is off the hook. For now."

"Blood of Christ!" Richard stood motionless in the doorway, shocked at sight of Gruffydd. The boy's face was covered with welts and bruises; one eye was swollen shut; dried blood had encrusted a gash across his forehead, matted his hair. He shrank back as the door opened, struggled to sit upright.

Richard had once come across a snared wildcat, crouched to earth, spitting fear and defiance as the huntsman moved in for the kill. He saw that same terrified rage now on Gruffydd's face, knew it would be a memory to trouble his sleep in nights to come. He had ever prided himself upon his analytical turn of mind. But however neglected his imagination was in consequence, he did not need to be told what the past three hours must have been like for Gruffydd, listening as his comrades were dragged to their deaths, expecting at any moment his own summons to the gallows, and he said furiously, "Who told you whoresons to maltreat him like this? And why is he gagged?"

"We had to, lord. It was the only way to shut him up. He got right abusive. As for his hurts"—the man pointed to his own blackened eye—"in truth, he gave as good as he got."

"Hand me a flask," Richard demanded, and he knelt by

Gruffydd, removed the rag they'd stuffed into his mouth. "Here," he said, "drink."

Gruffydd did, swallowing in gulps as if he could never get enough. At last he took one final mouthful, raised up and spat it into Richard's face.

Richard recoiled, and then raised his arm, slowly and deliberately wiped his face on his sleeve. "I came to tell you," he said, "that you will not be hanged."

Gruffydd did not react like one reprieved. His lips were drawn back from his teeth, and his unswollen eye blazed with such feverish hatred that Richard realized further conversation would be pointless. There was nothing he could say that Gruffydd would believe, and he sighed, reached for his dagger.

Gruffydd gasped, tried to squirm out of range. Richard had no liking for Gruffydd, but at that moment he found himself pitying Llewelyn's son as he'd never pitied anyone before. "I'll not hurt you, Gruffydd. I mean only to cut your bonds."

Leaning over, he slashed at the ropes binding the boy's wrists, and then hastily backed away. "I'll see that you're given balm for your bruises . . . and some wine."

Gruffydd made no response, and Richard beckoned to the guards, moved to the door. "I do not expect you to believe me," he said slowly, "but you'll not be harmed." Knowing that he lied, that Gruffydd had already suffered harm beyond healing.

Gruffydd did not move, did not reply, and Richard lingered a moment longer, then closed the door quietly behind him. At that, Gruffydd scrambled to his feet, grabbed for the tableboards, and tried to barricade the door. But it was a futile effort and he knew it. He slumped down on the bed, massaged the rope burns on his wrists, and listened for returning footsteps.

It was a long time before he let himself believe that Richard had not lied, that they would not be coming back for him. It was even longer before he could nerve himself to stand up, to walk to the window.

Below him the bailey was drenched in hot summer sun. A breeze had sprung up from the east, and the bodies swinging from the gallows were swaying gently back and forth. Gruffydd stood motionless, stared down at the slowly twisting bodies until the gallows blurred in a haze of hot tears.

John moved over to a table, selected a morsel of meat, and tossed it to one of the castle dogs. He and his son were alone in the hall; he had not even allowed the servants in to clean up, and the tables still gave cluttered testimony to their interrupted meal. He threw the dog another tidbit, said, "You might as well be the first to know. I'm calling off the Welsh campaign . . . at least for now. I cannot risk going into Wales until I'm sure I'd not be betrayed."

"I think that's most wise, Papa." Ah, Joanna, you truly did it, lass. You won a war. But not a victory the Welsh will ever want to celebrate. Richard glanced over his shoulder, toward the bailey. Jesú, no.

A glimmer of silver caught Richard's eye. Bending down, he scooped up a handful of pennies, for a moment studied them in puzzlement. And then he understood. This was the money John had ordered given to Joanna's messenger. He fingered the coins and then let them drop, one by one, back into the floor rushes.

"Since you mean to delay the Welsh invasion, you will not have any need of me for a while, then?"

"Mayhap not. Why?"

"Conisbrough Castle is but a day's hard ride from Nottingham. I should like to visit with my lady mother. Have I your permission to leave the court?"

"I see." John subjected his son to a thoughtful, probing scrutiny. At last he said, with obvious reluctance, "If that be your wish."

Until that moment Richard had not admitted to himself just how much he wanted to get away. "Thank you, Papa," he said, adding as casually as he could, "It'll not be dark till well past nine. I think I'll make use of the hours of daylight remaining, and leave now."

John merely nodded. But as Richard reached the door, he said suddenly, "Richard . . . you do mean to come back?"

Richard's hand tightened on the door latch. "Yes, Papa, of course I do." Wondering if he had a choice. Wondering, too, if he truly wanted one.

John moved to the window, watched Richard cross the bailey. He did not like this request of Richard's, not at all, but something in his son's face had warned him not to refuse. Not once had Richard met his eyes, not once.

Mayhap he should have tried to explain, to make Richard see why it had to be done. But why was it not obvious to Richard? Of what earthly value were hostages unless men knew they'd be sacrificed if need be? Now when he demanded hostages from Huntingdon and de Clare, from all those he suspected, they'd take great care to please him, to stay loyal. They'd learn from Llewelyn's fatal mistake.

He glanced over at the gallows. A moment later he was at the door, shouting for a messenger. He had not long to wait; he'd never been obeyed with such haste as he was in these hours after the hangings.

"I have a message for you to deliver, one of great urgency. You're to leave now for Wales."

The courier paled, guessing what was coming. "Wales, my liege? Llewelyn ab Iorwerth?"

John was indifferent to the man's alarm. "Yes. I want you to tell him of the hangings. I want him to know that his hostages are dead."

31

DOLWYDDELAN, NORTH WALES

August 1212

Joanna had moved a stool close to the bed, and for more than an hour she watched Llewelyn as he slept. His was the sleep of utter exhaustion; he'd not stirred for the past three hours, not even when Joanna removed his boots. The longer he slept, the more difficult it was for her to keep still. The urge to awaken him was becoming all but overwhelming, for they'd been apart for more than a fortnight, and never had her need to talk to him been so urgent.

But she dreaded it, too. What if she could not make him understand? In warning her father of the conspiracy against him, she'd been thinking of Llewelyn's safety as much as John's. Hers had not been an act of impulse. It was born of despair and fear and an anguish of spirit that only one who'd faced her choices could ever understand. If she did nothing, there was a very real possibility that her father might be walking into a lethal trap. Yet if she warned him of the danger, she might be taking from Llewelyn his only edge, the advantage that might spare his life, his realm. For she knew that if her father won this war, Llewelyn would die.

In the end, she'd sent the most trusted of her servants to John, because she could not do otherwise, because she loved her father, because there was a chance that her warning might stop a war. But now she had to tell Llewelyn what she'd done, and she was not at all sure he would forgive her.

Llewelyn's lashes flickered, and she leaned over, kissed him on the mouth. He opened his eyes, smiled at her. But then he glanced down, saw how shadows were chasing sunlight across the floor rushes.

"Why did you not awaken me ere this, Joanna?"

As he sat up, she slid her arms around his waist. "Do not get up, not yet."

There was nothing either of playfulness or seduction in her voice; she sounded so plaintive that he turned, held her close for a moment.

"I do not understand it, Joanna. I know John gave the command to gather at Chester on the nineteenth. Three full days ago. Yet my scouts report no movement on the roads, nothing." He had his boots on by now, and as he rose to his feet, Joanna's hand tightened convulsively on his arm. He gave her a quizzical look, and her fingers unclenched; she let him go.

He picked up his sword and scabbard, buckled it at his hip. "Did I tell you the latest word from the south? Rhys Gryg has taken and burned Swansea."

"Does it matter, Llewelyn? My father is not leading his army against Rhys Gryg or Maelgwn. It is Gwynedd he means to invade. It is you he means to destroy."

He glanced toward her, but said nothing. She knew she should have kept silent. That was not what he wanted to hear. He truly believed this was a war he could win. He had to believe that. She would to God she could believe it, too.

Llewelyn had reached the door. But something in Joanna's face made him pause, come back to her. "I know how you're hurting," he said, and Joanna put her arms around his neck, clung tightly. She'd rarely seen him look so tired; his dark eyes were bloodshot, swollen from lack of sleep, and his skin was rough and scratchy against her throat. She did not mind, but Llewelyn rubbed his chin, said ruefully, "I expect you'll want me to shave ere we go to bed tonight?"

"That depends upon what you do have in mind," she said, and he grinned.

"After a fortnight apart, need you even ask?"

Joanna managed an answering smile, but it was as strained as her banter. Mayhap she should wait, not tell him until after they made love. But the longer she delayed, the harder it would get. And if he ever found out from someone else . . . That thought was frightening enough to give her courage, and she said abruptly, "Llewelyn, we must talk."

"It will have to wait till night, *breila*. I've lost too many hours of daylight as it is."

Joanna did not argue; a delay not of her own making was a reprieve she could accept in good conscience. "Tonight, then," she agreed. "You still have not told me how long you'll be at Dolwyddelan."

"That will depend upon John," he said, and opened the door just as Ednyved came through the porch entranceway.

"Llewelyn, an Englishman has ridden in with a flag of truce and a right strange story. He says he has a message of urgency for you, that it comes from John."

"A royal courier?"

"No, that is what be so strange about it. He is not a courier at all, is a blacksmith from Shrewsbury. He claims he met John's courier in a Shrewsbury alehouse, that the man paid him to deliver John's message. Moreover, he insists upon telling his tale to you and only you. Do you want me to send him away?"

"No. Either he is telling the truth or he is willing to risk his life for a preposterous lie. Whichever it is, I want to know."

Ednyved nodded. "I rather thought you would. He is waiting below."

The man looked to be Llewelyn's age, in his late thirties, with the callused hands and heavily muscled forearms that were the inevitable badges of his trade. What was most distinctive about him was his extreme nervousness. He knelt, and when Llewelyn gestured for him to rise, he shifted awkwardly from foot to foot, darting sidelong glances from under lashes matted with dust and sweat, and then blurted out, "I thank you for seeing me, my lord. Men call me Ralph the Smith, for I've a smithy in Shrewsbury, not far from the church of St Alkmund."

The information appeared gratuitous, but was not; Llewelyn understood that the man was seeking to establish his credibility, showing that he was, as a man of property, one deserving of belief. "I understand you have a message for me?"

"My lord, I must ask you to bear with me, let me tell it my way. I fear you'll not believe me unless I explain how I happened to come by what I know. This past Saturday I'd stopped in a riverside tavern for a few tankards of ale. There was a stranger there . . . half drunk, a talker. He said he was King John's courier, and indeed he was wearing the King's livery. He was telling anyone who'd listen that the King had entrusted him with a message for you, a message he was loath to deliver. He was offering two pence to the man who'd take it for him, half now, half afterward. That was a day's wages, and I was not the only one who took an interest. But . . . but when he told us what the message was . . ." He paused, for the first time looked Llewelyn full in the face.

"It was not just the money, my lord. Not after I heard the message. You see, my first wife . . . she was of your blood. I am telling you this because . . . because I want you to understand. It seemed to me that you had a right to know. I kept thinking of my own boy . . ." His eyes were small and close-set, all but obscured by thick, shaggy brows, eyes brimming over with so much pity that Llewelyn's breath stopped.

"For Christ's sake, man, what do you have to tell me? Just say it!"

"Your son, my lord—he's dead. All the hostages are dead. King John hanged them last Tuesday at Nottingham Castle."

For a merciful moment, the words had no meaning for Llewelyn. But then his numbed brain absorbed the full impact of what he'd just been told. Gruffydd was dead. They were all dead. He'd given them up to John, and John had murdered them.

He turned away, without purpose or direction, stumbled against the table. The trestle boards tilted, spilled over onto the floor. He stared down at the wreckage, at the shattered flagon, and then picked up one of the broken clay shards. It was sharp-edged, sticky with wine, beyond mending. He tightened his fingers around it, squeezing until Joanna's hand closed over his own.

"My love, you'll cut yourself," she pleaded, and he opened his fist, let the shard drop back into the floor rushes.

"He died because of me. They all did."

"No, Llewelyn, that's not so!"

"Gruffydd was sixteen," he said, as if she'd not spoken at all. "Some of them were even younger. Twelve, thirteen. I thought . . . thought their youth would protect them, that John would be less likely to maltreat youngsters—" His voice thickened, broke. He pulled away from Joanna, walked rapidly from the chamber.

"Llewelyn, wait!" But when Joanna would have followed after him, Ednyved stepped in front of her, blocking her way.

"Let him go, Joanna. You are the last one who can help him now."

"I'm his wife!"

"You are also John's daughter."

Joanna took a step backward, stared at him. "I see. So you believe it, too. Well, it is not true, Ednyved. It is not true!"

Ednyved said nothing, but she saw his disbelief, and her eyes narrowed. "There is no evidence to support this man's story, none whatsoever. Have you not learned by now not to accept alehouse babble as gospel? You need only think upon the wild rumors that have been circulating all summer long. First we heard that the royal treasury at Gloucester had been plundered. But that turned out to be false, did it not? And then we got word that my father's Queen had been abducted and raped, their baby son killed. But that was not true, either. It was no more than vicious gossip, tales spread by men with nothing better to do than give grief to the unwary.'' She drew a bracing breath, said, ''And this ugly accusation is no different, Ednyved. This is no less a lie.''

''I know there has never been a true friendship between us, Joanna. But believe me now, that I am speaking as a friend. For your sake as well as Llewelyn's, leave him be.''

''Leave him be?'' she echoed incredulously. ''My husband thinks that his son is dead, and it's not true. I will not stand helplessly by whilst he breaks his heart over a lie, I will not! Now please move away from the door.''

He did. ''I hope you will remember,'' he said, ''that I did try to stop you.''

It was unnaturally still. The birds had muted their songs at Llewelyn's approach, and he heard only the sound of his boots on the wet gravel of the riverbank. It had been a dry summer, and the river was shallow and slow-moving; mossy rocks jutted up toward the sun, seeming to offer a safe passage to the far shore for those willing to take the risk. How many youths had stood on this bank, gathering up their courage to put those beckoning stepping stones to the slippery test? For risk-taking was the measure of a man. Had he not taught Gruffydd that from birth?

Llewelyn knelt, cupped his hands, and splashed river water onto his face. Yes, he'd taught Gruffydd about risk-taking and manhood and pride. But he'd not taught him how to die on an English gallows. Gruffydd would have fought them, knowing no other way, would have spat defiance until the rope choked off all breath. Llewelyn could hear his own breathing grow ragged; it was coming in harsh, uneven gasps, filling the quiet woodland clearing with strangled sound.

For a time he knelt motionless on the riverbank, and there burned behind his closed eyelids a gallows laden with bodies, bodies left to rot in the summer sun, because he had been a risk-taker.

His instincts for self-preservation had long since become second nature to him; when a branch snapped underfoot, his head jerked up. The sound came again. Someone was following the trail he'd taken from the castle. He rose swiftly, hand on sword hilt. A moment later a large black alaunt broke through the underbrush, bounded joyfully toward him.

At sight of the dog, Llewelyn's eyes filled with tears. Math was his son's dog, had been Gruffydd's veritable shadow, and when Gruffydd went away, the big dog's grieving had been heartrending. When he'd begun to refuse food, Llewelyn had taken over the dog's feeding, slowly coaxed the alaunt back to health, and in the past year, Math was never willingly far from his side.

Llewelyn bent down, gathered the dog to him. Math began to bark, swiped at his face with a rough, wet tongue, and he pulled back. Only then did he see his wife standing at the edge of the clearing.

Llewelyn was the first to speak. "Go back to the castle, Joanna. This is not the time to talk."

There was no emotion in his voice; he sounded like a stranger. Joanna hesitated, and then stepped toward him. "Llewelyn . . ."

"Not now," he said, much more sharply this time. He turned away, began to walk along the riverbank.

"Llewelyn, wait!" Hastening after him, she found she could not match his pace, and caught his arm, forcing him to stop.

"My love, you must listen to me. This one time you must believe me. Your grieving is for naught. Gruffydd is not dead."

"Joanna, no!" But she clung to his arm with surprising strength; he could not free himself without hurting her.

"You must hear me out, Llewelyn. Please, beloved, please listen. My father is not a good man. Mayhap not even a kind one. But he would never murder Gruffydd and the other hostages. He is not capable of a cruelty like that, Llewelyn. I know he's not, know—"

"No, you do not know! You've never known John, never!" Llewelyn jerked free, saying bitterly, "But I did. I knew how vicious he could be when cornered, how merciless, for I knew what he'd done to Maude de Braose. I knew all too well, and yet, God forgive me, I still turned my son over to him—" He broke off abruptly, turned to stare blindly out at the sun-glazed water.

" 'What he'd done to Maude de Braose.' What do you mean by that, Llewelyn?" Raising her hand to her forehead, Joanna found it damp with sweat. She was suddenly aware of the hot, humid air, utterly still, as all-enveloping as a shroud; the sun had begun to hurt her eyes. "What do you mean?" she repeated.

"Your stepfather told me Maude de Braose died in prison. Are you saying he lied?"

Llewelyn swung back to face her. "Maude did die in prison. What Hugh did not tell you was how she died." He paused and then said, "All right, then, the truth. Mayhap I should have told you long ago. John had Maude de Braose and her son cast into a dungeon at Windsor Castle, and then he starved them to death."

He'd never seen anyone lose color so quickly. Joanna's face was so ashen, her eyes so wide and unseeing that he took an instinctive step toward her, put his hand on her arm. But then she raised her chin, swallowed, and said, "I do not believe you."

His hand dropped to his side. "Christ Jesus, Joanna, do you truly think I'd lie to you about that?"

He did not wait for her answer, turned and walked away. Like most huntsmen, he knew how to make the woods his own, left no trace of his passing. Math had vanished, too. Joanna stood alone in the clearing.

Within his chamber, Llewelyn found Ednyved and Morgan awaiting his return. They rose as he entered; he was grateful when neither offered expressions of sympathy or commiseration.

"I must have been gone several hours. Has there been any further word from our scouts?"

"Nothing. More and more, it looks as if John means to delay the invasion, Llewelyn."

Ednyved was holding out a large goblet. Llewelyn caught the strong odor of fermented honey, and shook his head. "No mead. Not yet." After some moments of silence, he said, "On the morrow I must begin telling the parents of the hostages that their sons are dead. It would mean much to me, Ednyved, if you were with me."

Ednyved drew a sudden, sharp breath. "Ah, Llewelyn . . ." He coughed unconvincingly, and then said brusquely, "You do not have to do that. I'll take care of it for you."

Their eyes met, held. Llewelyn slowly shook his head. "No, Ednyved, I *do* have to do that," he said, and the other man nodded.

"I've sent for Rhys and Catrin." He hesitated. "Did Joanna find you?"

"Yes," Llewelyn said, "she did." He sank down in the closest chair, began to fondle Math's thick sable fur. The dog had been swimming in the river, and his legs were caked with dried mud, his tail matted with burrs. Llewelyn found himself remembering how Gruffydd would groom the alaunt by the hour, wielding his brush until Math's coat shone like ebony. "Morgan . . . fetch my daughters."

"Would you rather I told them, Llewelyn?"

"No. This, too, I have to do." Llewelyn glanced up at the priest. "It was in this same chamber that I had to tell Gruffydd his mother was dead. He was just five."

Morgan's throat constricted. "I know there are times, lad, when God's ways must seem—"

"No, not God, Morgan . . . John." No more than that, but on his lips a common Christian name became an unspeakable obscenity, became a vow of vengeance rooted not in reason, but in blood.

As Morgan opened the door, they heard footsteps on the outer stairs. Llewelyn stiffened at the sound. It was a shock to realize that the person he most loved was suddenly the person he least wanted to see.

But it was not his wife who entered; it was his fourteen-year-old daughter. Gwladys was panting so, she could hardly speak. She stumbled into the chamber, clutched at a chair for support.

"Papa . . . there's an Englishman in the great hall. I overheard him saying . . . saying that . . . Papa, it's not true? Gruffydd, he's not dead?" Her eyes searched Llewelyn's face. "No . . . no, Papa, no!"

Llewelyn reached her as she began to scream, caught her to him and held her as she wept. But he had no comfort for her, no more than on the morrow, when he would have to face the parents of the other murdered boys.

"Madame, thank God Almighty! I've been so uneasy. Where were you?"

"Where?" Joanna gestured vaguely. "I think . . . down there. By the river."

"Madame . . . are you all right?"

Joanna nodded, not convincing Branwen in the least. Her shyness notwithstanding, Branwen could be very stubborn. "Are you sure, Madame? In truth, you look ill." But Joanna seemed not to hear. She was turning away as Catherine and Rhys rode through the gateway into the bailey.

Catherine did not wait for her husband's assistance. Sliding from the saddle, she ran toward Joanna, disregarded protocol, and embraced her as a sister.

"Joanna, what can I say?" Catherine's fair skin was splotched, the blue eyes reddened and puffy. "I still cannot believe it. Where is Llewelyn?"

Joanna was reluctant to admit she did not know, and she was grateful when Branwen said, "He is in his chamber, Lady Catrin."

By now Rhys had reached them. Tragedy had not made him any the less taciturn; he greeted Joanna with his usual economy, moved toward the stairs. Catherine started to follow and then stopped, looked back over her shoulder.

"Joanna, are you not coming?" And when Joanna shook her head, she hastily retraced her steps. "Dearest, I do not understand. If ever Llewelyn needed you, it is now."

"He . . . he does not want me there, Catherine."

The other woman stared at her. "Joanna, what are you saying?"

"He believes it, Catherine, truly believes my father hanged Gruffydd and the other hostages. I could not bear to see him hurting so, and I tried to tell him, to make him see it was not true. But then he told me . . . he told me, Catherine, that my father starved Maude de Braose to death."

She saw first horror on Catherine's face, and then pity, and she said tautly, "You need not look at me like that, Catherine. It is not true."

"Joanna . . . Joanna, I know naught of politics. If you say it is not true, I want to believe you. But would Llewelyn lie?"

Joanna shook her head wearily. "He is not lying, Catherine. He believes it to be true. I know it is not, but I cannot convince him of that." Tears were spilling down her face. She made no attempt to wipe them away.

Joanna awoke with a gasp, did not at once remember where she was. She sat up, feeling queasy and disoriented. Beside her, Davydd and Elen slept soundly; in the other bed, Catherine lay between Joanna's stepdaughters, Marared and Gwenllian. Joanna rose quietly from the bed, stood looking down at Catherine. Catherine's coming had been a godsend; she'd been remarkably successful in consoling Gruffydd's sisters. Joanna had ached for the bewildered children, but she knew she'd been of little help to them. In the past twelve hours her sense of reality had become hopelessly distorted; she felt as if her emotions were somehow sealed off, under glass and beyond reach.

She did not remember the dream that had so frightened her, was thankful she did not. Moving to the table, she poured herself some wine, noting with odd detachment that her hands were shaking. She wore several rings; without stopping to think what she did, she slipped one from her finger, laid it upon the table. It was topaz and silver, a long-ago gift from her father. She stared down at it, telling herself that her gesture had no significance. She did not believe Llewelyn. She could not.

Elen stirred, whimpered in her sleep. Joanna stood by the bed until she was sure her child slept, and then she moved silently toward the nursery door. Outside, all was dark and still. The air was surprisingly cool against her skin. She crossed the bailey with quickening steps, gripped by the uneasy, irrational certainty that she was being watched, that the darkness was alive with hostile, unseen eyes.

Upon the table a candle was burning down toward the wick. Gwladys was curled up at the foot of the bed, having at last cried herself to sleep. Llewelyn was sprawled in a nearby chair, his head pillowed awkwardly upon his arm. There was an empty mead flagon on the table, another on the floor by his chair. From a shadowed corner, Math's eyes glowed like embers; his tail tipped slightly in acknowledgment of Joanna's right to be in the bedchamber, even at such an hour.

Joanna moved closer to Llewelyn, stood beside him for several moments. His face was in shadow. Only his mouth was touched by the candle light; it was tautly drawn even in sleep, communicated so much pain that Joanna began to cry again, silently, in utter despair. At last she dried her tears upon her sleeve, backed quietly toward the door.

When Joanna returned to her bedchamber, the sun was rising above the hooded silhouette of Moel Siabod, dispelling the dawn mists that overhung the valley like fallen clouds; already the day gave fair warning of what was to come, vagrant winds and sweltering heat. Gwladys was sitting on the bed, listlessly pulling a brush through her tangled dark hair. She looked up as Joanna entered, said tonelessly, "My father is not here. He has gone to see the families of the murdered hostages, to tell them that John hanged their sons."

Joanna was appalled, tried not to let Gwladys see it. Gwladys was the most passionate of Joanna's stepdaughters, the most like Gruffydd. It had been a slow and tentative endeavor, making a friend of this prideful, spirited girl, but Joanna had eventually coaxed from Gwladys what she'd never gotten from Gruffydd, acceptance. Her heart twisted with pity now at sight of the girl's grieving, and she said helplessly, "Gwladys, if only there was something I could do . . ."

"But there is." Gwladys flung back her hair; her eyes were as black as jet, and just as cold. "You can write to your father, Madame. You can ask him to return the bodies of those he murdered. Ask him to return my brother's body for decent burial."

Never had Joanna so wanted a day to end; never had one seemed so sure to drag on into infinity. She passed the hours as best she could, with her children, rising every ten minutes or so to stare out into the bailey. But by dusk, Llewelyn still had not returned.

"Joanna . . . do you want me to talk to Gwladys?"

Joanna gave Catherine a grateful look. She'd been badly shaken by her stepdaughter's hostility; that it was understandable did not make it less hurtful. "Thank you, Catherine, no. She is still too distraught. I can only wait till we get word from Nottingham, till it is proven that Gruffydd and the other hostages are safe and well. But Catherine, if it is not soon . . . Jesus wept, the suffering this evil rumor has caused!"

She rose, moved restlessly to the window. "Gwladys is not the only one blaming me, Catherine. I see it on other faces, too."

"I know," Catherine conceded. "But not all do feel that way, Joanna. Llewelyn's people know that John would never have agreed to a truce if not for your intercession. And what you did that day at Aberconwy, defying your father on Llewelyn's behalf, that won you more favor than you realize. There are many who do not blame you, Joanna, who are sorry for your pain."

"But I do not want that, either. I do not want them pitying me because they think my father is the . . . the Antichrist!"

Catherine did not know what to say to that. She watched in silent sympathy as Joanna turned from the window, began to pace.

"I find myself haunted by what Llewelyn said. I know it is not true, but I cannot stop thinking of it. It is such a vile accusation, Catherine; how can Llewelyn believe it? We are alone, and I can speak the truth with you. I think it very likely that my father did have Arthur put to death, as his enemies charge. Men do things in anger, give commands they might later regret. I think it happened that way with Arthur."

She stopped before Catherine. "But it would take hours to drag thirty hostages to the gallows, Catherine. There'd be time to relent. Even if my father had given such a command in a moment of rage, he'd not have carried it out. As for the other, what Llewelyn said about Maude de Braose, that could never be. Such a dreadful death as that would take days, even weeks . . ."

She shuddered, for she had the imagination to envision the full horrors of a death by starvation, Maude's slow realization that food would never be forthcoming, that none would heed her screams, that her dungeon was to be her tomb.

A silence fell. Joanna moved back to the window. Almost at once she tensed. "Llewelyn," she breathed, and suddenly she was very frightened.

Llewelyn had dismounted by the time Joanna reached the bottom of the keep stairs. She started toward him, then stopped at sight of Cristyn. Cristyn had ridden in that afternoon with Tegwared and Anghared, her seven-year-old twins, and her presence was just one more goad to Joanna's unraveling nerves. Even though she believed Llewelyn's physical intimacy with Cristyn was over, their continuing friendship occasionally gave her some uneasy moments; she would always be jealous of Cristyn, if only because the other woman had the power to make her remember what it was like to be fifteen, awkward and innocent and so desperate to please.

Cristyn was looking up intently into Llewelyn's face, her hand on his arm. Saying all the things I cannot, Joanna thought. Llewelyn put his arm around Cristyn; they stood for a moment in a quiet embrace. It was, Joanna knew, just what it looked to be, but she felt a pang nonetheless, found herself resenting Cristyn for being able to offer the comfort she could not.

Llewelyn had begun walking toward the great hall. He stopped when Joanna said his name, waited for her to reach him. She started to speak, but her words caught in her throat. His eyes were hollowed, his skin grey with fatigue; there was a bleak, bitter desolation in his face that went beyond grieving, that Joanna could not bear to look upon.

For a long moment, Llewelyn studied her face, searching for something he could not find. "You still do not believe me, do you?"

"Llewelyn, I . . . I cannot!"

"No," he said slowly, "I do not suppose you can. But to tell you the truth, Joanna, I do not know where that leaves us."

"Do not say that," she whispered. "You cannot mean that. Jesú, Llewelyn, we have to talk!"

"What would we say? I've just come from telling a man and his wife that their eleven-year-old son has been hanged, the son I took from them as a hostage. Do you truly think this is the time to defend John to me?"

"I'm not defending him, I'm not!" But he was no longer listening; he'd turned away.

Joanna stood as if rooted. She could feel eyes upon her, curious, gloating, pitying; they no longer mattered. At last she followed Llewelyn into the great hall, not knowing what else to do.

She paused uncertainly in the doorway. And then she saw the self-appointed courier, the Shrewsbury blacksmith.

"Why are you still here?"

He was flustered by her tone, and stammered, "The priest . . . he said your lord husband might have additional questions for me, said I should wait for him . . ."

"Wait for payment, you mean, wait for your blood money! Tell me, how much do you think my husband should give you? You've seen the grief you've brought upon us; what price do you put upon it?"

Joanna heard her voice rising, shrill, accusatory. Llewelyn was suddenly at her side, saying, "Joanna, that is enough."

"No, it is not! This man goes into a tavern, hears a drunken stranger babbling in his cups, and suddenly he becomes a man with a mission, suddenly he cannot rest until he's made sure that we've heard the latest alehouse gossip. Well, you've delivered your poisonous offering, you've had your moment of acclaim. But look around you and then tell me if it was worth it!"

"You're not being fair! It was more than gossip. I know the man spoke the truth."

"How could you possibly know that?" Joanna said, so scathingly that the man's face flushed a resentful shade of red.

He raised his chin, said defiantly, "The day the courier reached Shrewsbury, Robert de Vieuxpont hanged Prince Maelgwn's younger son. He was just a lad, not yet seven, and he died at the King's command. Why would I doubt, then, that the other hostages, too, were dead?"

The emotional upheavals of the past two days had left Llewelyn without the capacity to feel shock, outrage, to feel anything at all . . . or so he'd believed. "Are you saying John had a seven-year-old boy hanged?" he demanded incredulously, and the blacksmith nodded.

"I saw the boy's body with my own eyes, my lord."

Their voices were echoing strangely in Joanna's ears, growing faint and indistinct. The people, too, seemed to be receding, faces blurring, slightly out of focus. The scene before her had lost reality; she was in it but somehow no longer part of it. She turned, without haste, began to walk toward the door.

"Joanna!" Llewelyn caught up with her in two strides, but she did not stop until he put his hand on her arm. She looked up at him, her face so still and remote that he felt an inexplicable throb of fear. "Are you all right?" he said, very low.

"Yes." He'd shifted his hands to her shoulders; she had to resist the urge to pull away, not wanting to be held, to be touched. "I want to be by myself, Llewelyn. I just want to be alone for a while."

He hesitated, and then stepped back. "We'll talk later."

"Yes," Joanna agreed politely. "Later."

Joanna slid the bolt into place. Only then, with the world shut out, did she begin to tremble. Moving to the bed, hers and Llewelyn's, she lay back against the pillows. It came upon her without warning. Suddenly sweat broke out on her forehead, her face began to burn, and she was overcome by nausea. When it did not abate, she stumbled into the privy chamber. After some wretched moments, she vomited weakly into the privy hole.

She heard knocking on the door; Catherine called her name. Then it grew quiet again. After a time she was able to return to the bedchamber, where she washed her face, rinsed her mouth out with wine. But the more she tried to make sense of what she'd been told, the more agitated she became. Her thoughts took flight, too swiftly for coherence, ricocheting wildly off the outer parameters of belief. She sought desperately to seize upon fragments of fact, to patch them into an intelligible pattern, one that would enable her to understand. But the raw, graphic horror of the images filling her brain blotted out all else. A bewildered child being led up onto a gallows. A woman screaming alone in the dark.

A kaleidoscope of faces seemed to spin before her eyes. The florid, heavy face of the Shrewsbury blacksmith. Llewelyn's, lean and dark and terrifyingly aloof. John's, mouth quirking as if at some secret and very private joke. When she was little, their eyes would meet across a chamber, he'd wink, and she'd be flooded with happiness, reveling in the reassuring intimacy of their shared smiles. Had he smiled, too, as he gave the command to hang Maelgwn's son? He was just a lad, not yet seven. John had Maude de Braose and her son cast into a dungeon at Windsor Castle, and then he starved them to death. He hanged the hostages; they're dead . . . dead. She sank to her knees by the bed, but the voices would not stop. When she could endure them no longer, she fled the chamber.

Catherine was waiting out on the porch. "Ah, Joanna, I'm so sorry . . ."

"I want Llewelyn. Please, Catherine, bring him to me."

"I will, dearest," Catherine said swiftly, soothingly. "I will. But a man has just ridden in, and he . . . he was there, Joanna, at Nottingham the day the hostages were hanged. Llewelyn is with him now. I know he'll come to you as soon as he can."

"No!" Joanna shook her head vehemently. "No, I cannot wait!" She could hear her voice rising again, as it had in the hall. Her need for Llewelyn was an instinctive, blind groping toward the light, toward the only haven left to her, and she repeated, with the stubbornness born of shock, "I cannot wait. I must see him now."

Her eyes were clouded over, unfocused; they held a look Catherine had seen before, the dazed, defenseless look of a child half-awakening from a nightmare. Catherine had always been able to dispel childhood horrors with hugs and lit candles, but she had no comfort to offer Joanna, for her fears were not fantasy. She knew that Llewelyn would have no comfort, either.

Llewelyn was standing by the dais; men had clustered around him, intent eavesdroppers upon this eyewitness account of the August 14 hangings. Joanna did not yet know what she would say to him. In truth, she did not want to talk at all, for there was nothing he could say to change what was—that the whole fabric of her life had been founded upon lies. She asked no more now than to be held, asked no more than the reassurance of physical closeness, the familiar feel of his embrace.

She had almost reached Llewelyn when her gaze fell upon the man kneeling before him. Marc, the most trusted member of her household. Marc, whom she'd sent to Nottingham with a warning for John.

"Morgan . . ." Llewelyn's voice was husky, almost inaudible; he sounded stunned. "Tell my daughters." And then he was moving away from the dais, moving swiftly toward the door. He passed within several feet of Joanna, but seemed as oblivious of her as he was of the others in the hall. She stood in stricken silence as the distance between them widened; she'd begun to tremble again.

"Madame!"

Marc had risen to his feet, was hastening toward her. He

started to speak, but she did not give him the chance. "You told him. You told him about my letter."

He nodded. "Madame, I had to tell him. We're at war with John. Why would I be in England . . ."

Joanna was no longer listening. For a moment she closed her eyes. How could she face him? He might have understood yesterday, but now . . . . Lady Mary, what was she to do?

"Madame . . . did you not hear what I said about your stepson? He is not dead, Madame. He is not dead."

Llewelyn was standing by the window. He heard the door open behind him, but he did not turn, not until Joanna said his name.

"Marc told me," she said softly, "that Gruffydd is safe."

"Safe? Safe . . . oh, Christ!"

Joanna had never heard so much raw emotion in his voice, so much fear. Tears began to burn her eyes.

"Why did John spare him? Why?"

"I . . . I do not know, Llewelyn."

"Hanging is not an easy death. But there are worse ways to die, much worse."

They looked at each other, and the same thought was in both their minds: Windsor Castle and the agony of Maude de Braose's last days.

"I have no way of knowing if Gruffydd is even still alive. John could have had him put to death yesterday . . . or tomorrow. Gruffydd will never know which sunset might be his last. And I can do nothing for him, nothing."

"Beloved . . . ." But the right words eluded her. He'd spoken only the truth; how was she to dispute it? The silence was fraught with tension, with all that still lay unsaid between them. Moving to the table, she poured out a cupful of mead, all she could think to do for him.

He took it from her, drank slowly, keeping his eyes upon her all the while, and then he said, "Do you want to tell me now what was in the letter you sent to John, the urgent letter that was for his eyes alone?"

Her voice was little more than a whisper. "I . . . I warned him that he faced betrayal by his own men if he led an army into Wales."

She might have been a stranger of a sudden, a haggard, frightened woman looking up at him with eyes full of entreaty. "I trusted you," he said. "I've never trusted a woman as I trusted you."

"It was all I could think to do, Llewelyn. If my father feared treachery, there was a chance he'd not come into Wales, that he'd abandon the invasion. I did it for you. Beloved, I swear it!"

"Was this the first time? Or have you been keeping him informed all along? Have I been underestimating your talents? Loving wife, ardent bedmate—and John's spy?"

"No, Llewelyn, no!" Her voice broke and she began to weep.

He watched, saying nothing. He'd taken the mead on an empty stomach, and it was beginning to have an effect; so, too, was the lack of sleep, the guilt, the grieving. His anger ebbed away, leaving only exhaustion in its wake. Joanna's denial rang true, but it mattered little. Nothing mattered now but Gruffydd and what he faced at John's hands.

"Llewelyn, I would have told you, in truth I would. I meant to . . ."

"I do not want to talk about it. Not tonight."

"But you do not understand, you've not let me explain—"

"Joanna, not now!"

The world had become a bewildering place to Davydd. His brother was dead. But then he was not. His sisters had been weeping continually. For three days now, his mother had been sleeping with Elen and him in the nursery. His father seemed no happier after learning that Gruffydd was alive, while his mother wept quietly in the night, and near dawn she'd awakened them all with her screams. Davydd did not understand.

Sitting on the edge of his bed, he watched as his mother and Aunt Catrin folded his clothes into an open coffer. He was anxious, wanting to make sure they packed his favorite toys, his wooden horse and his whipping top.

"Mama had a bad dream," he told Catherine. "I dream about wolves sometimes."

"We all do, sweeting." Catherine straightened up, said softly, "Joanna, are you sure about this? I truly think you should wait till Llewelyn comes back . . ."

"I cannot, Catherine." Joanna drew Catherine aside, out of her son's hearing. "He might not let me go, and if I do not, I think I may truly go mad. I dreamed about her last night, about Maude . . . Catherine, I have to go."

She moved over to the table, picked up a letter. "I want you to give this to Llewelyn, Catherine—"

"Madame!" Branwen was standing in the doorway. "Madame, Prince Llewelyn just rode in. When he saw your coffers being loaded onto the pack horses, I . . . I had to tell him.''

''I understand, Branwen.'' Joanna leaned back against the table, gripped the edge for support.

''Papa!'' Davydd scrambled from the bed, ran to his father. ''We're going away, Papa, we're going to England! Did Mama tell you?''

''No, Davydd, she did not.'' Llewelyn's eyes flicked down to the open coffers, up to Joanna's face. ''Catrin, would you take Davydd outside?''

''I was going to leave you a letter.'' Joanna held it out, as if in proof; he made no move to take it.

''Where were you planning to go . . . to your father, to John?''

''No!'' She took a step toward him. ''I'm not going to my father, Llewelyn. You must believe me. I could not do that . . . not now. I'm going to my brother . . . to Richard.''

''For how long?''

''I . . . I do not know yet. Mayhap a month. Llewelyn, I have to go. I have to find some way to live with what I've learned. Nor can we continue like this. If we had some time apart, it . . . it might help.''

She'd feared that he might forbid her to go. Yet suddenly she wanted him to do just that, to tell her to stay, that their problems could be worked out, that he could forgive her.

A splash of red midst the floor rushes caught Llewelyn's eye; bending down, he retrieved his son's whipping top. He turned it over in his hand, fingering the wooden point, and when he looked back at Joanna, his eyes were bleak.

''I think you're right,'' he said. ''It is probably for the best that you go. I'll see that you have a safe escort.''

Not trusting her voice, Joanna could only nod.

''You may go, Joanna, if that be your wish. But not my children. They stay with me.''

''They are my children, too, Llewelyn!''

She sounded so panicked that he found himself relenting. ''You may take Elen, then,'' he said reluctantly. ''But not Davydd. Not my son.''

''But why? Do you want to hurt me as much as that?''

He slammed the wooden toy down upon the table. ''Do you think I'd ever willingly deliver up a second son into John's hands?''

She shrank back. ''But—''

"But what, Joanna? Are you going to assure me again that I've no cause for concern, that John would never harm a child?"

Joanna flinched, no longer met his eyes. "No," she whispered. "No . . ."

Llewelyn found he could not be impervious to her pain, however much he willed it. "I do not want to quarrel with you, Joanna."

"I'm not going to my father's court, Llewelyn, I swear I'm not. Davydd would be safe with me."

His mouth hardened again. "No. You may take Elen . . . for one month, no longer than that. But not Davydd."

He moved toward her, seemed about to speak, and then reached, instead, for the letter. Their fingers brushed, the meaningless, impersonal intimacy of strangers, and Joanna drew an audible breath. When she raised her eyes to Llewelyn's, her lashes were wet, fringed with tears.

"What I did was not an act of betrayal. I would never betray you, Llewelyn."

"I want to believe you," he said at last. "But even if I can, is that enough? Could we live with John's shadow ever between us?"

And Joanna had no answer for him.

32

GRANTHAM, ENGLAND

September 1212

Richard stood by a window in his bedchamber, staring out into the rain-drenched darkness. The storm had swept in from the north, scattering the manor livestock and soaking the oats and barley harvested and left out to ripen in the late summer sun. Lightning had seared the aged yew tree in the village churchyard, and the villagers were sheltering before their kitchen hearths, cheated of daylight hours precious to a people dependent upon rushes dipped in tallow and fires that gave off more smoke than light.

"Sweetheart, are you not coming to bed?"

"Soon." But he moved, instead, to the table.

Eve sat up, stifling a yawn. "Are you reading again that letter from your lord father?"

"Yes."

Another woman would have wanted to know if he planned to return to court. Eve was quite content to wait until Richard chose to tell her, and it was that which he valued even more than the pleasure she gave him in bed. That Eve was lacking in perceptiveness, even in simple curiosity, mattered little to Richard; what did matter was that she made no emotional demands, that she was placid and good-natured and easily relegated to the fringes of memory during their long separations.

He glanced down at the letter, at the phrases he already knew by heart. ". . . only twelve, so a plight troth might be advisable . . . bring you a barony, lordship of Chilham . . . an advantageous match . . ." Richard silently mouthed the words; an advantageous match, indeed. Marriage to Rohese de Dover would make him lord of Chilham Castle. With his lineage blemished by the bar sinister, with no lands of his own, he was no great matrimonial prize. And yet his father was offering him a barony.

434

"My lord." A servant stood in the doorway. "There's a woman seeking admittance out at the gate."

"I'd not turn anyone away in such foul weather, least of all a woman. Give her shelter for the night."

"My lord, you do not understand. This woman says she is your sister!"

Joanna had stripped off her wet clothes. Wrapped in one of Eve's bedrobes, she stood as close to the hearth as she could get, and when Richard handed her a goblet of hot mulled wine, she drank in deep, thirsty gulps. He watched uneasily, saying nothing. They were alone; Elen and Joanna's maids had been bedded down in an upper chamber, and Eve had uncomplainingly withdrawn so Richard might speak privately with his sister.

"How did you know I was at Grantham, Joanna?"

"I went to Conisbrough Castle. Your mother told me." Joanna set the goblet down, began to towel-dry her hair. There was an exaggerated and painstaking deliberation about her movements that Richard had occasionally seen in those who'd had too much drink or too little sleep. He moved closer, close enough to see that Joanna's face was free of all cosmetics, that the skin was discolored and smudged under her eyes, stretched so tightly across her cheekbones that it put him in mind of silk strained to the breaking point. It was an unsettling thought. Her tension was contagious; Richard could feel it constricting his muscles, eroding his composure. How much did she know?

"It worked, that warning you sent Papa. He has called off the invasion of Wales. He was truly shaken by your revelation, Joanna. He demanded hostages from all those he suspected. Most complied, how reluctantly you can well imagine. But Eustace de Vesci and his cousin Robert Fitz Walter fled the court, de Vesci to Scotland and Fitz Walter to France. To Papa, that is all the proof needed of their guilt. But he suspects that others, too, were involved in the plot, and as long as he does, I think it unlikely that he'll risk going into Wales."

A fortnight ago that would have been the answer to Joanna's every prayer; now it was salvation come too late. She could not rejoice, felt only a numbed sense of relief.

"Joanna . . . did you hear what I just said?"

"Yes, I heard." She turned from the hearth. "You were at Nottingham, Richard. You saw the hangings."

It was not a question, but he nodded, said reluctantly, "Yes, I saw them."

"I did not believe it, Richard. I tried to comfort Llewelyn by assuring him that it could not be true. I kept faith with my father, and all it cost me was my marriage."

"Joanna . . ."

"Papa had Prince Maelgwn's younger son hanged in Shrewsbury. Did you know that, Richard?"

"Yes . . . I heard."

"He was not yet seven. Did you know that, too?"

Her voice was low and so brittle that Richard sensed any answer would be the wrong one. "Papa did give the command to hang Prince Maelgwn's son; I cannot deny that. But he may have forgotten how young the boy was. He may not even have known—"

"Richard, no!" Joanna had begun to tremble again. Richard pulled a blanket off the bed, draped it about her shoulders. As their eyes met, she said softly, "Why did you not tell me about Maude de Braose?"

Richard expelled his breath in a sound much like a sigh. "I hoped you would never have to know."

"You should have told me, Richard. I had the right to know."

"I did not tell you, Joanna, for the same reason that Llewelyn did not. We wanted to spare you if we could."

"I know what Llewelyn told me is true. I have to accept it, to learn to live with it. But I do not know if I can ever understand it. How do I reconcile my memories with what Papa did at Nottingham . . . at Windsor? How, Richard?"

"I do not know," he admitted, and she reached out, grasped his arm.

"But you must. You've done it . . . somehow. Tell me, Richard. Tell me how you've done it." When he was silent, she cried, "For God's sake, help me! Papa never raised his hand to me, not once. He was oft moved to pity at sight of a crippled beggar, and he never refused alms to the needy. He liked to play with his dogs, and I once saw him rein in to berate a drover who was whipping his cart horse. Yet now I must believe that same man sent children to the gallows, gave the command to starve two people to death. How could he do it, Richard? Did he never awaken in the night, thinking of them? Did Maude's shadow never once fall across his table?"

"Joanna, do not do this to yourself."

"How can I stop? There are reasons beyond counting why men murder, but there can be only one reason for a death such as Maude's. Papa had to want her to suffer. He had to want to prolong her agony as long as possible."

"No," he said, "no."

"No more lies, Richard. Do you not think it time I faced the truth?"

"I'm not lying, Joanna. I've had months and months to think on this. All his life our uncle Richard did as he damned well pleased, with explanations or apologies to no one. But Papa is not like that; he needs to justify his actions, even to himself. He wanted Maude dead, but he had no right to execute her, and he knew it; all knew it. If he'd had her beheaded, there could be no doubt that it was done at his command. But prisoners are often neglected, often sicken and die. I truly think that is why he chose starvation and not the axe. Not to see Maude suffer. To enable him to deny responsibility for her death, to be able to claim it was not of his doing."

"Maude's guards misunderstood their orders? Forgot to feed her? Christ Jesus, Richard, who could ever believe such a fable?"

"Uncle Will believes it. He's managed to convince himself that Maude and her son died through neglect. He has to believe that. How could he continue serving Papa if he did not?"

"How, then—" Joanna stopped herself in mid-sentence, but he finished it for her.

"—can I continue to serve him? I do not often ask that question. And when I do, I tell myself it's because he is still my father. Because he is still the King. Because the only difference between Papa and other men is that he has the power to do what they cannot."

"You cannot truly believe that, Richard," she said, and he shrugged. "What of Isabelle?" she asked, after a long silence. "Think you that she knows?"

"About the hostages, yes. About Maude, not likely; who'd dare to tell her? You need not fret about Isabelle. She has very selective senses, sees and hears only what she wants to know."

"Was I . . ." Joanna swallowed. "Was I like that, too?"

"You loved him, Joanna. I doubt that anyone loved him the way you did." Richard hesitated. "When Papa decided to delay the invasion of Wales, he moved up into Yorkshire. But he expects to be back at Nottingham within the fortnight, wrote and requested that I join him there. I mean to do that, Joanna. Would you be willing to go with me? Mayhap if you talked to Papa . . ."

He felt no surprise, only a sad sense of futility when she said in a wretched whisper, "I cannot, Richard. I cannot . . ."

"I know," he conceded. "This is a de Warenne manor. You're welcome here as long as you like."

"I'll stay until you return to court. After that I shall go to stay at the White Ladies priory in Brewood Forest."

The White Ladies priory was a small Augustinian nunnery in Shropshire which had occasionally benefited from John's largesse. Richard knew Joanna had twice visited it with John, at age eight and then again a few months before her marriage to Llewelyn. He thought her choice of sanctuary a very telling one, and he ached for her, thinking it ironic that he, who had always valued competence as the highest virtue, should now feel so utterly ineffectual, able to offer such meagre comfort.

"Joanna . . . you have not left Llewelyn?"

She slowly shook her head. "No. I could never leave Llewelyn. But I'm not at all sure, Richard, that he wants me back."

"Mama, look!" Elen balanced precariously on the tree stump, and when she was sure she had Joanna's eye, she dived like an otter into the October leaves heaped about the stump. Joanna hastened to the rescue, anticipating scraped knees and sobbing, but Elen was already sitting up. She had dirt on her dress, leaves in her hair, and a satisfied smile on her face.

"Did you see me jump, Mama, did— Ohhh! What is that?"

Joanna followed the grubby little finger, saw two twitching ears protruding from a nearby thicket. "That is a rabbit or coney, Elen," she said softly. "Be still so you do not fighten it away."

"It's smaller than a hare," Elen observed, with the knowing eyes of a country child. "Do we have them back home? Can I pet it, Mama? Can I keep it?"

"I do not know if there are coneys in Gwynedd, Elen," Joanna admitted. "It is not native to England, was brought over some years back by the Normans for their sport."

Elen's other queries now became academic; the rabbit fled as soon as she moved. "Oh, Mama, it's gone!"

"I'm sorry, sweetheart." Joanna was, sorry for so much. These weeks at Brewood had not been happy ones for her daughter. Not a day passed that Elen did not ask when they were going home. Sometimes she sounded fretful, petulant, at other times unbearably plaintive, and at no time did Joanna have a satisfactory answer for her. "Soon" meant little to a homesick five-year-old who missed her father. It was coming to mean less and less to Joanna, too.

Several nuns were passing, lugging heavy oaken buckets of well water. They paused to beam upon Elen; she was a great favorite with them all, and when Sister Avelina offered to take her into the kitchen for bread and honey, she accepted readily. But she'd taken only a few steps when she stopped, whirled, and came running back to Joanna.

"Kiss me, Mama," she directed, and Joanna knelt, for a moment hugged her tight. Elen grinned, and then she was sprinting after the nuns, while Joanna stood very still, fighting her fear. If Llewelyn could not forgive her, she'd lose more than his love; she'd lose her children, too. When a marriage broke apart, the husband kept the children, and if he chose to deny his wife the right to see them, she had no legal recourse. Her own plight was even more perilous than that of most rejected wives, for her husband was a Prince, a Prince with the power to banish her from his domains, from their children's lives.

Joanna did not move until Elen's small figure was no longer in sight. And then she turned, began to walk away from the priory, under the leafy, rustling clouds of autumn oak and dappled elm. When her grandmother had divorced the French King, their two little daughters had remained with Louis. They were six and two then, and Eleanor did not see them again until they were women grown, in their twenties. Eleanor had apparently accepted the loss of her children as the price she must pay for Henry and the crown of England. But Joanna knew her own grieving would be beyond hope, beyond healing. The loss of her father she could, in time, accept. She could even learn to accept the loss of her husband. But not her children. Not Davydd. Not Elen. Not ever.

More than four weeks had passed since she'd come to the priory, six weeks since she'd ridden away from Dolwyddelan. Soon after her arrival at Brewood, she'd dispatched a man with a stilted and terse letter for Llewelyn, asking his permission to keep Elen in England beyond the month's grace he'd given her. In the weeks since, there'd been numerous sleepless nights when she'd labored over a second letter to her husband, a letter in which she sought his understanding, his forgiveness. Come dawn, she'd gather up her splotched and futile handiwork, feed it into the fire.

She was no less homesick than Elen. Her yearning for Davydd was like a physical ache, one that no herbs or ointments could ease. Her need for Llewelyn was no less intense; her body's thwarted cravings robbed her of sleep at night, and her memories wreaked havoc upon her daylight hours. But as much as she wanted to return to Llewelyn, she was terrified of doing so, terrified of having to face him and hear him say that their marriage was over. It was easier to do nothing, to cling to her

shreds of hope and tell herself that all would somehow work out
if only she gave them enough time.

In her despair, she'd convinced herself that Richard would
have the answers she needed. But Richard had failed her, and she
knew she was now failing herself. Unable to face her future,
unable to come to terms with her past. Grieving for the father
she'd lost, not to death, but to merciless, recurring dreams in
which she was walled up with Maude in that Windsor dungeon
and the bloated little body swaying from a Shrewsbury gallows
became Davydd's.

The woods were alive with the interior rhythms of its wildlife,
echoing to soft rustles and muted trills. Joanna stopped under a
maple tree, and the wind rained russet leaves down upon her.
One leaf spread its wings, revealed itself to be a butterfly mottled
in black and gold. The butterflies at Aber were the color of the
sky; from May to September they hovered over wildflower and
marsh grass, flickering blue flames to be extinguished at the first
frost. Joanna leaned back against the tree's gnarled trunk and
closed her eyes. Did Llewelyn, too, lie awake till dawn? How
was he dealing with his grief, his guilt? Had he learned to live
with his ghosts?

"Madame!" The scream was shrill, fraught with fear, utterly
out of place in a setting of such peace. Joanna tensed; the cry
came again, and she turned toward the sound. She soon saw a
blur of white, found a woman on her knees beside a fallen log.
She looked up as Joanna reached her, and Joanna recognized one
of the young novice nuns. Her habit was torn and dirtied, her
face scratched by her flight into the woods, and she had no breath
for speech, not even when Joanna grasped her shoulders, shook
her frantically.

"Has my daughter been hurt? For God's sake, tell me!"

"Oh, Madame, thank Jesus I found you!" The girl was on her
feet now, but had to lean on Joanna for support. "They took us
by surprise, rode into the priory as bold as could be. We thought
it was a raid, and Sister Avelina tried to hide your Elen in the
chancel. But one of the men called to her and she ran to him,
Madame, ran right to him. He demanded to see you, my lady,
and then our Prioress. We were so very frightened, Madame; all
know how godless the Welsh are. But . . . but they did not hurt
us. They talked to Prioress Alditha, then rode away, and . . .
oh, Madame, they took with them your daughter. They took
away your little girl!"

*   *   *

The quarter hour it took Joanna to reach the priory was the most terrifying time of her life. Running through the woods, she caught her gown repeatedly upon protruding branches, tripped over exposed tree roots and rocks, fought her way free of the thickets looming up in her path, seemingly set upon entrapping her forever in the midst of this God-cursed forest. By the time she was in sight of the priory walls, she was scratched and bruised and thoroughly disheveled, her ears echoing to the sobbing sounds of her own breathing, to the cry of "Elen!" that came to her lips of its own volition, that went unanswered in the strange silence that had enveloped the priory.

The guest house was to the north of the church, set apart from the nuns' dormitory and infirmary. It was there that Joanna shared a chamber with Elen. It would, she knew, be empty. She reached for the latch just as the door opened, and she all but fell into the room, into Llewelyn's arms.

He put his hands on her waist to steady her, said, "Are you hurt?"

She shook her head, and he released her. She was suddenly dizzy, and leaned back against the door. There was a sharp pain pressing against her ribs, cutting off her breath. "Elen . . . where is she?"

"On her way back to Gwynedd."

Joanna was too appalled for anger. "Jesus God, Llewelyn, did you have to do it like that?"

"I was thinking of her safety. I did not want her here should word get out that I'm at the priory."

The common sense of that could not be denied; some of Joanna's panic began to subside. But then Llewelyn said, "I made a mistake in letting you take her, Joanna. I thought she would be safe because of her sex. But the more I thought on it, the more uneasy I became. The risk was just too great. I'll not allow her to leave Wales again."

Pride had always been of paramount concern to Joanna. But not now. "I know you have the power to take Davydd and Elen from me. I can only beg you not to do that, to remember how much I do love them—"

"Whatever happens between us, I'd not deny you the right to see our children. I would still provide for you, would allow you to remain in Gwynedd to be near Davydd and Elen if you did not want to return to England. How could you think I'd do less than that?"

Joanna had no answer for him, for she could not explain her fear even to herself, an instinctive, elemental fear that had nothing whatsoever to do with logic or even love. She drew several shaken breaths. "Are you saying that our marriage is over?"

"I do not know, Joanna," he said, and there was in his voice a sadness that she found far more chilling than anger.

"Is it not dangerous for you to be here, on English soil?" she asked abruptly, and he shrugged.

"Probably. But I have no plans to tarry longer than necessary." He saw that she was not reassured, and added, "The borderland is quiet at present. John has ordered his army to disperse."

He was close enough to touch; Joanna's fingers brushed his sleeve, came to rest upon his arm. "Richard told me that twenty-eight hostages were hanged at Nottingham, all those who were being held at my father's court . . . save only Gruffydd. But there were others, mayhap a handful, who were being held elsewhere, and they still live. Richard promised me he would seek out their identities, then pass on that information to you."

"And he did, a fortnight ago. A curious letter, Joanna, for an English King's son to write to a Welsh Prince. He was cautious, made no promises that might compromise him, but he implied, nonetheless, that he would speak for my son if he could." Llewelyn reached out, traced the path of a scratch that marked her throat; at the unexpected touch, so like a caress, Joanna began to tremble. "He told me, too, that your warning saved Gruffydd's life."

"And do you believe him?"

"Yes," he said, "I do."

"Then . . . then can you not forgive me?"

"It is not a matter of forgiveness, Joanna. I would that it were." For a moment longer, his fingers lingered on her throat, and then he stepped back. "Did you see John? Did you see your father?"

"No! I swore to you that I would not. I did not lie to you."

"We have to talk about him, about John. I have to know what you feel toward him now. Joanna, I have to know."

She twisted her hands together, gripping her wedding ring as if it were a talisman. "I loved him, I believed in him. I married you to please him. And now . . . now I think of that little boy in Shrewsbury, I think of our Davydd and . . . and I know that I could not face him again. I cannot love the man he is, I cannot. But I remember how much I loved the man I thought he was . . . and it hurts more than I can bear. If he'd died, I'd still have had memories. But now even my memories are false. They do not comfort, they only torment . . ."

She closed her eyes, and then felt Llewelyn's fingers on her face, slowly wiping away her tears. She sobbed, and moved into his arms. She'd lost her veil, and he stroked her hair, smoothed the untidy ebony braids, brushed back stray wisps from her temples.

"You must not ever think," he said, "that I do not feel your pain." She made a wordless murmur, pressed closer. He caught the familiar fragrance of her perfume, felt her hands sliding up his back, and damned himself for a fool, for an unwary moment in which he'd almost believed that he meant only to comfort her, to hold her as she wept.

Joanna had raised her head from his shoulder. Her eyes no longer shone with tears; they were luminous, filled with sunlight, with such naked need that he caught his breath. Taking his hand in hers, she kissed each finger in turn, bit down gently on his thumb; her tongue circled his palm, and his free hand tightened on her hair.

For a moment that seemed endless to Joanna, he did not move. And then he lowered his head, brought his mouth down hard upon hers, not ending the kiss until they both were breathless. He'd begun to fumble with her clothing, swearing when the lacings of her bliaut resisted his impatient fingers. She raised her arms so he could pull the gown over her head; the chemise quickly followed. He kissed her again, caressing her belly and thighs until she moaned, arched against him. Pushing her down upon the bed, he unbuckled his scabbard.

When he lowered his body onto hers, he was not gentle, but neither was Joanna. That was not what she wanted from him now. For more than two months she'd slept as chastely as a nun, and her body had taken fire with the first touch of his fingers on her throat. She had no need of prolonged foreplay, and she entwined her arms tightly around him as he parted her thighs. "Now, love, now . . . oh, yes, now . . . ." She climaxed almost at once, with his third thrust, and then again when she felt him tense, groan, and jerk convulsively, gasping *"Siwan"* against her ear.

After a time, Llewelyn raised himself up, rolled over onto his back. Joanna was not yet ready to move. She knew it was a common belief that a woman's lust was greater than a man's, and for the first time she wondered if there might not be truth to that folk wisdom. She could only marvel now at the fevered urgency that had so utterly consumed her so short a time before. But she knew that she had given Llewelyn pleasure no less intense than he had given her. His breathing was still uneven and shallow, a pulse was beating rapidly in his throat, and his body glistened with perspiration. She leaned over, touched the tip of her tongue to a droplet of sweat trickling toward his chin. He did not respond, and a moment later he rose from the bed, reached for the clothing scattered about the floor.

Joanna's sense of languid well-being dissipated in the span of seconds, in the time it took Llewelyn to turn away from her. She was suddenly cold, confused, afraid. "Llewelyn . . . are you angry with me?"

"No, not with you, *breila*."

The endearment gave her little comfort; it was too obviously offered as a courtesy. Nor did his denial carry conviction. "You are angry," she said slowly, "and you were not angry ere we made love. Beloved . . . beloved, I do not understand. You cannot deny that you still want me, not now—"

"Of course I still want you," Llewelyn said sharply. "Our problems did not take root in our bed." He was already dressed; moving to the table, he pulled the laver toward him, splashed cold water onto his face, and then gave an abrupt, mirthless laugh. A pity he'd not thought to do that sooner!

He'd spoken the truth; he was angry with himself, not Joanna, and disconcerted by the realization of just how much he did still want her. In the six weeks since her departure, he'd had few restful hours, no peace of mind. Night after night he found himself lying awake in the bed he'd shared with Joanna, thinking of his son, thinking of the youths hanged at Nottingham, thinking of his wife—John's daughter. And in time he'd come to a decision, that if Joanna could not give him the answers he had to have, it would be better to end their marriage. To walk away from Joanna would be the most difficult act of his life, but he knew he could do it. However much it hurt, he could do it. But he could not send her into English exile against her will; he could never deny her the right to see their children. He'd sought to reassure her of that, promised she could stay in Wales, and now the full implications of that rash promise were all too clear to him. What would it be like to have her in Gwynedd, to have her so tormentingly close at hand and yet no longer his?

Joanna hastily drew her chemise over her head, followed him to the table. "What is it, then? Is it that you no longer trust me?"

Surprisingly, he shook his head. "I do trust you, Joanna. You told me you'd never meant to betray me. As hurt and angry as I was, I think I believed you even then. I must have, else I'd never have permitted you to take Elen. I know you were not choosing between us when you sent John that warning. You wanted to save your father's life, but you also wanted to stop a war, a war you thought I'd lose. And you did, *breila*." His mouth softened. "I might quarrel with your methods, but I can hardly take issue with your results. The English King's banner does not fly over Gwynedd . . . because of you. And my son has had a two-month reprieve . . . again because of you."

"You do not know how I've wanted to hear you say that, Llewelyn. But now you have, and it seems to count for naught. If you still trust me, what is it, then, that is keeping us apart? My love, I do not understand . . ." And then it came to her, the only possible answer, and she caught his arm, moved so she could look into his face.

"Unless . . . unless you can no longer love John's daughter? My God, Llewelyn, is that it?"

"Yes . . . it is," he admitted, and heard her indrawn breath, sharp as a blade. "Joanna. Joanna, listen and try to understand. John is going to kill my son. I've had to face that. It is only a matter of time; sooner or later he will give a command and Gruffydd will be dragged out to an English gallows . . . or worse. Gruffydd is going to die, and there is nothing I can do to stop it. Even if there were, I could not do it. I cannot buy Gruffydd's life with Gwynedd's sovereignty. Twenty-eight hostages died at Nottingham because I could not keep faith with John. I cannot bargain for Gruffydd over their dead bodies."

His voice was quite even, tautly controlled. But Joanna saw what that control cost him, saw the way the tendons suddenly stood out in his throat, saw the toll these past weeks had taken in the newly chiseled lines around his eyes, his mouth, and she was both awed and appalled by the strength of will that enabled him to forge such a resolve. There was nothing on God's earth that she would not have sacrificed for Davydd or Elen.

"For more than six years, Joanna, you have been torn between us, between your love for John and your love for me. You've never been able to give me all of your heart, never been able to pledge your loyalty to me utterly and unreservedly. No, lass, I am not blaming you for that. I understood, and I did my best to accept it. I taught myself to curb my tongue, to leave much unsaid. But no more. We can never go back to the way it was, Joanna."

"I know that, Llewelyn, but . . ." Joanna's voice trailed off. This was the nightmare that had held her in Brewood. So often had she anticipated this moment that it was as if they'd played

out this scene before, as if she'd always known the time would
come when she'd be listening to him explain, kindly but implaca-
bly, why their marriage had to end.

"For all of our marriage you've defended John, offered excuses for his cruelties, blinded yourself to the unholy truth about
him. But I can no longer indulge your love for this man. I'd learn
to resent you, and in time I might even learn to hate you, *breila*.
Rather than have it come to that, I'd sooner end the marriage
now, whilst we can still salvage friendship from it."

"But it does not have to be like that, Llewelyn. I would not
defend John. How could I? My loyalties are no longer divided, I
swear it."

Never before had Llewelyn heard Joanna call John by his
Christian name; it was always "my father" or "the King" or,
with intimates, "Papa." Was it an unconscious, anguished attempt to distance herself from John? Or a desperate denial of a
blood bond she knew he found abhorrent? He put his hands on
her shoulders, said quietly, "Joanna, you do not understand how
much I'd be asking of you. Do you truly think you could disavow
a lifetime of love? That you could remember the frightened
five-year-old who was taken to John at Rouen and then harden
your heart against him?"

"Yes," Joanna whispered, and he tilted her face up, kissed
her on the forehead.

"Beloved, I think not. I'm not even sure I'd have the right to
expect that of you."

"I give you the right. You are my life, you and our children.
Why will you not believe me?"

"Ah, Joanna . . . I want to believe you. But I know what
we'd be facing. I know what our future would be likely to hold.
You do not think that John has abandoned his plans to claim
Gwynedd for the crown? There will never be peace between us,
breila, not until one of us is dead. For now, John fears to cross
into Wales, but he's dispatched the English fleet to blockade our
coastal waters, and he's seeking to overthrow me with the aid of
the sons of my uncles, Davydd and Rhodri. They've been dwelling in English exile, and he hopes to make puppet Princes out of
them, promising them most of Gwynedd if they lead a rebellion
against me."

"He offered them most of Gwynedd?" Joanna echoed, sounding so shocked that he felt the need to reassure her.

"You need not fear. There is a world of difference between
being invested with possession in London and then taking posses-

sion in Gwynedd. John's grant is more symbolic than substantial, but it does show how utterly intent he is upon vengeance, upon seeing my head impaled on London's new bridge—"

Llewelyn broke off, for Joanna was no longer listening. She was staring past him with glazed amber eyes, and when he touched her shoulder, he found that her body had gone rigid with rage.

"Liar!" she spat. "That double-dealing liar! He promised me, he swore on his oath of honor that he'd safeguard Davydd's inheritance, that I need never fear for Davydd's future. And fool that I was, I believed him!"

"Does it truly surprise you so, Joanna? Davydd is my son."

"He is my son, too . . . and John's grandson."

To Joanna, it was the final betrayal. She turned away, moved to the window. Several of the nuns had gathered at a discreet distance. They were casting uneasy yet curious glances toward the Welshmen who were now loitering near the guest house, keeping an anxious vigil for Llewelyn. So turbulent had this past hour been that she'd all but forgotten the danger Llewelyn could be in, the risk he'd taken in coming into England. But the sight of his waiting men brought her fear back in a rush.

"Llewelyn, you must go!"

"I know." But he made no move to depart. Instead he stepped toward her, pulled her away from the window. "I do not mind you bedazzling my men, but I'd hate for you to disconcert those poor nuns!"

It was not the realization that she was clad only in her chemise that brought the blood up into Joanna's cheeks, it was the unexpected amusement in Llewelyn's voice. She started to ask him how he could be joking now, of all times, when she saw what he had in his hand, her discarded gown.

"You'd best make haste to dress, *breila*. We've a long ride ahead of us."

She raised her eyes to his face, and then closed the space remaining between them. He drew her into his arms, for a brief moment held her close.

"My love, you will not be sorry. You will not ever be sorry."

Llewelyn could not share her certainty. "We'll try, Joanna," he said softly. "At least we'll try."

33

DOVER CASTLE, ENGLAND

May 1213

Somewhere a dog was howling, a forlorn, haunting plaint that echoed eerily upon the sea-misted air, rending the fabric of Gruffydd's troubled dreams and jarring him into abrupt, uneasy wakefulness. He dreaded nights like this, dreaded the solitude and the silence, the hours alone with his ghosts.

He could think of few sounds as mournful as a dog's howling . . . or as disquieting. All knew it to be an ill omen, a harbinger of coming woe, and he instinctively fumbled for his talisman, the agate stone that gave the wearer strength, valor, the fortitude to prevail against his enemies. His guards had long since stolen his rings; he'd managed, though, to conceal the agate in his clothing, and in the months since Nottingham, it had been a secret source of comfort, a tangible link with Gwynedd. But his fingers plucked in vain at the torn wool tunic, the begrimed shirt. Fully awake now, he remembered. The agate was gone, lost on the road to Dover.

It was of no matter, he told himself resolutely. Dogs barked and men died, but the one happening need not presage the other. He lay back upon the pallet, began to whisper rapidly, "Sweet Lord Jesus defend me, grant me remission of all my sins and keep me from all peril. Lord, save me waking, save me sleeping, that I may sleep in peace and awake in Thee in the glory of Paradise." He felt better at that; soon after, he slept.

When he awakened again, sun was seeking entry through the arrow loops high above his head, and two men were standing over his pallet with drawn swords.

In answer to John's urgent summons to arms, the men of England began to gather in early May at Barham Downs in Kent. The response was heartening; the impending French invasion had vitalized public opinion in John's favor, and those unmoved by patriotism were motivated by the knowledge that to refuse to bear arms was to risk "perpetual servitude."

For the past week John had been staying with the Knights Templar in Ewell, and it was to Ewell that Richard was returning on this Tuesday morning in mid-May. Chilham Castle was less than twenty miles from Ewell, and Richard had taken advantage of his proximity to pay a courtesy call upon his young betrothed.

He invariably enjoyed his visits to Chilham. It was gratifying to spend a day riding about the manor demesne, to see the green fields and well-fed livestock and know it would all eventually be his. That Rohese de Dover was a gentle, biddable girl, shyly eager to please, only made his marital prospects all the more alluring.

But he'd had an ulterior motive for this particular visit to Chilham: to escape, if only for a few days, the oppressive atmosphere of his father's court. What John had most feared was at last coming to pass; the circle was closing.

Sparing Gruffydd had not sundered Llewelyn's alliance with the other Welsh Princes. The hangings of the hostages had unified the Welsh as nothing else could have done. Rhys Gryg had fallen into John's hands, was being held captive at the royal castle of Carmarthen. But Maelgwn and Gwenwynwyn were ravaging Norman settlements in South Wales, and Llewelyn had retaken the only two castles still in Norman control; he had now regained all of the Perfeddwlad, regained all he'd been forced to yield up to John at Aberconwy. The Welsh were a God-cursed, stiff-necked, and utterly vexatious people, John said bitterly, but they did have an inexplicable ability to rise phoenixlike from the ashes of defeat, to soar upward on wings too scorched for flight.

As troublesome an enemy as Llewelyn was proving to be, he did not pose a serious threat to John's sovereignty. But as winter thawed into a verdant spring, John found himself facing a more dangerous foe, one who had the power to do what Llewelyn could not, to bring his reign and his life to an abrupt and bloody end.

At Christmas the Pope had at last invoked his ultimate weapon, dispatched Stephen Langton to the French court with letters formally deposing John as King of England and freeing his subjects from their oaths of allegiance. Philip was more than eager to show himself a good son of the Church, and he immediately

announced plans to invade England and claim John's crown for a
more worthy aspirant, his own son Louis.

With a French fleet being rigged at Boulogne, John was forced
to acknowledge that time had finally run out, and he hastened to
send envoys to Rome. This eleventh-hour capitulation gained him
an extension of the Pope's deadline; the papal legate Pandulf was
now in England to accept his submission to papal authority.

By coming to terms with the Pope, John had thus been able to
deny Philip the opportunity to cloak himself in the mantle of the
Church, to sanctify his invasion as a holy war of retribution
against a renegade King. But if Philip's pretensions had been
sabotaged, his ambitions remained intact; the French fleet would
sail with or without the Pope's blessings. Which meant, Richard
thought bleakly, that his father would soon be fighting a war on
two fronts, trying to repulse a French landing in the south whilst
Philip's Welsh allies turned the Marches into a wasteland of
smoldering manors and charred fields. And if it came to that,
how long would John's disaffected barons hold fast? How long
ere men like Derby and Huntingdon and de Clare elected to
throw in their lot with Philip?

Upon his arrival at Ewell, Richard was surprised to find Isabelle walking in the garden with her two youngest children. He
had not seen much of Isabelle in recent months, still less of his
little half-brothers and sister, for John had become obsessed with
fears for their safety. After learning of de Vesci and Fitz Walter's
intriguing, he'd required armed bodyguards, not only for himself
but for his family, too; he'd even gone so far as to give orders
that no one be admitted to the presence of his eldest son and heir
without written permission.

Isabelle greeted Richard with unfeigned warmth, for they were
long-standing allies in a conspiracy of self-interest, one dedicated
to John's weal.

"Did my father meet with the papal legate?"

"Yes, they met yesterday in Dover." Isabelle gestured for the
nurses to take the children on ahead. "It did not go well, I fear.
Will told me that Pandulf was aloof, unable to conceal his
doubts, his suspicions that John was not acting in good faith.
And the terms offered were the very ones John had scorned for
these five years past. He had to agree to receive Stephen Langton
as Archbishop of Canterbury, to reinstate the clergy who'd gone
into exile when the Interdict was declared, and to recompense the
Church for its losses. But what I think John found hardest to

swallow was the Pope's insistence that he pardon Eustace de
Vesci and Robert Fitz Walter, restore them to favor.''

From their respective exiles in Scotland and France, de Vesci
and Fitz Walter had been loudly and persistently proclaiming
themselves martyrs to conscience, Christians who could not serve
an excommunicate King. Richard had not expected the Pope to
give credence to so spurious a rationale for treason, and he could
only shake his head in wonder, conclude that the name this
particular Pope had chosen for himself was uncommonly apt:
Innocent III.

"I thought I knew John so well, Richard, but I've never seen
him like this. Never.''

"What man would not be distraught, sore crazed with wrath?''

"But that is just it; he's not in a tearing rage. Richard, he is
. . . well, there's but one way to describe his mood. Do you
remember when Reginald de Dammartin gave John those weighted
dice? Remember how he kept winning every toss, until he finally
relented and showed us the trick? He is acting now just as he did
that day, like a man who knows he cannot lose.''

Isabelle glanced about, reassured herself that none were within
hearing range. "He has called a council meeting for this forenoon, and he means to summon Pandulf back to Ewell on the
morrow. I do not know what he has in mind. I can only tell you
what he said, that he has thought of a way to thwart Philip's
invasion plans, whilst gaining His Holiness the Pope as a steadfast ally.''

"Papa is more than clever; at times he can be utterly inge-
nious. But not even Merlin could manage that. The Pope would
never trust Papa again. Nor would he intervene on Papa's behalf
unless the Church had a stake in the war, and it does not.''

Isabelle shrugged. "I daresay you're right. But John is strangely
calm for a man beset on all sides. He— Richard, look. The
prisoner being escorted through the gateway . . . is that not
Llewelyn's son?''

Richard spun around. Gruffydd's guards were pulling him
from his horse. He stumbled, nearly lost his balance, and looked
in Richard's direction. Richard saw recognition on his face and,
for the briefest of moments, an involuntary appeal.

John glanced around the table at the few men he did not suspect
of complicity in the de Vesci–Fitz Walter plot. They'd listened
intently, without interruption, as he explained what he planned to

do, and why, and he'd seen their initial shock slowly give way to understanding, and then approval.

"Well?" he said. "Now that you know, what say you?"

"It ought to work," Chester conceded, and then added, with uncharacteristic enthusiasm, "For certes, Philip will be caught utterly off guard."

"So, too, will His Holiness the Pope." Will was beaming; it had been some years since John had seen such unqualified admiration in his brother's eyes. Pembroke, too, was nodding appreciatively. But it was Reginald de Dammartin, the fugitive Count of Boulogne, who echoed John's own opinion of his desperate ploy. Dammartin was a newcomer to John's inner circle; he'd fled to England the preceding year, after a bitter dispute with the French King. Aggressively independent, not overly scrupulous, and possessed of a brutally candid tongue, he had not found many friends at John's court. But as he was also utterly without self-pity, undeniably quick-witted, and a raconteur par excellence, with an inexhaustible supply of boisterous, bawdy tales as uproarious as they were unseemly, John had conceived a genuine liking for the man, quite apart from Dammartin's considerable value as a political ally. For not only was Dammartin Count of Boulogne by right of his wife, he also held the Norman fiefs of Aumale, Domfort, and Mortain, which John had lost to Philip in 1204.

Dammartin was grinning. "There is but one word for such an underhanded stratagem—brilliant."

The other men laughed. They were still laughing as the solar door opened and Gruffydd was thrust into the chamber.

His guards shoved Gruffydd forward, forced him to kneel before the English King. John pushed his chair back from the table, watched Gruffydd in unnerving silence, his eyes speculative, not easily read.

"You're looking rather bedraggled these days," he said at last, and some of Gruffydd's fear was lost in a sudden surge of hatred.

"I'll not beg. No matter what you mean to do."

"What I mean to do," John said blandly, "is to instruct your guards that you may have a bath upon your return to Dover."

Gruffydd's jaw dropped. To be offered the promise of future tomorrows when he'd been measuring his life in minutes was a shock not easily absorbed. "Why would you want to do a kindness for me?"

The corner of John's mouth twitched. "I see you have your father's impeccable manners. As it happens, I mean to do you a greater kindness than that. I've decided to allow you to write a letter to your father." He beckoned to one of the guards. "Cut his bonds, but make no mistake; he's not to be trusted. There is parchment and pen and inkwell on the table, Gruffydd. You do know how to write? If not, you can dictate to one of my scribes."

Gruffydd flushed. "I can write. I'm a Prince's son."

John's smile was sardonic, but he said only, "You may write what you please, within reason. I think you should assure Llewelyn that you are well, that you are not being maltreated or abused. You may tell him, too, that I am willing to let him send Joanna to my court in order to verify the truth of your assurances."

Gruffydd was surreptitiously rubbing his wrists, while trying desperately to make sense of John's sudden benevolence. In the nine months since the Nottingham hangings, he'd dwelt in death's shadow; not a day dawned when he did not wonder if it would be his last. What enabled him to endure was the intensity of his yearning for freedom—and for vengeance. But if a beneficent spirit had offered to grant his lesser wishes, he'd have asked for a hot bath and contact of some sort with his family. It seemed almost diabolical to him that John should have pinpointed his vulnerabilities with such uncanny accuracy.

"Well?" John was regarding him with amused impatience. "What are you waiting for? The sooner you write the letter, the sooner you'll get word from home."

Home. To Gruffydd's horror, tears suddenly filled his eyes. "No," he said huskily. "No. I'll write no letter for you, now or ever."

It had never occurred to John that Gruffydd might refuse. "Why ever not?" he demanded, sounding more astonished than angry.

"Because you want it written. I admit I do not know why. But if it serves your interests, it cannot be to my father's advantage. So I'll not do it."

It was suddenly quite still. Even to Gruffydd, his words rang hollow, not so much defiance as doomed bravado. John was slowly shaking his head. "Do not be a fool, boy. Surely you know I can make you write that letter."

Gruffydd's stomach knotted. "You can try."

John pushed his chair back still farther; wood grated harshly on the flagstones. "I cannot decide whether you're an utter idiot or merely foolhardy beyond belief." He made an abrupt gesture and the guards jerked Gruffydd to his feet. "Take him back to Dover, where he can think upon his lunacy."

Reginald de Dammartin was the first to break the silence that followed Gruffydd's departure. "Are all the Welsh as mad as that?"

"I would that they were," John said tersely. "If so, Wales would be an English shire by now." Rising, he moved away from the table and, for the first time, noticed his son. Richard had entered unobtrusively some moments before, after a futile attempt to coax Isabelle into interceding on Gruffydd's behalf; she'd parried with a cynical and unanswerable, "If John indulges me, it is because I ask only for what I know he's willing to give."

Gruffydd's intransigence had not surprised Richard any, but his father's forbearance had. He reached John just as Will said approvingly, "Your patience with the boy was commendable, John, in truth it was."

"That was not patience, Will. He called my bluff, pure and simple. The joke is that I doubt whether he truly knew what he was doing even as he did it!"

"What do you mean?"

"Think upon it, Will. How would you have me explain to my daughter that Gruffydd's assurances of good health were extracted under torture? Even if I resorted to more subtle means of persuasion, withheld food or sleep until he agreed to cooperate, there'd be no way to keep him from regaling Joanna with all the gory details afterward. It should be obvious by now that the damned fool is too simpleminded to scare!"

While there was understandable exasperation in John's voice, he seemed to be taking Gruffydd's defiance with remarkable equanimity. Isabelle was right, Richard decided; something was definitely in the wind.

John was shaking his head again, in disbelief. "I daresay if I'd told him he was free to return to Wales, he'd then have insisted upon staying in England! I ought to have reminded him of the fate of his granduncles; mayhap that would have shaken some sense into him."

"I know about as much of Wales as I do of the heathen kingdoms of Cathay," Dammartin drawled, "and I confess I find them of equal interest. What befell the boy's kin?"

"After my father lost the battle of Crogen to Llewelyn's grandfather, Owain Fawr, he took vengeance upon his Welsh hostages. Two of them were Owain's sons, Llewelyn's uncles. Their eyes were put out with red-hot awls."

Dammartin was not shocked, for Philip had been known to do

the same to captured English soldiers; while Norman knights and men of rank were routinely ransomed, it was not unheard of to mutilate common soldiers, thus rendering them unfit for further combat. But for Will, that was a jab into an old wound.

"I've never been able to understand how our father could have done that," he muttered. "It was not like him." He hesitated. "John . . . you'd never take vengeance of that sort upon Llewelyn, by blinding Gruffydd?"

Will saw at once that he'd made a monumental blunder. John's eyes were suddenly opaque; a muscle jerked in his cheek. "I told you why I hanged those accursed hostages! It was necessary to set an example, to remind my barons how much was at stake. I did what had to be done, and I'm bone-weary of being criticized for it. Christ, the utter hypocrisy of it all! Who spoke up for those blinded Welsh hostages? Or those hapless souls hanged by my sainted brother Richard at Châlus? He took his deathbed vengeance upon men, women, and children alike, and none called him 'butcher' for it. As for that double-dealing hellspawn on the French throne, his hands are as bloody as Richard's. I may treat my Jews like milch cows, milk them for all they're worth, but they've not been slaughtered by rampaging mobs as they were in Richard's reign, and I've never burned Jews at the stake the way Philip has—eighty at Brie-Comte-Robert, when a Christian was found slain."

John paused, breathless, realizing too late just how much he'd revealed. "Leave me," he said, in a tone that brooked no argument. Richard alone braved his displeasure by remaining.

"Why did you want Gruffydd to write to Llewelyn, Papa? What would you gain by that?"

John was standing by the window, watching as Gruffydd and his guards rode through the gateway, on their way back to confinement at Dover Castle. "Llewelyn did warn me, Richard. He told me plainly that Joanna was his hostage as Gruffydd was mine. But I did not believe him, not then."

Richard was suddenly sorry he'd stayed. "And now?"

"Twice in the past six months I've summoned Joanna to my court, and twice he has refused to let her come. The last time I even offered to provide hostages if it would ease his qualms. Hostages . . . for my own daughter! And all I got in return was a stilted letter from Joanna, saying it was not possible for her to leave Wales, a letter she obviously wrote at Llewelyn's direction."

Richard had learned to pick his way through conversations about his sister as if each one were a quagmire. But never had he so dreaded making a misstep. Knowing that John was too adept at reading faces, he busied himself at the table, pouring wine for them both. "So you thought Llewelyn might relent if you made it worth his while?" he ventured cautiously, and John nodded.

"But I did not reckon with his son's lunatic yearnings for martyrdom! It might be foresighted to look after that lad, Richard; what could better serve England than to have Gruffydd one day reigning as Prince of Gwynedd? Can you envision him ever humbling his pride to an English King as Llewelyn did at Aberconwy? When pigs fly and monks no longer like their wine!"

Richard was relieved that they seemed to be edging away from the precipice. To banish Joanna into the peripheral reaches of memory where she could do John no harm, he said hastily, "How long are you going to keep me in suspense, Papa? Isabelle says you've a scheme to outwit Philip and foil his invasion plans. What do you have in mind . . . a miracle?"

John laughed. "I am merely taking a page from Philip and Llewelyn's own book. Philip has had great sport these months past, posing as a pious champion of the Church; to convince the Pope that he was acting in good faith, he even went so far as to release the long-suffering Ingeborg from Étampes Castle! And Llewelyn, too, has had his fun at my expense, turning treason into a crusade for Christendom, all with the Pope's blessings. You ask what I mean to do, lad? I mean to show them that I can play that game, too, and with far greater skill."

Phillip was currently holding court in the sleepy village of Gravelines, and his restive barons were forced to seek livelier sport in the seacoast town of Calais, just twelve miles to the west. Hugh de Lusignan, Count of La Marche, and his younger brother Ralph, Count of Eu, rode into Calais just before dusk, headed for their favorite wharfside alehouse.

"Three days till Ascensiontide." Hugh shoved a drunk aside, claimed the table closest to the door. "Think you that John is keeping count?"

"I am, for certes. I've a wager with our cousin Geoffrey, am hazarding one hundred marks that the old hermit is right."

"Wishful thinking, Ralph. I'd have to be able to spit into John's open coffin ere I'd believe he was well and truly dead. He may have the scruples of a Scotsman and the morals of a rutting swine, but he has Satan's own luck."

"Anyone using the words 'swine' and 'Satan' in one sentence

can only be talking about John Plantagenet. John Lackland. John of the Devil's brood. John, the Pope's sworn man.''

The room was hazy with smoke from hearth and reeking tallow candles, and Hugh's eyes were stinging. He blinked up at the man weaving toward their table, said trenchantly, "In your cups already, Fitz Walter?''

Robert Fitz Walter straddled the bench, sat down without waiting to be asked. "I'm nowhere near as drunk as I hope to get. Since you're both still sober, I take it you have not heard yet? The papal legate Pandulf landed at Wissant on Saturday, wasted no time joining Philip at Gravelines. He carried a right interesting message for Philip, told him the Pope demands that he abandon the invasion of England. He said that if Philip does not heed the warning, the Pope will lay France under Interdict again and, if need be, will excommunicate each and every man who sets foot on English soil.''

Hugh and his brother exchanged startled glances. "If that's an example of your English humor, it's not much to my liking.''

"Philip did not find it very amusing, either.''

Hugh set his goblet down, sloshed red wine onto the table. "You are not jesting, are you?''

"In truth, it does sound like a diabolical jest of sorts, but it is not mine; John's the one who is laughing. Do you not want to know why the Pope is of a sudden backing John, taking such a protective interest in English affairs? England is now a papal fief, part of the patrimony of St Peter.''

They were staring at him, dumbfounded. Hugh found his tongue first. "You're daft or drunk, or both!''

"Pandulf told Philip that on Wednesday last John did freely surrender to God and the Holy Mother Church of Rome the kingdoms of England and Ireland, to hold them henceforth as the Pope's vassal.''

Fitz Walter helped himself to Hugh's wine, drank too deeply, and gave a harsh, spluttering laugh. "All know those tales told of men who sold their souls to the Devil. But John must be the first to turn a profit by selling his to God!''

"Wrath of God, man, how can you laugh about it?''

"What would you have me do? Rant and rave and sicken on my own bile like Philip? When I left him, he was venting his fury upon God, John, Innocent, his servants, his dogs, all within reach. But it'll change nothing. He's already learned what a confrontation with the Church can cost, is not likely to go that route again. I'll wager that he calls off the invasion as the Pope demands, and turns his rage instead upon a safer target, John's ally, the Count of Flanders. Whilst in England, John will continue to rule as arbitrarily as ever, except that the Pope will now have a vested interest in John's survival.''

''You're taking this rather well for a man who can now expect to live out his remaining days in French exile,'' Hugh said suspiciously, and Fitz Walter grinned.

''Did I forget to tell you? My cousin de Vesci and I are included in the Pope's peace. I will be returning to England as soon as my safe-conduct does arrive.''

Hugh snorted. ''And of course John will welcome you back with true Christian forgiveness in his heart! Just how long do you expect this papal 'peace' to last?''

Fitz Walter rose unhurriedly to his feet. ''Long enough to serve my purposes.'' His eyes fell upon a large calico cat, curled up contentedly upon an empty footstool. He kicked the stool, dumped the startled animal into the fetid, sodden floor rushes.

''You see,'' he said. ''Not even a cat lands on its feet every time.''

Pope Innocent III to John, King of England:

''Who but the Divine Spirit . . . directed and guided you, at once so prudently and so piously, to consult your own interests and provide for the Church? Lo! You now hold your kingdom by a more exalted and surer title than before . . .''

On Ascension Eve, a large pavilion was set up on the Kentish downs, and there John celebrated Ascension Day with impressive pomp and grandeur. Trestle tables were lavishly laden with food; jugglers and minstrels entertained the crowds that flocked to the meadow, and the day rapidly took on the festive atmosphere of a fair or market day. At sunset the pavilion was taken down and John returned in triumph to the Knights Templar at Ewell. It was, for many, a day of bitter disappointment.

It remained for Peter of Wakefield to serve as an object lesson for false prophets, would-be rebels. Five days later the aged hermit was escorted to Wareham in Dorset, where he was dragged to the gallows behind the sheriff's horse, and there hanged.

tence of Stephen Langton, Archbishop of Canterbury. But he'd
had just one terse letter from Joanna in the past twelvemonth, and
he interrogated Eleanor now at some length, seeking reassurance
that his daughter was truly well, that her prolonged silence was
indicative only of Llewelyn's rancor.

Eleanor caught the undertones of unease, but she did not
comprehend the cause. She wondered why he had sent for her.
She wondered, too, if she would ever find the courage to confront him about her brother's death, to demand that he tell her
how Arthur had died.

Satisfied at last that she had no more to tell him about Joanna,
John said, "My brother Will has already sailed for Flanders,
where he'll be joined by Dammartin and my sister's son Otto, the
Holy Roman Emperor. For my part, I shall land at La Rochelle.
Once I've secured Poitou and Anjou, we'll be able to move
against Philip on two fronts."

"God grant you victory, Uncle." Why was he telling her this?

Reginald de Dammartin sauntered over, held out a dripping
wine cup to John. "When you begin husband-hunting for her,
John, remember that I put in my bid first."

"I would, Reg," John said and grinned. "But I think your
wife might take it amiss."

Eleanor was dumbfounded. "Husband-hunting?" she echoed.
"Uncle, what does he mean?"

John did not reply at once, studying her over the rim of his
cup. She shared Arthur's coloring, he thought, but little else.
Arthur had been too brittle to bend, but Nell was malleable clay;
rebellion was not in her. "Well, you can hardly expect to rule
Brittany without a husband to give you support and guidance, can
you?"

Eleanor seemed dazed; she could only stare at him in disbelief.
"You . . . you mean to recognize my claim to the Breton
throne?" No sooner were the words out of her mouth than the
full implications of her question hit her; if he admitted she was
the rightful heiress to Brittany, he was admitting, too, that Arthur
was dead.

John smiled. "Your claim is for certes superior to your half-
sister's," he said, adroitly sidestepping the trap.

She could still ensnare him, she knew. She need only ask:
What of Arthur's claim? But John's gaze did not waver; his eyes
held hers quite steadily, hypnotically.

"Your sister and her husband have been French puppets;
Philip pulled the strings and they danced at his whim. After I

prevail against Philip, I shall want a more reliable regime in
Brittany. Naturally, I thought of you, Nell.''

Eleanor swallowed. She was not so innocent that she did not
understand what was being offered and what was not. It might
sound as if John was opening the door of her cage, but she'd still
be tethered to his will. If her sister was Philip's puppet, she
would be John's.

She laced her fingers together, sought without success to still
their tremors. His advisers would govern in her name. He'd pick
a husband for her, and she'd be given no say in it. But she'd
have a measure of freedom. And she was still young enough to
have children, to have the family she'd thought forever denied
her. She closed her eyes, and Arthur's name hovered on her lips,
like an unspoken prayer.

''Well?'' John put his hand on her arm, felt her quiver at his
touch. How fearful she was, as timid as a trapped doe. Her
vulnerability stirred his pity, her lack of pluck his contempt. He
tilted her chin up, forcing her to meet his eyes. ''What say you,
Nell? If I make you Duchess of Brittany, will I regret it?''

''No, Uncle,'' she whispered. ''You'll not regret it. I'll do
whatever you want.''

On February 14, John landed at La Rochelle. Taking advantage
of an early spring thaw, he moved into Isabelle's Angoulême,
and then the Limousin. When the de Lusignans scorned his offer
of a truce, he led his army into Hugh de Lusignan's county of La
Marche. Philip had been forced to split his army, dispatching his
son Louis against John while he headed north in an attempt to
halt Will and Dammartin's depredations in Flanders. But Louis
was an overly cautious commander, and March gave way to
April and then May, and it began to seem as if the lost Angevin
empire was John's for the taking.

On Whitsun Eve, May 17, John captured the de Lusignan
castle of Mervant. The next day he moved on to Vouvant, where
Hugh's uncle, Geoffrey de Lusignan, had taken refuge with his
sons. Upon their refusal to yield, John's men surrounded the
castle, and the siege began.

After filling in the moat with brushwood and dirt, they succeeded in setting fire to the wooden palisade, soon gained control
of the outer bailey. John then ordered his siege engines brought
up, and from dawn to dusk on Tuesday, the mangonels sent
heavy rocks slamming against the castle walls and keep. While in
La Rochelle, John had secured a relatively new siege weapon;

called a trebuchet, it was a high-trajectory sling, larger and more accurate than the mangonels, and by Tuesday afternoon, this, too, was in operation, hurling enormous boulders and the dreaded Greek fire and even the rotting carcasses of dead horses into the inner bailey of the besieged castle. By nightfall, John's soldiers were wagering upon the hour of the castle's fall, and John's was the sound sleep of a man already savoring the victory to come.

After breaking his fast the next morning, John summoned the Earl of Chester and together they went to inspect the siege tower that had been completed soon after sunrise. Fashioned from tree trunks, it soared more than sixty feet into the sky. As John and Chester watched, hides doused in vinegar were tacked in place, and then, at John's signal, the huge belfry began to roll slowly across the bailey.

Up on the walls, the defenders were shooting flaming arrows, but they glanced off the hides, failed to ignite. Under cover of their shields, men clambered down, knocked off the belfry wheels, and then lowered its drawbridge, settling it against the castle wall. De Lusignan's soldiers began to throw torches, but men were already scrambling across, leaping onto the wall. Others were emerging from the lower stories of the belfry, hastening to join their comrades on the drawbridge. The fighting was now hand-to-hand combat. Men grappled with each other, swearing and gouging and panting; some lost their footing and fell, or were pushed off the walls to their deaths. But as more and more men crossed the drawbridge, the castle's defenders were forced to give ground. Already some of the attacking force had lowered thong ladders, were climbing down into the bailey.

"Look!" John gave a jubilant shout, pointed. "Our men have the inner gatehouse; the portcullis is rising!"

By noon the de Lusignans and their surviving men had walled themselves up in the keep, and John's soldiers were readying themselves for the final assault. John had decided not to dig a tunnel to undermine the keep; while that was the surest method, it was also the slowest. "We'll try the battering ram first," he concluded, after a painstaking appraisal of the keep. "Remember, though, that I want the de Lusignans taken alive if possible. I promised myself I'd have the pleasure of hanging the whoresons," he added, and his captains laughed.

"Your Grace!" The Earl of Derby was gesturing. "A rider is coming in under a flag of truce, and damn me if he's not wearing Hugh de Lusignan's livery!"

Within moments an exceedingly nervous youth was kneeling in

the dirt before John. "Your Grace, my lord Count of La Marche most urgently requests a meeting with you. Will you grant him a safe-conduct so he might enter your camp?"

"Indeed I will," John said, and smiled. "Tell Hugh that if he makes haste, he'll be in time for the hangings."

They met in John's command tent within the hour. Hugh de Lusignan had not aged well in the twelve years since Mirebeau. His hair and beard were the shade of sea salt, his skin as splotched and sun-browned as well-worn leather, and his eyes put John in mind of his favorite peregrine falcon. But he came forward without apparent hesitation, knelt and said, "I thank Your Grace for seeing me. I think it time we talked."

"I offered to talk in March, as I recall. You said you'd sooner break bread with the Devil . . . or words to that effect."

"I was in the wrong," Hugh said stonily. "I seek your pardon, seek peace between us."

So did John. He needed the powerful de Lusignan clan to make good his conquest of Poitou. But he took his time, let Hugh suffer the suspense until he finally nodded, said, "So it shall be, then."

Hugh's eyes glittered. "I shall give you faithful service, my liege. Now . . . what of my uncle and cousins?"

John smiled coolly. "I'd planned to hang them, Hugh," he said pleasantly. "But if you can talk them into surrendering, I'll pardon them . . . as proof of the friendship I now bear you."

Hugh sighed audibly. "Again, I thank Your Grace."

John signaled for wine. His ploy had worked even better than he'd expected; Hugh's uncle had proven to be irresistible bait. He'd bought a truce with the lives of Geoffrey de Lusignan and his sons, a truce for today. But what of tomorrow? What was to keep Hugh from disavowing his oath once his kinsmen were safe? He needed more, needed some way to bind the de Lusignans to him, to entwine his fortunes inextricably with theirs. And after careful consideration, he thought he knew how to do just that.

"There has been bad blood between us for far too long, Hugh. Let's pledge a new beginning, bury our grievances here and now."

Hugh's smile was sour. "Is that not what we are doing?"

"I mean what I say, Hugh. But words are hollow. So I'll give you living proof of my good faith—my daughter."

"Jesú!" Hugh sat back, staring at him. "Are you serious?"

"Very serious. Isabelle and I have a daughter; you have a son.

What better way to heal old hurts than to cleanse them in a bond of blood?''

There was no need to say more. This time Hugh's smile was genuine, even reached his eyes. He held his wine cup aloft. ''To the wedding,'' he said. ''And to new beginnings.''

Isabelle was growing bored. Rising, she glanced about the chamber. They'd come to Parthenay for John to accept oaths of homage from the de Lusignans, and to secure their precarious peace within the sanctity of marriage. That morning Hugh de Lusignan's grown son and namesake had been betrothed to John and Isabelle's young daughter Joanna.

The little bride-to-be, still two months shy of her fourth birthday, had no comprehension of the ceremony that linked her life to Hugh de Lusignan, and she was now playing contentedly in a corner with a new doll. Across the chamber, Hugh de Lusignan and John were exchanging faintly barbed courtesies, while Eleanor was in animated conversation with Ralph de Lusignan and Hugh's son. Isabelle could not help noticing the changes four months at John's court had wrought in Eleanor. She'd shed much of her shyness; she was even flirting a little with Hugh's handsome son.

When she caught John's eye, Isabelle blew him a playful kiss, and then moved toward the door. Wandering out into the gardens, she picked a bouquet of white violets, settled herself upon a turf seat in the shadow of a flowering peach tree. She felt no surprise when, after a few moments, she saw the younger de Lusignan coming toward her; she'd noticed the way his eyes followed her when he thought no one else was watching.

''May I join you?''

''Why not?'' Isabelle reached for her flowers, cleared a space on the turf seat. ''How did you get away from Eleanor? She's rather taken with you, you know. When you're there, she loses that air of martyred melancholy, becomes almost vivacious.''

He grinned. ''How sharp your claws, Madame! A man who was the vain sort might begin to wonder why.''

To Isabelle's surprise, she was not affronted. Mayhap it was his smile, she decided; it was disarming, boyishly endearing, appealingly at variance with the knowing blue eyes. She wondered how old he was—thirty-three, thirty-four?

She laughed and, at his questioning look, said lightly, ''I was just thinking that if fate had been different, I'd have been your stepmother!''

Hugh laughed, too. "You'd have been wasted on my father." Taking her hand in his own. "Just as you've been wasted on John."

"That is dangerous talk," Isabelle said coolly. But she did not pull away.

"But true." He turned her hand over, tracked her life-line with his thumb. "You're so very beautiful, far more beautiful than I remembered. How is it that John has not locked you away from the world? I'd have thought he'd sequester you behind the highest walls, veil you like a Saracen woman."

Isabelle opened her mouth to say John trusted her, that she'd never given him cause for jealousy. Instead she heard herself say softly, "Is that what you'd do if I were your woman, Hugh?"

"If you were my woman . . ." he echoed, and for an unguarded moment the game-playing was forgotten. Isabelle was accustomed to court flirtations. She was both flattered and amused that men invariably found her so desirable, but it was never more than a harmless diversion; she never forgot where the boundary lines were drawn, had never been tempted to cross over. She was shaken now by what was happening with Hugh de Lusignan, shaken to realize that she was responding to this man's smile, to his touch. She looked down at the lean, sun-browned fingers caressing her own, and then jerked her hand from his, forced a brittle smile.

"I daresay others might think this a rather peculiar conversation for a woman to be having with her daughter's betrothed!"

He did not return her smile. "I'll settle for the daughter if I must," he said softly, "but I'd rather have the mother."

When their eyes met again, Isabelle found she could not look away. "I'm afraid the mother is already spoken for, Hugh," she murmured, taking refuge in flippancy, while longing to reach out, to trace the curve of his mouth with her fingers. She fought the urge, kept her hands tightly clasped in her lap, and then a shadow fell between them, and she turned, saw her husband standing several feet away.

"John!" Isabelle was on her feet before she could realize that she'd have done better to remain sitting. Hugh's reaction was just as instinctive; he, too, sprang up, backed away from Isabelle. Isabelle recovered her poise first, summoned a dazzling smile. "John, love, your ears must be burning, for we were just talking about you!"

To her relief, John returned her smile. She moved hastily to his side, linked her arm through his. "I remember you telling me your sister used to call you Johnny-cat. Now I can understand why; you approached us as quietly as any cat could, made no sound at all!'' She was talking too much and too fast, but she could not help herself. She was suddenly panicked at the prospect of silence, and she chattered on brightly and aimlessly for several moments, while Hugh shifted uneasily, and John listened with an indulgent smile. After an interminable time, Hugh mumbled an excuse, made a swift departure. Only then, alone in the garden with John, did Isabelle begin to relax.

"So you were talking about me? What were you saying, Isabelle?''

"Oh . . . nothing out of the ordinary, love. We talked about Joanna, the betrothal, and—'' Isabelle cried out as John grasped her wrist, jerked her roughly toward him.

John had been neither surprised nor perturbed when he saw Hugh de Lusignan rise, follow Isabelle out into the gardens. He was gratified, not threatened, by the awareness that other men desired his wife, that they envied him so. It was not jealousy or unease that had motivated him to join them, but rather a sense of prideful possession; he enjoyed claiming Isabelle as his before a man so obviously bewitched by his beautiful wife.

The shock was all the greater, therefore, for being so unexpected. It was not the sight of Isabelle and Hugh sitting together under the peach tree that jolted him so; it was the look on his wife's face. It was not the look of a woman engaging in an innocent flirtation; it was a look of yearning, a look both erotic and intimate, the look a woman would give her lover.

He tightened his grip on her wrist. "Tell me, Isabelle. What was de Lusignan saying to you?''

"John, you're hurting me!''

"Tell me!''

The pain was radiating upward from wrist to elbow; tears filled her eyes. "All right! I'll tell you. He was flirting with me, that's all. No more, I swear it!''

He released her so abruptly that she staggered backward, sank down on the turf seat, cradling her wrist. She'd always been scornful of women who cringed before abusive husbands, wondering how they could be so lacking in pride. But she had never been hurt before, had never been subjected to violence of any kind. Now she wept soundlessly, flinching as he stepped toward her. "Why are you so angry? Men always flirt with me; it means nothing. You know that, John, have never minded before.''

"Mayhap I should have.''

Isabelle forgot her pain in a sudden surge of fear. "My God, John, what are you saying? Surely you do not think I've been unfaithful to you? Never, John, never—I swear on our children's very lives! You must believe me!"

"Must I? Why? Why should you not have betrayed me, too? Why should you be any different from the others?"

Isabelle was terrified. "I would never betray you, never. John, I swear it. I'd have to be an utter fool to take such a risk!"

She saw his mouth twist, and realized she'd blundered; that was not what he wanted to hear. He was turning away, and she stumbled to her feet. "Oh, listen to me, please. There has never been any man but you. John, I love you, I do!"

"Do you, Isabelle?"

"How can you doubt it? I've been your wife for fourteen years; when have I ever failed you? I've shared your bed and your troubles, and I've given you three children." She wiped her face with the back of her hand, choked back a sob. "And . . . and there's something I have not yet told you. I was waiting till I was sure, but . . . John, I think I am with child again."

John did not react as she'd hoped. He gave her a cold, measuring look, a look that frightened her even more, and then said, very evenly, "Is it mine?"

Isabelle gasped. Tears streaked her face, smeared the kohl outlining her eyes. She sobbed again, caught his sleeve. "How can you ask that? How?"

Neither of them had heard the approaching footsteps, and they spun about as Hugh de Lusignan coughed. "Your Grace, do forgive me. I did not realize you and your lady were quarreling. I am indeed sorry for the intrusion." The words were properly remorseful, and Hugh ducked his head as if embarrassed. But he was a poor actor. John had seen how he stared at Isabelle, knew that Hugh hated him not just for that long-ago affront to his pride. His grievance was a festering, thwarted passion; he'd wanted Isabelle in his bed, he still wanted her, and could not hide the poisoned pleasure their quarreling gave him, his envenomed satisfaction that there seemed to be a snake in John's Eden.

Behind Hugh, John now saw Hugh's wife, Matilda, the wife he'd taken as substitute solace for Isabelle's loss. She was Isabelle's first cousin, but she'd not been blessed with Isabelle's beauty, was not a woman to make Hugh forget what could have been his, Isabelle and Angoulême. John drew a deep, deliberate breath as Isabelle said in a muffled voice, "We were not quarreling."

"There is no need to lie, Isabelle. We can be honest with Hugh." John's smile felt wooden, utterly artificial, but the words came of their own volition, even carried conviction. "We were indeed arguing, and I fear it was my fault. You see, Hugh, Isabelle just told me she is with child again. Naturally, I was delighted. But had I known of her condition, I'd never have allowed her to come with me to Parthenay, would have insisted she remain in La Rochelle, and I was disturbed that she did not tell me sooner."

The sudden fragrance of damask rose told John that Isabelle was now standing just behind him. He turned, slid his arm around her waist. She murmured, "You are sweet, love, to worry about me, but in truth there's no need." John could feel the tension in her body, but her voice had steadied, and now she smiled defiantly at Hugh, asked, "Are you not going to congratulate us, Hugh?"

"Indeed." Hugh's voice was toneless. "May God grant you a son, Madame."

When Hugh and Matilda withdrew, John at once released Isabelle, turned away from her. At the far end of the gardens was a large fishpond or stew, shaded by ancient yew trees. He walked toward it, stood for a time staring down at the sluggishly moving carp. His rage had ebbed away; he felt only emptiness, only a dulled sense of disbelief, of loss.

His faith in Isabelle's fidelity was born of circumstance: her extreme youth and innocence at the time of their marriage. As she matured into womanhood, he'd been her guide and mentor, shaping her thoughts and fantasies to fit his own needs. She was more than his wife, she was his creation, utterly unlike the other women in his life, and when she'd said she loved him, he'd taken it as his just due, had never thought to doubt her. Not until the moment he came upon her and the young de Lusignan seated on a turf bench and suddenly saw her not as his, but as a beautiful, passionate woman of twenty-six, a woman with a husband more than twenty years older than she.

"John." Isabelle had followed him. Stopping a few feet away, she pleaded, "John, please, we have to talk. You have to tell me if you truly meant what you said, if you truly doubt that this babe be yours."

John had picked up a handful of pebbles. Now he let them drop, one by one, watched the pond's peaceful surface fragment, rippling outward in ever-widening circles. "No," he said at last, "I did not mean it. I know the babe is mine."

Isabelle had not realized she'd been holding her breath. "Thank God," she sighed, utterly without irony. Her fear had been too great to allow her now the indulgence of resentment or outraged innocence, not when she thought of Eleanor's sixteen bitter years as Henry's prisoner, of Ingeborg's twelve wretched years in Étampes Castle, of the sinister silence that seemed to fall whenever mention was made of Maude de Braose and her disappearance into a Windsor dungeon.

"If the babe is a girl," John said, after some moments of strained silence, "we'll name her Isabelle."

Isabelle smiled wanly. "I should like that." Her fingers encircled her wrist, lingered over the darkening bruises, and then she moved toward him, into his arms.

"Promise me, John, that you'll never again doubt my love for you."

"I want to believe you," he confessed. She seemed about to speak; as her lips parted, he brought his mouth down on hers. "If I thought you'd ever taken another man to your bed, Isabelle . . ."

"I love you, only you." Her voice was husky, beguilingly soft. But her lashes had swept downward, veiling her eyes, her thoughts, and John felt a throb of fear. How would he ever know if she was lying or not? How could he ever be sure?

The dawn sky on Wednesday, July 2, was a sun-glazed, boundless blue in which a solitary eagle soared high above John's siege encampment at Roche-au-Moine. As men rolled, yawning, from their blankets, they gazed upward, took the eagle's flight as a good omen, for all knew that the eagle was king amongst birds, that old King Henry of blessed memory had ofttimes spoken of his sons as his eaglets. The sudden appearance of a golden eagle over the King's camp could only mean that he would prevail against the French King's son, that the day's victory would be theirs.

For a fortnight now, John had been besieging the castle of Roche-au-Moine, just a few miles to the north of Angers. Barricaded within its keep was William des Roches, Philip's Seneschal for Anjou, the same William des Roches who'd turned against John after Mirebeau. John's campaign had met with unqualified success to date; he'd won over the de Lusignans, captured castles and the strategic city of Angers, and his army had been swelled by the ranks of the Poitevin barons. When word came that Philip's son Louis was hastening north to des Roches's rescue, he chose not to lift the siege, chose instead to meet the French forces on the field of battle.

His scouts had reported that the French were approaching from the southeast, and the men now staring up at the circling eagle knew that battle was likely to be joined under that cloudless summer sky, that some among them would never see another dawning day. They were much heartened, therefore, when the eagle swooped lower, hovered for a moment above the tent of the English King.

Within, John was trapped in a dream of familiar horror, in which the very real fears of day merged with the secret terrors of the night, and he found himself naked and defenseless before his enemies, abandoned even by God.

"My liege?"

His eyes flew open; he looked up into the frightened face of a young squire. The boy backed away from the bed. "Forgive me, my liege, but you cried out . . . ."

"No matter, Simon, no matter." As John started to sit up, he found he was entangled in the bedcovers. He signaled for wine, wiped the sweat from his face with the corner of the sheet. He wondered if his servants gossiped among themselves, swapped stories of the King's troubled dreams, knew they did. Rumor was a servant's coinage, lavishly spent.

He could hear voices beyond the inner partition, the excited, uneasy laughter of men girding themselves for battle. He shared their unease, but not their excitement, for he had no love of war, no lust for battle glory. He had never been able to comprehend what perverse pleasure his brother Richard found on the battle-field, and when he fought, it was only because he could get what he wanted no other way.

The squire was back, offering bread sopped in wine. "An eagle alighted upon your tent this morn, lord, in sight of all!"

"Did it indeed?" John grinned, and the lingering darkness of his dream fled before the sunlight flooding his tent. "When Louis sent me his challenge, Simon, I replied that the sooner he came to Roche-au-Moine, the sooner he'd regret it. Today I shall make good my promise." And while there was a touch of bravado in that, it was also the pragmatic assessment of a battle commander who had picked the site, made the enemy come to him, and knew that numerical superiority was his.

The Earl of Chester was waiting for John, shared his breakfast as John was being armed.

"I understand couriers arrived with letters last night. Did Your Grace hear from Flanders, from your brother Salisbury and Dammartin?"

John shook his head. "I regret not, can only assume that they are still waiting for Otto and the Rhineland Princes to join forces with them. I did hear from England, though."

"From Pembroke?"

The Earl of Pembroke had remained behind in England; he and Peter des Roches, Bishop of Winchester, now John's Justiciar, had been entrusted with the government. Now John shook his head again. "No, the last letter I had from Pembroke spoke of his suspicions that Fitz Walter and de Vesci were stirring up trouble with the malcontent barons of the North. No surprise, that; when they refused to take part in our campaign, we knew they'd try to take advantage of my absence from the kingdom. But I think Pembroke and Winchester will hold them in check until I can return to deal with them myself. No, the letter was from my son."

Chester had developed a regard for Richard, and he smiled. "I know Your Grace wanted him to look to your interests in England, but I confess I'd have liked to have him with us today. He's a good lad, can be relied upon to keep a cool head."

John smiled, too. "That he can. Well, he'll be joining us next month, after his marriage to the little Chilham heiress." His squires had pulled his hauberk over a padded tunic, and were buckling his scabbard. "The truth, Ranulf. What are our chances?"

Chester could not recall John ever calling him by his Christian name. "Well, I'd not trade places with Louis for the surety of my soul!" he said, and John laughed. He was reaching for a wine cup when the shouting began.

"The King, where's the King?"

John yanked the partition aside just as the Earl of Derby burst into the tent. "Your Grace, you'll not believe it, what Thouars and the barons are doing—"

"Stop babbling and tell me, then!"

"The Poitevin barons, they're pulling out, my lord, deserting us!"

"Oh, Christ . . . ." For a moment John froze, unable to distinguish between daylight horrors and those of his dream. And then he shouldered Derby aside, ducked under the tent flap.

Men were clustered around the tent; they moved aside, quickly cleared a path. The Poitevins were already mounted, preparing to depart. John recognized Aimery, Viscount of Thouars, began to move toward him. They knew each other well; Thouars had long swung like a weathercock in a high wind, pledging fealty to John or Philip as circumstances seemed to dictate. He did not look defiant now, just uncomfortable, and before John could speak, he blurted out, "We were willing to join you in laying siege to Roche-au-Moine, but not to fight the French. That was never our agreement. Philip is our liege lord, too; we owe him—"

"You lying bastard! You've known for a fortnight that I meant to do battle with Louis, and you said nothing, raised no objections. No, you waited, waited till the day of the battle. Tell me, how much did the French pay you, Aimery? Did you get your thirty pieces of silver?"

Thouars flushed, began to bluster, but John was no longer listening. Even as he'd raged at Thouars, as embittered accusations and invective took shape upon his tongue, an inner voice sounded an instinctive warning. Something was very wrong. Thouars was unscrupulous and unreliable, but he was also weak-willed, shrank from confrontation. He'd have fled in the dark of night, on his own would never have found the courage for this diabolically timed desertion. John's eyes slid past Thouars, searched the faces of the others. And then he saw the de Lusignans, then he understood. His eyes locked with Hugh's. Hugh smiled and then leaned over, spat into the dust.

"You English have a proverb I've always fancied, John, the one that says revenge is a dish best eaten cold."

John jerked his sword from its scabbard. "You craven, cocksucking whoreson! God rot you, but you'll pay for this, I swear you will, if it takes me till Judgment Day!"

Hugh laughed. "Ah, but today is Judgment Day—for you. Good luck with the French."

With that, the de Lusignans spurred their mounts, signaled to their men. The other Poitevin barons followed, galloping out of the encampment to the jeers and taunts of the outraged English.

Chester came forward, stopped beside John. He waited, and after a time, John said softly, "And I gave him my daughter, my Joanna . . ."

"Your Grace!" The Earl of Derby was shoving his way toward them. "Your Grace, what mean you to do? The French will be upon us, and how can we fight now? We've just lost half our army!"

John turned, and then sheathed his sword. "We cannot fight. Give the command to retreat. Tell my captains to head for the Loire."

"But what of our siege weapons, the mangonels and trebuchet? What of our tents, your baggage carts, your—"

"Leave them." John's voice was without emotion, utterly flat, but Derby did not dare to argue. One look at John's face and he spun about, began to shout orders. The anger of their soldiers was now giving way to alarm, to the first stirrings of panic. Men began to run for their horses, and those who had no mounts began to scuffle with those who did. A few took advantage of the pandemonium to loot the tents of their commanders. Tempers flared, brawling broke out, and John's captains tried in vain to maintain some semblance of order. But the men had only one thought now, to flee before the French army arrived.

John did not move, even when his agitated attendants brought up his stallion, implored him to mount. He stood alone midst the chaos and confusion, watching the disintegration of his army.

Withdrawing to La Rochelle, John wrote urgently to his barons, earls, and knights, most of whom had remained in England, requesting that they cross the Channel and join him without delay, even promising that "if any of you should have understood that we bore him ill will, he can have it rectified by his coming." His son Richard, landing at La Rochelle in late July, caught up with John on August 2 at Limoges, where he had the unhappy task of telling his father that reinforcements were not coming, that John's hopes for regaining his continental empire now depended upon his brother Will and Reginald de Dammartin and the army they were assembling in Flanders.

It was a subdued gathering in the Abbot's solar that night. Eleanor was sitting in a window seat with John and Isabelle's five-year-old son, Richard; young Henry, as the heir to the throne, had remained in England, and little Joanna had been turned over to the de Lusignans for rearing at the time of her betrothal in May. Isabelle was moving restlessly about the chamber. When Richard appeared in the doorway, she held out her hand, beckoned him toward the settle.

"I'm so glad you've come. John is much in need of cheer."

Richard had noted his stepmother's pallor, the sleepless nights etched in the shadows smudged under her eyes, and he said, "I suspect that you are, too. Tell me about Joanna. The de Lusignans will not give her up?"

"No, of course not. They mean to honor the betrothal, Richard. She's their hostage, you see. As long as they have her, John cannot move against them, cannot punish them as they deserve."

Richard swore with unusual savagery. "Misbegotten, treacherous hellspawn, may the curse of God be upon them all."

Isabelle's lashes flickered. "Hugh's son was not at Roche-au-

Moine. It may be that he was not privy to their plans, did not
know what they meant to do.''

Richard's surprise was considerable. He might have expected
such naïveté from Eleanor, but never from Isabelle, Isabelle of
all women. "Have you been well? When is the babe due?''

"Not for months yet, not till December." Isabelle nodded to
her son's nursemaid, who rose to take the youngster off to bed.
Eleanor at once rose, too, offered to take him herself.

"You've been kind enough to read to Dickon all evening,
Nell, need not act as his nursemaid, too.''

Eleanor smiled at the child, who grinned back. "Oh, but I
enjoy it, Madame," she said, and did in fact look regretful when
the nurse led the little boy from the solar. She seemed about to
join Isabelle and Richard on the settle, but drew back into the
shadowed window seat as John entered the chamber.

Isabelle at once became solicitous, finding a cushion for him,
acting as his cupbearer. John accepted her ministrations without
comment. Richard was startled by how much he had aged in the
six months they'd been apart; the jet-black hair was rapidly going
very grey.

Giving Isabelle an oblique look that Richard could not quite
interpret, John said, "I expect Isabelle has been telling you about
the de Lusignans and our Joanna.''

Richard nodded. "You must not blame yourself, Papa. Many
a blood feud has been reconciled in the marriage bed. How could
you know what would happen?''

"I should have, though, for this was not the first time I gave
away a Joanna. And did marriage to my daughter bind Llewelyn
to me? Did it make of him an ally? I gained nothing, and lost a
daughter. No, Richard, I should have known . . .''

Neither Richard nor Isabelle knew how to answer, how to
comfort. Isabelle slid closer, began to massage the taut muscles
in John's neck and shoulders, but after only a few moments, he
impatiently signaled for her to stop. "Did you tell Isabelle,
Richard, of the news you brought me? This past May I instructed
Pembroke to levy a scutage tax of three marks per knight's fee
upon all those who'd balked at taking part in this campaign.
Scutage has always been paid in lieu of military service, since the
days of my great-grandfather. Yet Richard tells me that many are
now refusing to pay it, claiming they owe no service for wars
fought on foreign soil." John paused, before adding bitterly,
"And for this I can thank my great and good friend the Pope.
Had he not insisted I pardon de Vesci and Fitz Walter—"

Breaking off as the door opened, John turned, saw the Earl of Chester standing in the doorway. "Come in, my lord. We were just discussing the benefits of being the Pope's anointed. Since I became reconciled with God and the Church, nothing has gone right for me. What conclusion might I draw from that?"

But his sarcasm stirred no rejoinder. Chester had not yet moved from the doorway. He stood in shadow, saying nothing, and there was something about his stance, his utter stillness, that alarmed them all.

"Well?" John's voice was suddenly husky, full of foreboding. "What is it?"

"I've news, Your Grace. News from Flanders."

"Tell me," John said, and Chester came forward, knelt before the settle. "Your nephew Otto finally joined his army with that of your brother Salisbury. They were at Valenciennes, preparing to march on Paris, when their scouts reported that Philip had circled around, was now behind them. They swung about, and the two armies met on Sunday last near the village of Bouvines."

John's hand jerked; wine splashed upon his sleeve. "And the victory?"

"It went to Philip, Your Grace. The victory was Philip's."

John closed his eyes, gave himself up to the dark. But Chester's voice droned on relentlessly. "It was bloody work, my liege. Philip burned the bridge over the River Marque, so his men could not retreat. By battle's end, the dead numbered in the thousands. Your nephew fled the field when it became clear all was lost. But your brother and Dammartin scorned flight, fought to the last. Your brother led a desperate charge across the field to reach Dammartin's men. It was an act of great courage, Your Grace, and almost carried the day."

Chester's loyalties were not personal, were pledged to the monarch, not to the man. But as he looked now at John's face, his dark eyes softened, and he said, with some pity, "At least I can tell you that your brother still lives. He and Dammartin were both taken, are Philip's prisoners."

Isabelle reached over, gently pried the wine cup from John's fist. "Beloved, I'm sorry, so sorry . . ." When he did not respond, she tried to put her arms around him, but he pulled away, rose to his feet.

"It's over," he said, almost inaudibly. "It's all over."

"For now, yes. But there'll be other chances, Papa, other—"

"No, Richard. It's done."

John moved to the table, picked up an hourglass, put it down again. "Find out what Philip wants to ransom Will and Dammartin. Whatever it is, I'll pay it. Whatever it is . . ."

"I'll be honest with Your Grace. Philip may not be willing to free them—for any price. That's a possibility you may have to face, my liege."

John's head jerked up. "No! There must be a way to secure their release. You find it, Chester. No matter what it takes, you find it." What had begun as a command, even a threat, ended up quite differently, came as close as John could get to entreaty. "I cannot lose them, too," he said, and then turned abruptly, walked rapidly from the room. After a moment's hesitation, Isabelle followed.

Richard rose, too, then glanced back over his shoulder. "Is my father right, my lord Chester? Are Normandy and the other provinces well and truly lost to England now?"

Chester nodded. "Nor is that all we lost at Bouvines. Your lord father may have been defeated at a distance, Richard, but he was defeated all the same. You may be sure his barons back in England will seek to take full advantage of it."

Neither spoke after that; there was nothing to be said. The silence was at last broken by Eleanor. She'd sat, frozen, in the darkened window seat as Chester spoke of defeat and death. Now, as she began to comprehend what the battle of Bouvines would mean to her, she covered her face with her hands, wept bitterly.

35

ABER, NORTH WALES

December 1214

Joanna often dreamed of Llewelyn when they'd been apart for a while, but rarely had a dream been so vivid, so explicitly erotic, and she awoke with regret, reluctant to find herself alone in a cold, empty bed. But as she sighed and stirred, she felt Llewelyn's breath on her throat, felt his hands on her body, and she sighed again.

"Now I understand why my dream was so wonderfully wanton," she said drowsily. "But you're taking a great risk; my husband is expected back at any time."

He gave a low laugh. "Then I'd best make haste."

"If you do, I'll never forgive you." She slid her hands up his back, wrapped her arms around his neck. "Beloved, I'm sorry, so sorry. It was all my fault . . ."

"Later," he said, and kissed her lashes, her eyelids, and then her mouth. "Later . . ."

Rising from the bed, Llewelyn pulled a towel from a wall pole, rubbed himself vigorously. Returning to the bed, he pulled back the damp, rumpled sheet, and began gently to pat Joanna dry. "You know more than one way to set a bed afire," he said, and Joanna stretched provocatively, gave him a lazy, satisfied smile.

"We did strike some sparks," she agreed. "I truly missed you."

He smiled, too, and she touched her hand to his cheek. "How did your meeting with your cousin Madog go? Were you able to win him over?"

"Yes, quite easily. I think he's wanted for some time to disavow the English and throw in his lot with us. He just needed to know we bore him no grudge."

"You've been gone longer than I expected, fully a fortnight."

"After Madog and I came to terms, I got word that a Genoan merchant ship bound for Ireland had gone aground near Pwllheli. I decided to see for myself what cargo had washed ashore."

"I see." Joanna sat up, wrapped her arms around her knees. "I know that as Prince of Gwynedd you claim dominion over any ship that founders off your shores. But in the eight years we've been wed, Llewelyn, not once have you chosen to visit a shipwreck yourself. Was this merchant ship truly as richly laden as that?"

"No," he admitted. "But I thought it best if we had some time apart." He reached over, let his fingers follow the curve of her throat. "Else I might have been sorely tempted to throttle you, my love."

"I gave you cause. I'll not deny that I acted like the worst sort of shrew. The truth is that I think I wanted to provoke a quarrel with you." She smiled sadly. "And, by God, that I did."

"Your father's letter?"

"Yes." Joanna put her hand on his arm. "I fear you'll not like what I have to say, but I ask you to hear me out."

When he nodded, she drew an uneven breath. "I'd never gotten such a letter from my father before; I doubt if he'd ever written to anyone as he did to me that night at Woodstock. It began as a factual account of what has been happening since his return to England. He wrote that de Vesci and Fitz Walter met last month at Bury St Edmonds with the Earls of Clare and Norfolk and other barons who've refused to pay the scutage tax. He told me that they've changed their tactics, that they're now talking of a charter supposedly issued by the first King Henry. They claim this charter sets limits upon the King's authority, and they are demanding that John agree to be bound by its provisions. He is greatly troubled by this new stratagem, for he says it is like to find widespread support amongst his barons, even those who've so far held aloof. He thinks Stephen Langton's is the guiding hand behind it, for he says it is too subtle, too shrewd a maneuver for minds like de Vesci's and Fitz Walter's."

Llewelyn had been listening with some impatience, for she was relating facts already well known to him. With that last, though, he silently saluted John's insight, for he had been in contact with the rebel barons for several months, and this sudden emphasis upon a charter of liberties was indeed Langton's doing.

"It was not until he made mention of my uncle Will and

Reginald de Dammartin that the letter's tone changed, that his despair broke through.''

Llewelyn did not give a damn for John's despair, and he could not keep the coolness from his voice as he said, "I thought you told me John had been able to arrange Will's release."

"He did. When he besieged Nantes last summer, a cousin of the French King was amongst those taken captive, and Philip has agreed to exchange Will for his cousin. But he flatly refused to release Dammartin. He said Dammartin was a traitor, owed a debt of dishonor that was now due and payable. When my father wrote to me, he had just learned what Dammartin's fate is to be. Philip has confined him in a cramped, dark cell, chained to a log, and he shall be kept in that hellhole until he dies."

Joanna's voice faltered. "I know what you're thinking, Llewelyn, that my father has forfeited the right to sit in judgment upon Philip. There's no denying that he'll face Our Maker with sins no less grievous upon his soul. But Reginald de Dammartin was his friend, and I know how deeply he mourns, for I read his letter.

"I read his letter," she repeated, "and I wept. I knew how heartsick he was, sore beset on all sides. I knew, too, that he was ailing, for Richard had written me that he'd suffered a severe attack of gout, so painful that he'd been bedridden for days. Yet shall I tell you what I did, Llewelyn? I dried my tears, found pen and parchment, and wrote him an answering letter as cold as death. I'd have shown greater charity to a stranger on the roadside. I offered my condolences with lethal courtesy. I said I could not come to his Christmas court. And then I told him that if he truly loved me, he would prove it by releasing your hostages."

"Ah, Joanna . . ." Llewelyn had never hated John so much as at that moment, had never felt such utterly futile, frustrated anger. "God damn him," he said savagely. "Damn him forever and aye!"

"I think he is damned," Joanna whispered, "and . . . and if only I did not care! But I do, Llewelyn, I hated myself for writing that letter. And unfairly, unforgivably, I began to blame you."

She could feel tears burning behind her lashes, but she blinked them back. "Llewelyn, I swear I did not lie to you that day at the White Ladies Priory. I truly thought I could do what I promised you, that I could cut him out of my heart. You were right and I was wrong; I can never fully forget that lost little girl at Rouen Castle."

"I know."

"I cannot forgive him, Llewelyn. I cannot forget those children he murdered at Nottingham Castle. Until the day I die, there will be nights when Maude de Braose and a seven-year-old boy steal away my sleep. And yet . . . and yet I still cannot be indifferent to his pain. Not even for you."

Llewelyn felt no surprise, only a sense of weary wonderment that it had taken them so long to face the truth. She'd never be free of John. In a strange sort of way, she was as much John's prisoner as that poor lass, Eleanor of Brittany. Had he truly thought he could break that bond?

"Llewelyn? Llewelyn, talk to me. Tell me you understand, that you're not angry with me. Tell me what you're thinking . . ."

"I was thinking," he said, "that there's much to be said for marrying an orphan," and Joanna gave a shaken laugh, not far removed from a sob.

"I was afraid," she confessed, "so afraid you'd say that I'd broken my word, that you'd tell me again what you said at the priory, that you did not think you could love John's daughter."

"You were not the only one lying to yourself that afternoon, *breila*." He brushed her hair back from her face, breathed in the faint fragrance of lemon, the sandalwood scent of her perfume.

"Not that it's always easy loving you." His smile was at once tender and wry. "Welsh and Norman make for a spicy stew. And John casts a long shadow. I've never felt as close to any woman as I do to you, but I know that for all we share, there will always be secrets between us, drawbridges we dare not lower, because you are John's daughter."

Sliding his arm around her waist, he drew her into a closer embrace. "Yet I know, too, that I might not be alive right now if you were not John's daughter. He had me well and truly trapped when you came to him at Aberconwy. And still he offered a truce—because you asked it of him."

That was not a memory Joanna wanted to dwell upon. She did not doubt that her father loved her. It was a millstone around her neck, one that scraped her conscience raw.

"No more talk of John," she entreated. "Let's talk rather of our Norman-Welsh mélange. You like your food both sweet and sour; why not your woman?" Reaching up, she kissed him upon the mouth, a kiss at first soft and then seeking. "It's not always easy loving you, either. But it's worth the effort, my lord husband, well worth the effort." She made a protective sign of the cross over his heart, began to track with gentle fingers the scars of old wounds. "In truth, I'd lower my drawbridge for you any time," she murmured, and Llewelyn grinned.

"Scriptures talk of Heaven's gate, but for now I'd gladly settle for yours. Alas," he laughed, bringing her hand down, catching it between his thighs, "as you can see, if I were a flag, I'd be at half-mast."

Joanna laughed, too, slid lower in the bed. "I'd wager that I can raise a flag even faster than I can lower a drawbridge," she said, and was not long in making good her boast. This time their lovemaking had none of its earlier urgency; it was leisurely, playful, and curiously comforting in its very lack of intensity.

Joanna was drifting toward sleep; she stirred reluctantly as Llewelyn sat up, threw the coverlets back. "Can we not stay abed a while longer?"

"No, my lazy love, we cannot. I hear appeals from the commote courts this forenoon, afterward meet with my council." In council they would discuss an offer of alliance made by the rebel barons of England, discuss the resumption of war against his wife's father. Llewelyn pushed that thought from him. "A pity I cannot go riding this day; I should've liked to make use of my new saddle."

Joanna sat upright. "What saddle?"

"The saddle with ivory pommel and cantle, a silver girth buckle. The saddle over in yon corner, covered with a blanket."

"You wretch, that was to be your New Year's gift!" Joanna grabbed for a pillow. Llewelyn was laughing too much to defend himself, and she was able to deliver several blows before he could pin her down against the mattress.

"My lord, my lady, I'm so sorry!" Branwen was standing in the doorway, looking so flustered that Llewelyn and Joanna could not help laughing. But their laughter stilled abruptly at sight of the man standing behind Branwen, for he wore the colors of the English King.

Branwen was still blushing. "I did knock, in truth," she said faintly, stepping aside so the courier could enter.

Kneeling, he held out a sealed parchment. As Llewelyn reached for it, he said hesitantly, "It . . . it is not for you, my lord, but for your lady."

Llewelyn glanced toward Joanna. She'd lost color, made no move to take John's letter. After a moment, Llewelyn claimed it, laid it on the bed beside her.

"Are you not going to read it?"

Joanna shook her head. She rolled over, clutched the pillow to

her breast. She heard the door shut, heard one of Llewelyn's
wolfhounds whimpering for admittance. She closed her eyes.
What more did he want of her? Why would he not let her be?

"Joanna, I think you ought to read it. He must have answered
you within a day of getting your letter. That speaks of urgency,
breila."

"I cannot. I know that sounds foolish, but in truth I cannot.
You read it for me, Llewelyn . . . please."

She felt his hand touch her hair, and then he said, "As you
wish," broke the seal.

But as he scanned the first line, *"To my beloved daughter
Joanna, Lady of Wales, greetings,"* Llewelyn was suddenly
reluctant to read further, to read a letter never meant for his eyes.
"Joanna . . ."

"Please," she said, surreptitiously drying her tears against the
pillow, not wanting him to know that she could be so unnerved
just by the sight of John's handwriting.

Llewelyn was staring down at John's letter; he'd had to read it
twice before he could banish disbelief. "Jesus God," he breathed,
and there was in the look he now gave his wife no small measure
of awe. "He's agreed to your request, Joanna. He's agreed to
release my hostages."

"He did that . . . for me?" Joanna gasped, grabbed for the
letter. John's words soon blurred; the writing wavered, bled
black ink wherever her tears touched the page. Looking up at
last, she said softly, "But not Gruffydd."

She put her hand on his, half fearful he might pull away. He
did not move; he was staring past her, dark eyes blind to the
morning sunlight, the familiar furnishings of the chamber. For
four Welsh families this would be a Christmas never to be
forgotten, a time to give fervent thanks for the manifold mercies
of God. Their sons would be coming home.

But his son would not. Gruffydd would pass yet another
Christmas in an English castle, his fourth as a prisoner. Shut
away from the sun and sky, how long could a wild, free spirit
survive? How long could he live on hope? How long ere he
began to look upon death as a friend, as deliverance?

36

RHOSYR, NORTH WALES

March 1215

On January 6, 1215, Eustace de Vesci, Robert Fitz Walter, and the more recalcitrant of the English barons came armed to John's council in London, where they demanded that John confirm their traditional liberties, as embodied in the ancient laws of Edward the Confessor and the charter of Henry I. John played for time, refusing to give them his answer until Low Sunday, April 26, and the barons reluctantly agreed to wait. John at once dispatched a trusted agent to Rome. Eustace de Vesci followed soon after, for the barons, too, understood just how critical the Pope's support would be. Both sides then began to prepare for war.

Joanna leaned over her daughter's bed. Elen turned her face into the pillow, mumbled, *"Nos da, Mam."*

Joanna hesitated, but decided it was best to allow Elen her aggrieved sense of injury; Elen was seven, old enough for pride. "I bid you good night, too, dearest," she said gently, and then crossed the chamber to her son.

Davydd was wide awake, primed with questions to forestall bedtime. "Tell me why Papa has gone, Mama." His French was flawless, but Joanna knew that Welsh came more readily to his tongue, that Welsh formed his thoughts, and that realization had been a surprisingly unsettling one for her, as if a barrier had somehow been erected, leaving her on one side and her children on the other.

"Your father and the other Welsh Princes have gone to Rhyd y Groes to meet with the new Bishop of Chester and Coventry, who brings an offer of alliance from the English King."

The English King. But what else could she say? Your grandfather? When not a day passed that Davydd did not hear John vilified as a child-slayer, as Herod? Davydd was so young; how could she expect a six-year-old to understand what she herself could not at twenty-three? Was it not better to wait until he was older, until he began to ask questions? Mayhap by then she'd have some answers for him. Joanna reached out, playfully rumpled Davydd's dark hair, and hoped she was being honest with herself, that she was truly thinking of Davydd and Elen's pain and not her own.

Llewelyn returned that same night, shortly after Compline. As glad as Joanna was to see him, she was not eager to hear what he had to say, so sure was she that he'd spurned her father's olive branch. She delayed the inevitable with feigned cheer, with an animated account of all that had happened in his absence, and while he ate sparingly of smoked herring and rice, she told him that his Seneschal was still ailing, that Ednyved's wife had given birth to a daughter, and Elen had fallen from a tree, knocking out a tooth.

"Luckily it was one of her baby teeth. But I felt I had to punish her, Llewelyn, if only to keep her from breaking her neck, and now she's sulking." Joanna smiled ruefully. "I can always tell when I'm not in her good graces; she'll talk to me only in Welsh!"

Llewelyn laughed, pushed his trencher aside; they were less than a month into Lent, and already he was heartily sick of fish, yearning for forbidden foods: butter, milk, cheese, eggs, and, above all, meat. "I'll warn Elen that tree-climbing is one of the Seven Deadly Sins." Rising from the table, he moved toward Joanna. "We need not talk about it, *breila.*"

"How well you know me. But no, I was being childish. Tell me what happened. What did my father offer for your support against the northern barons?"

"Everything but eternal life everlasting. As always, John is profligate with his promises." Llewelyn turned back to the table, picked up a dried fig. "But you'll not believe what John's new Bishop told us. It seems that John is of a sudden afire with crusading fever, and on March fourth, he took the cross!"

Joanna stared at him, openmouthed. "My father?" But after a startled moment to reflect, she realized how clever a stratagem that was, and said so.

"More than clever, Joanna. To give the Devil his due, it verges upon brilliance. Whatever else John lacks, it's not imagination. Nothing could be better calculated to win the Pope's goodwill; Innocent has been striving for fifteen years to prod Philip and John into another holy war against the Saracens."

"I know," Joanna said, and for an unguarded moment there was in her voice the echoes of indulgent affection, of the love she'd once given to John in such free and abundant measure. "I remember the Pope's letters, but my father never found the prospect of dying for the Holy Land all that alluring!"

"Well, he's now seen the light . . . at a most opportune time, in truth. Since a crusader's person and possessions are inviolate, that puts his foes at a distinct disadvantage—the most Christian King and the infidel barons. De Vesci would have done better to bypass Rome, to spend these weeks fortifying his castle at Alnwick. For as long as John talks of Jerusalem, the Pope will buy whatever he has to sell."

It was a cynical assessment, but Joanna could find no fault with it. "What of Gruffydd? Did my father offer to release him?"

"Of course . . . after I help him prevail over the rebels."

"And . . . and you do not believe he would keep his word?"

"Do you, Joanna?"

"I do not know." Joanna averted her gaze. "Mayhap he might," she ventured, and Llewelyn's eyes narrowed.

"I see. Do you also believe that unicorns can only be caught by virgins? Do you believe, too, that the barnacle goose is spawned in the sea like a fish and may be eaten during Lent?"

"Llewelyn, stop! You asked me what I believed, and I told you. It's not fair to blame me because you did not like my answer. Would you rather I'd lied to you?"

A moment passed, and then another, before Llewelyn was able to summon up a taut smile. "How do you expect us to get a satisfactory argument going if you fall back upon logic?"

He stepped closer, let his hands rest upon her shoulders. "I know you want to believe that John would keep faith, set Gruffydd free. I would to God I could believe it, too, Joanna. But I know better. John promises gold and delivers dross. He'll never let Gruffydd go, never. Not unless he's forced to it."

Joanna said nothing. Llewelyn's way was not hers. She'd have bargained all that Heaven held, would never have risked the war that brought about twenty-eight deaths at Nottingham Castle. But Gwynedd was not her homeland, and Gruffydd was not her son.

"Joanna . . . there is something else I must tell you. William de Cornhill was John's sworn man long ere he was made Bishop of Coventry and Chester. He spoke for John, at John's bidding, offered to free Rhys Gryg, to buy our swords and let the dead bury their dead. But he warned, too, what we might expect should we make of John an enemy and not an ally. He was quite blunt, said that if I joined with the rebel barons, I would be excommunicated.''

Joanna gasped. "And you'd risk even that?" She knew that her father had not been greatly troubled by his own sentence of excommunication. But she knew, too, that Llewelyn's faith was not as tenuous as John's. "Llewelyn, beloved, think what you do. When you ride into battle, you'll be offering up more than your life. You'll be offering up your soul."

"I do not believe that, Joanna."

"But to be excommunicated is to be cast into darkness, eternal damnation—"

"For the sin of not supporting John? In my eyes, that is no sin, Joanna, and nothing the Bishop of Chester or the Pope says can convince me otherwise. Am I to believe that John Plantagenet is now the anointed of the Lord, the chosen of God? Not *my* God."

While Joanna shared Llewelyn's sense of outrage, she could not accept the comforting dichotomy he'd drawn between the stringent teachings of their Church and the infinite mercy of the Almighty. She believed in the Pope's power to damn her husband, however unjustly, for she was not like Llewelyn, not a rebel, and in despair she wondered how she'd find the strength to endure what lay ahead.

"So it will be war," she said softly. "War yet again."

On April 26, Robert Fitz Walter and Giles de Braose, Bishop of Hereford, led an armed force to Northampton. But John did not appear as agreed upon, and the next day the barons moved on to Brackley, where Saer de Quincy had a manor. At Brackley they set forth their demands in writing, calling for a return to "the old laws and customs of the realm," and warning that if John did not agree to their terms, they'd resort to force. John's reaction was pithy and predictable. "Why," he snapped, "do they not just ask for my kingdom?"

With John's refusal, events seemed to take on their own momentum. The arrival of letters from the Pope did nothing to diffuse the tension, for he commanded the barons to abandon conspiracies and render their customary service to their King. On May 3, the barons formally renounced their homage and fealty to John, and chose Robert Fitz Walter as the "Marshal of the Army of God and the Holy Church."

John did not respond as they expected. He stayed his hand, offered to submit their differences to the Pope and a jointly

picked council for arbitration. Despite the grandiloquent title
they'd bestowed upon Fitz Walter, the barons were well aware
that John had already preempted the high moral ground in this
coming war. Few were willing to gamble upon a papal judgment
against a crusader King, and their answer to John's offer was to
lay siege to Northampton Castle.

John had so far trodden with great care, had shown unexpected
restraint, and he now began to reap the benefits of his forbearance. The vast majority of the English baronage were neither
royalists nor rebels, and while many were sympathetic to the idea
of a charter of liberties, these same men were not as enthusiastic
about a civil war. The siege at Northampton was an embarrassing
failure. On May 12, John commanded his sheriffs to seize the
lands of all rebels. But just five days later the political landscape
was changed beyond recognition. For on Sunday, May 17, as
Londoners were at Mass, Robert Fitz Walter's friends opened the
city gates, and London, "the capital of the crown and realm,"
was surrendered to the rebels.

Although Shrewsbury was perilously close to the Welsh border,
its citizens trusted to the security of the Severn, for the town was
sheltered in a protective bend of the river. On three sides the
Severn acted as a formidable barrier, as a deep, natural moat; on
the north, the one landward approach was blocked by the stone
walls of Shrewsbury Castle. But the borderland was in turmoil
that May, and when rumors spread of a Welsh attack, people
panicked.

They had no luck in getting help from the Sheriff of Shropshire, for Thomas Erdington was a trusted agent of the English
King, and these days John's needs took precedence over all else.
Nor could they rely upon neighboring lords; Fulk Fitz Warin, the
de Hodnets, and the powerful Corbet clan were all allied with the
rebel barons and Llewelyn. Shrewsbury's common council met in
urgent session, took the only action open to them, the fortifica-
tion of the bridge that spanned the west bank of the Severn.

Known as St George's or the Welsh bridge, it was an imposing
structure, would not be easily assaulted. A tower blocked the
eastern entrance off the bridge onto the town's Mardevol Street; a
gatehouse with massive loopholed battlements barred entry from
the west. Trenches had been dug behind the bridge, sandbags
piled up. Frankevile, the little settlement on the opposite bank of
the river, was all but deserted. Frightened villagers had long
since driven their livestock into the hills, abandoning all they

could not carry. St George's and St John's, the two hospitals on the wrong side of the river, had been evacuated. To the men gathered now upon the bridge, all seemed in readiness, but the eerie stillness was not conducive to confidence. Each time birds broke cover along the riverbank, men flinched, tightened grips on sword hilts.

Richard Pride and his brother Walter had both served as provosts and thought it only natural that they should assume control of the town's defenses. The deputy constable of Shrewsbury Castle thought otherwise, and there'd been several heated exchanges. When the constable demanded that more men be deployed in defense of the castle, Richard Pride accused him of wanting to sacrifice the town for the castle, and they nearly came to blows. It took the intervention of Hugh de Lacy, Abbott of the influential Benedictine abbey of St Peter and St Paul, to restore order.

"Need I remind you whom the enemy is? It's madness to squabble amongst ourselves when Llewelyn ab Iorwerth and his cutthroat Welsh could come into sight at any moment."

The Abbot's acerbic rebuke sobered them all. John de Hibernia said uneasily, "Ought we not to send our women into the castle for safety's sake?"

No one answered him, for at that moment they heard the shouting. It came from behind them, from the town. The streets had been empty for hours; shops were boarded up, families barricaded within their houses. But as they turned, they saw a man running up Mardevol Street, running toward them.

"That's Lucas de Coleham," the constable said, needlessly, for Coleham was known on sight to all. The Pride brothers were already hastening to intercept him, with John de Hibernia and Hugh de Champeneys right at their heels.

"The Welsh . . ." Coleham was sobbing for breath; he reeled to a stop, grabbed at Richard Pride for support. "Llewelyn . . . he's at the bridge!"

"Lucas, are you drunk? We hold the bridge, hold—"

"The stone bridge . . . the English bridge! He's swung around to the east, is attacking from the other direction, from England!"

He saw horrified comprehension upon their faces. Someone swore; John de Hibernia muttered, "Holy Virgin Mother," and made an instinctive sign of the cross. The Abbot had reached them by now, clutched at Coleham's arm.

"My abbey," he panted. "What of my abbey?"

Coleham's throat was raw, his mouth parched. "It's afire, Abbot Hugh. It's burning."

"Spare the church!" Llewelyn's stallion shied as the wind sent sparks and cinders flying. He wheeled the horse in a semicircle, gestured to his right. "Burn the other buildings!"

Fire arrows had already embedded themselves in the thatched roofs of the laundry, the servants' dorters, the stables. Horses bolted in panic, several even floundering into the abbey fishpond. The Abbot's lodging had begun to burn; the guest house was already in flames. Dogs were barking frantically, and freed livestock milled about, but no monks were to be found, no resistance was offered. Most had fled as the Welsh rode into the abbey precincts; some had taken refuge in the nave of the church.

The Welsh had no time for the terrified monks. Just three hundred yards away was the English bridge, guarded by only a handful of men, men who were seeking desperately to raise its drawbridge. But they were too late; the Welsh were already on the bridge. Swords flashed, blood splattered upon the red grit stones. The one surviving English soldier whirled, plunged into the river; he did not surface again.

Llewelyn's stallion was maddened by the smoke, the scent of blood. It reared up wildly as a man darted into the street, swinging a chained mace. Llewelyn gave the horse free rein; it plunged forward, and the man went down under those flailing hooves.

Other men were emerging into the street, but the resistance the Welsh were encountering was sporadic, halfhearted. Women were screaming; some of the houses nearest the bridge were on fire. By the time Llewelyn reached Haystrete, he knew that Shrewsbury was his for the taking.

The High Cross was now in sight; ahead lay the sandstone walls of John's castle. A small group of men were clustered below the Cross. Their swords were sheathed, and they held up a makeshift flag of truce. Llewelyn recognized Hugh de Lacy, and he reined in his mount.

The Abbot came forward cautiously; his comrades kept a more prudent distance. "My lord, I speak for the Holy Roman Church, for the provosts and common council of Shrewsbury. We will surrender the town to you, offer no resistance if you'll give us your sworn word that no further harm will come to our people."

"What of the castle?"

The Abbot was close enough now to see the blood smears on

Llewelyn's sword. He could not bring himself to look toward the east, toward the billowing black smoke that overhung his abbey. What they were offering in peace this man could take by force, and then turn their town over to his men for their sport. "The castle, too, will yield, my lord. We ask only that no more lives be lost, that you spare the innocent."

"I'd not see men die for a prize already won. Your offer is a fair one; so are your terms."

The Abbot's shoulders sagged. His relief was such that he could not speak, could only sigh a fervent, "Thank God Almighty!"

Richard Pride was not as easily assured; he knew from first-hand experience what could befall a conquered city. "I do not mean to give offense, my lord, but are you sure you can control your men?"

"Yes," Llewelyn said laconically, "I'm sure."

No more than that. But Richard Pride was suddenly sure, too. Reaching for his sword, he held it out, hilt first, to the Welsh Prince.

"What now? Shall we take you to the castle?"

"First I think we'd best see to those fires," Llewelyn said. "I find I suddenly take a very personal interest in Shrewsbury's survival."

By noon the Welsh had gathered in the inner bailey of Shrewsbury Castle, where they watched as the royal arms of England yielded to the red-and-gold lions of North Wales. As Llewelyn's banner fluttered aloft above the keep, they cheered.

Llewelyn could have cheered, too. He felt the same excitement, the same jubilant triumph as he gazed upward, and he did not move until Rhys came to stand at his side.

"Shrewsbury was once the capital of the princes of Powys. You've retaken what was ours, Llewelyn."

"We cannot hope to hold it, Rhys; I know that. But I can hold it as long as it truly matters, until we've forced John to come to terms with us." Llewelyn reached out, impulsively embraced his friend.

"Passing strange," he laughed, "that the first English town I ever saw should have been Shrewsbury. I was just a lad of ten, but I remember it well, even after thirty years. And now . . . now Shrewsbury shall be my bargaining counter, Rhys. I shall make use of Shrewsbury to set my son free."

*   *   *

On June 10, John rode to the meadow called Runnymede, between Windsor and Staines. There he gave grudging consent to
the demands of his rebellious barons. The articles drawn up by
the barons were affixed with John's great seal, as proof that a
preliminary accord had been reached. It was then agreed upon
that negotiations would resume on Monday the fifteenth, using
the articles as the basis for a final settlement, a charter of liberties
that would also serve as a treaty of peace between the embattled
King and his disaffected subjects.

It was dark by the time John returned to Windsor Castle. He
dismissed his attendants, withdrew to his private quarters in the
upper bailey, and none dared intrude upon his seclusion, dared to
brave the Angevin temper on this, surely one of the most desolate
days of a troubled kingship.

It was Richard who finally resolved to breach John's defenses.
He was no more eager than anyone else to serve as scapegoat for
Fitz Walter and his Army of God and Holy Church, but he felt
honor-bound to offer his father some small measure of comfort,
if only a sympathetic ear.

"I'll go if you'd rather be alone, Papa."

There was in John's face the exhaustion of a man who'd lived
too long on nerves alone, and fury all the more intense for being
impotent. But he beckoned Richard into the bedchamber, said,
"No . . . I'd have you stay."

Several sheets of parchment lay scattered about the table.
Richard picked up one headed *Ista sunt Capitula que Barones
petunt et dominus Rex condedit*. That did, he thought, say it all:
"These are the clauses which the barons seek and which the lord
King concedes."

"The charter of Henry I that the barons set such store by,
Henry never held to it, Papa, He granted it and promptly disregarded it. Might it not be possible to treat the barons' charter in
the same way?"

"You're not familiar with all its provisions, are you? Look
upon the last page of the articles."

Richard had only a passing boyhood acquaintance with Latin,
and it took him some moments to make a laborious translation of
the clause dealing with "the form of security for the preservation
of the peace and liberties between King and Kingdom."

The more he read, the more astonished he became. The articles
provided for a committee of twenty-five barons to act as a court
of appeals against breaches of the charter provisions. If they
decided John was acting in defiance of the charter, they had the

power to seize his castles, lands, and possessions in order to force him into compliance, to do him injury in any way they could, sparing only his person and his family. Furthermore, all men were to be required to take an oath of obedience to these twenty-five barons, an oath to take precedence over oaths of allegiance to the King.

To Richard, this was an unheard-of constraint upon the inherent God-given powers of the crown, and a formula for disaster. He did not need to be told that Fitz Walter, de Vesci, and their supporters would constitute a majority on this committee of twenty-five. But it was the last sentence that shocked him so. It forbade John to seek the charter's annulment from the Pope and held that the Archbishop of Canterbury, the other Bishops of England, and the papal legate Pandulf must agree to deny John's right of appeal to the curia in a matter already before it, to compel John to forswear his own liege lord, the Pope.

As Richard looked up, his disbelief clearly showing on his face, John said grimly, "So you see, lad, whatever options I have, ignoring the charter is not amongst them." He joined Richard at the table, read again that last coercive clause, and then crumpled it in his fist, flung it to the floor.

"Much of what they want in the charter I could live with. In fact, many of their demands can be found in a charter granted the city of Bristol nigh on twenty years ago, a charter that eased distraint for debts, gave citizens the right to marry without the license of their lord, limited a lord's right of wardship. Do you know who granted that Bristol charter, Richard? I did, as Earl of Gloucester."

"I know you've ofttimes granted borough charters, Papa, and with generous privileges."

"Including one to London, giving them the right to elect a mayor . . . less than a week ere they opened the city gates to Fitz Walter!" John's rage was mounting; so was his sense of injury. "I may not always have dealt fairly with men I could not trust; I'll concede that much. I'd have been willing to redress individual grievances. But I'll not submit to force. I'll not surrender the traditional and ancient rights of sovereignty, rights that were my father's before me and will be my son's after me. I'll not turn my kingdom over to the likes of de Vesci and Fitz Walter!"

"But you put your great seal to this document, Papa. You agreed to grant them their charter of liberties."

"What else could I do? Fitz Walter holds London. Llewelyn razed Shawardine Castle to the ground, and then took Shrewsbury. There have been outbreaks in Northampton and Exeter. Lincoln is now in rebel hands. In South Wales, Reginald de Braose is laying siege to the castles I seized from his father. In the North of England, the Scots King dares to give open aid to the rebels. Christ, the country is in a virtual state of war! For nigh on a month, my revenues have been cut off, my government hamstrung. And each day sees more defections to the rebels. I'm no longer sure who's with me and who's not, and I do not know whom I can trust. Yes, I agreed to grant them their charter. At swordpoint! But the game is not over yet.''

"I've not read these articles, Papa. You say you can live with most of the provisions. Mayhap you could live with the charter, too, if you tried . . .''

"Never. This so-called peace treaty is utterly one-sided. There's no equity in it. They give up nothing, whilst I am compelled to free all hostages, to banish my foreign mercenaries and Poitevin bailiffs, to dismiss Peter des Roches as Justiciar. And then . . . then to submit to the judgment of five and twenty over-Kings, men who'd barter with the Devil to see me dead. But I am King by God's will, not Eustace de Vesci's. As King, I am responsible for my subjects, not responsible to them. I'd rather lose my kingdom fighting for it than see it whittled away piecemeal by men like de Vesci, Fitz Walter, and Llewelyn ab Iorwerth.''

"What will you do, Papa?''

"Whatever I have to do. I'll give them what they want, their Runnymede charter, and then we'll see; then they'll fly their true colors. Why do you think I've shown such forbearance, Richard? When have you ever known me to be so tender with traitors? But I've had to play to a larger audience than de Vesci and Fitz Walter. There are one hundred ninety-seven baronies in the realm. As far as I know, thirty-nine are in rebel hands. A like number hold fast for the crown. That still leaves well over a hundred that are unaligned, that have not committed themselves to either side. I daresay most favor a charter in some form or other, but how many of them would be willing to fight for it, to fight both crown and Church? Especially when they see how Fitz Walter and his five and twenty use their charter, as a means of feathering their own nests and settling old grudges . . . not all of them with me.''

"You mean, then, to ask the Pope to annul the charter?''

"If I have to, yes.''

"But what of this provision in the articles, the one expressly forbidding you to appeal to the Pope?''

"The Church will never accept such a stricture. It was naïve of Fitz Walter to think otherwise. However sympathetic Langton is to the concept of a charter, he cannot in conscience agree to foreclose a papal appeal. To do so would be to put the charter above the Church. I've talked to Langton and to Pandulf. The price the barons will have to pay for this great charter of theirs is to omit any mention of the Pope."

John sat down suddenly in the nearest chair. "Shall I foretell the future for you, Richard? It does not take a Peter of Wakefield to predict what is to come. I shall give them their accursed charter, for I have no choice. But they will not keep faith, with it or with me. The Pope will intervene on my behalf, invalidate the charter as an act of naked extortion."

John paused, glanced over at his son, and Richard saw that for once he was being utterly honest. "And then," he concluded bleakly, "we will have what none of us truly wanted—war. War to the death, no quarter given, and God pity England."

37

DOLWYDDELAN, NORTH WALES

June 1215

When Llewelyn rose to fetch Gwladys, Joanna experienced a moment of near panic. Ever since his arrival at Dolwyddelan, she'd been dreading the time when she would find herself alone with Reginald de Braose. Taking a bracing swallow of wine, she cast about frantically for a neutral topic of conversation, for a way to keep Maude's ghost at bay.

"I know your son Will. He once stayed at my husband's court. How does he? Will he be attending your wedding?"

"Not likely, Madame. As far as I know, he's still in France. Will's ever had a mind of his own, and now that he's nineteen . . ."

"His mother's death must have been hard on him," Joanna sympathized, trying all the while not to think of the deaths that must have truly devastated Will. Had Reginald been the one to tell him? How could you tell a fourteen-year-old boy that his grandmother and uncle had been starved to death?

"In truth, Madame, they were not that close." Reginald signaled for a servant to refill his cup; he did not seem to share Joanna's unease. "My daughter Matilda is a good lass, does what she's told. But Will and I . . . well, we always seem to be at odds. Part of the trouble, I think, is that he was my mother's favorite, and she— Jesú! Madame, are you all right?"

Joanna stared down at her broken cup, at the wine soaking the rushes. When she raised her eyes to Reginald's, they were blinded by tears. "I'm sorry," she whispered, "so sorry . . ."

Reginald was suddenly as flustered as she. "How stupid of me," he said at last. "I was thinking of you as Lord Llewelyn's wife, had all but forgotten you are John's daughter."

"I do not know what to say to you. I pray for Maude's soul, and for your brother's, but—"

"Madame, do not distress yourself so. I do not blame you. We are none of us answerable for the sins of our fathers."

That was not the creed of his House; few Marcher families had so bloody a history as the de Braose clan. But Reginald sounded sincere, and even if he was speaking only out of his need to gain Llewelyn as ally, Joanna was grateful for his assurance, was willing to take absolution upon any terms she could get.

She was spared the need to respond, for Llewelyn had just reentered the hall, was escorting his daughter toward them. Gwladys showed no embarrassment at being the object of all eyes. At seventeen, she had poise a much older woman might envy, a sure sense of her own worth as a Prince's daughter. We must get her a wedding gown of purest emerald silk, Joanna thought, a color vivid enough to set off those dark gypsy looks. Gwladys would make a very handsome bride and, thank God, a willing one. Joanna knew the girl would have preferred to wed a Cymro, one of her own people. But even the independent Gwladys would never have claimed the right to choose her own husband, and she seemed content enough with Llewelyn's choice.

Joanna, however, had yet to be reconciled to the match. She could see the shrewd political logic in such an alliance. She could even see why the union was advantageous for Gwladys. Reginald de Braose was an attractive man, not yet forty, with polished manners and a reputation for being more moderate and reasonable than most of his tumultuous kindred. And the bulk of the de Braose lands were situated in Wales or the Marches, so Gwladys would be spared the fate that had so daunted Joanna, the prospect of a life in exile. But to Joanna, all else was overshadowed by a bond of blood.

Llewelyn had sympathized with her reluctance to see her step-daughter wed to Maude de Braose's son. But he had not been deterred from making the alliance. Joanna knew he had balanced her discomfort against the good of Gwynedd, and she'd come up short.

"What are you thinking of, *breila?*" Llewelyn was smiling at her. She linked her arm in his, let him lead her aside.

"I was thinking," she said, "how thankful I am that we have years yet ere we must give our Elen away in marriage."

"What is this?" Joanna looked up as Llewelyn dropped a parchment scroll into her lap.

"I thought you might be curious about the Runnymede charter."

"Indeed I am, but I do not read Latin . . ." Unrolling the parchment sheets, Joanna stared in wonder at what she held, a French translation of her father's charter. "Llewelyn, you did this for me?"

"Well, one of my scribes did." Llewelyn pretended to stagger backward as Joanna jumped to her feet, flung her arms around his neck. "Had I only known I could gladden you so cheaply with a few pages of parchment, I might have saved a small fortune over the years, need not have given you all those moonstones and garnets and gold necklets."

"Laugh if you will, but the world is full of men who'd as soon share this charter with their serfs as with their wives, men who think a literate woman to be the Devil's handiwork."

"And with good reason, *breila*. Teach a woman to read and write, and ere long her head will be overflowing with unseemly and unwomanly ideas. She might even think to enter an enemy encampment, to negotiate peace terms on her husband's behalf."

"Have I ever told you," Joanna murmured, "that you have very taking ways?"

Llewelyn laughed. "I daresay the citizens of Shrewsbury would agree with you."

Joanna laughed, too, and sitting down upon the settle, she began to thumb through the document, reading at random. "I doubt my father was much troubled to agree that fish-weirs be banned from the River Thames! Nor by this provision that no free man shall be imprisoned or outlawed except by the judgment of his peers or by the law of the land; he offered that himself in his compromise proposal of May tenth. In fact, Llewelyn, much of this charter seems to state existing law. Take this clause: 'No one shall be taken or imprisoned upon the appeal of a woman for the death of anyone except her husband.' I thought that was already the law of the land, that a woman could testify only to the murder of her husband or to her own rape."

"It was, but apparently John has been somewhat lax about enforcing it, and his courts have been more responsive to women's pleas than the barons liked."

"That's true. I remember one case in which he even allowed a woman to testify against her own husband! She claimed he was in collusion with the plaintiff to defraud her of her land, and John found in her favor." Joanna very much needed to recall acts of compassion, equities she could balance against the horror of Nottingham Castle, the merciless vengeance taken upon Maelgwn and Maude de Braose. But Llewelyn was not the ideal audience for a testimonial to John's better nature, and she glanced nervously in his direction, seeking to gauge the extent of his forbearance.

Quarrels had been kindled by much less. But Llewelyn's mood had been euphoric for days now, ever since they'd gotten word of the settlement upon the meadows of Runnymede. He could not begrudge Joanna such meagre solace, and he nodded agreeably. Reassured, Joanna returned to the charter.

"I know men think it unfair that a woman has the right to engage a champion whilst an accused man must fight for himself. But I find this provision no less unfair, Llewelyn, for it could conceivably be interpreted to deny a woman the right to bring a rape charge. How glad I am that we have our own laws, that we are not subject to trial by ordeal or combat and a Welshwoman's oath is conclusive as to whether she was raped or not."

"When you said 'we,' did you speak from the heart? Have you come to think of yourself as Welsh, *breila?*"

Joanna hesitated. "No," she admitted. "I think of Wales as home, but that is because of you, our children. In all honesty, I have not your love of the land; people are all that matter to me. I do not have any attachment to England, either, have never felt the . . . *hiraeth* that you do away from Wales."

Llewelyn would have preferred another answer, but had not truly expected one. "I'd wager that most of Norman-French blood feel as you do. But I think that will change in time. The loss of Normandy casts a long shadow."

Joanna was intrigued. "You're saying that having lost their Normandy estates, men will come to give greater worth to their English lands?"

"Already you can see signs of it, Joanna. You Normans may not yet think of yourselves as English, but you've begun to draw distinctions of birth. One of the complaints against John's Justiciar, Peter des Roches, was that he was born in Poitou, not England. It was the loss of his Angevin Empire that brought John to Runnymede. But that same loss will one day forge a sense of unity amongst the English, Norman and Saxon alike. I only hope it will not be at the expense of the Welsh."

He sounded suddenly grim, and Joanna reached up, laid her hand on his arm. "Have you forgotten the story you told me, Llewelyn, of the Welsh sage and King Henry? Henry wanted to know if the royal army would prevail, and he said . . . ."

"He said, 'Lord King, I do not think that on the Day of Direst Judgment any race other than the Welsh, or any other language, will give answer to the Supreme Judge of all for this small corner of the earth.' "

"I do not think the Welsh need fear the future, beloved, not as long as the House of Cunedda rules in Gwynedd. But why do you link Normandy and Runnymede?"

"Because, Joanna, this charter is aimed as much at John's father as it is at John. John's government is not that different from Henry's. Granted, his word is worthless, but Henry was not slow to dissemble, either, when it served his purposes. Henry's barons chafed under his rule, too, fully as much as do John's. No lord wants an overly strong King, a government that truly governs. John is hated because men feel—rightfully—that they cannot trust him. But he might have been hated less had he been less effective a King . . . or had he not lost Normandy. Henry and Richard both ruled with a heavy hand, but they were gone from the kingdom for years at a time, occupied by events in Normandy, Anjou, Poitou. Those absences gave their English barons a needed respite, some breathing space. But for nigh on ten years, John has been anchored in England, riding the length and breadth of the realm, bringing his courts and his constables, collecting taxes, levying scutage, making enemies. To his hard-pressed barons, he must have begun to seem as ever-present as God, as inevitable as death . . . and about as welcome!"

Joining her on the settle, he stretched out, pillowed his head in her lap, and she leaned over, gave him a playful upside-down kiss. "This charter could only have been drawn up by lawyers, with their passion for complexity. The wardship of minors, debts to the Jews, bridge-building, intestate deaths, uniform measures of wine and corn; is there any subject they did not seek to address? So much of it seems unnecessary to me. Here it states that a widow shall not be compelled to marry again, provided she offers security that she'll not marry without the King's consent. I agree with the principle, Llewelyn, but it already is the practice. Widows often petitioned my father for the right not to remarry, and he almost always allowed them to purchase that privilege."

"Yes, he did. But that privilege depended upon the King's whim, his convenience. Now it will depend upon the charter. As a widow, which would you rather rely upon, Joanna?"

Joanna did not need to consider. "The charter," she conceded. "I see your point. You're saying that the true significance of this charter is that it changes privileges into rights?"

"And that it goes beyond the rights of individual petitioners. It's rather like a borough charter, one granting certain privileges to the citizens of a particular town. Except that this charter encompasses the entire realm. That is a novel concept. A pity it shall be as short-lived as the peace it warrants.''

''Are you so sure that the peace cannot last?''

''Read the last clause of the charter, Joanna. Then read the list of names affixed to the charter, the barons elected to the committee of twenty-five. And then tell me if you think John will ever accept their governance.''

Joanna did as he bade. ''God's wrath, look at these names! Eustace de Vesci, Robert Fitz Walter, Saer de Quincy, the Earls of Hereford and Clare—I count fully fourteen to be my father's sworn enemies, only two to be men he can trust. Llewelyn, they want war; it's as simple as that.''

''Nothing is ever that simple, love. I grant you that they mean to press their advantage to the utmost. They are not likely to keep faith with the charter. But I find it hard to fault them for that, for they know that John will not, either. He's bound to appeal to the Pope, and when he does, he will prevail. It cannot be otherwise, for his legal position is unassailable. Canon law holds that an oath given under duress is not binding. The Pope must annul the charter. John knows it, I know it, and I expect most of the barons know it, too.''

Llewelyn sat up, reached for the charter. ''You asked what I see as the true significance of the Runnymede charter. For me, it lies in two brief provisions, *breila*. One compels John to make restitution of Welsh lands, liberties, and rights seized unjustly by the crown, recognizes the supremacy of Welsh law in Wales. And the other . . .'' He did not bother to glance at the parchment, for he had long since committed the words to memory.

'' 'We will restore at once the son of Llewelyn,' '' he quoted, '' 'and all the hostages from Wales and the charters delivered to us as security for peace.' That is the heart of John's great charter, Joanna. My son is coming home.''

It was early morning; the July sun had not had time to assert dominion, and the air still held some of the dampness of night. Joanna's ladies were helping her to dress, and Llewelyn was about to submit himself to his barber's razor. It was then that the shouting began in the bailey, the sounds of celebration.

The scene that greeted Llewelyn was one of pandemonium. The bailey was thronged with men and women, barking dogs, excited children. In the midst of all the uproar, Gruffydd was struggling to control his stallion. He'd obviously not expected so joyful a welcome, and he smiled shyly at his well-wishers, acknowledging the greetings of friends shoving to reach his side. He was wearing a finely woven new tunic, but it was streaked with dust and sweat, offering Llewelyn poignant testimony to the urgency of his son's journey.

The crowd now took up Gruffydd's name, chanted it in triumphant unison. Gruffydd flushed under the acclaim, and then glanced up, saw Llewelyn standing on the stairs. As he slid from the saddle, the crowd hushed, parted before him. He moved toward the keep, stood looking up at his father.

"Gruffydd." Llewelyn's voice was suddenly husky. He came down the stairs, stopped when the space between them could be breached by an outstretched hand.

"It's really me, Papa." Gruffydd tugged self-consciously at his beard. "I must look like a right proper Norman. But they would not trust me with a razor, and once I was free, I was not willing to wait a moment longer than need be."

"I do not think," Llewelyn said slowly, "that a single day has passed in these four years when I did not envision this moment, imagine what it would be like, what I'd say to you. I meant to tell you how much I've missed you, and how very proud I am of you. And now you're here, and that's not enough. Christ, it does not even begin to be enough."

"It is enough for me, Papa."

Joanna had followed Llewelyn out onto the stairs. She stood very still, watching as her husband and his son embraced. She'd long had an unease of conscience where Gruffydd was concerned, for she remembered with uncomfortable clarity how she'd welcomed Gruffydd's banishment to the English court. It was a memory that often came back to haunt her in the months after Gruffydd's harrowing ordeal at Nottingham Castle, and she'd resolved that if the boy was ever given his freedom, she'd try to make peace with him. Not just for Llewelyn's sake. She owed it to Gruffydd. This was yet another of John's debts that she was somehow honor-bound to repay.

But her good intentions faltered now at sight of Gruffydd. Her pity had blurred Gruffydd's memory, and she'd had almost three years to recast her recollections in a more sympathetic mold, to convince herself that she could befriend Gruffydd if given a second chance. It was a shock, therefore, to confront reality, the flesh-and-blood man standing on the stairs. With his bright beard, broad shoulders, and flowing hair, he did not look like a proper Norman to her, more like a Norse pirate chieftain. She'd forgot-

ten the aura of danger that clung to Gruffydd. Even as a boy he'd
had it, and he was no boy now, was very much a man.

Neither Llewelyn nor Gruffydd seemed to want to end their embrace. When they finally moved apart, both had tears in their eyes
and both were laughing. Only then did Joanna start down the stairs.

"Welcome home, Gruffydd," she said, and smiled at him.

Gruffydd did not return her smile. She was his father's wife,
he could not forget that. But he could not forget, either, that he'd
forfeited four years of his life because of her, because she would
see her son as Llewelyn's heir. "Yes, Madame," he said softly.
"Gwynedd is indeed my home."

Gruffydd entered the stables, set his lantern upon a stall gate, and
knelt, holding out a savory beef bone. Math's tail twitched; he
snatched the bone from Gruffydd's hand, retreated with it into
the shadows. Gruffydd rose, but made no move to go. The
raucous celebration of his return had not died down with the
day's end, and after three years of solitary confinement, Gruffydd
was overwhelmed by all the noise, the press of people. He'd
once seen a young deer on the loose in Shrewsbury; he could
better understand now the panic a woodland creature might feel
in such alien surroundings, and he was not eager to return to the
hall, to take center stage again. Gruffydd did not feel like a hero,
not at all, just very tired, confused, and curiously let down.

The stable door creaked and he glanced up, saw a small boy
peering in at him. But he did not mind sharing his solitude with a
child, and he gave the boy an encouraging smile.

"See that alaunt in the corner? Math was my dog once; I was
sure he was the best dog in all of Christendom! I truly hated to
leave him, and whenever I'd get too homesick, it would help to
think of Math, to think how he'd welcome me home." Gruffydd
settled back upon a bale of hay. "But I was gone four years. He
does not even remember me."

The child came closer. He was a thin youngster, with a thatch
of untidy black hair, a shy smile, and a smudge of dirt on his
nose. "Here," he said, thrusting something into Gruffydd's hand.
"This is for you."

Gruffydd held it up toward the lantern light. "A penny?"

"It's my lucky penny."

"Then I cannot keep it, lad."

"But I want you to," the boy protested, and squatted down
beside Gruffydd. "I do not remember you, not at all," he
confessed, after some moments of companionable silence. "I

was too little when you left. But I'm six and a half now." He paused, waited expectantly. "Do you not know who I am? I'm Davydd—your brother."

Gruffydd's hand jerked; the coin fell into the straw. Davydd at once scrambled to retrieve it. "Here, you dropped your penny."

Gruffydd ignored Davydd's outstretched hand. Getting hastily to his feet, he stared at the boy. His brother. Joanna's son.

"I do not want it," he said roughly, saw Davydd's mouth quiver, saw only a small child, bewildered and hurt. But then Davydd stepped forward, and the lantern light fell full upon his face, upon the slanting hazel eyes. Accursed cat eyes. John's eyes.

Gruffydd drew an uneven breath. "Jesus wept, you even look like him! You may speak Welsh better than she does, but you've still got his eyes, his blood. God grant that I never forget it."

Gruffydd was badly shaken, and he took refuge now in rage, rage that would enable him to blot out memory of that moment, however fleeting, when he'd identified with Davydd's pain. If he ever gave in to weakness like that, he was lost, and so was Gwynedd. This was Joanna's son, John's grandson. "Go away," he said. "You had no right to do this, to seek me out. I do not want you here."

Davydd stood rooted. "Why are you so angry with me? What have I done? I've never hurt you—"

"You've never hurt me? I spent four years in an English prison because of you, you and your mother! Why do you think John wanted me as a hostage? Because he means to make you Prince of Gwynedd, a puppet English Prince to dance to London's tune!"

Davydd was struggling not to cry. "I did not want you to be a hostage! I was glad you were coming home, gave you my penny. And my mama was glad, too, when the English let you go; she told me so. You say such strange things, and they make no sense. Papa is Prince of Gwynedd. So why would the English King want me to be Prince? And I'm Welsh; how could I ever be an English Prince?"

"No, you are not Welsh," Gruffydd said bitterly. "They may give you a crown, but they cannot give you that. Welsh you'll never be."

Davydd gasped. "I am so Welsh! You take that back!"

"Ask your mother, your Norman-French mother. She was born in England, the daughter of the English King. If I mate Math to a spaniel, the pups will be neither alaunt nor spaniel, but mix-breeds, curs. Neither one nor the other. That's you, too, neither English nor Welsh, and you'd best learn to live with it."

*   *   *

Davydd was alone in the stables. Gruffydd had gone, taking his
lantern, and the dark was not friendly. Davydd still clutched his
penny; now he flung it away, into the blackness beyond him, and
moved closer to Math. The dog growled low in its throat. "I do
not want your bone, Math," Davydd said, but the dog growled
again. He'd find Mama, that's what he'd do. Mama could tell
him if there was truth in what Gruffydd said.

The great hall was overflowing with people. Davydd had to
squirm his way between them, trying not to tread upon the long,
trailing skirts, trying to avoid jostling elbows, spilling wine cups.
His neck began to ache as he craned upward, searching for
familiar faces. He could not find his mother, and he began to feel
a suffocating sense of panic. He wanted to get away from the
smoke and loud laughter, the bodies walling him in on all sides.
He wanted his mother.

But it was not Joanna that he found; it was Llewelyn. It had
never occurred to him to seek out his father for comfort. He
loved Llewelyn very much, but he was very much in awe of him,
too. His need was now so great, though, that he could wait no
longer. He had to know, and he edged his way forward until he
could pull at the sleeve of his father's tunic.

Llewelyn glanced down. "Should you not be abed, lad?" He
was turning back to the adults encircling him, when his son
tugged again at his arm.

"Papa? Papa, am I Welsh?" he said, and saw with relief that
he'd succeeded in catching his father's full attention, for that was
not always easy to do.

"Come with me," Llewelyn said, and led Davydd up the steps
onto the dais, sat the boy down in his own seat. "Now," he said,
"what would make you ask a question like that? Of course you
are Welsh."

"Is Mama Welsh?" Davydd asked, very low.

"No, lad. Your mother is of Norman-French descent."

"Then . . . then I'm not Welsh," Davydd concluded despair-
ingly, and Llewelyn swiftly shook his head.

"You are Welsh, Davydd. You are my son, and under our law,
that makes you Welsh, as Welsh as anyone in this hall, me included."

Llewelyn smiled at the boy, but Davydd ducked his head.
He'd begun to pull at the embroidery decorating the seat cushion.
"If Mama is Norman, I must be half Norman."

"That's right, you are. Welsh by law, and half Welsh and half
Norman by blood."

"But the Normans are your enemies, Papa."

"Yes, some of them are. But not all. I have many English friends, Davydd, men I'd trust far more than I would a Welshman like Gwenwynwyn. To have Norman blood is no shame, lad. After all, you are not ashamed of your mother. Surely you do not think less of her for being Norman?"

"No! I love Mama more than anything. But . . . but what of me, Papa? Mama is Norman; what am I? If I'm not fully Welsh and fully Norman, then I'm nothing!"

"Ah, Davydd, no. You could not be more wrong. Most people have only one heritage. But you have two, your mother's and mine. That gives you more than my other sons, makes you doubly blessed."

Davydd was silent for a time, plucking absently at the cushion threads. "I had not thought of it that way," he admitted. "But what of Math, Papa? If you mate him to a spaniel, the puppies will be curs."

Llewelyn reached out, brushed the hair back from Davydd's eyes. He did not doubt now that Davydd was mouthing something he'd overheard; no six-year-old would ever have drawn such an analogy on his own. "You know that roan stallion of mine, the one I bought at Michaelmas? I got him in Powys, because they are celebrated for the fine horses they breed. Horses of Spanish stock, crossed with sturdy Welsh mares. Crossbreeding can bring out the best of two strains, Davydd. In horses . . . and in men."

Had he said what the boy needed to hear? He was not yet sure, for Davydd's was not an easy face to read. "We should have told you ere this. But your mother finds it painful to talk about her father, and so we kept waiting . . . ."

"The English King is truly Mama's father?" Davydd had absorbed too many shocks this night for one more to have much impact. "He's a bad man, Papa."

"Yes, lad, he is. That's why it hurts your mother so."

"I'm glad, then, that I did not talk to Mama, that I talked to you." Davydd then astonished Llewelyn by saying, "To be both Welsh and Norman—is it like . . . like being a bridge, Papa?"

"Yes, Davydd, exactly like that." Llewelyn was that rarity among parents, one capable of making a realistic assessment of his offspring, tallying up both strengths and shortcomings. He was very fond of Tegwared, but saw him for what he was, a good-natured, amiable youth, both generous and feckless, equally lacking in ambition or malice. Marared and Gwenllian were eager to please, easy to content, neither as clever nor as stubborn as Gwladys. Elen was his free spirit, his secret favorite. And Gruffydd was his firstborn, the son wild and reckless and courageous and wronged.

But Davydd had remained an enigma. A quiet, self-contained child, he was little given either to confidences or complaints, and he was so well behaved that Llewelyn sometimes found himself wishing the boy would break free, put frogs in his sister's bath, or ink in the holy water. Such pranks were an exasperating but expected part of the rites of passage through boyhood, and it baffled Llewelyn to have a son so sedate, so unlike himself. This sudden glimpse into Davydd's mind was a revelation, therefore, the first intimation he'd had that this son could be special.

"Your brother Gruffydd is back in the hall. Let's go over and talk to him," he suggested, not noticing when Davydd lagged behind.

"Papa . . . Papa, will Gruffydd go away again?"

Llewelyn turned, smiled reassuringly at the boy. "No, lad, he'll not go away. Not ever again."

Davydd stopped on the steps of the dais, stood watching as his father crossed to Gruffydd. Davydd's sisters were already there, clustered around Gruffydd in an admiring circle. At the sight of Elen in Gruffydd's lap, Davydd felt a sharp surge of a hitherto unfamiliar emotion, jealousy.

Something nudged his leg, and he looked down to see Math, gratefully wrapped his arms around the dog's ruff. "I wish you'd bite him," he whispered, but without any faith that Math would. Gruffydd would give him bones and win him over. Why should Math be any different than Papa, or Elen and Gwladys? They all thought Gruffydd was wonderful, that he could do no wrong. He was the only one in all of Dolwyddelan who was sorry that Gruffydd had come home.

He heard his father say, "And you actually refused to write the letter? You turned John down?" He sounded so amused, so proud, that Davydd felt tears prick his eyes. Never had he felt so alone. But at that moment he saw his mother. Joanna was standing by one of the hall screens. She, too, was watching Gruffydd and Llewelyn. Davydd's unhappiness had honed his insight, and the look on his mother's face gave him sudden, surprised comfort. He was not alone, after all. Mama was sorry, too, that Gruffydd was back.

38

ABER, NORTH WALES

July 1215

"If it were me, I'd spit on his summons! Why should you be at John's beck and call? You're Prince of North Wales, not a lackey of the English King!"

It was suddenly very still in the hall. Llewelyn swung around in surprise, turned thoughtful brown eyes upon his eldest son. "For certes, I do not see myself as John's lackey. But the fact is, Gruffydd, that the princes of Wales are vassals of the English crown, and John is within his rights in summoning us to his court to renew our oaths of homage. That is the price we must pay for the concessions he granted us in the Runnymede charter. I'll not lie to you, lad. I'll not pretend that I like it any. But I have to do it nonetheless."

"I would not."

"You would," Llewelyn said evenly, "if you were Prince of Gwynedd."

Gruffydd's eyes flickered. "I should think a Prince could do as he pleased."

There was so much innocence in his son's arrogance that Llewelyn no longer had to strive for patience. "I'm doing this, too, lad, because the Archbishop of Canterbury asks it of me. I owe him, Gruffydd; he assumed personal responsibility for assuring your release. He's a good man, and Lord help him, but he truly believes a peace can be made between John and his barons. Which brings me to the third reason why I shall go to Oxford: it will afford me an opportunity to judge for myself how much time we have ere war breaks out."

"Well, it is your decision, Papa," Gruffydd said, managing to make a statement of simple fact sound as if he were making a concession of sorts. Llewelyn looked faintly amused, Ednyved pensive, while Joanna drew farther back into the shadows of the window seat so none could read her face.

"Ednyved, I'll need you with me, and Rhys, too. Morgan? Have you any yearning to see Oxford?"

The priest smiled, shook his head. "My bones are getting too old and brittle for journeys like that."

"What about you, Gruffydd? Would you be willing to come with me?"

Gruffydd raised his head. "The next time I cross the border into England," he said, "it will be at the head of an army."

It had gotten very quiet again. But Llewelyn said only, "As you will." He turned away, crossed the hall, and stopped before Joanna.

"What about you, *breila?*" he said softly, and with so much understanding that Joanna suddenly found herself blinking back tears.

"I cannot, Llewelyn. I just cannot face him—not yet."

As shadows began to spill out of the corners, John called for torches. Dusk was settling over the city, and the sight of that darkening sky filled him with dread. The pain was bad enough during the day, but at night it became intolerable. And there seemed to be little his doctors could do. They mumbled that gout rarely struck in summer, admitted they knew neither its cause nor its cure, had no greater comfort to offer than their assurances that such an attack usually ran its course within ten days.

With infinite care, John shifted position. He was among men he trusted: his Justiciar, Hubert de Burgh; the Earls of Chester and Pembroke; his cousin Warenne. But even with them he was unwilling to show weakness, to reveal the full extent of his suffering. "It's been over a month since we met at Runnymede. In that month I've released hostages, dismissed some of my Poitevin captains, granted Hertford Castle to Fitz Walter, Fotheringhay to the Earl of Huntingdon, Mountsorrel to that turncoat de Quincy. And what have they done? They've fortified their castles for war, defied officers of the crown, refused to give me a written pledge of their loyalty. And still they hold London!"

"We may be able to reach a compromise there, Your Grace. The Archbishop of Canterbury is sorely distressed by their intransigence, but he still thinks he can persuade them to yield control of the city in August, on the feast of the Assumption—provided that all have taken oaths of obedience to their twenty-five by then, and that you have satisfied their claims for disputed castles."

"You call that a compromise, Hubert? By those terms they could justify holding London till Judgment Day! Satisfy their claims, you say? There's no way on God's earth that I can ever do that. But what I can do is stop this charade."

John picked up a letter, threw it onto the table. "This arrived at noon. The Pope has commanded all of Christ's faithful to support me, and he directs Langton and Pandulf to excommunicate the barons if they do not come to terms in eight days. Langton is balking, contending that the Pope's letter was written without knowledge of the Runnymede charter. But he'll not be able to make that claim for long. I've appealed to the Pope, advising him of the shameful settlement I was forced into making at Runnymede and formally requesting that he annul the charter."

"John, I must talk—" Isabelle was already in the room before she took notice of the other men. "I did not know you were in council. I will come back later . . ."

John shook his head. "No, we'll continue this on the morrow." Her entry could not have been better timed, for his foot was beginning to throb again, and he was grateful that Isabelle had given him so plausible an excuse to cut the meeting short. All knew a pregnant woman had to be humored, and he'd far rather appear as an indulgent husband than as a crippled King.

As soon as they were alone, John pulled aside the blanket, stared down at his afflicted ankle. It was swollen to twice its normal size, so discolored by a dark purple rash that his skin seemed covered with blotched, ugly bruises; even the veins were distended, protuberant. John covered it with the blanket again, sagged back in his chair.

Isabelle placed a wine cup on the table within his reach, then lowered herself onto a nearby bench. This was the first of her five pregnancies to cause her so much discomfort. She felt bloated, her back ached all the time, and her queasiness was continuing although she was well into her fourth month. She wondered if it was because she'd become pregnant so soon after Isabella's birth. At the time she'd welcomed this pregnancy; what better way to offer John tangible proof of her fidelity? But in the sweltering heat of high summer, the child she carried was becoming more and more of a burden. She'd never felt so ungainly, so vulnerable.

John had closed his eyes, and as she studied his face, she felt a new and chilling fear. John, too, looked vulnerable. What if he was? What if he lost this war? What would happen to her?

"When we leave Oxford, I mean to send you and the children to Corfe. It's the strongest of my castles; you ought to be safe there." John reached for the wine cup, pushed it away after one swallow. "Send down to the buttery for hippocras; I cannot drink this swill. But first, what have you to tell me?"

"John . . ." Isabelle braced herself. "The Welsh Princes have ridden in," she said, and winced at his sudden smile. "My love, I'm so sorry, but . . . but Llewelyn did not bring Joanna with him. John, he came alone."

Whenever he stayed in Oxford, John held court in the palace known as the Domus Regis, the King's House; it was his birthplace and a favorite royal residence. But it was also situated outside the city walls, and for his July confrontation with the charter committee of twenty-five, he bypassed the more comfortable King's House for the greater security of the eleventh-century castle. It was there that he welcomed the Welsh Princes, and there that he accepted their oaths of homage and fealty.

As Llewelyn glanced about the chamber at the men mingling in apparent harmony, his sense of unreality intensified. He could almost believe he'd stumbled into some lunatic land in which nature's laws were mocked and madness reigned. The committee of twenty-five had been in session all week, hearing appeals of men who felt themselves wronged by John, and Oxford seemed populated by John's enemies. Giles de Braose alone was absent; he and his brother Reginald had balked at taking part in the Runnymede settlement, at making any peace with John.

Llewelyn was turning as a voice murmured just behind him, in Welsh, "Would you care to wager how long their Runnymede peace lasts?"

"Till Michaelmas?" Llewelyn hazarded, and Maelgwn gave a shrug, a twisted smile.

"I've just heard a story I can scarce credit, but Saer de Quincy swears it to be true. John was to arrive on Thursday last from Woodstock, but he did not reach the city till the morrow, and sent word that his illness would prevent him from leaving the castle. He wanted the barons to hold their council in his chamber, but they refused, insisted that he come to them."

Maelgwn drained his wine cup. "I would," he said, "have given a great deal to witness that."

Llewelyn would never think of Maelgwn as a friend, but in the three years they'd been allies, he had developed a grudging

respect for the other man. He'd watched as Maelgwn knelt before
John, received the kiss of peace from the man who'd murdered
his sons, and wondered if he'd have found Maelgwn's resolve
had Gruffydd, too, died at Nottingham Castle.

"I said Michaelmas, but it could be even sooner. John has as
many enemies as he has barons, and I truly think that at last he is
going to reap what he's sown. And when he does, Maelgwn,
Christ Jesus, what an opportunity for the Welsh! Once John is
hopelessly bogged down in a war with his own barons, we move
into South Wales, move against the Norman enclaves in Deheubarth
and Powys."

"We?" Maelgwn echoed, cocking a sardonic brow. "So the
Prince of Gwynedd will lead an army south to fight with us
against the Normans? Most magnanimous, my lord, but I wonder
what Gwenwynwyn will think of your generosity. I suspect he'd
say we might be exchanging one army of occupation for another."

"I daresay he will. But what of you, Maelgwn? What say
you?"

"Oh, I expect I will give you the benefit of the doubt. But
what I will not give you is Ceredigion."

Llewelyn laughed. "I prefer to make new mistakes, not to
keep repeating the same ones over and over. I learned a hard
lesson four summers ago at Aberconwy, but I learned it well.
Welsh disunity is the most potent weapon the Normans have, and
we alone can deny it to them."

"My lord . . . ." A servant was approaching, clad in the King's
livery. "My lord, the King wants to speak with you. Will you
follow me to his chamber?"

This was a summons Llewelyn had been expecting. "Like all
here in Oxford, I serve the King's pleasure," he said dryly, and
Maelgwn laughed for the first time since arriving at the English
King's court.

"I want no war with the Welsh. I want this peace to last." John
spoke slowly, drawing his words out for emphasis, to stress his
sincerity. "I would hope you believe that."

Llewelyn did; even John could handle only one war at a time.
This was the first close encounter he'd had with John since the
oath-taking, and he was startled to see what ravages three years
had wrought. John's eyes were bloodshot and puffy, his waist
thickening, his gestures abrupt. He looked more than ill, he
looked haunted, and Llewelyn suddenly remembered the judgment he'd once heard an Augustinian monk pass upon the En-

glish King. A great Prince, the monk had said, but scarcely a happy one.

A silence had fallen between them. John knew he had more dangerous enemies than the Welsh Prince, but there were few he hated as much, and rarely had anything come harder to him than this overture of peace. "To prove to you that I mean what I say, I am granting you two English manors, Bidford in Warwickshire and Suckley in Worcestershire."

Llewelyn was not impressed. How much English land did John think the lives of twenty-eight Welsh hostages were worth? "I shall hold the manors for my daughter Elen," he said coolly, "to be part of her marriage portion when she's of an age to wed."

John nodded. Assuming he'd been dismissed, Llewelyn rose, made an obeisance as meaningless to him as the oath of homage he'd had to offer to the English King. But as he reached the door, John could hold back no longer.

"I freed your son, just as I promised. So why, then, did you not bring Joanna with you? She's not seen me for three years; how could you keep her away?"

"I did not forbid Joanna to come. That was her choice."

"You expect me to believe that?"

"I do not much care what you believe."

"I know you've tried to turn Joanna against me. But I know my daughter, know she'd not believe your lies, your—"

"Lies?" Llewelyn moved away from the door. "There are twenty-eight families to testify to the truth of Nottingham Castle. To you, a Welsh death might count for less. But to Joanna, a child is a child. You murdered my hostages to take vengeance upon me, but you hurt Joanna, too. She still dreams of that lad you hanged at Shrewsbury, Maelgwn's son. Only in her dreams, it is Davydd, her son, on your gallows."

"I'll tell you who I blame for Joanna's pain—you! If you'd let her come to me, I could have explained, could have made her understand that I only did what I had to do. I hanged those hostages because you broke faith. They'd still be alive now, had you not betrayed them. Once you did, I had no choice. I had to set an example, but you forced me to it."

"It does not surprise me that you find it so easy to justify the deaths of children. But what of murder done in the dark? How do you justify starving a woman and her son to death?"

To Llewelyn's surprise, John flushed. Only then did he realize that this might well be the first time John had been held accountable for Maude's murder, for her family and friends had been exiled or intimidated, and John's family and friends did not truly want to know.

"They died in one of my prisons," John said, after a lengthy pause, "but I did not seek their deaths. Despite what you and others think, I am not responsible."

For a man nurtured on parental falsehoods, a man to whom lying was now not so much habitual as reflex, it was a surprisingly unconvincing defense. Llewelyn slowly shook his head. "Is that what you truly want me to tell your daughter?"

For once, John could think of nothing to say. The look on Llewelyn's face was one he'd seen before. The man who'd come to tell him that Maude and her son were dead was a trusted servant, a man who'd shown himself to be immune to conscience, impervious to scruples. Yet there'd been in his eyes something John had never expected, a look of judgment, of involuntary revulsion. And it was only then that John had realized the full measure of what he'd done.

He'd given in to Angevin rages before, said things better forgotten, given commands he later regretted. But he'd never done anything he could not afterward justify to himself. Not until he'd allowed himself to take an unforgivable vengeance upon Maude de Braose and her son. Not until he'd seen the truth in a soldier's eyes, that there were some acts nothing could justify.

He felt no grief for Maude, no remorse. What he did feel was harder for him to admit, to deal with—shame. He did not think he was any more cruel, any more vengeful than other men, than his brothers, his enemies. But he could not defend what he'd done to the de Braoses, could only put the memory from him as an aberrant act, a tragic mistake. All men have things in their pasts that they'd change if they could. All men. But that was not an argument he could make, not to Llewelyn ab Iorwerth. The Welshman's eyes had taken on the glitter of dark ice. If he was seeking absolution, he'd come to the wrong church.

"I should never have given my daughter to you. Of all the mistakes I've ever made, that must rank amongst the biggest."

"Is that the message you'd have me give Joanna? That our marriage was a mistake?"

"No, damn you, it is not! Tell Joanna . . . tell my daughter that she will always be that, my daughter, and she will always be welcome at my court."

*   *   *

In mid-August came a second letter from the Pope, castigating Stephen Langton and some of the English bishops for not giving John greater support against his barons and ordering the Archbishop forthwith to excommunicate all "disturbers of the King and kingdom." When Langton refused to comply, the papal legate Pandulf suspended him as Archbishop of Canterbury.

It was late September when the papal bull *Etsi Karissimus* reached England. Condemning the Runnymede charter as "shameful and base and illegal and unjust," as "concessions thus extorted from a great Prince who had taken the Cross," it declared the charter to be "null and void of all validity forever."

On September 30, a disloyal castellan surrendered the great royal fortress of Rochester to the rebels. On October 13, John seized the city and laid siege to the castle. By then, Fitz Walter and his cohorts had already opened negotiations at the French court, had offered the English crown to Louis Capet, the eldest son of the French King.

39

TYWYN, NORTH WALES

January 1216

Llewelyn led his army into South Wales in early December.
Joined by the other Welsh Princes, he laid siege to the Norman
fortress of Carmarthen, which had been for more than seventy
years the center of royal power in the Tywi Valley; it fell to
Llewelyn in just five days. The castles of Cydweli, Llanstephan,
St Clears, Laugharne, Narberth, and Newport were taken in rapid
succession. On the day after Christmas, the Welsh added Cardigan and Cilgerran castles to their list of conquests, and a jubilant
Welsh chronicler recorded that "the Welsh returned joyfully to
their homes, but the French, driven out of all their holds, wandered hither and thither like birds in melancholy wise."

Rarely had a winter been so mild. The sea was a placid blue, and
the beach glistened like powdered crystal, more than justifying
Tywyn's name—a shining seashore. Alison spun around in an
exuberant circle, arms and skirts flying. "It feels verily like
spring, Madame!"

Joanna, too, was enjoying the warmth of the sun on her face.
"Davydd? Would you like to help me build a sand castle?
Davydd . . . what's wrong?"

Davydd was cradling his arm at an awkward angle. "I fell,
Mama."

Joanna experienced a dizzying jolt of panic at first sight of the
blood soaking her son's tunic, but a hasty examination of his
injury reassured her that although the cut was deep, it was not
serious. Alison was already unfastening her veil, and Joanna's
bodyguard was holding out his dagger. Slitting Davydd's sleeve,
Joanna tied a makeshift bandage and then, seeing that Davydd

was on the verge of tears, she said swiftly, "Do you know why you bled when you cut yourself on that shell? There are conduits in your arm, called veins, which carry the blood from your liver."

As she had hoped, that interested Davydd. "Where's my liver, Mama?"

"I'm not truly sure; near your stomach, I think. I do know it is the source for love and carnal lust." She had an inspiration then, and jerked off her own veil. "Here," she said, and fashioned for her son a sling. "Now you look like a soldier coming home from the war. Do you think you can walk back to the monastery? If not, I can send Marc to fetch your pony."

"I can walk, Mama." Davydd handed Alison his collection of shells, and they started across the sand. Joanna had laughed when Llewelyn once asked her if Davydd was not too quiet for his age; with her, the boy was rarely still, was a veritable fount of questions and queries and curious non sequiturs. His injury had not bridled his tongue any, and he soon transformed their walk into an inquisition, wanting to know what caused high tide, why blood was red, why love sprang from the liver and not from the spleen, as laughter did.

"Show some mercy; one question at a time!"

Davydd grinned. "All right. Are there elephants in England?"

Joanna sighed; elephants were Davydd's newest passion, and he could happily discuss their odd ways for hours on end. "No, I think not. Elephants live only in faraway lands like Ethiopia and India."

"Are there dragons in England, then?"

So it was not elephants at all; it was England. "There have been reports of English dragons, but I've never met anyone who actually saw one, Davydd."

"Uncle Rhys told me he heard of a place in England, called Stroke or Stripe, where men are born with tails. Is that true, Mama?"

Joanna laughed. "You mean Strood, in Kent. That's but a folktale. Strood is close by Rochester Castle, and I was often there with my father. But I saw nary a single tail!"

Davydd looked disappointed. "Mayhap they hide their tails in their tunics." He stopped to pick up a shell. "Rochester Castle . . . is that not where the fighting was?"

Joanna nodded. "But the fighting is over now at Rochester." The castle had been surrendered to the King after a seven-week siege. "The King has headed north, into Yorkshire. The rebels

are allied with Alexander, the Scots King, and some of them
even did homage to him for lands in Northumbria. Alexander has
been raiding over the border, and my father wants to drive him
back into Scotland—also to punish the rebels.''

How much more should she tell him? She'd vowed that she'd
not keep anything from her children again, but how much truth
could a seven-year-old handle? Did Davydd need to know that
John's army was wreaking bloody vengeance upon the North?
Did he need to know that rebel manors were being torched,
livestock slain, that terrified towns were offering John lavish
sums to be spared the fate of Berwick upon Tweed, burned to the
ground, its citizens slaughtered?

"Is it a bad war, Mama?"

"To me, all wars are bad, Davydd, but that is a woman's
view. In war, soldiers sometimes do great evil, and the innocent
suffer. It need not always be that way, though. Your father
controlled his men at Shrewsbury. But my father would not—or
could not—control his men at Berwick, and many people died.''

"Will the King win his war with the barons?''

"I'm not sure, Davydd. Your father says the odds are in his
favor, since his army is made up of mercenaries, routiers. They're
seasoned soldiers, you see, men who earn their living by their
swords. Llewelyn thinks my father is likely to prevail, unless the
French give substantial aid to the rebels. They have offered the
crown to Louis, the French King's son, but Philip is loath to
incur the Pope's wrath again. Whilst he did allow Louis to send
seven thousand French troops to London, he is discouraging
Louis from coming over himself, and that is what the rebels truly
need, a Prince they can rally around.''

Davydd slanted her a sidelong glance. "Mama . . . do you
want the King to win?''

It had not escaped Joanna that Davydd invariably referred to
John as "the King," never as "your father." She knew the little
boy was confused by her relationship to John, but she did not
want to lie to him, and she said slowly, "You know that John
has committed grievous sins. But he is still my father, Davydd,
and so I have to say yes, I do hope he will prevail over the
rebels.''

"But . . but what if he wins, and then he makes war on
Papa?''

He'd gone unerringly to the heart of Joanna's dilemma. But as
she looked into his upturned face, she suddenly realized what he
was really asking, realized how threatened he felt by her kinship

to the English King. "I would hope it never comes to that,
Davydd. But if it did, I would want your father to win. You and
Elen and Llewelyn are my family, and Wales my home."

That was what Davydd needed to hear, and he reached up, slid
his free hand into hers. "Papa would win," he said confidently.
"He took all those castles from the Normans. He's a good battle
commander, is he not, Mama?"

"The best, love. This was the first time, Davydd, that all the
Welsh Princes banded together, offered a united front to the
Normans. And it was your father's doing, as is this conference
on the banks of the River Dyfi. All of the Welsh Princes have
gathered in answer to Llewelyn's summons, and that, too, is a
first. Your father is seeking to make a lasting peace in the south
between Maelgwn, Rhys Gryg, and their nephews, and to bring it
about, he has proposed an equitable partition of Deheubarth
amongst them."

"What of all they won from the Normans? Is Papa not going
to keep any of that land?"

"No, Davydd, he made no claims for himself. Do you know
why? Because your father is a very clever man. He's gaining
something from this peace that is of far greater value than land or
castles, something of historic significance. That is why he sent
for us, so that we could witness what is to happen."

Davydd's eyes had widened. "What, Mama?"

Joanna smiled. "You'll find out," she said, "on the morrow!"

A man standing on the bank of the River Dyfi could look north
into Gwynedd, south into Ceredigion, and Llewelyn had selected
the river estuary as an appropriate site for his peace conference.
It had taken all of his diplomatic and political skills and nearly a
week of wrangling among the participants, but in the end Llewelyn
had prevailed, and on a mild, sunlit morning in January, a formal
partition of Deheubarth was proclaimed.

Joanna had chosen an inconspicuous spot near Llewelyn's
tent, one that nonetheless afforded an unobstructed view of the
ceremonies taking place upon the white sands of Aberdyfi. As
the agreed-upon division of the various cantrefs and commotes
was read aloud to the assembled lords, Davydd lost interest,
began to fidget with his sling. Joanna had been unable to convince him that he did not need it; he'd even managed to fasten his
mantle so that the sling was still visible.

"If you do not stop squirming," she murmured, "you are going to miss the surprise."

"Well, when will it happen, Mama?"

"Now," Joanna said. An expectant silence had fallen; men were jostling to get closer to their Princes. As all watched, Maelgwn crossed the sand, knelt before Llewelyn, and swore an oath of homage and fealty to the Prince of Gwynedd. Rhys Gryg, who'd been freed from an English prison some months earlier; Llewelyn's cousin Hywel; his cousin Madog, Prince of upper Powys; Maelgwn's rebellious nephews, Rhys Ieunac and Owain—one by one they followed Maelgwn, acknowledged Llewelyn as their liege lord.

Gwenwynwyn was the last to approach Llewelyn. High color had mottled his cheekbones, and his eyes were slits of resentful rage, but he, too, knelt and did homage to the man who'd been his lifelong rival. Llewelyn half turned, and for a moment his gaze met Joanna's, a moment in which they exchanged a very private message.

"Do you know what this means, Davydd? The other Welsh Princes have just acknowledged Gwynedd's suzerainty, have just acknowledged Llewelyn as their liege lord . . . their Prince. He's too shrewd to lay formal claim to the title, knowing that would but alarm the English and stir up the jealousies of his allies. But from this day forth, your father is, in effect, Prince of Wales."

Davydd did not fully comprehend the significance of what he'd just witnessed, but he responded to the echoes of pride and jubilation in his mother's voice. "I'm glad Papa wanted me here, glad he's to be Prince of all the Welsh. Mama . . . will I be Prince of Wales, too, one day?"

Joanna did not answer at once, and as he glanced up at her, he saw that she was no longer watching Llewelyn. She was staring at the tall youth standing by Llewelyn's side, staring at his brother Gruffydd.

"Yes, Davydd," she said softly. "If I have any say about it, you will, indeed, be Prince of Wales."

Gwenwynwyn soon recanted, swayed by his jealousy of Llewelyn and the beguilements of the English King. A thirteenth-century Welsh chronicle set forth the denouement of this embittered rivalry:

In that year Gwenwynwyn, lord of Powys, made peace with
John, King of England, scorning the oath and pledge he had
given. . . . And after Llewelyn ab Iorwerth had learned that,
he felt vexed; and he sent to him bishops and abbots and other
men of great authority. . . . And when that had availed him
naught, he gathered a host and called the Princes of Wales
together to him, and made for Powys to war against Gwenwynwyn, and he drove him to flight into the county of Chester and
gained possession of all his territory for himself.

40

CORFE CASTLE, ENGLAND

June 1216

By spring, John's war seemed all but won. In three months he had brutally and effectively suppressed rebellion in the North and East of England. He was receiving formidable support from his brother Will, who'd led a punitive expedition into East Anglia, and the two most powerful lords in the realm, the Earls of Chester and Pembroke, were holding fast for the crown. The rebels still controlled London, but they were losing heart. By April, a number of them were seeking to make peace with John; even Eustace de Vesci was asking for terms.

It was not the prospect of fighting for John's kingdom that had discouraged Louis Capet from joining the rebels; it was his father. While Louis was quite willing to risk excommunication for the English crown, Philip was not. It took Louis until Easter to coax a grudging consent from the French King, but on April 24, Philip summoned the papal legate Guala to a council at Melun. There the French monarch and his son contended that John was no rightful King, having been charged with treason by his brother Richard and having been condemned by a French court for the murder of his nephew Arthur. Guala was not impressed, and warned them that John was the Pope's vassal and England part of the patrimony of the Holy Roman Church. But Louis was deaf to all but the seductive sirens of kingship, and he declared his intent to claim the crown that was his by right, his wife being niece to John and granddaughter to Henry.

John remained sanguine in the face of the impending French invasion, for he, more than any other English King, had appreciated an island kingdom's need for naval supremacy and had spared no expense in building England's first fleet. He felt confident that his ships would be able to keep Louis bottled up within Calais harbor. There was one aspect of successful kingship, however, that John had always utterly lacked—luck. Fortune now delivered a stunning blow. On the night of May 18, a sudden storm raked the Kentish coast, and John's galleys were scattered, driven onto the rocks or out to sea.

When coast watchers at Thanet reported sails on the horizon two days later, John allowed himself the indulgence of optimism, allowed himself to hope that some of his fleet had ridden out the squall. But the ships that sailed into Pegwell Bay flew the golden fleur de lys of France.

Pembroke and Chester advised against an immediate confrontation; too many of John's mercenaries were French, and John owed them too much in back pay to trust them in an encounter with their liege lord's son. John agreed, unwilling to risk all upon a single battle, one that might be decided by treachery, and he withdrew toward the west.

He'd hoped that the invasion of a foreign Prince would rally his subjects to his side. The opposite happened. Louis' presence upon English soil acted as a catalyst for the rebel cause. Men flocked to his banners, even men who'd so far been loyal. John's support began to bleed away. To stave off a lethal hemorrhage, the papal legate Guala invoked the moral authority of the Church on John's behalf, and on Whitsunday he publicly excommunicated Louis and his followers, placed London under Interdict. But that did not deter Londoners from giving Louis a joyous welcome just four days later.

Stunned by the acclaim and acceptance the French Prince was encountering, John abandoned Winchester as Louis moved into Hampshire. On June 14, Louis took the ancient city of Winchester, set about besieging the royal castle. John retreated southward, reaching the security of Corfe Castle on June 23. That was the day he learned of the defections. The Earl of Arundel, the Count of Aumale, and John's own cousin, William de Warenne, Earl of Surrey, had gone to Winchester, where they had disavowed allegiance to John and acknowledged Louis as their King.

Corfe Castle dominated the Dorsetshire peninsula known as Purbeck Isle. Its history was a grim one, for it was often used as a royal prison. Here the ill-starred prophet Peter of Wakefield had passed the last months of his life. Here twenty-two knights taken captive after John's victory at Mirebeau had overpowered their gaolers,

barricaded themselves within the keep, and starved to death
rather than surrender. Here, too, John held four of Maude de
Braose's grandsons, children of the son who'd died with her in a
Windsor dungeon. But Corfe was also a favorite residence of the
Angevin Kings. John had constructed lavish living quarters in the
inner bailey, just east of the great keep, where Isabelle and their
children awaited his coming.

Isabelle stirred, reached sleepily toward John's side of the bed.
"John? Why are you not abed?"

John turned from the open window, from the summer dark. "It
has begun to rain," he said. "Go back to sleep."

Instead she sat up, wrapped herself in the sheet. "I've missed you
so. We've never been apart like this, not in all the years of our
marriage. Pour me some wine, love, and talk to me. I just do not
understand why this is happening, John. It makes no sense. Louis has
no right to the English crown. His claim is a . . . a bad joke. What
is he, after all? The husband of a daughter of one of your sisters!"

John paused in the act of pouring her wine, slammed the cup
down on the table. "Did I tell you what lame arguments they
offered Guala at Melun? Whilst it's true Richard did charge me
with treason, that was five full years ere he died! All of Christendom knows that we reconciled, that Richard named me as his
heir. As for that out-and-out lie about Arthur, no French court
ever sat in judgment upon me. Since when am I accountable to
the French King?"

"You're not, love," Isabelle said hastily. "Of course you're
not."

"Do you know what the Pope said when he was informed of
Philip's claim? He said that Arthur was a traitor who'd invited
whatever end he might have met. And he did, in truth. Whatever
regrets I might have, Arthur is not amongst them."

That was, she knew, as close as he'd ever come to a confession, to an admission that Arthur had died at his command. But
she did not care; Arthur's fate had never preyed upon her peace.
"John . . . is it true that Rochester Castle has been lost?"

He nodded. "It held out against me for nigh on two months,
but yielded to Louis without offering any resistance at all. Which
makes me wonder what will happen when Louis lays siege to
Windsor Castle, to Dover. Will they try to hold out? Or will their
castellans betray me, too?"

He swung about, back toward the bed. "Have I been such a
bad King, Isabelle?"

"John, no!"

"Then why," he asked, very low, "have my subjects forsaken me? Why are they so willing to support a foreign Prince?"

"John, that's not so. Many of your subjects are still loyal. For certes, the townspeople are. What king ever did as much to promote trade? Or granted as many borough charters? Let craven lords like Arundel and Surrey barter their honor to Louis. The towns will still hold fast for you."

"As London did?" he asked bitterly, and she had no answer for him, could only entreat him to come back to bed. After a time, he did. But he did not sleep.

John was seated before a table cluttered with parchment sheets, ink, maps, books. He was surrounded by people—several scribes, a mud-spattered courier, Peter des Roches, Robert de Vieuxpont— all competing for his attention. He scrawled a hasty signature for one of the scribes, reached for the courier's message as he said to de Vieuxpont, "I want you to go north again, Rob, am counting upon you to hold Cumbria and Westmorland for me."

Seeing him so preoccupied, the boys hesitated, but Isabelle prodded them forward into the chamber. "John, can you spare some moments for your sons?"

John had not seen his children for months. As he pushed back his chair, beckoned them to approach, he could not help noticing their shyness, their lack of ease. His baby daughters did not know him at all. Even to his sons, he was a stranger. Henry was eight, Richard seven, but he'd never been able to find much time for them, to make them part of his life as he had with the children now grown, born out of wedlock and before his kingship.

Isabelle took her youngest from the nurse, held the baby out toward John. Nell was entering her seventh month, and John had seen her for the first time yesterday, upon his arrival at Corfe. All of Isabelle's three daughters had inherited some of their mother's beauty; Nell had dark blue eyes and hair like cornsilk. John smiled at the child, but she ducked her head, hid her face against Isabelle's shoulder.

John was still holding the courier's letter. Breaking the seal, he rapidly scanned the contents, and at Peter des Roches's questioning look, he said, "It's from the Earl of Chester. Gwenwynwyn has died."

Henry edged closer. "Who's that, Papa?"

"A Welsh Prince, Henry, an ally of mine. But he's been living

in exile in Cheshire since the spring, when Llewelyn—your sister
Joanna's husband—drove him out of Powys.''

"But . . . but I thought Joanna was living in France, Papa."

"Not France, Aquitaine. I expect you're too young to remember your older sister. I lost two Joannas, lad, one to the de
Lusignans, the other to Llewelyn."

A servant had followed Isabelle into the chamber. "My liege,
your son, Lord Richard of Chilham, has just ridden in. Will you
see him?"

"At once." John glanced toward de Vieuxpont and des Roches.
"I sent Savaric de Mauléon to Winchester with an offer for
Louis, that I'd order the castle garrison to surrender if Louis
would agree to spare their lives. Richard was with him, will be
bringing word."

Richard had not waited for a servant's summons; he was
already standing in the doorway. One glance at his face, and
John stiffened.

"What is it?" he said sharply. "You might as well tell me
straight out; I'm getting used to bad news."

"It is bad, Papa, as bad as it could be. I do not know how to
tell you . . ." Richard was not easily discountenanced. John had
never seen him so shaken. It was with relief, then, that he heard
Richard say haltingly, "At Winchester . . . amongst those who've
gone over to Louis . . ."

"I know already, Richard, know that your Uncle Warenne has
broken faith, has done homage to Louis. But I do not want to talk
about it, not now."

"No . . . no, you do not understand. I'm not talking about my
Uncle Warenne. It's . . . oh, God, Papa, it's . . ."

John's mouth went dry. "Not Chester?"

"No, not Chester." Richard swallowed. "It's your brother.
Papa, it's Will."

"No," John said. "No, you're lying. Not Will."

"Papa . . . Papa, I saw him at Winchester with Louis. I saw
him!"

Isabelle gave a choked cry, thrust her baby at the nurse. John
was on his feet. He turned as Isabelle moved toward him. His
eyes were blind, focused upon her without recognition. But she
was too panicked to be able to respond to his pain, to be aware of
anything except the ground giving way under her feet. "Will
would never betray you unless it was truly hopeless, unless he
knew you could not win! What shall we do now? What will

happen to me? John, I'm so frightened! What if they besiege
Corfe? If you lose . . ."

She'd caught his arm, was clinging as if he were her only
anchor. But her words struck John like stones. He jerked free,
shoved her away with such force that she stumbled backward,
careened into the table.

"Mama!" But Henry did not move. He stayed where he was,
petrified. The other children had begun to cry. None of the men
moved, either.

"If you're so fearful for your future, why wait? Why not go to
Louis now, strike your deal with him? That's what you want to
do, is it not? Get out, all of you! I do not need Will, do not need
any of you! Go to Louis and be damned!"

The servants had already fled, and the nurses now gathered up
the weeping children, hastened them from the chamber. Peter des
Roches put his arm around Isabelle's shoulders; she had begun to
sob, and offered no resistance as he led her toward the door.
Richard had gone very white, but he stood his ground. "Papa,
I'd not betray you. Nor would Isabelle. She loves—"

"Get out—now!" John's voice cracked. He spun around,
fighting for control. When he turned back, Richard, too, had
gone.

There were two large clay flagons on the table. He reached for
the closer one, pulled it toward him. It was filled with a strongly
spiced red wine; he drank directly from the spout, until he
choked and tears burned his eyes. Picking up the second flagon,
he hurled it toward the door. It shattered against the wood,
sprayed dark wine all over the wall, the floor. He drank again,
cleared the table with a wild sweep of his arm.

The rain had ended before dawn, and sunlight was pouring in
from every window. He moved from one to the other, pausing to
drink from the flagon as he jerked the shutters into place, as the
room darkened.

The floor was littered with debris, with books and documents
and broken clay fragments. He stumbled over a brass candelabra,
sank to his knees midst the wreckage of his morning's work. The
flagon was half empty by now; his head was spinning.

"Why, Will?" he whispered. "Name of God, why?"

Johnny.

He froze, the flagon halfway to his mouth.

Thank God you've come, Johnny. Thank God.

He could not see into the shadows. "Papa?" he said softly.
"Papa?"

Stay with me, Johnny. The pain is always worse at night. Stay with me.

He grabbed for the flagon, drank deeply, spilling as much as he swallowed. "I did not understand, Papa." His voice echoed strangely in his own ears, sounded muffled, indistinct. "I was but one and twenty. At that age, we think we'll live forever . . ." He set the flagon down, waited. But no one answered him. His voices were silent, his ghosts in retreat.

He was never to know how long he knelt there on the floor of his bedchamber, alone in the dark. When at last he lurched to his feet, he moved unsteadily toward the windows, fumbled with the shutters until the room was once more awash in sunlight.

A book lay open, almost at his feet. He reached down, picked it up. He took an uncommon enjoyment in reading, always carried books with him, even on campaigns. This was one of his favorites, a French translation of the Welsh legend of King Arthur; but several pages were torn, the cover smeared with ink. He blotted the ink as best he could with his sleeve, replaced the book upon the table.

"Damn you, Will! I trusted you. More fool I, but I truly trusted you. You think I'm beaten. You think Louis has won. Well, not yet. As Christ is my witness, not yet."

41

CIRENCESTER, ENGLAND

September 1216

"I understand you will not be staying with us after all, Madame?"

Isabelle did not enjoy the company of clerics. Too often she found them dour and disapproving, for if women were all daughters of Eve, born to lead men astray, a woman as worldly as Isabelle must be the very incarnation of Jezebel. But Alexander Neckam was no unlettered village priest. He was Abbot of the prosperous Augustinian abbey of St Mary, a man erudite and cultured, a man entitled to royal courtesy, and she found a smile for him.

"No, I regret not. My lord husband the King has decided it is too dangerous for me to accompany him any farther, and my son and I will be returning to Corfe whilst he goes to raise the siege of Windsor Castle."

"We heard the King spent part of the summer along the Marches. Was he able to win over the Welsh?"

"He did hire some Welsh men-at-arms, but he had no luck with the Welsh Princes, with Llewelyn or Maelgwn. Nor with Reginald de Braose."

Neckam seemed to sense her preoccupation, for he made no attempt to prolong their conversation, but murmured, instead, of duties elsewhere. She was not long alone, however; Richard was coming up the pathway. Falling into step beside her, he followed her into the abbey gardens.

Some yards to their right, John was walking with his son. When Richard started toward them, Isabelle laid a restraining hand on his arm. "No," she said. "Give them time to say their farewells. And whilst we're still alone, tell me the truth. Can John win?"

"Had you asked me that in June, I'd have said no. Now . . . now I'm not so sure. There are straws in the wind, a growing discontent with the French. Some of the rebel barons are belatedly beginning to recognize reality—that should Louis prevail, they'll have a French King, a French court. Already they're seeing what that would mean; each time Louis has taken a castle, he's given it to one of his French followers. Lastly, I know no man more dangerous to underestimate than my father."

Isabelle nodded. "When I'm with John, I cannot but believe that he will prevail against his enemies, that all will be well for us. But when we're apart, I . . . I lose faith. I think of what could happen to us should evil befall John, and I become so frightened, Richard, so—"

"Mama!" Henry was running toward them. "Papa says he's going to give me one of his falcons! Papa, you'll not forget?"

John, following at a more sedate pace, smiled and shook his head. "I'll give the order tonight, Henry. Richard . . . I've decided I do not want you to come with me. I'd rather you escort Isabelle and Henry back to Corfe, then return to Wallingford Castle, hold it for me till further notice."

"If that is truly your wish, Papa."

Turning, then, toward the child, John smiled again at his son. "Henry, stay here and talk to your brother. I want a few words alone with your lady mother ere you depart."

Taking Isabelle aside, John led her toward a trellised arbor. As soon as they were within, Isabelle moved into his arms. The air was sun-warmed, fragrant with honeysuckle; she could almost convince herself that summer was not dying. "I'm so glad I had these ten days with you. But . . . but when will we see each other again?"

"I do not know," John admitted. "Louis has been besieging Dover Castle for some six weeks now, but to no avail. Windsor, Lincoln, and Barnard castles are also under siege. If they can hold out for me . . ."

Isabelle shivered. "You must promise me, promise you'll take care. John, I . . . I'd be lost without you!"

Her fear was more than disheartening, it was contagious. John tightened his arms around her, kissed her on the mouth, the throat. She clung to him, but without passion, and when he kissed her again, he tasted her tears.

"Papa!" The voice was Henry's, high-pitched, excited. John and Isabelle moved apart, moved back into the sun. Henry was sprinting toward the arbor, gesturing. "A courier, Papa, with urgent news from the North!"

One of the black-garbed Augustinian canons was standing a few feet away. "There's a man seeking to talk with you, my liege. He says he's from Barnard Castle, from Hugh de Balliol. May we bring him to you?"

"At once." John had paled. As Isabelle clutched his arm, he said tautly, "If Barnard Castle has fallen . . ."

A messenger was being ushered into the abbey gardens. He was disheveled and travel-stained, but John saw only his smile, the triumphant smile of a man bearing tidings sure to please. "The Scots King and his army assaulted the castle, my lord, but we drove them off."

"Thank God!"

"In truth, my liege. Shooting down from the battlements, one of our bowmen loosed an arrow at Eustace de Vesci. The Almighty guided his aim, lord. It struck de Vesci in the head; he was dead ere he tumbled from the saddle."

John caught his breath. And then he began to laugh. "I want the name of the bowman. That arrow of his is worth its weight in gold to me!" As he swung around, back toward Isabelle and Richard, they saw that his eyes were ablaze with light. "What better omen than this? I think my luck is about to change for the better—at long last!"

The Wash was a wide bay of the turbulent North Sea, fed by four rivers, extending more than twenty miles inland into the counties of Lincoln and Norfolk. The seaport of Lynn had grown up where the River Great Ouse emptied into The Wash. In early October its citizens were alarmed when they got word of an advancing rebel force. But by then John had reached Lincolnshire. He swung south again, detoured toward Lynn, and the rebels fled at his approach. On Sunday, October 9, the grateful townspeople of Lynn welcomed their King, and on the following day a feast was given in John's honor at the Benedictine priory of St Mary Magdalene, St Margaret, and All Virgin Saints.

However boundless their goodwill, their resources were limited; they could not hope to equal the exotic fare that had been set before John in happier days. But they did what they could with what they had, and John, whose expectations were minimal, was pleasantly surprised. Ample helpings of stewed pomegranates and pears were served, to much jesting, for all knew such fruits were aphrodisiacs. Tarts filled with marrow, sugar, and ground pork were offered next, followed by a roasted peacock; the cooks had labored hours to strut the bones and refit the skin and feathers so as to give the illusion of life everlasting. A pig had been slaughtered and cut in half, the hindquarters stuffed with suet and egg-yolked bread crumbs, then carefully sewn together with the head and forepart of a capon, thus creating a wondrous beast to delight both the appetite and the eye. But what amused John the most was the subtlety, a sensual mermaid sculptured of marzipan, tail dyed green with parsley juice, her flowing hair a spill of saffron.

As entertainment, there was an acrobatic act and an alarmingly inept juggler who seemed continually in danger of stabbing himself with his own knives. But for the townspeople, the true attraction of the evening was the presence of their King, and they listened, spellbound, to a rare firsthand account of the momentous happenings in the world beyond the marshy Fens, beyond Lynn.

"Upon reaching Windsor, I found I did not have enough men for a direct attack, but I was able to end the siege by acting as bait. As I moved north out of the Thames Valley, the French abandoned the siege and set out in pursuit. Rather halfheartedly, since they soon gave up and returned to London. Which surprised me not in the least; Louis seems willing to fight to the last Englishman."

As John had expected, that drew laughter. "I continued north, for we knew that the Scots King had come to Dover to do homage to Louis. It was my hope that I could intercept him on his way back into Scotland. Unfortunately he managed to elude our scouts, but we were able to wreak havoc upon the lands of our enemies in the shires of Cambridge and Lincoln."

Swallowing the last of his wine, John pushed aside the stale trencher that had served as his plate. "Does your almoner save these for the poor?"

"Yes, sire."

Glancing about at his men dining at the lower tables, John said loudly, "Let no one throw his trencher to the dogs," and signaled for more wine before resuming. "On the Thursday ere Michaelmas, we entered the city of Lincoln. I know there were those who thought Nicholaa de la Haye no fit castellan for Lincoln Castle, but she has shown herself to be as steadfast, as stalwart as any man in holding the castle for the crown. The townspeople had not her courage, however, and yielded the city to the rebels. They had no stomach for fighting, though, fled even as we approached. We pursued them north, and then headed back when we heard you were in need."

"And thankful we are for it," the Prior said fervently, and others in the hall took up the refrain, expressing their gratitude in terms so sycophantic that one of the young monks laid his bread down in disgust, his appetite utterly gone.

Brother Thomas was incensed that his Prior should make welcome a blasphemer, a man with such mortal sins upon his soul. The Angevins were ungodly, evil men. Thomas, who had been named after the holy martyr Thomas à Becket, did not doubt that Henry and his sons were burning in Hell. John, too, would feel the flames of perdition. Nothing could save him, for there was no contrition in his heart. When the land was laid under Interdict, he had shamelessly mocked the clergy, men of God, arresting the hearthmates and concubines of village priests, demanding that the priests ransom their illicit loves. He had heaped scorn and contempt upon Stephen Langton, a man of Thomas's own Lincolnshire and, like Thomas, of Saxon blood. Nor had John mended his ways after making peace with the Holy Father. Thomas had been appalled to hear that John had allowed his soldiers to stable their horses in St Andrew's priory church during his siege of Rochester Castle. And not three weeks ago he had burned and plundered the Benedictine abbey at Croyland.

No, such a man was damned forever and aye, as surely as if he were a Jew or infidel Saracen, and Thomas cursed his own cowardice, the fear that froze his tongue and kept him from crying out in ringing, clarion tones that liars are loathsome to the Eternal and the wrath of God is fearful to behold.

"I shall have to depart on the morrow, but I'll leave one of my most trusted captains, Savaric de Mauléon, in Lynn to see to your safety. Not that I expect the rebels to threaten you again," John added, sounding so cheerful, so confident that Thomas could endure no more.

"You said a number of disloyal lords had returned to their true allegiance, disavowed the French," he blurted out, half-rising from his seat. "Was one of these lords your brother Salisbury?"

His words seemed to echo endlessly in his own ears. All heads turned in his direction. Those seated beside him drew back so precipitantly that, in other circumstances, their recoil might have been comical. Thomas sat alone, seeing through a blur the shocked and outraged faces of his Prior, the townspeople, aware—as he'd never been aware of anything before—of the sudden and utter stillness of the King.

It seemed forever to those watching before John moved, completed an action frozen in time and space at mention of Will's name. Bringing his cup up to his mouth, he took a swallow of verney. The sweet white wine burned his throat like vinegar. Setting it down, he glanced toward Thomas, saw only a fearful youngster, beet-red and speechless, as if in belated realization of his gaffe.

"No," he said, his voice very measured and remote, "the Earl of Salisbury was not amongst them."

There were relieved murmurings among the people at that. The Prior, who knew Thomas as John did not, gave the errant monk a scorching look that promised retribution at the earliest possible moment, and fumbled for a more suitable topic of conversation. It was John's old friend and comrade Peter des Roches who came to their rescue. He was not deceived by John's icy demeanor; he knew the monk had lacerated anew a wound that had yet to show any signs of healing, and he acted now to turn attention away from John and to himself.

"We shall need your help, Prior Wilfrid," he said swiftly. "We encountered some difficulty in crossing the River Wellstream yesterday. Can you suggest a safer passage?"

"Indeed, my lord Bishop. The safest way is to ford the river at Wisbech, fifteen miles to the south. There is a castle there, so the King's Grace will have suitable lodgings for the night. But since your baggage train is so much slower and cumbersome, I would suggest you dispatch it by the shorter route, between the villages of Cross Keys and Long Sutton. It's some four miles across the estuary, but when the tide is out, much of the sand is exposed, and with local guides who know where the quicksands lie, it can be safely forded."

John had been only half listening to the Prior's long-winded explanation. He looked up, though, as a man rose and approached the high table.

"My liege, might I have a word with you? I am Roger of the Bail, and I—"

"I know a Lincoln man by that name, Peter of the Bail. At Michaelmas, I appointed him as city bailiff. Are you kin?"

"We are cousins, Your Grace." Roger beckoned, and two other men brought forward an iron coffer. As he lifted the lid, the torchlight fell upon a multitude of shimmering silver coins. "This is for you, my liege, from your subjects in the township of Lynn. It's not as much as we could wish—one hundred marks—but we wanted to give you tangible proof of our loyalty. Use it, with

God's blessing, to fight the French invaders and drive them back
into the sea.''

John was touched, for that was no small sum for these merchants and fishermen to have raised. "I thank you; your offering
shall be well spent." He gazed about the hall, heartened by sight
of so many friendly faces. "In the past I've granted many a
borough the right to elect a mayor, London and Lincoln amongst
them. A while back it pleased me to confer such a privilege upon
Lynn." Rising, he unsheathed his sword, handed it, hilt first, to
the young merchant. "Here," he said when Roger made no
move to take it. "Your mayor shall need a ceremonial sword."

Whatever else he might have said was lost in the sudden
explosion of sound, the wave of cheering that engulfed the hall.
When John could make himself heard again, he laughed and
signaled for silence. "I will drive the French invaders into the
sea," he said, "and then I shall come back to Lynn and celebrate
my victory with those who stood by me when my need was
greatest."

The sun rose at 6:20 A.M. on Wednesday, October 12, but
heavy mists overhung the marshes, did not begin to burn
away until midmorning. John crossed the River Wellstream at
Wisbech, turned north along the embankment toward the village
of Long Sutton. The cold was damp and penetrating, and the
wind whistled eerily through the billowing salt grass. Birds cried
mournfully, invisible in the mist, and occasional splashes heralded the passage of unseen animals.

"I hate the fenlands," John said grimly, "hate these barren,
accursed swamps. What man in his right mind would live here of
his own free will? Only a water snake could thrive in these
stinking bogs."

He'd been in a vile mood all morning, but his companions
understood why. He'd been taken ill the day they left Lynn, had
spent a sleepless night at Wisbech. He was still queasy this
morning, and at Peter des Roches's troubled queries, he finally
admitted that he felt as if one fox were gnawing at his belly,
another at his bowels. But he'd refused to lay over at Wisbech,
or even to slow their pace, although he'd twice had to dismount
while he vomited into the marsh grass.

"It's no surprise to me that you're ailing, John. I've been with
you these six weeks past, have seen firsthand the way you've
been abusing yourself. It's a rare day when you do not cover
forty miles; there've even been a few fifty-mile days! And then

you spend half the night tending to matters of state. You keep burning a candle down to the wick, my friend, and it gets harder and harder to light.''

"How profound," John said caustically, and spurred his stallion forward to ride beside John Marshal, the Earl of Pembroke's nephew. They began to trade marshland folklore, arguing whether it was true that men born in the Fens had webbed feet, whether the flickering swamp lights known as will-of-the-wisps were truly the souls of unbaptised babies. Peter des Roches started to urge his mount to catch up with them, but after a few strides he let his horse slacken pace. What good would it do? John was not about to listen.

When they reached the village of Long Sutton, the tide was out and the sands lay naked to a pallid autumn sun. Hungry gulls circled overhead, shrieking. The few houses huddled by the estuary did nothing to lessen the bleak desolation of the scene. There was no sign as yet of John's baggage train. But the wind was biting, and John's stomach was churning, and he let Peter des Roches persuade him not to wait, to press ahead toward Swineshead Abbey.

They turned west, and after a few miles John consented to stop for his first food of the day. The little hamlet of Holbeach was no less dismal than Long Sutton. The awestruck villagers shyly offered John shelter and what meagre hospitality they could. But as soon as he stepped inside one of the wattle-and-daub huts, he was assailed again by nausea; the second room of the cottage was used as a stable, and the rank animal odors sent him reeling back into the icy sea air.

One of the peasants produced a blanket, and John's servants unpacked a basket of wheaten bread and cheese. John could manage just a mouthful, but even though the villagers could offer only ale and goat's milk, he could not get enough to drink; he was as thirsty, he said bemusedly, as if he'd gorged himself all week on nothing but salted herring.

Sitting back on the blanket, he studied the cottage. "Cruck frame, thatched roof. As hard as it is for me to believe it, my daughter Joanna passed the first five years of her life in a house not much better than that one." He waved away a proffered chunk of bread. "What were you telling me about the tides, Jack?"

John Marshal took the bread John spurned. "The Prior told me low water is at noon, high water at six. The half-tide comes in about three or so, so they'd have to cross between twelve and two." He squinted upward, shook his head. "I've yet to see enough of the sun to hazard even a blind guess as to the time now. But I see no cause for concern, Your Grace. The local guides know these waters better than the fish do, know where the sinkholes and quicksands lie."

John yearned to lie back upon the blanket; his body ached for rest. But the wind was blowing sand about with such abandon that it had even begun to encrust the rim of his cup. "I want to go to Nottingham next week to confer with Philip Marc. And when we reach the abbey tonight, I ought to send a courier to Hubert de Burgh."

"You need not vex yourself over the Dover siege, John." Peter des Roches had no liking for Hubert de Burgh, who'd replaced him as Justiciar, but his wish to ease John's mind prevailed over jealousy, and he said, quite truthfully, "I know men call Dover 'the key to the kingdom.' But de Burgh has one hundred forty knights and a full garrison at Dover Castle. I'd wager he can hold out against Louis till Judgment Day if need be."

"My lords!" One of the villagers was pointing. "A rider comes!"

The men were already on their feet, swords half drawn. The rider wore John's colors, was one of the men left behind to wait for the baggage train. At sight of John, he jerked his lathered stallion to an abrupt halt, spraying sand in all directions.

"I waited and waited, my liege, and then ventured out onto the sands in search of them . . ." He swung from the saddle, leaned against his horse, sobbing for breath. "They—oh, Jesus, my lord, they're bogged down! They're out there in the river, caught in the quicksand, and the serfs say the tide is coming in!"

The villagers of Long Sutton were clustered upon the bank of the Wellstream, kneeling as their priest offered prayers for the souls of the doomed men trapped out in the estuary. They scattered as the horsemen came galloping out of the mist. The priest waved his arms frantically, ran after them, shouting that the incoming tide would turn the sands to quickmire and they'd all drown. John swerved his stallion just in time to avoid trampling the man, but he did not slow down; the horse plunged onto the sands. Most of John's companions followed.

The sounds reached John first, as the wind carried to him the cries of fear and rage, the shrill neighing of the sumpter horses. But until he saw the trapped wagons and animals, he did not—

could not—realize the full extent of the catastrophe. The heavy
carts and wagons were hopelessly mired down in midriver; the
more the terrified horses struggled, the deeper they sank. John
knew at once what had happened. The vanguard had become
bogged, but the baggage train was more than two miles long, and
those coming up behind were unaware of the disaster until they
stumbled onto the lead wagons. And by that time, retreat was
made impossible by the rearward. As more and more carts became bogged, men and horses began to panic, and the sight
meeting John's horrified eyes was one of utter and complete
chaos.

Rescue was beyond mortal men; the tide was already sweeping
in from the north. John could not see it yet, but he heard it, a
low, relentless rumble, getting louder. "Cut the traces!" he
shouted. "Free the horses!"

John Marshal was beside him now, gesturing. "We've got to
turn back! Or we'll drown, too!"

Some of the men had heard John's shouts, were slashing at the
harness traces. Most had abandoned the wagons by now, were
floundering in the river. John gave one despairing backward
glance and then swung his mount about, followed after John
Marshal as they raced the tide for shore.

Their horses were battlefield destriers, bred for stamina; but
they were capable of great speed in short bursts, and they were
within yards of safety when Peter des Roches's stallion splashed
into quicksand. The horse lurched to its knees, scrambled desperately to free itself as its rider clung helplessly to the saddle
pommel. Des Roches had enough presence of mind, however, to
wave John away when he saw the other man turning back. "No,
John, no! Go on!"

"Jump clear and I'll pick you up!"

"Your horse cannot carry us both!"

John Marshal had also wheeled his mount about. "Go back,
sire! I'll save him, I swear!"

But by then it was too late; the tide was upon them. John had
time only to turn his horse so the water did not strike them
sideways. As he was swept downstream, he caught a last glimpse
of Peter des Roches. The force of the surging waters had freed
the stallion, only to engulf both horse and rider. John saw Peter's
head break the surface, but the current was too swift to fight. His
stallion was swimming strongly now, striking out for the embankment; he could do nothing but give the horse its head.

John's stallion came ashore several miles south of Long Sutton. As he slid from the saddle, John found himself alone in a vast, empty marshland. The ground squished under his boots, his footprints filling with water. He shouted, in vain. Even the swamp birds were suddenly stilled. After a time, he heard a cry, saw a man struggling toward shore. Wading back into the shallows, he helped the man scramble up the embankment. Then they both slumped down upon the muddy ground, too exhausted even for speech. Out in the river, men and horses were drowning, but their death cries were muffled by the tide, muted by the rising wind. An unearthly silence blanketed the Fens.

John Marshal was the first to find them, followed by some of the villagers. John accepted the mantles they offered without comment, ignored their pleas that he come back with them to Long Sutton. But within the quarter hour he saw Peter des Roches limping slowly along the embankment. The elegant Bishop of Winchester was covered with fetid swamp mud and slime; even his hair was matted with it. But he was alive and smiling, and he and John embraced like brothers.

"The Almighty never showed me greater favor, John. I grabbed my horse's tail, held on so tightly that I could scarcely unclench my fists once we reached the shore!"

He gratefully accepted a wineskin, drank in deep, noisy gulps. "There are some of our men downstream. A few who knew how to swim. A few more who had the wits to clamber up onto loose sumpter horses. They told me those in the rear of the train may have made it back to Cross Keys ere the tide came in. But most of the horses drowned, for certes, and too many men. How many we'll likely never know; only Christ All-merciful can say where or when their bodies will wash up."

"What of my treasure?" John said huskily. "Think you that any of it can be recovered at the next low water?"

No one spoke; he had his answer in their averted eyes. The village priest at last said, "Some of it might be salvaged eventually. But most of it is gone, my lord."

He spoke so matter-of-factly that it was obvious he had no idea what John had just lost. His treasure, jewels, gold plate, coronation regalia and crown, his wardrobe, his chapel, holy relics, tents, furniture, siege weapons, supplies, books, documents of state, written records of his reign—all lay buried in the quicksands of the Wellstream. It was as if his very history were blotted out, his past swallowed up by the rising tide that had claimed his ill-fated baggage train.

"John . . ." Peter des Roches touched his arm, lowered his

voice for John's ears alone. "We'll leave men here to do what must be done. But we've got to get you to shelter, and with no delay. I beg you, do not argue with me on this. You're soaked through, and half frozen. A night out here in the Fens could be the death of you."

John was not about to argue, for never had he been so cold. He clenched his jaw until it ached, but even that did not stop his teeth from chattering. The pain in his intestines, constant throughout this day of horrors, was now as piercing as a knife blade, as penetrating as the wind blowing off the marshes. For the first time since he'd been stricken at Lynn, he remembered that his brother Henry had died of such a flux of the bowels, and when Peter suggested that they ride back toward Wisbech Castle, he shook his head, said reluctantly, "I think it best if we head for Swineshead Abbey, Peter. It's more likely they'll have a doctor there."

By the time he reached Swineshead Abbey, John was burning up with fever. He grew steadily worse on Thursday, but insisted, nonetheless, upon continuing the next morning to Sleaford Castle. Hearing that the Abbot of an abbey of White Canons at Croxton was skilled in the arts of healing, Peter des Roches sent urgently for the man, passed some anxious hours until his arrival at Sleaford on Saturday afternoon. He was with John now, while Peter and John Marshal waited in the solar for word.

"If only he'd rest!" Marshal burst out suddenly. "But no, he lies in there, as weak as a mewing kitten, and what is he doing? Dictating letters, giving pardons, acquittances, safe-conducts. Mayhap if you talked to him . . ."

"He's never been one for listening," Peter said dryly, spun around as the door opened.

"Well? How does he?"

The Abbot appeared to be choosing his words with care. "I bled him, and that seemed to ease him somewhat. I'm going to prepare a mustard poultice now to draw off the pain."

"You can speak plainer than that, can you not?"

The Abbot flushed at the peremptory tone. "Very well, my lord. The truth is that I can attend to the King's spiritual needs. But more than that, no; it's too late."

"You were not with him very long. How can you be so sure?"

"He is passing clotted blood," the Abbot said bluntly, and they no longer doubted, stared at him in bleak silence.

As he entered John's chamber soon afterward, Peter des Roches

wondered why he'd needed a stranger to tell him John was dying.
He had only to look into John's face. The shocking gauntness,
the relentless wasting away of flesh, the ominous ashen cast to
his skin—the signs were there for all but the blind to see,
attesting to an illness that was mortal. Only the eyes were still
John's, hollowed and feverish but utterly lucid, all too penetrating.

John struggled to sit up at sight of Peter. "I'm not overly
impressed with Abbot Adam. But I expect you'll want him to
accompany us to Newark on the morrow?"

"Newark? Jesus God, John, you cannot! That's twenty miles
from here!"

"And a damned sight safer, so let that be an end to it. Now
fetch me some wine, Peter. You'd not believe the noxious concoction your Abbot would have me drink—egg yolk in rosewater!"

Peter laughed, approached the bed. As he did, John reached
up, grasped his wrist. "Tell me," he said, "what you're keeping
from me. I heard servants talking, know a courier arrived from
Hubert de Burgh. Why did you not want me to see him, Peter?
What message did he bring?"

Peter hesitated, but John had never been easy to lie to. "The
news is bad, John. Hubert de Burgh has asked Louis for a truce
whilst he consults with you. Their supplies are running out. He
says if you cannot come to his aid, he may have to surrender
Dover Castle to the French."

John's grip loosened; he sank back upon the bed, and then
turned his face toward the wall. He heard Peter's footsteps
retreating, heard the door quietly close. He shut his eyes, but the
tears squeezed through his lashes, seared his skin like hot rain.

To the Abbot, Adam of Croxton, the world as he knew it was
encompassed within the white walls of his abbey of St John the
Evangelist. If his was a narrowed focus, he felt no lack, had
never yearned to break free of the familiar, to embrace the
unknown. He had not welcomed the summons from the Bishop
of Winchester, for he was not a man of worldly ambitions, and
his every instinct warned him that no good could come to him at
the King's court.

His instincts were sound. He found himself treating a dying
man, while fearing that he might be held accountable for that
death. His medical experience had been confined to the treatment
of the canons and lay brothers of his abbey, local villagers,
people who were in awe of his expertise, docile and submissive.
Nothing had prepared him for a patient like John. Arrogant,

irreverent, willful, he had yet to show any of the virtues that the
Abbot expected of a dying Christian. He was not humble, not
noticeably repentant, and he seemed thoroughly preoccupied with
secular concerns, seemed to be devoting all his waking thoughts
to his earthly kingdom at a time when he should be concentrating
only upon the Kingdom of God.

The Abbot had been appalled by John's determination to ride
north to Newark Castle. He'd have sworn John was too weak
even to mount a horse, but John did, somehow managed to stay
in the saddle for more than four miles. Even after he collapsed,
he remained stubbornly set upon reaching Newark, and his men
finally cut willows by the roadside, wove them into a makeshift
litter, for however weakened his body was, John's will was not
to be thwarted. Go to Newark he would, and go to Newark he
did, at a cost in pain the Abbot preferred not to dwell upon.

Newark Castle was nominally in the hands of the Bishop of
Lincoln, but in actual fact it was a royal stronghold, and its
constable, Robert de Gaugi, did all in his power to make the
King comfortable. John was lodged in the Bishop's private quar-
ters on the uppermost floor of the three-story gatehouse. For two
days now, the Abbot had divided his time between John's cham-
bers and the chapel of St Philip and St James. As he entered
John's bedchamber, he was not surprised to find a scribe at
John's bedside, to find John dictating a letter to Falkes de
Breauté, instructing him to free some servants of William de
Warenne, Earl of Surrey.

"Witness ourself at Newark on Tuesday, the eighteenth of
October, in the eighteenth year of our reign," John concluded,
and glanced over at Peter des Roches to explain, "Rumor has it
Warenne is ripe for switching sides again. A gesture of goodwill
costs us little, and might just push him off the fence."

The Abbot watched in silent disapproval as John turned back
to the scribe, began another letter, appointing Nicholaa de la
Haye and Philip Marc as joint sheriffs of Lincolnshire. It both
baffled and troubled him that John should be squandering his last
hours in sordid political dealings, and he marveled that a man in
such intense pain could be so coherent, so cynical, and so
singleminded. In all respects, he was finding John utterly beyond
his ken.

John was still dictating, this time to Engelard de Cigogne, his
constable of Windsor Castle, directing him to accept his son
Henry as liege lord and to hold the castle for him. His voice had
weakened over the past hours, for he'd been dictating similar

letters since dawn to his sheriffs, constables, and castellans. The effort he was making to talk was obvious to all in the room, and when he paused for breath, the Abbot stepped forward, held out a cup of dark liquid.

"Drink this, sire," he entreated, and tried to mask his annoyance when John demanded to know what was in it. "My own mixture: sumac, gall, pomegranate rind, and opium. It will ease your pain, my lord."

John was panting, but he shook his head stubbornly. "It'll make me sleep, too. And time is all I have." When the Abbot would have protested, he flared into sudden rage. "My son is nine years old. Are you so stupid that you do not know what that means? A child King and a kingdom at war, with half the realm under French control. A right loving bequest to leave my son, is it not?"

The Abbot shrank back, speechless. Peter des Roches moved toward the bed, said with as much conviction as he could muster, "John, I understand your fear. But you must not despair. I truly believe men will rally to your son. He's but a child, has offended no one. Even men who are your sworn enemies might well forsake the French, return their allegiance to Henry."

John could almost believe him—almost. "To hear you tell it, Peter, the best thing I can do for my son is to die." His outburst had exhausted him; he lay back against the pillows, fighting nausea. When he opened his eyes, the Abbot and Peter were bending over him, and he saw in their faces their relief that he still breathed. He swallowed with difficulty. He'd known for days that he was dying, but death was so very close now, was in the chamber with them, no longer willing to wait.

"I always thought, Peter, that I'd . . . I'd fear to die . . ." His tongue seemed to have swollen, was so rough and dry that he had to labor just to shape his words. "But . . . after a week of this pain, I'm beginning to see it as . . . as a release . . ."

Peter reached for a wine cup, held it to his lips. "Shall I hear your confession now?"

John managed a ghostly smile. "I think not. Better the Abbot be the one to absolve me of my sins. You see . . . you know me too well, would not . . . not believe me when I said I forgave my enemies . . ."

The Abbot looked shocked, but Peter was smiling through tears. John waved the Abbot away from the bed, plucked at Peter's sleeve. "You must take messages for me . . . Tell Pembroke that I entrust Henry into his care, that he must safeguard my son's crown. Tell Isabelle that she can rely upon Pembroke and Chester, that she can trust them . . . and you. Tell Pembroke, too, to reward those who . . . who were with me at the last.''

Peter could barely hear him now; he leaned forward, his ear to John's mouth. "Tell Llewelyn ab Iorwerth . . . tell him to take care of my daughter. And tell Will . . .''

John's voice trailed off, and Peter prompted gently, "Tell him what, John?''

John closed his eyes. "Nothing," he whispered. "Nothing . . .''

As the afternoon ebbed away, the sky darkened long before dusk and the wind intensified. The Abbot stood by John's bed, watching the uneven rise and fall of his chest. He was amazed that John still lived, for he'd been fearful that John might die before he could hear his confession, give him the holy Viaticum, and perform the rite of Extreme Unction. But John had rallied briefly, had once again shown an inner resilience that somehow defied all claims upon mortal flesh. Having administered the Sacraments, the Abbot had to believe that John was now in a state of grace. Yet dark doubts he could not acknowledge gnawed at the outer edges of his faith.

John had given the correct answers to the Seven Interrogatories, had received the Body and Blood of Christ, had shown the proper contrition. But after he was absolved, shriven of his earthly sins, he'd said softly, "Do not the Scriptures say there shall be greater joy in Heaven over one sinner that repenteth than over nine and ninety just persons?" Then he'd slept, and the Abbot did not know if he'd been sincere and seeking solace, mocking himself, or even mocking God.

John awoke to blackness and burning pain, to panic. He could not see, and when he cried out, no one answered him. His mind clouded by sleep and the Abbot's draught, he could not remember where he was or why he was suffering, and he tried to rise from the bed but had not the strength, lay there helplessly in the dark until the door opened and the Abbot entered.

He saw at once what had happened, began to offer profuse apologies. "The shutter blew open, my lord, and the candles guttered out. I went to fetch a lamp, did not think you'd awaken.''

The lamp was a crude one, no more than a wick floating in a bowl of fish oil, but its feeble light was the most welcome sight John had ever seen. For once he submitted willingly to the

Abbot's ministrations, let the monk squeeze water onto his swollen lips, bathe the sweat from his forehead.

"Fetch the Bishop," he whispered, saw the Abbot look away in sudden distress.

"My liege, he . . . he's gone. He and John Marshal left hours ago. They said it was urgent they reach my lords of Pembroke and Chester as soon as possible, in order to see to the safety of the young K—of your son." He flushed, then added remorsefully, "You were so ill, my lord, and it seemed so unlikely you'd recover your wits . . ."

"I understand . . ." And John did. Peter des Roches was his friend. But when a king died, his power died with him. He mumbled something too low for the Abbot to hear. He could not be sure, but it sounded as if John had said, *"Sic transit gloria mundi."* Thus passes the glory of the world. He gave John a look of surprised approval, glad that John seemed to be focusing his thoughts now as he ought, upon the Hereafter, and then stammered, "Your Grace, I . . . I have a great favor to ask of you. Not for me, but for my abbey."

That came as no surprise. How tired he was, so very, very tired. He roused himself with an effort, said, "Ask, then. Let yours be the last favor I grant . . ."

"My liege, if you only would . . . I know that you said you wanted to be buried in the Benedictine priory of St Mary at Worcester, before the shrine of St Wulfstan. But I wondered if . . . if you might consider . . . if we could have your heart and bowels for burial at Croxton?"

John's eyes opened—wide. "What?"

"If you'd consent, my lord, it would be such an honor. We'd bury them at the High Altar and say Masses for your soul—" He broke off, dismayed and bewildered, for John was laughing. His laughter was unsteady, rasping and harsh, but it was unmistakably laughter.

"If only I'd known there'd be . . . be such a demand," he gasped, "we could have auctioned off the . . . the choice parts . . ." The horrified look on the Abbot's face only made him laugh all the more, until he could not laugh and breathe at the same time, began to choke.

Thoroughly alarmed, the Abbot propped him up with pillows, hastened to give him wine. As the spasm passed, he lay back, closed his eyes. "I think I always knew . . ."

"Knew what, my liege?"

John turned his head, looked at him for a long time without answering. "I always knew," he said, "that I'd die alone . . ."

Joanna reached the Benedictine priory of St Mary at Worcester shortly after dark on Friday, November 18. The hospitaller was awaiting her at the priory gateway; so, too, was her brother. Richard helped her to dismount, kissed her cheek. The hospitaller was looking askance at Joanna's Welsh guards, but when she asked if he could accommodate her men, he nodded. "But of course, Madame. It is an honor to serve the sister of King Henry."

Joanna said nothing, but Richard saw her flinch. He took her arm as the hospitaller assured her that all was in readiness to commemorate the late King's month-mind with a solemn Requiem Mass. "Joanna, do you want to go to your chambers now?" he asked, and she shook her head.

"I want to go to him first. Will you take me, Richard?"

They walked in silence for a while. It had been snowing sporadically throughout the day, began again as they crossed the courtyard. Joanna's hood fell back; she seemed not to notice as droplets of snow dusted her hair, melted upon her mantle. As they entered the south walkway of the cloisters, she said, "Tell me," and Richard did, told her all he'd learned of their father's final days.

"A violent windstorm struck Newark ere he died. That's not uncommon for the season, but the fool servants took fright. Word spread that the Devil was coming to claim Papa's soul, and some even fled." They'd stopped by the church door. He saw the anguished question in her eyes and shook his head. "No, Papa never knew. The Abbot who tended him wrote to Isabelle, said that by the time the storm reached its height, Papa was no longer conscious. He died soon after midnight."

"And did they strip his body of his clothes and rings? Did they take all of value, as they did when his father died at Chinon?"

Her bleak insistence upon knowing the worst troubled Richard, but he did not lie. "Yes. But his soldiers kept faith, the routiers whom men scorned as base mercenaries, paid hirelings. They alone did not forsake him, Joanna, escorted his body to Worcester. Bishop Silvester officiated at the burial, but it was done without much ceremony, and in haste. The main concern was with getting Henry crowned as quickly as possible."

"I heard it was done at Gloucester. Were you there, Richard?"

He nodded. "On the twenty-eighth. The Bishop of Winchester

crowned him, since the Archbishop of Canterbury is still in Rome, under suspension. But then, even were he not, Westminster is in rebel hands. They did not even have a crown, Joanna, had to use a gold circlet provided by Isabelle.''

"Where are they now?''

''The younger children are still at Corfe. Henry and Isabelle are at Bristol with Pembroke. They reissued Papa's Runnymede charter last Saturday, with some of the more objectionable provisions deleted, that committee of twenty-five being the first to go. It is a shrewd concession, allows the barons to save face, and I think all but the very proud and the very embittered will come to terms with Pembroke and Chester. Peter des Roches told me that during Papa's three days at Newark more than forty couriers arrived from rebels seeking to make peace with Papa. But by then it was too late . . .''

They were still standing in the cloisters. Joanna's face looked chalky in the lantern light; nor had Richard liked the flat, brittle tone of her voice. "Joanna . . .'' He sighed, not knowing what to say. "I am truly sorry you had to come alone like this to Worcester.''

"I had no choice. My husband is at war with England.'' Joanna drew an audible breath. "Nor do I think I would have wanted him with me . . . not here.''

He started to speak, but she'd turned away, was moving ahead of him into the nave of the church. Vespers was done, and the monks were now at supper in the refectory; Joanna and Richard found themselves quite alone. Torches flared in the choir, and a dark object before the High Altar was ringed with white syze candles, with flickering light. Joanna moved up the aisle, until she was close enough to touch her father's stone coffin.

"But he wanted to be buried with St Wulfstan,'' she whispered. "He often told me so . . .''

"Bishop Silvester and the Prior assured me that his wishes will be honored. They plan to move the shrines of St Wulfstan and St Oswald from the crypt, to place them on either side of Papa's tomb.'' Richard smiled sadly. "Papa would have liked that—sleeping with saints.''

Joanna was still staring at the tomb. "Richard, would you mind leaving me alone for a time?''

He started to object, thought better of it. "I'll await you back at the Prior's lodgings.'' He turned toward the shadowed nave, then stopped. "Peter des Roches told me something I think you'd want to know, Joanna. He said that whilst Papa was at Lynn, he made a grant to Margaret de Lacy, Maude de Braose's daughter. He gave her one hundred eighty acres of land in the royal forest of Acornbury, to found a religious house in memory of Maude, her husband, and her son.''

The candles encircling John's tomb wavered, swimming before Joanna's eyes in a dizzying blur of brightness. She stood very still, listening as Richard's footsteps faded. And then she moved forward. She knelt in the coffin's shadow for an endless time, until her knees ached and she trembled from the cold. But she could find no comfort in prayer.

"You're proving to be a merciless ghost, Papa. I should have expected it, knowing you as I do.'' Her tears were coming faster now. ''What do you mean to do, Papa? Shall you haunt me for the rest of my days?'' Her voice broke; kneeling on the icy tiles before John's coffin, she wept bitterly.

BOOK TWO

BOOK TWO

1

WINDSOR, ENGLAND

September 1217

At the time of John's death, Louis exercised authority over half of John's realm. London was his, and his ally, the notorious pirate and freebooter Eustace the Monk, claimed dominion of the seas, operating at will from his base in the Channel Islands. But an anti-French antagonism was taking root in the country, and John's death gave many disgruntled rebels the excuse they needed to abandon Louis. Among those who acknowledged the boy King as their sovereign was John's brother Will, Earl of Salisbury.

John's alliance with the Church now stood his young son in good stead. Wales had been under Interdict since November. Louis and the rebel barons had been declared excommunicate, and the papal legate Guala did his best to elevate the conflict into a holy war, encouraging Henry's supporters to wear the white crosses of crusaders. Coming under such intense pressure from the Holy See, Philip was fast losing all enthusiasm for his son's English adventure. But Louis was not, and the war dragged on through the winter and early spring.

It began to seem as if neither side could score a decisive victory. Then, in mid-May, the Earl of Pembroke learned that Robert Fitz Walter, Saer de Quincy, and a French force were besieging Lincoln Castle. Pembroke saw his opportunity to engage them while Louis was occupied in another siege of Dover Castle, and by dawn on May 20, a royalist army was in sight of Lincoln's city walls.

Although the castle's hereditary castellan, Nicholaa de la Haye, had been waging a gallant defense, the town was securely in rebel hands. But Nicholaa sent her lieutenant constable out to the royalists with the welcome word that she could give them entry into the castle through a small postern door. Once in the castle, Peter des Roches made a daring reconnaissance into the city itself and discovered a gate along the western wall, blocked but unguarded. Returning to his companions, he shared this discovery with Chester, Pembroke, and Will, the leaders of the expedition.

While the royalist vanguard sought to batter down the north gate, another force gained entry through Peter's hidden gateway, and soon the steep, narrow streets of Lincoln had become a battlefield. By 3:00 P.M. it was over. The French commander was dead, Fitz Walter and Saer de Quincy were taken prisoner, along with three hundred French knights, and the rest of the French were in flight.

Amazingly enough, only five men were slain in the actual fighting. More died, however, on the chaotic retreat back toward London. And when the triumphant royalists sacked the city, many women and children drowned while trying to flee in small boats that capsized in the River Witham.

Their victory was so complete that the jubilant English dubbed it "the Fair of Lincoln," as if it had been a tournament. But it did not end the war. Louis still believed the English crown was within his grasp, was not willing to concede defeat.

Joanna reined in, shocked, at first sight of Windsor Castle. She remembered apple orchards, groves of hazelnut and filbert, lush vineyards nurtured since the days of her grandfather's reign. But she saw only scorched, mangled tree stumps, barren and pitted earth where rocks launched from mangonels had gone astray. As she passed into the lower bailey, there, too, she found scars of the castle's three-month siege. There were gaping holes in the ground, the outer timber palisades were blackened, and the stone walls of the middle and inner baileys were gouged and battered.

Even the great hall had not been spared; a section of the roof had suffered a direct hit. Joanna stopped her mare. It had been more than eleven years, but she even remembered the day of the week: Tuesday, May 2, in God's year 1206. She'd stood with her father here in the bailey, struggling to bid him farewell without tears, still unable to believe that in just nine days she would be the wife of a Welsh Prince. She'd thought she had managed to hide her fear from John, but when they embraced, he hugged her tightly, saying, "You'll have no regrets, sweetheart, I promise."

"No regrets," Joanna echoed now, a lifetime later, and then she laughed, a laugh so strained, so lacking in mirth that her men gave her looks of curiosity, even of sympathy. After a time, her mare began to fidget. Only then did she bestir herself, shake off her father's spell, and cross the drawbridge into the middle bailey.

The timber buildings constructed by Henry II for his Queen's comfort were ranged along the north wall of the upper bailey, and they alone seemed unscathed. Joanna was escorted across a grassy courtyard and into the chamber where Isabelle awaited her.

They were alone; Isabelle had dismissed her own attendants and Joanna's maid. There was genuine affection in their greetings, animation in their first moments of sharing, but there was a slight wariness, too, as if their intimacy needed to be rediscovered, to be tested anew after a five-year separation.

"Henry had an earache, so I had to put him to bed with a vervain poultice. He is so excited by your coming, so eager to see you," Isabelle said and smiled. "Being an only child myself, I confess I cannot comprehend his passion for siblings. But nary a day goes by when he does not make wistful mention of Dickon, even of Nell and Isabella, and they're just babes."

"They're still at Corfe?" Joanna's disappointment was sharp, for she'd yet to meet her little sisters.

"Yes, for safety's sake. In fact, dearest, I was not at all sure Llewelyn would allow you to come halfway across England, safe-conduct or not."

"Llewelyn does not know. He's waging war in South Wales, was besieging Haverford the last I heard from him."

"Well, whatever enabled you to—— Joanna, you do not yet know, do you? How could you, being on the road all week? There was a great sea battle fought on St Bartholomew's Day. The war is done, for Louis' hopes sank with his ships. And one of the heroes of the day was your brother!"

"Richard? Or Oliver?"

"Richard. Ah, Joanna, it was a glorious triumph. Robert de Courtenay was bringing reinforcements to Louis; they had a fleet of ten galleys and seventy smaller craft, under the command of Eustace the Monk. They meant to sail up the Thames to London, but our ships caught up with them at the mouth of the estuary. Richard brought his ship alongside Eustace's, and a cog commanded by John Marshal came up on the other side. The Monk had an enormous galley, but it was carrying horses and a heavy trebuchet, and was riding so low in the water that the deck was almost awash. Our cog was to windward, and the sailors threw down pots of powdered quicklime onto the French, temporarily blinding them. Richard and his men at once boarded the galley, and in the fighting that followed, all of the French knights—thirty-six—were taken captive. Eustace the Monk was found hiding in the hold. He offered a thousand marks for his life, but Richard had him beheaded on his own deck.

"After that, it was a total rout. Although we were greatly outnumbered, the French panicked once the Monk's ship was taken. Some of the galleys made it back to Calais, but all of the smaller ships were sunk or captured. Only the highborn knights were spared, all others being thrown into the sea. Much booty was taken and shared amongst our sailors afterward, with some set aside by the Earl of Pembroke to found a hospital in honor of St Bartholomew. The day's glory belonged to Hubert de Burgh, who commanded our fleet—and to Richard." Isabelle at last paused for breath. "John would have been very proud of him."

"Yes," Joanna agreed softly, "he would."

"Pembroke sent Robert de Courtenay to Louis." Seeing Joanna belatedly react to the name Courtenay, Isabelle nodded, said dryly, "Yes, he's my uncle, my mother's brother. He brought back word from London that Louis is now willing to make peace, to depart the kingdom. He meets on Tuesday with Pembroke and Hubert de Burgh to discuss terms."

"I'm glad."

"Are you truly, Joanna? After all, Llewelyn is allied with Louis . . ."

"But Henry is my brother. Of course I want him to win."

"What is troubling you, then? Is it that you think Llewelyn may not be willing to make peace with Henry?"

"No, it's not that. Llewelyn will eventually come to terms with the English . . . once they make it worth his while."

Isabelle had rarely heard Joanna sound so cynical, but she was amused nonetheless. "Your husband can charm, but he can also calculate finely enough to split hairs. In that, he's always reminded me of John," she said, and laughed. But Joanna did not. "Joanna . . . what is it? Is it Llewelyn?"

Joanna hesitated. "Yes." Rising, she moved restlessly to the window. "It began this summer, when Reginald de Braose submitted to Henry. To the Welsh, that was a betrayal. Llewelyn was furious, made up his mind to teach Reginald a sharp lesson. But I . . . I could not see it in the same light. I could think only of Gwladys—torn between husband and father. We quarreled, and he departed with angry words between us. As it turned out, he brought Reginald to heel in short order. He swept into

Brecknock, and as soon as he crossed the border into Gower, Reginald hastened to meet him at Llangiwg, humbled his pride and yielded up the castle of Swansea to Llewelyn. It was a quick and bloodless triumph for the Prince. But an utter failure for the father.''

"Was Gwladys very distraught?"

"No," Joanna said reluctantly, and then managed a rueful smile. "In truth, she was not. Llewelyn can do no wrong in her eyes, and she thinks he was perfectly justified. To Gwladys, there is but one side to any quarrel—the Welsh."

"I see. Well, then, do you not think you may have . . . overreacted somewhat?"

"You need not be so tactful. Say what you mean, that I was really reacting to past pain of my own. Of course I was. But that does not change the fact that Llewelyn put political aims above his daughter's welfare."

"Darling, men do that all the time. At least, ambitious men do . . . and is there any other kind?" Isabelle rose, too, followed Joanna to the window. "I am sorry, though, Joanna. I've known a few women who were well and truly in love. But you were the only one in love with her own husband! I admit I never thought it would last, yet I hoped for your sake that it might."

Joanna had been listening in surprise. "I once told Llewelyn that I did not always like him, and this summer was for certes one of those times. But I still do love him, Isabelle . . . and fear for him. Over the past eleven years, I've learned to live with his wars, with the knowledge that a well-aimed spear or arrow could make me a widow at any moment. But now . . . now he is under sentence of excommunication, and that pushes my fear beyond endurance. I'll not deny I find it hard, knowing he is always going to put Gwynedd first. But he found it hard, too, being wed to John's daughter. And no matter how angry he makes me, I could not envision my life without him . . . even now, when our marriage is admittedly at low tide!"

"I am glad, Joanna," Isabelle said, and meant it, although she remained convinced that a love so intense was no gift of God. "Now tell me," she said, because she knew it would please Joanna, "about Elen and your Davydd. From your letters, I suspect that he is your favorite, no?"

"No!" Joanna protested swiftly, if not altogether convincingly. "I love Elen dearly. But . . . I just cannot understand her as I would like. No matter how I try, there remains a barrier between us, one I've not been able to breach. With Davydd it's different, mayhap because I see so much of myself in him. I know what he is thinking and feeling and dreaming; even without words, I know."

"And what of the snake in your Eden? What of Gruffydd?"

Joanna's reaction was a revealing one. Her mouth tightened noticeably, and her eyes darkened; at that moment she looked very like John. "Davydd will be nine in November. Gruffydd is one and twenty . . . and has a large following amongst Llewelyn's people."

"Not surprising. He's a handsome youth, and there's something utterly compelling about his sort of recklessness. It's rather like watching an avalanche; you do not want to get caught up in it, but for certes you cannot ignore it, either. You're saying, then, that the Welsh regard him as Llewelyn's rightful heir?"

Joanna nodded. "If it were left to the Welsh, it would be no contest, would be Gruffydd by acclamation. And Llewelyn loves him very much, puts up with outrageous behavior he'd not tolerate from another living soul because of that love. As for Gruffydd, I sometimes think his hatred of England borders upon madness, for it is so impassioned, so . . . so utterly implacable. He despises me, of course, and is wildly jealous of Davydd. You want the truth, Isabelle? I think I was not so much angry with Llewelyn over Gwladys as over Gruffydd. You see, when Llewelyn led his army into Reginald's lands and then against the Flemings in Rhos, he was not just risking his own life. He was risking Davydd's, too."

"I do not know what to tell you, Joanna," Isabelle said and sighed. "I know what John would have said, though. He'd have said this was one of God's more macabre jests. Your son's danger will not cease till the day Gruffydd draws his last breath. Yet Gruffydd lives because of you. John spared him for you, because he thought you wanted that. He'd have sent Gruffydd to the gallows in a trice if you'd only asked . . ." Isabelle sighed again. "I so wish you'd come to him at Oxford, Joanna. It hurt him grievously that you did not."

"I could not!" Joanna's face was flaming. "I had no choice, had to put my husband and children first, and I'll not feel guilty about it!"

"Then why," Isabelle said coldly, "are you so angry?"

Joanna said nothing; her throat was suddenly too tight for speech. She turned abruptly away, back toward the window. She was still in profile; Isabelle could see how long it took for the color to fade from her face, and her own anger ebbed away. She reached out, touched Joanna's shoulder. Joanna spun around and they embraced, clung together in one of the most intense yet ephemeral of bonds, the solidarity of a shared loss.

"I'm sorry, Joanna. I never meant to hurt you." Isabelle's cheek was wet with Joanna's tears; she wiped them away, gave the younger woman an apologetic hug. "But I need to talk about John, and you're the only—"

"I cannot." Joanna's voice was muffled, all but inaudible. "Isabelle, I cannot . . ."

"I know you're grieving. But Joanna, so am I. These last months have been the most wretched of my life!"

Joanna had rarely heard Isabelle speak with such emotion, with such stark sincerity, and she felt shame for having assumed Isabelle's grief would be so easily assuaged.

Isabelle had begun to pace. "John was a . . . a law unto himself, was not an easy man to understand . . . or to live with. Especially these last few years. But I think I made him happy, and I . . . I loved being his Queen, Joanna. As far back as I can remember, I could turn heads, attract attention, but that was only because men found me fair to look upon. When I was Queen, it was different; I truly mattered. People sought to please me, to court my goodwill—because they knew John loved me. And now . . . now I might as well be a deaf-mute for all the heed they pay me. Without John, I count for naught."

"Surely you exaggerate," Joanna said slowly, and Isabelle gave a vehement shake of her head.

"I know I'm no Eleanor of Aquitaine. It never occurred to me—or to anyone else, obviously—that I should act as regent. But I ought to have some say in my son's upbringing, and I have none at all. Nor will I, as long as Chester and Pembroke have the government. They like me not, Joanna, think I'm frivolous and vain and foreign, a bad influence upon Henry. Yes, that is what I said—foreign. For suddenly my birthplace has become a liability. People now look at me askance because my mother is a first cousin to the French King, as if that somehow makes me suspect!"

"Isabelle . . . might you not be oversensitive, seeing slights when none was meant?"

"Then why did the Pope feel the need to issue a stern warning last February, forbidding people to harass me or molest my property and goods?"

Joanna's emotions were too ambivalent to allow for dispassionate analysis. The realization that Isabelle grieved more for the privileges and prerogatives of queenship than for the man who'd made them possible had done much to sour her sympathy for the other woman. And yet she could not help but identify with Isabelle's isolation, her sense of alienation, for she, too, had suffered for the sin of foreign birth.

Isabelle had stopped before a small table. It was littered with jars, with belladonna and kohl and marigold balm, casting-bottles of jasmine and violet perfumes, vials of rosewater; Joanna had never seen such an assortment. Isabelle was picking up jars at random; she seemed suddenly—and uncharacteristically—uncertain. Jerking off her wimple and veil, she loosened her hair, shook it free about her shoulders. Although it was not as pure a shade as in her early youth, and owed something now to rinses with lemon water, her hair was still soft and shimmering, evoking in Joanna an unexpected and nostalgic memory of her mother Clemence, so many years dead, Clemence with her swirling cloud of bright blonde hair.

"I might as well say this straight out, know no other way to tell you." Isabelle leaned back against the table, as if bracing herself. "I asked you to come to Windsor because I think of you as a sister, Joanna . . . and I wanted to bid you farewell."

"Farewell? I do not understand."

"I am more than the widow of a dead King, Joanna. I am Countess of Angoulême in my own right, and I have decided to go home, to go back to my own lands, my own people."

Joanna was stunned, at a loss for words. It did not surprise her that Isabelle should, even after seventeen years, have so little loyalty to England, for she did not feel truly bound to her own husband's homeland. But Isabelle would never be allowed to take her children. In abandoning England, she was abandoning Henry, Dickon, Nell, and Isabella, and Joanna could conceive of no circumstances, however wretched, under which she would willingly forsake Davydd and Elen.

Although she said nothing, Joanna's shock showed plainly in her face, and Isabelle frowned, said defensively, "It is for the best, Joanna. It's not as if they'll want for anything. Moreover, I have another daughter. Joanna—your namesake—is seven now, and I've not seen her since she was four."

"But the de Lusignans have custody of her. Will they let you see her?"

"I think so. Hugh is a reasonable man, after all. Why would he not agree?"

"Reasonable?" Joanna echoed incredulously. "Hugh de Lusignan?"

Isabelle laughed. "No, I was speaking of his son, of the younger Hugh." She'd picked up a mirror, was gazing pensively at the image it reflected, at the beauty not even polished metal could distort. "No," she repeated softly, "I do not think Hugh will refuse me."

2

DOLBADARN, NORTH WALES

February 1218

Situated on a rocky knoll eighty feet above Llyn Padarn, Dolbadarn
Castle commanded the route from Caer yn Arfon to the Conwy
Valley. This was Joanna's first visit to Dolbadarn since Llewelyn
had constructed the two-story circular keep, and she was dazzled
at sight of mountains mirrored in the deep blue depths of a
snow-fed lake. She stood now at the window in the upper chamber, gazing out at the regal heights of Yr Wyddfa, a stark,
snow-shrouded pinnacle framed against a cloudless winter sky.

"I wonder if I'm falling under the spell of Wales at long last.
Or does it seem so spectacular merely because I'm so happy?
Shall I tell you why? Last night I had a letter from my brother
Richard, telling me that his wife has given birth to a daughter.
And this morning Llewelyn gave me a gift of immeasurable
value. He has agreed to make peace with Henry, which means no
more war—for a time, anyway—and a chance to visit my brother's court, and most blessed mercy of all, the papal legate Guala
will now restore Llewelyn to God's grace. Oh, indeed? Well,
that might not mean much to you, but it means everything to
me!"

Her audience, a small, amber-colored spaniel, yawned again,
and Joanna laughed, scooped up the puppy. "I know I'm silly,
but I feel like being silly this morn. What shall we do now? Go
play in the snow?"

The castle bailey seemed carpeted in crystal, so brilliant was
the sunlight upon the drifts of ice and snow. Joanna's puppy ran
in circles, barking joyously, and Joanna wished suddenly that she
were not twenty-six, that she were still young enough to make

angels in the snow, to spin till she was dizzy, drunk on the utter purity of the icy mountain air.

"Topaz!" The puppy was barking at a woman crossing the bailey. Joanna called again, hastened to retrieve her errant pet. The hood of the woman's mantle shadowed her face, and Joanna did not recognize her until they were several feet apart. When she did, her exuberance vanished as if it had never been. Grabbing for the dog, she politely greeted Gruffydd's bride.

"Good morrow, Madame."

Joanna opened her mouth, shut it again. She'd twice suggested that Senena call her by her given name; what more could she do? It annoyed her that she should find conversation so difficult with this girl; she'd thought she'd long since prevailed over the anxieties and insecurities of her own girlhood.

Seeing Senena glance down at the dog, she said, "Topaz is a gift from my husband. I'd had a dog for nigh on thirteen years, did not think I wanted another when Sugar died. But Llewelyn was right, and I find Topaz a joy."

"I like dogs," Senena said. Hers was a breathless, little-girl voice that made her seem even younger than seventeen. So, too, did her size; she was barely five feet tall, looked incredibly fragile and tiny when standing next to her husband. She was not a beauty, was too pale, with unfashionable freckles and thick eyebrows she refused to pluck. Her eyes were undeniably her best feature, wide-set and compelling, a dark sea-grey, but to Joanna, they were too watchful, too unrevealing.

Joanna had made one or two halfhearted attempts to befriend Gruffydd's young wife, but she was not altogether sorry when Senena did not respond to her overtures. She was a quiet girl who rarely spoke in company, and Joanna had assumed she was shy. She was no longer so certain that was the case, was slowly concluding that Senena's reticence was not so much timidity as it was wariness. More and more, she reminded Joanna of a cat put down in strange surroundings, cautiously learning the lay of the land.

Senena was still studying Topaz. "I prefer a larger dog, myself," she said in the colorless little voice that made it so difficult to determine whether she meant to give offense. "I think dogs should be useful, not just decorative. If you'll excuse me now, Madame, Gruffydd awaits me in the great hall."

"By all means." Joanna stood watching as Senena walked away, not moving until Topaz pawed at her skirt. "Well, Topaz, I'm afraid you've just been dismissed as a decadent Norman trinket. Like me, no doubt.'' But she felt no real surprise. Senena was Gruffydd's cousin. She was also his choice; their marriage had come about because he wanted it so. It was only to be expected, therefore, that he and Senena shared more than a bed, that they shared a common outlook, a common enemy.

Senena had a surprisingly lithe, athletic stride, was already passing the West Tower. As she did, a small figure darted out behind her. Senena did not notice. But Joanna did, sharply cried out her daughter's name.

Elen whirled. She flushed at sight of her mother, hid her hands behind her back, but not before Joanna caught a glimpse of the snowball in her daughter's fist.

By the time she reached Elen, Senena had disappeared into the hall, apparently oblivious of the thwarted ambush. Joanna took Elen's arm, drew her aside.

''Elen, what am I to do with you? If you must throw snowballs, at least pick your victims with greater care. Believe me, Senena would not have been amused.''

Elen shrugged. ''I do not like her.''

''Why ever not?''

''Because . . . because she's Gruffydd's wife.''

Joanna stared at her daughter. ''But you've always been very fond of Gruffydd, and he of you. Have you quarreled?''

Elen looked down at the ground; her hair was loose, windblown, fell forward to hide her face. Joanna suddenly understood, drew a sharp, dismayed breath.

''It's Davydd,'' she said, and Elen nodded.

''Gruffydd hates him.'' She no longer sounded sulky, looked up at Joanna, brown eyes full of bewilderment. ''The day ere we left Aber, I was playing at the waterfall. Gruffydd and Senena were walking by the river. When they did not see me, I hid in the rocks so I could surprise them. I did not mean to eavesdrop, Mama, not really. They were saying mostly silly things, the way grown people do. Laughing and kissing, you know. But then Gruffydd began to talk about you and Davydd. He was telling Senena that you meant to deprive him of his rightful inheritance. He was saying hateful things about Davydd. Mama, he . . . he even said Davydd should never have been born!''

Joanna bit her lip. It was so unfair, so unjust that Davydd—and now Elen—should be caught up in adult passions, in ambitions and antagonisms beyond their ken. They were too young, she thought, too young! But she had no comfort for her child, could not lie. ''I am so sorry, Elen,'' she said, after a troubled silence. "I truly wish you could love both Davydd and Gruffydd. But since you must choose, I'm very glad you chose Davydd."

"I had to, Mama. Gruffydd has Gwladys and Marared and Gwenllian. But Davydd has only me."

Never had Joanna felt so inadequate, so unequal to the task of motherhood. "The hardest part of being a mother, Elen, is that we want so much to protect our children from all evil, all hurt. And we cannot . . ."

"I do not need to be protected, Mama," Elen protested indignantly. But when Joanna put her arm around the girl's shoulders, Elen did not pull away, and she stayed by Joanna's side as they walked together toward the great hall.

They had not yet entered the hall when they heard shouting and quickened their steps, for they recognized the voices as Gruffydd's and Llewelyn's.

"But you turned down the English last September, rightfully refused to take part in the peace between Henry and the French Prince. Why have you changed your mind, Papa? Why should you now be willing to submit to the English?"

"I do not consider it submission," Llewelyn snapped. "When they offered peace last autumn, it was conditioned upon our surrender of all the lands we'd taken from them in South Wales. Of course I refused, and then I waited. It was well worth the wait, Gruffydd. Yes, I have now agreed to do homage to Henry. But in return, Guala will absolve me of excommunication and lift the Interdict from Wales. Our past conquests will be recognized. I will be invested with custody of the royal castles they call Carmarthen and Cardigan, will hold them until Henry comes of age. The English have even agreed to acknowledge my authority in Lower Powys until Gwenwynwyn's sons reach manhood. Moreover, they—"

"Acknowledge? Who are they to acknowledge or legitimize your rights? You're a Welsh Prince, are not dependent upon the whims, the indulgence of the English crown!"

"For the love of Christ, Gruffydd, when will you—" Llewelyn stopped abruptly. This was not the way, and for certes not the place. "Come outside where we can talk in private," he said curtly, and turned without waiting to see if Gruffydd was, in fact, following him. By the time he'd reached the bailey, he was once more in control of his temper and determined that this time it would be different, this time he would somehow make his son understand.

"Gruffydd, listen to me. I know how you feel. When I was

your age, I felt just as you do, wanted what you want—an utterly
independent Wales, free of all foreigners, united under my control.''

"Is that so foolish a dream?'' Gruffydd challenged, and Llewelyn
slowly shook his head.

"No, lad, it is not. But it's a dream beyond our reach. God
has decreed otherwise. We're too sparsely populated, too conten-
tious, and we dwell in the shadow of England, a country some
twenty times the size of ours. We will always have to seek some
sort of accommodation with the English. The realities of power
dictate that, Gruffydd.''

When Gruffydd started to speak, he said, "I am not done; hear
me out. I fought against believing it, too, Gruffydd, refused to
admit that my horizons could be limited, my dreams denied. I
followed my heart and not my head, let my pride lure me into
disaster, into a near-fatal confrontation with the King of England.
It was only by the luck of the angels that I survived it, that I did
not lose all, that Gwynedd did not become an English shire.'' He
paused, put his hand upon Gruffydd's arm.

"I see so much of myself in you, Gruffydd. But in just three
days I shall be forty and five, and you're not yet twenty and two.
I want you to be able to benefit from my years, my experience. I
do not want you to make the same mistakes I did.''

"Whatever mistakes you may have made in the past, Papa,
they are nothing when compared to the one you're about to make
now.'' But the emotion in Gruffydd's voice was no longer anger,
and as he looked at Llewelyn now, his green eyes were misty,
almost pleading. "England has a boy King, Papa. This is a
God-given opportunity for us, and you're throwing it away.
You're throwing it away and I cannot understand why!''

Llewelyn's hand slipped from Gruffydd's arm. "No,'' he said
at last, "you truly cannot, can you?''

"Papa, you're not a coward. I'd kill any man who called you
one. But why, then, must you make the craven choice, demean
yourself before men not worthy of your piss? Why will you
not—''

"This discussion is done, Gruffydd. I go to Worcester next
month to meet with Henry. And this time you shall go with me.''

"No! Never!''

"You will have to live with the lords of Henry's court, have to
deal with Pembroke and Chester and Peter des Roches. So it is
time you met them, learned what manner of men they are.''

"No, Papa. I will not go.''

"Yes,'' Llewelyn said, "you will,'' and Gruffydd's eyes were the first to waver. He swung about, all but fled across the bailey. Llewelyn let him go, for he knew he'd won. But it was not a victory to give him joy. He stood motionless, staring down at Gruffydd's footprints in the snow, and suddenly he was remembering a childhood mishap, remembering that long-ago encounter with Walter de Hodnet.

"God help you, Gruffydd," he said softly, "but you'd never have done what Walter demanded. You'd have forced him to break your arm, to leave you maimed for life."

Llewelyn found Joanna by the river wall in the Bishop of Worcester's gardens. It had been a wet, chill March, and nights of killing frost had wreaked havoc among the Bishop's early-blooming crocus plants. Joanna was bundled up in a fur-lined mantle, but as Llewelyn reached her, she exclaimed, "Listen to that. A curlew, a sure harbinger of coming spring."

"My teeth are chattering too much to hear it. Are you not ready to come back to the Bishop's palace?"

"Well . . ." Joanna hesitated. "What I'd truly like to do now is to go into the church, to light a candle for my father." Although she knew she did not have to ask permission, her voice rose questioningly, nonetheless. Seventeen months after his death, John was still a sensitive subject between them.

"That's probably a good idea," Llewelyn said dryly, leaving unsaid the rest of his thought, that John's soul was in need of all the prayers he could get. "Come on," he said, sliding his arm around Joanna's waist. "I'll walk over with you."

Joanna was very pleased. "Admit it," she teased, "it did bother you, all those months when you could not enter a church. It had to, for how could you be sure God was on your side?"

"Just between you and me, *breila*, I've always suspected that the Almighty was Welsh," Llewelyn said, and they both laughed. They were still laughing as they entered the north door of the church, moved into the nave. But their laughter stopped abruptly a moment later, for they were face to face with Joanna's Uncle Will and his wife.

Joanna had known such a meeting was inevitable, but she'd been dreading it all the same. Her feelings for Will were hopelessly entangled. She could not reproach him for deserting her father, not when she felt herself to be guilty of the same sin. But she could not help remembering what Isabelle had told her, how devastated John had been by Will's betrayal, and that memory drained all warmth, all vivacity from her voice.

Her greeting was so lame, so unlike her that Will flushed. "I see," he said flatly. "So you, too, judge me."

"No," Joanna said, without much conviction.

"Isabelle and Richard blame me. But I expected you to be fairer than they, Joanna. After all, you made a choice, too, did you not? You disavowed John to please your husband, and if you ever cared about the grief that gave John, he never knew it!"

The words were no sooner out of his mouth than Will would have given anything to recall them. Joanna looked so stricken that he was swept with remorse. No matter how raw his nerves had gotten, there was no excuse for taking out his pain upon the lass, and he started to tell her so, to offer his apologies.

But Llewelyn forestalled him, saying scathingly, "Joanna was estranged from John over a matter of conscience. She could not stomach the murder of children. You, however, seem to have had no such qualms. For three full years after the Nottingham hangings, you continued to keep faith with John, to benefit from his favor. You did not abandon him until he seemed sure to be beaten, until you thought Louis likely to—"

"No!" Will had flushed even darker. "That's not so," he said in a choked voice. "It was not self-interest. It was because of what John did to my wife, to Ela. It was only then that she told me . . . told me that whilst I was a prisoner in France, John sought to seduce her."

It was suddenly very quiet in the church. Llewelyn and Joanna both appeared dumbfounded. Will swallowed. "I'm sorry, Joanna," he said miserably. "I did not mean to tell you that . . ."

Joanna was staring, not at him, but at Ela. For a long moment their eyes held, and then she said, "It's all right, Uncle Will. I know you did what you thought you had to do."

There was an awkward pause, and then Ela stepped forward, kissed Joanna on the cheek. Will wanted to do likewise, but felt too discomfited. He patted his niece on the shoulder, then made haste to lead his wife from the nave.

Joanna moved on into the choir, toward her father's tomb. Llewelyn followed more slowly. The irony did not escape him that he of all men should find himself cast as John's defender, but he did not have to strive for conviction; for once, he thought John truly deserved the benefit of the doubt. *"Breila,* I do not believe Will. I'm sure your Aunt Ela is a good, pious woman, but I cannot see her as a siren. John was no fool, would not risk so much for so little. From what you've told me, his women were invariably young and fair to look upon, and Will's Ela is no Eve.''

"You need not seek to persuade me, Llewelyn. I know it's not true. I saw it on Ela's face.'' Joanna's smile was sad, tremulous, but still a smile of sorts. "You're right; Ela is no Eve. But she is the mother of eight children. If she could salvage her family's future with a lie, I daresay she thought that a small price to pay. And how can I blame her? For loving her children? If my father had not earned himself such a vile reputation, men would not have been so quick to suspect the worst of him, and Will could never have convinced himself that Ela spoke true. What you said about Will was right; he is a weak man. But he's a decent man, too, and he deserves some peace of mind.''

She reached up, kissed him softly on the mouth. "Thank you for speaking up for me, beloved. Now I want to light a candle for my father. If you do not mind, I'd rather do it alone.''

Llewelyn watched as she turned away. If you can forgive Will, *breila*, why can you not forgive yourself? But the question was a silent one. They could not talk about John; that was a terrain too fraught with pitfalls and remembered pain. It troubled him, though, that Joanna seemed unable to talk about her father with anyone at all, even Catrin or Richard. At first he'd thought she only needed time to be able to come to terms with John's death. But he was beginning to realize that her grieving was interwoven with guilt— guilt she would not even acknowledge—that the normal healing process was ineffectual. Her grief was still raw, and he did not know how to help her.

He glanced down at John's coffin, and his mouth twisted in a bitter smile. John had been no easy foe to defeat, and as a ghost he was even more formidable, defying all attempts at exorcism. In death he was causing as much pain and turmoil as ever he had in his accursed lifetime. Joanna was not his only victim. Gruffydd, too, was one, Gruffydd who could not outrun his memories of English prisons.

The talk in Worcester was all of the coming crusade to capture the Egyptian city of Damietta. Both in England and in France, an impressive roster of wellborn barons had taken the cross, among them Robert Fitz Walter, Saer de Quincy and his eldest son, John's illegitimate son Oliver Fitz Roy—even Hugh de Lusignan. But the plans of one crusader in particular interested Llewelyn, and he deliberately set about encountering the Earl of Chester alone on the east walkway of the priory cloisters.

They greeted each other with the wary regard that men reserve for adversaries worthy of respect. Llewelyn at once came to the point. "I hear you mean to join the crusade. Is that true?"

Chester nodded. "I took the cross with King John, received a dispensation until the French were defeated. Now that the realm is at peace, I can fulfill my vow."

"Tell me," Llewelyn said with a faint smile, "have you no qualms about leaving your holdings in Cheshire? With you in the Holy Land, men might see your manors and estates as fruit ripe for the picking."

Chester thought Llewelyn's jest a rather dubious one, but he made a polite attempt to reply in kind, saying wryly, "It is good of you to be so concerned on my behalf. Of course, if you truly want to ease my mind, you can always offer a truce for the length of my absence."

As he expected, Llewelyn laughed and shook his head. But then he said, "Actually, what I had in mind was not a truce, but an alliance."

Chester stopped dead in the walkway. "Are you serious?"

"Very."

"We've been enemies for most of our lives. Yet now, when you have an opportunity to raid into Cheshire with impunity, you are offering to make peace? Why?"

"I'll not deny that your absence would enable me to seize an advantage. But it would be short-lived. You're right, we have been enemies, but by geography, not by choice. We each wield a great deal of power. If we joined together, how much greater that power might be, great enough to protect our common interests, to give us a formidable say in the King's council."

"Yes," Chester said slowly, "it would indeed."

Although he was sure he already knew the answer, Llewelyn took care to observe the formalities, asking, "Well? What do you think?"

"I think," Chester said, "that we ought to talk."

Gruffydd was utterly wretched at Worcester. The suffocating sensations of confinement had come back to haunt his sleep. He awoke in an English bed, craving Senena's warmth, dreading the daylight hours when he must mingle with men he despised, speak their alien tongue, watch as his father humbled himself before John's son.

As he crossed from sun into shadow, he paused, blinking as his eyes adjusted to the loss of light. He was not sure what drew

him so often to the priory church, but on three different occasions
he'd found himself standing before the High Altar, before the
tomb of the English King. It gave him a curious kind of comfort
to touch the cold marble of John's coffin. Once he'd even spat
onto it, knowing the gesture was childish and not caring in the
least.

But as he moved now into the choir, he came to an abrupt halt,
for he was not alone. Two young boys were standing by John's
coffin, a lone wall sconce spilling light onto their bowed heads,
one bright as flame, the other black as jet. His brother Davydd
and the boy King.

Having offered a prayer, Henry carefully crossed himself, then
reached out, ran his hand over the smooth surface of the tomb.
Davydd, too, started to touch the coffin, but so tentatively that
Henry said encouragingly, "Go ahead. Papa would not mind.
You're his grandson, you have the right."

At that, Davydd drew back. My grandfather, he thought, and it
did not seem real to him, not at all. "Do you miss him?" he
asked, and Henry nodded.

"I did not see him all that often, but I always knew I would
sooner or later. Now, when I think that I'll never, never get to
see him again, sometimes it . . . . it scares me."

Davydd gave Henry a look of sharp pity. "You must miss
your mother, too. Why did she go?" He did not mean to be rude,
but he found Isabelle's mysterious departure very disturbing; it
made him wonder if his own mother might not one day go back
to England, leave him as Isabelle had left Henry.

"I do not know," Henry admitted. "She—" His head came
up. "Davydd," he whispered, "someone is watching us. Over
there, see?"

Davydd peered into the shadows. "It's my brother," he said,
but the sudden tautness in his voice and stance communicated to
Henry an inexplicable sense of unease.

"Let's go," he urged, tugging at Davydd's sleeve.

Davydd wanted to go, too, but he did not want Gruffydd to
think he was running away. He circled around to the far side of
the coffin. "Do you like your brothers, Henry?"

Henry smiled at the silliness of the question. "Of course I do.
I like Richard and Oliver best, and I love my little brother
Dickon; he's nine, like you."

"We Welsh have a saying about brothers," Davydd said, so
loudly that Henry flinched. "*Gwell ceiniog na brawd.*"

"What does that mean?"

"Better a penny than a brother."

"I do not understand."

"Gruffydd does."

"Not so loud," Henry cautioned, "lest he hear you. I do not like being watched. Think you that we can slip out without him seeing us?"

"No," Davydd said, but then he sighed. "It's all right. He's gone."

One of the monks was moving sedately up the cloister walkway, toward the south door of the church. He stumbled backward as Gruffydd burst through the doorway, his box of candles spilling onto the cloister tiles. Gruffydd did not offer assistance; he'd not even noticed the man. He continued rapidly up the walkway, not pausing until he neared the Chapter House. At this time of day it would be empty, would be a good place to be alone. He was reaching for the latch as the door swung open and his father and the Earl of Chester emerged onto the walkway.

Llewelyn had often deplored his eldest son's sense of timing, but never more than now. "Were you looking for me, Gruffydd?"

Gruffydd shook his head. They'd been laughing together; he even thought he'd heard his father call Chester by his Christian name, call him Ranulf as if he were a friend, a comrade-in-arms.

"You know my son, of course, Ranulf," Llewelyn said, and Gruffydd stiffened. Ranulf. So he'd not imagined it. Ranulf.

"Indeed. I was present at Dover Castle the day he defied King John. I've never forgotten it, for that was one of the most courageous acts I've ever seen." In Chester's considered opinion, it was also one of the most foolhardy, and he might have said that to Llewelyn. But not to Gruffydd—he knew instinctively that this was one young man who'd never learned to laugh at himself.

"You might as well be the first to know," he said, and smiled. "Your lord father and I have pledged to forget past differences, to act as allies from this day forth." He heard Llewelyn's indrawn breath, and knew at once that he'd blundered, even before he saw the shock on Gruffydd's face.

"Papa . . . Papa, tell me he's lying. Tell me you'd not do this, you'd not befriend this . . . this Norman butcher!"

"Hold your tongue! The man speaks our language!"

"And slaughters our people! How often has his sword been smeared with Welsh blood? What else does he want from you? Are you to stand guard over his lands whilst he's in the Holy Land, act as his lackey, his—"

Llewelyn grabbed Gruffydd's wrist, shoved him back against the door, into the Chapter House. "Do not ever shame me like that before a stranger! You understand, Gruffydd? Not ever!"

Gruffydd had never seen Llewelyn so angry. Unnerved in spite of himself, he took a backward step. That there was some justification for his father's rage, he could not deny. "I ought not to have spoken out in Chester's hearing. In that, I was in the wrong. But . . . but my God, Papa, think what you do! Ever since you took that Norman witch into your bed, you've—"

Llewelyn was incredulous. "Have you lost your wits? Joanna is no witch!"

That was a very serious accusation to make, and Gruffydd realized he'd gone too far; he had no proof whatsoever that Joanna had ever used the Black Arts to ensorcell his father. "Mayhap she's not," he conceded, "but she is still to blame. She's gotten you to betray your birthright, to—"

"I've heard enough from you, more than enough. Go back to the guest hall, gather your belongings. I want you gone from here within the hour, want you back in Wales ere you bring further disgrace upon me."

"Gladly!" Gruffydd spun around, strode toward the door. There he paused for the briefest of seconds. But whatever he'd meant to say, he thought better of it. He shoved the door back, let it slam defiantly behind him.

Llewelyn sat down upon the closest wooden bench. Leaning back against the wall, he closed his eyes, rubbed his fingers over his throbbing temples; his anger had turned inward, and he felt suddenly sick. He'd lost track of time when the creaking of the door jolted him upright; he'd hoped Chester would have the common sense to leave him alone. The door opened wider. Not Chester. Morgan.

Llewelyn's mouth twitched, in what was almost a smile. "You always know when I have need of you. What have you—second sight?"

Morgan shook his head. "Gruffydd has gone."

Llewelyn closed his eyes again, then felt the priest's hand on his shoulder. "What can I do, Morgan? He's my son. Christ Jesus, but what can I do?"

3

DOLWYDDELAN, NORTH WALES

April 1220

Joanna was accustomed to having her bedchamber appropriated whenever her husband required a particularly private meeting place. She was not accustomed, however, to being present at such times, and was attracting more than her share of curious, covert looks. When Ednyved sauntered over to her window seat, she murmured, "If I tell them I'm here at Llewelyn's bidding, will they stop staring at me as if I'm a Norman spy in their midst?"

"Even after fourteen years in Wales, do you still know so little of our ways? They've never thought of you as a Norman spy—but rather as an English one."

Joanna bit her lip, but once more he'd won; she was unable to suppress a smile. She gestured for him to join her in the window seat, marveling—not for the first time—how unlikely and yet how dear a friend this man had become. Not that he'd changed any; he still had a sharp tongue, a sardonic eye, and spared none the cutting edge of his humor. But now she caught the glint of amusement behind the heavy lids, caught the echoes of affection. Now she knew that Ednyved was her ally, that he alone of her husband's friends did not want to see Gruffydd as Prince of North Wales.

"Did Llewelyn tell you why he wants us all here like this?"

"You know Llewelyn better than that, Ednyved. When he's truly troubled, he keeps his own counsel." And Llewelyn was troubled, that Joanna knew. So did Ednyved. They shared that awareness with no need of words, then glanced expectantly toward the door.

But it was not Llewelyn. At sight of her son, Joanna half rose.

"Davydd, you'd best come back later, after your father's council is done."

"But Papa told me to come, Mama. He said I ought to be here." Davydd glanced uncertainly about the chamber. He knew all in the room very well, but he was somewhat self-conscious nonetheless, and was grateful when his mother slid over, made room for him beside her in the window seat. As flattered as he was to be here, he was nervous, too, as nervous as the first time Llewelyn had taken him hunting. Gruffydd had spoiled that memory for him; Davydd still flushed sometimes, remembering Gruffydd's scorn when he missed his target, shot his arrow a full foot over the roebuck's withers. But Gruffydd was not here now to mar his pleasure in this, his first inclusion into the world of politics and statecraft, into the world of men.

"What does Papa want to tell us?" he whispered, and Joanna shook her head.

"I would that I knew!"

Llewelyn entered as she was speaking. He stood for an unusually lengthy time in the doorway, as if reluctant to enter, and once he was in the room, he seemed in no hurry to begin. He crossed to the table and picked up a wine cup, only to set it down untasted. The people in this chamber were those closest to him, those who'd celebrated his triumphs and endured his defeats, those who had the right to know what he meant to do. His eyes moved slowly from face to face. His brother Adda. Rhys. Morgan. Ednyved. Joanna. He could only hope they'd try to understand . . . and try to forgive.

His gaze lingered the longest upon his son. Davydd was now in his twelfth year, poised for entry into the uncharted terrain that lay between boyhood and manhood. A child and yet not a child, this youngest son of his. When he finally spoke, it was to Davydd.

"What can you tell me, Davydd, about the English laws of inheritance?"

Flustered to find himself suddenly the cynosure of all eyes, Davydd blurted out, "The eldest son gets all," only then to be seized with doubts, with the sinking sensation that he'd misfired another arrow. But his father nodded, as if satisfied.

"You're right, lad. That is the crux of it, the heart of the matter." Llewelyn's eyes left the boy, shifted toward the others. "I think we'd all agree that ours is a more just way. We do not leave younger sons to gain their bread as best they can; we divide a man's holdings equally amongst all his sons. But Scriptures say a kingdom divided against itself shall be made desolate. Is that not so, Morgan?''

He did not wait for confirmation. ''I've ofttimes spoken to you of my grandfather, Joanna. But I've not said much of his brother. There was naught but envy and dissension between them, a sharp rivalry that lasted the whole of their lives. And when my grandfather died, his sons fought for Gwynedd, not against the English, but against each other. My father was slain by his own kindred.''

He turned away from the table, moved toward the center of the room. ''Ours is a bloody past, but no bloodier than that of Powys and Deheubarth. There, too, a prince's death inevitably brought about the same slaughter, brother against brother. Verily, a man reading our history might well conclude that Cain and Abel, too, were Welsh. That is the ugliest of our legacies, that the sons of our princes must seize power over the bodies of their brothers. It is not a legacy I want to leave my sons.''

''What you say is true, Llewelyn. It is not in man's nature to share a kingdom. And because it is not, Welsh princes love their brothers not. Indeed, had I been born whole of body, the affections of our boyhood might not have survived the ambitions of our manhood. A disquieting thought, that, but who is to say? Yet there is nothing to be done about it. Our ways are not always easy, but they are ancient and revered, and above all, they are ours.''

''You're wrong, Adda. There is something I can do. Amongst God's Commandments, which one says that the laws of Hywel the Good cannot be changed?''

A shocked silence greeted so blasphemous a suggestion. Why were men so set upon clinging to the past at all costs? Why did the phrase ''as it's always been done'' give them such false comfort? Llewelyn's was an old and familiar impatience, made all the sharper now by his anxiety, and he said abruptly, almost defiantly, ''I do not expect you to agree with me. But so be it. I summoned you here to tell you that I have decided to bequeath my realm to one son, as the English kings do.''

Davydd heard his mother whisper, ''Oh, dear God,'' and there was so much fear in her voice that he was suddenly afraid, too, both of what his father would say next and of shaming himself before an audience of adults. He sat very still, scarcely breathing, thinking not of crowns and kingdoms but of Gruffydd, the first-born son, the Welsh-born son, the best-loved.

''Our people love you well, Llewelyn. But in this you ask too much. I do not think they'll willingly forsake a custom so deeply rooted in our past, accept in its stead the practice of our enemies. To men reared on the concept of equality amongst sons, such a change would be both alien and offensive.''

Even before Morgan had finished speaking, both Rhys and Adda were nodding in vigorous agreement. Ednyved, too, looked exceedingly dubious. ''There's truth in that, Llewelyn. It will not be easy.''

''I know,'' Llewelyn conceded. ''That is why it must be done in my lifetime. People will need time to come to terms with it, as with any new idea. But I think they can be made to see that it is for Gwynedd's good. Surely none amongst you can argue that it benefits a kingdom to have it split asunder by civil war.''

''The common sense of what you say cannot be denied,'' Adda said, and then smiled thinly. ''But men heed other voices than reason. I see, however, that your mind is set upon this, upon naming Gruffydd as your sole heir, and so—''

''No,'' Llewelyn said. ''Not Gruffydd. Davydd.''

''Me?'' Davydd gasped, sat suddenly upright, then flushed as he realized they were all staring at him. Joanna reached over, squeezed his arm, but her eyes never left Llewelyn's; he had seen such a look upon her face once before, the very first time he'd kissed her. Ednyved was smiling, but Rhys and Adda looked appalled, and Morgan, who understood, looked neither surprised nor judgmental, just unutterably sad.

''Do not speak of this yet, not even to your wives,'' Llewelyn said before either Adda or Rhys could recover, could burst out with impassioned arguments upon Gruffydd's behalf. As he'd hoped, they were constrained by Davydd's presence. Ednyved now cued the others by rising; they reluctantly followed suit.

''Papa . . .'' Davydd was still dazed. ''Papa, I'll make you proud, I will.''

''You'd better,'' Llewelyn said, and the boy gave him a radiant smile. He looked slight, almost frail, when compared to Gruffydd at the same age. Although Davydd was still quite young, Llewelyn did not think it likely he'd ever approach Gruffydd's uncommon height, and he could never hope to match Gruffydd's strength. But he'd once punctured his hand upon a nail, and when his playmates panicked, he calmly walked a half-mile for help, with the nail protruding from his palm. And Llewelyn had known for several years now that of his eight children, Davydd had by far the best brain.

Davydd was the last to depart. Joanna stood for a moment with him upon the porch, not speaking, just sharing. Then she turned, went back into the chamber where Davydd had been born, where Llewelyn awaited her.

They both moved toward each other at once, came together in the middle of the room. "Beloved, what can I say? I know that my joy is your pain—know, too, how very difficult a decision it was. In truth, Llewelyn, you are a remarkable man."

Llewelyn tightened his arms around her. "No," he said, his voice muffled in her hair. "No, I am a man who is going to lose his son."

Llewelyn had dreaded nothing—not even his surrender to John at Aberconwy—as much as he dreaded telling his son. And it proved to be even more of an ordeal than he expected. Gruffydd listened in unnerving silence, never taking his eyes from Llewelyn's face, eyes filled with such stunned disbelief that Llewelyn found his throat tightening, his own eyes stinging.

"The cantref of Meirionydd has been mine since my cousin Hywel's death. I am giving it now to you, Gruffydd. Also the lordship of Ardudwy. And in time, mayhap even—"

"Why?"

"As I told you, lad, Gwynedd has to be kept intact. It is the only way we can hope to resist English incursions, to—"

"Why Davydd? Why Davydd and not me?"

"Davydd is the nephew of the English King. That will afford him some degree of influence at the English court, for Henry gives great weight to blood ties. And they are of an age, have taken a liking to one another. That, too, might one day work to our advantage."

"I know you love her. But you loved my mother, too. I am your firstborn. And lest you forget, I was four years as an English prisoner—for you, Papa, for you!" Some of Gruffydd's control cracked. "Does that now count for nothing?"

Llewelyn flinched, but he did not relent. "I know you suffered on my account. But I cannot allow that to unbalance the scales, not when so much is at stake."

"Do not do this to me, Papa. All my life I've sought to please you, to make you proud of me. And I . . . I thought you were!"

"I am proud of you. There is no man in Christendom I'd rather have by my side in a battle." Llewelyn drew a constricted breath. "But I cannot let you rule in my stead. I cannot let you destroy yourself in a war you could never win." His voice changed, steadied. "And I cannot let you destroy Gwynedd. I will not prove my love by the loss of Welsh independence."

"What independence? You've turned Wales into an English fief, and yourself into an English lackey!"

"I know what I've taken from you, do not begrudge you your anger. But your bitterness will change nothing, Gruffydd, and that is what you must try to understand, to accept."

"Must I indeed? I think not, my lord Prince, I think not! You're not just denying me my birthright. I have a son of my own now, or have you forgotten? What of Owain, what of his right?"

Gruffydd was blinded by tears, but they were tears now of rage. He turned away, and Llewelyn caught his arm.

"Gruffydd, wait!"

Gruffydd wrenched free. "Tell your woman and her half-breed son to savor their victory whilst they can!"

Llewelyn made no further attempt to hold him. "When your anger cools, I hope you will remember what I am about to say now—that you will always have a place at my court, in my life, in my heart."

Gruffydd was already at the door. "Rot in Hell," he said, and sobbed. "Rot in Hell!"

As Joanna and Llewelyn left the abbey, crossed the stone bridge into Shrewsbury, Joanna felt uncomfortably conspicuous. It seemed strange to her that they should be riding so peacefully along a route Llewelyn had once followed in war. Llewelyn, however, did not share her self-consciousness. He was indifferent to the stares of the townspeople, had been amused that they should be staying in the very abbey guest-house once fired by Welsh arrows. As they turned onto the street called Altus Vicus, he nonchalantly pointed toward the High Cross, telling her that was where he'd accepted the surrender of Shrewsbury.

"Of course, that wall was not there then," he said, gesturing toward the structure in progress; stones were being mortared in horizontal layers under the supervision of masons, while men hoisted buckets of rubble up onto the scaffolding to fill in the space between the inner and outer faces of the wall. "The citizens of Shrewsbury can thank me for their new wall. In the past, the crown was never willing to put up the money needed to wall the city in."

"So you're saying you did the townspeople a favor by attacking them?" Joanna was delighted by Llewelyn's laughter, for she'd heard it so seldom in the past month, not since Gruffydd had left the court. "I was so proud of Davydd yesterday," she

confided, seeing again in her mind's eye the ceremony in which
Henry formally took his nephew under the protection of the
English crown, acknowledged Davydd as Llewelyn's heir. "Henry
seemed to enjoy it, too. He has quite a liking for pageantry,
cannot wait till his coronation on the seventeenth. I think he felt
cheated before, not being crowned at Westminster like our other
kings."

"*Their* other kings, if you please, Madame," Llewelyn objected, but he was smiling. "Should you like to attend the
coronation, Joanna?"

"I would indeed!" Joanna guided her mare closer to Llewelyn.
"May I take Davydd and Elen?" And when he nodded, she
experienced a surge of heartfelt happiness. "I'm very fond of
Henry. There's a sweetness about him, a vulnerability that can be
quite touching. I see in him Isabelle's extravagance and generosity, her love of surprises and compliments and secrets. But I can
find in him nothing of my father. Tell me, Llewelyn, what sort of
King do you think he'll make?"

"I agree with you that he's a likable lad. But he has two traits
that do not augur well for kingship. He is rather timid, and yet
inflexible, too, loath to compromise. In truth, I do not think he'll
make a good King for the English. He may well, however, prove
to be a very good King indeed for Wales."

Joanna joined in his laughter. "I suspect," she said, "that you
intrigue even in your sleep. I know you truly do like Henry, but
you're deliberately cultivating his goodwill, too. Sometimes you
look at him as if he were a fallow field, just waiting for your
plow!"

Llewelyn grinned, did not deny it. They had just crossed
through the arched gateway into the inner bailey of the castle,
and Llewelyn himself helped Joanna to dismount. "I do not tell
you nearly as often as I ought," he murmured, "but you hold my
heart." She gave him so loving a look that he almost kissed her
right then and there. "Come on," he said, taking her arm, "lest
these English think I'm besotted with my own wife!"

Davydd was waiting for them upon the steps of the great hall.
He had spent the night with Henry at the castle, and Llewelyn's
smile faded at sight of him, for he could not help thinking of his
other son, the son who would have socialized with the English
King only at swordpoint.

Davydd looked troubled. "Something is wrong," he said.

*   *   *

As they entered the great hall, Llewelyn paused to greet Pandulf, who'd recently replaced Guala as the papal legate, and Stephen Langton, restored to favor by the new Pope; as Archbishop of Canterbury, it was he who would crown Henry eleven days hence. Llewelyn addressed both prelates with marked respect, as genuine men of God. He did not hold the urbane, luxury-loving Bishop of Winchester in the same esteem, but Peter des Roches was deserving of notice, too, if for altogether different reasons. With Pembroke dead and Chester still on crusade, Peter des Roches was undeniably the most powerful man in England, the one with the most influence upon the young King.

Peter was flanked by Hubert de Burgh, the Justiciar, and William Marshal, who'd succeeded his father as Earl of Pembroke. His greeting to Llewelyn was noticeably cool; the Pembroke holdings in South Wales were extensive and it was inevitable that the young Earl, who was not the statesman his late father had been, should feel threatened by Llewelyn's growing power. Llewelyn was equally cool to him in return, before saying to Peter, "My son tells me a disturbing letter has come from the Queen."

Pembroke was affronted that Llewelyn should feel so free to meddle in affairs of the crown. But he was not in high favor at Henry's court, for he'd been one of those lords who'd abandoned John for Louis, while Llewelyn was brother-in-law to the King. He was aggrieved but not surprised, therefore, when Peter des Roches responded as if Llewelyn had a right to know.

"It's my fault, in part. I should have read the letter ere I passed it on to Henry. The Queen's never been one for writing letters, but I just assumed it concerned Hugh de Lusignan's death. You did hear he died on crusade?"

Llewelyn nodded. The latest endeavor to free the Holy Land had taken a heavy toll of Christian lives, among them Saer de Quincy and his eldest son and Joanna's half-brother Oliver, although those who lost loved ones on crusade at least had the consolation of knowing the slain were admitted at once into Paradise.

"Prepare yourself for a startling piece of news," Peter said. "It seems Queen Isabelle has married Hugh de Lusignan's son, her daughter's betrothed!"

Joanna had joined them just in time to hear Peter's improbable announcement. "She what?"

She sounded so amazed that Peter smiled; unlike Pembroke and de Burgh, who appeared genuinely shocked by Isabelle's wayward behavior, he seemed more grimly amused than anything else. "Here, my lady," he said, infuriating Pembroke by handing the Queen's letter to Joanna. "Read it for yourself."

Llewelyn followed Joanna to the window, where the light was better. Although his outdoor sight was still eagle-keen, as he moved into his late forties he was becoming increasingly farsighted. Knowing that, and knowing, too, that he was somewhat sensitive about it, Joanna elected to read Isabelle's letter aloud.

"She says that after the deaths of Hugh de Lusignan and his brother, the young Hugh remained alone and without heirs in Poitou, and he felt he could not marry her daughter because of her tender age. His friends counseled him to take a French wife by whom he could beget an heir. She writes: 'If he had done this, all your and our lands in Poitou and Gascony would have been lost. When we, however, saw the great peril which might arise should that marriage take place, we married the said Hugh, Count of La Marche, and let Heaven witness that we did this rather for your benefit than for our own. Wherefore we ask you, as our dear son, to be pleased with this, as it greatly profits you and yours.' "

Joanna raised her eyes from the letter, saw her husband struggling not to laugh, and she smiled ruefully. "She is not very convincing, is she? Isabelle, the martyred mother, bravely sacrificing herself for her son's sake. The rest of the letter asks Henry to give them her dower castles of Niort, Exeter, and Rockingham, and three thousand five hundred marks she says my father bequeathed to her."

"Does she mention her daughter at all?"

Joanna scanned the letter again. "At the end. She says she and Hugh will send Joanna back to England if Henry desires it. Llewelyn . . . I just remembered something very intriguing. When I last saw Isabelle, she spoke very kindly of this same Hugh de Lusignan, sounded as if he'd already made quite an impression upon her."

"Mayhap he had," Llewelyn said dryly, "but she's been back in Angoulême for two years now, and you notice she did not marry him until his father died, until he became the new Count of La Marche. Our Isabelle might look like gossamer and gold dust, but when it comes to practicality, she'd put a French peasant to shame."

"Nonetheless, I mean to cling to my romantic illusions," Joanna said and laughed. "What's more, I wish Isabelle well, hope she finds contentment in her new marriage."

"I wonder what the Pope will make of it. Isabelle was plight-trothed to Hugh's father, and Hugh to Isabelle's daughter. The truth, *breila*—does that not sound somewhat incestuous?''

But Joanna was no longer listening to his banter, for Henry had just entered the hall.

Henry turned as Joanna joined him in the window recess. He was an attractive youngster, with his mother's striking blue eyes; they were reddened now, suspiciously swollen. ''You heard?'' he mumbled, and Joanna took a sister's liberty, kissed him sympathetically upon the cheek.

''I know it was a shock, dearest. But it was only to be expected that your mother would one day wed again. She's been a widow for more than three years, and although thirty-two doubtless seems ancient from your vantage point, she ought to have many years ahead of her. You'd not want those years to be lonely or empty, Henry, I know you would not.''

''You do not understand.'' Henry had checked his tears, but his voice still quavered. ''Do you not see what this marriage means, Joanna? Now Mama will never come home.''

In the early years of the twelfth century, the English King had encouraged the settlement of large numbers of Flemings in South Wales. The settlements thrived, and in time Dyfed lost much of its Welsh character; Welsh was no longer spoken there, and the area came to be known as ''Little England beyond Wales.'' There was much bitterness between the displaced native-born Welsh and the Flemings, and the Welsh had been complaining to Llewelyn that the Flemings were burning their churches and running off their cattle. Llewelyn was quite willing to intervene on behalf of his countrymen, to punish the Flemish intruders, for that was how he viewed them. That the Flemings were tenants of the new Earl of Pembroke had not escaped his attention, either.

On August 16, Llewelyn was waiting in the city of Chester to welcome the Earl of Chester home from the crusade. Just a few days later, Llewelyn led an army south into Dyfed. Accompanied by most of the Welsh Princes, he destroyed the castles of Narbeth and Wiston, burned the town of Haverford, and did extensive damage to the Earl of Pembroke's lands in Rhos.

Pembroke vowed vengeance, but for the time being he was unable to act upon his anger, and the Welsh Prince's year closed in triumph.

But Gruffydd and his wife and infant son had withdrawn from Llewelyn's court, and Gruffydd still spurned all of Llewelyn's attempts at reconciliation.

4

ABER, NORTH WALES

July 1221

Rhys, Adda, and Morgan were seated at the high table in the great hall of Llewelyn's palace at Aber. Llewelyn had not yet returned from Shrewsbury, where, meeting with the young English King and the papal legate Pandulf, he'd agreed to a truce with the Earl of Pembroke and Reginald de Braose. It was a truce none expected to last; the interests of the Welsh Prince and the Marcher border lords were too antithetical to reconcile for long.

In Llewelyn's absence, Adda was accorded the place of honor, but he'd barely touched the food ladled onto his trencher. Neither Rhys nor Morgan had much appetite, either.

"Are you sure we ought to wait till Llewelyn returns from Shrewsbury?"

Adda nodded. "We can be that merciful at least, can give him a few more days ere he has to know about Gruffydd."

Rhys could not quarrel with that. Picking up a piece of bread, he occupied himself in cleaning his knife for the next course. "I still do not understand why Llewelyn took his wife with him. A council chamber is no fit place for a woman."

"Llewelyn thinks otherwise," Morgan said composedly. "He told me he felt certain he would benefit from her presence at Shrewsbury, even said—only half in jest—that he considers Joanna his ambassador to the English court."

Rhys looked rather skeptical, but then he startled them by saying, "I would that I'd gone to Shrewsbury, too, with Llewelyn and Ednyved."

It had been more than six years since Llewelyn had chosen Ednyved to replace the ailing Gwyn ab Ednewain as his Seneschal, and Ednyved had made the most of the opportunity; he'd

become Llewelyn's mainstay, wielding far more political power
than his predecessor. But Rhys had never before given the slightest sign of jealousy, given any indication that he nurtured political ambitions of his own or begrudged Ednyved his ascending
star, and Morgan and Adda were not sure now whether his
remark was an oblique admission of envy for his cousin's privileged position.

Rhys was unmindful of their speculative looks. He swallowed
a mouthful of gingered carp before concluding morosely, "If I
had, I'd not yet know about Gruffydd, would not be sitting here
wondering how to tell Llewelyn that his son is in rebellion
against him."

"You're sure it was Gruffydd? There can be no mistake?"

Llewelyn's voice was quite even, but Morgan was not deceived; he found it very hard to continue, to take away Llewelyn's
last shred of hope. "A fortnight ago Gruffydd led an army from
Ardudwy into Eifionydd. Our people took refuge in Cricieth
Castle, and he swung into Lleyn, burned your manor at
Pwllheli. Before retreating into Meirionydd, he crossed into Arfon,
harassed the monks at Beddgelert when they balked at emptying
their larders for his men."

Adda rarely laid his emotions open for others to see. But he'd
loved Gruffydd too much to be dispassionate now. "There is no
mistake, Llewelyn. Gruffydd is known on sight throughout most
of Gwynedd. Nor did he seek to conceal his identity. To the
contrary, he flaunted his banners for all to see. He wanted you to
know, Llewelyn, went to some pains to make sure you would."

Llewelyn turned toward Ednyved. "I want a courier to depart
at dawn for Meirionydd. He is to tell Gruffydd that I command
him to appear before my court to answer for his actions."

Ednyved nodded, then gave Llewelyn the only comfort he had
to offer—privacy. Adda and Morgan followed him from the
chamber, leaving Joanna in a quandary. Her every instinct counseled her to remain, but she was at an utter loss for words.
Gruffydd—no less than John—had always been an exceedingly
dangerous subject, to be broached only with the utmost caution.

"Do you think Gruffydd will obey your summons?"

"No," Llewelyn said, "I do not."

"Then . . ." Joanna paused. "What will you do, beloved?"

At first she thought Llewelyn did not intend to answer. He
moved away from her, stood for some moments staring at her

newest acquisition, a wall hanging of heavy linen embroidered in brilliant shades of worsted yarn.

"You look at that hanging and what do you see, Joanna? Unicorns and birds of paradise, Eden. But up close the pattern becomes thousands of individual threads. Pull just a few, and the entire pattern can unravel."

"I do not understand what you are saying, Llewelyn."

"Authority is no different, unravels just as easily. Men obey me for a number of reasons, one of which is that they fear the consequences if they do not."

"You're telling me that you cannot afford to let Gruffydd's raiding go unpunished. But can you do that, Llewelyn? Can you truly make war upon your own son?"

"I do not know," he admitted. "And that is what frightens me so, Joanna. I just do not know."

Fording the River Mawddach at Cymmer Abbey, Llewelyn led his men south. They were deep in Meirionydd now, having reached the mile-long lake called Llyn Myngul. It was a beautiful valley, but narrow and deep, and although Llewelyn's scouts had been able to allay his fears of ambush, he was relieved nonetheless as they left the lake behind, moved onto more open ground.

"Did I ever tell you about the time I climbed Cader Idris?" Ednyved gestured toward the towering summit on their right. "There's a lake hidden away up there as dark as ink, and local folk say it has no bottom, say that a creature of terrifying mien lurks in its depths. Mind you, I never saw it myself, but . . ."

Llewelyn turned in the saddle. His eyes rested for a long moment upon the other man, a plain face made more so by a disfiguring scar, a familiar face showing little of the sharp, pragmatic intelligence that made his advice so valuable, his friendship so dear. Llewelyn knew that Ednyved's son Tudur was one of Gruffydd's most trusted companions. He knew, too, that Ednyved had been unable to track down Tudur's whereabouts, might well find him with Gruffydd. And yet he'd said nothing of his own anxiety, instead had been doing his utmost to keep Llewelyn from dwelling upon the coming confrontation.

You are indeed the friend lauded in Scriptures, he who sticketh closer than a brother. But Llewelyn dared not say it aloud, lest his emotions break free. He had twenty-five years of memories he must somehow keep at bay, memories that stretched from Gruffydd's first spoken word to his last choked "Rot in Hell."

"Look!" Ednyved pointed, but Llewelyn already saw; one of their scouts was coming up from the southwest, coming fast.

"They've gathered near Craig Aderyn," he gasped out as soon as he was within hearing range. "I saw your son's banners, my lord. They're waiting for us, waiting to do battle."

Craig Aderyn was a breeding ground for peregrine falcons, and they were circling overhead, airborne and uncaring witnesses to the human drama about to be enacted below them. From time to time a man would glance upward, as if wondering what the sleek birds of prey portended. Tudur suspected that to many, the falcons seemed suddenly as unlucky as ravens, feathered omens of ill fortune.

Warfare as they knew it usually consisted of raids and sieges. Pitched battles were a rarity, and as he moved among the men, Tudur could sense their unease. But it was more, he knew, than their lack of battlefield experience. Although Gruffydd was their lord, Llewelyn was their Prince. Most of them felt very strongly that Gruffydd had been grievously wronged. Few of them were eager, however, to take up arms against a man who was already becoming something of a legend in his own lifetime.

Moreover, this war had split families asunder. Tudur and Gruffydd were not the only ones facing blood kin across a battlefield, and Tudur was not alone in his dread of what was to come. He felt torn in two, and he was not here now in Gruffydd's encampment by choice. It was simply that he had not known how to tell Gruffydd that he wanted no part in Gruffydd's war.

"Amlyn, ought we not to say a prayer ere the battle begins, ask God's blessing upon us?"

The other man nodded. "Tudur, I do not like this, not at all. I just tried to talk to Gruffydd, but I do not think he heard a word I said. He's acting right strange, Tudur. Not once did he take his eyes from Llewelyn's banner, not once."

Gruffydd was astride his favorite destrier, a black stallion so temperamental that none but he could ride it. The horse bared its teeth now at Tudur's approach, and Tudur's mount shied away. "Gruffydd? Gruffydd, we have to talk whilst there's time. Do you still want Amlyn to lead the vanguard?"

He waited, and then repeated, more urgently, "Gruffydd, do you not hear me? Gruffydd, answer me!"

Even then, Gruffydd did not respond, not until Tudur reached out, grabbed his arm. Gruffydd's stallion reared, and he reined it in a semicircle until he'd gotten it back under control. His face was drained of all color; Tudur had never seen him look so shaken.

"Gruffydd, what is it?"

"I cannot do this, Tudur." Gruffydd's mouth twisted. "God help me, but I cannot!" And with that, he suddenly spurred his horse forward, ignoring Tudur's shocked protest, the baffled cries of his men. As if racing his own regrets, he set the stallion at a dead run toward his father's camp.

"Llewelyn!"

Llewelyn was conferring with two of his captains, spun around at Ednyved's shout. All around him men were pointing, staring at the lone rider galloping toward them. Ednyved was now at Llewelyn's side; he, too, had recognized Gruffydd, and he said hastily, "Do not do anything rash, Llewelyn. Make sure it is not a trick of some kind."

But Llewelyn was not listening. He'd already turned, was swinging up into the saddle. "Hold our men here," he said, then gave his stallion its head, rode out to meet his son.

When Gruffydd was fifty yards away, Llewelyn reined in his mount, waited for his son to come to him. Gruffydd had some trouble in stopping his horse. He'd always had a heavy hand, in his agitation jerked too hard upon the reins and the stallion reared up again, sending sand and clods of grass flying.

"I assume you want to talk." Llewelyn was startled at the sound of his own voice; it sounded so cold and unyielding, revealed nothing of his inner turmoil.

Gruffydd had acted on impulse, had not thought out what he wanted to say. He could only blurt out the truth. "I thought I could fight you, Papa. I truly did."

"And now you cannot?"

"No." Gruffydd shook his head helplessly. "I saw your banners and I knew . . ." Unsure what to do next, he slid from the saddle, waited as Llewelyn dismounted, too. Although they were now close enough to touch, still the words would not come. Gruffydd was well aware of the magnitude of his offense, but he was not able to humble himself, not even now, with so much at stake. He slowly unsheathed his sword, held it out toward Llewelyn. "I submit myself unto your will, Papa," he said, in unconscious echo of Llewelyn's own submission to John at Aberconwy, adding tautly, "What mean you to do?"

Llewelyn took the sword, and then handed it back. "I mean," he said, "to forgive you," and Gruffydd's pride dissolved in a surge of anguished emotion.

"Christ, Papa, I'm sorry. I never wanted it to come to this, I swear it."

"Neither did I, Gruffydd." And stepping forward, Llewelyn embraced his son, while hearing the distant shouts of both armies, the reprieved cheering of brothers and cousins spared a war none of them had truly wanted.

Llewelyn's encampment at Llyn Myngul was a scene of reunions and rejoicing. Campfires flared like beacons in the dark, and the summer wind carried the sounds of singing for miles as the two armies mingled, celebrated far into the night.

Ednyved had been looking for Llewelyn for some time, at last found him walking alone by the lakeside. It was a night of rare beauty; the sky was filled with stars, and the placid waters of the lake reflected an infinity of shimmering pinpoint lights, the luminous sheen of a crescent moon. But Llewelyn appeared oblivious to his surroundings. He seemed deep in thought, started visibly as Ednyved came up beside him.

"Will Gruffydd come back with us to your court?"

Llewelyn nodded. "Yes. We talked about it and he's agreed to return. I do not plan to leave Meirionydd yet, though. I want to do some further scouting in the Dysynni Valley, look for a suitable site for a castle."

Ednyved was quick to comprehend. "I see. You mean, then, to reclaim Meirionydd and Ardudwy."

"Yes." Llewelyn stopped, turned to face the other man. "I have no choice, Ednyved," he said bleakly. "I love my son. But I can no longer trust him."

5

LLANFAES, NORTH WALES

October 1222

"No! No, I'll not do it. I'll not marry him."

"Elen, what are you saying?" Joanna rose, moved quickly toward her daughter. "We thought you would be elated. The Earl of Chester has no children; his sister's son John is his sole heir. Do you not realize what that means? Upon his father's death, John became Earl of Huntingdon, and he'll one day inherit the earldom of Chester, too. You'll be marrying into one of England's greatest families. Moreover, John is a first cousin of the Scots King. Your father and I could not hope to make a better match for you."

"But I do not want him!"

"Elen, I am trying to understand, I truly am. But I do not see why you would balk at the marriage. John is not a stranger to you; you met him at Shrewsbury two years past. He's a personable youth, well mannered and agreeable. You're nigh on fifteen and he's almost seventeen, so your ages are quite suitable. And this marriage will make you Countess of Huntingdon, and eventually Countess of Chester. So why, then, are you so reluctant?"

Elen said nothing, but her mouth was still set in mutinous lines, and Joanna reached out, turned the girl to face her. "Elen, listen to me. I'll not deny that this marriage is very important to your father. But we want you to be happy, darling. If you have a valid reason for opposing the marriage, now is the time to tell me. Why do you not want to marry John the Scot?"

"I do not like him, Mama."

Exasperation and bafflement—familiar emotions to Joanna where her daughter was concerned. "But you do not know him well enough to make a judgment like that," she pointed out, striving for patience.

Elen tossed her head. "His eyes are too close together. And he has a weak chin."

"Elen, for the love of God! What does that have to do with marriage?"

Elen knew her mother was right; marriages were based upon pragmatic considerations of property and political advantage. Unable to defend her position, she could only fall back upon accusation, upon raw emotion. "I should have known you'd not understand! You never do!"

"As it happens, Elen, I understand more than you realize. It is only natural that you might feel qualms. When I married your father, I—"

"Oh, Mama, that was different! You love Papa!"

"I learned to love him, Elen. The truth is that I did not want to marry your father, to live in Wales, and I was utterly wretched when we were first wed."

But Elen's image of Joanna was still circumscribed by childhood boundaries, and she found it impossible to identify her mother with a fearful fourteen-year-old bride. "You're happy with Papa. But I'd not be happy with your John the Scot, and he can just look for a wife elsewhere."

"Elen, it is not that simple. I do not think you understand how much this alliance means to your father. What are you going to tell him, that you do not like John the Scot's eyes?"

Elen flushed. "Do not laugh at me!"

"Believe me, child," Joanna said wearily, "I find nothing remotely amusing about this."

"I am not a child. In three weeks I'll be—"

"Fifteen. I know; I was present at your birth, remember?" Joanna could hear her own sarcasm, but could not help herself. Her anger was rising, fueled by insidious misgivings that defied all logic, all common sense. She knew this marriage was for her daughter's good; why, then, was she suddenly plagued by doubts?

"I had good reason for reluctance—marriage to a man I'd never even seen, a man more than eighteen years older than I, from an utterly alien world, my father's enemy. None of that is true for you, Elen. I just cannot comprehend your attitude. Why must you always be so willful? Your sisters were quite content to let your father choose their husbands, did not—"

"They would! Gwenllian and Marared have as much spirit as . . . as sheep," Elen said scornfully, while prudently making no

mention of Gwladys. "But I'll not be wed against my will to a
Scots-Norman coxcomb. And you cannot make me, Mama. Welsh
law states that 'every woman is to go the way she willeth,
freely.' A Welshwoman has the right to pick her own husband,
unlike the women of your blood, who pass with the land like
serfs!"

"That is not precisely true, Elen," Joanna snapped. Her daughter's taunt had stung, more than she wanted to admit. "A Welsh
widow may indeed marry again—or not—as she freely chooses.
But a young girl, a maiden, is still in her family's care."

"Mayhap if you spoke better Welsh, Mama, you'd have learned
more of our ways. You're right; the family of a virgin maid can
prevent her from marrying a man not of their choice. But they
can do nothing whatsoever about it if she is no longer a virgin.
So I need only lose my maidenhead and I will be utterly free to
wed or not as I wish."

Joanna's reaction was all Elen could have hoped for; she'd
rarely managed to render her mother speechless. But her moment
of satisfaction was fleeting—and costly. She spun around as the
door slammed, gasped at sight of her father.

Llewelyn had always shunted the onus of discipline off onto
Joanna, at least where his daughters were concerned; Elen had
long ago learned which of her parents was more likely to laugh
away a minor misdeed. But there was nothing of the familiar
indulgent father about Llewelyn now. He looked no less incredulous than Joanna, and a good deal angrier.

"I cannot believe what I just heard you say," he said, and
Elen blushed.

"I did not mean it, Papa, truly!"

"I would hope to God not. If I ever thought a daughter of
mine would so shame herself—"

Joanna interrupted hastily. "I'm afraid, Llewelyn, that Elen
does not want to marry John the Scot."

"I gathered as much. But what I do not understand is why.
Suppose you tell me that, Elen. Tell me why you'd scorn an
earldom."

"I . . . I do not like him, Papa. He seemed so staid and
proper; I thought him a bit of a prig. And he has no sense of
humor, none!" Elen's eyes suddenly brimmed over. While her
distress was real enough, her tears might not have flowed so
readily had she not so many memories of times when she'd won
her way by tears. Her father was frowning; she put a hand upon
his arm, looked up entreatingly into his face. "Please, Papa. Do

not make me wed John the Scot. I'd be so unhappy, Papa, I just know I would.''

For a long moment Llewelyn studied his daughter. Joanna watched, holding her breath. And then, to her utter astonishment, he said, "I'll not force you, Elen."

Elen flung her arms around his neck, bestowing grateful, haphazard kisses. "Thank you, Papa, thank you!"

"Llewelyn?" Joanna was staring at her husband in disbelief. He gave her an oblique glance, one she could not interpret at all, then turned back to Elen.

"I want what is best for you, Elen. Your mother and I would not see you hurt, not for all the political gains under God's sky. John the Scot is Chester's nephew and heir. But he is also a decent young man, would never use you ill. You could be content with him, Elen, I have no doubts of that."

"But . . . but Papa, you said you'd not force me!"

"Nor will I. I am not ordering you to this, lass. I am asking it of you, asking you to trust my judgment. It is that important, Elen. I need not tell you, a Welshwoman, what is the most binding of all bonds, that of blood."

Elen sensed that she was being outflanked. "I know that, Papa. But there is no need for this marriage. You and Chester are already allies."

"Yes, lass, we are. But I am forty and nine, and Chester even older. What happens when my power passes to Davydd, and Chester's earldom to John the Scot? The alliance is too valuable to leave its survival to chance. If I no longer have to fight the Earl of Chester—whoever he may be—I am then free to act in South Wales. The Welsh princes will always have to defer to the English crown. But we can prevent further Norman encroachments into our lands. We can make sure that there are no more Flemish settlers moving in to displace the Welsh, that men like Pembroke build no more Norman towns on Welsh soil. We can still safeguard the future, and this marriage will help to do that."

Elen's breathing had quickened. "You're not being fair, Papa," she said, almost inaudibly. "I do not want to marry him."

"I know, lass." Llewelyn's voice had softened, too. "And I understand. How could I not? For much of my life I've had to do things that I did not want to do. But they had to be done nonetheless, because so much was at stake."

Elen was silent. But the sudden droop of her shoulders was more expressive than any words she could have uttered. Llewelyn brushed the tears from her face. "I trusted you to make the right

decision, Elen. I knew I could. Can you not trust me as much?
You'll have no regrets, lass, I promise you.''

John had once made the same promise to Joanna, under identical circumstances, and he'd been right. Joanna closed her eyes,
said a silent, fervent prayer to the holiest and most merciful of
mothers that Llewelyn, too, might be right.

''I'll do as you wish, Papa.'' But it was a stranger's voice, did
not sound like Elen at all, and suddenly Joanna found herself
wishing passionately that her daughter could be a child again,
with a child's choices and the easy comfort to be found within a
mother's embrace. She moved forward, put her arm around
Elen's shoulders. The girl stiffened at the touch; pulling away,
she fled the chamber. She stumbled several times, bumped into
the table as she turned, and that, too, was unlike Elen.

They let her go. Llewelyn sat down abruptly in the nearest
chair. He was the first to break the silence. ''Was I wrong,
Joanna?''

She shook her head. ''No, love, you were not. I do believe
what I told Elen, that we could not make a better match for her
than this.''

Crossing to his chair, Joanna put her arms around his neck,
rested her cheek against his hair; although she teased him at times
about going grey, it was still thick and dark, showed silver only
under fullest sunlight. But he looked his age at the moment,
looked so careworn that she leaned over, kissed the corner of his
mouth. ''I'll talk to Elen,'' she promised. ''I'll go and look for
her right now.''

''I wish you would, *breila*. There's no logical reason for Elen
to oppose this marriage, and once she's wed, finds herself the
Countess of Huntingdon, she'll see it was for the best. I know
that, Joanna. And yet . . . yet I still feel as if I'd been hunting
for roebuck and instead shot someone's tame fawn.''

Llanfaes was one of Joanna's favorite manors. She liked the
relatively mild island climate, loved to walk along the shore, to
gaze across the narrow strait toward the lofty range called Eryri
by the Welsh and Snowdon by the English. She knew that Elen,
too, loved the dramatic contrast of sea, sky, and mountains, and
she headed for the beach. As she expected, there she found her
daughter, standing alone by the water's edge.

Elen was clutching her veil; it was crumpled, wet with tears.
But her eyes were dry as she turned to face Joanna; they held no

tears, only anger. "Go away, Mama," she said. "I do not want to talk to you."

"Darling, I know you're hurting. But it will pass, I swear it will. Elen, I know."

"You've felt like this, Mama? You've felt trapped? Trapped and helpless?"

"Yes, Elen, yes. God's truth, I did. You must believe me, darling."

"I do, Mama. I believe you. And that is why I cannot forgive you." Elen's voice was coldly accusing. But all the while she was twisting and knotting the veil with hands that shook.

"I know Papa loves me. But he is a man and cannot possibly understand how it feels to be bartered to the highest bidder like a prized filly. You, though, Mama, you should have understood. You should have spoken up for me. But you did not, did you? And now you tell me you know how I feel. Well, that just makes your failure all the more unforgivable!"

"Elen, I could not argue against this marriage. I believe it is right for you. John can offer you a good life, can offer you all I've ever wanted for you, and more. And he—"

"But what of me? What of what I want?"

"You're fourteen, Elen. You're not in a position to make a decision that will affect your entire life. Nor was I, at your age. A young girl cannot choose her own husband. Darling, you know that. This is how marriages are made. This is how it's always been done."

"Just because something has always been done a certain way does not make it right. But you cannot see that, can you, Mama? You'll not talk to Papa. You'll not try to change his mind."

"No, Elen," Joanna said softly. "I cannot do that."

Elen dropped her veil, watched as the wind carried it away, an incongruous splash of color against the drifting sand. "Then we have nothing more to say, have we? I'll marry your John the Scot, Mama. And you may be right; I may in time be reconciled to it, to him. But what if I'm not? Have you thought of that? What if you're wrong?"

Llewelyn and Chester selected Tuesday, November 22, as the date for the wedding, three weeks past Elen's fifteenth birthday, five days before the beginning of Advent, when the marriage Mass would be prohibited. Elen and John the Scot were wed in the city of Chester, in the same abbey church in which Llewelyn and Joanna had been wed sixteen years earlier. The wedding was a social event of impressive proportions, attracting the highborn of Wales and England alike. Rhys Ieunac had died that past August, but his brother Owain was present, as were his uncles Maelgwn and Rhys Gryg. So, too, was Llewelyn's cousin Madog, lord of Upper Powys. Henry could not attend, but he'd sent his younger brother, Dickon, and his seven-year-old sister, Nell, in his stead. And as Joanna glanced now around the great hall of the Earl's castle, she saw most of the Norman nobility.

"I was astonished when Hubert de Burgh accepted his invitation," she confided to Richard. "He and Chester have been at odds for months now, and I would not think he'd want to socialize with a man who likes him so little."

"The English court thrives on such feuds," Richard said dryly. "The very fact that de Burgh mistrusts Chester would guarantee his presence here; he'd want to make sure Chester and Llewelyn were not conspiring against him. I daresay that if he were not in Ireland, even Pembroke would have attended the wedding."

"I'm right glad he did not. The last thing I want is a brawl, thank you. Speaking of which, I was not heartbroken when Gruffydd refused to come. But he and Senena are the only ones absent. That's Tegwared, Llewelyn's other son, standing over there with my Davydd. You've never met Tegwared, have you? I do not know him well myself, for he was with Cristyn till he was seven, and was then reared in Ednyved's household as a foster son, in accordance with custom. The lass with him is his betrothed, one of Ednyved's daughters." Joanna's smile was fleeting. "At least that is one marriage we need not worry about."

Richard followed the path of her gaze, across the hall to where Elen and her new husband were standing, surrounded by well-wishers. "Is it strange for you, Joanna, being back at the scene of your own wedding?"

"Somewhat strange, yes. Sixteen years does not seem so very long, but a surprising number of our wedding guests are now dead. Hugh Corbet. His brother Robert, just last month. Stephen de Hodnet—you did not know him, a friend of Llewelyn's."

Fearing that she was about to name Maude de Braose next, Richard sought to distract her, saying hastily, "And of course Isabelle is not here. I miss her, Joanna, more than I'd have expected. Does she write to you?"

"Isabelle? Not likely! But I did have news of her just a fortnight ago. Although it's less than a year since she gave Hugh a son, Henry says she is with child again."

Joanna paused, looking about the hall. The feasting was now done, and the trestle tables were being dismantled to allow for dancing. "I'm rather glad Thomas Corbet is not here; I remember him stirring up trouble at my wedding. So, too, did Fulk Fitz Warin; he kept going on about the bedding revels at the top of his voice! But he was not invited, either; he's siding with Pembroke these days. So, too, is Baldwin de Hodnet, even though Llewelyn once gave both men refuge at his court. They are just about the only Marcher lords not present, though. All the Fitz Alans are here, and more de Braoses than I can count."

It surprised Richard that she sounded so nonchalant, almost flippant. "Are you more comfortable now, Joanna? Being with the de Braoses?"

"The truth, Richard? No, I am not. But that is a problem I'm learning to live with. What other choice do I have, with three of my husband's daughters wed into the de Braose clan?"

"Three? Gwladys and Reginald de Braose, of course. And then—what is her name—Marared and Reginald's nephew Jack. Who else?"

"Last year Gwenllian was wed to William de Lacy, half-brother to Hugh de Lacy, Earl of Ulster, and Walter de Lacy, Lord of Meath. Walter is husband to Margaret de Braose, Maude's daughter."

"Ah, Joanna, what a tangled coil." But after a moment Richard started to see the perverse humor in Joanna's predicament. His mouth twitched, and he coughed, trying to camouflage a laugh.

Joanna gave him a look that was quizzical, half resentful. But there was something contagious about his amusement, and she was soon laughing, too. "I know—it's ludicrous," she admitted. "I'm bloody well surrounded by de Braoses; any day now I expect to find one under my bed!"

Their laughter had been a spontaneous, almost involuntary reaction to the absurd, and it ended as abruptly as it began. Much sobered, Joanna said quietly, "It is not so bad with Reginald, for I do not see much of him anymore; he and Llewelyn have not been on good terms for several years now. But Jack de Braose is often at our court. We're polite to each other, Richard, too polite. But I cannot look into his face without remembering that his father and grandmother died in a Windsor dungeon, that he spent eight years in confinement at Corfe Castle. And if it is so uncomfortable for me, how must it be for him?"

Richard knew it was not the place, but the opportunity might not arise again. "Joanna, I hope you'll not take amiss what I'm about to say. Your problem is not with the de Braoses. It's with Papa. Until you face the truth about him, about the manner of man he was and how you feel about that, you're going to continue doing this to yourself, and I hate to see it. Jesú, we earn enough guilt and remorse of our own in this life without taking on the sins of others."

"I have faced the truth! Do I deny the cruelties Papa committed, do I defend him? What more do you want of me?"

Joanna's voice had risen; several people were looking in their direction. Richard leaned over and, in a rare gesture of public affection, kissed his sister on the cheek. "I'm sorry," he said, and was. He had no answers for Joanna. What had worked for him—distancing himself from John—obviously did not work for her. "I just want you to be happy, that's all."

"I am happy, Richard, in truth I am," Joanna said, and then she smiled. "I think you are, too; I've rarely seen you look so relaxed. It must suit you, being Lord of Chilham, sheriff of Berkshire and Staffordshire."

"It does indeed. Whatever else may be said of Papa, he did right by us in our marriages."

"Yes," Joanna said, "he did. I only hope Llewelyn and I did as well for Elen."

She was still thinking of that a few moments later, as she made her way across the hall toward Gwladys. How could a parent ever know which marriage would flourish and which would fail? Marared seemed utterly content with Jack de Braose, had given him a son upon whom they both doted. But Gwladys and her husband treated each other with the cool politeness of strangers, and after seven years, their marriage was still barren.

"I'm so glad you were able to come, Gwladys," Joanna said warmly, for she'd not been at all sure that Reginald would agree to attend the wedding; he was rarely seen these days in the same company as his nephew. The feud between Reginald and Jack had been dragging on for several years now, ever since Jack had regained his freedom and laid claim to the bulk of the de Braose lands, as the heir of Will and Maude's eldest son. Nor had Llewelyn eased the tension any by siding with Jack, allowing him to wed Marared.

Joanna had found it difficult to forgive Llewelyn for that, for putting additional strain upon his daughter's troubled marriage. But Gwladys kept her own counsel, and if she had regrets, none but she knew. She and Reginald seemed to find no lack of reasons for increasingly long absences apart, and now she said, quite composedly, "I'd have come with or without Reginald. Surely you do not think I'd ever miss Elen's wedding?"

Both women turned, gazed across the hall. Elen was clad in a gown of Alexandrine velvet, a brilliant blue-green shade that set off to perfection her free-flowing black hair, gleaming like polished ebony against a gossamer gold veil.

"She makes a lovely bride," Gwladys said, and Joanna nodded slowly.

"Yes . . . but not a happy one."

"I do not think you need fret about Elen, Joanna. She's so volatile that she needs a steadying hand. I expect John will be good for her."

Gwladys accepted a wine cup from a passing servant, clinked it against Joanna's. "To Elen," she said. "And speaking of volatile spirits, my husband's wayward son has decided to put in an appearance after all."

"Will? He's here?"

"Indeed he is. And how like Will; he misses the wedding entirely, but arrives in time for the celebration. I am sorry about this, Joanna, hope you do not mind too much."

"No, I . . . I do not mind. You just caught me by surprise, for he did turn down the invitation. Did he bring his wife?"

"No, thank God!" Gwladys said, and laughed at Joanna's startled look. "You do not know her, do you? Take it from me, the Lady Eva Marshal is a bitch, every bit as haughty and obdurate as her brother Pembroke."

Joanna was only half listening; she had no interest whatsoever in Will's wife. She'd not expected this, that she'd feel so flustered at the thought of seeing Will de Braose again. She did not truly know him; theirs had been a brief afternoon encounter more than twelve years past. But she'd thought of him often since learning of Maude's fate, and she knew suddenly that of all the de Braoses, it was Will she'd always most dreaded to face.

"You do not like Will, do you, Gwladys? Would you tell me why?"

"Well, he did oppose my marriage to his father, so from the beginning there was tension betwixt us. But it's more than that, Joanna. I think he's a dangerous man, the sort that breaks hearts and heads with equal ease. Down in Deheubarth, the Welsh call him Gwilym Ddu."

"Black Will?" Joanna echoed in surprise. "That's passing

strange, for I remember his hair as being very light, a flaxen color.''

"It still is,'' Gwladys said, very dryly.

"I see. He's not very well thought of, then?''

"That depends upon whom you ask. Men do not like him much, women generally like him too much. There's been more than one scandal involving an angry husband, an errant wife. Will's not trustworthy, Joanna. Local legend has it that he once sold the same piece of land to three different buyers, and whilst I cannot vouch for the truth of that, I'd not put it past him. He cuts with a sharp blade, does our Will, leaves himself no margin for error.''

The dancing had begun; a circle was forming for the carole, and Elen and John the Scot were soon coaxed into the center. They danced well together, won themselves a round of applause when the figure was completed. Elen then shook her head and John led her back toward the sidelines. He had a naturally ruddy complexion, even more flushed now from the dance, and the same unruly, sandy hair as his cousin the Scots King, but he did have an engaging grin, which he flashed as he caught Joanna's eye.

Elen, however, had no smiles at all to offer. Although she was standing beside John, her hand in his, she seemed set upon acting as if their proximity were mere coincidence. She was watching the other dancers, looking so aloof that Joanna wanted to take her aside, to shake some sense into her. Remembering how she'd labored to hide her own reluctance from Llewelyn, it seemed to her that Elen was behaving very badly, and she started toward them, intent upon having a brief word in private with her daughter. For better or worse, Elen was now John's wife, and she must be made to see how important it was that she make an effort to please him.

So engrossed was Joanna in her concern that she did not notice the man until he moved into her path, so suddenly they almost collided. She stepped back, looking up at a stranger, a very attractive stranger, with bright blond hair and beard, clear grey eyes, an unsmiling, sharply sculptured mouth. The fourteen-year-old boy Joanna had remembered was utterly gone. But she still recognized him and smiled, said, not altogether truthfully, "I am glad to see you again, Will.''

"Are you, Madame? Are you indeed?'' he drawled, and while the words themselves were innocuous, he invested them with so much hostility that the blood surged up into her face.

Her reaction was instinctive, purely defensive. "Of course I am, Will," she heard herself say archly. "We'll talk later, I hope?" She managed another smile, polite but dismissive, and moved away before he could respond.

Joanna was more shaken by the encounter than she should have been; dimly she realized that. She did not doubt that Will was voicing what all the de Braoses thought; he just happened to be the only one who did not need her husband's favor, who could afford to be honest. So why, then, did it hurt so?

She sought without success to catch Elen alone, had no more luck in tracking down Llewelyn. She danced several times, but could find no pleasure in it, for by then she was aware again of Will. He made no approach, but he never took his eyes from her—a cool, challenging stare that she could neither ignore nor acknowledge. She endured it as long as she could, and then her anger broke through. Draining her wine cup, she turned, walked directly toward Will.

"I think," she said, "that it is time we talked."

She'd rarely seen eyes so compelling, or so cold. "What do we have to say?"

"If you do not want to talk to me, why are you staring at me? Why are you following me about the hall?"

"Was I?"

"You know damned well you were!" She heard her own voice, sharp-edged and shrill, and took several quick breaths. "I do not want to quarrel with you. Surely we can talk without anger. You once told me that you did not believe in blood guilt for women, remember?"

Something flickered in those grey eyes, too elusive for analysis. "Yes," he said, "I do remember. But your father taught me otherwise."

Joanna waited until she was sure she could trust her voice. "It seems I was mistaken. I have nothing to say to you after all."

The porch of the great hall connected directly to the chapel in Caesar's Tower; the chamber above it had been set aside for Joanna's little sister. But Nell had shown herself to be as strong-willed as the grandmother after whom she'd been named, resisting bedtime until she was half asleep on her feet. Only then had she yielded, allowing Joanna and her nurse to put her to bed.

Joanna lingered longer than necessary, sitting on the bed and stroking Nell's hair, sunlit ringlets that curled around her fingers like finely spun silk. There had been no need for her to accompany Nell, just as there was no need for her to remain. But she was in no hurry to return to the hall. As miserable as her own wedding had been, her daughter's was proving to be no less an ordeal.

She could delay only so long, though, for it was almost time for the bedding revels. Soon she would have to help put Elen to bed, as she'd just done with Nell. But unlike Nell, Elen would not be sleeping alone. She swallowed the last of her wine, moved reluctantly toward the door.

The spiral stairway was not lit; the cresset light had burned out, and she'd forgotten her candle. She'd had too much to drink, was feeling lightheaded and had to stop repeatedly, groping her way blindly in the darkness, a few steps at a time.

She had no warning, nothing to alert her that she was no longer alone. She simply turned a bend in the stairwell and there he was, looming over her, barring her way. She recoiled against the wall, a scream starting in her throat, and he swiftly put his hand over her mouth.

"Jesú, but your nerves are on the raw," he muttered, and Joanna sighed with relief, recognizing his voice.

"You startled me, Will!" she said indignantly. "How did I know who it was? What are you doing here? Did you follow me?"

"Would you believe me if I said I was looking for a privy chamber?"

"No, I would not." Joanna was becoming aware now of the untoward aspects of this encounter, becoming acutely aware of Will. She was standing on the step above him, but he was still taller than she, and so close that she could smell the sugared wine on his breath. "I think you'd best let me pass," she said, her voice suddenly husky, and he laughed.

"You wanted to talk, did you not? Well, here I am."

"You're drunk, Will. Let me by."

"Suppose . . . suppose I do not want to do that," he murmured, and when Joanna pushed against him, he did not move.

"What do you want from me?" she whispered, feeling behind her for the wall, seeking to orient herself in this eerie black well.

"I do not know." He, too, was whispering now, his breath hot against her cheek. And then his hand was on her throat, and his mouth on hers. She'd been expecting violence, but he was surprisingly gentle with her, and the kiss was unhurried, almost tender. It was that which held her immobile for several seconds, which kept her from struggling at first. But the spell did not last.

With a gasp, she tore her mouth from his, shoved against his chest.

Again he surprised her; when she pulled free, he let her go. She stumbled, nearly lost her balance on the stairs. Her head was spinning; she could not seem to catch her breath.

"Have you lost your wits? Jesus God, my husband would kill you if he knew!"

"Are you going to tell him?"

To her fury, he did not sound particularly impressed. But as much as she wanted to tell him yes, she was going to Llewelyn, common sense prevailed. "No," she said, as coldly as she could. "No, I'd not do that to Elen, would not stain her wedding day with blood."

Her words sounded hollow to her, even a little pompous. Will apparently thought so, too, for he laughed. He was above her now; the way below was clear, and she turned away, started down the stairs. He stopped laughing, for the first time called her by her name. She ignored him, lifted her skirts and plunged around the final bend in the stairwell, into the light. He caught up with her at the bottom of the stairs, reached for her arm, saying, "Joanna, wait."

She jerked away. "Do not touch me," she spat. "Not ever again, do you understand?"

Some of the guests had overflowed from the hall, several couples seeking privacy in the empty chapel. They turned toward the stairwell at sound of voices, and Will faded back into the shadows. Joanna stood there alone for a moment, leaning against the wall. And then she scrubbed the back of her hand vigorously across her mouth, stepped out into the torchlit chapel. Will watched from the stairwell as she reentered the hall.

The bedding revels were not as raucous as they might have been, due in large measure to Llewelyn's presence in the bedchamber. Even the most obstreperous of wedding guests tended to be somewhat circumspect, to curb their cruder jests in the hearing of the bride's father. But Joanna still found the experience exceedingly painful. The sight of her daughter naked in bed with an unwanted stranger tore at her heart. She no longer cared at that moment about the cogent, convincing arguments that could be made in favor of this marriage, not when she looked at Elen's face. Elen had lost her air of defiance; she clutched the sheet against her breasts, looking unbearably young to Joanna, utterly vulnerable. When she leaned over the bed to kiss her daughter Elen clung to her, for the first time since agreeing to the marriage.

"It will be all right, darling," Joanna whispered, but there was nothing more she could do. She and Llewelyn had made this bed, and now it was for Elen to lie in it.

The wedding party trooped back toward the great hall under a cloudless, star-studded sky. Traces of the first snowfall still lay unmelted upon the bailey ground, and some of the younger men began to pelt one another with snowballs, to chase the women, who fled into the hall, shrieking with laughter. Joanna was enveloped in a fur-lined mantle of Lincoln wool, but she could not stop shivering, not even after reaching the huge center hearth. She was soon joined by others, found herself in the midst of a boisterous, bawdy argument as to who felt the greater lust, men or women.

Joanna was in no mood for ribald jests, for jokes about bitches in heat and rutting stags, and she turned away, pushed toward the edge of the crowd, only to stop abruptly at sight of Will. She spun about, but not in time; she knew he'd seen her blush. She brought her hand up to her cheek, felt the heat burning her face and throat. She could still taste Will's kiss. It was a disconcertingly intense memory, even though she was sure she knew why—she had never been kissed before by any man but Llewelyn. Damn you, Gwilym Ddu, she thought, fighting the urge to cry the words aloud. Damn your arrogance and your audacity and your mocking grey eyes, damn you, damn you!

"There you are, Joanna." Llewelyn was smiling at her. "What are you doing so far from the hearth?" Catching her hand, he shoved his way through the crowd, into the coveted inner circle. There was some grumbling, which stilled as men recognized him, grudgingly gave way. Joanna followed reluctantly in his wake. She'd seen very little of him all night. Where had he been when she truly needed him? If he'd been more attentive, Will would not have dared to follow her into the stairwell. Llewelyn knew how she felt about the de Braoses. Why in God's name could he not have found other husbands for his daughters? Why could he not have put her needs first, just once?

The sexual argument was still going strong. Hubert de Burgh had claimed center stage, was insisting that it was not open to dispute; women were more lustful because they were imperfect. As the imperfect always yearned for union with the perfect, it only stood to reason that woman's desire was greater. Undaunted when the women in the audience hissed good-naturedly, he said complacently, "You cannot deny what is set down in Scriptures. 'All wickedness is but little to the wickedness of a woman,' Ecclesiasticus. The noted theologian Tertullian put it even plainer. Woman, he said, is the gate of the Devil, the first deserter of Divine Law, responsible for the loss of Eden."

Joanna had never liked de Burgh. But never had he seemed so odious to her as he did now. In truth, he looked like a sleek, well-fed cat, insufferably well-pleased with himself. The braggart. And who in the world was Tertullian?

"But the final word ought to go to the great Aristotle. He proved conclusively through his writings that the female state is one of deformity, albeit a common one. When the man's seed is perfect, it produces a male child; when flawed or imperfect, a female. You might even say," he quipped, "that the female is merely a misbegotten male!"

Joanna had not meant to speak out. But with that, the same imp that had once beguiled her into defying Maude de Braose again took possession of her tongue. "I do hope, my lord, that you will at least grant us poor 'misbegotten males' one small virtue. You will admit that without women, your Aristotle and Tertullian would never have been born?"

There was laughter, and some of the women cheered; spirited debates were always a favored form of entertainment.

Hubert de Burgh was smiling, quite unperturbed. "Indeed I will, Madame. But even as a breeder, woman is of secondary importance in the divine order. All know that the child belongs more to the man than to the woman, since the fetus forms from the male's seed. You need only think of a tree sending forth roots. The father is like the tree, the mother like the earth that nurtures it. Whilst it cannot exist without the two, it clearly belongs more to the tree from whence it sprang than to the earth where it was planted."

It may have been the smugness of his smile. It may have been the memory of a bloody birthing chamber, those endless hours of agony and fear. It may only have been the proverbial last straw in a day of emotional turmoil. Suddenly Joanna was trembling, as angry as she'd ever been in her life. But Llewelyn had been alerted by her first outburst, had known at once that this was no game. Now he saw how her eyes narrowed, saw the pupils contract, like the eyes of a cat about to pounce, John's eyes in a blazing Angevin rage, and he said swiftly, with just enough sardonic inflection to be insulting, "You surprise me, my lord de

Burgh. Surely you have not forgotten the Lady Mary, mother of
Our Saviour? If Our Lord Jesus was not ashamed to be born of
woman, why should you be?''

De Burgh's smile froze. ''I never said I was!''

''Mayhap you should learn to choose your words with greater
care, then,'' the Earl of Chester observed coolly, ''for I, too,
took that as your meaning.''

The crowd had fallen silent. Even the most politically naïve
among them were aware that the conversation was heading for
deep waters, pushed by currents that had nothing whatsoever to
do with the Virgin Mary or the failings of women.

De Burgh had reddened, but he was too well mannered—and
too intelligent—to provoke an open row while a guest under
Chester's roof. He could wait. ''It grows late,'' he said tersely.

He heard someone in the crowd, one of the Earl's partisans
safely cloaked in anonymity, mutter, ''Later than you think,''
and there was some scattered laughter.

It was Joanna's Uncle Will who acted to defuse the tension, to
avert a confrontation. Will was not as friendly with Chester as
he'd once been, and he had yet to forgive Llewelyn for that scene
in Worcester Abbey. But Joanna was still his niece, and for her
sake he raised his wine cup high, saying loudly, ''It is indeed
late, and for certes we want this evening to conclude upon a
cordial note. Let's drink, then, to the happiness of the bride and
groom. To John the Scot and the Lady Helen!''

The ploy worked; others took it up, until John and Elen's
names rang from the rafters. People began to make ready to
depart, those who were not bedding down in the castle. Llewelyn
and Chester were talking together; Joanna heard them laugh. So,
too, did Hubert de Burgh.

''Mama, that was wonderful, the best part of the whole
wedding!'' Davydd was grinning. ''I was so proud of you.''

''You should not have been, Davydd. If not for your father,
I'd have caused a scene that they'd have been talking about for
the next twenty years.''

''Really? I wish you had! Hubert de Burgh went red as a
radish; it was so hard not to laugh. Why do he and my lord
Chester hate each other so much?''

''The usual cause, Davydd—power. Chester was on crusade
when the old Earl of Pembroke died, and when he returned, it
was to find that de Burgh was now clinging closer to Henry than
a limpet. Chester feels that he was shunted aside, that de Burgh
usurped his rightful place as Henry's chief counselor. And be-

cause de Burgh feels threatened by Chester, he is beginning to side with Llewelyn's foe, the Earl of Pembroke. Does any of this make sense to you?''

Davydd nodded. ''Oh, yes, Mama. You have to counter your opponent's moves, try to guess what he'll do ere he does it. Just like chess!''

Llewelyn was coming toward them now, and Joanna moved to meet him. ''Ought I to thank you?'' she murmured, and he shook his head.

''No need; I enjoyed myself thoroughly!''

''You do thrive on turmoil, I'll grant you that. Llewelyn, I want to go back to the abbey. If this night does not end soon—''

''No, not yet. I've a surprise for you.'' Ignoring her protests, he put his arm around her waist and escorted her across the hall, into the solar, toward a corner stairwell. As she followed him, still objecting halfheartedly, she found herself thinking of her stairwell encounter with Will de Braose, and she wondered how long it would take for that memory to fade.

As they reached the top of the stairs, the door swung open. ''Morgan?'' Joanna was utterly baffled by now. ''What are you doing up here? What is—'' She broke off, gazing about her in wonder. The chamber was ablaze with light, with scented wax candles. The floor rushes were freshly laid, and across the bed coverlets were scattered the last flowers of the season: marigolds, lilies of the field, even a few Christmas roses.

''It looks like a bridal chamber, Llewelyn,'' Joanna exclaimed, and then, ''Good Lord, it is! This is the chamber in which we passed our wedding night!''

Llewelyn was laughing. ''I decided it was time to rectify a wrong. Sixteen years ago we neglected to get the nuptial blessing for our bed. But if you'll come over here with me, *breila*, Morgan is prepared to remedy that.''

Joanna took Llewelyn's hand, knelt with him by the bed as Morgan made the sign of the cross, rapidly intoning a brief prayer to God Eternal, seeking His blessings upon His servants, Llewelyn and Joanna, that they might live in good accord in His divine love, and that their offspring might increase till the end of the ages. He then sprinkled holy water about, made a discreet departure.

Llewelyn rose, started to help Joanna to her feet. ''*Breila*? Are you crying?''

Joanna gave a shaken laugh. ''Hold me,'' she entreated. ''Just hold me close. Your timing could not have been better. You'll never know how much this means to me, never . . ."

Llewelyn pulled off her veil, began to loosen her hair. "It was not a good night for you, was it?"

"It was an absolutely wretched night . . . until now."

"It gets better," he said, and picking her up, he carried her to the bed, where they lay together midst the flowers, made love by candlelight in the bridal chamber where their marriage had begun.

The chamber was dark, utterly still. Through a parting of the bed hangings, Joanna watched the dying embers of the hearth burn lower and lower and at last flicker out.

"Joanna?" Llewelyn propped himself up on his elbow. "Can you not sleep?"

"I was thinking of you, of our belated nuptial blessing. I do not know you as well as I thought I did, never suspected you had a romantic streak."

"Just make sure no one else suspects," he warned. "There are some secrets to be shared only betwixt man and wife, and only in the dark, only in bed."

Joanna laughed softly. "Ah, Llewelyn, you do know how much I love you?"

"I might have an inkling or two." Her hair was caught under his arm and he shifted so she could pull free. "But you were not thinking of me, *breila*. You were worrying about Elen."

"Yes . . . I was. How did you know?"

"Because," he admitted, "so was I."

6

LUDLOW CASTLE, ENGLAND

July 1223

The Earl of Pembroke had been attending to his Irish estates since November of 1222. Early in the new year, Llewelyn took advantage of Pembroke's absence and struck at the Earl's allies in Shropshire, capturing castles from Fulk Fitz Warin and Baldwin de Hodnet. Hubert de Burgh persuaded the young King to mount a punitive expedition into Wales, and by March 7 they were assembling an army at Shrewsbury. But the Earl of Chester now interceded upon Llewelyn's behalf, persuaded Henry that Llewelyn's dispute with Pembroke could be settled by peaceful means.

The Earl of Pembroke thought otherwise. Arriving back in South Wales in mid-April, he laid successful siege to the castles of Cardigan and Carmarthen, which Llewelyn had held since the winter campaign of 1215. Llewelyn was just as swift to retaliate, and in early May Gruffydd led an army south. After taking and burning the Norman town of Kidwelly, Gruffydd and his men clashed with Pembroke at Carmarthen Bridge. What followed was a bloody day-long battle in which many men died but neither side could gain the advantage.

At this point Stephen Langton, Archbishop of Canterbury, intervened. Henry was now in his sixteenth year, and although not of a martial nature, he had his share of Angevin ambition. But his dreams of conquest centered upon the recovery of Normandy, not all-out war with his sister's husband, and he was quite willing to heed Langton, to act as peacemaker. While Llewelyn was skeptical, he yielded to Henry's request, agreed to attend a July council at the border castle of Ludlow.

* * *

In an upper chamber of the castle keep, Llewelyn was meeting with Henry, Stephen Langton, and Hubert de Burgh, while Joanna awaited his return in the great hall. Although Henry had welcomed them with genuine warmth, Joanna was not comfortable at Ludlow. This was unfriendly territory, the great hall filled with hostile Marcher lords, men with extensive Welsh holdings, with very strong reasons for wishing Llewelyn ill.

But Joanna was not alone for long. Within moments her young son-in-law approached, holding out a wine cup. She smiled, touched that he should feel the need to look after her in Llewelyn's absence. "Thank you, John. Did I tell—oh, no!"

John swung about, but could see no cause for alarm. "What is amiss?"

"Across the hall. Ralph de Mortimer and Thomas Corbet just walked up to Gruffydd." Seeing that he did not comprehend, Joanna added impatiently, "I know Thomas Corbet. He's up to no good, means to bait Gruffydd into a fight. And believe me, it'll not take much!"

"You need not fret; I'll see to it," John assured her, but then he smiled. "It seems the Bishop of Winchester has the same idea," he said, and they watched as Peter des Roches adroitly herded the malcontent Marcher lords safely away from Llewelyn's son.

"Thank Heaven for Peter's sharp eye," Joanna sighed. "My father often joked that Peter might not be as innocent as the dove, but he was verily as guileful as the serpent! John, tell me. I could not help but notice how cordial Peter suddenly is toward your Uncle Chester. The Welsh have a proverb: The enemy of my enemy is my friend. I was wondering if Peter might not be taking that to heart."

There was surprise in the look that John gave Joanna, a startled and reluctant reappraisal. It had baffled him that Llewelyn would make use of a woman for delicate diplomatic maneuverings, that Joanna so often acted as his envoy to the English court. But her questions showed a shrewd perception of political undercurrents, and suddenly Joanna's presence here at Ludlow did not seem so inexplicable after all. How much, he wondered, did she cull from careless male speech? How many men would think to guard their tongues, to be wary of a comely woman?

"Peter des Roches is not the only one with a sharp eye," he conceded. "You are quite right. Des Roches is a man quick to tend to his own pastures, and he suspects Hubert de Burgh of grazing on the wrong side of the fence. There is no love lost

betwixt them these days. But de Burgh still holds the ear of the
one who matters most, our young King.''

Joanna nodded. ''John . . . I do not mean to interfere between
a man and his wife. But I've gotten a disturbing letter from Elen.
She wrote that you forbade her to visit us—'' She stopped in
mid-sentence. ''You did not?''

''Indeed not,'' he said indignantly. ''I would never act to cut
Elen off from her family. I did tell her that I did not want her to
go into Wales this summer, but only because war seems imminent. I know how homesick she is, but I had to put her safety
first.''

''Yes,'' Joanna agreed slowly. ''Of course.'' If this youngster
was not speaking the truth, he was as skilled an actor as any
she'd ever seen at Christmas mummeries. And Elen had ever
been capricious and headstrong. But however Joanna sought to
rationalize, one fact still stood out starkly—that some seven
months after her marriage, Elen was not happy with the husband
they'd chosen for her.

At that moment there was a sudden stir; Henry and Llewelyn
were reentering the hall. Joanna hastened toward her husband.
Gruffydd and Ednyved were also converging upon Llewelyn. He
met with all three of them in the center of the hall, gave them the
bad news they could already read in his face.

''Shall I tell you their terms for peace? I am to yield up the
castles I took from Fitz Warin and de Hodnet. But Pembroke
gives up nothing, gets to keep my castles of Cardigan and
Carmarthen.''

Gruffydd swore under his breath. ''What did you tell them,
Papa?''

''What do you think I said?'' Llewelyn paused, looked directly
at Joanna. ''You'd best go and bid your brother farewell. I told
him we'd be leaving Ludlow within the hour.''

Joanna was dismayed, but she knew better than to argue when
Llewelyn sounded like that. She nodded, did as he said.

Henry gave her no chance to speak, took her arm and led her
toward the window recess. ''Joanna, you must talk to your
husband, must get him to see reason.''

''Henry, there is nothing I can do.''

''I do not want war with the Welsh, you must know I do not.
But I had no choice, Joanna. Cardigan and Carmarthen have too
much strategic importance to leave them in the hands of a Welsh
Prince. Surely you can see that.''

"Yes, of course I can. Why should a Welsh Prince have any right to castles on Welsh soil?"

Henry had vivid blue eyes, a drooping left eyelid that gave him a drowsy, appealingly vulnerable look. But both eyes opened wide now, showed so much hurt that Joanna was at once remorseful.

"I am sorry, Henry. I do love you," she said softly. "But I love my husband, too, and I am so very tired of always having to choose . . ."

Henry watched as she moved away, back to Llewelyn. When Hubert de Burgh joined him, he said, "I never meant to hurt my sister, Hubert. I was so sure I could make her understand. You said she would."

"It cannot be helped, my liege. It is no easy thing to be a King, to find the courage to make difficult decisions. You must be strong, lad, must—"

"I am!" Henry cried, stung. "I'll do what must be done. But that does not mean I have to like it."

Gwenwynwyn's two young sons had been living in England as wards of the crown. On the same day that Llewelyn rode away from Ludlow, Henry ordered the boys to be brought to his court at Gloucester in hopes of winning away from Llewelyn the allegiance of the men of Powys. He then sent the Earls of Pembroke and Salisbury into Wales.

While Llewelyn sought to cut off their supply lines, Gruffydd sprang a lethal ambush in a hilly pass of Carnwyllion. But Pembroke and Will were able to fight their way free, began to lay waste to the countryside of Dyfed. Once more, Wales was at war.

Llewelyn's siege of Buellt Castle was in its second week. The Welsh had at last been able to cross the deep wet moat, to breach the outer curtain walls. But they'd been repulsed when they sought to assault the inner defenses, had been driven back in disarray.

Llewelyn and his captains were conferring behind the shelter of the outer curtain wall, mapping out a new plan of attack. "Do you want to try the battering ram again, Llewelyn?"

"Yes. But first I think I'll go up on the wall, see if I cannot find a weak spot in their defenses, a section that seems undermanned."

"May I go with you, Papa?"

"No, Davydd, you may not." The boy's disappointment was all too obvious, and Llewelyn knew he was not being fair. But he had no intention of relenting. Although he'd gone cheerfully off to start a rebellion at fourteen, with nary a thought for his own mortality, he'd discovered that his views on fourteen-year-olds and warfare had moderated considerably over the years, at least when the fourteen-year-old in question was his son.

The fighting for the outer bailey had been fierce, and the dank, scum-covered moat had taken on a sinister reddish cast. Always fetid and foul-smelling, the water now hid decomposing bodies in its murky depths, even the partially submerged carcass of a horse, bloated and black with flies. The stench was overpowering, followed Llewelyn even after he'd crossed their makeshift bridge, climbed a thong ladder to the top of the wall. Here, too, bodies lay exposed to the sun, crumpled along the parapet, sprawled in the bailey.

Below Llewelyn, the bailey was a scene of disorder and commotion. His soldiers had put up sheds to shelter themselves from the English crossbows, and they scurried back and forth, readying the battering ram for another run at the barbican, while panicked animals—goats, sheep, cattle—milled about in their midst. But as chaotic as it was in the outer bailey, Llewelyn knew it must be infinitely worse within the cramped inner ward, for Reginald de Braose had to shelter not only his own people, but the villagers who'd fled to the castle at the outset of the attack.

Gruffydd and Ednyved had followed him up, were in a huddled colloquy with several Welsh bowmen. Llewelyn continued along the walkway, stepping over the body of an English soldier, a broken sword scant inches from his outstretched hand. The more Llewelyn studied the inner defenses, the more dubious he became. Reginald de Braose had refortified Buellt in 1219, to impressive effect. Llewelyn knew he could eventually starve the garrison into submission, but he was not sure he'd have the time. Pembroke and Salisbury were already in Wales, and Henry was said to be gathering an army at Gloucester.

He happened to glance down, saw Davydd standing by the moat, staring up at him. Davydd looked so forlorn that Llewelyn felt a conscience qualm. It was one thing to make sure Davydd was kept well away from the fighting, quite another to try to shield him from any and all risks. Leaning over the embrasure, Llewelyn signaled to his son, beckoned for Davydd to join him on the wall. Davydd grinned, began to run.

Llewelyn would never know what prompted him to turn away from the embrasure at that precise moment. It may have been a sixth-sense awareness of danger; it may have been sheer luck, of the sort he'd had all his life. He caught a blur of motion as the Englishman lunged at him, and he stumbled backward under the impact. But the broken blade struck only a glancing blow, instead of burying itself in his back.

Llewelyn had no time to draw his own sword, grabbed for the man's arm as he raised the blade again, thrusting downward as if it were a dagger. They grappled desperately for control of the weapon. It was only inches from Llewelyn's throat when he managed to wrench the man's wrist down against the stone battlement. The man grunted in pain, but did not—would not—drop the sword. His face was very close to Llewelyn's, a young face, freckled and dirt-smeared, a face not to be forgotten. Dried blood had caked in his hair. His lashes were very fair, almost white, his lips peeled back from his teeth in a grimace of pain and hate. Llewelyn could smell his sweat, hear his rasping breath, a sound so loud as to blot out all else.

They struggled silently on the narrow walkway, each man seeking to kill, to survive. Llewelyn slammed the other man's hand onto the battlements again. This time he cried out and the blade slipped from fingers gone suddenly numb. Llewelyn reeled backward, fumbling for his sword. But the English soldier was staring past him, making no move to defend himself. His mouth contorted and he caught at the embrasure for support. His eyes were already glazing over by the time his knees buckled. As he fell forward, almost at Llewelyn's feet, Llewelyn saw the arrow protruding from his back.

During the timeless span of their struggle, it had seemed to Llewelyn that they were alone on the walkway, alone in the world. But now he saw men running toward them, swords drawn. Llewelyn slid his own sword back into its scabbard, leaned against the battlement. It hurt to breathe, and he winced as he ran his hand over his ribs. But the chain links of his hauberk had deflected the blow; although he'd be badly bruised, he was not bleeding.

Gruffydd and Ednyved came panting up. No one spoke; they stared down at the body, at that quivering arrow shaft. Hastening across the parapet from the opposite direction was a bowman as young as the man he'd shot. He was grinning, flushed with pride and excitement, utterly unprepared for what was to come. As soon as he reached them, Gruffydd grabbed his arm, shoved him roughly against the battlement.

"You stupid, foolhardy dolt! Of all the lunatic stunts I've ever seen . . ." Gruffydd was all but incoherent in his rage and the youngster shrank back, too flustered even to offer a defense.

Llewelyn tended to agree with Gruffydd. The young bowman had taken an enormous risk; it was not unheard of for an arrow to pin a rider to his horse. But he knew, too, that Gruffydd's anger was spurious, was actually fear masquerading as fury, and he said, still laboring for breath, "Let it lie, Gruffydd."

"Christ, Papa, he could have killed you! What if he'd missed, if he'd hit you instead?"

Llewelyn preferred not to dwell upon that. "What's your name, lad?"

The bowman swallowed. "Trefor, my lord," he mumbled. "Trefor ab Alun."

"You're a good shot, Trefor. I'll remember."

Trefor beamed, but dared not linger. Gruffydd's anger counted for more at that moment than Llewelyn's approval, and he hurried to rejoin his comrades.

Ednyved picked up the broken sword, flung it out into the moat. "It seems to me, Llewelyn, that you're the one who needs the nursemaid, not your Davydd!"

Llewelyn's smile was wry, faintly discomfited. "I should have known better," he admitted. "But it did prove one thing, that I was right about these Norman hauberks. Without it, I'd have been skewered like a stuck pig."

"Papa . . ." Davydd was standing several feet away. He'd lost all color, was so shaken that Llewelyn knew at once he'd witnessed the fight.

As Llewelyn climbed down the scaling ladder, he began to appreciate the extent of his injuries; his muscles were already exceedingly sore and tender. But he knew how very lucky he had been, and as soon as he and Davydd were standing on firm ground, he said, "I'm glad you saw that, lad. I hope to God you remember, for it might save your life one day. I did something very foolish up there. I saw a man lying on the wall, just took it for granted that he'd been killed in the morning's assault. But on the battlefield you can take nothing for granted, Davydd, nothing. Careless men do not make old bones, lad."

"I was so scared for you, Papa. Were . . . were you scared, too?"

Llewelyn turned, looked into the hazel eyes upturned to his,

Joanna's eyes. "Not whilst we were fighting, Davydd. You do not have time to be afraid during a battle, are too busy trying to stay alive. But afterward, when you think about it, about all the loathsome ways there are to die, I suspect most men feel fear. I have, for certes."

Davydd no longer met his eyes. "I've heard men say that Gruffydd knows no fear."

"Do not measure yourself against Gruffydd, lad. I chose you as my heir because I saw in you qualities of leadership." Llewelyn hesitated, for it was not easy to say. "I did not find those qualities in Gruffydd. I trust you not to repeat that to anyone else. But I trust you, too, to remember it."

"Llewelyn!" Ednyved was leaning over the wall embrasure. "De Braose wants to talk, says he'll send his son out if you'll warrant his safety."

"Agreed." Llewelyn looked at Davydd and then grinned. "Tell him I'll even invite him to dinner!"

The tents of English kings were opulent, even sumptuous, spacious enough for privacy as well as comfort. Llewelyn's tent was of a more modest scale, for even if he'd had the resources to indulge himself, no Welshman could have respected a commander who went to war with feather mattresses and silver plate. Llewelyn contented himself with a pallet, and when dinner was served, he and his guests sat in a circle on the ground, just as his men did around their campfires.

If Will de Braose thought Llewelyn's accommodations spartan, it did not show in his face. The Marcher lords tended to be a hardy lot, as robust and tough-minded as the Welsh they fought and befriended, and Will ate with gusto, even knowing that he was being served one of his own beef cows. As much as it irked Gruffydd to hear Normans pervert his tongue, it offended him even more to hear one speak such fluent Welsh, and he was hard-pressed to manage even a semblance of politeness. He would never understand how his father could bring himself to eat and drink with their enemies, never.

"It scarcely seems fair to repay your hospitality with what I have to tell you now." Will reached for another piece of bread. "But my father and I thought you had a right to know. Your daughter Gwladys is within the castle."

There was a moment's silence. Then Llewelyn laughed derisively and Gruffydd spat, "Liar!"

"My son speaks bluntly, but true . . . which is more than you

do. Do you think I'd besiege Buellt without first making sure of
my daughter's whereabouts, her safety? Gwladys is many miles
to the north, at my court on the isle of Môn.''

Will did not seem at all abashed. He shrugged, said with an
unrepentant grin, ''Well, you cannot blame a man for trying, can
you?''

Llewelyn shifted his position with unwonted care; neither mutton fat nor a lanolin ointment had done much to ease his discomfort. ''You'd not be here lest you had an offer to make. What is
it?''

''Seven hundred head of cattle if you ride away on the morrow.''

That was a fair offer. But there was more to consider than
profit, more at stake than cattle. ''I'll think about it,'' Llewelyn
said noncommittally. He'd noticed that Will kept glancing over at
Davydd, had noticed, too, that it was making the boy uncomfortable. ''You do know my son Davydd?'' he said pointedly, but
Will did not take up the challenge.

''I suppose I was staring,'' he conceded calmly. ''It's just that
he looks so much like his mother. It's not often a blood kinship
shows so plainly as that.''

Gruffydd set down his wineskin. ''I always thought Davydd
looked verily like John, God rot him.''

Will's eyes cut toward Gruffydd. ''I'll drink to that, to John,
King of England . . . and of Hell.''

Even in the subdued lantern light, Llewelyn could see the color
rising in Davydd's face. It did not surprise him; if Joanna at
thirty-two could not resolve her relationship with John, how could
Davydd at fourteen? For his son's sake, he acted to end the
conversation. ''I'll give you my answer on the morrow.''

But Will did not move. ''You must have hated John even as
much as I did. Christ knows, he gave you reason enough!''

Llewelyn looked over at Davydd, then nodded slowly. ''Yes, I
hated John.''

Will leaned forward. ''Then . . . then how could you live in
contentment with John's daughter?''

Llewelyn was astonished. But as he studied Will's face, he
saw that the younger man had not meant to offend. His grey eyes
held Llewelyn's own; he seemed truly to want to know. Llewelyn
had no intention, however, of answering a question so intensely
personal. ''I fail to see,'' he said coolly, ''how my marriage is of
concern to you.''

Will's eyes flickered; he was the first to look away. ''You're right, of course. It is not my concern. If my curiosity has led me astray, I apologize.'' His smile was self-mocking. ''If there is one thing we de Braoses pride ourselves upon, it is that we never offer an unintentional insult!''

Llewelyn was not taken in by Will's nonchalant disclaimer. He did not know Reginald's son well at all, but one thing he did not doubt, that the mere mention of John had touched a very raw nerve indeed. It was Davydd who told Will what he wanted to know. Davydd could not bear to have his mother associated in any way with the cruelties of the English King, and he said abruptly, ''My lady mother and King John were estranged for the last four years of his life.'' ·

Gruffydd opened his mouth, but for once discretion prevailed. Llewelyn had risen, and this time Will took the cue and rose, too. They were exchanging ironic courtesies when one of Llewelyn's men ducked under the tent flap.

''My lord, one of our scouts has just ridden in, says it is urgent that he speak with you.''

The man was unshaven, begrimed, had obviously passed a full day in the saddle. He knelt before Llewelyn, but wasted no further time on protocol. ''My lord, I bear evil tidings. The English King and the Justiciar marched out of Hereford at dawn this morn, heading toward the Gwy Valley—toward Buellt.''

''How large an army?''

''Too large, my lord. Mayhap twice the size of ours.''

Llewelyn turned aside. He heard Gruffydd cursing softly, damning the English to a particularly vile quarter of Hell; rarely had his son's sentiments so perfectly mirrored his own. It was at that moment that Will de Braose did something as provocative as it was impolitic. He laughed.

He at once regretted it, found himself the focus of icily measuring eyes. His hand dropped instinctively to his sword hilt, but he put greater faith in his privileged status, a guest at Llewelyn's hearth. ''Need I remind you that you swore to my safety?''

''No, you need not. Just be thankful a Welshman's word is not as worthless as you Normans claim.'' Llewelyn turned to the closest man, said curtly, ''Escort de Braose back to the castle.''

Will did not press his luck, held his tongue. But no one objected. Not even Gruffydd had seriously considered harming him, for it was understood that there were promises that could be broken and promises that must be kept; John might not have been so hated had he not blithely broken both kinds.

Once Will had gone, they could give vent to their disappointment, their rage that their prize was to be so rudely snatched from their grasp. But they could not long afford to indulge their anger, not with an English army less than a day's march from Buellt. "Give the order to break camp," Llewelyn said grimly. "We are done here. De Braose has won . . . this time."

After raising the siege of Buellt, Henry and Hubert de Burgh continued north, feeding their troops with Welsh cattle, burning and pillaging. By September 30, they had reached the border castle of Montgomery. Soon thereafter, they made use of their ultimate weapon—the Church of Rome. Llewelyn was excommunicated again, and warned that if he did not capitulate, his subjects would be absolved of all oaths of allegiance.

But Llewelyn was not a man to repeat his mistakes; he'd learned when to fish and when to cut bait. He sent word to Henry that he and the other Welsh Princes would come to Montgomery on the eighth of October, submit themselves to the English crown.

October 8 was a Sunday, God's day. An autumn sun shone upon the surrounding hills with a mellow warmth, burning away the mists that had shrouded the valleys for days and revealing blazing oaks, maples dappled in russet and saffron. But the day's beauty only deepened Davydd's forebodings. His unease intensified with each mile that brought them closer to Montgomery. He could think of nothing but the tales he'd heard of his father's surrender at Aberconwy. How could he watch as Papa humbled himself to Henry? What would the English demand of Papa? Would men blame him, too, remembering he was Henry's kin, half Norman?

When the sun-silvered waters of the Severn came into view, Davydd could endure no more. Urging his mount forward, he reined in beside Llewelyn. "Papa, do you have to do this? Is there no other way? Why can we not withdraw up into Gwynedd?"

Llewelyn signaled for his companions to drop back. "Whilst it is true that my own domains are not endangered, that cannot be said of my allies. If we do not come to terms with the English, Maelgwn and Rhys Gryg and Owain risk losing all. And although Gwynedd is not yet threatened, my influence in Powys and Deheubarth is. By making peace now, we can still salvage something from this debacle. Henry has agreed to restore to the other Princes the lands they'd lost to Pembroke, and to—"

"But what of you? You'll have to yield up those Shropshire

castles, and Carmarthen and Cardigan, too! It's not fair, Papa, you know it's not!''

"I cannot pretend that I like losing those castles, Davydd. But I do not see that I have a choice . . . just the dubious consolation that we Welsh take as a tenet of faith, the understanding that no matter how grievous our troubles are, they can always get worse.''

"Jesú, Papa, how can you jest? You've told me how John sought to shame you, to—''

"Is that what you fear, another Aberconwy? Ah, no, lad. This is no life-or-death struggle; we're talking about a couple of castles, a loss of face, no more than that. Most importantly, Henry is not John.''

Davydd was still dubious, but upon their arrival at Montgomery he discovered that his father was right, an astute judge of men. While Henry would later reveal his fair share of human failings, vindictiveness was never among them. He was genuinely glad to accept Llewelyn's submission, had no intention of turning the occasion into an ugly object lesson for the Welsh. Llewelyn was his sister's husband and therefore entitled to err. Henry pardoned the Welsh with artless generosity, with an ingenuous simplicity that was both his strength and his weakness, that he would never entirely outgrow.

Nor did Llewelyn's foes gloat openly over their victory, Pembroke because his antagonism toward Llewelyn was impersonal and thus without rancor, and Hubert de Burgh because he was dangerously dependent upon Henry's goodwill.

The Archbishop of Canterbury had already restored Llewelyn to God's grace, lifted the Interdict from Wales. All that remained to be done was to acknowledge the supremacy of the English crown, and this Llewelyn did, kneeling and pledging oaths of homage and fealty to the sixteen-year-old King. It was nowhere near as painful as Davydd had expected, and he watched with great relief, grateful that Henry had not his father's vengeful nature, that Llewelyn's English allies—Chester, John the Scot, Jack de Braose—were there to lend moral support.

As Maelgwn and Rhys Gryg came forward to swear fealty to Henry, Llewelyn crossed the hall, moved toward his son. "You see?'' he said. "No lasting scars.''

Davydd nodded. "I'm learning, Papa,'' he said, and Llewelyn grinned.

"I'm counting upon that, Davydd.'' But as he glanced about the great hall, his smile faded. "Where's Gruffydd?''

"He walked out, Papa.''

Llewelyn said nothing, for what was there to say? How long, he wondered, would he keep expecting more than Gruffydd could deliver? How long ere it stopped hurting?

Henry and Hubert de Burgh were planning to erect another castle at Montgomery, and construction had already begun at the new site, a mile to the south of the existing motte and bailey. As he wandered aimlessly about the bailey, Gruffydd heard the boisterous sounds of returning workers, miners and carpenters coming back from their day-long labors. Already trees and underbrush had been burned away, scarring the land; the hill was being cleared, made ready to receive a new Norman fortress.

Gruffydd had walked out of the hall because he did not trust himself, did not think he'd be able to keep silent, to watch passively as his father shamed himself before their enemies. That was a harsh judgment to pass upon Llewelyn, upon a man he still loved, and it gave him no small measure of pain. But he could interpret Llewelyn's behavior in no other way. They could have withdrawn into the mountain fastness of Eryri, fought the English on their own land, their own terms. Papa need not have yielded, need not have come to Montgomery. To Gruffydd, this was a dishonorable and indefensible surrender, one he could neither understand nor forgive.

He knew he could not remain indefinitely out here in the bailey, and braced himself to go back into the hall. But his good intentions were forgotten as he approached the steps, saw his brother standing in the sun.

Gruffydd stopped abruptly, staring up at Davydd. "Why are you not inside with your English kindred? You cannot tell me that you needed to get away as I did. Not you, Henry's nephew, John's grandson. Why should you care if Welsh pride is trampled into the dust?"

"I care."

To Gruffydd's exasperation, that was all he got. No matter how he prodded Davydd, he could never break through the boy's defenses. When Davydd felt threatened, he simply withdrew into himself, and that only strengthened Gruffydd's contempt, his conviction that Davydd was utterly unfit to rule in Llewelyn's stead.

He moved closer and Davydd backed up a step. But the knowledge that Davydd feared him did not give him any satisfaction. Christ pity Gwynedd, he thought, and suddenly he could keep silent no longer, the truth was bursting forth of its own accord, in a scalding surge of bitterness.

"Prince Davydd. The heir apparent. The favorite. The usurper! Tell me, are you enough of a fool to believe that will ever come to pass?"

He saw Davydd's jaw muscles tighten. But the boy's voice was colorless, devoid of emotion. "Papa will not change his mind."

"I know," Gruffydd admitted, and that was the hurt beyond healing. "But Papa will not live forever," he said roughly. "And then we shall see. I could not fight Papa. But I shall take great pleasure in fighting you, in claiming what is rightfully mine!"

Davydd swung around, started back into the hall. He was cautious by nature, as deliberate of action as he was quick of thought. He'd learned to turn silence into a shield, understood Gruffydd far better than Gruffydd understood him. Gruffydd's were volatile and impassioned rages, outbursts of heat and elemental energy, summer lightning in a cloudless sky. Davydd's rages were rare, seldom seen, and long-smoldering; as slow as he was to anger, he was even slower to forgive. Now, as he reached the door, he stopped, turned to face Gruffydd.

"You are right," he said. "Papa will not live forever. But neither will I be fourteen forever. And then, just as you said, we shall see."

7

SHREWSBURY, ENGLAND

August 1226

In January Henry fell gravely ill, and it was feared he might die. He did recover, but his Uncle Will of Salisbury was not as fortunate. Sailing from Gascony back to England, Will was shipwrecked, for a time was presumed lost. Although he survived several harrowing weeks at sea, his health declined. He died on March 7, much mourned, and was buried with great honors in the partially constructed cathedral church at Salisbury.

Henry watched complacently as Joanna scanned the letter he'd just handed her. "You see? Nell is quite content now with Pembroke. Did I not tell you that wedding was for the best?"

"And it seems you were right," Joanna conceded. This buoyant, sprightly missive was a far cry from the tear-splotched, forlorn letter she'd gotten from Nell two years ago, pleading with Joanna to intercede for her, to persuade Henry not to make her marry the Earl of Pembroke. But Pembroke had been very kind to his child bride, indulging her every whim, and the little girl seemed to have found in her husband the father she could not remember.

"I've something else for you, too, an early birthday present. I'm giving you the manor of Condover in Shropshire."

Joanna was delighted. Until Henry had given her an English manor the preceding year, she'd not realized what a secure feeling there was in being a property owner, in having land of her own. "You spoil me as much as Pembroke spoils our Nell," she said, and Henry laughed.

"I try. I just like to make people happy, to surprise them. And this ought to do both." Henry was holding out a parchment scroll. But as Joanna reached for it, he snatched it back. "How could I forget? You do not read Latin, do you? Ah, well, mayhap I could be coaxed into reading it to you.''

"Please do," Joanna said, utterly intrigued by now. Llewelyn and Davydd were no less curious. Only Elen did not join the circle, but stayed where she was in the window seat.

Henry was thoroughly enjoying the suspense, took his time in unrolling the scroll. "You'll observe the papal seal, no doubt. I had it in my hands two months ago, but I wanted to wait, wanted to see your face, Joanna. Are you ready? 'Dispensation to Joanna, wife of Llewelyn, Prince of North Wales, daughter of King John, declaring her legitimate, but without prejudice to the King and realm of England.' ''

Their response was entirely satisfactory; they were staring at him in obvious astonishment. "Henry, I . . . I do not understand," Joanna said at last. "How can this be?"

"Does it matter? Is it not enough that I asked and His Holiness the Pope obliged?"

"But there had to be more to it than that, Henry!"

"Ah, Joanna, it is not such a mystery. Papa's marriage to the Lady Avisa was dissolved, declared to have been void from its inception. That meant he was free to enter into another marriage or plight troth up to the time he wed my mother. Suppose he had pledged his troth with your mother. If that were so, you'd have a claim to legitimacy, would be entitled to recognition.''

"But, Henry, he did not plight troth with my mother!"

"Since she's dead and Papa's dead, who is to say?" Henry grinned, held out his arms. "Are you pleased, Joanna? Did I surprise you?"

"That you did, for certes!" Joanna moved into his embrace, while Llewelyn studied the papal dispensation.

" 'Without prejudice to the King and realm of England,' '' he quoted. "I take it that means Joanna's legitimacy is qualified, bars her from any claim to the English crown?"

"I knew you'd catch that straight off!" Henry laughed. "It seemed for the best. No offense, Llewelyn, but you've shown yourself to be too adroit at taking a weak claim and making of it an irresistible one!"

They all laughed at that, and Joanna kissed Henry again. Henry was so delighted at the success of his stratagem that it was some time before Joanna was able to disengage herself, to join Elen in the window seat.

"Darling, are you all right? Why are you sitting over here by yourself?"

"I'm fine, Mama, truly." Elen summoned up a smile. "So . . . tell me. How does it feel to be legitimate after all these years?"

"I'm not sure. My father would likely have found this hilarious, but I doubt that my mother would have seen the joke. How could she?"

"Speaking of jokes, what did Papa say to make you laugh so?"

Joanna grinned. "Oh, that. He asked me if conditional legitimacy was like being somewhat pregnant. He— Elen, what is it?" For Elen had not been able to turn away in time; Joanna had seen the sudden tears well in her daughter's eyes.

"Elen . . ." Rising, Joanna caught Elen's hand, drew her reluctant daughter to her feet. "Let's go out into the gardens, where we can talk."

"I have nothing to say, Mama."

"Well, I do," Joanna said, propelling Elen toward the door.

The garden at Shrewsbury was enclosed by whitethorn hedges; within the flowery mead were several wooden benches and a small fountain. Joanna and Elen halted before the fountain, while Joanna searched for the right words.

"Elen . . . sometimes men act kindly toward their wives in public, seem to be loving husbands. But these same men then treat their wives very differently in private. Most women have no choice but to suffer in silence. But that is not true for you, darling. I know you are unhappy. If that is why, if John is abusive or cruel to you, for God's sake, tell me. We can help, Elen. But we can do nothing as long as you keep silent."

Elen had plucked a briar rose, was dropping the petals, one by one, into the fountain. "Oh, Mama, do you not know me better than that? Do you truly think I'd stay with a man who beat me?"

"Well, then, what is it? Is he openly unfaithful? Has he brought a mistress into the castle keep?"

"Are those your standards for sympathy, Mama? If he beats me or flaunts his sluts, I'm deserving of pity. If not, I bear my lot as best I can."

"Elen, I did not say that!"

Elen picked up a daisy this time; it soon joined the shredded rose in the fountain. "No," she admitted after a long pause, "you did not, did you? To answer your question, I cannot say with certainty that John is faithful, but he is discreet. You and Papa were right about him. He is indeed a good man—pious, courageous, steadfast, and honest." She turned away from the fountain, began to pace. "What woman could ask for more in a man? What woman would have the right to ask for more?"

Joanna followed her across the grassy mead. "Yet you are not content."

Elen shook her head. "No. I feel . . . feel trapped. I expect that sounds right foolish, but it's true all the same. Do you remember that caged magpie I had as a child, how fond I was of it? I will not permit my maids to keep pet birds on any of our manors, cannot abide them now . . ."

Joanna caught her breath. "Ah, child, why did you not confide in me ere this?"

Elen shrugged. "I did once, Mama. I told you I did not want to marry John, and what did that avail me?" As always when she was distraught, she could not keep still, but moved restlessly back and forth, heedlessly trampling flowers underfoot. "John and I never quarrel. Would you believe me if I told you that in nigh on four years I've never seen him well and truly wroth? He believes in control, you see. He does not argue, he analyzes. He even explains my own emotions to me, patiently shows me not only how I erred, but why. So you need not fear, Mama. He hardly sounds like an abusive husband, does he?"

"No," Joanna said slowly. "Just an unloved one," and Elen turned her head away, surreptitiously brushed the back of her hand against her cheek.

"At first I was glad when I did not get with child; that may be sinful, but I was. After a time, though, I could not help wondering why I did not become pregnant. And . . . and then I began to want a baby, my baby. For the first time in my life, I took an interest when other women talked of birthing and children and the marriage bed, of the ways a barren wife might conceive. So I put mistletoe over our bed. I drink feverfew and anise in wine. I pray to St Margaret. And each month I count the days, dread that first spotting of blood . . ."

"Darling, you must not give up hope. Isabelle was barren for six full years ere she finally conceived. But she then was able to give my father five healthy children, and four so far to Hugh de Lusignan. Nor is she the only—"

"Mama, I know you mean well. But that is no comfort. Better I should face the truth, that my marriage is barren." Elen laughed suddenly, mirthlessly. "Barren in every sense of the word!" Choking back a sob, she spun about, fled the garden.

Joanna reached out, caught the edge of the fountain for support. This was her fault, all her fault. When she'd wept upon

being told she must wed a Welsh Prince, Isabelle had sought to
comfort her, assuring her she'd learn in time to be content with
Llewelyn. Isabelle had been right; most women did adjust, did
find a measure of contentment in all but the most wretched
marriages. But not Elen. And she should have realized that,
should have known the marriage was doomed. When had Elen
ever learned to compromise? Did it even matter that she brought
so much of her unhappiness upon herself? How could she blame
Elen for the nature God had given her? It was like blaming her
for having brown eyes. But if anyone should have foreseen this,
it was she. For who knew better than she how stubborn Elen
could be, how passionate and, for all her bravado, how easily
hurt?

   And what was she to do now for her daughter? What could she
do? Leaning over the fountain, Joanna splashed water upon her
face, and a memory surfaced. St Winifred's Well—Gwenfrewi in
Welsh—was a holy shrine in North Wales, close by Basingwerk
Abbey. It was celebrated for its cures, and the ailing and infirm
made painful pilgrimages to avail themselves of its restorative
waters.

   Joanna felt the faintest stirring of hope. There was something
she could do. She and Elen would make a pilgrimage to St
Winifred's Well, implore the saint to heed their prayers, to give
Elen a child.

8

CRICIETH, NORTH WALES

August 1228

Of all the diseases that ravaged the countries of Christendom, none was so feared as leprosy. The Church sought to ease the suffering of those afflicted by proclaiming it a sacred malady, an admittedly agonizing means of achieving salvation. But Scriptures said otherwise. According to Leviticus, the leper was unclean and defiled, to be shunned by his fellow men, and people were only too willing to obey that harsh dictum, to banish the leper from their midst, stifling the voice of conscience with the comforting belief that the leper's fate was deserved, God's punishment for sins of the flesh, for lust and lechery and unholy pride.

In England, lepers fared better than in other countries; the English were generally more tolerant, more sympathetic toward the leper's dreadful plight. An English leper was not taken to the cemetery and forced to stand in an open grave while a priest declared, "Be thou dead to the world, but alive again unto God," as was often done in France. But the English leper was still subject to banishment, was escorted to the church as if he were a dead man, where he knelt under a black cloth as the congregation chanted, "*Libera me, Domine.*"

For the leper, there would be no release but death. No longer could he enter churches, markets, inns. He must wear his distinctive leper garb, a dark hooded cloak, and carry clappers or bell in order to warn others of his approach. He must shun the company of all but his fellow lepers, and when he died, he would be buried as he'd lived, alone.

What befell him once he'd been stigmatized depended upon his own resources and the loyalty of family and friends. If he was wealthy and well loved, he could sequester himself in his own home. Or he could seek to enter a leper hospital, a lazar house. Life in a lazar house was not easy; the leper was compelled to bequeath his possessions to the hospital, to forswear such worldly amusements as chess and dicing, to take an oath of chastity, poverty, and obedience. But few balked, for the alternative was to be cast out upon one's own, to survive by begging, to face the hostility of people who shrank from the disfigurement and the ulcerated sores, and, as the disease took its gruesome toll, eventually to starve.

There was deep mourning, therefore, at Llewelyn's court when Iorwerth, one of Ednyved's sons, was diagnosed as having the disease of Lazarus. For Iorwerth, of course, there would be no hut by the roadside, with alms-dish nailed to a pole. He had a manor at Abermarlais, had a father wealthy enough to provide for his needs, influential enough to soften the strictures of his exile. He would not want for food or comfort or medical care. Ednyved could provide him with ointments, juniper oil, viper potions, even so exotic a remedy as the blood of a turtle from the faraway Cape Verde Islands. He could aid Iorwerth in making pilgrimages to the shrine of St Davydd's and the holy well at Harbledown, near Canterbury. He could even coerce Iorwerth's reluctant wife into keeping faith with her marriage vows, for while the Church did not recognize leprosy as grounds for divorce, Welsh law did. But what Ednyved could not do was to command a miracle, and nothing less would save his son. Knowing that, he could only grieve for his doomed child. And his friends could only grieve with him.

They could not even offer the meagre comfort of forced cheer, could not seek to console Ednyved with false optimism, fabricated tales of wondrous cures, for he would not speak of his son. Even with Gwenllian he refused to share his grief, for Iorwerth was not hers, but was a son of Tangwystl, the mother who'd died giving him birth. And so the bleak Lenten season dragged on under the heavy burden of Ednyved's frozen silence, and when it was spring, fate dealt another blow, no less cruel.

It was Easter, and Davydd Benfras, son of Llewelyn's court bard, Llywarch, was entertaining the court at Aber. He was reciting a lively account of a long-ago battle, when Rhys suddenly stumbled to his feet. Rhys looked quizzical, surprised rather than alarmed, but then he reeled backward, his clutching hands seeking support and finding only the edge of the tablecloth. He dragged it down with him, sent platters and dishes and tureens of soup clattering to the floor. Llewelyn was the first to reach him, cradled his head as Rhys fought for breath. But he was dead by the time Llewelyn's physician could be summoned.

Catherine was so bereft that they feared for her very sanity. Nothing could comfort her, not her children or her Church or her friends. At Joanna's insistence, she stayed for several weeks at Llewelyn's court, but then she went back to the manor house she'd shared for so many years with Rhys. In the months that followed, she withdrew into the past, into her memories and her regrets, until even to those who loved her, she seemed no more than a pale wraith, a wan, frail shadow trapped in a time no longer hers.

Llewelyn and Ednyved were stunned by Rhys's sudden death, for they'd lost more than a cherished friend, companion of boyhood and manhood. Standing in the shadowed choir of Aberconwy Abbey before Rhys's coffin, the same thought was in each man's mind, that it could have been him.

That thought, too, had been Joanna's. Common sense told her that she was likely to outlive Llewelyn, but she'd never allowed herself to dwell upon that likelihood, upon that eighteen-year difference in their ages. She knew their life together was bound to change as he aged, but not yet. Merciful Lady Mary, not yet.

Llewelyn's hair had begun to silver. His sight was no longer as sharp as it had been, and he tired more easily, complained of slowing reflexes. But he could still put in a day's hard riding. His health was excellent. Like all the Welsh, he'd taken good care of his teeth, and he still had a handsome smile, a young man's smile. Although he and Joanna no longer made love as frequently as in the early years of their marriage, Joanna had no complaints about their love life. She found it hard to believe that twenty-two years could have passed since the day of their wedding, and time seemed to be treating Llewelyn so kindly that it was surprisingly easy to pretend it was also standing still.

But then Rhys had died in seizure upon the floor of Aber's great hall, Rhys who was four and fifty, a year younger than Llewelyn. And a few weeks later, word reached Aber that Reginald de Braose had died at Abergavenny Castle. Like Rhys, Reginald had been in apparent good health, and he, too, was younger than Llewelyn. Joanna began to look upon her husband with new eyes, eyes haunted and full of fear.

Her anxiety was all the greater because the news from England was not good. After five years of peace, the Marches were once more in turmoil, and Joanna passed this, her thirty-sixth summer, in growing dread, for it was beginning to seem more and more likely that Llewelyn would be riding again to war.

Stephen Langton had died early in July, and with his death an irreplaceable voice for peace and conciliation was stilled, the last check upon Hubert de Burgh's growing ascendancy, for Peter des Roches had departed England the preceding year to fulfill a crusading vow, Chester had been stymied, Will was dead, and Pembroke was in uneasy alliance with de Burgh. Flourishing a new title, Earl of Kent, de Burgh now turned his eyes and ambitions westward—toward Wales. In April, Henry agreed to give him the castle and lordship of Montgomery.

The local Welsh reacted with alarm, laying siege to the castle and pressing their attack with such vigor that Henry and de Burgh were compelled to lead a royal army to the rescue. So far Llewelyn had not taken up arms himself, but he was deeply mistrustful of de Burgh's motives, and Joanna feared he would eventually be drawn into the fray. She was to meet Henry later in the month at Shrewsbury in hopes of preserving their fragmenting peace, but she was not optimistic of success, for the interests of her husband and brother were at heart irreconcilable.

August found Llewelyn's court at his seaside castle of Cricieth. On Tuesday, the Assumption of the Blessed Mary, Joanna spent the afternoon dictating letters to Elen, Catherine, and her young sister Nell. A brief letter was also dispatched to Gwladys, who'd returned to South Wales to settle a dispute over her late husband's lands; Reginald's son Will was contesting her dower rights. Joanna was just completing the last and most important of the lot, informing Henry that she had received his safe-conduct and would be meeting him in a fortnight's time at Shrewsbury.

Branwen and Alison had long since departed Joanna's service, had been found husbands and were raising families of their own. Glynis, Joanna's latest maid, had grown bored and wandered to the window, where she stood gazing out to sea. "The sun has just broken through, Madame. After nigh on a week of rains, I'd all but forgotten what it looked—" A loud blaring noise intruded over the sound of rolling surf, the raucous gulls. It blasted again and Glynis exclaimed, "Did you hear that, my lady? A hunting horn. Your lord is back from the hunt!"

By the time Joanna reached the bottom of the stairs, Llewelyn was already dismounting. The bailey was thronged with laughing men, lathered horses, and barking dogs; even before Joanna saw the deer carcasses strapped to the sumpter horses, she knew their hunt had been a rousing success.

Giving his reins to a groom, Llewelyn reached for Joanna as she came within range, bending her backward in a playful embrace. He was begrimed and sweaty, and when he kissed her, she tasted mead on his breath; they'd apparently begun celebrating on the way back to the castle. That meant, she knew, dinner would likely be a rowdy, boisterous affair. But she did not mind in the least, for this was the first time since Rhys's death that she'd seen Llewelyn in such high spirits.

"What were you doing?" she chided. "Chasing deer through a mud wallow?"

"Is that the thanks I get for putting venison on your table?" He gave her a sudden squeeze, laughing when she squealed. "Come, I'll show you the prize kill of the day, a fine ten-point buck brought down by Davydd. Unfortunately, two of the brachet hounds were hurt—"

Llewelyn had stopped, was gazing across the bailey. Joanna turned, saw at once what had caught his eye. Several horsemen had just been ushered through the gateway. But it was the horse being led that was drawing such admiring glances. The destrier was always larger than the palfreys used for daily riding, but this particular stallion was one of the largest Joanna had ever seen, standing almost seventeen hands high. It was a magnificent animal: broad chest, lengthy flanks, a powerfully muscled body and small head, a sweeping silvery tail and a coat as white as the foaming breakers crashing down upon the beach. Joanna smiled at her husband, said indulgently, "Go ahead, go take a closer look."

Llewelyn was not the only one to be captivated by the cream-colored stallion. It had attracted a crowd of admirers, men who looked on enviously now as one of the riders handed over the reins to Gruffydd.

"I bought him in Powys last month," Gruffydd said proudly, as Llewelyn came up beside him. "What do you think, Papa?"

"He's a beauty, in truth." Llewelyn circled around to get a better look, taking care not to get too close. One reason the destrier was rarely ridden except to war was that its natural gait was a rather jarring trot. But the other reason was that it was notorious for its fiery nature, and the other men, too, were giving the horse respectful room.

"I had to pay nigh on forty pounds for him," Gruffydd volunteered, and several men whistled. "As soon as I saw him, though, I knew I had to have him. You know what he put me in mind of, Papa? That white stallion you gave me for my twelfth birthday, remember?''

''I remember. That was a well-bred palfrey, but I doubt it could hold a patch to this one. I'd say he's cheap at twice the price.''

Gruffydd smiled. ''I'm glad you're so taken with him, Papa. You see, I bought him for you.''

''You're serious?'' Llewelyn turned to stare at his son. ''What can I say, Gruffydd? I think you're too generous for your own good; a horse like this does not come along that often.''

''Nonetheless, I want you to have him.'' Gruffydd watched as Llewelyn reached out and lightly stroked the stallion's arched neck; it snorted, flung its head up. ''However, I'm afraid you cannot ride him just yet. The man I bought him from said he was somewhat skittish, no easy horse to ride. What I'd like to do is to school him myself, until I'm sure he's a safe mount for you.''

''A safe mount for me?'' Llewelyn echoed incredulously. But his astonishment yielded almost at once to irritation. It was not just that he prided himself upon his horsemanship; it was also that he knew himself to be a much better rider than Gruffydd, who tight-reined his horses, seemed to take a perverse pride in high-strung, half-broken mounts. ''I hardly think that necessary, Gruffydd. I expect I've been riding long enough to know how to handle a skittish horse.''

Gruffydd was still smiling. ''I know you have in the past, Papa. But you were much younger then; the danger was less. I do not mean to offend you, but aging bones are brittle, break more easily. What you were once able to do might now be beyond you, might—''

''Lead the stallion over to the horse block,'' Llewelyn cut in sharply. Men at once moved back, cleared space, and took up positions to watch. Gruffydd shrugged, stepped aside. And Davydd felt a sudden chill.

Llewelyn did not mount right away; instead he stood quietly, letting the horse become accustomed to his scent, the sound of his voice. As he studied the stallion, his anger ebbed and his eyes grew wary. He was close enough now to see the knotted ridges on the horse's withers, the marks of abuse. When he ran his hand over the stallion's shoulder, it flinched. Somewhat skittish, Gruffydd had said. More than that, he suspected, much more. The stallion's head and neck were held well down; the position of its tail told him that so was its croup, while its back was arching like that of a cat. Even more than the laid-back ears, these were the signs of a restive animal, a likely bolter.

"Papa." Davydd had decided to trust his instincts. Following Llewelyn to the horse block, he said quietly, "Papa, I wish you'd reconsider. I have a bad feeling about this horse."

"So have I."

"Then why risk it? You always told me that horses can best be tamed with patience, that in any contest of brute force, the horse is bound to win."

"I know, lad. But if I back down now, I take an even greater risk, that men think me afraid to ride him."

"Jesú, Papa, who could doubt your courage?"

Llewelyn gave the boy a twisted smile. "Do not deceive yourself, Davydd. When a man reaches a point where he has nothing left to prove, he's either dead or dying." Davydd looked so troubled that he added reassuringly, "There's no great trick to handling a bolting horse. I need only get him turning in circles, let him tire himself out."

Unbuckling his scabbard, Llewelyn handed Davydd his sword. Taking the reins, he waved Davydd and the groom back, then gripped the pommel and swung up into the saddle. He was expecting some sort of resistance, but what he got was bottled lightning. The stallion shot forward, but instead of bolting, it began to buck wildly, kicking out in a frenzy, coming down with such force that Llewelyn felt as if his spine would snap in two.

Men had scattered in all directions, were shouting encouragements. But Llewelyn knew there could be but one outcome, knew he could absorb only so much of this punishment. He was half blinded by his own sweat, tasted blood where his teeth had torn his inner lip, and his legs were cramping in painful spasms; he was finding it harder and harder to throw his weight into his heels, to maintain his grip on the saddle. But the stallion had yet to show any signs of tiring, was twisting and plunging as if crazed, so desperate to free itself that at times all four feet were off the ground.

The castle dogs were going berserk, making excited dashes at the panicked horse, and they only frightened it all the more. When a large alaunt cut directly in front of it, the stallion reared up suddenly, and Llewelyn felt his first jolt of real fear. It was not that he expected the horse to throw itself backward. For all the folklore he'd heard of outlaw stallions that deliberately sought to crush their riders, he'd never encountered such a rogue killer, did not know a man who had. What he feared now was not so

much the stallion's intentions as the muddy bailey; the ground
had not had time to dry, was still slippery and rain-soaked. He
slackened the reins, leaned forward, but the stallion was already
scrambling, starting to slide. For several terrifying seconds the
animal struggled to keep its balance, and then it was going over
backward and Llewelyn kicked his feet free of the stirrups, flung
himself sideways as the stallion fell.

The ground was soft, but Llewelyn landed at an awkward
angle, his leg twisting under him. He lay stunned for several
moments, conscious but dazed, aware at first only of pain. There
was mud in his mouth; he spat it out, started to sit up. But the
bailey began to spin, and he lay back, closed his eyes. When he
opened them again, Joanna was kneeling beside him, cradling his
head as he'd done for Rhys. He recognized other faces now,
Davydd and Ednyved and Gruffydd, faces white and taut, the
faces of men looking into an open coffin, and he swallowed,
said, "How is the horse?"

They stared at him and then burst into unsteady laughter.
Joanna laughed, too, or perhaps she sobbed; he could not tell
which, for she was leaning forward, had begun to cover his
mud-streaked face with kisses. Llewelyn braced himself on his
elbow, started to sit up again. Now that his head had cleared, he
was concerned that he might have broken a bone, and it was with
some trepidation that he ran his hand over his throbbing left leg.
Once he concluded that he'd done no more than pull a muscle, he
closed his eyes again, silently giving thanks to the Virgin for
protecting him on this, the holiest of her days. As he turned his
head, he saw that the stallion had regained its feet. It, too,
seemed to have been accorded a measure of divine mercy, for it
had also escaped serious injury. It was standing quietly, sides
heaving, head down, looking—for the moment at least—like the
most docile of palfreys.

Llewelyn looked from the horse to his eldest son. "Somewhat
skittish, Gruffydd?" He said it with deliberate wryness, as if it
were a jest, and a number of people laughed. But Gruffydd did
not. Nor did Davydd.

"Before God, Papa, I did not know he was so wild. And I did
try to discourage you from riding him . . ."

Llewelyn heard Davydd draw a sharp, hissing breath. But he
kept his eyes upon Gruffydd, saw the color mount in the younger
man's face. At last he said abruptly, "Help me up, Davydd." It
was painful to bear weight upon his left leg, but not enough for
alarm. He glanced down at himself and grimaced, for his tunic

was soaked with sweat and caked with mud. "See to the stallion for me, Gruffydd. Right now I need a long, hot bath. And whilst I soak, I shall try to decide who best deserves to own such a remarkable beast. Pembroke's a possibility, but I'm more inclined to offer it to Hubert de Burgh."

As he expected, that got a laugh, gave him the opportunity to make an unhurried, graceful exit. But Joanna was not deceived; she knew him too well, knew he was playing to their audience, that only when they were alone would she find out the full extent of his injuries.

Entering their bedchamber, Joanna discovered that Llewelyn had not bothered to summon his squires; he had simply flung himself down upon the bed. She moved toward him, stopping several feet away. "I have to tell you," she said slowly. "That was one of the most foolhardy things you've ever done."

Llewelyn's mouth twitched. "No, *breila*. That was the most foolhardy."

He held out his hand and Joanna caught it between her own. "Let me summon a doctor, Llewelyn. I'll not rest easy until I hear him say you are well and truly unhurt."

"If you must. But not now, not yet." He allowed Joanna to help him strip off his tunic and his muddy boots; then he lay back against the pillows, his eyes closing again. She stroked his hair, pressed her lips to the pulse in his throat. He was drenched in perspiration; she could hear the rapid pounding of his heart, and her own took up a quicker cadence. But he did not seem to be in great discomfort; she read exhaustion in his face more than pain.

"You look so . . . remote, so far away. What are you thinking of?"

"A day twenty years past, the day I gave Gruffydd that white palfrey." His eyes remained closed, but he seemed to sigh. "What a twisted road we've traveled since then . . ."

"Llewelyn . . . do you believe Gruffydd? That he truly did not know the stallion was so wild?"

"He knew." Llewelyn turned his head on the pillow, met her eyes. "He wanted to see me take a fall," he said softly. "To see me fail."

Joanna's suspicions were uglier than his. But she said nothing, for she knew now that he'd not walked away unscathed, after all. Knowing that he'd insist upon eating in the great hall, she said, "I'll go to the kitchens, instruct the cooks to delay dinner. Try to rest, beloved; I'll be back."

Ednyved was waiting for her on the outer stairway of the Great Tower. "How does he, in truth?"

"He has no hurts you can see. Where is Gruffydd?"

Usually, grooms had to resort to a lip twitch in order to handle the white stallion. But this time it had submitted meekly, too shaken by its fall to summon up a spirit of defiance.

Gruffydd was still shaken, too. He lingered in the stable long after the grooms had gone, slumping down on a large bale of hay. It was quiet, and the smells of horses and hay and manure were comforting in their very familiarity. He sat there for some time, alone in the semidarkness, listening to the soft nickering of the animals, trying to make sense out of emotions that were as contradictory as they were compelling. His senses were normally acute, but he'd let himself be lulled into incaution, and he did not hear the footsteps in the straw, jumped when a voice spoke suddenly out of the shadows.

"How disappointed you must be."

The voice was familiar, and yet it was not. It sounded like Davydd, but it held none of Davydd's vaunted control, the icy indifference that Davydd had learned to wield like a whip. This voice was uneven, raw with rage, throbbing with hatred. Gruffydd got slowly to his feet, and one of the shadows moved, revealing that it was indeed his younger brother. But this was a Davydd he'd never seen before, and he instinctively dropped his hand to his sword hilt.

"I do not know what you mean."

"Yes, you do. You deliberately goaded Papa into riding that stallion, knowing full well that the horse was not broken!"

"That is not true. I did not know."

Davydd's lip curled back. "Liar!" he jeered. "No man buys a horse without riding it first. And you even claim you were warned it was skittish. You'd never have resisted a challenge like that, not you! You tried to ride that stallion, and if there were any justice, you'd have broken your worthless neck! Was that when you got the idea? When you found you could not master him yourself?"

Gruffydd took a swift, threatening step forward. He towered over the younger man, but Davydd stood his ground. Gruffydd had flushed. Lying did not come easily to him, and he made no more false denials, instead fell back upon the truth, as he perceived it to be. "Even if I did know about the stallion, I had no evil intent in mind, never meant for Papa to be hurt."

"I'll grant you that. You were more ambitious, were hoping for more than a broken leg. I think you've grown weary of waiting, think you wanted him dead!"

Gruffydd gasped, then lashed out. Davydd saw the blow coming and recoiled, but he was not fast enough. Had he not pulled away, it might have broken his jaw. As it was, it had enough force to snap his head back, to stagger him. He stumbled and Gruffydd swung again, buried his fist in Davydd's stomach. He doubled up, fell to the floor just as Joanna and Ednyved entered the stable.

"Jesus God, no!" Joanna gave Gruffydd one incredulous look of horror, knelt by her son. He was bleeding profusely, and she was afraid to touch him, afraid to find a wound that might be mortal.

Ednyved, too, had whitened at sight of Davydd's blood. "Christ, what have you done?" he demanded, grabbing Gruffydd roughly by the arm.

Gruffydd jerked free. "What do you think, that I stabbed him?" Outraged, he drew his sword halfway up the scabbard. "Do you see any blood on the blade? I hit him, that's all."

"He's lying, Ednyved, has to be. Jesú, look at all this blood!"

"Mama . . ." Davydd coughed, struggled to sit up. "Mama, I'm not hurt."

Gruffydd let his sword slide down the scabbard. "Your precious nestling has a nosebleed, Madame," he said scornfully. "No more than that . . . this time."

Joanna could see now that Gruffydd spoke the truth, that this frightening rush of bright red blood was indeed coming from Davydd's nose. Forcing him to lie flat, she sought to stanch the bleeding with her veil. Gruffydd stood watching for a moment longer, then turned and stalked out.

As soon as the bleeding ceased, Davydd insisted upon sitting up. "I need some water," he muttered. "I cannot go out there with blood all over me." Ednyved found a drinking pail, but when Joanna tried to help, Davydd snapped, "I am not a child, Mama, do not need to be coddled!"

"Davydd, that was not my intent!" But Gruffydd's taunt came back to Joanna then—"your precious nestling"—and her hand slipped from Davydd's sleeve. She would have protested, though, when he turned to go. But Ednyved caught her eye, shook his head.

"It's best to let him be," he advised, once Davydd was out of hearing. "His pride is sore, and that's not a hurt a mother can heal."

Joanna did not agree, but she had not the energy to argue. Reaction had set in and she was trembling again. She looked about in vain for a stable workbench, dropped down upon the bale of hay. "Till the day I die," she said numbly, "I'll never be able to forget that sight, Davydd crumpled on the ground, drenched in blood, with Gruffydd standing over him, hand on sword hilt. Can you blame me, Ednyved, for thinking what I did?"

Ednyved sat beside her on the bale. "No, for I thought it, too."

"Llewelyn thinks Gruffydd wanted to see him take a fall. I would that I could believe he had nothing more in mind. Tell me the truth, Ednyved. Do you think Gruffydd was hoping Llewelyn would be badly hurt, mayhap even killed?"

He seemed in no hurry to respond. "I saw his face when Llewelyn was thrown. If he was not fearful for Llewelyn, he's a rather remarkable actor, and acting has never been one of his talents."

"But he had to know the risk!"

"Joanna, you're asking me what only Gruffydd can answer. It may be that even he does not know for certes. If you're asking whether Gruffydd hates Llewelyn, I think he has learned to hate him. But in a strange way, I think he still loves him, too."

"How can he hate and love Llewelyn at the same time?"

Ednyved shrugged. "Probably the same way you hate and love John," he said, and Joanna jumped to her feet, began to pace.

"Gruffydd has no intention of honoring Llewelyn's wishes, of accepting Davydd as his liege lord. As soon as Llewelyn is dead, he means to lay claim to the crown."

"I know that, and I know, too, what you fear. But you're seeing Davydd with a mother's eye. Do not underestimate the lad, Joanna. He is stronger than you think."

"I am not saying Davydd is weak! I am saying he is young, too young. He's just nineteen, Ednyved, and Gruffydd is thirty-two, with years of battlefield experience. Can you honestly tell me you believe Davydd could hold his own against Gruffydd?"

"Not now," he conceded. "Not yet." A silence fell between them. He watched Joanna pace, finally said, "I can think of only one way to solve the problem Gruffydd poses. But I doubt you could bring yourself to do it, not even for Davydd. Hire men to arrange a killing."

Joanna recoiled, and he said dryly, "You see? I knew you could never do it."

"Neither could you." Joanna moved toward him. "But you've given me an idea, Ednyved. What if Gruffydd were banished from Llewelyn's court, banished from Wales?"

He looked thoughtful, nodded slowly. "Yes, that might well give Davydd the time he'd need. But you'd best think this through, Joanna. You're talking about causing Llewelyn a great deal of pain."

"I know." She shook out her crumpled veil, stared down at the bloodstains. "Will you help me, Ednyved? If not for Davydd, for Gwynedd?"

"Yes," he said. "I'll help you. How?"

"I do not know yet," she admitted. "But I'll find a way. Somehow I'll find a way."

Joanna's mission to Shrewsbury met with surprising success. She was able to patch up another peace, to stave off a confrontation between Llewelyn and the English crown. But she was not sanguine about the long-term prospects of this truce, suspected it would be of fleeting duration, for Hubert de Burgh was not content with his acquisition of Montgomery Castle, was casting covetous eyes upon the neighboring Welsh commote of Ceri.

Gruffydd reacted with predictable fury to Llewelyn's announcement of a truce, and after quarreling bitterly with Llewelyn, he withdrew from his father's court for several weeks. Joanna usually welcomed his absences, but for the first time she found herself waiting impatiently for Gruffydd's return. She had finally hit upon a plan, likely to be successful by its very simplicity. She meant to exploit Gruffydd's own weaknesses, to let his blazing temper be the instrument of his downfall.

A midday sun was stalking shadows across the rush-strewn floor of Aber's great hall. In one corner a spirited dice game was in progress. Davydd Benfras was replacing a horsehair string on his favorite harp. All around him men were working at various chores, with differing degrees of enthusiasm, rubbing saddle leather with goose grease, mending harnesses, whittling wooden combs for wives, toys for children. Women were churning butter, spinning wool, while dogs wandered about, hunting for discarded bones midst the floor rushes.

The scene seemed to be one of perfect domestic tranquillity, but rarely had Joanna been so tense. She and Glynis had spread a

length of wool upon a trestle table, were cutting out a gown for
Catherine. But she could not keep her mind on the task at hand,
could not keep her eyes away from Gruffydd.

Gruffydd was putting a keener edge upon his sword, set the
sharpening stone aside at Senena's approach. She brought him a
brimming wine cup, then lingered to talk, and Joanna's nerves
grew more taut by the moment. First she'd had to wait for
Gruffydd's son Owain to leave the hall, not wanting a child to
witness the ugly scene to come. And now Senena was unwittingly acting as saboteur.

Gruffydd was laughing, reached out and tweaked one of
Senena's long brown braids. Although many Welshwomen still
cut their hair fairly short, more and more of them were following
the Norman fashion, following the example set by their Prince's
wife, and Joanna was grimly amused that Senena, too, had
adopted the style of a people she so despised.

As she watched them bantering together, Joanna found herself
thinking that they were a mismatched pair. They put her in mind
of a brilliantly colored linnet and its dowdy, drab brown mate.
Senena was not so much plain as overshadowed, an ordinary
woman with an uncommonly handsome husband. Joanna felt sure
that Gruffydd strayed from time to time, just as she knew Llewelyn
had occasionally strayed. But if Gruffydd was like Llewelyn in
that he could have his pick of very willing women, he was like
Llewelyn, too, in that he seemed to have no need of numerous,
ever-changing bedmates. He was content with one woman, with
the wife who obviously adored him, who was as fiercely protective of him as any lioness could be.

That was a better analogy, Joanna decided, Gruffydd as the
tawny-maned male lion, awesome to behold but actually dependent upon his less flamboyant mate, the rangy lioness who did
the hunting. Senena of the watchful cat-eyes, Senena who was
more calculating than her tempestuous husband, and thus more
dangerous. But no, she was being unfair now, letting her dislike
of Senena lead her astray. How could she blame the woman for
being loyal to her husband, her children? They had three now:
nine-year-old Owain, six-year-old Gwladys, and a second son
born just that spring, named after Llewelyn.

Joanna frowned, brought her mental ramblings to an abrupt
halt. Why was she going on like this? Yes, Gruffydd was a
caring husband, a loving father. What of it? Why was she culling
out his virtues from amongst his failings, searching for those few
traits she might justifiably honor?

After some moments of conjecture, she thought she knew. It was as if she were seeking to reassure herself, to show that she was not acting out of malice, that her hatred of Gruffydd played no part in what she was about to do. Well, mayhap her motives were not as pure as she'd have liked, but she'd not be lying when she answered to the Almighty for this, when she avowed that she could see no other way, no other choice.

At last Senena was moving away. Joanna laid her scissors down, stood up. Her eyes searched out Ednyved. He nodded almost imperceptibly, started toward the door. Joanna braced herself, then crossed the hall, sat down beside Gruffydd in the window seat.

Gruffydd could not hide his surprise. "Yes, Madame?" he said coldly, warily.

"I thought you might want to congratulate me. I did avert a war, did I not?"

This was so unlike Joanna that Gruffydd's suspicions kindled like sun-dried straw, and he responded with uncommon caution. "No, you did not. You did but delay it. You did my father no service by your meddling, for Hubert de Burgh will take our restraint as weakness. He'll be all the more likely now to move into Ceri, because we failed to halt him at Tre Faldwyn . . . or as you Normans call it, Montgomery."

"I'm sorry you take that view. But I cannot say I'm surprised. After all, you have such a limited understanding of political matters. How fortunate for Gwynedd that Davydd and not you shall rule in Llewelyn's stead."

Gruffydd caught his breath. "Just what do you want from me?"

This was not going as she'd hoped it would. Gruffydd was furious, but so far he was keeping his voice as low as hers; they'd yet to attract attention. Moreover, she was finding it harder than she'd expected to provoke a quarrel in cold blood, to insult without the excuse of anger.

"There is no mystery, Gruffydd. You remember that day last month at Cricieth Castle, that day you deliberately baited Llewelyn into riding that crazed stallion? I knew that was not mischance, knew what you had in mind, letting a poor dumb brute do your killing for you. I just could not prove it . . . until now."

Gruffydd was on his feet before she could finish speaking. "That's a lie, an accursed Norman lie!"

Joanna rose, too. Heads were turning now, swiveling in response to Gruffydd's shout. From the corner of her eye, she saw Llewelyn and Ednyved entering the hall. But she saw, too, that Senena was hastening toward them. She reached out, put a hand upon Gruffydd's arm, as if seeking to placate him, and said softly, "As I said, I have proof. One of the grooms came to me, confessed he found a spiked burr under the stallion's saddle—"

She got no further. Gruffydd's outrage, his sense of injustice and injury overrode all else, swept aside the last shreds of his restraint. He'd always suspected Joanna of trying to poison Llewelyn's mind against him, but in his worst imaginings he'd never expected her to concoct so blatant, so brazen a lie. Had she been a man, he'd have already exacted his vengeance. But his was a society in which women were not to be subjected to violence. Even now the ingrained discipline of a lifetime held, and he did the only thing he could do, flung the contents of his wine cup into Joanna's face.

Joanna gasped, no longer had to feign anger. "You're a lunatic, an utter and absolute lunatic!" she cried, backing away, frightened by his fury. The hall was in pandemonium; through a roaring in her ears, she heard voices rising, saw a blur of shocked faces, most registering stunned disbelief of what they'd just seen. And then Llewelyn had reached her side, and she forgot the pretense, forgot she had sprung this trap herself, threw herself into his arms with a heartfelt, "Thank God you're here!"

"You're not hurt?" He waited only for her to shake her head before he swung around to confront his son. "All your life I've made excuses for you, found reasons to explain away your deranged behavior. I cannot even begin to count the times I've overlooked your tempers, your blunders. But no more. This time you'll answer for what you've done."

"But it was not my fault!"

"It never is, is it? You're always the injured innocent, never accountable for your own actions. It's as if your entire history begins and ends with those years you spent in English prisons. Well, that was thirteen years ago, Gruffydd, and my patience has at last run out."

Senena was tugging frantically at Gruffydd's arm. "Do not argue with him, love, I beg you. Do not say what you may later regret!"

Gruffydd ignored her, did not even hear her. "Your patience? What of mine? You talk of making excuses for me. What do you think I've had to do for you? I've watched for years as you shamed yourself, shamed us all, watched and could do nothing about it. I do not know why this last surrender surprised me so.

You're so eager to stay in the good graces of the English King that nothing else matters to you . . . least of all, pride. I once accused her"—he pointed toward Joanna—"of bewitching you, and you denied it. But how else explain your actions? You demean yourself before the English King, allow de Burgh and Pembroke to humiliate you, to—"

"That is enough, Gruffydd!"

"What do you call it, if not humiliation? You can posture all you want, boast that you're a brother sovereign of the Scots King, but the truth is that you've shackled us to the English throne, made us vassals of John's son. And yet we're likely to look back upon your reign as the Golden Age of Gwynedd, in comparison with what would befall us under Davydd! Christ, Papa, you must see him for what he is, a craven weakling, a pampered milksop who'd panic at the first hint of trouble, and yet you'd have him over me! You'd forsake your firstborn, abandon our ancient laws of inheritance, and all to please a Norman-French bedmate!"

"I do see Davydd for what he is, and I see you for what you are, irresponsible and willful and foolish beyond belief. You talk of governing Gwynedd, and yet you cannot even govern your own temper. You're a child, Gruffydd, a child at two and thirty, and it is time you faced the truth. I would never have turned Gwynedd over to you. Should evil befall Davydd in my lifetime, I'll choose Tegwared then, or even Adda's son. But not you, never you, for you'd blunder into a war you could never win, destroy the work of a lifetime in less than a twelvemonth."

Gruffydd was stunned. "You'd do that? You'd truly choose Tegwared over me?"

"Yes." Llewelyn's voice was very cold. "If it came to that, I would."

In the silence that followed, Gruffydd could hear the ragged, labored sound of his own breathing; it seemed so loud to him that he feared others, too, might hear. Senena was plucking again at his sleeve; her eyes were wet with tears. "Beloved, please. Come away now."

"Not yet." His voice sounded strange to him, as if coming from a distance. "So you do not think I'm fit to rule? Well, go ahead, have Davydd acknowledged by the English, by the Pope, the Marcher lords. The Lord Jesus Himself can anoint him, for all I care. For it will avail you naught, old man. Your power stops this side of the grave. Once you're dead, I'll take what is rightfully mine. I'll take Gwynedd and I'll take my vengeance."

Llewelyn had gone very white. "Do you think I'd let that happen?"

Gruffydd forced a laugh. "How can you stop me? You'll be safely gone to God, remember?"

A muscle had begun to jerk in Llewelyn's cheek. "Courage such as yours is not always a blessing, Gruffydd. Sometimes it can be a curse." He no longer sounded angry, sounded oddly dispassionate and distant, and then, as Gruffydd puzzled over the cryptic meaning of his words, he raised his hand, said, "Seize him."

Llewelyn's household guards looked utterly appalled, but they did not hesitate, at once surrounded Gruffydd, drawing their swords. Gruffydd's reaction was as instinctive and as explosive as his white stallion's had been; he made a dive for the window seat, for his sword. But although the sharpening stone still lay untouched, the sword was gone, for Ednyved did not believe in taking undue risks and had quietly appropriated the weapon. Trapped in the window seat, Gruffydd drew his dagger, turned to face his pursuers. They advanced warily, nervously aware that Llewelyn's command had been to seize him, not to slay him, and they made no attempt to stop Senena when she darted between them.

"Gruffydd, you cannot fight them! Beloved, save yourself, I beg you!"

Gruffydd had friends in the hall, had men sworn to him. With a bitter sense of betrayal, he saw now that none of them was going to come to his aid, that they'd not go against Llewelyn. He knew Senena was right, but he knew, too, that he could not yield. "Senena, I cannot . . ." he said huskily, and then, "Christ, no! Owain, get back!"

His son had entered the hall unnoticed, had stood transfixed until the scene erupted in violence. The boy did not understand what was happening, saw only that his father was in danger, and he sprinted forward, crying, "Papa!" Sobbing, he began to flail out at the men encircling Gruffydd, until Llewelyn grasped him by the arms, pulled him away. Even then, he continued to struggle. There was no sound in the hall but that of his sobs. No one moved. And then Gruffydd's shoulders slumped; he dropped the knife into the rushes.

"You win, Papa. What now? Are you going to do Davydd's killing for him?" That was sheer bravado, though, for Gruffydd felt certain Llewelyn would never put him to death. "I can only tell you what I told John, that I'll not beg."

Llewelyn released his grandson, watched as Owain ran to his father. "Alun," he said, still sounding like a stranger to Gruffydd, one remote and unrelenting and beyond reach, "you are to escort my son to Deganwy Castle. He is to be confined there until I personally give you orders to the contrary. He is to be well treated at all times, and his wife and children may join him there. But he cannot be trusted, and is to be closely watched. If you fail me, you'll long regret it. You understand?"

"Indeed, my lord." Alun gestured, and Gruffydd found his arms being forced behind his back. He no longer resisted, for he had too much pride to let himself be dragged, bound and helpless, from the hall. But at the door he halted, his voice rising in a defiant shout. "You've just bought Davydd some time, no more than that! You'll have to kill me, old man, and I doubt that you can do it, that you—" His guards shoved him forward; the rest of his words were cut off by the closing door.

Senena had stood very still. Now she turned, crossed to Llewelyn, and dropped to her knees before him, a supplicant's posture belied by the blazing grey eyes. "Gruffydd will not beg, my lord, but I will. You must not do this. Confinement will kill Gruffydd, you know it will. He's your son, your firstborn son. Let him go. We'll leave Wales, I swear it, will never return. Just let him go."

"I cannot do that. He would never accept exile, and you know it, Senena."

Senena rose to her feet. "It would have been a greater mercy if you'd killed him, then." Reaching for her son, she said, "Dry your tears, Owain. We go to Deganwy Castle to be with your lord father."

A path cleared at once; no one seemed to want to touch her, even to meet her eyes. Head high, she started toward the door, leading her son by the hand. But she stopped as she reached Joanna, and then whirled, spun around to face Llewelyn.

"Do you want to know whose fine hand brought about my husband's downfall? She did it, your so innocent and right loving wife! She sought Gruffydd out in the window seat, deliberately goaded him to violence, to his ruin. None of this need have happened if not for her!"

After seeking Llewelyn in their private chamber and the chapel, Joanna was at a loss as to where to look next. But as she approached the stables, a young groom came hurrying out at sight of her.

"Madame, how thankful I am to see you! My lord Prince first told me to saddle his chestnut palfrey, then ordered me to go, saying he'd do it himself. And when I tried to tell him that I was right glad to serve him, he lashed out in a fury, told me to get out, to . . ." The groom trailed off in despair. "My lady, I did not mean to displease him, do not even know what I did. And now he's so wroth with me . . ."

"No, he is not. You need not fret; you've done nothing wrong. Just go about your other duties. All will be well, I promise you."

As she entered the stable, Joanna could feel inquisitive equine eyes upon her. Horses were poking their heads over their stall doors, and her favorite roan mare gave a welcoming nicker. But Llewelyn was nowhere to be seen. She paused uncertainly before the stall of his chestnut palfrey, and then moved toward the far door, out into the stable yard. He was not there, either, and she crossed to the shed where the stable gear was kept.

"Llewelyn?" The shed was dark; coming from sunlight, she could see no more than a man's silhouette. "Llewelyn, I've been looking all over for you. You left the hall so suddenly . . ." She came closer, said hesitantly, "Beloved, I was worried about you . . ."

"Did Senena speak the truth? Did you deliberately goad Gruffydd into that rage?"

When Senena had accused her in the great hall, she'd responded with an instinctive, heated denial, indignant enough to carry conviction. But alone now with Llewelyn in the darkened shed, Joanna found she could not lie to him.

"Yes . . . I did. I wanted him to show you his true nature, to show you how dangerous he is. I thought you might banish him from your court, into exile. But I never meant for this to happen, Llewelyn. I never thought you'd be forced to imprison him, I swear it."

She waited, at last entreated, "Are you not going to say anything? It is bad enough that I cannot see your face, but your silence is worse. I did it for Davydd, Llewelyn, for our son. Surely you can understand?"

He brushed past her, moved out into the yard. As he stepped into the sunlight, Joanna was shocked at the sight of him. His face looked ravaged, as if he were bleeding from an internal wound, one that could drain away a man's lifeblood before his physicians even diagnosed the danger. She ran to catch up with him, followed him back into the stable.

"Llewelyn, you must listen to me. I know your pain, know—"

"Do you?" But he turned away before she could answer, entered the chestnut's stall, where he took undue care in bridling the horse. Joanna watched helplessly as he laid a sweat pad across the animal's back, passed the crupper under its tail.

"Will you not talk to me? Llewelyn, this serves for naught!"

He positioned the saddle, began to adjust the girth buckles. "Senena was right. Killing Gruffydd would be kinder than caging him."

"Ah, Llewelyn . . . what else could you do? He forced you to it, gave you no choice."

He swung around to face her, and she shrank back. Never had he looked at her like this, a look that went beyond anger, that came perilously close to denying a lifetime of love. "You blame me for what happened? Llewelyn, that's not fair! I know how this hurt you. But I had no choice, either. I had to put Davydd's life above all else. I had to do whatever I could to protect him. How could you expect me to do less?"

"I would have expected you to come to me! Davydd is my son, too. Do you think I'd not have done what I could to safeguard his life, his inheritance?"

"But I knew you would not have banished Gruffydd! You yourself admitted you've always indulged him, forgiven him. I was sure talking would do no good, that you had to see for yourself just how untrustworthy he truly is. Be honest, Llewelyn. What would you have done had I come to you with my fears, my suspicions?"

"We'll never know, for you never gave us the chance. Had you trusted me enough to confide in me, mayhap I could have found another way. At the least, I'd not have had Gruffydd taken by force at high noon in the great hall, whilst his nine-year-old son looked on!"

"I am sorry about that, truly I am . . ." Joanna said haltingly. "But I thought I was acting for the best."

"By going behind my back? By lying and conniving? You said I had no choice. You're right, for you saw to that!"

"Why will you not try to understand? Jesus wept, I did it for Davydd!"

He shoved the stall door back, led the stallion out into the row. "I do understand, more than you think. This is not the first time, after all, that you've lied to me. When you sent John that secret warning, you justified that just as easily, swore you'd done it for me. And now Davydd. Who are you to make my decisions for me, to decide what I ought to do?''

He was leading the stallion toward the door. Joanna hastened to keep pace, grabbed his arm. "I did not believe you'd banish Gruffydd unless forced to it. I still believe that! How can I not, when you've forgiven him time and time again?''

He pulled free, swung up into the saddle. "To give credit where due, your scheme worked admirably. You duped me into doing exactly what you wanted, like a master puppeteer. My congratulations, Madame. I daresay John would be very proud of you!''

Joanna flinched as if from a physical blow. "Damn you!'' she cried. "Damn you, damn you!''

Llewelyn spurred his stallion forward. Joanna did not try to stop him. Standing in the stable doorway, she watched as he cantered across the bailey.

9

TREGARNEDD, NORTH WALES

October 1228

Joanna waited for Catherine's servant to move out of earshot before continuing. "Davydd returned the next day from Bangor, and when he learned what had happened, he was furious. He accused me of having no faith in him, insisted he needed no help in thwarting Gruffydd's ambitions, and how could I argue?" She smiled, but without humor. "At Davydd's age, a mother's fear is taken as a mortal insult."

"And what of Llewelyn? You could not reconcile?"

"No. I've never seen him so angry. But by then I was no less angry myself. In the days that followed, we avoided one another whenever possible, no longer spoke unless absolutely necessary. It was dreadful, Catherine. And then on the fourth day came word that Henry and Hubert de Burgh had invaded Ceri." Again that bleak, mirthless smile. "For once, Gruffydd was actually in the right; he'd predicted as much. I was still angry, still hurt. But I did not want Llewelyn to ride to war with harsh words or unhealed wounds between us. I swallowed my pride, sought to make peace . . . to no avail. Llewelyn rebuffed me so sharply that he kindled our quarrel all over again."

Joanna sighed, picked listlessly at the food set before her. "And now it has been three weeks since he and Davydd rode south. They are waging war in Ceri, fighting Henry and de Burgh, but I know no more than that. Not a single message has Llewelyn sent me, nary a word."

Putting the bread down, Joanna gave Catherine a speculative look. "You've heard me out in virtual silence. Surely you understand why I acted as I did? We're talking about nothing less than Davydd's very life!"

"I am myself a mother. Of course I understand. But I can understand Llewelyn's anger, too. If only you had come to him first . . ."

Resentment flickered, failed to catch. Was Catherine's caution truly so surprising? Joanna doubted that in all of her married life she'd ever acted independently of Rhys. Moreover, she looked ghastly, looked frail and thin and colorless, had aged shockingly in these months of widowhood. "I did not mean to burden you with my troubles, Catherine. We'll talk of them no more," Joanna promised, and kept to that resolve for the remainder of her stay.

When Joanna returned to Aber at dusk the following day, she was tired and dispirited. With each visit to Catherine, she could see the distance between them widening, could see in Catherine only a gentle ghost of the lively, loving woman she'd once been. But she did not know how to arrest the drift; her every lifeline seemed to fall short of Catherine's indifferent fingers.

Her mood did not improve on finding her bedchamber in disarray. Not only had Madlen taken advantage of her absence to sleep in Joanna's feather bed, she'd neglected to make it up afterward. Moreover, several of Joanna's more expensive gowns were spread helter-skelter about the chamber, and Joanna doubted Madlen's glib explanation that she'd been sorting them out; trying them on was more likely. Joanna was annoyed, but Glynis was outraged and began to berate the younger girl for such unseemly behavior.

Madlen was quite unperturbed by Glynis's ire. Nor was she apprehensive of losing her place in Joanna's household; she was comfortably confident that Joanna would overlook all but the most egregious of impudences, for she was a cousin once removed of Ednyved. But Madlen still had no liking for reprimands, and she sought to avoid one now with a tried-and-true tactic, diversion.

"Madame, I have wondrous news for you! A letter arrived this forenoon from your lord husband. He says the war is going very well for us. The English are running low on food, are sore beset by our men, and they're losing their will to fight, are squabbling amongst themselves. Lord Llewelyn has cut off their supply lines, even captured a great Norman lord when he ambushed a foraging party, one who'll bring a goodly ransom. He writes that he expects the war will soon be over, that Hubert de Burgh will have to abandon the castle he hoped to build at Pen y Castell and withdraw from Wales."

"I am not going to ask how you know the contents of my husband's letter . . . not yet. Right now I just want you to fetch it for me, and be quick!"

"Madame, I would not pry into your letter! I cannot read! Lord Adda shared it with us in the great hall."

Joanna could not hide her dismay. "The letter was to Adda? Not to me?"

"No, Madame, not to you." Not spiteful, just oblivious, Madlen added blithely, "Oh, but Lord Llewelyn did include a message for you in the letter. He sent that captive Norman lord to us for safekeeping, but he says the lord is to be treated as a hostage of high rank, not as a common prisoner, and he is to be given the freedom of the court, as he pledged his knight's honor he'd not try to escape. Yet our lord would as soon rely upon a more tangible barrier than an enemy's honor, and he thinks it best to put a swift current betwixt the lord and temptation. That was his message, that you should at once move the court to the isle of Môn."

Joanna spun about, moved to the window so she'd not betray herself with burning color. Almost immediately, though, she recoiled, having caught sight of Senena crossing the courtyard. "What is she doing here, Madlen?"

"The Lady Senena? She came back yesterday, is making arrangements to send some of Lord Gruffydd's household goods to Deganwy: his favorite feather bed, wall hangings, and the like." Madlen gave Joanna a look of avid curiosity, wishing that just once Joanna might confide in her, share those intimate details about which she could now only speculate. But Joanna was silent, and she began to pick up the discarded dresses with a sigh of frustration. So much excitement—Lord Gruffydd's confinement, Lord Llewelyn's quarrel with her lady, war with the English—and she was at the very heart of it all. But what good did it do her when her lady hoarded her secrets like a miser?

Joanna's anger had not yet abated by the time she entered the great hall. In truth, she welcomed her resentment, her sense of injury, for it kept her fear at bay. Llewelyn's silence was becoming more and more ominous. For the first time she found herself thinking the unthinkable: What if Llewelyn could not forgive her?

Much to Joanna's relief, Senena was not in the hall. She started toward the dais, while Madlen chattered on cheerfully at her side. "There is the Norman lord, Madame. I think he's very handsome, in truth. And I've never known a Norman to speak

such perfect Welsh; he sounds verily like a Welshman. Not that I
mean to say your Welsh is so faulty, but— Madame?'' Madlen all
but bumped into Joanna, so suddenly had she stopped. ''Madame, you look so queer of a sudden! Why, I'd almost think
you'd seen a demon spirit of some sort. You know Lord de
Braose?''

Joanna swallowed. ''Yes,'' she said. ''I know him.''

As Llewelyn's daughter by marriage, the mother of his grandchildren, Senena had every right to be at his court, however unwelcome Joanna found her presence. Senena made no more accusations,
managed a brittle, courtesy in response to Joanna's strained
civility. But she watched Joanna constantly, with narrowed grey
eyes full of accusation and implacable hate.

Will de Braose's manners were less forced. To be taken captive in warfare was not an uncommon occurrence, and while
costly, it was not shaming. Will accepted his plight with the
fatalistic sangfroid of a man sure he'd eventually be able to
purchase his freedom. If at Chester Castle he could see Joanna
only as John's daughter, he took care to accord her now the
public politeness due Llewelyn's wife. But like Senena, he, too,
followed her with his eyes, eyes no less grey than Senena's, and
although not as overtly hostile, somehow even more disquieting.

Joanna had always enjoyed their stays on Môn; she liked the
island climate, loved the magnificent views of the mainland
mountain ranges. But now she began to feel as if Môn were as
much her prison as Will's. She came to dread the evening meal,
when she could neither avoid nor ignore her unwelcome guests,
and she did whatever she could to make the dinner hour her only
point of contact with Will and Senena. She took to riding the
eight miles to Tregarnedd, passing the mornings with Catherine.
In the afternoons she and Glynis went for long walks around
Rhosyr, and when Glynis fretted that Llewelyn would not approve of their wandering about unescorted, Joanna then refused
even Glynis's company, continued her walks in defiant solitude.

Ordinarily she walked in the meadows near Rhosyr, taking
care not to venture into the marshlands that lay off to the west,
where the River Cefni wound its way to the sea. But on this
particular afternoon she wandered down to the beach. The strait
was rough, the winds coming not from the usual southwest but
from the east, what the Welsh called *gwynt coch Amythig*, the red
wind of Shrewsbury. Joanna was just about to turn back when
she rounded a sand dune, saw Will de Braose standing by the

water's edge. She spun about, but not in time. Topaz had begun to bark, and she heard Will calling her name.

He was panting slightly by the time he reached her. "Why are you so set upon avoiding me?"

His smile was challenging enough to sting her into a rude rejoinder: "Possibly because I do not like you much."

Unfazed, he laughed. "Do you know what I think? I think you're afraid of me."

Even after so many years in Wales, Joanna knew but one Welsh obscenity. She used it now, snapping, *"Twll dy dîn,"* and then turning on her heel. Will caught up with her in two strides and, still laughing, put his hand upon her arm.

Joanna gave him no chance to speak. She pulled free, faced him with such fury that his laughter stilled. "If you ever touch me again, I will have you taken by force to Dolbadarn Castle and confined there till my husband's return."

He arched a brow. "I do not think your husband would like that. He gave orders that I was to be well treated."

At this moment Joanna did not much care what Llewelyn liked or not, and she almost blurted that out, catching herself just in time. "You've had one warning," she said coldly. "That is all you get." And this time when she turned away, he made no attempt to stop her.

On one of her walks, Joanna had come upon an abandoned hut. A simple wattle-and-daub structure, circular in shape, it put Joanna in mind of the *hafods* she'd seen so often on the mainland, rudely built houses occupied only during those summer months when the Welsh drove their flocks to higher pastures. It surprised her to find a *hafod* here on the flatlands; she could only surmise that some unknown herdsman had once sought to fatten his sheep on the salty marsh grass. Whatever the reason for its existence, Joanna was grateful for the discovery, for October was a month of sudden rains and the hut provided welcome shelter, a solitary refuge from the antagonisms and tensions swirling about Rhosyr.

As the days drew closer to October 19, Joanna was caught up in a treacherous tide from her past, a backwash of painful memories. John always weighed heavier on her thoughts as the anniversary of his death approached, but never so oppressively as this. Suddenly she found herself yearning to make a pilgrimage to Worcester, to pray in the shadow of her father's tomb and have a Requiem Mass said for his tormented soul. So very strong was the urge that it invoked in her a sense of superstitious unease; what if John himself was struggling to reach her, beseeching her help in escaping the sufferings of Purgatory? But even if it was truly so, she was powerless, trapped in Wales by yet another of her husband's wars.

That was unfair to Llewelyn and she knew it, knew this latest war had been Hubert de Burgh's doing. But she was not particularly concerned about fairness, not on this grey October noon after yet another sleepless night, a night of tallying up grievances, marital debts long overdue. How fair was Llewelyn being to her? Was it fair to send Will de Braose to their court, knowing how she dreaded contact with any member of Maude's family? Was it fair to let a full month of silence go by? And when he returned, what then?

Would he expect her to beg his forgiveness, to disavow the action that might well have saved Davydd's life? Yet if he was still angry, what choice would she have? She'd have to placate him, to be properly remorseful and contrite, if that was what it took to heal her marriage. And while she did not question the cost, for she loved her husband, she could muster up no eagerness for a reconciliation such as that.

Glynis had insisted upon packing a basket for her, and when it began to rain, Joanna spread a blanket upon the *hafod* floor, prepared to eat a picnic meal under Topaz's hopeful eye. The sun soon broke through the cloud cover, spangling the dripping trees with iridescent light and giving false promise of abiding summer warmth. However brief this respite from the rain, it was heralded by a resurgence of meadowland music, the trills of thrush and wren, the raucous cawing of jackdaw. Joanna even thought she heard the nightjar's whistle and quickly crossed herself, for it was known to the Welsh as the *Aderyn corff,* the corpse bird.

When Topaz bounded up, darted for the door, Joanna rose, too. Although she reached for her eating knife at sound of the dog's barking, hers was a gesture more of inbred caution than of alarm, for she knew there were neither wolves nor boars on the island, and she did not fear men; it was inconceivable to her that any Welshman would dare to offer insult or injury to Llewelyn's wife. "Topaz, come!" she called, and the dog came frisking back into the *hafod*. A moment later a man's shadow fell across the doorway, blocking out the sun.

"Jesú, but you're a hard woman to track down," Will complained, bending over to pat the spaniel, who was—to Joanna's intense annoyance—fawning upon him as if he were family.

"You admit it, then?" she demanded. "You were following me?"

"Of course I was. I had no choice, what with you bound and determined to shun me at court. I thought if I could find you alone, mayhap you'd not be so quick to bolt."

Joanna was infuriated by the imagery his words suggested, that she was a skittish, high-strung filly to be gentled with soft words and sugar lumps. She was also faintly afraid, instinctively sensing danger of some sort. "I do not want you here. And if you do not leave, I shall."

He shrugged and moved aside so he no longer blocked the doorway. Nor did he attempt to touch her as she brushed past him. But as she stepped out into the sunlight, he said softly, "You truly are afraid of me, Joanna. Why?"

Joanna stopped, turned reluctantly back to face him. "Just what do you want from me?"

"To talk. I think I owe you an apology." He was standing in shadow, and she moved cautiously back into the *hafod* so she could see his face. He did not seem to be mocking her, but she was still assailed by doubts; who knew the depths of those inscrutable grey eyes?

"You said you like me not. I expect I gave you cause, that night at Chester Castle. But you do not strike me as a woman who'd nurse a grudge. Can we not agree that I was in my cups and put it behind us?"

"Yes . . . if I could be sure you mean what you say."

"I do." He smiled, ever so slightly. "I cannot say I regret kissing you; that would be both unchivalrous and untrue. But I do regret hurting you, and I regret lying to you."

Joanna took a step closer. "Lying to me? When?"

"When I told you I now believed in blood guilt for women. For I do not, Joanna, not for you."

Joanna bit her lip, said nothing. Rarely had she been so torn, so pulled by ambivalent emotions. Will's words could not have been better calculated to disarm her defenses; she wanted to believe him, to believe Maude's ghost could be exorcised at long last. But a second self stood apart and jeered: What was this if not the sugar lump? She wavered, and then chose to heed the voice of her heart. "I would rather bury a grudge than nurture it. If you truly want that night forgotten, it is, then."

Will smiled. "Let us say, then, that we are friends reunited for the first time in many years, that we last met on that beach at

Cricieth. Agreed?'' And when she nodded, he gestured toward the basket. "Have you enough for two? I'm famished."

Taking her consent for granted, he sat down on the blanket, began to root in the basket. "Glory to God, roast chicken!" he exclaimed, with such boyish exuberance, such irrepressible enthusiasm that Joanna could not help herself; she sat down, too.

Will pushed the basket toward her. "Now that I think on it, I lied to you once before. You remember asking me why I'd come to your rescue that day on the beach? I told you it was because I wanted to do Gruffydd an ill turn, and that was true enough. But it was more than that. I was rather taken with you, Lady Joanna, thought you quite the most alluring, exotic creature I'd ever seen!" He grinned suddenly. "Every lad should have a memory like that tucked away, remembrances of a beautiful older woman who helped to guide him along the way to manhood. Regrettably, we never reached that road, but . . .''

Joanna suspected she should be offended, but in all honesty she was not. Instead she felt a certain guilty pleasure in knowing Will found her desirable, even now at thirty and seven. But she did not think it wise to allow the conversation to take too intimate a turn, and she said hastily, "Will, I think I'd best say this plain out. I know that for many wives the line between friendship and flirtation blurs, but not for me. I want a friend, not a lover."

Will laughed. "Who has been telling tales on me—Gwladys?" He was one of those men who talked with his hands, and as he gestured now, he brought his drumstick too close to Topaz's nose. She took that as an invitation, snatched it as Will gave a startled yelp and Joanna cried, "Stop her, Will! A chicken bone can choke her!"

It took several chaotic moments before they managed to retrieve the bone from the disgruntled dog. Will finally collapsed, laughing, on the blanket as Joanna stripped the bone of meat and hand-fed it to Topaz. "I cannot believe all this bother about a dog. Are you always so tender toward those you love? If so, your husband is indeed a lucky man."

"Yes," Joanna said very evenly, "he is." Will was sucking on a finger, claiming the dog had bitten him. His hair had tumbled down across his forehead; it shone like silver where the sun touched it, and she wondered how it would feel. "I ought to be getting back," she said abruptly, and he sat up at once, began to protest.

"Not yet. If you go, I'll have nothing to do but return to Rhosyr, brood about the exorbitant ransom your husband will

demand for my release. Or try to coax a civil word from the
sour-tongued Senena. On my first day here, I did but bid her
good morrow, and she drew back her skirts as if she'd just come
across a pox-ridden beggar!''

Joanna had to laugh. "You have not changed as much as I first
thought," she said, and Will grinned.

"By all accounts, that holds true for Gruffydd, too. He was
God's greatest fool at fourteen, is no less of one today. Tell me,
Joanna, just how did he end up at Deganwy Castle? I've been
indulging in some discreet eavesdropping, enough to gather you
had a hand in it."

Joanna's jaw muscles tensed. "Yes," she said defiantly. "I
did. I deliberately provoked Gruffydd into a heedless rage, hoping he'd force my husband into banishing him. Why? Are you
going to stand in judgment upon me, too? I suppose you think a
woman has no right to meddle in the concerns of men, that I
ought to have done nothing, just let my son lose—''

"Do I get a chance to speak? I think you ought to be proud of
yourself."

"Truly?" Joanna said uncertainly. "You mean that?"

"Indeed I do. I'll grant you, I might feel differently if you
were my wife and pulled such a trick on me. But since you are
not, I am free to give credit where due. It was a deed well done,
Joanna. Just think upon what befell Rhys Gryg last year. His own
son lured him to Llanarthneu, took him prisoner, and held him
till he agreed to yield Llandovery Castle. Gruffydd may be half
mad; in truth, I think he is. But so is a woodhound, and if it bites
you, you're like to die."

"You do understand! I had to give Davydd time to reach
manhood, Will, had to put him first."

He nodded. "Is this why you've been so unhappy, Joanna?
Because your husband blames you for what happened?"

Joanna had no intention whatsoever of discussing either her
unhappiness or Llewelyn's anger. "My husband does not blame
me, Will. If I've seemed disquieted, it is because of Senena."
Casting about for a safer topic of conversation, she said hurriedly, "But I do not want to talk of her. I'd rather hear about
you. I know you wed the Earl of Pembroke's sister. And I seem
to remember Gwladys telling me you have daughters. How old
are they? What are their names?"

"Daughters I have, indeed, in overabundance," he said ruefully. "No less than four! My oldest is nigh on nine, the young-

est still in her cradle. We christened them with the family names
of de Braose and Marshal: Isabella, Eva, Eleanor . . . and Maude.''

Maude. Of course he'd have named a daughter after the grandmother he loved. Fool that she was, had she truly thought they
could ever be friends? Joanna rose, sought to busy herself in
brushing off her skirt. ''I have to go,'' she said, not meeting his
eyes.

He rose, too. ''Joanna, wait. There is something I must ask
you. Your son Davydd told me that you and John were estranged
during the last years of his life. Is that true?''

''I do not want to talk about it, Will.''

''Joanna, I want—nay, need to know.''

Joanna's throat had tightened. ''Why? What does it matter
now?''

''It matters,'' he said grimly. ''You could not have loved him,
not a man like that. What sort of father could he have been? The
Angevin temper was one with legend. The Devil's brood. And
John . . . John was the worst of the lot. You had to have suffered
at his hands, to have feared him.''

''No, Will. No, it . . . it was not like that. My father was
always good to me.''

''I do not believe that, do not believe you. Why do you defend
him to me? Christ, if any man knows the truth about John, I do!''

''I am not defending him! I am not denying what he has done.
You have every reason to hate him. But I will not lie to you.
Whatever evil he may have committed, he was still a kind father,
even a loving one.''

''A loving father? God in Heaven, do you hear yourself? He
was accursed, utterly evil and beyond redemption, and for you
to—''

''No!'' Joanna's voice was shaking. ''My father repented his
sins, died in God's grace. His soul is in Purgatory, not in Hell.
The Almighty says there is forgiveness for all, that—''

''Not for John. Never for John!''

''Do not say that!'' Joanna was appalled. ''He did repent ere
he died, and God will forgive him. He was not utterly evil, he
was not! He was capable of kindness, too, and the Almighty will
take that into account when judging him.''

''Kind? Because he gave you hair ribbons and sugared quince?
Do you truly think such trifles can be balanced against the
gallows, the rotting bodies?''

''I was not talking of trifles!'' Joanna drew a labored breath,
sought to call to mind John's acts of charity, of compassion.

''My father truly loved England, as his father and brother did not. And he cared for his subjects' weal. He was the most accessible of Kings, was hearing appeals even whilst fighting for his throne, that last fortnight of his life.''

When Will would have interrupted, she cried, ''No, hear me out! You asked for particulars and you shall have them. The son of a friend was recently stricken with leprosy. I know I need not tell you the horrors of such a fate. Yet, as pitiful as the leper's plight is, it can be even more wretched if his king or lord lacks pity. Under such lords, lepers have ofttimes been burnt, even buried alive. But my father did pity them, Will, and he did whatever he could to ease their travail. At Shrewsbury he entitled the lepers to a portion of all flour sold at market. At Bristol he granted lepers a settlement of their own, where they could dwell under the protection of the crown. He even founded St Leonard's Hospital at Lancaster long ere he became King, when he was but two and twenty! Do such acts sound like trifles to you? Would a man utterly evil care for the least of his brethren?''

''You want to talk of John's pity? Let's begin, then, at Windsor Castle. I am sure my grandmother and uncle were fearful, for they knew John well. But I doubt even they could have guessed what he had in mind for them. They were dragged to an underground dungeon, thrust into the dark, and left to die. They were given no candles, no water, no food but a basket of oats and an uncooked ham. For ten days they were left alone in that hellhole, with the door barred against their screams. On the eleventh day the guards entered the cell, found them both dead. There was no way of knowing just when they'd died, how long their suffering had lasted. The guards could tell, though, that my uncle had died first and that my grandmother had gone mad at the last. Shall I tell you why, Joanna? Shall I tell you how they knew that?''

''No,'' she whispered. ''No, please . . .''

''Because my uncle's cheek was bitten and chewed, as if gnawed by a rat. But it was not a rat who'd eaten his flesh, it was his own mother. Those were her teethmarks in his face. That was what she'd been driven to in the final hours of her life, by your father, by the man you call kind!''

He'd grasped Joanna's wrist, forcing her to listen. When he released her, she stumbled backward, fled the hut. Her stomach was heaving and she fell to her knees on the grass, lay prone as the trees whirled above her head, spinning in sickening circles. She clutched tufts of grass, clung as if the earth itself were falling away from her. She was weeping as Will knelt beside her.

Gathering her into his arms, he held her as if she were a child, and for a time there was no sound but that of her choked sobbing, the whimpering of her spaniel.

"I'm going to take you back inside now." The voice was so gentle that she wondered if it was truly Will's, but she obediently put her arms around his neck and he lifted her up, carried her back to the shelter of the *hafod*. "Here," he said, handing her his flask. "Drink." She did; the liquid was warm and so heavily spiced that she choked anew. It burned her throat, set her head spinning. She drank again, at his insistence, but shook her head weakly when he offered the flask a third time.

The last of her tears squeezed through her lashes. "Will, I'm sorry, so sorry . . ."

"So am I, Joanna. I ought never to have told you that. There've been times," he confessed, "when I'd have given up my chances of salvation if only I'd not known, if only I could forget . . ."

Joanna shuddered. "How could your father have told you? Why did you have to know?"

He reached out, touched her tearstained face. "You were weeping for me? For that fourteen-year-old boy?"

Joanna shuddered again, and when he put his arm around her, she did not move away. "There was no need for you to know, no need . . ." She turned so she could look up into his face, into eyes fringed with surprisingly long, fair lashes. "You were so young. How could you live with pain like that?"

"By learning to hate. Not just John. The men he trusted, the men who waxed fat on his favor, men like Hubert de Burgh and Peter des Roches. Your Uncle Salisbury."

"And me?"

"I wanted to hate you, thought I did . . . until I saw you again at Chester Castle. But you know that, Joanna. You know how much I wanted you, how much I want you right now."

"Will, I cannot . . ." But he was leaning toward her, covering her mouth with his. His breathing had quickened, but there was no urgency in his kiss, not yet. It was both unexpected and reassuring, this gentleness; he had about him such unsettling undertones of violence that it was startling, somehow, to find he could be so tender a lover. Joanna knew she had to protest now, while there was still time for protesting, for thinking. But when he kissed her again, she found herself responding, kissing him back.

He was too practiced for awkward fumbling with clothing, slid his hand into the bodice of her gown. She gasped as he cupped her breast, and he gave a low laugh. "God, how I want you! It'll be so good, I promise you . . ." And for Joanna there was only that moment, the feel of his hands on her bared skin, and an urgency to match his own. When he lowered her back onto the blanket, she reached up, drew him down into an impassioned embrace, and it was not long before he was murmuring, "Now, love. Spread your thighs for me. Ah, yes, yes . . ." There was a tense moment in which they feared he was too ready, too eager. But he was able to keep control, moving slowly at first, deliberately, until Joanna moaned, dug her nails into his neck, and then he did lose control, but it no longer mattered; there was for them both a shattering release, convulsive and complete.

Will was the first to move, shifting his weight off Joanna and sitting up. She lay still, her head turned away, until he tugged gently on her braid, compelling her toward him. Leaning over, he kissed her possessively on the mouth. "You were worth waiting for," he said, smiling, and Joanna flushed even darker.

"What have I done, Will?" Her voice was muffled, almost inaudible. "My God, what have I done?"

He tilted her chin up, forcing her to meet his eyes. "What you wanted to do. For you did want me, Joanna, just as much as I wanted you."

Joanna's lashes swept down, shadowing her cheek. Sitting up, she pulled her skirt down, began relacing her bliaut. Her fingers were unsteady, but when Will reached over to help, she shook her head. She was on her feet now, retrieving her mantle from the floor. "Will . . . I have to go."

He rose without haste, draped her mantle about her shoulders. "Give me a minute to make myself presentable, and I'll walk back with you."

"No!" She pulled away, staring at him with such wide, frightened eyes that he was both touched and amused.

"What do you fear, Joanna? That people need only glance at us now to know?" Laughing, he caught her by the shoulders, drew her back into his arms. "My love, it does not show in your face. You look no different."

"I feel different. I feel . . ." Joanna's mouth twisted. She turned away, moved rapidly toward the door.

"Joanna." She paused, with obvious reluctance, and he said "I shall be here at noon on the morrow."

"No," she said. "No."

"I'll be waiting for you."

His words stayed with her as she walked back toward Rhosyr. *I'll be waiting for you.* He'd smiled, as if her denial meant nothing, as if sure she'd come to him. Joanna stopped abruptly, stood motionless for so long that Topaz began to whine. Kneeling there on the path, Joanna put her arms around the dog. "What am I to do?" she whispered. "Lady Mary . . ." But she could not pray. Hers was a mortal sin. She had betrayed her marriage vows, betrayed her husband. And on the morrow, what then? For Will was right. She had wanted him, was as much to blame for what happened as he. She did not understand it, could not fully believe it even now, but she could not deny it. She did want Will.

Will reached the *hafod* well before noon. Joanna had been too distraught to think of the blanket and basket. The blanket lay as they'd left it, still rumpled from the weight of their bodies, but the basket had been overturned, emptied by scavenging animals. Will righted the basket, smoothed the blanket, and sat down to wait. At half past twelve he left the *hafod*, stood for some moments squinting up at the sun. He was turning to go back inside when he heard a dog bark. Several birds broke cover, went winging over the hut. The spaniel appeared first, with Joanna following much more slowly.

She was so tense, her approach so hesitant that Will instinctively stayed quite still. She reminded him of a woodland creature, untamed and poised for flight, and he said very quietly, "I was beginning to fear you were not coming."

"I did not think I was."

They regarded each other in rapt silence until Will deemed it safe to move. Stepping toward her, he took her hand. "I thought about you half the night. I kept remembering how you wept, wept for my pain." He smiled, his familiar smile of self-mockery, but to Joanna, unexpectedly suggestive of sadness. "Over the years, many women have wept because of me. But I honestly could recall nary a one weeping *for* me . . . just you."

Joanna had wept again at night, lying alone in Llewelyn's bed. But she did not know whether her tears were for the boy Will had been, or for this madness that had so suddenly come upon her, that had brought her back to the *hafod*, to Will. She closed her eyes, but could still see him behind her lids: tousled hair streaked by the sun, thin mobile mouth, golden lashes and beard, details she'd not even been aware of noticing—a small scar on his right temple, a shaving scratch on his throat. He was very close now; she could feel his breath on her cheek. Her lashes lifted and she saw his mouth soften, curve just before he kissed her.

In the days that followed, Joanna felt as if she were drifting farther and farther from shore, from the sureties of the world she knew, the world she was terrified of losing. She had no appetite at mealtimes, and sleep eluded her; she lay awake some nights till dawn, rose hollow-eyed and racked with guilt, unable to understand why she was jeopardizing her marriage, perhaps even her life, for a man she did not truly know—and yet unable to stay away from him. She knew she did not love him. The sexual attraction between them was undeniably intense, and had been since that night at Chester Castle, for she could see that now, could acknowledge that it had first flared on a darkened stairway in Caesar's Tower. But could she be so foolish as to risk so much for that, for lust? Why, then, had she never been tempted ere this? Why had she never even fantasized about any man but Llewelyn?

Llewelyn. What would he do if her sin was found out? Joanna thought of the French Queen Ingeborg, held fast at Étampes Castle for no fault of her own. She thought of the innocent Lady Alys, confined by Richard in Rouen for six long years. And she thought of the look on Llewelyn's face should he ever learn of her infidelity. But each afternoon she found herself walking in the meadows, toward the *hafod* where Will awaited her.

They would make love on the blanket, and for a brief while Joanna could forget her fears, even her guilt. Sometimes they would eat food Will smuggled from Rhosyr, and they would talk. Lying with his head in her lap, Will was relaxed enough to let down some of his defenses, to trust her with an occasional truth. He spoke of his boyhood at Bramber and Buellt, of his exile in France, conceded he'd earned his reputation for reckless risk-taking. He was intelligent, ambitious, and could be very amusing. He was also cynical and not overly burdened with scruples, was quite candid in admitting that when he wanted something, he set out to get it, rarely counting the cost. But every now and then Joanna would catch glimpses of another Will, glimpses of the boy he'd been and the man he might have become, and at such moments she would feel the sadness of loss, and yet, at the same time, a curious sense of vindication.

She encouraged him to talk about Maude, and as painful as it was, she forced herself to listen attentively, prompted by a hazy hope that dwelling upon happier memories might somehow help him to forget the other, the horror. He talked sometimes of John, with such venom that she suspected he was testing her. She listened in silence to these embittered outbursts, without protest. It shamed her to remember her yearning to visit Worcester, to pray at John's tomb. Each time she thought of what had happened in the darkness of that Windsor dungeon, she was overcome with revulsion and self-loathing. To love a man capable of such cruelty was to condone it, even to make herself an accomplice of sorts. And yet she had loved him, loved him and then grieved for him. Topaz rings and Maltese lapdogs and honeyed words. How cheaply she'd sold herself. How little it had taken to claim her heart.

"How could you have been so rash? Whatever were you thinking of, Will?"

At first Will had been amused by Joanna's anger, but he was beginning to lose patience. "This is ridiculous, Joanna. All I did was to greet you when you entered the hall. I kissed your hand. Why should that give rise to gossip?"

"You kissed my palm, a lover's kiss! Jesus God, Will, what if someone had seen?"

He shrugged. "But no one did, so why are you so fretful?"

"Because Senena was standing not five feet away! You know how she hates me. If she ever suspected—"

He stepped toward her, silenced her with a lingering kiss. "Forget about Senena, love. Let's not waste time quarreling."

"I do not want to quarrel. But it frightens me, Will, that you would take such a risk, and it frightens me even more that you seem to find it amusing." Will was not listening, though, had pulled her back against him, encircling her within his arms, kissing her throat. Joanna yielded, allowed him to draw her down onto the blanket. "Promise me," she said huskily. "Promise me you'll not be so reckless."

It may have been the quarrel, the fact that they'd resolved nothing. It may have been her realization that Will was excited by the danger of discovery, by the very risks she found so frightening. But for the first time the magic failed to take. She could not shut off her thoughts, could not surrender unconditionally to her body's needs, was unable to reach climax. And afterward she was caught up in despair, hers the panicked sensations of a swimmer swept far beyond her depth. She turned on her side so Will would not see that she wept. Never had her sense of foreboding been so strong, a terrified certainty that this could end only in tragedy. The Lord God was a God of wrath, would punish her for so great a sin, would punish her and Will as they deserved. But what of Llewelyn? He would also suffer for her sin, and where was the fairness in that?

Will had been disappointed by their lovemaking; he was too experienced not to know when a woman's response was genuine and when it was feigned. He was irked now by her prolonged silence, and he wondered why women had to complicate things so unduly, why they had to bring so much baggage into bed with them, remorse and regrets and, inevitably, recriminations. Such qualms rarely stopped them from sinning, he thought, just from truly enjoying it. He'd hoped Joanna might be different, should have known what a frail hope that was. Knight's widow or King's daughter, there was not a one of them who seemed capable of taking her pleasure as she found it, not even a woman like Joanna, as passionate as any he'd ever bedded.

"Are you still vexed about Senena? Or are you having conscience pangs?"

"Is that so surprising? Need I remind you that adultery is a sin?"

Will sighed, raised himself up on his elbow. "What kind of sins are there, Joanna?"

"What kinds? Mortal and venial," she said, sounding puzzled, and he shook his head.

"No, my love. There are secret sins and found-out sins, and it is foolish to worry about the first until it becomes the second. Think on it, Joanna. Who are we hurting as long as no one knows?" Leaning over, he nuzzled her neck. "You're not the fool most women are; you ought to have learned that lesson by now."

He meant that as a compliment, for he truly did think she was more intelligent than most of her sex, and he was taken aback by her reaction. She sat up abruptly, gave him a look of utter outrage.

"And just how am I to have learned such a lesson? By practice? You think I've done this before?"

"You're saying you've never taken a lover? I'm the first?" Will was surprised and pleased, but somewhat skeptical, too, and it showed in his face. Joanna jumped to her feet, began tugging at her disheveled clothing. He rose, too, put a hand upon her arm.

"I did not mean to offend you, love. I just did not expect it.

You are a beautiful woman, after all, and must have had more than your share of offers.''

"And you think that is what determines infidelity—opportunity?'' Joanna was even angrier because she saw he was not taking her anger seriously. "By your measure, the only wife to be trusted would be one as plain as homespun. How does your own wife figure in your calculations, Will? I hear she's a handsome woman; am I to assume, then, that she takes lovers?''

"No.'' His voice was suddenly sharp. "No, she does not.''

"I see.'' Joanna reached for her mantle, fumbled with the catch. He stepped in front of her, barring her way.

"Joanna, you do not understand.''

"You explain it to me then, Will. Explain why it is right for me to dishonor my marriage vows, and wrong for your wife.''

"This is such an absurd argument, so utterly needless. Your pride is too tender, love; you see insults where none was intended. If you say I am your first lover, of course I believe you. And in truth, I'm very flattered.'' He sought to unfasten the catch of her mantle. "Do not go, not yet.'' The mantle slipped from her shoulders, fell to the floor at her feet. "Stay with me,'' he said coaxingly. "Do you not want to?''

"Yes,'' Joanna confessed. "I hate to quarrel. But can you not see why I was upset? I know what we are doing is wrong, cannot pretend otherwise. And for all your talk of secret sins, you know it, too, Will. If adultery is a sin for your wife, it is no less a sin for me. And if—''

"Will you forget about Eva? I was not saying that Eva is more virtuous than you. If her circumstances were like unto yours, she, too, might stray. That is all I meant, love, I swear.''

Joanna was not mollified, for he had inflicted a hurt no less painful for being unintentional. "How are my circumstances so different from Eva's?''

Ignoring her challenging tone, he put his arms around her, drew her close. She stood irresolute for a moment, and then, as his hands slid up from her waist to her breasts, she sighed softly, rested her head against his chest.

"Well, to begin with, your blood runs much hotter than Eva's.'' He laughed, and Joanna bit her lip to keep from laughing, too.

"You have a wicked tongue,'' she chided. "A man should not talk so of his wife.''

"Not even to his mistress? I do but speak the truth. You are more passionate than Eva. Fairer to look upon. Far more exciting in bed. I do not doubt Eva could have been quite content in a nunnery. Could you say the same, sweetheart?'' he teased, and to his delighted amusement, Joanna actually blushed. ''No, my love, you could not. It's more than a waste, it's a crime against nature to fetter a woman like you to an aging husband.''

Joanna wrenched free. ''How dare you!'' Her voice was low, but so full of rage that for a moment Will merely stared at her in surprise.

''Joanna?'' He moved toward her, but she backed away, out of reach. He'd never seen eyes as green as hers, and he found himself thinking suddenly of the tales he'd heard of her fabled grandmother, the outrageous and autocratic Eleanor of Aquitaine. But he was rapidly tiring of these displays of Angevin temper. ''Now what's wrong? Jesú, but your nerves are on the raw today! I did but speak another truth, that you are wed to a man much older than you. Nigh on twenty years older. I am being blunt, but not unkind. A man cannot be blamed for growing old. But neither can a woman for wanting what he can no longer give. So what harm if we—''

''You fool!'' Joanna all but spat the words. ''You vain, boastful fool. You talk so glibly about truths. Let me give you one, then. Yes, Llewelyn is five and fifty and you're but two and thirty. But for all that, he is twice the man you could ever hope to be, in bed or out!''

''Is he now?'' Will had gone rigid, first incredulous and then infuriated. ''Then suppose you tell me this. If you're such a satisfied wife, why have I been able to tumble you all week long on the floor of this stinking *hafod?*''

Joanna had begun to tremble. ''I do not know,'' she admitted, sounding not so much angry now as despairing. ''God help me, I do not know. But no more. May the Blessed Mary be my witness, no more!''

Snatching up her mantle, she whirled, ran from the *hafod*, ran until she was sobbing for breath, ran until the meadows were misted by a light, warming rain and she saw ahead the distant timbered walls of Llewelyn's manor.

Joanna left Rhosyr that same afternoon, was gone by the time Will returned to the manor. Catherine showed no surprise at her unexpected arrival, welcomed her as if hers was a visit planned long in advance. She found some comfort in Catherine's quiet company, but Catherine could not give her the advice she most needed, could not tell her what to do about Will. Joanna dared not confide in her, could not even risk confessing to her chaplain.

Until she could find a way to confess in anonymity, she must live with a mortal sin upon her soul. As frightened as she was at being denied absolution, she was even more fearful of blaspheming her vow. She had sworn to the Blessed Virgin that she would not bed with Will again. And she had to keep that vow. She had betrayed Llewelyn, betrayed herself. She could not betray the Lady Mary, too. But could she trust herself? She must pray for strength, must find it in her to resist temptation. And she must somehow see to it that she and Will were never alone again.

Joanna passed three days at Tregarnedd, returned to Rhosyr with great reluctance. The sun had been elusive all morning, making weak forays through the clouds rolling in off the Irish Sea, and by the time Joanna dismounted in the manor bailey, she could no longer see her shadow.

"Have Madlen see to the unpacking, Glynis. I'm sure she's done not a stitch of work whilst we were gone." Topaz was sprinting toward her, and Joanna bent down, gathered the whimpering little animal into her arms, absurdly grateful for at least one heartfelt welcome.

"Mama!"

"Davydd?" She straightened up, watched wordlessly as her son hastened toward her. As he'd grown into manhood, he'd become less and less given to public displays of affection. But he showed no such reticence now, embraced Joanna warmly.

"When did you get back? Davydd, why did you not send word to Tregarnedd?"

"We rode in last night, would have dispatched a messenger this morn."

"But why are you back so soon? Your father . . . he's not hurt? Davydd, tell me if—"

"He's fine, Mama, truly. He's in the great hall, discussing ransom terms with Will de Braose. All is well, could not be better. We won, Mama. The war is over."

"Llewelyn . . . Llewelyn is with Will?"

Davydd nodded. "Have you no questions for me? Do you not want to hear how we triumphed over the English? We gave them no respite, harassed them day and night, finally forced them to make peace. We met with Henry and Hubert de Burgh and they agreed to dismantle Hubert's new castle, to withdraw at once from Ceri, whilst Papa agreed to assume the costs of the expedition. That was truly clever of him, Mama, for Henry is now grateful to Papa for helping him save face, and he's begun to blame de Burgh for the entire debacle." Davydd grinned. "Papa can put a fox to shame at times. And the best part of the jest is this. The three thousand marks Papa is to pay Henry—that is the amount he is demanding for Will's release!"

"And Will agreed to this? He is to be freed?"

"Well, there's more to it than that, but I'll let Papa tell you the rest. Come on, let's tell him you're here." When Joanna did not move, Davydd turned back with a quizzical smile. "Mama? Are you not coming?"

"No, I . . . I want to change my gown first. I was not expecting . . ." Joanna's voice trailed off in confusion, but Davydd just laughed.

"Mama, you look fine," he insisted, as Glynis chimed in, assuring Joanna that the gown was quite becoming.

"But . . . but it's green," Joanna said, very low, and both Davydd and Glynis looked at her in surprise.

"Mama, green is your favorite color!"

Joanna said nothing. Green was her favorite and most flattering hue. It was also the symbolic shade of fidelity. Abandoning further protests, she allowed Davydd to lead her into the hall.

Davydd was still talking about their campaign, laughing as he told her de Burgh's half-built castle was now known as "Hubert's Folly." But Joanna was no longer listening. Llewelyn and Will were seated together by the open hearth; they seemed surprisingly at ease with one another, were talking with animation, and as she watched, they exchanged smiles. And then they were turning, getting to their feet as she walked toward them.

Joanna's mouth was suddenly parched; she sought to shape it into a smile, said as calmly as she could, "Welcome home, Llewelyn." Had they been alone, she would have waited for his rejoinder, taken her cue from that. But with Will's eyes upon her, she felt she had no choice but to step forward, to kiss Llewelyn lightly on the mouth. His response told her nothing; even if he was still furious with her, he'd never have been so churlish as to rebuff her in public. His face was impassive; as well as she knew him, she could not read his expression.

"You look pale," he said. "Have you been ailing?"

She shook her head, started visibly when Will chose that moment to interject himself into the conversation. "I'm glad you're back, Madame. I confess it was rather lonely here the past few days, what with both you and the Lady Senena gone." And then, before she could anticipate him, he caught her hand, brought it up to his mouth, with impeccable manners and laughing eyes.

Joanna's reaction was instinctive and vehement; she jerked her hand away. They were all staring at her now, Will with poorly concealed amusement, Davydd with surprise, and Llewelyn with a look that brought the blood up into her face, a look of curiosity . . . and conjecture. "Actually, you were right, Llewelyn," she said unsteadily. "I do not feel well. If you'll excuse me, I think I shall go and lie down." Not waiting, not daring to wait, she turned and walked swiftly from the hall, feeling their eyes upon her all the while.

Upon reaching her bedchamber, Joanna dismissed her maids. She'd decided she really would lie down, hoping in that way to avoid a discussion with Llewelyn, should he seek her out. She stripped to her chemise, began to unbraid her hair. But her fingers had become infuriatingly clumsy; she kept dropping hairpins and brush, even a small glass bottle of her favorite scent. Glass was very much a luxury, and this perfume vial was of a particularly delicate design, the handiwork of a Genoan master craftsman. With a cry of dismay, Joanna knelt, began to search the rushes for the broken shards. But once she'd salvaged the fragments, she saw the bottle was beyond repair. She stared down at the glass splinters, and suddenly her eyes were brimming over with tears. Sitting on the floor in the middle of her bedchamber, she began to cry.

Llewelyn found himself hesitating before the door, not at all sure what sort of reception he would get. The memory came to him then of another quarrel with Joanna, another occasion when he'd stood before a bedchamber door, reluctant to go in. The memory was very vivid for being more than twenty years old; it had been their first true quarrel, but a memorable reconciliation, leading to the consummation of their marriage. He no longer hesitated, reached for the latch.

"Joanna?" He was beside her at once, brushing back the cascading dark hair that hid her face. At his touch, she fell forward into his arms, buried her face in his shoulder. Her sobbing was spasmodic, out of control, but he was more alarmed by her violent trembling, like one with the ague. He was baffled to discover that she was clutching several broken pieces of glass; he had to pry her fingers loose before she'd drop them. In all the years of their marriage, he'd never seen her weep like this, as a maltreated child might weep, helplessly, utterly without hope.

When he lifted her in his arms, she felt as light as a child, too, frighteningly fragile. After putting her down upon the bed, he started to rise, but she clung to him and he sat beside her, holding her as she wept.

At last her sobs began to subside. She no longer sounded so incoherent and he leaned over, put his lips to her forehead. Although she did not feel feverish, he was not yet reassured. "Shall I summon my physician?"

Her head moved on the pillow, tossed emphatically from side to side. He rose, crossed to the washing laver, and came back to the bed. Joanna stirred when he gently wiped her face with a wet cloth, lay looking up at him with tears silently trickling from the corners of her eyes. "I'm sorry," she whispered. "I'm so sorry. I love you, I do. I never meant for it to happen, I swear it . . ."

"I know that, *breila.*"

"You . . . you know?"

"Why should that surprise you so? You wanted to see Gruffydd banished, not imprisoned. That was no part of your plan. Did you think I doubted that?"

"Gruffydd." Joanna closed her eyes. "No," she echoed faintly, "that was no part of my plan . . ."

Llewelyn regarded her in silence for several moments. The signs of strain were much more apparent now than they'd been in the hall, the hollowed cheekbones, the smudges that lurked like bruises under her eyes, the way her fingers plucked aimlessly at the coverlets. "I thought I knew you so well," he said, saw her flinch. "But I could not have misjudged your mood more. I knew you were angry with me, and upset. But I did not understand how truly troubled you were." Their time apart had been for the best, or so he'd thought, for it had given him the opportunity to come to terms with his own anger, with resentments he alone could resolve. But Joanna's face told him a far different story, told him their estrangement had done much more damage than he'd realized.

Tears still seeped through Joanna's lashes. She had been angry with Llewelyn, very angry. She'd blamed him for his stubbornness, for his unwillingness to understand, for words spoken in anger, slights to her pride, and above all, for that last taunt flung at her as he'd ridden out of the stable. But how insignificant those complaints seemed now, how trivial when weighed against the enormity of her sin, her betrayal.

"Can you forgive me, Llewelyn? In all honesty, can you forgive me?"

"I'll not lie to you, Joanna. You were wrong. You should have come to me, and I'll never fully understand why you did not.'' But he spoke without anger, for he'd concluded that he had no choice but to forgive her. If he did not, the grievance was likely to fester, an untreated wound dripping daily poison until, in time, the marriage itself would be infected.

"Yes," he said, "I do forgive you," and it was easier than he'd thought it would be; her contrition was balm in and of itself.

Joanna struggled to sit up. "Hold me," she implored. "Hold me so tightly that I can believe you'll never let me go."

He obliged with a smile, held her close, listening to the shuddering sounds of her breath, smoothing her long, tangled hair. "No more tears," he murmured, "lest we both become waterlogged."

"I never wanted you to be hurt, Llewelyn, never. You must believe that, beloved."

Llewelyn did not want to talk about Gruffydd, did not want to think about Deganwy Castle. "Hush, *breila*, hush." He pressed his mouth to her swollen eyelids, continued to stroke her hair. Her perfume was beguilingly familiar; he'd missed her scent, her softness, missed waking up beside her in the morning, reaching for her in the night.

"Are you feeling better now?" When she nodded, he ran his fingers caressingly along her throat. "Then how would you like to give me a proper welcome home? I did win a war, after all."

He laughed, leaned over to kiss her, and was utterly taken aback when she recoiled, gasping, "No!"

"We've played some intriguing games in bed, but I cannot say this one appeals to me, Joanna, would as soon we save it for another time." He frowned. "Unless you truly are ailing?"

"No, beloved, I am fine." Joanna's reaction had been both involuntary and irrational. But for one panicked moment, she'd actually found herself thinking that Llewelyn had only to kiss her to know she'd been unfaithful. "I did not mean to cry out like that. I am not ailing and it is not the time of my flux. Of course I want to make love with you; when do I not? It's just that . . . that I was expecting Glynis to come in at any moment. If you would but bar the door, my love, I'm sure we can find a game more to your liking."

She lay back against the pillows. But by the time he returned to the bed, she was beset by a new fear. She felt frozen, numbed, emotionally drained. What if she could not respond to him?

At first she did find it difficult to relax, to blot out all but the feel of his hands and mouth on her body. Llewelyn was in no hurry, though. He'd long ago learned that pleasures could be all the sweeter for being prolonged, but as his body's slowing reflexes compelled him, of necessity, to pace himself more prudently, he'd discovered that delay could act upon a woman as an aphrodisiac; the more drawn out and deliberate their lovemaking, the more excited his wife became, and he no longer regretted having lost the immediate and urgent arousals of early youth.

He took his time, and slowly, skillfully, he kindled a fire between them, one that burned hot and bright and eventually became all-consuming. Joanna drifted back to reality with reluctance. Their lovemaking had been more than a physical bonding, a source of intensely intimate and perfect pleasure. For her, it had been a catharsis. For the first time she dared hope that she need not lose her husband. She would never forgive herself, but mayhap it was not too late. If she was well and truly contrite, mayhap the Almighty would show mercy, would let hers remain one of Will's secret sins. If so, she would devote the rest of her life to making Llewelyn happy. She would gratify his every whim, be the wife he deserved, bedmate, companion, confidante, whatever he wished.

"What are you thinking of, *breila?* You look very far away."

"No farther than this," she said, taking his hand and holding it against her heart. "I'd tell you it beats just for you if I were not fearful you'd think me maudlin, hopelessly lovesick. See? You're laughing at me already."

"Just a little." Llewelyn settled himself more comfortably, propped pillows against his back as Joanna rose from the bed, padded barefoot across the chamber to fetch wine. He'd been utterly thankful that she'd been spared the travails of yearly pregnancies, having come so close to losing her in the birthing chamber at Dolwyddelan. But as he looked at her now, he was thinking that there were other benefits, as well, to her subsequent barrenness, for her body had retained the supple muscle tone, the lissome and willowy grace of her youth. His eyes followed the fall of her hair, from breast to hip, and up again to her face. Feeling his gaze upon her, she glanced over her shoulder, smiled radiantly, and he said, "Joanna, what is there between you and Will de Braose?"

Joanna would never know how she managed to continue pouring wine, how she kept her hand steady. Very carefully she set the flagon back on the table. "What do you mean, Llewelyn?"

"The tension in the hall was hard to miss." His voice was dry, his eyes unwavering upon her face. She gripped the wine cup between her palms, took one quick swallow, and then walked

back to the bed. Why had she not foreseen this? Who knew better
than she how keen his eye could be?

"You are right," she said slowly. "I suppose I was not very
good at hiding my feelings. I'm sorry if I was rude. But I find it
very difficult to be in Will de Braose's company. You know how
I feel about his family. And with Will, it is more than I can bear,
for he loved Maude well, and his hatred of John is still green,
still very raw. He told me . . . told me that Maude died mad."

Her shudder was not feigned, was all too real. It did not
escape Llewelyn, nor did the sudden reversion back to "John."
He slid over and she got into bed, handed him the wine cup. "I
thought it was something like that," he said. "Ah, lass, I am
truly sorry."

Joanna forced herself to lift her head, to look into his eyes,
dark eyes full of intelligence and affection . . . and faith. He
loved her, would never suspect her of so base a betrayal. He
trusted her. She'd have to bear that to the end of her days, the
burden of his trust.

Llewelyn put his arm around her shoulders, drew her down
against his chest. "Would it be easier for you if I moved the
court back to Aber, whilst keeping Will here at Rhosyr till his
ransom is paid?"

"Jesú, yes! Oh, yes, please." She kissed his throat, blinking
back tears. She'd thought she'd reached the nadir of shame and
self-loathing on that last day in the *hafod*, raging at Will, at her
incredible folly. But it was infinitely worse now, having to lie to
Llewelyn, to look into his eyes and take such despicable advantage of his love.

"Joanna, I do understand your feelings for the de Braose
family. I know you've never been at ease with any of them. And
I would that I could promise you need never set eyes upon Will
again. But I cannot."

"Llewelyn . . . what are you saying? What are you trying to
tell me?"

She sounded suddenly so frightened that he frowned, bit his
lip. "I want Buellt Castle, *breila*. I've got to have it, for it
commands the upper reaches of the Gwy Valley."

"I . . . I do not understand. Davydd said Will had agreed to
pay you three thousand marks. Surely he'd not yield up Buellt,
too?"

"No, of course not. But he is willing to give it as his
daughter's marriage portion. That is what I am trying to tell you,

Joanna. Will and I have agreed upon an alliance, one secured by
wedlock, the marriage of his eldest daughter and our son.''

"Davydd . . . Davydd is to wed Will's daughter?''

"In time. Isabella is but a little lass yet, so I expect they'll
only plight troth for now." Llewelyn leaned over, tenderly kissed
Joanna's upturned face. "I know this does not please you, love,
and I am sorry. But it cannot be helped.''

Joanna turned her head into his shoulder, brought her hand up
to her mouth, bit down on her fist. She must not laugh. If she did,
she'd not be able to stop. Like her mother. So many years ago,
but Joanna could still hear her, hear peal after peal of that shrill,
hysterical laughter as her mother looked at her, at her bastard
child, her "mistake." *We pay and pay for our sins*, she'd
gasped. *We pay and pay.*

10

DEGANWY, NORTH WALES

September 1229

Llewelyn's grandsons were standing on the stairs of the keep, watching as he rode through the gateway into the inner bailey. The younger boy, his namesake, was a dark, solemn child, a toddler clutching a bedraggled toy. But Owain could have been a ghost from Llewelyn's past. His hair was redder, brighter than Gruffydd's, and his eyes were grey, but for all that, he looked enough like his father at age ten to evoke memories better left buried.

Whether by inheritance or empathy, Owain had adopted his father's body language as his own; the squared shoulders, the jutting little chin were wrenchingly familiar. "Why have you come?" he demanded. "We do not want you here. Go away!"

"Owain, hold your tongue!" Hastening down the stairs, Senena grasped her son by the shoulders. "How dare you speak to Lord Llewelyn like that? He is your Prince and your grandsire, and you owe him respect!"

"But Mama . . ." The boy looked so bewildered that Senena felt a conscience pang; he was, after all, only parroting what he'd heard in their private chamber. She could not risk antagonizing Llewelyn, however, and she said sharply, "See to your little brother. I shall expect you to apologize to your grandfather ere he leaves." Moving forward, then, to greet Llewelyn, she mustered a taut smile. "It was good of you to come."

Llewelyn dismounted, tossed the reins to the nearest man. "You sent word that Gruffydd was asking to see me. Did you think I'd refuse?" He signaled for his men to await him in the great hall, glanced toward Senena once and then again, much more searchingly. "Senena? Gruffydd did ask for me?"

"No." Reaching out, she clutched at his arm. "I lied. I had to lie. It was all I could think to do. Llewelyn, you must see him, talk to him. Please say you will!"

Llewelyn slowly shook his head. "I think it better if I do not, Senena. If he does not want to see me, what would it serve?"

"Wait, please. At least hear me out. You want the truth? I'll tell you, tell you whatever you want to know. I've tried so hard to help Gruffydd, to raise his spirits, to keep him from despairing. But he, of all men, cannot abide confinement. Some days he'll not talk to me at all, and he spends hours standing at the window, never taking his eyes off the horizon, those soaring seagulls." Llewelyn made an involuntary movement, and her hand tightened on his arm. "If you could just see him, Llewelyn, if you could but talk together, mayhap then . . ."

Llewelyn knew better, knew that talking would change nothing. But as he looked into his daughter-in-law's face, he could not refuse her. "Your loyalty does you great credit, lass. I'll talk to him. Just do not expect too much to come of it."

Senena heard only the consent, not the qualification. "Thank you," she sighed, and he followed her up into the keep. Gruffydd's chamber was on the uppermost floor. Pausing on the threshold, she gave Llewelyn a look of anxious entreaty. "It might be better if I spoke to him first. If you'll wait . . ." He nodded and she slipped inside.

The door was ajar. Llewelyn could see a marble-top table, the sweep of velvet bed hangings. Senena had not stinted in making Gruffydd's captivity as comfortable as possible, as if enough luxuries might somehow compensate for the guards at the bottom of the stairwell. The table was cluttered with the evidence of Gruffydd's struggle to fill empty hours, to vanquish the enemy that time had become: a chess set, a draughts board, a stack of books. It was the books that Llewelyn found most poignant, for Gruffydd had never been a reader. He backed away from the door. A mistake. This was a grievous mistake.

"No! I'll not see him!" Gruffydd's voice carried clearly into the stairwell. Senena's response was softer, less distinct; she seemed to be pleading with him. Her importuning was in vain; Gruffydd's voice came again, raw with the rage of impotence. "Would you have me grovel to him? And for what? He's not going to relent, and I'll be damned ere I'll give him absolution. Tell him if his conscience wants easing, he can seek it elsewhere. Let his Norman slut console him, let her whelp—" Llewelyn heard no more; he turned, moved into the shadows of the stairwell.

The guards stepped aside respectfully, let him pass. His spurs clinked, struck sparks against the stones, and then he was emerging into the sun, into brilliant, blinding light. Owain had disappeared, but the younger boy was sitting on the outer stairs; when Llewelyn said his name, he smiled up at the man with innocent camaraderie, heartrending trust.

"Llewelyn, wait!" Senena was flushed, breathless. She ignored her son, caught up with Llewelyn at the foot of the stairs. "Do not go, not like this. I know you heard Gruffydd, but . . . but can you blame him? I'll not apologize for his pride and I'll not make excuses for his bitterness. He is still your son, your firstborn. How can you turn your back on him like this? Do you hate him so much?"

"Hate him?" Llewelyn swung about, pointed toward the little boy. "Do you think you could ever hate Llelo? Or Owain? How can I hate the man as long as I remember the child?"

"You want to free him!" Senena cried, and it was both a challenge and a plea. "I can see that now. You truly do. Why will you not do it, then? Llewelyn, I beg you. Let him go."

"And then what? Can you honestly tell me he'd willingly go into exile? That he'd accept Davydd as my heir? You know he would not. Within hours of my death, Gwynedd would be at war. He'd never yield to Davydd, would die first. And if he won . . . if he won, Davydd would be the one to die. He'd put Davydd to death, disavow all allegiance to England, antagonize the other Welsh Princes, goad the Marcher lords and the crown into an invasion, and as for Joanna . . . how do you think she would fare at his hands, Senena?"

"What are you saying, then? That you can never let him go?"

"No . . . I am not saying that. When I feel confident that Davydd can stave off any challenge to his authority, that he can safeguard what I've won, I'll give Gruffydd his freedom."

"And you think that should give me comfort? That day will never come! Davydd will never be able to hold his own against Gruffydd!"

Llewelyn was not vulnerable from that quarter. "You are wrong, Senena," he said quietly, with such calm certitude that Senena's rage spilled over.

"This is Joanna's doing, all of it! She's set you against your own, scrupled at nothing to get what she wanted—the crown for her son! How could you be so taken in? My God, if you only knew—"

"If I only knew what, Senena?"

The coldness of the query brought her up short. What could she tell him? She had nothing but suspicions, needed more than afternoon disappearances, Joanna's obvious unease, and her own instincts. Not only would Llewelyn not believe her, he'd never forgive her.

"I do not mean to offend you, my lord. But I love your son, and who will speak for him if I do not? If you do not free Gruffydd in your lifetime, he will never be freed. If he is still confined at your death, he will remain caged for the rest of his days. Davydd will never let him go. Can you do that to him? Can you condemn him to a life in shadow, away from the sun and the changing seasons? Can you—"

Llewelyn had no answer for her. He turned away in silence.

At Michaelmas, Davydd and his sister Gwladys departed for London, where Davydd was to do homage to Henry. Joanna had decided not to accompany her son, in part because she did not want to take any attention away from Davydd's first diplomatic mission and in part because she did not want to leave Llewelyn for very long. He'd been sleeping badly since his return from Deganwy; all too frequently of late, she would awaken to find him staring into the dark, and she could offer only the most evanescent and ephemeral of comforts, winding her arms around him and holding him close, able to sympathize with his pain but not to share it.

She did agree to meet Davydd in Shrewsbury upon his return, and she arrived at the Benedictine abbey on a mild afternoon in October. Later that day a plainly dressed woman entered a Shrewsbury church, asked the priest to hear her confession. That she was a stranger did not surprise him, for there was a lamentable reluctance even among the truly devout to confess their more serious sins to their own parish priests. She followed him toward the chancel, seated herself on the shriving stool, where she could be seen by all yet not heard, and in a very low voice confessed to the sin of adultery. Afterward, Joanna walked back to the abbey with a lighter step, for the first time in a year feeling at peace with herself.

Davydd and Gwladys rode into the abbey precincts the following morning, laden with gifts and London news. Joanna was delighted to discover they were accompanied by Elen and John the Scot. But her smile froze at sight of the man riding at Elen's side, at sight of Will de Braose.

In accordance with Norman custom, dinner was served in the

forenoon. The meal was less stressful, however, than Joanna had expected, for Will was on his best behavior; even Gwladys thawed toward him, enough to laugh heartily at his maliciously accurate imitation of Hubert de Burgh at his most pompous. Not surprisingly, the London visit was the focal point of conversation and the talk was easy, often amusing, the dinner passing without incident.

Afterward, Davydd took Joanna to the stables, where he proudly displayed his London purchase, a superb red-gold stallion. "I remembered those stories Papa would tell me of Sul, his first horse, so I named this one Sulwyn. You think Papa will like him?"

Joanna was not deceived by Davydd's offhand manner, knew he'd gone to great pains to find this particular look-alike for Sul, to give his father this substitute solace. "Nothing could please him more, darling," she said, and Davydd smiled. Linking her arm in his, he led her toward a beckoning sheen of blue, toward the placid waters of the abbey fishpond.

"Does Will plan to return with us to Aber?" Joanna asked as nonchalantly as she could, felt a dizzying rush of relief when Davydd shook his head. "Davydd . . . I'd like to talk to you about Will and the plight troth. How do you feel—truly—about taking his daughter to wife? Darling, if you'd rather not, it's still not too late. Your father and I made a mistake with Elen, would not—"

"Mama, I appreciate your concern, but there's no need. I've no objections to this match. Why should I? How many brides bring their husbands a prize like Buellt Castle?"

"You are sure, Davydd? The girl's youth does not matter?"

Davydd picked up a pebble, sent it skipping across the surface of the pool. "I know it'll be years ere Isabella can be a true wife to me, but in all honesty, Mama, I see that as no disadvantage." He gave her a sideways glance, a self-conscious smile. "There is a girl, you see . . ."

Joanna did see. "Do you love this girl, Davydd?"

"I think so," he admitted. "But you need not fret. I've always known mine must be a marriage of state. Mari knows it, too, never expected more of me than I could give. But I'd not see her hurt if I could help it. A marriage like this would be easier for her, would give her no cause for jealousy."

It came as something of a shock to Joanna to realize Davydd could be so pragmatic, so dispassionate even about passion. How unlike her children were! She yearned to know more about this mysterious Mari, but knew she'd never ask; this was not a part of a man's life that he'd share with his mother. She wondered suddenly if it had been like this for Llewelyn, too, if he'd felt the same uneasy blend of pride and loss upon seeing his son for the first time as a man grown.

"But what of Isabella's lineage? You have no objections to wedding a girl of Norman blood?"

"I think of myself as Welsh, Mama. For certes, my loyalties are to Wales, to Papa's people. But I am no less your son than Papa's, and to disavow my Norman blood would be to disavow you. When I was but a lad, Papa told me I was luckier than most, having two heritages to draw upon. I came to see that he was right, that a man who can claim descent from both Owain Fawr and Eleanor of Aquitaine is indeed blessed with a remarkable family tree!"

Joanna was deeply touched, but too wise in the ways of motherhood to embarrass her son by letting him know. She contented herself with a smile, a kiss upon his cheek, and a necessary lie. "Now that I know it is truly your wish to wed Isabella de Braose, my mind is greatly eased."

"Mama, I must talk to you about Henry. I wanted to be the one to tell you, made the others agree to that, for I know how fond you are of him. He has been forced to delay his expedition against the French, for when he arrived at Portsmouth, he found less than half the expected ships in the harbor. I had remained in London, but Elen's husband was at Portsmouth, and his account can be trusted, however unlikely it first sounds to you; John could not embellish a tale in the telling to save his very soul. He says Henry flew into a wild rage, blamed Hubert de Burgh for failing to assemble enough ships. He lost all control, cursed de Burgh as a traitor, as a pawn of the French, even went so far as to draw his sword."

"He did what?"

Davydd nodded. "John says it was a right ugly scene, says his Uncle Chester had to step between them, intercede for de Burgh— Chester, of all men! When they were at last able to calm Henry, the rupture was somehow patched over. De Burgh is to continue as Justiciar, but I doubt that he'll forget. Nor will the men who witnessed it. It showed Henry in no favorable light, Mama, made him look unsteady of purpose, unreliable of temper . . . and not a little ridiculous."

"This sounds so unlike him. His is a gentle spirit, Davydd, not given to violence . . ."

"It seems he has more of the Angevin temper than men thought."

Joanna frowned. "You mean his father's temper. But you're wrong in that, Davydd. John would never have thrown such a tantrum. He once put a sword to Llewelyn's throat, but that was very deliberately done. He'd not have drawn a sword upon one of his own councilors, not unless he fully meant to use it. Whatever men may say of John, he was never inept."

Davydd had developed a morbid fascination with the Angevin King, the grandfather he'd never known. Even now, in his twenty-first year, he found it impossible to identify with John in any sense, to acknowledge a blood bond with a mortal enemy of the Welsh. He found it equally hard to associate his mother with such a man, and he loved Joanna too much to indulge his curiosity at her expense. He wanted to take advantage of this sudden breach in her defenses, to ask those questions only she could answer. But he did not want to hurt her, and he hesitated.

"They sound as unlike as chalk and cheese, Mama. Henry is well-meaning but weak, and John . . ." He paused, watching her intently. But she was already pulling back; the moment had passed.

"And John was neither," she said, with forced flippancy. "Well-meaning or weak, I mean. Let's go back, Davydd. I want to talk to Elen, see if I cannot coax her into returning to Aber with us for a time."

"I think she— Will? What are you doing out here? Were you seeking us?"

Joanna spun around, saw Will ambling toward them. "Yes, I was," he said, favoring them with a lazy smile. "I need to talk to your mother, Davydd. Would you mind if I borrowed her for a few moments?"

Davydd felt some reluctance, knowing Joanna was never fully at ease with a de Braose. But he could not refuse without rudeness, without offending the man who was to be his father-in-law. "Of course, Will. I'll go and find Elen, Mama, shall await you back at the guest hall."

As Davydd moved away, Joanna began to walk rapidly along the water's edge, not waiting for Will. But he had no difficulty in keeping stride, fell into step beside her. "Come now, Joanna, surely you cannot object to us meeting like this, in a monastery garden in the middle of the afternoon? What could be more innocent? Moreover, the plight troth did make us kin of sorts. Of course, we were already linked by an earlier marriage, that of my father and Gwladys. I once sought to figure our relationship out, did only give myself a right sharp headache! It's a tangled coil, in truth; see what you can make of it. Gwladys is your step-daughter and was, for nigh on thirteen years, my stepmother. Now my question is this. As the stepmother of my stepmother, does that make you my step-grandmother?''

Joanna gave an involuntary splutter of laughter. "Jesú forfend!''

Will was grinning. "I thought I could coax a smile if I truly tried. Am I forgiven, then?''

Joanna stopped, for the first time looked him full in the face. "I am not angry with you, Will. I do not blame you for what happened. I want only to forget.''

"I'd rather remember,'' he said, plucked a sprig of honey-suckle from the closest vine, and handed it to her. She took it, but then began to walk again.

"I would like to thank you, Will, for your kindness at the time of Catherine's death. I know I never answered your letter, but it did help.'' Not at first, though; she'd been terrified when Will's messenger was ushered into the great hall, handed her the letter in full view of all. She'd broken the seal with unsteady fingers, but her fears were unrealized; the contents did not compromise her in any way. Will had written a graceful letter of condolence, explaining that he'd only recently heard of Catherine's death, and expressing his sympathies to Joanna and Catherine's family. She'd been able to pass the letter over to Llewelyn without the slightest qualm. "It was a kind thought,'' she repeated, bringing the honeysuckle up to breathe in its fragrance.

"I knew you were very fond of her. Was she ill for long?''

"I loved her,'' Joanna said softly. "And no, not long at all . . .''

"Did you ever tell her about us?''

"No.''

"Just as well. But what of your maid . . . Glenna? Can you trust her?''

"Glynis? Yes, I believe so. Why?''

"No . . . it was a foolish whim, much too risky. However trustworthy she seems, it would be madness to put yourself into her power like that. A pity, though. To have had an entire night together . . .'' He shook his head regretfully. "Well, we'll just have to make do with what we can. At least we'll have an afternoon. What about tomorrow? I know an inn not far from Shrewsbury, a bit on the shabby side but no hovel. It can provide what we most need, clean sheets, decent wine, and privacy.''

"No, Will. No.''

"Think on it, love; just us and a soft bed." Will's smile was wry. "I might as well confess; I'm past the age where I enjoy rolling about on dirt floors, like my comforts with my pleasures. I want to be able to take my time, to undress you myself . . . very slowly. I want you to unbind your hair so I can feel it against my chest as I kiss you, and then—"

"Will, stop, please stop! I cannot, not ever again!"

"Why not?" He sounded truly surprised. "You need not fear discovery, love. I'll take care of it, arrange everything—"

"No. I love my husband." To Joanna's dismay, her voice was unsteady. "I do, Will, I do!"

"I no longer doubt that," he said hastily. "You made that quite clear the last time we were together in the *hafod*. You love him, well and good. But you still want me, Joanna." She was shaking her head and he stepped closer. "Look me in the eye then and say you do not. Tell me you do not want to go to that inn, do not want to be in my arms right now, do not want me to make love to you."

Joanna's face was burning. But she raised her chin, met his eyes. "I do not want to go to an inn with you. I do not want to bed with you. It's over, Will. It's done."

His eyes shifted from her face, followed the rapid rise and fall of her breasts. "Now why," he murmured, "do I not believe you?"

Joanna backed away. "You act as if this were some sort of game! Have you never thought what would happen should my husband find out about us?"

He shrugged and she began to understand. "I once told you that you could not trade upon being fourteen forever. But that's what you're still doing. Only now it's your name, your family's power."

He was no longer smiling. "And what does that mean?"

"Tell me the truth, Will. How many unhappy husbands have suspected you of cuckolding them and yet looked the other way? How many of your vassals were unwilling or unable to act upon their suspicions?"

He shrugged again. "What does it matter? That has naught to do with us."

"But it does matter! Can you not see that? Do you truly think Llewelyn, too, would turn a blind eye? That being a de Braose, a highborn Norman lord, would save you? It would not, Will; believe me in this, it would not. Llewelyn would kill you if he knew. As simple as that. He would kill you."

"He need never have to know, Joanna. Why can I not convince you of that?" He glanced about, saw no one in sight, and caught her hand, brought it up to his mouth. "If you do not want me, darling, why does your pulse jump so when I touch you? Why does your breath come so quick?"

Joanna jerked free. "Yes," she gasped, "yes, I do want you. Is that what you would have me say? But it will avail you naught, for I will never act upon it. I will not destroy my marriage for you!"

She'd dropped the honeysuckle on the path and Will picked it up, crushed it between his fingers as he watched her move away. She was all but running in her haste to put distance between them, did not look back.

11

ABER, NORTH WALES

April 1230

Joanna and Gwladys were seated at a table in the great hall, making up the guest list for Gwladys's upcoming marriage to Ralph de Mortimer. This was no less political a match than the other marital alliances Llewelyn had forged with his Norman-French neighbors. Ralph de Mortimer was an influential Marcher lord, baron of Wigmore, his a family that had long been hostile to Llewelyn. But antagonism had yielded to expediency, and he'd shown himself eager to ally with the Welsh Prince, to wed Llewelyn's eldest daughter. Joanna was not all that impressed with Mortimer, a brash, forceful man, noted both for his candor and his quick temper. Gwladys, however, obviously saw something in him that Joanna did not; she had suggested the match to Llewelyn, after meeting Mortimer during her London visit, and now, with the wedding but weeks away, she gave every indication of looking forward to her new life as Ralph de Mortimer's lady.

"Shall we begin with the Marshals, Gwladys? My sister Nell will attend, of course, but Pembroke will have sailed with Henry for Brittany by then. I think we ought to invite Pembroke's younger brothers, though; they are—"

"Joanna . . . I'd rather we wait. I asked Senena to join us."

Although Joanna said nothing, hers was an expressive face. Gwladys leaned across the table. "Let us speak plainly. I do not blame Papa for keeping Gruffydd at Deganwy, for Gruffydd gave him no choice. Nor do I blame you. It is only natural that you should try to safeguard Davydd's rights. Gruffydd has a man's courage, a man's will, but a child's grasp of the world we live in. Yet I still love him, I still feel his pain, and I would never forsake him. When he asks me for something, I try to oblige, and he asked me to include Senena in my wedding plans. She needs this, Joanna, needs some pleasure in her life. I want to do this for Gruffydd, want you to do it for me. Will you?''

Such a question could have but one answer. Joanna nodded. ''I'll try,'' she said grudgingly. ''In all honesty, I cannot promise that she'll not provoke me, but I will try.''

''Fair enough.'' Gwladys half rose, beckoned to her sister-in-law. ''Ah, there you are, Senena. Joanna and I were just discussing those who cannot attend. Chester, too will be sailing with the English King and Pembroke. I doubt that Gwenllian and her husband will come from Ireland. But at least Marared and her husband will be present. What of Elen and John the Scot, Joanna?''

''I think not,'' Joanna said regretfully. ''They're visiting the court of John's cousin, the Scots King, will not be back in time. But my brother Richard and his wife will come for certes, and mayhap my aunt, the Countess of Salisbury.''

''May I assume you do mean to squeeze in a few Welsh midst all these Normans?''

Joanna dropped her pen, splattering the parchment with ink. Gwladys said hastily, ''The Welsh will be well represented, Senena. Here is our list. Have you any suggestions to make?''

Senena gave the list only a perfunctory glance. ''What of Will de Braose and his wife? Surely you do not mean to overlook them. Or have you already given Will an invitation, Madame?''

''No, I have not!'' Joanna drew a deliberate breath. She could not do this to herself, could not allow her suspicions and her guilt to color the most innocent of utterances; in that way lay madness. ''Of course I mean to invite Will and Eva de Braose; they are Davydd's kin now.'' And, picking up the pen, she inked in the names of her lover and his wife.

Gwladys laughed suddenly, none too happily. ''That man always did have a diabolical sense of timing,'' she said, as Joanna turned with foreboding, saw Will de Braose being ushered into the hall.

He greeted the three women in turn, and then smiled at Joanna. ''I suppose I ought to have sent word ahead, but I took it for granted that you could accommodate me.''

How long, Joanna wondered in sudden despair, was it to be like this? How long ere she could talk to this man and not feel a shamed sense of intimacy? ''You are ever welcome at my husband's court,'' she said reluctantly, stressing the words ''my husband'' in the vain hope that Will would understand the emphasis, abandon the chase. "But neither Llewelyn nor Davydd is here. They are meeting in Bangor with the Bishop, and I do not expect them to return until the morrow. Mayhap you would rather continue on to Bangor, join them there?"

"Bangor is but six miles," Gwladys chimed in, no more eager than Joanna to have Will at Aber. But he was shaking his head, saying that only a churl would give up an opportunity to pass an evening with three charming women, and Joanna could only pray that neither Gwladys nor Senena caught the mockery beneath the good manners, that none but she could read the message in those amused grey eyes.

Dinner should have been a festive occasion, freed as they were of the monotonous menus of Lent; the table was bountifully set, and afterward there was music and dancing. But for Joanna, the evening was an ordeal. Will was in recklessly high spirits; he insisted upon dancing with Joanna and Gwladys, even attempted to coax Senena into joining the carole, and he flirted outrageously with Glynis, who seemed both flustered and flattered by his attentions. And all the while Joanna could feel Senena's eyes upon them, upon her and Will.

Joanna was standing alone, watching the dancers. When Will materialized unexpectedly at her side, her nerves betrayed her and she splashed half of her wine into the floor rushes. "Shall I fetch you another cup, Lady Joanna?" Will asked, so solicitously that she yearned to slap him.

"No. You've had enough wine tonight for both of us. You can do something for me, though. You can stop trying to bedazzle Glynis. Let her be, Will. There's no sport in seducing such an innocent."

Will laughed so loudly that he turned several heads in their direction. " 'Jealousy is cruel as the grave,' " he quoted softly. "Do you recognize that, Joanna? The Song of Solomon. Who'd ever expect to find so erotic a love poem in Scriptures? Shall I recite it for you? 'Behold, thou art fair, my love. Thy lips are like a thread of scarlet. Thy breasts are like two—' "

"Will, hush!" Joanna was truly frightened now. "When the stakes have become life or death, it is no longer a game. Have you not noticed how Senena keeps watching us? She puts me in mind of a stalking cat, makes me feel like a bird with a broken wing."

"The cat eyes are yours, love, not Senena's."

"Will, stop! Listen to me . . . please. You must leave me alone. If you do not, I'll have no choice but to denounce you,

accuse you of making unwelcome advances. Do not make me do
that, Will. I do not want you to come to harm!"

Will grinned. "Nor do I, darling!" But as he studied her face,
his smile changed, became softer, more sympathetic. "I wish I
could convince you, Joanna, that you're distressing yourself for
naught. Why should you care what Senena suspects as long as
you have Llewelyn's trust? But if it will ease your mind, I'll
strive for discretion. Now . . . tell me quickly whilst we're still
alone. Where can we meet . . . and when?"

Joanna gave a strained, shaken laugh. "You never hear me, do
you? I do not know what else to say to you, how to convince
you . . ." Shoving her wine cup into his hand, she said, "I do want
more wine, after all, Will. Would you mind?" And as soon as he
moved away, she turned, crossed the hall to Gwladys.

"I know you like Will's company no more than I do, but I
need you to act in my stead for the rest of the evening. Will you
do that for me?"

Gwladys gave a mock grimace. "I cannot pretend I'm thrilled
at the prospect. But I do owe you a favor. Go along, then; I'll see
to the hall and our guests."

As Joanna hurriedly departed the hall, Senena came to stand at
Gwladys's side. "It is rather early for bed, is it not?"

Gwladys shrugged. "Joanna does not find it easy, being with a
de Braose." Senena laughed; Gwladys did not like the sound of
it, and she said with far less friendliness, "I am not asking you to
sympathize with her predicament, Senena, merely to understand
it."

"But I do." Senena was smiling. "I do understand, Gwladys.
I understand very well, indeed."

One of the windows in Joanna's bedchamber was unshuttered,
and the sounds of laughter and music carried on the quiet April
air. Glynis was dutifully brushing out Joanna's hair, but she kept
casting such wistful glances toward the window that Joanna at
last relented.

"Never mind," she said. "You need not braid my hair into a
night plait. Would you like to return to the hall?"

"Oh, yes, Madame, thank you!"

"But Glynis . . . do take care. Do not pay too much heed to
Will de Braose's honeyed words. His promises are counterfeit
coins; they look genuine until you seek to spend them."

Glynis blushed and then grinned impishly. "I know that,

Madame, I do. But it's like our trips to the Shrewsbury market; I
can enjoy looking without necessarily meaning to buy!''

Joanna smiled, waved the girl out. Alone now in the bedchamber, she felt calmer, safe both from temptation and exposure.
Talking to Will would do no good whatsoever. The more she said
no, the more intrigued he became. She could not trust him, and
in all honesty, she was still not sure she could trust herself. She
and Will must never be alone. She must avoid him whenever
possible, and if that meant open rudeness, so be it. She could
only hope Davydd would understand. But even if he could not,
that changed nothing.

She took several books and a candle with her to bed—and
Topaz, for the spaniel always took shameful advantage of
Llewelyn's absences, abandoning its sleeping basket for its mistress's feather bed. Joanna removed her bedrobe, gave the dog an
indulgent pat, and reached for the books.

The first she discarded at once, a romance of the ill-fated love
of Tristan for his uncle's wife, the beguiling Iseult. There was a
perverse comfort in attributing adulterous passion to a love potion; Joanna wryly wished she could so easily explain away her
own infidelity. But she was in no mood for an object lesson—
however lyrical—in the inevitable wages of sin, and she chose
instead a French translation of a lengthy English poem, *The Owl
and the Nightingale*.

Even this selection was not as innocuous as it first seemed. A
cynical couplet could have served as John's epitaph: "The dark
way he so fully knows, that in the bright he never goes." Other
lines struck too close to home. "A woman may sport beneath the
sheet, in wedded love or lustful heat." "For sure it is a better
thing, for wife to love her husband pure, than wanton with a
paramour." Joanna dropped the book into the rushes, blew out
the candle.

She was almost asleep when Topaz began to whine. The door
creaked; she heard the bolt slide into place. Glynis. She pulled
the pillow closer. But Topaz continued to whimper. She was
rolling over, a drowsy reprimand forming on her lips, when the
bed hangings were drawn back. A candle still burned on the
table; framed in flickering light, a man was standing by the bed.
Llewelyn? Joanna sat up, blinking sleepily. But then he moved,
and the candle caught the sheen of flaxen hair. Joanna gasped,
grabbed for the sheet. "Will?"

"Did you think I was not coming? I did not want to be too
obvious, love, waited nigh on an hour." He grinned. "And I

know what you're going to ask now. But no one saw me; it's full dark.'' As he was speaking, he was unfastening his mantle. Tossing it onto a coffer, he began unbuckling his scabbard and sword.

"Will, no! My God, you're mad! Someone could come in at any moment!"

"Who'd dare enter your private chamber at such an hour? Only Glynis, love, and she's over in the great hall, dallying with my squire. Sometimes the more unlikely a trysting place, the safer it actually is.''

Unbelting his tunic, he pulled it over his head, and Joanna's fear suddenly gave way to outrage. "You truly think I'd do this to Llewelyn, that I'd lay with you in my husband's own bed? Get out, get out ere I start to scream!''

He dropped the tunic onto the floor, stared at her in surprise. "What game are you playing now, Joanna? You know you w꜠nt me. Why did you depart the hall like that if you did not expect me to follow—''

"I expected nothing! I'll take no blame for your mistakes, for your accursed, overweening pride. For months now I've told you that it was over. And even if I were utterly besotted with you, I'd never have invited you into Llewelyn's bedchamber, never!''

Will gave a half-angry laugh. "You make it sound as if we're about to defile a sacred shrine!'' Yet he was not as irked as he might otherwise have been; she was clutching the sheet up to her breasts, but the material was soft, clinging, adhered to the curves of hip and thigh, and her hair spilled over her breasts, onto the pillow in a midnight cloud. "Mayhap I did misread you, Joanna,'' he conceded. "But I'm here now, and I cannot believe you truly want me to leave. You admitted it yourself at Shrewsbury, how much you still wanted me. You remember how it was between us . . .'' He leaned over the bed, his mouth seeking hers, and Joanna screamed.

Will never had more reason to bless his quick reflexes. As stunned as he was, he reacted instinctively, swiftly clasping his hand over her mouth, choking back her cry. He'd encountered resistance from women before, but it was usually playfully offered, a lover's game. Joanna was struggling in earnest, in panic, trying to bite his hand, to scratch, to roll off the bed. He realized at once that he could not restrain her without truly hurting her, and when he loosened his grip on her mouth, she succeeded in giving another muffled scream.

Never had Will's desire diminished so rapidly; never had he

lost an erection with such speed. He was no longer aware of the soft female body thrashing under his, was aware only of that unshuttered window, her hysterically barking dog.

"Joanna, calm yourself. I do not want to hurt you. Joanna, listen to me! Do you know what will happen to me if anyone heard your scream? Christ Jesus, I'll be gelded with a dull knife! I'll not force you, I swear. If I take my hand away, let you up, do you promise not to scream?"

She nodded, after an unnervingly long pause. He released her then, very cautiously. She was gasping for breath, but she did not cry out, and he relaxed somewhat, enough for anger. "Whatever possessed you? Good Christ, woman, you almost got me killed!"

Joanna was too shaken for speech, half blinded by her own hair. She pulled the sheet up, panting, rubbing her wrists. But when Will took a step toward the bed, she cried, "If you dare to touch me again . . ."

Her voice had risen and he hastily backed away. "What do you think, that I had rape in mind? At your own court, in your own bedchamber? What kind of a bloody fool do you think I am?"

They glared at each other, but his protest had the ring of truth. Joanna acknowledged that by reaching for the spaniel, seeking to quiet it. Will moved to the table, poured himself a double measure of mead. "I cannot remember when I've felt death so damned close," he confessed. "Between you and that wretched dog, I expected half the court to come bursting in at any moment."

"You're luckier than you deserve. I want you out of here . . . now!"

"You do want me to dress first? I'd look somewhat conspicuous, wandering about the bailey in my shirt and chausses." Will set the cup down, studied Joanna with baffled, angry eyes. He still could not believe he'd not have been able to bring her around, if only he had enough privacy and time. But not here, not now, not when a single scream could bring a dozen men on the run.

"Here," he said, moving warily toward the bed. "Take the rest of this mead. If your nerves are half as frayed as mine, you need it."

Joanna did, but she shook her head. "Just put it down and get out."

She was still rubbing her wrist, and he said, "Are you hurt? In truth, Joanna, I did think you were expecting me, that I was welcome in your bed. I suppose every man has coerced a consent

at one time or another. But I would never, in this lifetime or the
next, force a woman like you. A Prince's wife, the King of
England's sister? That mad I am not! I frightened you, I know.
But you gave me a turn, too. Let's call it check and mate,
and—"

"I do not want to talk. I just want you to go."

"All right. I'll go." It was for the best; she was too distraught
to be trusted. But on the morrow he'd have to find a way to talk
privately with her, to mollify her somehow. Women could be
vindictive, unforgiving, and she was in a unique position to do
him harm, to poison the King's mind against him. "I'll go," he
repeated, but instead he turned, moved swiftly toward the window.

Joanna sat up in alarm. "Now what are you about? Get back
lest you be seen!"

"Something is amiss." Very cautiously, he peered around the
shutter edge. "People are coming out of the hall. I cannot be
sure, but I think I hear your name, hear 'Siwan.' "

Joanna heard it too, now, a confused babble of voices, barking
dogs. "What is it, Will?"

"I do not know, mayhap a fire . . ." He risked another look,
and then drew back hastily. "Christ, it's Llewelyn!"

Even then, Will kept his wits about him. Llewelyn was dismounting in front of his lodgings, but if the door was thus
eliminated as a means of escape, that still left a side window.
Will darted toward it, began jerking at the shutter latches. "Joanna, hide my clothing and sword!" But Joanna was incapable of
moving. She sat frozen, staring at the door.

"Joanna? Joanna, are you all right? Unbar the door!" The
voice was Llewelyn's. She heard other voices, too; someone was
pounding on the door, and Llewelyn was shouting for the key.
Will had the latches up by now; he jerked the shutters open, and
then recoiled.

"Jesú, there are men outside! Quick, Joanna, where can I
hide?" But Joanna did not reply, and as he swung about, he saw
the latch begin to move. As they watched, it was slowly, inexorably pushed upward, and then the door was thrust open.

Llewelyn was not alone, and the chamber was cast into eerie
brightness by the sudden flare of torches. But Joanna saw none of
the men. No one existed for her but Llewelyn. She watched,
stunned, as he strode into the room, watched as he came to an
abrupt halt, watched as his face changed, watched as her world
fell apart.

Llewelyn looked from Will to Joanna, and despite the irrefutable evidence of infidelity, there was still a moment in which he half expected Joanna to offer a rational, convincing explanation for Will's presence, half dressed, in their bedchamber. But she had yet to utter a word, and all the color had drained from her face. She looked up at him in stricken silence, silence more damning than any confession could have been, and he could read in her eyes only horror, despairing entreaty, and an admission of a betrayal beyond forgiving.

Will stood very still. He'd talked his way out of awkward corners before, but none like this. He'd seen the disbelief on Llewelyn's face give way to a far more frightening emotion, and he thought, Christ, he loves her! He'd always prided himself upon his glibness of tongue, but as he looked at Llewelyn, he knew suddenly that it would not avail him now, that nothing would.

He no longer had enough saliva for swallowing, had to try twice before he could get the words out. "I know this looks bad, but—" He got no further; Llewelyn's sword was already clearing its scabbard. He had nowhere to run, felt the wall at his back, and knew the last sight he'd ever see was the light reflecting off that gleaming steel blade.

Joanna was petrified, averted her eyes. But she made no sound. Her throat had closed up; even if Llewelyn turned the sword upon her next, she'd not have been able to cry out.

"Llewelyn, wait!"

Joanna opened her eyes, saw that Ednyved had stepped between Llewelyn and Will, "No," he said grimly, "not like that. It's too easy. Give him the death he deserves. Hang him."

Will drew an audible breath. No one else spoke. And then Llewelyn slowly lowered his sword. "Yes," he said in a voice Joanna had never heard before. "You're right. It is too quick this way. Take him."

For the first and only time in his life, Will panicked, made a sudden lunge for the window. But Llewelyn's sword came up with eye-blurring speed, and Will froze, his stomach muscles contracting, anticipating that first thrust into the belly or groin. There'd be nothing easy or quick about such a death, not with Llewelyn wielding the blade. Better to take his chances with the hanging, for there was a hope—however slight—that enough political pressure might reprieve him.

He no longer resisted, therefore, when Llewelyn's men laid hands upon him, but they treated him roughly all the same, jerking his arms behind his back and shoving him toward the door. He did not struggle, realizing that Llewelyn had only to say the word and they'd gladly hang him then and there, over the bed. He stumbled, nearly fell, and for a moment his eyes found Joanna.

"I ought to be gallant and say you were worth it, darling," he said huskily, "but no woman is worth hanging for."

His words meant nothing to Joanna; she never even heard them. "Llewelyn . . ." She had yet to take her eyes from her husband's face. "Llewelyn, I'm sorry . . ."

Llewelyn moved toward the bed. When he brought the sword up, he heard gasps. Joanna's lips parted; her breath quickened. Tears had begun to streak her face. He knew suddenly that this was the way he would always remember her, clutching a sheet to hide her nakedness, dark hair falling about her face in wanton disarray, kneeling in the middle of the bed, the bed in which she'd betrayed him. Her deathbed. One downward stroke of his sword and the sheets would be soaked with blood. His hand tightened on the hilt, and then he thrust the sword back into its scabbard, turned to face the others.

"I want de Braose's men taken prisoner, too. See to it."

Men hastened to obey. Llewelyn became aware now of their audience, of the people crowding into the antechamber. "Get them out of here," he snarled, and the antechamber cleared as if by magic, while through the open window he could see Will de Braose being dragged across the bailey.

"Llewelyn . . . Llewelyn, I did not ask him to come to me. It was over between us. Beloved, I swear it, I swear I never would have brought him here, into your bed . . ."

If her words had registered with him, Joanna could see no indication of it in his face. He turned away from her, and as he moved through the doorway, Joanna sobbed, begged him to wait, to listen, but he did neither.

"Llewelyn . . ." Joanna sobbed again, collapsed upon the bed. He was gone and he would not be back. She'd lost him, lost all, all . . . She did not think it was possible to feel pain greater than this. But then she heard her son's voice, heard Davydd say, "Why, Mama, why?"

"Davydd?" Her voice broke. "Davydd . . . you saw? My God, oh, my God, no . . ."

He moved from the shadows of the antechamber, stood there staring at her as if he no longer recognized her. "Glynis sent word that you'd been taken ill, that the doctors feared a rupture . . ." He sounded dazed, his words labored, coming as uncertainly as if he were speaking a language not his own. "She said . . . said you might be dying. Papa, he . . ." He shook his head, as if to clear it. "We half killed our horses, and when we rode into the bailey, no one knew, no one . . ." The words trailed off raggedly, his mouth contorting.

"What have you done, Mama? Jesus God, what have you done?"

Davydd had gone. Joanna was alone. She would never know how long she lay there in the darkness. Upon the table a solitary candle still sputtered, burning down toward the wick. When at last it flickered out, Joanna rose from the bed, groped her way across the chamber. She did not bother with stockings or chemise; finding a gown in one of her coffers, she pulled it over her head, began to search for her shoes. She did not braid her hair, merely brushed it back over her shoulders. She had to see Llewelyn. She had to tell him that she'd not lain with Will in his bed. Nothing else mattered. He could never forgive her, she knew that. But let his grieving be for those October afternoons in the *hafod*. Not for this, not for a betrayal in his own bedchamber. She could at least do that for him. She could give him the truth about tonight and hope it might in time help to heal some of his pain.

Once she was dressed, though, she found herself standing motionless by the door. How could she find Llewelyn? The thought of entering the great hall in search of him was terrifying. She wanted only to stay here in the dark, never to have to face others again. But she must somehow find the courage to do this, for Llewelyn's sake if not her own. She braced herself and then opened the door, only to find her way barred by armed guards.

HERE BE DRAGONS

12

ABER, NORTH WALES

April 1230

The men came for Joanna the following morning. She had no
warning; they entered without knocking, announced brusquely
that she was to accompany them. "Where are you taking me?"
she asked, the composure of her question utterly belied by the
tremor in her voice, and one of the men laughed.

"Did you not hear the hammering? Carpenters have been
laboring since dawn to erect a gallows . . . for two."

Even before she saw the startled looks on the other faces,
Joanna was sure the man lied. If Llewelyn meant for her to die,
she'd have died last night in her own bed. He would never hang
her; she knew that with such certainty that she found the assurance now to challenge their authority. "I want to know where I
am to be taken."

"Do you indeed? Well, I'd not give a fig for what you want,"
he jeered, and Joanna stiffened, for that expression had long
since taken on obscene connotations. "You've no right to ask
questions. You forfeited all rights the day you chose to play the
whore for a Norman lord."

No one had ever dared speak to her with such contempt, and
Joanna felt as if she'd been torn, naked and defenseless, from a
cocoon of privilege and power, with no skills for survival in this
harsh new world. But indignation was an indulgence no longer
available to her. All she could do was to salvage what dignity she
could. "Very well. I will come with you as soon as I braid my
hair."

Her tormentor stepped toward her, took the brush out of her
hand. "No, you will come now," he said, and she had no choice
but to obey. When Topaz sought to follow, he thrust the dog

aside impatiently, and Joanna had no choice but to accept that, too.

Just as they reached the door, a terrifying thought came to her. What if he was not lying about the gallows? What if she was being brought out to watch as Will was hanged? Merciful Jesus, let it not be so, she was praying wordlessly, desperately, as they opened the antechamber door.

As early as it was, the bailey was thronged with men and women. They watched in unnerving silence as Joanna emerged into the sunlight, but as she was led forward, they began to murmur among themselves. Several spat deliberately upon the ground; one bolder than the rest called out loudly, "Norman slut!" Joanna flushed, suddenly seeing herself through other eyes, hostile eyes. How she regretted dressing last night in such haste; without stockings or chemise she felt half naked, slatternly, and with her hair loose, tumbling down her back, blowing untidily about her face, she must look as if she'd just been roused from a man's bed, a lover's embrace.

There was a sudden stir; Glynis broke through the crowd, ran toward Joanna. "I did not do it, Madame," she cried. "I sent no message, I swear by Our Lady I did not!"

"I know, Glynis, I know." Joanna's eyes swept the crowd. "Where is Senena?"

"Gone, my lady. She left nigh on an hour ago for Deganwy Castle."

That came as no surprise to Joanna. Senena would want to tell Gruffydd with no delay. Glynis was gazing at her in sudden comprehension. "Madame, you think it was she . . . ?"

"Who else? But you must go back now, Glynis, lest the others think you too sympathetic, lest they suspect you of aiding and abetting me in a liaison with Will."

Glynis looked frightened, but she stayed resolutely by Joanna's side for several strides. "Go with God, my lady."

The crowd's anger was growing, and as Joanna feared, some of it was now directed at Glynis. But most of the abuse was reserved for Joanna, and as she heard herself called "whore" and "harlot," she began to comprehend at last the political implications of her adultery. Their outrage was in fact rooted in fear, the fear that she'd made Llewelyn ridiculous in the eyes of his English enemies. Nor was the fear ill-founded. The aging husband with a wanton young wife was a stock figure of fun, found in innumerable comic tales and guild mummeries, and for a Prince, nothing could be more injurious to authority than laughter, the mockery of other men. As Joanna came to this appalled understanding, she realized, too, that her sin was twofold in the eyes of Llewelyn's countrymen, for not only had she betrayed her husband, she had betrayed him with a Norman, with one of her own.

She faltered, and the heckling increased. She knew she must not weep, must not show fear. For Davydd's sake, she must be strong enough to endure their scorn. As a child in London, she'd once seen a harlot doing public penance through the city streets; the hapless woman had been followed by a jeering crowd, pelted with mud and rotten apples, and that memory came treacherously back to haunt Joanna now. The insults were getting uglier. Would they dare subject her to the same harsh treatment?

Another memory came to her then, this one more merciful, for it enabled her to find the courage she so needed, the memory of a woman more than twenty years dead, the memory of a woman who'd also been an unfaithful wife, a woman who would have faced down such a hostile crowd with haughty indifference, her father's mother, her grandmother, Eleanor of Aquitaine.

Joanna squared her shoulders, nerved herself to get through this ordeal with what grace she could. But her resolve carried her no farther than the great hall, for there Gwladys awaited her.

Gwladys had passed a sleepless night; her shock was only now yielding to a raw and very bitter rage. "You made a fool of my father, made fools of us all. You even turned me into an accomplice of sorts, taking care of your duties in the hall whilst you took care of Will de Braose, and in my father's own bed!"

"Gwladys, no! That's not so, I swear it!"

"And upon what do you swear, your honor as a faithful wife, a devoted mother? Gruffydd and Senena were right about you, right all along. What grief we might have been spared, had we only heeded them!"

Gwladys no longer trusted herself, whirled and plunged back into the hall. Joanna forgot all else; intent only upon telling Gwladys the truth about Will's presence in her bedchamber, she started after her stepdaughter, and the most hostile of her guards grabbed her by the arm, swung her about so roughly that she cried out, as much in shock as in pain.

"Get your hands off her . . . now!" At sight of Davydd, the crowd fell silent. To many, he was an object of sincere if embarrassed sympathy. But to others he was still the *alltud*—the foreigner—who had usurped the rightful place of Llewelyn's more deserving son, his Welsh son. The guard was one of these, and although he obeyed Davydd's command, released Joanna, he did so grudgingly.

"I am but following orders," he said with a belligerence he'd never have dared to show if not for Joanna's disgrace.

"Not any longer. You have just been relieved of your duty."

The man's eyes flickered. "My lord Ednyved told me I was to take the woman from Aber," he said stubbornly, and Davydd stared at him, incredulous.

"Are you defying me?"

There was in Davydd's voice the arrogance of one accustomed to unquestioning obedience, the arrogance of a Prince's son. But was he? How could they ever be sure now? The taunt never left the man's lips, though, checked in great measure by fear of Llewelyn, but in part, too, by what he saw now in Davydd's eyes.

He had not misread Davydd; for a moment, he'd truly found himself hoping the guard was defying him, giving him justification for what he'd wanted to do since first walking into his mother's bedchamber, seek to ease his pain and disbelief in a killing rage. It unnerved him now to realize how precarious was his self-control, for after that stable confrontation with Gruffydd, he'd vowed never to allow his emotions such free rein again.

The guard yielded, turning away in sullen, resentful silence, and Davydd raised his voice. "Bran!" A man at once detached himself from the crowd of onlookers. The other guards were shifting uneasily, no longer sure what was expected of them. "You are to answer to Bran, to take your orders from him." Davydd paused and then said very deliberately, speaking for the benefit of all within hearing, "The Lady Joanna is to be treated with the respect due her as the King of England's sister . . . and my lady mother. Bear that well in mind, for the man who forgets it will have cause to regret it."

Davydd paused again, to make sure that his warning had taken effect. And then Joanna stepped forward, touched his arm.

"Madame?" It was said with such cold, remote formality that to Joanna, it was as much of a rebuff as a physical recoil. Her hand slipped from his sleeve; he heard her indrawn breath.

"Davydd . . . where am I to be taken?"

"My father has commanded that you be ferried across the strait to Llanfaes, held there until he decides what should be done."

Llanfaes! Joanna had not dared admit until now just how truly

frightened she was, how much she dreaded the thought of incar-
ceration in a darkened castle dungeon. But Llanfaes held no
dungeons; it was a seacoast manor. She deliberately dug her nails
into the palm of her hand, for Llewelyn's unlooked-for leniency
threatened to shred her composure as even the crowd's hostility
could not. "Davydd, I must speak with your father. I must see
him, if only for a few moments."

But Davydd was already shaking his head. "He is gone. He
rode out at first light."

"Can I not wait till he returns?"

"It would serve for naught. He'll not see you." Davydd
gestured abruptly and Bran touched Joanna's arm, politely but
firmly indicating that she was to follow. She did, but gave
Davydd one last despairing look over her shoulder, and Davydd
cried out, "Wait!"

Beckoning to the nearest man, he gave a terse, low-voiced
order, one that earned him a look of surprise. But the man
obeyed, hastened across the bailey toward Joanna's lodgings,
reemerging a moment later with Topaz straining upon a leather
leash.

Davydd stood motionless, watching as Joanna moved to claim
her dog, as she was then escorted toward the gateway. He
ignored the stares, the whispers. Even the most probing eyes
could read nothing in his face, and many marveled that he could
be so impassive a witness to his mother's banishment from his
father's court, his father's life. None was close enough to see the
tears welling in his eyes.

As Joanna's guards carried the coffer chests into her bedchamber,
Glynis said apologetically, "They would not allow me to take
your jewelry, Madame. But I was permitted to pack your clothing and your harp and your bath vials and—"

"That is more than I expected, Glynis." And more than she
deserved. During Ingeborg's years of confinement at Étampes
Castle, it was said that Philip had denied her warm blankets, a
physician's care. But I, Joanna thought bleakly, I am to do
penance in my own bedchamber, with silver brushes and bath
oils. Her guilt suddenly seemed more than she could bear. For
the first time, she could understand why repentant sinners sought
to expiate their wrongdoing with hair shirts, with sackcloth and
ashes. Such gestures no longer seemed extravagant or suspect;
theirs was actually the easier way, mortifying the flesh in order to
mend the spirit.

As the men withdrew, Joanna moved toward the younger woman. "It was kind of you to come, Glynis. But you need not stay with me."

"I know that, Madame. Lord Davydd said that if I did not want to come to Llanfaes, he'd find another to serve you. But I told him it was my wish to be with you."

Joanna felt tears prick her eyes, but she blinked them back, fearing that if she started to cry, she'd not be able to stop. She hugged Glynis wordlessly, and the girl said shyly, "Madame, will you tell me how this came to be? I do not understand, for I know you love Lord Llewelyn."

"Yes . . . I do. And I will try to answer you, Glynis. But there is something I must do first. Did you bring parchment, pen and ink?"

Glynis nodded sadly. "They were the very first items I packed, my lady."

It took Joanna most of the afternoon to compose the letter to her husband. Again and again she had to scrape the parchment clean, but at last the words began to come. She did not try to make Llewelyn understand her infidelity; she knew that was hopeless. She gave him, instead, a factual account of the chronology of her brief liaison, swore that it was over long before Will's foolhardy intrusion into her bedchamber. She told him she loved him, would always love him, and she begged him to do what he could for Davydd, and to find the right words when telling Elen. And then she sent Glynis in search of Bran.

"Will you take this letter back to Aber, to Lord Llewelyn?" Seeing him about to refuse, Joanna hastily pulled a ring from her finger. "I would like you to accept this garnet ring as a token of my gratitude."

He eyed the ring with longing, but still he hesitated, and Joanna realized that he feared to face Llewelyn, to be the bearer of an unfaithful wife's plea. "Take the letter to Lord Davydd. Tell him I ask that he give it to his father."

He reached for the ring, and then the letter, and after that, Joanna could do nothing but wait. He was back sooner than she expected, shortly after dusk. At sight of the letter she felt a sudden throb of hope, for she'd not thought Llewelyn would answer her. What mattered was that he would read her letter, learn the truth. But as she turned it over, she saw her own seal, unbroken, intact.

Bran averted his eyes, made uncomfortable by what he saw

now in her face. "As you see, Lord Llewelyn would not open it, and Lord Davydd said . . . he said it will avail you naught to write again. He said his lord father will not read your letters."

Joanna was standing at the window, gazing up at a spring sky as brightly blue as the Irish Sea; clouds drifted by like floating islands, trailing fleece in their wake. The meadows would be ablaze in gorse, a brilliant yellow flower she'd picked by the armful in springs gone by. How strange that something so simple as a walk on the beach could suddenly mean so much.

"Glynis, is this a Thursday or a Friday? When I awoke this morn, I could be sure neither of the day nor the date."

"This is a Friday, Madame, the third of May."

"May third," Joanna echoed, and then, "eighteen days." She turned abruptly from the window. A week from the morrow would be the anniversary of her wedding. Twenty-four years since that fourteen-year-old girl had shyly clasped Llewelyn's hand upon the steps of St Werburgh's abbey church, twenty-four years. She almost spoke her thoughts aloud to Glynis, caught herself just in time. She was learning that to yield to memories was to embrace pain beyond endurance, was the surest route to madness.

There was a knock upon the bedchamber door. Bran opened the door but did not enter; instead he stepped aside, allowed Ednyved to stride into the room.

Ednyved was brutally blunt. "I've come to tell you that Will de Braose was hanged yesterday at Aber." He was watching Joanna intently, but whatever reaction he might have expected, it was not this; she merely looked at him, showing no emotion at all, and he said curtly, "You did hear me?"

"Yes." He seemed to be waiting, and Joanna wondered what he wanted her to say. Was she supposed to show surprise? She'd known from the moment Llewelyn walked into her bedchamber that Will was a dead man. Was she supposed to grieve for Will? Mayhap one day she might, that he should have died at four and thirty, died so needlessly. But she would have to forgive him first, and she could find no forgiveness in her heart.

Ednyved moved farther into the chamber. "I think he did not truly believe it, up to the last expected Llewelyn to relent. But when he realized there was to be no reprieve, he died well, with courage."

"Yes," Joanna said again. Will had never lacked for courage. If only he had, he'd still be alive, and she'd be at Aber with her

husband and son. She swallowed, said softly, "Ednyved . . . tell
me. How is Llewelyn?"

"Bleeding."

His answer was so graphic, so unexpectedly expressive that
Joanna shuddered. Turning her back upon Ednyved, she moved
blindly toward the window. He followed, grasping her shoulders
and compelling her to face him.

"What would you have me do, sugar the truth for you? Nay,
no tears. The time for tears is past. Ere I go, I want you to tell
me why. You weep for Llewelyn and not for de Braose. You did
not love him?"

He was hurting her, his fingers digging into her flesh, but she
neither protested nor pulled away. She shook her head and he
released her, stepped back, staring at her in baffled bitterness.

"That only makes your betrayal all the more unforgivable.
Sweet Jesus, woman, why? I've watched as you struggled and
schemed and fought to secure the succession for Davydd, only
then to play into Gruffydd's hands like this! And for what? A
tumble in bed with a swaggering cock, a rakehell not worthy of
Llewelyn's spit!"

"What . . . what do you mean that I've played into Gruffydd's
hands? Whilst I daresay he is taking great satisfaction in my fall,
the shame is mine, not Davydd's."

"You think not? When you've given Gruffydd's supporters a
weapon they'd never dreamed within their grasp, an opportunity
to cast doubts upon Davydd's paternity?"

Joanna gasped. "But . . . but that is the most outrageous of
lies! And utterly impossible. Will was just a lad when Davydd
was born, could not possibly—"

"You truly do not see, do you? A woman's honor is verily like
her maidenhead, in that once it is gone, it cannot be regained.
Now that you've been taken in adultery with one man, there will
be those who'll think de Braose was not the first, that there must
have been others."

"My God . . ." No more than a whisper. "My God, what
have I done?"

"Madame . . . Madame, sit down." Glynis was beside her,
putting a protective arm around her shoulders. "Just sit there and
I'll fetch some wine."

A cup was hastily thrust into Joanna's hand; the stem felt cool
to her fingers, wet and sticky with wine. She drank deeply,
without tasting, holding the cup with both hands. "Llewelyn . . .

Llewelyn does not believe this? Tell me he does not, Ednyved,''
she pleaded. ''Tell me he knows Davydd is his!''

''No . . . he does not believe it. I am sure of that.'' Answering
her unspoken question then, he added, ''Nor do I. Nor would
most people, I'd wager. Given your extreme youth at the time of
Davydd's birth, I think it unlikely that such a suspicion would
gain widespread belief.'' His voice hardened. ''But do not deceive yourself. There will be some who'll give it credence, if
only because they want to believe it. Davydd's enemies—and he
does have them—will seek to use it against him, as they'd use
any weapon at hand.''

''And I . . . I gave it to them,'' Joanna said, sounding so
dazed, so devastated that Ednyved felt a flicker of unwelcome
pity. But he did not contradict her.

''Well, I've had my say,'' he said, thinking Llewelyn was
wise in refusing to see her, to spare himself yet more pain. For as
easy as it was to hate what she had done, it was not as easy to
hate her, not as easy as it should have been.

''Ednyved, wait. There is something you must know. I did
allow myself to enter into an intrigue with Will de Braose, in a
moment of weakness, of madness if you will, during that time
Llewelyn and I were estranged, whilst he was waging war in
Ceri. But I ended the affair almost ere it began. I did not ask Will
to my chamber that night, and nothing happened between us,
nothing.''

When he did not reply, she fumbled for her crucifix chain.
''You do not believe me? I'll swear it, then, swear it upon the
lives of my children, upon their very—''

''That is not necessary. I think I do believe you, if only
because your version makes more sense. I've known men like de
Braose; they scorn the merlin hawk nesting free in the heather,
must have the one under guard in another man's mews. But
women rarely share that lust for risk-taking, and I could not see
you bringing a lover into Llewelyn's bed, not unless you were
love-blinded . . . or bewitched.''

''Will you tell Llewelyn, then? Will you tell Davydd?''

''I will tell Davydd. I cannot tell Llewelyn.''

''But why? I am not asking this for my sake; I know he cannot
forgive me. But if he knew the truth, his grieving might not be so
great. Can you not see that?''

''It is you who do not see, Joanna. Llewelyn is not about to
believe anything you say, not now. Yours was the one betrayal
he never expected. I truly think he'd have killed any man who

dared come to him with suspicions, would never have believed it of you. And now . . . now he will not allow your name to be spoken in his hearing. Only once has he mentioned you, saying you were dead to him . . . and the measure of his bitterness is the measure of the love he once bore you.''

DOLWYDDELAN, NORTH WALES

DOLWYDDELAN, NORTH WALES

May 1230

Leaving Aber soon after Will de Braose's hanging, Llewelyn began a wide circuit of his domains, maintaining a highly visible presence to discourage speculation and set gossip at rest. He was at Dinbych Castle by mid-May, where he was overtaken by a Cistercian Abbot who'd often served as an emissary of the crown; the Abbot was bearing letters from the English King and his Chancellor, and Llewelyn agreed to meet with the Chancellor at Shrewsbury in June. From Dinbych, Llewelyn moved south into Powys, and then on to the Cistercian abbey of Strata Florida. He did not linger, however, and the last days of May found him back in Gwynedd, in the heartland of his realm, the mountain citadel he most loved, his castle at Dolwyddelan.

He'd been traveling so rapidly, spending so many hours in the saddle that he'd outdistanced most couriers, and the table in his bedchamber was strewn with letters that had only recently caught up with him. He was sorting through them, dictating responses to a scribe, as Davydd entered the chamber.

"Papa . . . ." Davydd was unsure how to identify Richard, but after a moment's reflection, he realized it was immaterial; announcing him as Richard Fitz Roy would not make him any the less Joanna's brother. "Papa, my Uncle Richard has just ridden in. Are you willing to see him?"

Llewelyn was not, but he was even less willing to admit it, so he nodded.

The exchange of greetings was awkward for them all. Richard looked fatigued, and not a little embarrassed. "It is good of you to make me welcome."

"You are Davydd's uncle," Llewelyn said dispassionately,

but Richard was not deceived, saw Llewelyn's courtesy for what it was, an icy exercise in self-control.

Richard had given much thought to what he would say to Llewelyn, but he realized that was time misspent. To offer this man sympathy would be to offer a mortal insult. Although he'd never lacked for courage, he did not find it easy now to make mention of his sister's name. "Davydd tells me that Joanna is at Llanfaes. Have I your permission to see her?"

"Yes," Llewelyn said, still in those dangerously soft tones, and Richard thanked him, thinking all the while that Will de Braose must have been one of God's great fools . . . second only to his sister.

"I'll see that my uncle and his men are fed and bedded down in the great hall," Davydd offered, and when Llewelyn nodded, he ushered Richard toward the door. But within moments he was back, glancing first at the stacked parchments and then at Llewelyn's scribe.

"It grows late, Papa, and Celyn looks tired. Can the letters not wait till the morrow?"

"Your concern for Celyn's well-being is commendable," Llewelyn said dryly, but then he smiled at his son. "Very well, lad. That will be all, Celyn."

"Shall I summon your squires, Papa?"

Llewelyn resisted the temptation to ask if Davydd wanted to keep vigil by his bedside till he slept. "No, Davydd, that's not necessary. Go back to the hall now, make sure that our guests are looked after."

Gathering up the correspondence, the scribe made a discreet departure; those who served Llewelyn this spring had, of necessity, learned to be as prescient as soothsayers, as unobtrusive as shadows. Davydd paused in the doorway. "God grant you a restful night, Papa," he said, and Llewelyn thought it might be for the best, after all, that Richard had come to his court. Mayhap Richard might be able to do what he could not, talk to the lad about Joanna. That Davydd had such a need, he well knew. A man might disavow a wanton, cheating wife. But a son could not be expected to disavow his mother.

Reaching for a flagon, Llewelyn poured himself a cup of malmsey. He drank slowly, rationing himself, for he was not such a fool as to think he could drown his dreams in wine. Picking up the cup, he crossed to the bed, lay down upon it fully clothed. The dreams had a numbing sameness, differing only in detail. Most often the dream did but reflect reality; he would

walk into his bedchamber, unsuspecting, and find his wife with
her young lover. More than once, though, the dream took an
even uglier turn, and he would enter the chamber while they were
making love, naked bodies entwined together in his bed, so lost
in their lust they did not perceive their danger until it was too
late, until he had sword in hand. Sometimes he heeded Ednyved,
took a more calculating, cold-blooded vengeance; sometimes
Will died at once, there in the bedchamber. But not Joanna, for
even in his dreams he could never bring himself to thrust the
sword into her breast.

As harrowing as these dreams were, they were not as rending
as the others, the dreams of days gone by, those that recreated his
world before his discovery of Joanna's infidelity. Like most
dreams, they were an incongruous blend of the fanciful and the
commonplace, dreams in which a man might get saddle sores
from riding a unicorn. But in them all, Joanna was the one
constant. Taking a bath, she'd splash him with soapy water,
giggling like a little girl. Or she'd look up at him over a Welsh
grammar lesson, grimace and vow she'd master his tongue if it
took her a lifetime. She was there to welcome him home from
war, and there beside him in the night, and the seductive lure of
memory was such that he would awaken in drowsy arousal,
reaching for her. And then he would remember.

Llewelyn took a deep swallow of malmsey. Upon his first
night at Dolwyddelan, he'd been crossing the bailey, had come
upon some of his soldiers squatting by the door of the great hall,
passing a flask back and forth as they discussed his wife's
betrayal, her lover's death. They tempered their abuse of Will de
Braose with a grudging acknowledgment of his gallows courage,
but they spared Joanna nothing, damned her in language as
coarse as it was colorful. When Llewelyn stepped out of the
darkness, they scrambled to their feet, staring at him in stricken
silence. All save one youngster, drunker than the rest, who
blurted out, "I do not understand your forbearance, my lord.
You must hate her now, you must! So why have you not punished her as she deserves?"

Appalled, his more sober comrades made haste to intervene,
sought to turn aside Llewelyn's anger with a babble of apology
and excuse. Llewelyn looked at the boy, younger even than
Davydd, trying in his muddled way to empathize with his lord's
pain. How easy it would be to make a scapegoat of this imprudent
youth. Easy and understandable and unjust. "I do not suffer fools
gladly," he said curtly, "but luckily for you, lad, I have more

patience with drunkards. Go sleep it off.'' The soldiers did not press their luck; they scattered.

But the boy's question stayed with Llewelyn in the days to come. Why had he not punished Joanna as she deserved? Why had he sent her to Llanfaes? Why had he made hers such a comfortable confinement? He'd done it for Davydd's sake. That was the obvious answer, the easy answer. But was it the only answer?

His last memory of Joanna had yet to fade; he had only to close his eyes to bring it into sudden, sharp focus, to see the tangled dark hair, the rumpled sheets, even the sweat trickling down her throat, into the hollow between her breasts. That woman he could hate, and did, the woman who'd taken a Norman lover, made him a laughingstock, betrayed his trust, jeopardized Davydd's succession. Blood will tell, the soldiers had jeered; who should be surprised that John's daughter showed herself to be a shameless wanton? Harlot. Whore. Harsh, ugly names. The woman who'd taken Will into his bed deserved them all.

But what of the seventeen-year-old girl who'd almost died giving birth to Davydd? Or the woman who'd stood in this chamber, pleading with him to let her intercede with John? What of the woman who'd curtsied to him that day at Aberconwy, salvaging his pride, defying her father for his sake? Did she, too, deserve to be called slut?

Llewelyn drained the last of the wine, threw the cup across the room, watched it shatter against the wall. It was an act of impulse, one he at once regretted. Come morning, the servants would find the broken clay shards upon the floor; they would make no comment, would clean up the wreckage with impassive faces. And they would not understand.

No one did. Morgan had come the closest to comprehending; in his one attempt at consolation, he'd counseled endurance. "Give yourself time, Llewelyn, time to grieve. Try to remember that pain does pass. Think upon Tangwystl and how you mourned her. But the hurt did eventually heal . . . and so will this.''

At least Morgan could understand that it was possible to grieve for an unfaithful wife; few others did. But he was wrong to equate Tangwystl's death with Joanna's betrayal. This was a different sort of loss, and in its own way, more painful, for he'd lost more than Joanna, he'd lost their life together, too. In destroying their future, Joanna had also poisoned their past.

Closing his eyes, Llewelyn lay back against the pillow. But no

man could ever fully master memory. The tides ran higher at
night, and he found himself engulfed without warning, carried
back in time to an October afternoon, to the cloistered silence of
the White Ladies Priory. Joanna was standing again before him,
disheveled, breathless, a russet leaf clinging to her hair, turning
up to him a face streaked with tears.

Llewelyn gave a sudden, bitter laugh, for what greater irony
could there be than this, that the one person able to understand
exactly how he now felt should be Joanna, Joanna who'd cried
out in such despair, "If he'd died, I'd still have had memories.
But now even my memories are false. They do not comfort, they
only torment . . ."

"Richard!" Joanna's book thudded to the floor; in three strides she
was across the room, in her brother's arms. "How glad I am to
see you, how very glad!" He did not return her embrace, merely
patted her awkwardly on the shoulder, but he'd always been
sparing with physical demonstrations of affection, and she reached
up, kissed him on the cheek before stepping back to smile at him.

"I'm not sure what I expected, Joanna. But not this," he said,
glancing about the bedchamber. "One might think you were still
Princess of Gwynedd."

Joanna's smile vanished; his voice was very cold. "Would you
rather have found me in a dungeon at Cricieth, Richard?"

"Of course not," he said impatiently. "But I cannot help
marveling at Llewelyn's leniency."

"You've seen him, talked to him? Tell me how he is, Richard.
How does he?"

"How do you think he does? The man loved you, Joanna."

"I know," she whispered. "I know . . ."

"How could you do it? How could you shame yourself, shame
your family like this? At first I thought it had to be some sort of
macabre hoax! And if I could not believe it, I would not even
attempt to imagine what Llewelyn—"

"Richard, enough! I do not need you to tell me of the pain
I've caused those I love. I was there, I saw, and those are
memories I'll have to live with for the rest of my life. I do not
deny that I have committed a grievous sin, and I'll willingly
answer for it to my husband, to my children, to the King, and to
God. But not to you, Richard. Least of all to you!"

"You do not think I've a right to be angry? Disappointed?"

"I do not think you've the right to pass judgment upon me. I think you forfeited that right when you refused to pass judgment upon John."

"What mean you by that, Joanna?"

"You knew, Richard. You knew about Arthur, about Maude de Braose and her son. You saw the hangings. But you stood by John even then, even after watching those Welsh children die at Nottingham. So I do not think it is for you to judge me. Unless you can explain why adultery is a greater sin in your eyes than murder."

"I see it was a mistake for me to come."

"Mayhap it was," Joanna agreed, and he turned, walked out.

But no sooner had he gone than Joanna's anger was gone, too. She sat down upon the closest coffer, feeling weak, empty, and alone, utterly alone. Why had she sent Richard away? Who else did she have? Henry would be no less shocked than Richard, no less judgmental. An unfaithful wife was a creature utterly beyond her Aunt Ela's ken. She was not close to her other brothers. Two of her three sisters were strangers to her, and Nell was but fourteen.

Even her dead would not have understood. Catherine had been her dearest friend, but Catherine had been Llewelyn's friend, too. Her grandmother? Eleanor would have been indifferent to the immorality of her adultery, but would never have forgiven the stupidity of it. Her mother would have been horrified, with the peculiar intolerance of the onetime sinner. Her father? Hating Llewelyn as he did, how could he not have been delighted by her infidelity? But her mockery went awry, for she knew better. John would not have forsaken her. The man who had murdered Maude de Braose was the same man who had loved her enough to forgive her any sin.

She had sent Glynis to gather gorse and wood sorrel, and she was grateful now to hear footsteps in the antechamber, grateful for Glynis's opportune return; hers were not thoughts she cared to dwell upon. She rose, moved toward the door. But it was not Glynis, it was Richard.

His smile was tentative, almost but not quite apologetic. "I would not have gotten so angry if there were not some truth in what you said. But I was halfway to the ferry ere I would admit it to myself."

"You came back, Richard. That is what matters," Joanna said, and this time their embrace was mutual, comforting and conciliatory. Drawing him down beside her upon the settle, Joanna entwined her fingers in his. "I will answer your questions as best I can. But first you must tell me if you spoke to Davydd, if he gave you any message for me.''

He shook his head. ''He's not yet able to talk about you, Joanna. Mayhap in time . . .'' He tightened his grip upon her hand. ''How much have you been told? You do know Will de Braose has been hanged?''

''Yes,'' she said, startling him by her matter-of-fact tone. If she could sound so indifferent to Will's fate, then all his assumptions had to be in error.

''I can offer no excuses, no explanations for my conduct, Richard. But there is this you must know. My liaison with Will was a brief one, and long over. But Will was not accustomed to a woman telling him no and meaning it, thought he would be welcome in my chambers. He was not.'' Richard was looking at her so strangely that she felt sudden dismay. ''You do not believe me?''

''How could I have been so stupid? I actually believed you must have been beguiled by this man, had become so infatuated you'd lost all common sense. Knowing you as I do, how could I have been so blind?'' He rose to his feet, began to pace. ''Why did I not see the truth ere this?''

''What are you talking about?''

''I think you know, Joanna. But if you'd have me elaborate upon the obvious, I am willing. Where shall we begin? With Llewelyn? You love your husband, you truly do. You have a marriage that was tested in fire and found true, a marriage that by rights ought to have foundered years ago, and yet it not only survived, it somehow flourished. You're no fool; you well knew the consequences of a wife's infidelity, knew you risked divorce and disgrace, mayhap even death. You knew, too, that adultery is a mortal sin. Yet despite all that, you still decided to take the risk, to take a lover. And of all the men in Christendom, whom did you happen to choose? Surprise of surprises, none other than Maude de Braose's grandson! Need I say more?''

Joanna's protest was immediate—and indignant. ''What are you saying, that John's sins led me to sin in atonement? That is ridiculous, Richard. I am not responsible for my father's cruelties!''

''I know,'' he said. ''I've been seeking to convince you of that for nigh on twenty years.''

Joanna opened her mouth to argue, to insist he was wrong. Instead she surprised herself by saying, ''I do think it was important to Will that I was John's daughter. I think he found a perverse satisfaction in that. He learned to hate too young. But he had cause, Richard, more cause than you know . . .''

She did not finish the sentence, said abruptly, "What of Henry? Does he know?"

Richard nodded. "He got word ere he sailed for St Malo." He sat down beside her again. "I'll not lie to you, Joanna; it's better that you know. Sentiment is very much on Llewelyn's side, even in England. Men feel he was justified in acting as he did, that Will de Braose well deserved to die. More than eight hundred people gathered to witness his execution, and not all of them Welsh. Will was too familiar with too many bedchambers; even amongst his own family, he does not seem to have been much mourned."

Joanna linked her fingers in her lap. She found herself thinking, now, not of the man who'd brought disaster upon them both, not even of the man who'd been her lover, but of the youngster who'd come to her aid with boyish, good-natured gallantry, who'd put her in mind of Llewelyn at fourteen. "To die alone and unloved," she said softly. "What a sad fate . . ."

Richard shrugged. "It is your fate that concerns me now. I'll admit I was none too sanguine ere today . . . ere seeing this," he said, gesturing about the bedchamber. "But I am beginning to believe all is not as bleak as I first thought."

Joanna bowed her head. "Llewelyn says . . . he says I am dead to him, Richard."

"Yes, I know. But have you not noticed the startling discrepancy between what Llewelyn has said and what he has done? I do not mean to inflict further hurt, Joanna, but few men would treat an unfaithful wife as indulgently as he has so far treated you. I think his forbearance bodes well for the future. Whilst it is true that the Church does not formally recognize adultery as grounds for divorce, Llewelyn will have no trouble in—"

"Welsh law does provide for dissolving a marriage upon a wife or a husband's infidelity," Joanna interrupted, and despite herself, she could not help remembering the night Llewelyn had told her that, the night they'd first shared a bed as man and wife.

"A husband's infidelity, too?" Richard echoed, so surprised he almost allowed himself to be sidetracked. But the oddities of the Welsh legal system would have to wait. "Joanna, listen. I've been giving it much thought. As I see it, Llewelyn has three choices open to him. He can continue to keep you here, at Llanfaes. He can compel you to enter a nunnery. Or he can banish you from his domains. I expected him to select the second alternative. You're something of an embarrassment, you know . . . both to the Welsh and to the English, and a cloistered embarrassment would fade more quickly from men's memories. But now that I've seen your confinement, I think we might reasonably hope for the best, that he might agree to your return to England.''

"Mayhap he might. I do not know, Richard. Nor do I much care,'' Joanna confessed, and Richard smiled.

"Not now, no. But even the most benign captivity is still that, captivity. You need only think of our cousin, Eleanor of Brittany, comfortably kept at Bristol and Corfe castles for nigh on thirty years. In time you will care, Joanna, you'll care passionately.''

Joanna said nothing, and he reached out, patted her hand. "You must be patient, though. It would be disastrous to pressure Llewelyn now. We can only wait, first for the divorce and then for his decision. But Henry will not forsake you. You're family, and that matters more to Henry than scandal. I do believe that eventually you will be set at liberty, and once that happens, you'll have a home with my wife and me, a home at Chilham Castle.''

"Thank you, Richard,'' Joanna said, because it was expected of her. But his offer seemed no more real than did the future he envisioned for her. Rising, she moved to the table, opened a small casket.

"I've written letters to Elen and Davydd, to Henry and Nell. Will you take them, Richard? Will you engage couriers for me?''

"Of course. And I shall write to Llewelyn on your behalf, ask him if you cannot be allowed to leave these rooms occasionally. I think he might agree, if only for Davydd's sake.''

"I would like that,'' Joanna admitted, "to be able to walk on the beach.'' She hesitated, reluctant to make a request that might be misconstrued. "There is one thing more you can do for me, Richard. I would like to have Masses said for Will, for the repose of his soul.'' And when he made no comment, but merely nodded, she sighed, said quietly, "I cannot mourn him. I'm not even sure I can forgive him. But at least I can pray for him.''

14

LLANFAES, NORTH WALES

June 1230

Richard read Llewelyn correctly, and an order did arrive in due course, allowing Joanna the freedom of the manor compound and the nearby beach. Her guards objected to this new duty in vain, protesting that they felt foolish trailing after a lone woman and an aging spaniel. Lady Joanna could not swim; did Bran fear she could walk on water? But Bran remained adamant. Would any of them want to face their lord if she disappeared? Or if harm befell her? For so baffled were they about what their duties actually were, uncertain whether they were gaolers or bodyguards.

It was a warm Sunday in late June, too warm for walking, and when Joanna came upon the debris of an ancient wreck, she sat down upon a salt-encrusted spar. The guard following at a discreet distance stretched out on the sand, began to doze. So, too, did Joanna's spaniel.

Joanna spent many hours like this, gazing across the strait toward Aber. She knew Llewelyn was no longer there, so even this last tenuous link had been sundered, but she found herself drawn to the beach nonetheless. It was an uncommonly clear day; the wind was still and the Eryri Mountains had shed their cloud haloes. She was able to recognize individual peaks, Llewelyn's lessons in geography having at last taken effect, and she realized suddenly how much she would miss these familiar soaring silhouettes, miss the stark splendors of her husband's realm. "You were right, love," she whispered. "You always said I'd come in time to see the grandeur of your homeland . . ."

Topaz had begun to bark. From the corner of her eye, Joanna glimpsed a woman crossing the sand. "Hush, girl," she soothed. " 'Tis only Glynis." But the dog knew better, was already caper-

ing about in eager welcome. Joanna turned and her heart skipped
a beat, then began to race. Flustered and not a little fearful, she
stood very still, watching as her daughter walked toward her.
This was the confrontation she'd most dreaded. Davydd might in
time forgive her, but Elen? They'd been too often at odds, never
quite connecting, theirs an erratic sort of intimacy, one with
boundaries, self-imposed constraints, vast areas left uncharted,
unexplored by mutual consent. What could she say to Elen now?
How could she expect Elen to understand?

"Well, I will say this for you, Mama. No half measures; when
you decide to come down off your pedestal, you do so with a
vengeance."

The words were tart, but surprisingly the tone was not; it was
more rueful than reproachful, almost whimsical. Joanna stared at
her unpredictable daughter, saying at last, "I am glad you've
come, Elen."

"I would have come sooner, but John and I had gone north
from Edinburgh, were doubtlessly the last to know." Elen glanced
over at the sleeping soldier before sitting down upon the sea-
warped driftwood. "Your guard is out of hearing range. Sit with
me, Mama, so we can talk."

"Did you get my letter?" Joanna asked, sighing with relief
when Elen nodded.

"Yes, it finally caught up with me, and just in time. Papa's
letter had been sparing of details, and I was well nigh going mad,
trying to envision circumstances under which you'd have taken a
lover into Papa's bedchamber. I could only conclude you were
sore crazed with love, and yet you'd showed no symptoms of it
at Shrewsbury. When your letter came, I could only wonder why
I'd not guessed the truth. That was so very like Will, after all."

Elen finally paused for breath. "All this did clear up one
mystery for me, though. Will was notorious for his roving eye,
and yet with me he was always quite circumspect, could not have
been more respectful had I been a nun. At least now I know
why!"

"Elen . . . I will never understand you. How can you jest?"

"I guess . . . guess because I'm nervous. I just did not know
what to say to you." Elen mustered a wan smile. "You will
admit, Mama, that my lessons in the social graces never covered
a situation quite like ours."

She did not wait for Joanna's response, leaned forward and
touched her mother's hand. "I do have some good news for you.
I asked Papa if the priest from St Catherine's could say weekly

Mass at the manor, and he agreed. Mama . . . does that not please you? Why do you look at me so strangely?''

"I . . . I never expected sympathy, Elen.''

Elen withdrew her hand. "Why not? Why should you think I'd be less understanding than Davydd?"

"Davydd does not understand, darling. I can only hope that he will in time, as I'd hoped you might. But I would not have blamed you for being bitter. We've so often been at cross purposes, and I know . . . I know how much you love your father.''

"Yes, I do. I love Papa dearly. But what would you have me do, Mama? Disavow you because you made a mistake? Would that change anything? Would it make Papa's hurt any the less?''

"A mistake,'' Joanna echoed, dismayed. Had Elen so misconstrued her letter? "Elen, I thought you understood. I was unfaithful to your father.''

"Yes, Mama, I know. You broke your marriage vows. But a few afternoons in an abandoned *hafod* do not make you the whore of Babylon. You sinned and then were sorry. I daresay the same can be said of Papa. Papa is a remarkable man, in truth, but he wears a crown, not a halo. Surely you know he has been unfaithful to you?''

Joanna was both disconcerted and defensive. "Yes . . . I know. But when I compared my lot with that of most wives, I had no cause for complaint. Llewelyn never kept a mistress at court; he even put aside Cristyn for me. Whilst we never discussed it, I knew he did bed with other women, but only when I was not available, only when we'd been long apart.''

"As when he was waging war in Ceri?''

"Elen, I do not see the point of this. What would you have me say? Of course I would rather Llewelyn shared no bed but mine. But I could not realistically expect him to abstain for weeks at a time.''

"You did.''

"Why are you being so perverse? You cannot equate Llewelyn's occasional lapses with my adultery. Infidelity is a greater sin for a woman; so it has always been.''

"Yes, so men keep telling us,'' Elen said dryly, and Joanna found herself staring at her daughter as if at a stranger.

"I once told my father that blood breeds true,'' she said slowly. "I spoke greater truth than I knew, for none could ever doubt you are Eleanor of Aquitaine's great-granddaughter. It frightens me to hear you talk like this, for I do not think you realize the danger in it. Elen . . . Elen, you've never . . . ?'' She let the sentence trail off, and Elen gave her a smile of gentle mockery.

"You ought not to ask a question, Mama, unless you are sure you truly want to know the answer."

"Oh, Elen, no . . ." Joanna whispered, sounding so horrified that Elen flushed, sprang to her feet.

"What are you going to do, Mama? Lecture me on morality? I should think that would be rather droll, coming from you!"

Joanna, too, was on her feet now. "Elen, you must listen to me. I am not passing judgment upon you, ask only that you hear me out. Walk toward the water with me, so we may be sure we cannot be overheard. Please, darling, you do not know what you risk!"

Elen hesitated. "Very well, Mama. But I'll hear no sermons from you!"

"I said I was not judging you. I want only to ask you a question. Mine could have been a far different fate. But your father has shown me remarkable leniency. Why do you think that is, Elen?"

This was not the question Elen was expecting. "I . . . I suppose he did it for us, for Davydd and me. And then, he did love you. Mayhap he finds it hard to hurt you, even now . . ."

Joanna flinched, but then she nodded. "You are right. But I think there is yet another reason for his restraint. I think his response might have been different had he not been Welsh."

Elen came to an abrupt halt. "I do not understand. Welsh law holds adultery to be a grave sin indeed. So why . . ."

"Because the Welsh look upon women in a different light. A Welshman does not think of his wife as his property; she has rights of her own. But a Norman wife does not, and that makes her betrayal all the more unforgivable in her husband's eyes. Elen, I know of what I speak, for I am Norman-French born and bred; their ways are mine. I know no Norman lord capable of treating an unfaithful wife as Llewelyn has so far treated me, not even the men of my own family. My darling, your husband is a good man, but he does not share your heritage, and you must ever bear that in mind. Promise me that, Elen, promise me you'll not forget."

Elen's resentment had ebbed away as Joanna spoke. "You've no cause for fear, Mama. That question you almost asked? The answer is no, I have not."

Joanna looked into her daughter's beautiful brown eyes, eyes that held hers quite candidly, and realized she had no way of

knowing whether Elen spoke the truth. Even if she had, what of
tomorrow? Elen was entrapped in an unhappy marriage, a barren
marriage. How long would it be ere she sought satisfaction
elsewhere, ere that rebellious spirit led her astray?

"Ah, Elen . . ." Her voice wavered. "How could we have
meant so well and done so wrong? I truly thought you could learn
to love John the Scot, but I should have known, should have
seen . . ."

"I no longer blame you, Mama." Elen stooped to pick up a
cockle shell. "None of us is given a warranty of happiness, not
in this life. Even if I'd wed another man, who's to say we'd have
found contentment together? Sometimes even love is not enough.
After all, you loved Papa, and where did it get you?"

"To Llanfaes," Joanna said tonelessly, and Elen dropped the
shell, moved to close the space between them.

"Mama, I'm sorry! I do not know why I said that. Why must
my accursed tongue inflict wounds I never mean?"

"It does not matter, Elen . . . truly."

"But it does! I swore to myself that this time I would not do it,
that I'd say nothing hurtful or harsh." Elen turned her back,
stood staring out over the water. When she spoke again, her
voice was indistinct, pitched very low. "But I've sworn that
before, only to hear myself provoking yet another quarrel with
you, stirring up strife betwixt us . . ."

"Why?" Joanna reached out, touched her daughter's arm.
"Why, Elen?"

"I would that I knew! Frustration, resentment, mayhap sheer
perversity. You do not bring out the best in me, Mama. But then
I hardly need tell you that, do I? I've always been a disappointment to you, as far back as I can remember—"

"Darling, that's not so! Elen, I love you, I do!"

Elen kept her eyes stubbornly set upon the distant mountains,
but her lashes were wet, tangled. "That may be so, Mama, but
you do not approve of me. I used to wonder how Davydd did it,
how he knew so unerringly just how to please you, for I . . . I
never did, you see. I did try, though. You may not believe that,
but I did.

"I was about seven the first time I realized you were not like
the mothers of my friends. Your father had freed some of Papa's
hostages, merely because you asked it of him. People were so
joyful, so grateful, and I was so proud of you. I wanted to be a
great lady, too . . . just like you. And as I grew older, I watched
as you acted for Papa at the English court, I saw how much Papa

loved you, and I tried to be what you wanted, to be like you. But you were so controlled, so serene, so sure of yourself, and I . . . I was none of those things, Mama. In truth, I was not in the least like you, at best could only hope to become an imperfect copy of a perfect original, and that seemed rather pointless to me, even at fourteen. And so I stopped trying to gain your approval. Only I . . . I could not stop wanting it.''

Elen had not intended to reveal so much and she forced an abrupt, self-conscious laugh. "I did not mean to babble on like this. I guess I've been like a bottle corked too long. One inadvertent touch, and the contents spew out in a great gush. Let that be a lesson to you, Mama. There are few questions so full of risk as a seemingly simple 'why.' ''

Joanna had been listening to her daughter's outpouring in astonishment. "Is that how you truly saw me, Elen? As controlled, serene, sure of myself? God in Heaven!" She caught Elen's arm, turned the younger woman to face her. "Elen, look at me. Truly look at me. I was a King's bastard. Under our law, I had no claims to anything, least of all to my father's name. My father loved me, but he could not legitimize my position at his court; I was there on sufferance and all knew it. And then at fourteen, I became a foreign wife, the English bride, the outsider once more.''

Elen's eyes had widened. "I never knew you felt that way, Mama. You always seemed at home in Wales.''

"That is what I am trying to tell you, Elen. I learned at a very early age to hide my fears, to appear what I was not. Pride, no less than charity, covers a multitude of sins. I was very fortunate, found with your father what had been denied me in John's world, and in time I did gain greater assurance; the poise was not entirely pretense. But scrape away the surface gloss, dig through the glaze to the raw clay, and you'll find a little girl forbidden to play with the other village children, a little girl who'd lie for hours in the heather above Middleham Castle, wanting only to belong.

"And that is what I wanted to give you, a sense of belonging. You were so impulsive, Elen, so . . . so rash. I did try to curb your spirits, to teach you to adapt to the world you'd one day have to live in, as the wife of a Norman lord. I did want you to conform; I cannot deny it. And I was disappointed when you would not. But only because I loved you so much, because I feared for you. My darling, you seemed so heartrendingly vulnerable, so open to hurt. I wanted to spare you that if I could, to

show you how to construct a woman's defenses, how to make
castle walls out of courtesy, to distance yourself whilst still
preserving the inner keep, the secret self that is Elen.''

Elen was blinking back tears. "I daresay you're right, Mama."
She gestured toward a tiny bird skittering along the water's edge.
"Life probably would be easier for me if I had protective coloring, if I could blend into my background like that little sandling." She smiled tremulously. "But I'm not a sandling, Mama,
am more akin to the magpie, I fear, curious and conspicuous and
too venturesome for my own good!"

Joanna stepped forward, touched her hand to Elen's cheek.
"As it happens," she said, "magpies have ever been one of my
favorite birds," and Elen came into her arms, clung tightly.

Joanna was reluctant to end their embrace, kept her arm around
Elen's waist. "Passing strange, that you should have drawn that
analogy to the sandling, for your father once made a surprisingly
similar comparison. He, too, talked of protective coloring, told
me I cloaked myself in the muted earth tones of a wellborn
Norman lady. But he knew it was camouflage, knew me so
well . . ."

He'd never been taken in by her act. Right from the first he'd
seen through it, had seen the frightened little girl behind the
bridal silk, the brittle smile. Joanna's eyes filled with tears.
"Elen . . . Elen, I've made such a bloody botch of things. Tell
me the truth. How badly have I hurt Llewelyn? I do not mean the
man; that I know. But what of the Prince? How much damage
have I done?"

"Not as much damage as you fear, Mama. I'll not deny the
potential was there for disaster, that you threw a burning brand
into a sun-dried field. But Papa acted to contain the fire, seems to
have quenched it in time. Not so surprising, at least not to
anyone who knows Papa. He holds all Wales in the palm of his
hand, has for nigh on fifteen years now. It would take a brave
man to challenge him, an even braver one to mock him. Mayhap
if he'd showed weakness . . . but he hanged Will de Braose at
high noon before eight hundred witnesses. Men will remember
that, Mama."

"And Davydd?"

Elen did not pretend to misunderstand. "Again, the answer is
not as much damage as you think . . . or as there could have
been. Papa has made a point of keeping Davydd close by his
side—conspicuously so. When he met the English Chancellor in
Shrewsbury last week, Davydd was with him, and will be with

him again when he meets with Maelgwn next month. It is an effective strategy, Mama, will do much to discourage speculation, to still all but the most vicious tongues."

"I would to God I could believe that . . ."

"I'm not offering false comfort, Mama. Papa is a man well able to take care of himself, to look to his own interests. He was never a defensive battle commander, preferred to take the war into enemy territory. And that is what he has done. He is no longer calling himself Prince of Gwynedd, has begun to make use of a new title—Prince of Aberffraw and Lord of Eryri."

After more than twenty years in Wales, Joanna at once grasped the significance of the change. Aberffraw was the ancient capital of Gwynedd, and in Welsh lore, the Prince of Aberffraw held a position of dominance. Although he was shrewd enough to do it by indirection, with a subtlety to allay the suspicions of his English neighbors and the jealousies of his Welsh allies, Llewelyn was, in effect, claiming for himself the title of Prince of Wales.

Joanna bit her lip. "How very like him that is," she said, and there was in her voice such a poignant blend of pride and pain that Elen felt as if their roles had suddenly been reversed; she found herself yearning to comfort Joanna as a mother might comfort a hurt and helpless child.

"Let's go back to the manor, Mama. You look so careworn; you've not been sleeping, have you?"

"Not much," Joanna admitted. She whistled for Topaz and they began to walk along the shore. "We'd best wake Ifan up ere we go; I think he might be discomfited if we just went off and left him. Tell me about Gwladys and Ralph de Mortimer. Were they wed as planned?"

"No, the wedding was delayed. But it has been rescheduled for next month." Elen's eyes rested pensively upon her mother's face. She'd not exaggerated; the strain was telling upon Joanna. She sighed, knowing what she had now to say would only lacerate an overburdened conscience even more.

"I know no other way than to say this straight out, Mama. Papa and the de Braose family have decided to honor the plight troth."

Joanna stared at her daughter in disbelief. "Davydd . . . Davydd is still going to wed Will's daughter?"

Elen nodded. "Papa wrote to Eva de Braose and her brother Pembroke, told them that whilst he'd had no choice but to put Will to death, he was still willing to consider a marital alliance. Will's widow and Pembroke showed themselves to be no less pragmatic than Papa. Not only did they want the marriage to take place, they wanted it to be celebrated as soon as possible, despite Isabella's tender years. The wedding is to be held at Cricieth in Michaelmas week.''

Joanna closed her eyes, but the sun still burned against her lids, dried the tears on her cheeks. How could Llewelyn bear to do this? How could he look at Isabella de Braose and not think of Will? ''And Davydd . . . he's willing?''

''Yes, Mama, it seems he is. In part, I think, because he wants so much to please Papa. If Papa were to suggest he wed with a mermaid, I daresay Davydd would start scouring the beaches for one. But there's more to it than that. People ofttimes misjudge Davydd. He's more like Papa than men realize; theirs are differences more of style than substance. Davydd knows his own mind, Mama, knows what he wants—and obviously that is Buellt Castle.''

Elen, like Llewelyn and Davydd, spoke French with Joanna, partly from habit, partly for the greater privacy it accorded their conversations, and partly because their French was more fluent than Joanna's Welsh. She was surprised now to hear her mother murmur, as if to herself, *''Un pechod a lusg gant ar ei ol.''*

''One sin draws a hundred after it? Ah, Mama, you're too hard on yourself.''

''Am I? I think not, Elen.'' Joanna turned away, stared blindly out to sea. ''That poor little lass,'' she said softly. ''How bewildered she must be, how fearful . . .''

15

CRICIETH, NORTH WALES

September 1230

Will de Braose was not entirely unmourned. There was one who
grieved for him—his ten-year-old daughter. Isabella's was a
world of restrictive boundaries, a life of absolutes and order,
subject at all times to the stringent, exacting disciplines laid
down by Eva de Braose. A timid child, Isabella had learned
obedience at an early age, but she had also learned to fear her
mother. Eva was the bedrock to which their family clung, anchor
and mainstay, and she ruled her small domain with a tight
rein—in Will's absences. For into this cloistered citadel of enforced serenity, Will would burst like a flaming comet, trailing
the real world in his wake like celestial vapors. He invariably
disrupted daily routine, unsettled the servants, and took malicious
pleasure in disobliging his coolly competent wife. Isabella—quite
simply and unknowingly—he bedazzled.

To a child nurtured upon reprimands, starved for affection, it
was not difficult to unearth evidence of love in Will's benign
neglect, to magnify his careless kindnesses to epic proportions.
Isabella treasured his smiles, the small gifts he would occasionally bestow, kept a lock of his bright blond hair in her birthday
locket. His death had devastated her, and her grieving was all the
greater for its secret, unsanctioned nature. That her mother did
not mourn Will, the child well knew, and fear made her mute,
for she could not risk Eva's disapproval. Now that Will was
dead, Eva's favor was all the more precious, was all she had.

Eva had spared her eldest daughter none of the sordid circumstances of Will's death, but that account was too brutal, too
degrading for the child to accept. In self-defense, she set about
weaving Eva's ugly facts into a softer pattern, one that reflected

the colors of romance and high tragedy. All the minstrel tales that so enthralled her celebrated the splendors of illicit passions, celebrated star-crossed lovers like Arthur's Queen and the brave Lancelot, Tristan and the fair Iseult. So it must have been for Papa and the Lady Joanna, she decided, and she found comfort in casting Will as the gallant knight who died for love, Joanna as the tragic beauty who'd loved him as Eva did not. And then her mother called her into the solar at Abergavenny Castle, told her that the plight troth still held, that she must wed Llewelyn's son at summer's end.

Although Eva de Braose had no qualms about marrying her daughter to a son of the man responsible for her husband's death, she did feel it would not be seemly for her to attend the wedding. As the Earl of Pembroke was in Brittany, it fell upon his young wife Nell and Gilbert, another of Eva's brothers, to escort Isabella to Cricieth.

Nell slowed her mare, dropped back to ride at Isabella's side. "We're but a few miles from Cricieth Castle, will be there by noon." Isabella's was by nature a pale, delicate complexion, but it showed now such a waxy whiteness that Nell grew alarmed. Poor little bird, she thought, and sought for words of cheer. "I shall be your aunt twice over come the morrow, for not only is my lord husband brother to your lady mother, the Lord Davydd is my nephew. Passing strange, I know, for he is a full seven years older than I! But he is a good man, Isabella, will treat you kindly." Would he, though? How could she be sure? In truth, she did not know Davydd well at all, could only wonder what had motivated him to make such a marriage as this.

Isabella swallowed. "Cricieth . . . is this where my father died?"

"No, lass. That was at Aber."

"He's buried there . . . at Aber?"

"Yes," Nell said, all the while heaping mental curses upon the head of her sister-in-law. Whatever ailed Eva? Had she told the child nothing?

"Aunt Nell . . . will they let me visit Papa's grave?"

"Jesú!" Nell turned sharply in the saddle, stared at the child. Merciful Christ, the lass loved her father! Damn Eva de Braose for this! How could she not know? Or was it that she did not care? "Yes, sweeting, I am sure they will," she said hastily, making a silent vow that she'd somehow see to it.

"I dared not ask Mama about her . . . about the Lady Joanna. Aunt Nell, will you tell me what befell her? Will she . . . will she be at Cricieth?"

Nell was getting in over her depth. She ought never to have agreed to this. She may be the child's aunt, but she was also Joanna's sister. At least, though, she could reassure the lass on this one point. "No, dearest, Joanna is not at Cricieth. You need not see her, not ever, for she has been sent away in disgrace."

"Oh . . ." An involuntary sound, a quavering sigh that communicated to Nell the unlikeliest of emotions, disappointment. Nell subsided into a baffled silence. She pitied Isabella, but was perplexed by her, too. She'd never known her own father, for John had died before her first birthday. But she had tried to imagine how she'd feel if she were being forced to marry into a family responsible for her brother Henry's death, and that only showed her how deep and divergent were the differences between her and Isabella de Braose, for she would never have agreed to the wedding, would have had to be dragged kicking and screaming to the altar.

She glanced reflectively at Isabella's profile. A pity the lass did not have more pluck. A lamb to the slaughter, in truth, and what could she do to help? "Isabella, I'm going to speak right plainly. As you're to be Davydd's wife, all you can do now is seek to make the best of it."

"Will they . . ." Isabella's voice was tremulous, faltering. "Will they hate me?"

"No, of course not," Nell said, somewhat impatiently, for that was a question she'd never have asked. The hatred would have been hers. But she could sense in Isabella only fear.

As they entered the great hall, Isabella balked suddenly, and Nell slipped a supportive arm around her waist. "When we reach the dais, remember to make your curtsy. Lord Davydd is the one at Lord Llewelyn's right, and those are Davydd's sisters, the Lady Elen, Countess of Huntingdon, and the Lady Gwladys de Mortimer. Come forward now, Isabella, and greet them." Still Isabella did not move; she was trembling so violently that Nell could only hope she'd not shame them by fainting. She murmured soothing words of reassurance, and when they had no effect, she hissed, "Isabella, show some spirit!" And that worked; Isabella had been taught unquestioning obedience. She followed Nell toward the dais, clinging to her arm.

It did not surprise Llewelyn that Isabella was so fair, for both

Will and Eva de Braose had flaxen hair. Still, the sight of the
child's blonde braids triggered a sudden, sharp memory. He
could see again her father standing on the gallows, the sun
gilding his hair with a silvery sheen. He'd never looked so
young, so vital and alive as he did then, in his last moments of
life. And as Llewelyn had watched, all he could see was that
blond head cradled in Joanna's lap. He shook off the past with
difficulty, moved down the steps of the dais.

"Look at me, child," he said quietly. Isabella did as he bade.
To his relief, she did not have Will's smoke-grey eyes; hers were
a soft misty blue. "You are very welcome at my court, Isabella.
I hope in time you'll come to feel at home with us." But his
words sank like stones into the depths of the child's fear, left no
impression, not even a ripple.

Davydd had no better luck. He was not particularly at ease
with children, and found himself at a loss now. Feeling rather
foolish, he murmured conventional words of welcome, handed
Isabella her bride's gift, an opal pendant set in silver; it might
better, he thought, have been a doll. Isabella mumbled an all but
inaudible "Thank you." She did not even unfasten the velvet
wrapping until prompted by Nell.

"Look, Isabella, how lovely it is. Here, let me clasp it about
your neck."

Llewelyn was faintly amused by Nell's purposeful, take-
charge manner, so at variance with her ethereal blonde beauty.
For she was a beauty, as young as she was, was very much Isabelle
d'Angoulême's daughter. But he could see nothing in her of John
or Joanna. Never had he been so aware how fleeting time was, how
unfairly and heartrendingly finite, looking now at Nell and realizing she was the same age as Joanna at the time of their wedding.

"Should you like to see the chamber made ready for you,
Isabella?" he suggested, and Isabella nodded quickly. She was,
he suspected, so anxious to escape their company that she'd have
acquiesced no less eagerly had he offered a tour of the stables.
But when Gwladys volunteered to take her, she hung back, blue
eyes imploring Nell not to desert her, not to forsake her so soon.

"I'll be along shortly, Isabella. I promise," Nell said, and the
adults watched in troubled silence as Gwladys led the girl away.
Nell's eyes, no less blue than Isabella's but a good deal more
vivid, flicked from face to face. A deal struck in theory could
prove to be quite different in fact, in the flesh-and-blood embodiment of a terrified ten-year-old. Did they, she wondered, still
think Buellt Castle was worth the price of purchase?

Gilbert Marshal cleared his throat, said with overly hearty assurance, "I daresay she just needs a little time. She's a gentle, biddable lass, and it's not as if she had a particular attachment to her father—"

"That's simply not so," Nell interrupted. "The girl thought the world of Will. And you need not glower at me like that, Gilbert. Better that they know the truth. Davydd, you will bear that in mind, and watch what you say to her?"

Her tone was a shade too peremptory for Davydd's liking. "Yes . . . Aunt Nell," he said dryly, but Nell was oblivious to the sarcasm, so single-minded was she in the pursuit of her own ends.

"Llewelyn, I must talk with you . . . about Joanna."

She at once felt the change in atmosphere, the sudden chill. Llewelyn's eyes grew guarded, gave away nothing of his thoughts, at once remote and utterly aloof. Davydd looked no less distant. Elen, too, had tensed. Gilbert hastened into the breach, said sharply, "Nell, you have no right—"

Nell refused to retreat. "Yes, I do. Who will speak for my sister if I do not? Llewelyn, it has been more than five months now. How much longer do you mean to hold Joanna at Llanfaes?"

Nell was the first one to put that question to Llewelyn; until now, no one else had dared. It may have been the challenging thrust of her query, as if he had to defend what he'd done. It may have been that he was unaccustomed to being interrogated by a fourteen-year-old girl. Or that he had no answer for her. But whatever the reasons, the result was a sudden flare of anger, intense enough to prevail over the constraints of courtesy, and he said curtly, "As long as I choose."

No one spoke. Nell flushed, lost some of her aplomb, showed herself vulnerable, after all, to the insecurities and misgivings of adolescence. "I'll . . . I'll go and see to Isabella now," she said, sounding so subdued that Elen, too, excused herself, followed Nell from the hall.

They walked in silence for some moments. Nell at last gave Elen a look that was both apologetic and embarrassed. "I did not help Joanna much, did I?"

"No," Elen said tartly. "For certes, you did not."

"I meant well, truly I did," Nell said, and sighed. "Henry says I'm too forthright for my own good. I suspect that's a polite way of saying I talk too much. But Elen, do you not think it strange that your father has not yet divorced Joanna?"

"Yes," Elen admitted, and she, too, sighed. "Yes . . . I do."

Elen had persuaded her husband to come back to Wales for Llewelyn's Christmas court at Aber. She understood the political considerations behind Llewelyn's choice; he could not let his subjects think him reluctant to return to his chief residence. But it was a political decision undertaken at great personal cost; never had Elen seen her father look so haggard, so bone-weary, so suddenly aged. Aber's atmosphere was proving oppressive to them all. An aura of gloom overhung the court, and the Christmas revelries were muted, lacking spontaneity or any genuine sense of joy.

Elen was standing with her husband John, and with Gwladys and Ralph de Mortimer, for Gwladys, too, had felt the need to be with her father on this particular Christmas Eve. As Elen watched, Isabella bade Davydd good night and made an unheralded, unnoticed departure from the hall. "That poor little lass," she said sadly, unconsciously echoing Joanna's prophetic judgment. As difficult as it was for Papa and Davydd to be back at Aber, might it not be hardest of all upon Will's daughter? "That child flits about like a wraith, does not even seem to cast a shadow. John, what say you we have her with us for a time?"

"Another bird with a broken wing, Elen?" John's smile was indulgent. "Mayhap in the spring," he temporized. But then Isabella was forgotten. A few feet away a woman in blue velvet was holding forth to a small but attentive audience; John recognized her as the Lady Gwenllian, wife to Ednyved. She had a loud, carrying voice, a distinctive laugh, and her words came clearly now to John's ear, words of venomous contempt, words that brought a rush of hot color into his wife's face, and he said hastily, "Let it lie, Elen. You do not want to cause a scene."

"No? Just watch me." Elen evaded his restraining hand, pushed her way through those encircling Gwenllian. An embarrassed silence fell at sight of her; few had realized she was within hearing range. Even Gwenllian was slightly discomfited, but too proud to show it. She smiled archly, said, "Lady Elen?" and Elen very deliberately tilted her wine cup, poured the contents onto Gwenllian's velvet gown.

Gwenllian screamed loudly enough to turn heads, stared at her wine-stained skirt as if she could not believe the evidence of her own eyes. Shock gave way almost at once to outrage, and she cried, "You've ruined my gown, you spoiled, willful—"

Gwenllian choked off further utterance so abruptly that Elen knew there could be but one reason why, and she turned, found Llewelyn was close enough to touch. She felt no surprise that he should have materialized with a suddenness that a sorcerer might envy; she was all too familiar with his uncanny sense of timing. He took in the situation at a glance, said without emotion, "How careless of you, Elen."

Gwenllian opened her mouth, closed it again. She saw her husband standing at the edge of the crowd, but he did not contradict Llewelyn; his face was impassive, and Gwenllian yearned to rake her nails across that dark, weathered skin, to damn Elen as she deserved, to spit and scratch and call down the wrath of the Almighty upon the lot of them. She did nothing, though, for greater than her fury was her fear of public humiliation. She bit down until her jaw muscles ached, until she could trust herself to say, "No matter. Who amongst us has never spilled a little wine?" She even managed a grimacing smile of sorts, but dared not let her eyes meet Elen's. Or Ednyved's. She'd saved face. But she would not forget, would not forgive.

"Elen." Llewelyn's voice was very low. As people drifted away, began to disperse, his hand closed on Elen's wrist. "I would talk with you," he said, and Elen could gauge the full extent of his anger by the unremitting pressure of those hard, bruising fingers. She followed him to a far corner of the hall, with Ednyved but a step behind. "Well?" Llewelyn said coldly. "You do owe me an explanation."

"I think I'm entitled to one, too," Ednyved interjected, no less coldly.

"I could not help it, Papa. She . . . she called Mama a slut."

Llewelyn's mouth thinned, twisted down. He glanced toward Ednyved. The other man nodded, said, "I'll see to it."

Llewelyn looked at his daughter, and then he did something he'd not done since she was a child; he tilted her face up to his, and kissed her upon the forehead, with enough tenderness to bring tears to her eyes. But when she started to speak, he shook his head, then turned and walked away.

Across the hall, Elen caught her husband's eye. John slowly shook his head. He was too well-bred to berate her before witnesses, but she knew she'd earned herself a long lecture on decorum and propriety. Gwladys and Davydd were making their way toward her; they, too, looked judgmental.

"When," Davydd said, "will you learn not to act upon your emotions?"

"Never, I hope," Elen said, and saw that her brother was not as disapproving as he'd have her think.

"Elen, do not mistake what I am about to say." Gwladys paused, intent upon choosing just the right words, for Joanna was a sensitive subject between them. "I am not defending Gwenllian, not at all. But there's more to her bad manners than sheer malice. Gwenllian and Ednyved's youngest son made up a bawdy, satiric song about Joanna and Will de Braose, and then he was fool-hardy enough to boast of the authorship. As you'd expect, Papa was enraged; so, too, was Ednyved. Gwenllian thought it prudent to pack her son off to Ireland for a stay, to give Papa's anger time to cool. But the incident put some noticeable cracks in her marriage, and she finds it easier to blame Joanna than to blame her son."

Ednyved had nine sons in all. Most of them were comparative strangers to Elen, and when she asked Gwladys for the rash poet's name, it meant nothing to her. But it would from now on. Gruffudd ab Ednyved. She would remember him. She would make a point of it.

Gwladys soon wandered away. Elen and Davydd stood alone for a time, watching the dancers circle back and forth. Elen loved to dance, but she could find in herself now not the slightest desire to join the carole. "I would have expected Papa to be wroth with Gwenllian; his pride would demand as much. But I saw more than anger in his face. Davydd, he still loves her."

"I know," Davydd said. "And how much easier it would be for him if he did not. I would that there were some strange alchemy to change love into hate, to blot out memories, to banish yesterdays . . ."

"Are you speaking for Papa? Or for yourself?"

"For Papa, Elen." Davydd sounded annoyed, and a silence fell between them. But then he said very softly, "I could never hate Mama."

"Papa looks so tired. I worry about him so much, Davydd . . ." Elen's eyes searched the hall, seeking her father. "Who is that woman with him? The one in green."

"You mean . . . Hunydd?"

"If that be her name. Who is she, Davydd? I've never seen her before." She looked at Davydd expectantly, was surprised to see color mount in his face.

"It has been over eight months, Elen." But even then she did not understand, not until he added defensively, "What did you expect Papa to do, take holy vows?"

Elen's eyes narrowed, focusing upon Hunydd with sudden, probing intensity, subjecting the older woman to an exacting scrutiny, one that was far from friendly. Hunydd's were quiet attractions—a smile of singular sweetness, a tranquil composure. There was nothing gaudy or obvious about her appearance, nothing garish in her dress. She was listening attentively to Llewelyn, but she was not clinging to him, was not giving herself proprietary airs. That mattered little to Elen; she still found herself seething with resentment, with a child's sense of betrayal and loss.

Davydd was watching her. "The marriage is dead, Elen," he said quietly.

"I know." Elen tore her gaze from Hunydd. "But tell me the truth, Davydd. Tell me it does not bother you to see that woman in Mama's place."

Davydd beckoned to a passing servant, claimed a cup of mead. He drank, glanced at his sister, and drank again. "It bothers me," he said, and passed the cup to Elen.

They looked at one another. All around them swirled the sounds of music, of harp and *crwth*. The hall was bedecked with evergreen boughs and Christmas holly, lit by blazing torches, flickering rushlights, gilded candelabras. But to Elen it seemed as festive as a wake. "Davydd . . . is it always like this?"

"No," he said, giving her a bleak smile. "Sometimes it is not nearly so cheerful."

At low tide, the white sands known to the Welsh as Traeth Lafan lay exposed and men could venture out upon them with little risk. Davydd stood at the water's edge, watching as his sister was ferried across the strait, and as the boat touched bottom, he strode forward, held out his hand to help her alight upon the sand.

"Dismiss your men," he said, "and I'll escort you back to Aber." Elen linked her arm in his, and they began to walk up the beach. "Tell me," he said, after a few moments, "how is Mama?"

"The truth? Wretchedly unhappy."

"Did you give her my letter?"

"You know I did." Elen stopped, put her hand imploringly upon his arm. "Summon the boatmen back, Davydd. Go and see her. It would mean so much to her if you—"

"No," he said hastily. "No . . . I cannot."

She stepped back, stared at him. "How can you be so

self-righteous, so unwilling to forgive? Jesú, Davydd, Mama would have forgiven you any sin under God's sky!''

"I know," he admitted. "Do you not think I want to see her? But I cannot, Elen. I cannot do that to Papa."

"But Davydd, Papa knows I go to Llanfaes. I've made no secret of it; nor has he ever attempted to dissuade me."

"You're not his son."

"Davydd, he would not—"

"You just do not understand. You do not see Papa every day, as I do. All his life, Papa has been the most decisive of men. Yet now he does nothing. Men expected him to divorce Mama months ago. But he has not. He cannot bring himself to do it . . . not yet. The wound is still too raw. It's not healing as it ought, Elen, and till it does, I'll do nothing that might add to his pain."

"Ah, Davydd . . ." But she did not know what to say, and they walked the rest of the way in silence.

"Am I intruding, Papa?"

Llewelyn shoved his chair back, smiled at his daughter. "An opportune intrusion, lass. As you can see," he said, gesturing toward the chessboard, "Ednyved has maneuvered me into a right perilous position."

Elen closed the door, came forward into the bedchamber. As she did, she could not help envisioning the desperate drama that had been played out in this chamber at Eastertide, and she thought, How can Papa bear to sleep here? "Papa, we do need to talk . . . about Mama."

Llewelyn's smile froze, and when Ednyved started to rise, he said, "There is no need to go. Elen, I've told you this before. There is nothing to say."

"But there is, Papa, and I beg you to hear me out. Not only for your sake, for Davydd's."

Llewelyn pushed his chair back still farther, got to his feet. "Davydd?"

"Papa, he is being torn in two. He thinks he cannot be loyal to you unless he disavows Mama."

Llewelyn frowned. "I never wanted that, would never have asked it of him."

"I know, Papa. But until you act, Davydd is not free to act, either. He cannot reconcile with Mama, will not even go to Llanfaes. Papa, do you not see? To go on like this, month after month, with nothing resolved . . . it only causes greater pain. It is not fair to you, to Davydd, to me . . . or to Mama."

"Fair to Joanna?" Llewelyn's voice had taken on a cutting edge, and Elen's resolve began to waver; she'd never found it easy to gainsay her father.

"Please, Papa, hear me out. I'm not defending what Mama has done, but I do not think she's forfeited all claims to fairness. She was your wife for nigh on twenty-four years. All the love and loyalty she gave you cannot be blotted out as if it had never been, not for one wretched mistake."

"Mistake?" he echoed incredulously. "That is rather a quaint way to describe adultery, Elen."

Elen was too deeply committed now to recant. "A mistake, Papa. She let herself be seduced at a vulnerable time in her life, at a time when you and she were estranged. She erred. But she repented of it, she—"

"Indeed?" he said scathingly. "Was that what she was doing with Will de Braose in my bed—penance?"

"Nothing happened that night, Papa—nothing. They were together, yes. But it was Will's doing, not Mama's. She did not lay with him."

Llewelyn's face was very still, suddenly unreadable. Elen took a step closer, and then he said, "Do you expect me to believe that?"

"I believe it, Papa."

They'd all but forgotten Ednyved. He spoke up unexpectedly, laconically. "For what it's worth, Llewelyn, so do I."

Llewelyn glanced toward Ednyved, and then away. Could there be any truth to Elen's claim? Could it be that Joanna had not brought de Braose into this chamber, into her marriage bed? But why did he care? Why did he want so to believe it?

He swung back toward his daughter, said roughly, "That changes nothing. She has never denied laying with de Braose. Does it matter when . . . or where? She was unfaithful. She betrayed me. Do you think I could forget that? Or forgive?"

"No," Elen admitted. "No, I do not. Nor does Mama. Even though she always forgave you."

"Just what do you mean by that?"

Elen had never meant to go so far. But she could no longer control her tongue, heard herself say, "I mean, Papa, that you were not always faithful to Mama. She knew that, too . . . and yet loved you no less."

Llewelyn's anger was tempered by disbelief. "What are you saying, Elen? Are you truly likening my occasional lapses to Joanna's adultery with de Braose?"

Elen smiled wanly, sadly. "Those were Mama's very words—'occasional lapses.' She agrees with you, Papa, sees her sin as unforgivable. But I . . . I find myself wondering why marriage vows are only for women. Why is it so one-sided, Papa? Why is it so damnably unfair?"

"Because," Llewelyn said bluntly, "if it were not, how would a man ever know if a child was his?" He saw at once, though, that his daughter had given his words a meaning he'd never intended. Elen paled, then held out her hand in instinctive entreaty.

"You do not doubt that, do you, Papa? You do believe that Davydd and I are yours?"

Llewelyn drew a sharp breath. "Ah, Elen . . ." He swiftly closed the space between them, took her in his arms. "I know you are, lass. I've never doubted that, not even for a moment."

"Papa, I want only for you to be happy again. I think I understand why you've not yet divorced Mama. It's . . . it's like repudiating your past, like an amputation of the soul. But sometimes amputation is the only way. You've seen enough battlefield injuries to know that."

Elen had rehearsed her plea often enough so that it came readily to her lips now, but she could not altogether stifle a sense of guilt at what she was doing, urging her father to forsake Joanna. Yet what else could she do? If Papa could not forgive Mama, he had somehow to forget her. But however much she told herself that, she still felt that hers was at once an act of healing and betrayal. Raising up, she kissed Llewelyn on the cheek, then all but ran from the chamber.

Ednyved rose without apparent haste. "Let's leave the rest of the game till the morrow."

He had almost reached the door when Llewelyn said, "What would you or Rhys . . ."

He regretted the impulse in mid-sentence, let the words trail off into oblivion. Ednyved stopped, gave him a pensive, searching look. "I've thought on that," he conceded. "I daresay there's not a man at your court who has not. I suspect Rhys would have slain them both, Catrin and her lover. I'd have hanged the man, divorced Gwenllian." He paused. "But then Rhys loved Catrin too much, and I love Gwenllian too little."

Llewelyn said nothing. Ednyved reached for the door latch, glanced back over his shoulder. "I'd not presume to advise you, Llewelyn. But whatever you decide, my friend, do it soon. One way or another, lay your ghosts to rest."

Llewelyn stood motionless in the center of the room, staring at the bed, the bed in which Joanna had lain with Will de Braose. Or had she? He swore under his breath. The silence was illusory; so, too, was his solitude. He swore again. "Lay my ghosts to rest. Christ, if only I could . . ."

16

LLANFAES, NORTH WALES

January 1231

Joanna drew the shutter back, gazed up at a sky opaque and dark. Clouds had begun to drift over the island shortly after dusk. It was unseasonably mild for late January, and the air was damp and drizzly. She caught muffled echoes of thunder, a sound as ominous as it was uncommon; winter thunderstorms were ill-starred occurrences, often portents of coming grief, untimely death. Joanna crossed herself, pulled the shutters into place, closing out the sounds of night and sea, but not those forebodings born of superstition . . . and solitude.

Loneliness was an unrelenting foe, one that Joanna had come to know well in the past nine months and thirteen days. It could never be conclusively defeated; at best, she could hope for a stalemate, but in the last week it had gained hard-fought ground, for Glynis had departed for a fortnight's visit with her family.

If loneliness was the enemy, time was its ally. Never had the hours in a day seemed so interminable to Joanna. For more than twenty years, hers had been a life of constant activity and unremitting responsibilities. In learning Welsh, she'd taken up the obligations of a woman of rank, and from dawn till dusk she'd been occupied in the management of her husband's vast household, acting as consort, wife, mother. Hers were supervisory skills; she was not expected to turn her own hand to domestic chores. But it was for her to see that those chores were performed, that soap was made and candles were dipped and bread baked, that salt was hauled in from Cheshire brine springs and Spanish cottons from the great fairs at Winchester and Smithfield, that meat was salted for winter and linen woven from flax, that no man was turned away hungry from Llewelyn's hearth, be he highborn lord or lowborn beggar. Any free time was given over to the universal female pastime, sewing, for not even queens were exempt from the demands of needlework.

There was an embroidery frame in one corner of the bedchamber, but it collected only cobwebs; Joanna had no one to sew for. Now she filled her days with vain regrets, played listless games of chess, merels, and tables with Glynis, read and reread her meagre library, and yearned for her freedom. For Richard had been right; jeweled fetters were no less onerous for being gilded, and she was no longer indifferent as to what her future might hold. But she had decided not to accept her brother's offer, did not want to dwell at Chilham Castle upon his charity. Llewelyn could banish her from Wales, but not from the Marches. She had a Shropshire manor at Condover and a hunting lodge near Ellesmere, and she meant to put down roots in the shadow of her husband's realm, as close as she could get to her son.

There was a Welsh proverb by which Joanna put great store these days: For every wound, the ointment of time. She fervently hoped it would prove true for Davydd, that eventually the breach between them could be mended. But until she was free, she could do nothing to effect a reconciliation, and it was this aspect of her confinement she found most crippling. How much longer did Llewelyn mean to hold her here? Why had he not divorced her ere now? She was baffled by his failure to act, for by rights he ought to have repudiated her months ago. He had ever been a man to cut his losses, to jettison useless cargo, and for a Prince, what greater encumbrance could there be than an unfaithful wife?

There was an hourglass on the table, but the sands seemed to have frozen. No matter how often Joanna glanced at it, she could detect not the faintest trickle of time. After unbraiding and brushing out her hair, she wandered aimlessly about the chamber, at last settling down with her harp. The one benefit she'd gained from these months of enforced leisure was that her harp playing had improved dramatically since her first halting efforts under Llewelyn's tutelage. Striking a chord, she began to sing softly.

"In orchard where the leaves of hawthorn hide, the lady holds a lover to her side. Until the watcher in the dawning cried, 'Ah, God, ah, God, the dawn! It comes how soon.' " The song had five additional verses, but she did not continue; the melody was too plaintive, the lyrics too easy to identify with.

Next to the hourglass was her most cherished possession, a small ivory casket of letters, her only link with the world beyond Llanfaes. Lifting the casket lid, she took inventory of these much-handled keepsakes: four letters from Elen, two from Richard, one from Nell, and one—heartbreakingly brief and stilted—from Davydd. Sliding the candelabra toward her, she picked a letter at random, one of Elen's, began to read aloud passages long since memorized.

Her head jerked up at the sound of Bran's footsteps in the antechamber; she knew he would not come to her at such an hour unless he had news of grave import. Her breathing quickened, for these months in isolation had honed her nerves to the breaking point. All too often she tormented herself with morbid visions of Llewelyn lying ill and feverish, refusing to send for her, damning her with his dying breath, never knowing that she loved him still. She'd become obsessed with this fear, that death would end their estrangement, that as it had happened with John, so, too, would it happen with Llewelyn, and she rose hastily to her feet as the door opened.

Bran's somber face did nothing to reassure her. "Madame," he said, "my lord is here to see you."

Joanna stared at him, doubt giving way to dawning joy, for Bran was Davydd's man and it did not occur to her that he could mean anyone but her son. When Bran stepped back, she was stunned at sight of her husband.

Llewelyn closed the door with deliberation, but he did not slide the bolt into place. There was a part of Joanna's mind that noted this, for she seemed suddenly able to focus only upon irrelevancies, and she found herself noting, too, that the wool of his mantle was dry. The storm must still be nigh, she thought, and then: How tired he looks, and thinner; he's not eating as he ought.

"Well?" Llewelyn said, and the challenging, hostile tone of his voice brought her abruptly back to the realities of their respective positions. "Have you nothing to say to me?"

Joanna swallowed. "These months past," she said huskily, "I've begged the Almighty for but one favor, that I might see you once more, have the chance to explain. Now . . . now you are here and suddenly I do not know where to begin."

"I want the truth from you. Not what you think I'd rather hear, or what you'd have me believe. Can I trust you for that much, for the truth?"

He'd turned words into weapons, each one inflicting a wound of its own. Joanna nodded. "Yes," she whispered. "I will tell you the truth." But what was it? If only she could think coherently, calmly. Why had he not forewarned her of his coming,

given her time to prepare? She knew why, though. His was first
and foremost a military mind, trained to take advantage of surprise. He'd removed his mantle, flung it carelessly across a
coffer, but she read tension in his stance, in every line of his
body, and she changed her mind as she watched him. There'd
been nothing premeditated about this visit; his was the taut
wariness of a man acting on impulse, acting against his better
instincts.

He had yet to unbuckle his scabbard, had yet to move away
from the door. Over the years she'd seen his moods range across
the emotional spectrum, had seen him enraged, jubilant, disheartened, sardonic, playful, calculating, and occasionally frightened.
But never had she seen him so obviously ill at ease.

"Elen told me that you did not bring de Braose to our
bedchamber that night. Is that true?"

"Yes," Joanna said. "I swear it." But how could she make
him believe that? Her eyes strayed from his face to the open
casket, and then she was rummaging through the letters, scattering them about the table in her heedless haste. "This letter
explains it better than I could. Will you read it, Llewelyn?
Please?" She held out the sealed parchment to him; their fingers
brushed as he took it, and she was jolted by even so brief and
casual a contact as that. Did he feel it, too? She could not tell,
for he was turning away, shifting so that she could not watch his
face as he read.

The few moments it took him to scan her letter encompassed
an eternity for Joanna. "I tried to tell you," she said. "And
when I could not see you, I wrote that letter. But you sent it back
unread . . ."

Llewelyn glanced again at the letter and then dropped it onto
the table. "It would not have mattered. I'd not have believed
you."

"Do you believe me now?" she asked, but he did not answer
her. Moving to the far side of the table, he reached for the
flagon, splashed wine into an earthenware cup. Joanna watched,
bracing herself for whatever was to come. His first question,
though, was utterly unexpected.

"Do you blame me for his death?"

She gave a startled shake of her head. "No, of course not.
You had the right."

His eyes had narrowed. "You did not mourn him?"

She shook her head again, and he took a step toward her.

"And what you said in your letter, it was true? You did not love him?"

"No, never." She drew a sharp, shuddering breath. "In all honesty, I am not sure I even liked him . . ."

His mouth twisted. Striding forward, he grasped her by the wrist and jerked her toward him. "Then why did you do it? If you did not love him, why did you lay with him? What did you get in his bed that you could not get in mine?"

She gasped and he loosened his grip. But although she'd later find buises upon her wrist, now she did not even feel the pain. Was there no limit to the damage she'd done? That Llewelyn of all men, Llewelyn who was so confident, so secure in his sense of self, secure in his manhood, that he should have succumbed to doubts of this dark nature . . . Jesú, if only she had those October afternoons to live over! Her infidelity could not have been better calculated to penetrate her husband's armor, to strike with devastating effect at his one vulnerability, that he was a man wed to a much younger wife. A wife who'd then taken a lover of thirty-two.

"Beloved, no, it was not like that! No great passion burned between us. I swear it, Llewelyn, swear upon all the saints," she cried, for at that moment she was willing to perjure herself even to the Almighty if only that would give Llewelyn a measure of comfort. "You must believe me. Will was never able to pleasure me as you did," she said, and realized that she was not lying, after all; those feverish, urgent couplings with Will had never been more than flesh unto flesh, lacking utterly the deep and abiding intimacy of her lovemaking with Llewelyn.

"You must believe me," she repeated. "Think back upon our lovemaking in the months after your return from Ceri. Did I want you any the less? You know the answer to that, know how hot my blood ran for you. Ah, Llewelyn . . . we've shared so much, overcome so much. What man could hope to compete with memories such as mine? What man could hope to compete with you?"

"Will de Braose."

"He meant nothing to me! Why do you find that so hard to believe? What of the women you've bedded with? I always told myself that yours were infidelities of the flesh, never of the heart. Was I wrong? What happened between Will and me did not touch upon the love I have for you. It . . . it was . . ."

She faltered and he said sharply, "Was what? If it was not for love and not for lust, just why did you do it, then? Christ, Joanna, why would you risk so much for so little?''

''I . . . I do not know if I can make you understand. I am not sure I fully understand it myself . . . even now. But this I can tell you—it would never have happened if he had not been Maude de Braose's grandson.''

She had so often rehearsed this very speech, as an act of faith. But she found herself fumbling for words, so fearful was she that he'd not hear her out. ''There . . . there was a strange sort of bond between Will and me. No—not carnal, not like that!'' She could no longer meet his eyes, for she was now getting into an area of half-truths and equivocation, denying a sexual attraction that had been magnetic, fateful . . . and mutual. But that was a secret she would take to her grave, and she said hastily, wretchedly, ''I never meant for it to happen, Llewelyn. I was seeking only to comfort him, to—''

''I see. And in offering your sympathy, it seemed only natural to offer yourself as well? A veritable angel of mercy. Tell me, Joanna, what of Will's cousin? Jack de Braose suffered, too, at John's hands, even more than Will, for he lost both father and grandmother in that Windsor dungeon. What of his grieving? What did you feel obliged to do for him?''

Patches of hectic color stood out suddenly along Joanna's cheekbones. ''Do you truly believe that, Llewelyn, believe I had other lovers? That Will was not the first? Or did you say that just to hurt me?''

Llewelyn stepped back, gave her a long, measuring look. ''No,'' he said softly. ''No, I do not believe there were others.'' And then he slowly unbuckled his scabbard, sat down at the table.

For Joanna, that simple act was fraught with significance. She took a seat across from him, knowing now that he would listen to her—truly listen—and she'd never asked for more than that.

''Richard thinks it was an . . . an act of atonement. I told him that was lunacy, of course, but now I am not so sure. I've never pitied anyone in my life as I pitied Will that day. He told me, you see, told me just how his grandmother and uncle died. Maude went mad at the last. Will told me she . . . oh, God, Llewelyn, they found her teethmarks in her son's face! And Will was not spared that. He was but fourteen, and still they told him . . .''

Llewelyn had not known the gruesome details of Maude's death. But it stirred in him no pity for Will, only outrage that he should have shared so grisly a secret with Joanna, the one woman least able to bear such a burden. He reached for the wine cup but did not drink, pushed it, instead, across the table toward Joanna. He was beginning to understand. A clever man, de Braose. God rot him, too clever by half. Starvation and seduction . . . and John again. Always John.

Joanna drank deeply, gratefully. She was perilously close to tears. "I sometimes dream of Maude, that Windsor dungeon. Once or twice I've even awakened screaming. And I keep wondering if John knew, or if he would have cared."

"You cannot blame yourself for John's cruelties, Joanna."

"I know. And I do not. But I can blame myself for loving him. For I did love him, Llewelyn. There's a part of me that still does . . . even now. I think that's what I find hardest to admit or to understand, that I could still love him . . ."

Llewelyn found himself responding to the pain in her voice. Reclaiming the cup, he, too, drank deeply. Joanna reached out; her fingers stopped just short of his. But then she drew back, said quietly, "I am not making excuses, Llewelyn, truly I am not. But I wanted you to understand that mine was not a betrayal of the heart. In some ways it was almost adultery by mischance, for it would never have happened had even one of the circumstances been different. If Will had not been sent to Rhosyr. If we had not quarreled so bitterly over Gruffydd. If I had not known Will as a lad, had not been able to identify so readily with his pain. If you had not—"

Llewelyn set the cup down with a thud. "What?" When she hesitated, he said, "Tell me, Joanna. We agreed this would be a night for truths. Tell me."

"I am afraid to tell you, afraid you'll think I am blaming you."

"What are you talking about?"

"About the de Braose marriages." She saw him stiffen and she leaned across the table toward him. "You can so easily misconstrue what I'm about to say. I shall risk it, though, ask only that you hear me out. Llewelyn, I understand why you sought those alliances, I truly do. You did not act lightly, had compelling reasons for wanting the marriages. But that did not make it any easier for me. Four times I had to stand by as you married your children into the de Braose clan, four times I—"

"You said you understood why, understood I was acting for Gwynedd's good."

She nodded. "And I did understand. But . . . but I think I

needed—just once—for you to put me first. When you did not, I was hurt . . . and aggrieved. More than I knew. I truly thought my anger was over, quenched. But there were embers still smoldering, and I can see now that they fueled our quarrels. Unacknowledged anger acts like flint to tinder, can spark fires where we least expect them."

Llewelyn shoved his chair back. "What are you saying? That your anger led you into adultery?"

Joanna rose as he did, hastened around the table toward him. "No, that is not what I am saying. I did not take a lover to spite you. Does that sound like me?"

Her eyes were riveted upon his face, eyes full of entreaty. As he looked into those eyes, his mouth softened. "No," he admitted. "No . . . it does not."

"I did not knowingly act upon that anger, Llewelyn. That I swear to you upon the surety of my soul. Nor did I ever seek to justify my infidelity by tallying up grievances of my own. I knew from the beginning that there was no justification for what I was doing. But I am trying to be honest with you, honest with myself . . . and I'll never be sure I did not unwittingly let that resentment taint my judgment, my—"

She stopped abruptly, for he was shaking his head. "Since that is not a question you can ever answer, Joanna, what point is there in dwelling upon it? Can you not see the folly in holding yourself accountable for thoughts you are not even sure you had?"

The corner of his mouth quirked; it was only a phantom, fleeting shadow of the smile that could invariably catch at her heart, but it was still a smile, and she responded to it. It seemed almost miraculous to her that they could be talking together like this, without rancor or recriminations, and she hesitated to say or do anything to jeopardize this fragile, astonishing accord. But she had to know.

"Llewelyn . . . why have you not yet divorced me?"

He looked at her, saying nothing. She reached out; her hand brushed his sleeve. "Will you tell me this, then? Will you tell me what you mean to do?"

"Until tonight," he said, "I did not know."

"And now?"

But even as she spoke, the storm broke. A sudden gust of wind blew the shutter back, quenching candles and scattering her letters about the floor. Rain was slanting in through the window, and they both flinched as thunder cracked directly overhead.

They exchanged startled looks, and then sheepish smiles.
"Christ, but that one was close," Llewelyn said, and moved
hastily to relatch the shutter while Joanna gathered up her letters,
sought to comfort her cowering spaniel.

"Llewelyn, stay here tonight. Please do not attempt a crossing
of the strait in weather this vile."

"All right."

"You mean it? You'll stay?"

He shrugged, gestured toward the window. "What choice do I
have?"

Joanna nodded slowly. "Yes," she echoed, "what choice?"
More fool she, to read so much into his ready assent; what else
could he do, in truth? "Llewelyn, there is something I must say
to you. I'd not blame you if you did not believe me, but I must
say it all the same. I love you. I've loved you since the summer
of my fifteenth year, and divorce will not change that. Nothing
will."

He stood very still, for one of the few times in his life at a
loss for words, troubled in no small measure to realize how much
he wanted to believe her.

Joanna awoke sometime before dawn. The chamber was dark,
but the hearth log still burned. Taking care not to disturb Llewelyn,
she rose from the bed. He did not stir, not even when she settled
down beside him again, having placed a candle in one of the
headboard niches. His breathing was even, deep. He seemed to
have shed years in his sleep, and looked so peaceful that she
found herself blinking back tears.

If not for the fact that they were still clothed, this could have
been one of a thousand nights she and Llewelyn had passed in
this bedchamber, in this bed. But it would be the last. Come
morning he would awaken, arise, and walk out of the bedchamber, out of her life. She had two, mayhap three hours at most.

Leaning over, she drew the coverlets up around his shoulders.
How had he been able to fall asleep so easily? She'd lain awake
for hours. That was not an uncommon experience for her; there'd
been many a night in these past months when her body's cravings
had banished sleep, when memories of their lovemaking would
set her to trembling. The needs of the flesh were not always easy
to subordinate to enforced, involuntary chastity, and she was
finding it increasingly difficult to be so tantalizingly close to
Llewelyn now, to be sharing his bed but not his embrace.

His lashes flickered; opening his eyes, he looked up at her. As always, she marveled at his ability to shift so smoothly from sleep to wakeful alertness; his dark eyes showed no disorientation, no surprise at sight of her. "Is it dawn?" he asked, and she shook her head.

"No, not yet. Go back to sleep."

He raised up on his elbow, glanced upward. "Why the candle?"

Color crept into her cheeks, but she gave him an honest answer. "I wanted to watch you."

His mouth curved. "It is not sporting to watch a man whilst he sleeps." Pushing the pillow back against the headboard, he regarded her in silence for several moments. "It ought to feel strange, waking up beside you after so many months. But it does not feel strange at all, feels very natural."

"I'm glad," she said rather breathlessly, "so glad you came." He had yet to take his eyes from her face, and her color was deepening. "Do you know now what you will do . . . about me?"

"I've always known what I ought to do." He reached for a strand of her hair, entwined it about his fingers. "But now . . . now I know what I want to do."

"What?" she whispered, not daring to move, to risk breaking the spell.

"This," he said, and leaned toward her. The kiss was very gentle, almost tentative. But then her arms went up around his neck, and he felt her tears on his face. When he kissed her again, her mouth clung to his, and it was as if they'd never been apart. Theirs was suddenly a world bounded by bed hangings of Tripoli silk, a world without yesterdays or tomorrows, just the here and now and two halves made whole—all too briefly.

Joanna's breathing had yet to slow; it still came in loud, uneven gasps. She heard Llewelyn panting, knew his climax had been no less intense, no less overwhelming than her own. When he started to withdraw, she tightened her arms around him, "No," she entreated, "no, not yet." He shifted so that his weight no longer bore down upon her, and then he laughed, a sound Joanna had never thought to hear again.

"I was just thinking," he said, "that there's more to be said for laying one's ghosts to rest than most people realize."

She kissed the corner of his mouth. "Llewelyn . . ."

Their eyes met, held. "No, *breila*," he said. "Not now."

She nodded, disappointed but not surprised. She was afraid to

attach too much significance to their lovemaking. It was too easy
to explain it away as a one-time occurrence, a natural male
response to intimacy and opportunity. Common sense warned
that there was no place in a Prince's life for a discredited, sullied
wife. But lying now in Llewelyn's arms, his breath upon her
cheek, his hand upon her hip, she could not help but hope, and
she settled back against him, closing her eyes. After a time, the
change in his breathing told her he slept. She watched the hearth
log burn down, listened to the lulling rhythm of rain upon the
slate roof. Shortly before dawn, she fell asleep, too.

When she awoke, the rain had stopped, the room showed the
shadowy half-light of early morning, and she was alone. She sat
up, pushing her hair out of her eyes, her brain clouded with
sleep. "Llewelyn?" Reaching over, she jerked the bed hangings
all the way back; the chamber was empty. If not for the sight of
her discarded clothing scattered about the floor, she might almost
have believed she'd dreamed it all. The fire had gone out and the
air was chill; she shivered, fumbled for her bedrobe, and began
numbly to follow her routine upon rising, as she'd done every
morning for the past nine months.

Five minutes later she halted her brushing in mid-stroke, sat
down in the closest seat. She'd known that what happened between a man and woman in bed was not a reliable indication of
intent. But however acute his morning-after regrets, how could
he have left her like this, without even a word of farewell?

A knock sounded at the door and a young man entered,
carrying a tray. "Where shall I put this, my lady?"

Joanna had never seen him before. "Who are you?"

He was staring past her at the bed, at its telltale dishevelment,
his eyes wide and wondering. When he turned back to Joanna,
his expression made it clear he thought her a practitioner of
sexual sorcery, a Norman-French Circe. "I am Phylip, Madame," he mumbled. "I came over last night with my lord; he
ordered me to fetch this from the kitchen." And only then, as he
set the tray upon the table, did Joanna see that it held food for
two.

Although she caught the enticing aroma of hot baked bread,
Joanna did not stir. She was still sitting there, the tray untouched
before her, when Llewelyn returned. One glance at her face and
he crossed swiftly to her side. "Joanna?"

"I thought . . . thought you'd gone," she said, and he drew
her to her feet, his hands tightening on her shoulders.

"Gone? What did you think that was for?" With a jerk of his

head toward the canopied bed, the rumpled sheets. "Old time's
sake? Hiraeth?"

"I did not know what to think," she confessed. "I was afraid
to expect too much."

"I told you once that you held yourself too cheaply, *breila*. It
seems you still do," he said, and slipped his arm around her
waist. "Let's eat first, and then you can finish dressing. Do not
bother about packing; we'll send for your belongings later."

"You . . . you want me back, Llewelyn?"

She sounded so dumbfounded that he smiled and shrugged.
"After twenty-four years, you're a hard habit to break, Joanna."

She did not return his smile. Her eyes searched his face
intently, incredulously. "Can you do that, Llewelyn? Can you
truly forgive me? Could you live with the shadow Will would
cast?"

He tilted her face up to his, touched her cheek. "In all
honesty, I do not know, Joanna. I can make you no promises,
can only say I am willing to try. I do know this, that after living
without you for nigh on ten months, I think it's worth the risk."

The Llanfaes ferry had suffered storm damage, and they had to
ride west, to cross at Abermenai. The sun shone with a lucent,
incandescent brilliance for Joanna; never had she been so dazzled
by the sapphire of the sky, the turquoise of the strait, the snow-
glazed summits of Eryri. The wind was brisk, the road mired in
mud, and her mantle was soon spattered, but she did not care in
the least. Her only regret was that she could not ride pillion
behind Llewelyn, for her sense of reality seemed dependent upon
physical contact with her husband; only he could dispel her
disbelief, and she kept her mount so close to his that once his
spur even caught in the skirt of her gown.

She was still in a state of dazed euphoria as they approached
Bangor. Ahead, a herdsman and his dogs were seeking to corral
several stray cows. The cattle were milling about, blocking the
road, and their master's impatience changed to chagrin at sight of
his sovereign.

"Good morrow to you, my lord. God blight these contrary
beasts, but I'll have them clear in a trice, will—" His jaw
dropped; his words choked off into an unintelligible splutter.

Llewelyn appeared indifferent to this peculiar behavior. Glancing over his shoulder, he beckoned to one of his men. "Seth,
give this fellow a hand."

The herdsman did not even acknowledge his lord's kindness,

for he could not take his eyes from his lord's wife. He was gaping at Joanna as if she were an apparition, one to be warded off with incantations and henbane. Only then did Joanna comprehend the true magnitude of what Llewelyn meant to do.

"Llewelyn, wait!" She urged her horse forward, caught at his sleeve. "Llewelyn, this is madness. Your people scorn me as an adulteress, feel I betrayed you both as wife and consort. They'll never understand, never accept me."

"They may not understand, but they will accept you," he said, and his voice was suddenly grim.

Joanna bit her lip, stared at him in despair. "But . . . but what if they will not? They hate me now, Llewelyn, and that hatred might well spill over onto you if you take me back. There will be those who'll say I've bewitched you, and . . . and others who'll think you've grown soft, weak . . ." There was no need to continue; she saw that. She was warning him of dangers he knew far better than she. When had he ever acted without considering the consequences? She'd been the blind one, the selfish one.

"How can I let you do this? How can I let you risk so much on my behalf?" She saw his face—dark, haggard, but still handsome—through a haze of tears. "I know . . . know what I ought to do. But I am not strong enough, beloved, cannot give you up . . ."

"The decision is mine, Joanna, not yours. You bear no responsibility for it." He held up his hand, halting his men upon the pathway, and taking the reins of Joanna's mount, he led her off the road into the woods.

He drew rein in the shadow of a silver birch, stripped naked by winter winds. The ground was covered by decaying leaves, broken branches. Joanna inhaled the scent of spruce, the scent of the sea. "You said our reconciliation was worth the risk. But is it, Llewelyn? Is it truly worth what you might lose?"

He did not answer at once; his eyes swept the horizon, tracked a cormorant's shooting dive into the sea. "When I came to you last night, it was not—knowingly—with thoughts of reconciliation. I was seeking answers only you could give me, Joanna, seeking to cauterize a wound that would not heal. But as I listened to you, I found myself able to understand why it had happened. It was not my wife who lay with Will de Braose; it was John's daughter. Once I realized that, I could balance the scales without bitterness, balance a marriage against a mistake—albeit a monumental one." His last words were sardonic; his smile was not. "I want you by my side again, in my bed, at my table, as my lady, lover, wife.''

"They will never understand," she said unsteadily, and he nodded.

"Probably not. I daresay I'll forfeit a great measure of goodwill. There will be men who'll think I've lost my wits, am in my dotage—I know that. But they'll govern their tongues in my hearing. That," he said coolly, "I can damned well guarantee."

"Llewelyn . . . are you sure? Am I truly worth it?''

"Do you remember what you said last night about the de Braose marriages?" He leaned over, dried her tears with the back of his hand. "This time, Joanna, this time I do mean to put you first.''

Neither Welsh culture nor Welsh topography had been conducive to the development of English-style towns and villages. Small settlements had sprung up, however, around Llewelyn's manors at Aber, Llanfaes, and Trefriw, and monasteries often served, too, as beacons for community life. So it was for the cathedral church of St Deiniol at Bangor Fawr yn Arfon, episcopal see for the diocese of Bangor.

Although official fairs and markets were unknown in Llewelyn's domains, informal markets thrived wherever people tended to congregate, and this was such a market day in Bangor. Stalls had been set up in the churchyard, and the marketplace and street were crowded with those who'd come to barter, to browse, and to gossip with their neighbors. Vendors sold hot pies and rolled out kegs of ale for the thirsty; itinerant pedlars loudly hawked their wares; animals offered for trade added to the clamor. It was the sort of chaotic market scene Joanna had often seen in England, but with a distinctly Welsh flavor, boisterous bedlam that ceased within moments of her arrival in their midst.

Llewelyn was known on sight to all in Bangor; to many, he was the only Prince they'd ever known. He'd first gained political power at twenty-one, and now, in his fifty-eighth year, he was well enshrined in local legend, eclipsing even his famous grandfather in the folklore of his people, the uncrowned Prince of Wales. As word circulated that he'd just ridden into the town, men and women deserted the market stalls and the wrestling and archery bouts; some even abandoned a bloody cockfight, those with no money on the outcome.

But the cheering stopped abruptly as the people recognized Joanna. She heard shocked murmurings spreading through the crowd, heard the name Siwan repeated in growing wonder. As men doffed their caps, Llewelyn held his stallion to a stately canter, and then slowed to a walk. Joanna paced her mount with his, but her mouth was dry, her heart pounding. She knew that men ofttimes drew false courage from crowd companionship, knew, too, that the Welsh were more outspoken, less awed by rank than the English, and she waited now for the jeers, the shouts of derision.

None came. Llewelyn reined in before one of the vendors. "My throat is right parched. What have you for such a thirst?"

"Wine, my lord. But it is poor stuff, not fit for Your Grace," the man protested, while fumbling for a clean, uncracked cup.

"It will do," Llewelyn said, and smiled at the man. He drank slowly, keeping his eyes upon the crowd; he found none willing to meet his gaze. "Here, love, drink," he said, in Welsh, not French, and held the cup out to Joanna.

She could not swallow, but she obediently put the cup to her mouth. Llewelyn never carried money himself, but he gestured now and one of his men tossed a coin to the vendor. It was eerily still. Llewelyn urged his mount forward; Joanna followed. The crowd fell back, watching in stunned silence.

The road to Aber wound its way along the seacoast, offering a superb view of the strait, but Joanna had eyes only for her husband. She was still astonished at their reprieve, so sure had she been that men would rail at her, call her slut and harlot. She glanced again at Llewelyn's profile. *Not in my hearing,* he'd said, and it was not bravado. What had happened in Bangor was as much a testament to his personality as to his power. But then, she thought, the two were one and the same.

"I only hope you can cast such a spell upon the folk at Aber," she said, mustering a strained smile; Aber was now less than five miles distant. She slowed her mount, earning herself a quizzical look from Llewelyn. But then he, too, eased his chestnut. Joanna stared at the road ahead; did Llewelyn ever think of that desperate midnight ride in answer to Senena's false summons? Davydd's words seemed to echo on the wind: *We half killed our horses . . .* Only to arrive at Aber and discover—

"Joanna, that serves for naught."

She gasped, then gave a weak laugh. "Jesú, what are you, a warlock?"

"I know you," he said simply.

She hesitated, then realized the folly in that; silence could cripple no less effectively than suspicion. They had to be able to

talk about it. "It was not Glynis, Llewelyn. It was Senena who
sent you that message."

"I know. She later admitted it."

"I can well imagine her satisfaction," Joanna said bitterly.
"Senena had guessed, gambled, and gotten lucky beyond belief,
and all it had cost was a man's life."

"At first, mayhap. But her satisfaction soon turned sour.
She'd somehow convinced herself that I would then free Gruffydd.
As if I'd been holding him just for your pleasure . . ." Llewelyn
shook his head. "I ought to warn you, though, *breila*. Senena is
at Aber." He heard her sharp intake of breath, said dryly, "It
should be a memorable homecoming."

Within moments of their arrival at Aber, the bailey was packed
with people. Joanna was gripping the saddle pommel so tightly
that it was digging painfully into her palm. Never had she seen a
crowd assemble so fast. Many of the faces were familiar to her;
all shared a common expression, one of utter disbelief.

Llewelyn had dismounted, was reaching up to help her from
the saddle. Setting her down, he tilted her face up to his. The
kiss was lingering, very deliberate. And then he turned to face
his countrymen.

No one spoke. The silence was even more absolute than in
Bangor. Llewelyn had known there would be no overt defiance,
not at his own court. The sheer audacity of his act would
paralyze dissent. There was a sudden stir. People were stepping
aside. Ednyved had his wife's arm in an inexorable grip;
Gwenllian's body was stiff, resistant, but she followed him as he
moved toward Llewelyn and Joanna.

Reaching for Joanna's hand, Ednyved brought it to his mouth.
"Welcome home, Madame."

Gwenllian's face was a study in frustrated fury. "Yes," she
said tonelessly, while her eyes bored like gimlets into Joanna's.

There was nothing for the others to do then but to follow the
example of Llewelyn's Seneschal. One by one they came forward, mumbled grudging words of welcome, made awkward
obeisances. Joanna had retreated into her public persona; her
answers were automatic, and to many, she appeared aloof, unrepentant. She saw Senena standing some distance apart, but it was
the hostility of the others that she felt most keenly. Adda's
greeting had been edged in ice. How can I bear it? she thought.
How can I live surrounded by so much hatred? But then Llewelyn touched her arm and she turned, saw her son.

Joanna forgot all else. She started toward Davydd; he quickened his step and they met in the middle of the bailey. "Your father has forgiven me," she said softly. "Do you think you can forgive me, too, Davydd?"

"Yes," he said, "oh, yes."

Ednyved had remained at Llewelyn's side, and he seized this opportunity now to say, very low, "Well, you've just set tongues wagging from Cricieth to Colchester. They'll be gossiping about naught else for the next six months, on both sides of the border. Are you sure, Llewelyn . . . truly sure?"

Llewelyn's eyes were fastened upon his wife and son. As he watched, they embraced. He glanced back at Ednyved. "Yes," he said. "I am sure."

"Are you certain she'll be at the waterfall, Davydd?"

"Not really. But she does play there sometimes, and I know not where else to look." Davydd gave Joanna an oblique, inquiring glance. "Are you positive you want to do this now, Mama?"

"I do not want to do it at all," Joanna admitted. "In truth, I dread facing the child. Does she blame me, Davydd, for her father's death?"

"I could not say. Isabella is a timid little lass, keeps very much to herself. I confess I know naught of what goes on in her head. I think she fears Papa. I suspect she fears me, too."

"Does she look . . . ?"

"Like Will? No, she favors her mother."

They were within sight of the cataract; it had been known to freeze during exceptionally bitter winters, but now it shimmered in the January sun, patterned the mossy rocks below with lacy foam and spray. Davydd pointed. "There she is. Isabella!"

The girl whirled, and even at that distance Joanna could see how she flushed, as if caught in some flagrant misdeed. Davydd moved toward the rocks, beckoned to her. "Isabella, come here. I want you to meet my mother."

"The Lady Joanna?" Isabella lifted her skirts, scrambled up the rocks. "You've come back!" The change in her was startling; her face was eager, expectant. "I prayed you would, I prayed so hard, and the Almighty heeded me, He brought you back!"

Joanna reached out, took Isabella's hands between her own. Her heart went out to this lonely little girl, but the last thing she'd expected was to be hailed as Isabella's saviour. She smiled at the child, and then Isabella gave her the poignant answer to the puzzle.

"You're so pretty," she breathed, and raised up to whisper shyly, "No wonder Papa loved you so."

Over the girl's head, Joanna's eyes met her son's in mutual dismay, if for different reasons. Davydd was thinking that Isabella's attachment to his mother might prove politically embarrassing, only fueling gossip all the more. Joanna was thinking that to keep faith with Isabella, she'd be obliged to live a lie. It seemed the ultimate irony to her that she should be given the responsibility of rearing Will's child, but it was both a penance and a privilege. Putting her arm around Isabella's shoulders, she said gently, "Let's go home, darling."

Joanna was standing in the antechamber, staring at her bedroom door. Hours after her arrival at Aber, she had yet to cross that threshold. During her months at Llanfaes, Will's ghost had mercifully kept his distance. But if she were to encounter him at all, surely it would be here, and she reached reluctantly for the door latch, dreading that first onslaught of memory.

Within this bedchamber she'd passed much of her married life. It looked as she remembered it, and yet it did not, familiar but somehow foreign, too. It took a moment for her to realize why; all traces of her had been erased. Gone were her favorite silver candlesticks, her carefully tended violets and gillyflowers, even the wall hangings embroidered with unicorns.

Joanna's eyes filled with tears. It was not Will who'd haunt her peace; it was the memory of her husband's face as he walked into this chamber, found her with Will. How could she ever forget that moment of horror? How could she forgive herself?

"Joanna."

She spun around, saw Llewelyn standing in the doorway. "I'm afraid, beloved," she whispered. "Suddenly I am so afraid. Not just of the hostility I know I must face, not even of my memories. I'm afraid, too, of tomorrow. No matter how expertly a thing is mended, Llewelyn, the break is ever visible thereafter . . ."

"Yes," he said, "I know. A scar signifies past pain, a wound that did not heal as it ought. But it testifies, too, to survival, *breila.*"

Joanna looked at him, and then she held out her arms. He closed the door, moved toward her.

17

ABER, NORTH WALES

July 1234

Joanna stared down at the parchment, daunted by its blankness. Letters to her cousin Eleanor were never easy; she kept up the contact partly from habit and partly from pity. But this letter was particularly difficult to compose, for so much time had elapsed since she'd last written. The days when Eleanor had been welcomed at John's Christmas court were long gone; for some years now, her horizons had extended no farther than the outer bailey walls of Bristol Castle. Joanna could not be sure what, if anything, Eleanor knew of the momentous events of the past three years.

Had Eleanor heard of Hubert de Burgh's fall from power? Did she know that Llewelyn had fought two bloody and successful wars against the English? Did she know of the Peace of Middle, concluded just three weeks ago? Did she know of all the deaths?

Joanna glanced toward the window seat where her sister Nell was plucking a harp; she played badly but with characteristic concentration. Her husband's sudden death in April 1231 had devastated Nell; so impassioned had her grieving been that she'd even taken a holy oath of chastity, an emotional extravagance against which Joanna had argued in vain. And just as she had feared, Nell's mourning ran its course in time, but the oath endured, locking Nell into a lifelong widowhood.

The political consequences of Pembroke's death were no less far-reaching, for he'd held the wardship of Will de Braose's daughters, and with the wardship went control of the de Braose estates. When Henry imprudently bestowed the wardship and lands upon Hubert de Burgh, Llewelyn reacted with alarm, for de Burgh already held the lordships of Cardigan, Carmarthen, Gower,

756   *Sharon Kay Penman*

and Glamorgan. The igniting spark flared at Montgomery Castle, where de Burgh's garrison beheaded Welsh prisoners, and in June Llewelyn swept southward, leveled Montgomery to the ground. He then pressed on into the de Braose lands, burning and pillaging on such a scale that the English bishops excoriated him as a "despoiler of churches."

This was the third time that Llewelyn had been excommunicated for what he saw as political sins, and he would later joke about installing a turnstile for his private chapel. But Joanna had never seen any humor in it, and her relief was inexpressible when Llewelyn was restored to God's grace in December, after a botched campaign by Henry and de Burgh.

The following year was one of uneasy truce along the Marches. Peter des Roches, Bishop of Winchester, was back from his Holy Land pilgrimage, and he was so successful in blaming Hubert de Burgh for the Welsh fiasco that in July Henry stripped de Burgh of his high office, demanded an accounting; by November, he was being held at the Tower. But 1232 was also the year in which death claimed the man who'd shown himself to be Llewelyn's most steadfast ally; in October, Ranulf, Earl of Chester, died at his manor of Wallingford in his sixty-third year.

The precarious peace of 1232 did not long endure into 1233. As Nell and William Marshal had been childless, the earldom of Pembroke passed to William's brother Richard. But the relationship between Henry and Richard Marshal had gone sour from the start, fraught with suspicion and mutual mistrust. After months of misunderstanding and strife, Henry yielded to Peter des Roches's urgings, proclaimed Marshal a traitor, thus making of the man a reluctant rebel, a rallying point for dissent. A civil war erupted and Llewelyn was not long in entering the fray upon Richard Marshal's behalf, even though Marshal was a partisan of the disgraced Hubert de Burgh. Llewelyn's objective was always the same, to weaken the power of the English crown in Wales, and he saw in Richard Marshal's rebellion an opportunity that would not come again.

Once again the Marches took fire, and once again Joanna had to watch helplessly as her husband and son rode to war. But the outcome was not long in doubt. Henry was no general, and found himself facing two of the most experienced battle commanders in his realm. In November 1233, he fled in disarray as the royal encampment at Grosmont was overrun by Marshal's Welsh and English allies. In January 1234, Llewelyn and Richard Marshal ravaged Shropshire to the very gates of Shrewsbury, and Henry found himself under increasing political pressure to come to terms. In March he agreed to a truce, and in April he capitulated to Marshal's demands, dismissed Peter des Roches and his other Poitevin advisers, and vowed to keep faith with the Runnymede charter.

But Richard Marshal never knew he'd won. He'd crossed over to Ireland to see to his estates there, and in early April he was wounded in a skirmish with Henry's supporters, taken prisoner, and treated so harshly that he died within days. It was left to Llewelyn to gain reparations for the followers of his fallen ally. On June 21 the Archbishop of Canterbury met Llewelyn at the Shropshire village of Middle, and peace returned to Henry's realm.

The Pact of Middle was the crowning achievement of Llewelyn's reign, the culmination of a lifetime's struggle against the English Kings. But on this, the eve of the festivities planned to honor her husband's triumph, Joanna was thinking not of Llewelyn's victory celebration but of their dead. So many deaths. William and Richard Marshal. Llewelyn's sons by marriage, Jack de Braose and William de Lacy. Chester. Maelgwn. Maelgwn's brother, Rhys Gryg, slain at the siege of Carmarthen Castle. Morgan, dead nigh on a twelvemonth now. Llewelyn rarely talked of him; he could not. She gazed down at the parchment. So many deaths. And each time she looked into Llewelyn's face, she could not but wonder how much time remained to them. How precious days and hours became with the realization of how few they were.

"You look so solemn, Joanna. What are you thinking of?"

"That Llewelyn and I have been wed twenty-eight years. That sounds so long, Nell, but in truth it passed in a blur of light, days into months into years . . ."

"Your mind takes the most morbid turns," Nell admonished. "Fretting about time's passing will not slow it down one whit. Let's talk instead of tomorrow's revelries. Have all the guests arrived? I hope none of the Marshals will be coming; I did tell you, did I not, how disagreeable they've been since William's death, begrudging me my dower rights?"

"Repeatedly," Joanna said, and smiled to soften the sting. "I ought to find Isabella; I promised I'd help her decide what to wear tomorrow."

"Come to my chamber first. I want to show you the gown I bought in London at Whitsuntide, a samite silk of willow green."

"I'd love to see it," Joanna said, remembering in spite of herself the ceremony in which Nell placed a gold band upon her finger to symbolize her marriage to Christ, adopted a nun's habit of homespun. She still wore the ring, but she'd long since put aside the homespun, resumed her rightful place at her brother's court.

As if reading her thoughts, Nell said suddenly, "I know people were quick to judge me when I began wearing bright colors again. But I've not abjured my oath, and that should be what matters to the Almighty, should it not? It vexed me beyond bearing to think of others gossiping behind my back, poking their noses into my life. And when I think how it must have been for you . . . How did you endure it, Joanna? Were you not enraged at their impudence, their effrontery?"

As always, Joanna was amused by Nell's uncalculating candor. It was, Joanna thought wryly, not a trait she'd inherited from either of her parents. "I think I felt not so much resentful as uncomfortable. But you speak as if the disapproval was all in the past. I would that it were."

"Even after three years . . . ?"

"Oh, it gets easier, Nell, with each passing year. But for some, three lifetimes would not be enough time for me to expiate my sins. They've accepted me because Llewelyn gave them no choice, but they will never truly forgive me. I've had to face that, to learn to live with it, even though that includes some of my husband's own family. His daughter Gwladys, his brother Adda. My family, too. Our Aunt Ela for one. Elen's husband for another. John will never understand how Llewelyn could take me back."

Joanna had been sketching aimlessly as she spoke; the letter to Eleanor was covered with interlocking circles. She looked down at her handiwork, put the pen aside. "Nor do I think I'll fare well at the hands of Welsh historians. I ought not to mind what's said about me once I'm safely dead, but I'm afraid I do." Her smile was rueful. "I never hungered for fame, much less notoriety, but I seem fated to be remembered as Llewelyn's wanton foreign wife."

Nell did not dispute her; she knew how swiftly gossip became enshrined as gospel. "What matters, Joanna, is that you and Llewelyn have been able to salvage your marriage. In all honesty, I was not so sure you could."

"In all honesty, neither was I," Joanna confessed. "At first we were so wary with one another, so painstakingly polite we'd have put a couple of saints to shame! And God pity us, but we went on like that for weeks, so anxious not to tread amiss that we

could scarce move at all. Luckily a day came when I had a right
sharp headache, a day when I walked in and found Llewelyn
ransacking our bedchamber for his privy seal. The room looked
as if a whirlwind had struck; I regret to say neatness has never
been one of Llewelyn's virtues. And as I stood there surveying
the wreckage, Llewelyn demanded to know where the seal was—as
if I stored the blasted thing under my pillow. I lost my temper,
snapped at him; he snapped back, and as quickly as that, we
found ourselves in a flaming row, like any husband and wife on a
bad day. That realization hit us both at once, in mid-shout. We
stopped, looked at each other, and then, as if on cue, we burst
out laughing." And in remembering, Joanna laughed again. "It
was then," she said, "that I truly began to believe we might
make it, after all."

Joanna was standing beside her brother, bringing him up to date
on the happenings at her husband's court. "Llewelyn's cousin
Madog is here, as is Maelgwn's son. Gwenllian is still in Ireland,
but Llewelyn's other daughters are present, and Tegwared and
his wife; they've given Llewelyn and Ednyved four grandchildren
so far. Gwladys, too; did you know? After thirteen barren years
with Reginald de Braose, she found herself with child within a
twelvemonth of marrying Ralph de Mortimer, has two sons by
him now. There's Glynis; you remember her from Llanfaes?
Llewelyn and I made a most advantageous marriage for her, and
I stood godmother to her firstborn. That is Marared over to your
right; did I tell you she's to marry Walter Clifford?"

Richard had been listening indulgently, having no real interest
in Welsh weddings and birthings. But an alliance with a Marcher
lord like Clifford was of no small significance, and he said
admiringly, "So Llewelyn has entangled another Norman fish in
his nuptial nets. He's pulled in quite a catch over the years:
Chester, de Braose, de Mortimer, de Lacy . . . and now Clifford.
Had he only a few more daughters and a sister or two, he might
have won over the Marches by marriage!"

"Strange you should say that. Morgan, may God assoil him,
once told Llewelyn the same thing, almost word for word."

"I heard he'd died."

She nodded. "Last year. No great surprise, for he'd been
ailing, and he'd reached a venerable age. But Llewelyn took his
death hard, still misses him sorely."

A sudden burst of laughter drew their attention. They turned
to discover that Nell was displaying the same magnetic allure for

males that her mother had so often demonstrated; she was surrounded by bedazzled admirers, a vision in willow green, and Richard murmured, "Jesú, how like Isabelle she is. The man on her left, the one gazing at her as if bewitched, damn me if he does not look remarkably like the Earl of Winchester."

"That's because he is. And the man laughing is his younger brother, Robert de Quincy." Richard did not comment, but Joanna felt a need to elaborate further, to explain why the sons of one of their father's bitterest enemies were guests at her hearth. "Saer de Quincy," she said. "How Papa hated him. And how long ago it all seems. Roger and Robert de Quincy came with John the Scot and Elen. They are kin to John; his aunt was once wed to their uncle."

"You owe me no explanations, Joanna. As you say, it was a long time ago. Seeing Nell brings it back, though, for she could be Isabelle at eighteen, in truth she could. Do you ever hear from her—from Isabelle?"

"Not for years. What with Hugh de Lusignan's intrigues and Isabelle's yearly pregnancies, when would she find the time to write?"

Richard grinned. "I've lost count; how many children has she borne de Lusignan? Seven? Eight? For certes, we know what they do when they're not plotting against Henry or the French King." Nell's laughter came to them again, and he shook his head. "That chastity oath of hers was an act of arrant lunacy, Joanna. She'll never hold to it. How can she? Look at her, she's the most beautiful woman in the hall."

"Not so." Neither had heard Llewelyn's approach; they turned as he said, "Elen is the most beautiful woman at Aber . . . and that's because she so resembles her mother."

Fair coloring was prized no less by the Welsh than by the English, was valued even more for its rarity, and that awareness made Llewelyn's gallantry all the more endearing to Joanna. She touched her lips to the rim of her wine cup, then handed it to him. He smiled, put his mouth to the imprint of her kiss, and drank.

Watching their byplay, Richard felt both amusement and awe. He'd not been sanguine about their chances for reconciliation; Llewelyn's bloody rending of the de Braose lands in 1231 had given incontrovertible evidence of the sort of wound that infidelity could inflict. But there was such intimacy in the look that now passed between them that he no longer doubted, and he could only marvel at what he could not understand.

There'd been a lull in the dancing; John the Scot was calling for silence. As conversation hushed and heads turned, he strode up onto the dais. "I hope our Welsh brethren will not take it amiss if I speak French; my father's Gaelic enabled me to understand your tongue, but I speak it too poorly for public utterance." Glancing toward Llewelyn, he said, "In the recent strife betwixt King Henry and your Prince, I was sorely tried. I had to hold with my King, but I am bound to Lord Llewelyn, too, both by choice and wedlock. I can say, therefore, in all certitude that few welcomed the Treaty of Middle more whole-heartedly than I."

He raised his wine cup high. "I drink to peace between our peoples . . . and to your Prince. Wales has had its share of strong-willed, able rulers, men like Hywel the Good and Owain the Great. It is my pleasure now to honor a man whose feats equal if not eclipse theirs. A man who is my ally, friend, father by marriage, a man whose memory will burn brightly for genera-tions to come amongst the Welsh, a man who well deserves to be remembered by history as Llewelyn the Great."

It was a memorable tribute, one that Llewelyn had not been expecting. "Llewelyn Fawr?" he echoed, then shook his head and grinned. "I do not know, John. Although I can say for certes that no one will ever call me Llewelyn the Good!"

Midst the ensuing laughing, his eyes met Joanna's. She saw how deeply he'd been pleased, put her hand upon his arm, her happiness spilling over in full and intoxicating measure. But it was then that her gaze happened to fall upon her daughter. Elen was watching her father and husband, and there was on her face an expression of unutterable sadness, a look of yearning and of despair.

"Lady Joanna? I saw you leave the hall, feared something might be wrong."

"Not at all, Isabella. I am but returning to my bedchamber to tighten a garter."

"Shall I fetch your maid? Or mayhap I could help you myself?"

At times Isabella's emotional dependence could be cloying, but Joanna's fondness for the girl was genuine, and she smiled, shook her head. "No, darling, there's no need; you go back to the hall," she said, and she would ever after thank God fasting for that casually made decision to go unaccompanied to her bedchamber.

The night was warm, starlit, and scented with honeysuckle, Joanna's favorite fragrance, but she was too preoccupied to notice. Ere the evening was over, she'd have to find time alone with Elen. But would Elen confide in her?

Entering the antechamber, she was reaching for the door latch when she heard it, a sound so unexpected, so chilling that her fingers froze on the ring—the sound of a man's laughter. She stared at the door, disbelieving, caught up in a surge of superstitious fear, for what man would dare intrude into Llewelyn's private chamber? There was but one answer to that question, an answer that raised gooseflesh on her arms, sweat on her forehead. No mortal man.

"Will?" she whispered as the laughter came again. All knew ghosts walked at night, evil spirits come to tempt the unwary, incubi to lay with women whilst they slept. But as she stood there, she suddenly remembered a night when she'd awakened Llewelyn with kisses, and he'd pretended to believe she was a succubus, intent upon stealing his seed. It was an incongruous, bawdy memory, but it stiffened her spine, gave her the courage to do what she knew Llewelyn would have done, confront the unknown. She groped for her crucifix, gripped the latch, and thrust the door open.

They sprang apart, turned startled faces toward her, faces that mirrored her own fear. Her daughter and Robert de Quincy. "Mama!" Elen's voice was uneven, breathless. "What are you doing here?"

Joanna moved forward into the room. "I might well ask you the same question, Elen."

Robert de Quincy stepped into the light cast by Joanna's lantern; she had not paid him much mind in the hall, had noted only that he had a ready laugh. She saw now a thatch of dark hair, high hollowed cheekbones, a full mouth, and intensely blue eyes, eyes full of anxiety. "Do not blame Elen, Madame. I lured her here, told her—"

"That's not so. This was my doing, Mama, not Rob's." Elen put her hand upon his arm. "Go back to the hall, Rob, ere you be missed. I'll talk to my mother."

"You're sure?" he asked, and the intimacy of that brief exchange was enough to confirm Joanna's worst fears. She looked from her daughter to de Quincy, with a sinking certainty that they were lovers.

"Yes," Elen said, "I'm sure." But before he reached the door she cried, "Rob!" He stopped and she flung her arms around his neck, kissed him full on the mouth. And then she turned defiantly back to face her mother.

The door closed; Joanna put her lantern down. "Well?" Elen said. "Go ahead, Mama. Say what you will. But ere you do, you might remember what Scriptures say about sins and casting the first stone."

"What can I say?" Joanna sat down upon the bed. Never had a headache come upon her so suddenly; her temples were throbbing, her vision blurring. "You must love him. I cannot believe you'd take such a risk if you did not. But to bring him here . . . Jesus wept, Elen, what were you thinking of?"

Color rose in Elen's face. "It was folly, I know," she admitted. "But I had to be alone with him, if only for a few moments, and I dared not bring him to my own chamber . . ." She moved toward the bed. "I do love him, Mama," she said softly, "and he loves me."

Elen had not dared to light candles, and the only illumination came from Joanna's lantern; she stared at it, a weak, flickering flame in a sea of shadows. "What mean you to do, Elen?"

Elen shrugged. "What can I do? Even if John would agree to a divorce, we have no grounds the Church would recognize. Till death us do part; was that not what the vows said, Mama?"

She was back at the table, like Joanna, drawn by the light. "You remember how often you berated me for my impulsiveness, my lack of caution? Well, Rob is like me, too quick to act, heeding his heart, not his head. He'd run away with me tomorrow if I agreed."

Joanna caught her breath. "Elen . . . you would not?"

"How could I?" Elen had begun to pace. "That would make John a laughingstock. I could not do that to him, not when I remember how Papa—" She broke off abruptly; a silence fell.

"I would not hurt John if I could help it." Defiance had crept back into Elen's voice, as if she expected disbelief. "Nor would I ever willingly hurt Papa. If I ran away with Rob, Papa's alliance with John would come apart like cobwebs. And you'd be hurt, too, Mama. Men would say 'Like mother, like daughter,' would rake up all the old gossip about you and Will de Braose. We'd all be spattered with the mud, Mama, not just Rob and John and me, but you, too, and Papa, even Davydd."

She came back to the bed, sat down beside Joanna. "I might be willing to risk all that, might be selfish enough to put my happiness first; I'll never know. But I could never risk Rob's life. John is not a vindictive man, but he is a prideful one. If I ran away with his cousin, he'd not rest until he'd avenged himself upon Rob, avenged his honor.''

Joanna reached over, took Elen's hand. "If you love him, Elen, let him go."

"I cannot," Elen said, "I cannot." And after that, there was nothing left to say.

Llewelyn raised himself up on his elbow, watching as Joanna brushed her hair. "Are you sure nothing is troubling you, *breila?*"

"Very sure, Llewelyn." What would it serve to tell him? She'd only be burdening him for naught; there was nothing he could do. To forestall further questioning, she hastily slipped off her bedrobe, climbed into bed. He put his arm around her shoulders, drew her close. She was relieved when he seemed content only to hold her; after her scene with Elen, she was not in the mood for lovemaking. She pillowed her head against his chest, felt his hand on her hair, gently stroking.

"Joanna, we do need to talk."

She shifted so she could see his face. He sounded so grave; could he possibly have guessed about Elen and Robert de Quincy? "Talk about what?"

"On the morrow I am going to Deganwy Castle." The body he held was suddenly rigid; the muscles in her back contracted, stiffened under his hand. He kissed her on the forehead. "If Gruffydd can give me the assurances I must have, I mean to set him free."

"Llewelyn, no!"

"Joanna . . . Joanna, you must try to understand. When I confined Gruffydd at Deganwy, Davydd was nineteen and untried. He is now twenty and five, has fought at my side in three wars. I've secured for him the recognition of the Pope, the English King, my Welsh allies, and when I die, he shall inherit a united realm, a legacy no other Welsh Prince has been able to leave his son. But I've done all I can. What I bequeath him, he—and he alone—will have to hold. I have every confidence that he can."

"I have faith in Davydd, too. But why risk civil war?"

"Because," he said slowly, "I cannot condemn Gruffydd to a lifetime shut away from the sun."

And that she could understand. She reached out, touched his cheek. Would there ever be a time when she was not torn between those she loved? For so many years, her father and her husband. And now . . . now her husband and her son. How

could she blame Llewelyn for wanting to set his son free? But
Davydd's right to the succession could be guaranteed only by
Gruffydd's continuing captivity.

"Joanna . . . can you accept my decision?"

"I shall have to accept it." She lay back beside him, closed
her eyes. What else could she do? The last time she'd intervened
on Davydd's behalf, she'd come close, Jesú, so close to destroying her marriage. Llewelyn was right; it was for Davydd to
safeguard his inheritance. He was a man grown, no less ambitious
than Gruffydd, and twice as clever. He would prevail. But the
words rang hollow. She could not stave off a sense of dread, of
coming calamity. Lady Mary be merciful, it was beginning all
over again.

Llewelyn returned to Aber at dusk the following day, and Gruffydd
rode by his side. Joanna had not expected Llewelyn to act so
swiftly, had thought she'd have more time to prepare herself for
Gruffydd's return. As people surged out into the bailey, she
followed slowly, her mind echoing to the refrain of a French
chanson, one that warned against allowing the wolf into the fold.

Had so much not been at stake, she might have been able to
summon up sympathy, for Gruffydd showed the rigors of long
confinement. He had a pronounced pallor, the beginnings of a
double chin, and hair cut so carelessly that it was obvious he'd
long since become indifferent to appearance, while the deep
grooves around his mouth told Joanna more than she wanted to
know of his years in Deganwy's great keep.

Senena, however, looked radiant; an uninformed bystander
might well have identified her as the released prisoner. Their son
Owain rode beside her, and the sight of him was a shock to
Joanna. The younger children had often stayed at Llewelyn's
court, but Owain, never. The nine-year-old boy she remembered
was a gangling youth of fifteen, awkward in his newfound manhood, a flesh-and-blood ghost from Gruffydd's troubled past.

Llewelyn had dismounted. His smile was dazzling, and Joanna yearned to be able to rejoice with him, to be truly and
wholeheartedly happy that his son was free.

"Madame." Gruffydd was bending over her hand. His demeanor was scrupulously correct; captivity had taught him caution if nothing else, Joanna thought, and she, too, took refuge in
courtesy, in the most formal of Welsh greetings, a hollow "May
God prosper you."

Gruffydd's eyes shifted to her face; in their depths she saw a raw flame flicker. "I wish no less for you, Madame."

Almost at once Gruffydd was surrounded by family, friends, and well-wishers, embraced by his sisters, his uncle. He was greeted far more coolly by Elen and Tegwared, but enough people were clustering about him to give his return the aura of a hero's homecoming. Joanna turned, walked away.

Elen soon joined her. "Nothing has changed," Joanna said tonelessly. "Nothing."

Elen shook her head. "You think not? Watch," she said, and Joanna followed her daughter's gaze, saw that her son had just ridden into the bailey.

If Davydd was surprised by Gruffydd's early arrival, it did not show in his face. He reined his stallion in, waited for Gruffydd to come to him. After a conspicuously long pause, Gruffydd did. They exchanged but a few terse words before Gruffydd swung about, stalked back to his wife and sisters. Llewelyn moved swiftly toward his youngest son. Davydd slid from the saddle. They spoke softly together for several moments and then Davydd smiled, nodded. But he kept his eyes upon Gruffydd all the while.

As Joanna watched, a memory stirred, elusive, perplexing. She frowned, seeking to bring it into focus. There was something so tantalizingly familiar about this scene, about Davydd's cool composure, his detachment, the way his hazel eyes narrowed as they took the light, took Gruffydd's measure . . . and then the memory broke through, with such vivid clarity that time blurred, the years fell away, and she exclaimed, "Mirebeau!" in startled revelation.

"Mama?"

"Do you see how Davydd is watching Gruffydd? So distant and yet so deliberate. I knew I'd seen that look before, and now I remember. I once saw my father watch Arthur in that very same way."

The little church of St Rhychwyn was cool and still. Not even the parish priest was there to disturb Joanna. Kneeling before the altar, she was alone with God, alone with her dead. She prayed first for her father, for his need was greatest. And then she prayed for the others: Clemence, Eleanor of Aquitaine, Will of Salisbury, Catherine, Rhys, Morgan, Chester, Arthur, Maude de Braose, Will. She concluded with prayers for those who'd died in

Llewelyn's compulsive war against a ghost, the war that had brought such devastation to the de Braose lands.

The sun was beginning its slow descent toward the west by the time Joanna emerged from the church and started back to Llewelyn's hillside manor at Trefriw. She'd stopped to gather bell heather when she heard Elen's voice; a moment later her daughter came around a bend in the path.

"They told me you'd gone up to Llanrhychwyn, Mama, so I thought I'd walk up and meet you. But why did you not go to St Mary's? Papa had it built for you, after all, to spare you this walk."

"I do attend St Mary's for morning Mass. But now and then I need the solitude of Llanrhychwyn, need that time alone to pray for loved ones . . . and to remember."

They walked in silence for a time; it was too hot for haste. Pine woods rose up on both sides of the path, dark and shadowy and primeval. "Look," Elen said, stooping to pick a daisy. "Did you ever play that game, Mama, plucking the petals to see if love will last?" Her eyes shifted from the flower, up to Joanna's face. "Were you praying for your father?"

Joanna nodded. "Elen . . . we can talk about him if you like. You have the right, darling; he was your blood kin, too."

"Can you talk about him, Mama . . . truly? You pray for him. Does that mean you've forgiven him?"

Joanna was quiet. "No," she said at last. "That is for the Almighty to do. But I have forgiven myself for loving him, am no longer ashamed of that love, and mayhap that's as much as I can hope for."

They'd almost reached Trefriw. Joanna stopped, touched Elen on the arm. "Elen, I am so glad you agreed to stay for a time with us. But I want you to promise me that you'll turn to us if ever you need help, if ever—"

"Mama, I will. But you need not fear." Elen smiled impishly, held out the daisy. "See," she said. "I just pulled the last petal, and it promises that love will prevail!"

Dismounting in a clearing within sight and sound of Rhaeadr Ewynol, Llewelyn walked to the edge of the cliff, stood gazing down at the cataract, a surging spillover of foam and flying spray. Joanna had remained a prudent distance from the precipice, and at last he heeded her entreaties, joined her on the grass under an ancient oak.

Joanna and Elen had returned to Trefriw just as Llewelyn and

Davydd rode in after a day's hawking, and when Llewelyn suggested they ride over to Rhaeadr Ewynol to see the results of recent heavy rains, Joanna had accepted with alacrity; except in bed at night, they'd had little time alone this summer. Now she leaned back against the tree and Llewelyn stretched out beside her, pillowing his head in her lap.

"I had another talk with Ednyved," he said. "He's still set upon making that pilgrimage to the Holy Land, says he can begin laying plans now that Gwynedd is at peace."

That would be a strenuous, dangerous undertaking for a man of any age, and Ednyved was past sixty. Joanna frowned, stopped stroking Llewelyn's hair. "Do you not think you can dissuade him?"

"No," he said regretfully, "I do not." A comfortable silence settled over the glen. When Llewelyn spoke again, he sounded lazily content. "John the Scot gave me a remarkable book Chester picked up in France, written by a man who'd gone on pilgrimage to the Holy Land. It's an account of his adventures, interspersed with suggestions for his fellow pilgrims. I think Ednyved might find it right useful, for he tells the reader how to deal with Venetian money-changers, which ports are best for engaging passage to Palestine, that syrup of ginger helps to ease seasickness. He even includes a vocabulary of foreign words and sentences, those phrases a man would be most likely to need, like 'Where is the inn?' 'How much?' And one so utterly essential I thought it best to commit it to memory: *'Marrat nyco.'* "

When Joanna gave him a quizzical, curious look, he laughed. "That is Arabic for 'Maiden, wilst thou sleep with me?' "

Joanna laughed, too. "You've just convinced me how fortunate I am that you're not going on pilgrimage with him!" But a pilgrimage was more than a propitious opportunity for spiritual salvation; it offered, too, a rare chance for great adventure. "Llewelyn . . . you would not want to accompany Ednyved?"

"No, *breila*. I've thought of pilgrimage; what Christian has not? But I do not think I'd transplant well, need to keep my roots in Welsh soil." His eyes began to gleam; he added, "Furthermore, as much as I would like to see the Holy City wrested away from the Saracens, even more would I like to see Wales free of you English."

Joanna tugged at his hair. "If you must be insulting, at least be accurate. Norman-French, if you please."

"I stand corrected. Although I think English will win out, if not in Davydd's lifetime, mayhap in his children's. Now that you've lost Normandy, the day might well come when English, not French, will be the language even of the court."

"Be serious," Joanna said, and tossed an acorn to a small red squirrel. "I only wish the crusaders had been as successful in their quest as you've been in yours; there'd not be a mosque left intact in all of Jerusalem."

"You make it sound as if I've won my war, Joanna."

"Beloved, you have! You've outwitted or outfought two English Kings, unified your people, secured the succession for Davydd, and engendered a sense of shared identity amongst the Welsh, an awareness of their common destiny. Llewelyn, those are remarkable achievements."

"Yes," he said, "but will it last?"

Joanna had been able to find a curious sort of comfort in that courtyard scene at Aber, in that sudden glimpse of Davydd in a new and unnerving guise, as a man utterly intent upon claiming a crown. She opened her mouth now, ready to reassure Llewelyn that Davydd would triumph, and then realized he was not speaking of Davydd's succession, but rather of Wales. Her smile was both wry and resigned; whilst she worried about people, his concern would ever be for empires.

She very much wished she could foretell for him the future of Gwynedd, assure him the Welsh would continue to thrive in the shadow of a stronger neighbor. Since she could not, she leaned over, kissed him tenderly, then made him laugh by calling him Llewelyn Fawr, for they'd turned John the Scot's lavish praise into a private bedtime joke.

The sun was very low in the sky, the river reflecting the red-gold of a summer sunset. Joanna sat up reluctantly. "We ought to be getting back," she said, but Llewelyn shook his head.

"No," he said, "not yet. We have time." And so they lingered awhile longer in the clearing, watched together the passing of day.

EPILOGUE

Joanna died in 1237 and was buried, at her own request, at Llanfaes, where Llewelyn established a Franciscan monastery to honor her memory. He died three years later and was succeeded by their son Davydd. But Llewelyn's triumph was ephemeral, for it was personal, and his dream of a united, independent Wales was not destined to be.

AUTHOR'S NOTE

In seeking to resurrect a time more than seven centuries distant from ours, I often found that research would take me only so far. It was necessary to rely upon imagination to a greater extent than in my earlier novel of fifteenth-century England, for Llewelyn's world was not as well chronicled as that of the Yorkist Kings. But the structure of *Here Be Dragons* is grounded in fact; even the more unlikely occurrences are validated by medieval chroniclers. Joanna's secret warning to John did reach him at Nottingham as Llewelyn's hostages were being hanged. Llewelyn and Gruffydd did reconcile on the battlefield. And Llewelyn did indeed return unexpectedly to Aber on an April night in 1230, to discover Joanna and Will de Braose alone in his bedchamber. I took but one factual liberty: Llewelyn captured Mold Castle in January of 1199, but I placed the siege in April, the better to integrate the Welsh and Norman story lines.

All of my major characters in *Dragons* actually lived, with the exceptions of Morgan, Rhys, and Rhys's wife, Catherine; whenever possible, I also cast my secondary characters from real-life molds. Although history has preserved for us the identity of Tangwystl, the mother of Llewelyn's son Gruffydd, other female figures remain in shadow. Llewelyn's concubine lived, but Cristyn is a name of my choosing. Little is known of Joanna's mother, other than her Christian name; I gave her a surname and a family background to reflect the skeletal known facts and the most common circumstances of illegitimacy.

Llewelyn's third son, Tegwared, has been utterly eclipsed by the embittered rivalry between his brothers Gruffydd and Davydd; most historians make no mention of him whatsoever. I discov-

ered him in the remarkable *Welsh Genealogies,* a life's work by
Peter C. Bartrum. From *Welsh Genealogies,* I was able, too, to
determine the name of Llewelyn's brother, Adda. Like Tegwared,
Adda has been relegated to the outer reaches of historical obscu-
rity. I knew Llewelyn had a sibling, as a letter of his refers to his
nephews, but until I consulted Mr. Bartrum's work, I had no luck
in tracking down this elusive sibling. As I sought to dramatize in
Dragons, the Welsh system of inheritance all too often fostered
fratricide. Adda, therefore, is an anomaly, neither Llewelyn's
rival nor his active ally. So unusual was his absence from the
political arena that I could only explain it in terms of a disability
of some sort.

Little is known of Llewelyn's early years. It is believed he
passed his childhood in Powys and England; by his fifteenth
year, he was challenging his uncles for control of Gwynedd.
Historians have long been cognizant of his kinship to the Corbet
family; he often stayed his hand, spared Corbet lands, and a letter
of his addresses William Corbet as "uncle." In the nineteenth
century, historians speculated that Llewelyn's mother might be a
hitherto unknown Corbet daughter, but Marared ferch Meredydd's
identity has since been established beyond any doubt. Marared
must therefore have made a second marriage after Iorwerth's
death in 1174. In researching the Corbet family, I was able to
eliminate Robert Corbet without difficulty. His brother William
was the "uncle" of Llewelyn's letter. Walter Corbet was a
monk. By the process of elimination, Hugh Corbet had to be
Marared's second husband, Llewelyn's stepfather.

I made use of Welsh spellings and place names wherever
possible, except when referring to the Norman towns and castles
in South Wales. While "Llywelyn" is the purest Welsh form of
the name, I chose a slightly Anglicized version, knowing that
most readers would be unfamiliar with Welsh. The same reasoning governed my spelling of Davydd; although the modern Welsh
alphabet contains no letter *v,* it was in use in the Middle Ages,
and I thought a phonetic spelling might aid in pronunciation. For
consistency, I called Llewelyn's Seneschal and friend Ednyved
by his family name—ap Cynwrig—but he is more commonly
known as Ednyfed Fychan; readers of *The Sunne in Splendour*
might be interested to know he is the ancestor of Henry Tudor.

Lastly, I made use of "Norman" as an inclusive term for all
people of French descent, e.g., Normans, Angevins, Poitevins,
etcetera. To have referred to them as "French" would have
created endless confusion, and it seemed the lesser sin to opt for

clarity. In the same way, I referred to those of Anglo-Saxon descent as Saxons, not as English, the term they would have used, thus enabling me to stress the divisions still so prevalent in King John's England.

John was much maligned in the lurid tales told of him after his death, and a compelling, colorful legend gradually took root— John, Nature's Enemy, John of the Devil's Brood. Only in the twentieth century have the myths been stripped away, permitting historians to judge John's reign without passion or prejudice, to judge John himself—as a king, as a man—a judgment I sought to convey in *Dragons*. History's judgment upon Llewelyn echoes that of his contemporaries, to whom he was Llewelyn Fawr— Llewelyn the Great.

As a point of interest, the title of this book has its roots in the common practice of medieval cartographers; when a mapmaker had drawn upon all of his geographical knowledge, he would neatly letter across the void beyond: Here be dragons. I found the symbolism hard to resist, given how very little the English of the thirteenth century knew of Wales and the Welsh. Then, too, the national emblem of Wales is a winged red dragon, much like those heraldic dragons once emblazoned upon the banners of her princes.

S.K.P.
OCTOBER 1984